D1516276

# LETTERS TO JOEY

*Spirituality and Transformation in the Catholic Church Today*

by Fr. Robert B. Mattingly

ii

Although about real issues and real lives, this is a work of fiction. Names, characters, businesses, places, events and incidents are either the products of the author's imagination or used in a fictitious manner. Any resemblance to actual persons, living or dead, or actual events is purely coincidental.

# Table of Contents

# IV. Living the Journey:
## The Practice of Second Half of Life Spirituality

# V. The Journey and the Church:
## Challenges and Choices, Spirituality and Institution

# VI. The Journey Onward for Individuals and the Church:
## Present, future, hope and caution

# PREFACE

I am a retired priest incardinated in the Diocese of Venice in Florida. In 2006, my doctor recommended that I retire "early" at the age of sixty-eight because of heart disease. My bishop compassionately accepted my doctor's recommendation, and he granted me an early retirement. The ensuing years of retirement opened the door for me to explore and appreciate an understanding of religion, spirituality, priesthood, and friendship that though ancient and perennial, was new for me. Paradoxically, and gratefully, I found that in my old age I was being reborn again.

The event that awakened, and inspired me to make good use of my retirement years, occurred in 2011, when I attended the "Loving the Two Halves of Life" conference in Albuquerque, New Mexico. The presenters were Fr. Richard Rohr, Fr. Ronald Rolheiser, and Ms. Edwina Gateley. The paradigm on spirituality that they presented, based on developmental transformation, deeply moved me and served to open my heart, mind, and soul, to a new way of life. Thus, I began a spiritual journey of questioning so much of what I had taken for granted earlier in life, resulting in an abundance of discoveries and newfound joys, worth far more than the pains of letting go.

After the conference, upon my return home, I met with Gina and Bill Iacone, parishioners at the church from which I had retired. I shared with them my excitement about what I had heard at the conference, and they were eager to listen and ask questions. Gina and Bill were also looking for a deeper faith-life, so our dialogue and common interest in spirituality had united us over the years in this shared quest. After many months of discussion, Gina suggested I write a book based on what I had come to learn and experience as a result of the conference. When she first made this proposal, my primary reaction was fear. But her idea, and the challenge it represented, stuck with me, and before long the call to speak outweighed the fear, and I began writing this manuscript.

What I present in this book, although significantly different at times from what I learned in seminary, has helped me to be more aware of, and accepting of, those who have ideas that I may not agree with or understand. I now see better the significant role of personal experiences in shaping who we are and how we see the world. Further, I now better appreciate the importance of dialogue, the acknowledgment of mystery, and the foolishness of thinking I have absolute certitude regarding so many diverse issues. In sum, I see that change, lifelong change, is to be embraced, and that by accepting this transformative view of life, many conflicts and misunderstandings may be softened or even resolved.

Regarding the text itself, if the reader finds any faults, the responsibility, of course, is mine alone. But the positive contributions of others I wish to make explicit. Two close friends, Gina Iacone and Dr. Pamela Stagg-Jones have been reading the various drafts, and they have continually encouraged me to produce the final product. I am especially grateful for Dr. David W. Robinson, who has been a close confidant throughout the effort, and has been what I could fairly call an informal editor. I am deeply grateful to Marilyn Hill, who proofread the final draft. Each week for five years, David and I have worked together on this book, discussing both big themes and significant details. David's creative mind and rich background in spirituality, religion, and depth psychology have greatly helped to put this book into its final form.

The book is fictional, presented as a dialogue in the form of letters between a retired priest and his seminarian great nephew. Although presented as fictional, many of the stories recounted in the missive have actually taken place as told, or reflect a merging of several persons and events from both my own life and the lives of those whom I have known. Following convention, I share these stories using fictional names and altered places. Numbers were added to the letters for easy reference.

Usually in retirement, a priest is expected to "help out" the priests in the local parishes. This enables the institutional church, amidst the current decline in vocations, to continue to deliver the graces the Church offers. It is rare that a priest has the opportunity in retirement to study, write, question, and relearn because of financial pressures and the need to work. This is most regrettable both for the individual priest and the community at large. I believe that as we age we need to be allowed, no, encouraged, to go deeper in our understanding of religion and spirituality if we are to become fully human and fully alive. Yes, I love the Catholic Church and I am grateful for my life as a priest. But, I have witnessed that encouragement of this "wisdom journey" is rare in the institutional church. This observation is connected to the sadness I feel regarding the broader phenomenon of people who no longer find the Church relevant in their lives. With unbroken loyalty, I have committed my life to service in the Church, and it is this spirit that underlies my conviction that change is now necessary in the institutional church. Otherwise, if the status quo prevails, for many people the Church will become irrelevant and obsolete, and for them, the Church will die. In this way, the Church itself becomes diminished, to what extent only time will tell. This book is thus my offering to the widespread movement of many voices aimed at keeping the Church not just relevant and alive but dynamically prophetic. I do believe with God all things are possible (Matthew 19:26).

Fr. Robert B. Mattingly
Port Charlotte, FL
July 4, 2020

# INTRODUCTION

On May 18, 2017, I, Robert Mattingly, received in the mail a large package, wrapped in brown paper, sent from Cincinnati, Ohio. I wondered who I knew in Cincinnati. The return label simply said, "Stone and Waters Law Firm."

When I opened the package, there was a letter addressed to me from one of the firm's attorneys. The attorney was writing as the executor of the will of Rev. Matthew Scott who had passed away and, curiously, had left to me a collection of personal letters. It took a few moments for me to recall that Fr. Matthew was my second cousin, the child of my dad's long-deceased aunt. Matthew was six years older than me, and I only met him when we were children when our parents lived in Oxen Hill, Maryland. Matthew's parents, Regina and William moved to Detroit, post-war, so I lost track of Matthew.

The executor's letter outlined, in cursory fashion, that Fr. Matthew had passed away on February 11, 2016, after suffering a fatal stroke while asleep. His body had been discovered by his neighbor, Jim, when he failed to respond to Jim's text messages.

The executor of the will explained that Matthew had been a teacher for many years as well as a pastor in local churches. He had apparently carried out a robust correspondence, with numerous friends and strangers alike, including a five year exchange with his grand-nephew, Joey. While living in retirement, for reasons still not clear to me, Fr. Matthew had directed in his Last Will and Testament to leave me his collection of letters, complete with explicit permission for me to use his letters, if I so desired, and in whatever manner of my choosing. The only stipulation was that the letters be used to help others in their spiritual journeys. This of course piqued my interest.

I received the package on a Thursday, and I spent the whole weekend reading over the sixty-six letters of correspondence spanning five years from January 2011, until January 2016. I couldn't put the letters down. The letters dealt with numerous aspects of spirituality, life in the church, and practical problems of being a priest. At the beginning of their correspondence, Joey was twenty-five years old and Fr. Matthew was seventy-seven years old. Joey addressed his grand-uncle as simply "uncle" in his letters, and Fr. Matthew simply addressed his grandnephew as "nephew."

I realized that the letters share a little-known paradigm, model, or pattern about spirituality that simply says that the human spiritual journey could be divided into two halves which could be labeled the practice of first-half of life spirituality and the practice of second-half of life spirituality. It was Doctor Carl G. Jung who first popularized the phrase: "the two halves of life" to describe two major tasks in life. First half of life spirituality, often defined by the religion we embrace, has its own goals, signs that indicate its presence, and its own images of God. Normally we are taught to practice a religion, when we are in the first half of life. By way of analogy, to build a home, we must first create a foundation, a base upon which a wonderful home can be built. The practice of first half of life spirituality is like pouring a foundation for a home.

Transitions occur in our stages of human development. In the early part of life, we are dependent upon others. In adolescence, we desire to be independent of others. Later in life, we become aware of the values and rewards of living interdependently with others. The same thing happens in the spiritual journey. In the first half of life, we are dependent upon our ministers, parents, and teachers for handing us down a religion; a spirituality. But we go through stages when we question our religion, we ask how it really pertains to us personally. We want to think independently. As we question, we gradually become aware of the need for a new spirituality, a new religion, that matures with new insights and understandings.

By way of analogy, the awareness that we have reached the stage of needing an adult spirituality is like going home to find that our dwelling, the end product of our first half of life spirituality, is still solidly built but no longer serves our needs. We find that changes to the dwelling become necessary both because it is aging and because we have different needs. We must gradually effect these changes in order for it to remain in good shape and to fit us more properly.

As I read through the letters, it struck me that many individuals could benefit from these letters, so I decided to edit these letters into a book, with the permission of Fr. Matthew's grandnephew, Joey, so as to share this paradigm with others.

Audience:

If there were a general target for this work, it would be every soul open to the movements of the Holy Spirit. This book can be helpful to any person who knows that no one has fully lived up to the glory of God and that our individual lives remain partial, unfulfilled, and not yet complete. We all would like to become fully human and fully alive. This book is for anyone humble enough to see the limitations of what has gone before, and who is hungry for something still greater, unexpected, and yet to come in their own lives.

More specifically this book targets Roman Catholic seminarians and priests with whom I have lived and worked for the nearly half a century, as a fellow seminarian and priest, and for whom I have great respect and admiration. "How beautiful on the mountains are the feet of those who bring good news, who proclaim peace, who bring good tidings, who proclaim salvation, who say to Zion, 'your God reigns'" (Isaiah 52:7).

1. Individuals who desire to be fully alive:

St. Irenaeus, one of the great saints of the second century said, "The glory of God is a human being who is fully alive!" Yet psychologists say that the average person achieves only ten percent of his or her potential to live, learn, and love. Jesus said, "I have come that they might have life and have it to the full" (John 10:10). I am convinced that we are not able to become fully human and fully alive unless we have an opportunity to become aware of and practice second half of life spirituality. When our images of God are based on truthfulness, we have a better opportunity to become fully human and fully alive. When our passion in life is to love our neighbor instead of just being focused on our own well-being, we become fully alive. When we become the "bread of life" for others, we become fully human and fully alive. When we give up our tendency to be dualistic thinkers, we become fully alive. If we remain practicing first half of life spirituality during the second half of life, we risk being held back from becoming fully human and fully alive.

2. Individuals who desire to be good shepherds:

The purpose of this book is to help all those consciously on a spiritual journey to become good shepherds, not in the sense of paternalistic lords, but as soul-friends and wise mentors along the journey. Jesus was the good shepherd. As members of the Body of Christ, all of us are brothers and sisters in Christ, so God calls all of us to be good shepherds for one another. An awareness that God calls us to be good shepherds can help us to better practice love of neighbor. This book can help lay Catholics, other Christians, and those who are spiritually independent to discover a spiritual road map that gives an overview of the process involved in becoming a good shepherd.

3. Catholics who are designated as "alumni Catholics:"

Today, we do have a large number of "alumni Catholics" in this country. There are many young and older laypersons who were once baptized as Catholics who no longer attend the Catholic Church on a regular basis. Many people have not only disaffiliated but never affiliated with a religious tradition and are also described as "the Nones", the fastest growing religious demographic in the United States. Many young people feel shamed because they know they are not living according to the norms of their religion, especially in the area of sexuality. But as we shall see in Fr. Matthew's letters to his grandnephew, Joey, perhaps their reluctance to attend mass indicates that they are beginning to transition into the practice of second half of life spirituality.

Many older Catholics no longer attend Mass on a regular basis because they experience that the Church is not fulfilling her purpose of bringing good news to them. The practice of first half of life spirituality often tells us what not to do or else. The practice of second half of life spirituality stresses what we are capable of doing, good news! When young and older non-practicing Catholics discover that perhaps they are practicing some aspects of second half of life spirituality, they may see the many benefits that their religion offers. When alumni Catholics find out that there is an adult side to religion, an adult spirituality, they are often excited and encouraged to work for change in the Catholic Church rather than just staying away.

4. Catholics who are dealing with scrupulosity:

There are many older Catholics, in their second half of life, that suffer scrupulosity. Scrupulous individuals can be tormented by unnecessary feelings of guilt and shame. They may repeatedly confess the same sins and shortcomings since they are overly concerned about punishment when they die. They want to be above reproach. Absolution provides them with comfort, but soon their fears return. In some ways they are like children. They live in constant fear of displeasing God. They painstakingly worry about their imperfections and often they cannot distinguish normal human behavior from sin. And so they become preoccupied with whether or not they have sinned and offended their image of a Vengeful God.

This book could help scrupulous individuals to realize that there is another adult way of looking at reality called second half of life spirituality. Once a person realizes that there are more truthful images of God that usually come later in life, their excessive fear, worry, and scrupulosity can be reduced.

As I mentioned, the practice of first half of life spirituality focuses on what is right and what is wrong. Thus, we are aware of our sinfulness. This is necessary as part of the process of becoming a whole person. The practice of second half of life spirituality focuses on God's compassion and unconditional love. If we are to imitate Christ in this life, our images of God determine to a large degree our desire to be a friend of the historical Jesus who was the image of the invisible God.

5. Catholics who have faced terrible tragedies:

There are many Catholics who no longer attend church because of some personal tragedy they faced, such as the loss of a child for no just or discernible rationale. Their child may have suffered a fatal disease such as cancer or died in a terrible automobile accident, or died of a drug over-dose. As a result, they are often unconsciously angry with God. Somehow, they blame God for taking their child. Their image of God locks them into a state of constant anger. A positive, healing relationship with God is foreclosed.

When we practice first half of spirituality, we form images of God that may serve us well if we do not experience major tragedies. However, some Catholics retain these early images of God when they are older, in their second half of life. They are never consciously led to reshape their images of God in a way that reflects a deeper reality so as to serve them as adults by leading them to a different spirituality that makes it possible to better handle the major tragedies of life.

6. Individuals who desire to trace their own spiritual journey:

This book could serve as a stimulus for readers to trace their own spiritual journey in a way that provides clarity and guidance. Soren Kierkegaard, the nineteenth century Danish philosopher and theologian said, "Life can only be understood backwards; but it must be lived forwards."

The practice of second half of life spirituality provides us rich opportunities to understand our younger years, our first half of life. Father Matthew shares so much with his nephew, Joey, that traces his own spiritual path whereby he could accept himself with both his gifts and failures, his accomplishments and defeats. By taking time to look at our paths of growth, we can discover many blessings and encouragement for forward movement. Paradoxically, out of our apparent failures, we can discover growth and blessings. C. G. Jung said, "The gold is in the darkness."

7. Older Catholics who no longer find the Church exciting:

The paradigm of the two halves of life could benefit older Catholic laypersons who have never been encouraged to move into the practice of second half of life spirituality. Too often at liturgies, retired people seem to be present only out of an obligation instead of joyfully participating. When people are joyless, it often indicates that they are in a rut where they either are not encouraged to change or they are unwilling to change. Could it be that many older laypersons in the Church try harder and harder with the practice of first half of life spirituality, and they are not finding the fulfillment they expected? They are perhaps discovering the spiritual unease that comes from an inadequate spirituality and underlying world view. C. G. Jung astutely wrote in his book Modern Man in Search of a Soul: "I have treated many hundreds of patients. Among those in the second half of life-that is to say, over thirty-five, there has not been one whose problem in the last resort was not that of finding a religious outlook on life. It is safe to say that every one of them fell ill because he had lost that which the living religions of every age have given their followers, and none of them has really been healed who did not regain his religious outlook."

"Religious outlook" for Jung in the paradigm of the two halves of life spirituality refers to viewing life with an adult spirituality. Therefore, devout, well-intentioned people can end up sad and frustrated if they either are unwilling or have not been encouraged to move into the practice of second half of life spirituality. Those who never progress beyond the practice of first half of life spirituality can end up judging themselves by the fulfillment of the law that they could never fully keep. They miss the joy and fullness of life that Jesus promises so they never became fully human and fully alive.

8. Individuals who are spiritually independent:

The paradigm of the two halves of life can be helpful to spiritually independent individuals who are desirous of exploring perennial wisdom. Those who are spiritually independent are open to the wisdom from whatever religion it may come. However, they are free from having to believe everything held in that religion.

According to a Pew Research Center survey, a third of adults in the United States under thirty are religiously unaffiliated today. As I mentioned above, they are labeled " the Nones," a negative label. However, most Nones are not rejecting spirituality or God, but they are asking good questions. They do not confine their search for answers to any one religion. In this book, perennial questions are explored and most of the responses to these questions are based on actual experiences without claiming certitude and instead pointing to mystery.

The cost of change:

It should be clearly acknowledged that being transformed in and through the practice of second half of life spirituality involves not only joy, but also pain and discomfort. This suffering of the soul takes place in many forms, but certainly one aspect may be thought of as the loss of what is familiar, simple, and safe. Fr. Matthew in his letters that follow will slowly and methodically reveal to his nephew, Joey, that when we obey the call to second half of life spirituality, we indeed do pay the price of our innocence.

Ironically and often tragically, when we try to be too "good," too often, too soon, and too long, we may retain a form of innocence, through repression and denial, but at the cost of denying our bigger self found in mystery. This mystery is discovered by opening one's heart and mind to a sense of wonder, a sense of inquisitiveness, and the fearless asking of questions. Along the way we find that the answers point to further questions. We learn that we can apply reason and intellect within a certain limit, and it is important to do so in order to discover the limits for oneself. But beyond that limit, the intellect is not only not useful, but it can even mislead us. We cannot know the direct and concrete answers to all our questions so we are faced, at some distant point, not with certitude but with mystery. We need not be fearful of this mystery.

Unless we are willing to change, to be changed, we can end up relying on our own will-power to be "good" instead of moving into a spirituality whereby we know that we need God's grace to be good. The emphasis of one's spirituality shifts as we move from the practice of first half to second half of life spirituality from an egocentric preoccupation for self-perfection to a passion for living, sharing, and witnessing divine life.

Conclusion:

It takes a long time to experience life, or rather, to consciously understand that life-experiences are our primary teachers. That is, if we let them be so. If we learn from our joys and sorrows, we may eventually transition into the practice of second half of life spirituality and appreciate the insights of perennial wisdom. The soul is not mathematical in nature but rather follows its own course as we grow in age.

Churches, as human constructions, are normally first half of life institutions which serve an important social and spiritual function. Difficulties often result when there is a clash between church leaders who practice first half of life spirituality and parishioners who practice second half of life spirituality. If more could be done to encourage the transition to and understanding and practice of second half of life spirituality, there would be fewer conflicts, attendance at worship services would likely increase, parishioners would be more joyful, the wisdom of the ages within and outside of Christianity would be better respected, and better shepherding would naturally occur.

The practice of second half of life spirituality is meant for adults not children. St. Paul said, "When I was a child, I used to talk like a child, think like a child, reason like a child. When I was a man, I put childish ways aside" (1 Corinthians 13:11).

So let's begin with letters of exchange between Joey, a seminarian, and his beloved Uncle Matthew, a retired priest.

# I.  The Journey Begins:
# The Formation and Practice of First Half of Life Spirituality

Letter #1
Friday, January 28, 2011

Dear Uncle Matthew,

I got up early this morning, before morning prayer, to write a letter to you for the first time. I felt an urge to communicate with you. I like it here in the seminary, and I would like to share with you what is going on in my life.

I was thinking that it would be very helpful to me if I had a wise person to guide me while I am in the seminary studying to become a priest. My spiritual director is good, but he will be leaving the seminary soon and returning to his diocese. I would very much like to correspond with you on a regular basis since you are my uncle, a priest, and someone whom I can trust. You have known me since I was born. I have always regarded you as a man of integrity. I know you are a busy man in your retirement years, but you could be a great help to me if you would offer me insights and reflections as I study to become a priest. I would like to be able to ask you questions from time to time. We have a good formation program here, but if you would share some of your pastoral experiences with me, that would greatly supplement my academic studies. During my college days, I met some young men with progressive ideas about religion. You would be a great help if you would share the plurality of thought in the Church today.

Today is my twenty-fifth birthday. I was born on this day, the feast of St. Thomas Aquinas, in 1986. I pray that St. Thomas Aquinas will bless me in a special way as I study to become a priest since the Church regards him as a model teacher for those studying for the priesthood.

Entering the seminary last fall was a big move for me since it changed my area of study and in general turned my life upside down. My degree in engineering from Virginia Tech and my work at the National Security Agency (NSA) enables me to have a scientific world view. Now, in pre-theology, I am being trained to have a religious world view. This is a difficult yet rewarding transition for me.

I do like my studies in pre-theology. I believe that a major in philosophy will help me to better appreciate different ideas regarding the answers to the important questions we ask in life. For example, I am enjoying our History of Philosophy class. We are studying Aristotle who was so brilliant. He and the other Greek philosophers delved into the deepest questions of life.

You said on the phone that last week you attended a wonderful Conference in Albuquerque. You mentioned that the speakers shared many good insights about religion and spirituality that might be of some benefit for me. If you wish to correspond with me on a regular basis, could you share with me what you learned at the Father Richard Rohr Conference? I am trying to understand the teachings of the Catholic religion, so I'm sure your insights on religion would help me.

I look forward to hearing from you.

Peace,

Joey

Response to Letter #1
Monday, February 7, 2011

Dear Joey,

I would enjoy corresponding with you on a regular basis. We have been close to each other over the years. I remember when you were born. My nephew, Steve, married Marie and later you and Paul were born. So you are my grandnephew. Steve and Marie were so grateful to God for you when you were born. Your dad told me he was so proud to show you off to everyone.

I remember well your graduation from Virginia Tech in 2008. Your parents were so proud of your academic and athletic accomplishments. Yes, your entry into the seminary last fall was a major step requiring many changes. You have the benefit of being supported by your family. I'm excited that you are enjoying your studies. Yes, a different world view may be difficult to grasp, but we all have to be exposed to different world views so as to eventually establish our own world view. Hopefully, St. Thomas Aquinas will inspire you in your studies.

Last month, I attended the Conference in Albuquerque, "Loving the Two Halves of Life." The presenters were Fr. Richard Rohr, Fr. Ronald Rolheiser, and Ms. Edwina Gateley. I learned for the first time about this particular paradigm that brilliantly explains the spiritual journey. This Conference blessed me to see this paradigm as a roadmap for an adult spirituality.

Do you remember, Joey, when you were in high school we watched the movie, Close Encounters of the Third Kind? Steven Spielberg directed the science fiction film based on a true story of a man who claimed he saw an unidentified flying object (UFO). Once he saw the object, his life radically changed. He couldn't explain what he saw to others because people couldn't understand. The man who saw the UFO was totally convinced of the validity of his experience.

That is how I felt after I attended the Richard Rohr Conference. The paradigm he presented changed my life. The Conference introduced me to a treasure that brought new excitement and meaning to my life. The Conference gives me the tools to look at the past and better understand what happened. The Conference also gives me the tools to better understand the present because it helps me to be a better minister of the gospel. I feel like the man in the parable of the treasure hidden in a field. Now that I have located the treasure, I am willing to do anything to keep it and share the treasure with you (Matthew 13:44).

Corresponding with you, using the Socratic Method, would not only benefit you as you discern your vocation in life, but it would help me to clarify my own thoughts and ideas on religion and spirituality. I have kept a detailed journal over the years, so I do have many stories of a pastoral nature that could be helpful to you. I am aware of the plurality of thought in the Church. I don't agree with some theologians, but I'll be happy to share different world-views.

Earlier in my life, I made a Profession of Faith. According to Canon Law, pastors, professors in seminaries, and those about to be ordained deacons, must make a Profession of Faith. If and when you make a Profession of Faith, you will promise not to question or call in doubt anything contained in what is called the "deposit of faith." In my preaching over the years, I have never said anything in public that would deny or question anything proposed by the Magisterium of the Church.

In my letters to you, I will try to honestly and vulnerably answer your questions and address your concerns. I will share, if you so desire, some of my own experiences in life as well as the experiences of others. I will not try to change your mind or your belief system, but at your request, I will share with you what others think about various topics so that you can better appreciate mystery rather than presuming certitude. By questioning what we assume to be true, we deepen our faith. The Conference is already motivating me to think, question, and study. As you learn in your formation program our basic Catholic beliefs, I hope to broaden my own outlook on religion and spirituality. Our correspondence will be like a diary that shows our common quest for an adult spirituality.

From what I learned at the Conference, it seems that if the Church is going to survive in the decades to come, the Church must be willing to dialogue and change. I read that the second largest denomination after Roman Catholicism is former Roman Catholics.

You mentioned earlier that you had a conversion experience when you worked at the NSA. I wish you would share your conversion experience with me. I have a special interest in the stories people share about their conversion. I know something big must have happened to you to change your vocation and to embrace a celibate path of life which is a major change in your world view!

I have been helping out in four parishes since I retired. I spend a lot of my time preparing homilies and celebrating masses. I am taking more time to journal, read, listen quietly to the quiet whispers of the Holy Spirit, and re-learn so much of what I learned when I was your age in the seminary.

In the seminary, your formation program is largely designed to help you to know and appreciate your Catholic religion which is like a container (a foundation, an identity), that you can build upon as you age. Religion gets us started in life so that we have a relationship with God, people, and the world. The religion we practice is influenced by our teachers, family members, social circles, and the wider culture. As you know, there are many religions in the world (Christianity, Judaism, Hinduism, Buddhism, Islam, etc), and each religion has its own world view along with its own teachings.

I took some notes on the concerns that we have in the first half of life. These concerns I will refer to as goals. These goals will help you to be aware of what we need to achieve so as to become fully human and fully alive. I wish someone had shared these goals and objectives with me earlier in life.

Essential goals to accomplish in the first half of life:

Notice that I do not say that these are goals we practice in first half of life spirituality because these essential goals are much broader. We all can agree that these goals are essential regardless of whether we practice Hinduism, Judaism, Buddhism, Islam, Christianity, or New Age (often this category includes those who are spiritually independent), or no religion. To become fully human and fully alive, we need to accomplish these essential goals.

Four traditional and essential goals:

First, it is essential to develop a strong ego. At the Conference, the speakers used the term "ego" to describe that part of the mind that is the center of consciousness, and it is what we refer to when we use the term "I" or "me." When we are in the first half of life, our ego helps us to be in control, to name, fix, and acquire certitude. The ego helps us to achieve and compete so that we are successful. The ego gives us a continuing sense of identity so that when we wake up tomorrow we realize we are the same person that we were yesterday.

The ego strives to establish our identity, vocation, and gender-preference. The ego strives to make us look good so that we will succeed. Religion can assist the ego in meeting these goals or religion can create problems.

The ego must develop so as to control our diet, sexual desires, physical exercise, study, social life, and religious worship. Already before entering the seminary you learned how to be self-disciplined, orderly, and in control. In the first half of life, we must learn to obey the laws of civil society. In the seminary, you will learn the Catholic Church's beliefs that you will later be expected to defend and teach. The ego helps us to live by boundaries determined by God and other people. The ego will benefit from your Catholic training so as to help you with impulse control. That means that just because you feel like eating, drinking, or spending money doesn't mean it is good for you or for other people.

Second, it is essential to acquire an identity. We need to answer the question, "Who am I?" During the first half of life, the foundational development of character, spirituality, and maturity occur. Otherwise, we can go through life blinded to the truth about others and ourselves. We need to develop self-esteem and a healthy self image. To accept who we are, we must become aware of our ego and how it works. We must recognize our compulsions, obsessions, and virtues. Religion can greatly help us to know who we are.

Your patron saint, St. Thomas Aquinas said, "Self-love is the form and root of all friendship. To know and appreciate your own worth is no sin."

Dr. Carl G. Jung said in his book, Memories, Dreams and Reflections, "Acceptance of oneself is the essence of the whole moral problem and the epitome of a whole outlook on life."

The American theologian, Reinhold Niebuhr wrote the Serenity Prayer: "God grant me the serenity to accept the things I cannot change, the courage to change the things I can, and the wisdom to know the difference." This prayer helps us to discover what is not working in our lives.

Your philosophy courses will help you to know yourself because the perennial questions that philosophy asks will be discussed and answered with various view-points. In future letters we can discuss how self-acceptance takes place. Self-acceptance overcomes any toxic shame that may later in life bind us. Non-acceptance creates an inner rupture and conflict.

The educational process (high school, college, graduate studies) serves to assist us in our identity by broadening our knowledge of the world, career opportunities, others, and self.

We discover our sexual identity and gender preference so as to answer the questions, Who am I attracted to? Whom might I marry? How will I express my love?

Part of acquiring an identity is to discover what success means to us although we each define success differently. We answer the questions, Am I looking good to others and to myself? How do I compare with others my age? How can I make it to the top?

When we identify what makes us successful, we discover what makes us happy. We answer the questions, What will make me happy? How will I be happy? Does my happiness come through accomplishments in sports, politics, friendships, academic achievements, etc.?

Establishing our identity includes discovering and exploring our instincts and emotions so that we learn that they are precious gifts that help us rather than hinder us.

Third, we need to provide for security and establish boundaries. We need to trust that the world is a good place and we can trust other people. In the quest for security and establishing boundaries, we try to answer the questions, Do my parents love me? Am I safe here? Do I have enough food and money?

While working at the NSA, you were making a salary, renting an apartment, and you were able to take care of your physical needs. Now you have decided to study for the priesthood. The means for providing for your security needs have changed. But, generally speaking, we all must choose a vocation. We need to make money so as to live in this world. We need to obtain health insurance, life insurance, and money for retirement. Providing for security in the first half of life ensures stability and opens the door for us to have many opportunities later during the second half of life. For survival, we need to preserve and enhance our assets, physical, social, spiritual, and mental. We need to acquire some material possessions such as a car, home, bank account, etc.

Fourth, we need to develop an informed conscience. Rev. Charles Curran says in his book Conscience that conscience is "generally understood as the judgment about the morality of an act to be done or omitted or already done or omitted by a person." We form our conscience by our experiences in our culture, family, and church. When we are young, we are impressionable. We tend to think that what we see is good and truthful. As we age, we have more experiences so that we can better discern right from wrong. Forming a conscience involves an evolution during our whole life.

Many people who practice their Catholic religion simply do what the Church teaches without question. The Eternal Word Television Network (EWTN) is a good example of a religious network that stresses the formation of conscience based on church teachings found in the Catechism of the Catholic Church. Your studies in the seminary will inform you about the process of forming your conscience.

Our sense of morality, the formation of our conscience during the first half of life, is influenced by our images of God. Father Richard Rohr in his book, What the Mystics Know says that our images of God are ninety percent a mixture of the images we have of our mother and father. Our images of God are largely the products of what we heard from church leaders.

During the first half of life, our images of God greatly impact our ability to achieve our goals and they influence our motivation for our actions and inactions. When we practice our religion in the first half of life, we may do the right thing for the wrong reason because our images of God are elementary.

Your success in life:

Success in your life as a priest or as a layman will be determined by the completion of these four essential goals and many other goals. Completing these goals will contribute to the aliveness you will enjoy. You are blessed to be in the seminary where you have so many advantages "to see" and "to hear." Jesus said, "Be awake." Your courses are all about becoming better aware of reality. That is the purpose of religion and your formation, to help you to see and understand reality as it is within a Catholic world view.

When you have accomplished your formation program and are knowledgable about the teaching of the Catholic Church, you might think that your spiritual journey is complete, adequate, and coherent. Religions often offer rewards and punishments if we complete or fail to complete the essential goals that I indicated above. But the truth is that your spiritual journey has just begun!

Enjoy your studies in philosophy. I'm so excited that you have this opportunity in the seminary to enjoy the luxury of having a few years to pray, study, and to be gradually transformed into a fully human person. The Church is wise to require seminarians to have a background in philosophy since many of the challenges society faces today are rooted in some particular philosophy or world-view.

Peace,

Uncle Matthew

Letter #2
Tuesday, February 22, 2011

Dear Uncle Matthew,

I am so happy that you are willing to correspond with me on a regular basis. I read over the four goals that I should accomplish in the first half of my life. These goals are very helpful. Thank you. You were able to summarize very well these concerns/goals. Accomplishing these goals will make life so much better in the second half of life of my life.

Since I am older than many of the seminarians and I have a college background plus two years of working experience at the National Security Agency, I think I am making good progress in accomplishing the goals that you mentioned. I can tell that you have thought a lot about religion and spirituality. Apparently, teachers like Fr. Richard Rohr have helped you, and so many others, to grow spiritually!

How old are you now, Uncle Matthew? I can't remember what you told me earlier. I admire your stamina and pursuit of the intellectual life. We were off yesterday for Presidents' Day, so I had a relaxing day in the seminary.

You asked me to share my conversion experience that occurred while I was working at the NSA in Fort Meade, MD. My experience was simple, but very powerful for me.

Here is my story. I spent the weekend with my parents who lived at that time in Washington, D. C., and I decided to organize my bedroom closet. I noticed a stack of old catechisms that I used while attending faith formation in high school. I was discarding them one-by-one when I saw an etching of a young man who was at a crossroads in his life. To his left was a flat road laden with flowers, but at the end of which stood Satan. To his right was a hilly narrow road with thorns, rocks, and at the end of which stood Jesus. It struck me in an uncanny way that I was also at a crossroads in my life. I had to make a choice about my path in life. I realized that I was on the road leading to Satan.

After a short period of time, I went down to the living room where my parents were entertaining my Aunt Rose and Uncle Harvey. I blurted out to all of them that I wanted to become a priest. I recall that my parents' reaction was one of caution. They were worried that I was making a major decision too quickly. Of course this sudden decision meant giving up my girlfriend, Dolores, and radically changing my career. After I shared the news with Dolores, she said she would wait a year for me, if I were to change my mind. After waiting a year, since I was still committed to becoming a priest, she started dating Fred whom she later married. She later gave birth to twin boys. We are still in contact although she and Fred have moved to Albany, NY.

Can you explain to me what new insights you learned at the Rohr Conference? Also, I'm still a bit confused regarding the difference between religion and spirituality. You described religion in your last letter. I never thought about spirituality but only about the knowledge and practice of my religion. I'm also interested in signs that individuals show when they are accomplishing first half of life goals.

Peace,

Joey

Response to Letter #2
Monday, March 7, 2011

Dear Joey,

Thank you for sharing your conversion story. That few minutes in
your life turned your life upside down! Hold on to that experience.
Write it down. In times of temptation to leave the seminary, read
over your story so as to recall your precious calling.

I am now seventy-seven years old. I will be celebrating my
birthday on March 17, the feast of St. Patrick.

I will not only be willing to share with you the notes I took at the
Fr. Richard Rohr Conference in January, but I will also share
insights that I have learned over the years. One lesson I learned
at the Rohr Conference was that all of us have a responsibility to
think, question, and make assumptions, but always with the
humility to be corrected, if necessary.

 Insights:

I'll share five insights that helped me so much.

First, I realized the title of the Conference, "Loving two halves of
life," describes a little-known paradigm, (like a spiritual
roadmap), which says our religion, with its beliefs and practices
that were suitable, even necessary, early in life, is best to be

outgrown as our life unfolds.

At the Conference they quoted the passage when Jesus spoke about wineskins and wine because, by way of analogy, it seems to very well describe this paradigm. In the first half of life, we acquire a religion that is like a wineskin, (a container, a foundation), that helps us to live in this world. The wine inside, by way of analogy, is our spirituality. In the second half of life, we need to re-examine our religion and our spirituality and become aware that we need to make changes. We need a new wineskin and new wine. Jesus said, "People do not pour new wine into old wineskins. If they do, the skins burst, the wine spills out, and the skins are ruined. No, they pour new wine into new wineskins, and in that way both are preserved" (Mark 2:22).

At the Conference, they shared a quote from Dr. Carl Jung, "One cannot live the afternoon of life according to the programs of life's morning; for what was great in the morning will be of little importance in the evening, and what in the morning was true will at evening have become a lie."

One of the tasks in the second half of life, is to assume the responsibility to ask questions, to accept the uncomfortableness of doubt, to lose the security of assuming that we have certitude, and to be more open to the gift of faith.

Second, I realized at the Conference that there is a difference between religion and spirituality. You mentioned that you are confused about the difference. Religion has been with us for a few thousand years, but spirituality has been with us from the beginning of humankind. There are many religions. Not everyone has a religion, nor does everyone practice a religion. But everyone has a spirituality.

Spirituality pertains to the inner experience of how we think and feel and choose to relate to God. It addresses our unconscious, our desires, and our passions. There are signs of a spiritual person: compassion, selflessness, forgiveness, and humility. Spirituality is something we do. We serve others, pray, study, and create a sense of union with God. Our images of God are important because they impact our spirituality. For example, in our relationship with God, if we have an image of God as a mean dictator, it will have an enormous impact on our spirituality, our relationship with God, our morality, our self-image, and our style of prayer and worship.

I'll try to explain with an example. Nelson Mandela was the president of South Africa from 1994-1999. He dismantled apartheid, and he forgave those who incarcerated him for twenty-seven years. He was awarded the Nobel Peace Prize. When Nelson Mandela died in December 2013, his spirituality inspired the world; not his religion. His spirituality went beyond the dogmas and practice of any religion. He could forgive, heal, radiate inner peace, and unconditionally love his neighbor. The point is that some people may practice a religion but have an underdeveloped spirituality. Other people may not practice any religion, but they have a developed and inspiring spirituality.

The late Jesuit priest Anthony de Mello, in his book Awareness, said spirituality means being willing to wake up, listen to new ideas, practice self-observation, and unlearn almost everything we have been taught. To be spiritual for the Hebrews meant to be alive in the world and alive in God. Spiritual did not mean to be simply pious or otherworldly. The German theologian and mystic, Meister Eckhart, said that spirituality is not to be learned by flight from the world, by running away from things, or by turning solitary and going apart from the world. Rather, spirituality penetrates all things, and we find God there.

Author and counselor John Bradshaw, in his book Healing the Shame that Binds You said, "Spirituality is about expansion and growth. It is about love, truth, goodness, beauty, giving, and caring. Spirituality is about wholeness and completion."

A good way to understand spirituality is to realize that twelve-step programs, such as Alcoholics' Anonymous, practice a profound spirituality, but they do not practice any religion. There is a lot of wisdom in the insight, "Religion is for people who are afraid to go to Hell and spirituality is for those who have already been there."

Third, I realized at the Conference there is a need to make this material simple so that more people can benefit from this paradigm which could assist all of us in becoming good shepherds. How can we combine the metaphors of wineskins and wine with religion and spirituality? Why not look at it in this way? We could simply say that in the first half of life, we practice a religion and a spirituality that I am going to call "the practice of first half of life spirituality." In the second half of life, we practice a modified religion and spirituality that I am going to call "the practice of second half of life spirituality."

Fourth, I realized at the Conference that religion and spirituality often come into conflict when religious authority figures try to control and determine a person's individual spirituality. Unfortunately, institutions can become self-interested.

For example, in many churches today, authority figures give the impression that if we stick with our religion and learn what is taught in the Catechism of the Catholic Church, attend Mass every Sunday, and avoid breaking the Commandments, we will have a wonderful spiritual life that will last us for a lifetime. This impression goes against the paradigm of "Loving the two halves of life." This impression also goes against the tradition of the mystics in our Church.

Fifth, I realized at the Conference that the practice of first and second half of life spirituality does not necessarily follow chronologically. Someone in their twenties may show signs of practicing second half of life spirituality, and someone who is eighty may show signs of practicing first half of life spirituality.

I now wish someone had shared with me these insights so that I could have had an overview of the spiritual journey earlier in life. I wouldn't have made so many mistakes and endured so much unnecessary suffering.

Signs indicating the practice of first half of life spirituality:

I really should end this letter now, but you asked me to share with you some signs that individuals show when they are accomplishing the goals found in the first half of life. That is a big question. I don't want to disappoint you, so I'll share the following signs that are more personal and psychological.

I am generalizing when I share these signs to help you see reality. It is important to remember that these signs that individuals show when they are accomplishing the goals found in the first half of life are actually showing the practice of first half of life spirituality. These signs are good, helpful, and sometimes necessary, during the first half of life. But if individuals show some of these signs in their second half of life, the signs could indicate a failure to practice a new spirituality which I am calling second half of life spirituality.

1. The ego demands satisfaction:

As I said earlier that developing a strong ego is one of the goals of first half of life spirituality. A noticeable sign that you are developing a strong ego is the ego's demands for satisfaction. For example, you want answers to your questions. When you were studying to become an engineer, you wanted to solve the problems in physics and math. You want to "settle the dust." In the seminary, you might ask your professor, "Father, tell me is it right or wrong to do this?" In sexual matters you may ask, "How far can I go before committing a mortal sin?" In so far as the Eucharist, you may ask, "Father, do you really believe the bread and wine after the consecration are the actual body and blood of Jesus?"

Your desire to have your questions answered stems from internal uncertainty. During the first half of life, you are searching for truth. When you experience something new, you want to know what to believe as true and what to reject as false.

2. Social pressure affects our motivation:

When we practice first half of life spirituality, we are influenced by social pressure. We want to be accepted. We fear rejection. We want to avoid shame. Our actions at times are heavily influenced by our parents, church teaching, and peer pressure. In college we probably act in ways that please our best friends. Often in the practice of first half of life spirituality, our actions are motivated by ignorance, passion, fear, force, and/or habit, so when we act out, we feel guilty.

3. We cling to our private moral superiority:

In the practice of first half of life spirituality, we show signs that we want to protect our ego. To do so, we tend to share with others our private moral superiority. The ego in its desire for acceptance and self-indulgence without guilt will tend to hide imperfection and true sinfulness. While there may be confession of sins of commission, there is a tendency to protect the ego by including, "I haven't missed mass. I haven't used the Lord's name in vain. I said my morning and evening prayers. I tried to be good to everyone." When we practice first half of life spirituality, we rarely see our root sins. We may confess, "I missed mass twice" but we do not try to figure out why. Again, these signs are normal during first half of life spirituality.

4. We tend to be egocentric:

We show signs of practicing first half of life spirituality when we focus in on what is good for us, self-interest. We are basically very egocentric. For example when we practice first half of life spirituality, universal health care, minimum wage increase, fair pensions, environmental issues, and immigration issues are not our concern unless they hurt us in some way. We may hear about the poverty in Haiti, but we are more concerned about the local Catholic school providing playground equipment for our children. People who are greedy on Wall Street are most likely locked up in the practice of first half of life spirituality. The ego tends to think that the world revolves around fulfilling its self-interest. We can think we are entitled; that the world owes us something.

Sadly, so many parishioners who are in their second half of life still show signs of first half of life spirituality. This tendency to be absorbed in self-interest shows up also in politics.

5. We tend to shame others:

We show signs of practicing first half of life spirituality when we shame others so that our ego feels superior. For example, if a child doesn't want to attend Mass, a parent might shame the child by saying, "God will punish you. Don't you know that you are breaking my heart when you do not go with us to Mass?" Those with addictions sometimes shame their parents, friends, or spouse for their problems instead of assuming responsibility.

6. We live our false self:

You mentioned that you read a book by the late Fr. Thomas Merton who was a great spiritual writer and a deceased Cistercian monk. He is credited to be the first to use the term, the false self  to clarify what Jesus surely meant when he said that we must "lose ourselves to find ourselves" (Mark 8:35).

We could define the false self as who we think we are. The false self is good and necessary in the first half of life. Fr. Richard Rohr calls the false self our relative identity; our "container." The false self pertains to our job, education, body image, successes, and gender identity. Many of the signs of first half of life spirituality flow from the false self. Jesus would call the false self our "wineskin."

Fr. Thomas Merton says in his book, New Seeds of Contemplation, "It is then the false self that is our god, and we love everything for the sake of this self." That is why the false self is like the grain of wheat that must die (John 12:24).

We show signs the we practice first half of life spirituality when the false self is easily offended by the words and actions of others. Sometimes at funerals, I have noticed that older individuals who are still practicing first half of life spirituality are still carrying a grudge over some situation that occurred many years ago. Those who are easily offended when they are in their second half of life show signs that they are still living with their false self that is inherently needy and fragile.

Later you will learn that you want to live your true self which is like a clear eye, an eye without any obstruction. Jesus said, "Take the log out of your eye, and then you will see clearly" (Luke 6:42). We think we see clearly when we practice first half of life spirituality, but later we realize that we were not fully conscious of our ego with its duplicity, fears, worries, and insecurity.

7. We have a primitive understanding of the Bible:

We show signs of practicing first half of life spirituality when we tend to accept the Bible as both literally and historically true. We assume to be historically true the stories in the gospels about the birth of Jesus with the star, the crib, and the shepherds. In the Hebrew Scriptures, we think of Jonah and the whale as being a true story.

Those who practice fundamentalism are comfortable staying in the practice of first half of life spirituality. Fundamentalism appeals to certainty, authority, and absolute truth. Thus we find Christian fundamentalism, Muslim fundamentalism, Hindu fundamentalism and Jewish fundamentalism. Fundamentalism relies on authority that provides absolute truths that cannot be questioned or doubted.

8. We think dualistically:

We show signs of practicing first half of life spirituality when we tend to see reality dualistically: secular/spiritual, hot/cold, up/down, right/wrong and good/bad. For example, St. Paul speaks of the dualism of the spirit versus the flesh. "What I do, I do not understand. For I do not do what I want, but I do what I hate....So now it is no longer I who do it, but sin that dwells in me" (Romans 7:15-19).

When we continue to see reality dualistically during the second half of life, we show signs of still labeling people as "we" versus "they." We judge people as "rich or poor," "friend or enemy." We stereotype individuals according to the color of their skin, their age, their education level, their religion, and their country of origin.

9.  Our understanding of "church":

We show signs of practicing first half of life spirituality when we use the word "church" to refer to hierarchical authority. When the word "church" is used, we think, "What does the bishop say? What does the pastor want? What has the pope said about this issue?" There is stress on obedience and submission. In the priestly ordination ceremony, the bishop will say to you in 2016, "Do you promise to be obedient to me and my successors..."

I have noticed that priests who practice first half of life spirituality tend to focus on issues of belonging and believing. They emphasize church teaching that must be believed. They give the impression that beliefs pertaining to the Trinity and Eucharist are definable and understandable. They are concerned with issues involving membership requirements and penalties. For example, "Who can receive the Eucharist? Who can be baptized in our church? Who can be buried in our church?"

10.  We tend to be arrogant:

Beware of arrogance. When we practice first half of life spirituality, we can be arrogant which manifests itself when there is a perceived judgment,"I'm right and you are wrong" without a willingness to dialogue and thereby understand the issues. Instead of attempting to understand the "what" and "why" of another's actions, we tend to judge with an arrogant attitude.

11.  We attempt to convert others:

We show signs of practicing first half of life spirituality when we try to convert others to our way of thinking so as to feel superior. The ego will do almost anything to feel superior over other people. The tendency to convert others can come through apologetics or through the Internet. Politicians use negative advertising on television whereby they say something negative about their opponent. People send us emails with attachments to articles in the press. Sometimes we sense that those who sent the articles are trying to convert us to their way of thinking. Political jokes are sent by email. Usually the joke uplifts their candidate and puts down their opponent.

12.  We attempt to manipulate God:

We show signs of practicing first half of life spirituality when we think we can achieve grace when we do charitable acts and say special prayers. We think that we can manipulate God and receive heavenly rewards. We show signs of thinking that God is a good daddy in the sky who will give us what we want, if we pray the right prayers and make the right sacrifices. In a local church, I picked up a little card that read, "Fridays during Lent are really special! You can gain a Plenary Indulgence on each Lenten Friday by reciting the prayer (on the others side of the card) before a crucifix."

13.  We stress externals:

We show signs of practicing first half of life spirituality when we emphasize externals such as creeds, flags, trophies, badges, correct rituals, Bible quotes, and special clothing. All of these are largely substitutes for actual spirituality. Some priests are caught up in issues like: "Should we have pews with kneelers or not? Should we encourage silence in church or some talking?" Some priests put up signs in their churches telling the people not to speak in God's house. Some priests are concerned as to whether visiting priests during the offertory part of the mass pour water into each chalice or say all the words in the Eucharistic Prayer correctly.

In my next letter to you, I'll apply some signs that are more characteristic of the practice of first half of life spirituality and apply them to the institutional church.

Peace,

Uncle Matthew

Letter # 3
Tuesday, March 29, 2011

Dear Uncle Matthew,

Thank you for explaining to me the meaning of the paradigm of "Loving the Two Halves of Life." I also better understand now the distinction between religion and spirituality. The Biblical quote about the wineskins and wine made it very clear to me why from now on you will be simplifying things by concentrating on spirituality; the practice of first and second half of life spirituality. Since I have an engineering background, I would describe the practice of first half of life spirituality as building the foundation for a house. The practice of second half of life spirituality is the building.

I am familiar with Alcoholics' Anonymous. When I was in college, my roommate told me about his dad's sobriety through AA. I often stayed with my classmate's family on weekends. The family was not religious (church goers), but they respected and helped one another which to me meant that they all practiced some form of spirituality.

Thank you also for sending me signs that indicate the practice of first half of life spirituality. I appreciated that you said these signs are normal and good in the first half of life. I can use these signs as a test to look at my own behavior and character.

You seem to be telling me that the overall goal of the paradigm of "Loving the Two Halves of Life" is to provide a spiritual roadmap that will greatly assist people to see the value of pursuing a rich spirituality which will transform them to become fully human and fully alive. I like the concept of wholeness. I met guys in college who spent a lot of time going to the gym to develop their bodies, but they were not socially developed. At the NSA, I met some men with PhD's in electrical engineering, but they were arrogant and lacking in compassion. In the seminary, some men are very clerical, almost rigid in the way they adhere to doctrines, which shows that they lack wholeness. I do want to be fully alive whereby I know how to use all my God-given talents in a good way. I have met many young men who cannot cry and many old men who cannot smile. That is a sign of a lack of wholeness.

I never knew that there are different spiritualities. Also, your reflections have alerted me that once I know all about the Catholic religion and develop a solid spirituality here in the seminary, later I will have to build upon or modify my religion and spirituality so that it is meaningful and helpful to me as an adult. This transition requires a willingness to change which is necessary in almost every aspect of life if we are to become fully human.

I hope you had a wonderful birthday on the 17th. I prayed for you at mass. I was saddened about the terrible earthquake in Japan that caused that tsunami on March 10. I was unfamiliar with tsunamis until that occurrence made international news.

When I was reading over the personal signs we show when we practice first half of life spirituality, I wondered if the institutional church practices and promotes first half of life spirituality. What do you think? I await your reply with anticipation.

Peace,

Joey

Response to Letter #3
Friday, April 15, 2011

Dear Joey,

Yes, that tsunami was terrible in Japan. We prayed for the victims in our church. Hopefully, good will come out of this tragic situation.

This Sunday we will celebrate Passion Sunday. I've always liked that liturgy with the proclamation of the Passion. Soon, Easter will be here. I hope your Lent is going well. Today Federal taxes are due. I submitted my tax forms last month. Not that the liturgy and paying taxes have anything in common except that it confirms that life is constantly a mixture of the sublime and the mundane.

I just finished reading Fr. Richard Rohr's new book, Falling Upward-a Spirituality for the Two Halves of Life. It is outstanding. He shares so much food for thought and spiritual growth. I have on my bookshelf thirteen of his books. He has spiritually fed me and so many others for many years with his tapes, CD's, books, conferences, and DVDs. Somehow Rohr in each of his works brings some new insights to me. He is amazing!

Most of us when we are in the first half of life think that if we achieve the goals I mentioned earlier, we are set for life in the area of religion. It is a rude awakening, accompanied by suffering in one form or another, to realize that later in life we must strive to accomplish new goals, and some of the goals we accomplished during the first half of life have to be changed, modified, or discarded. That's why I find this paradigm on the two halves of life to be so insightful.

Now, you find your religion to be exciting because you are in an atmosphere of growth. You are secure. But later in life when you are not in an atmosphere of growth and lack the security of good health, children who love you, and a safe home, you will be challenged. Unless you have the "armor of God," as St. Paul said, to cope with the many new challenges in life, you risk getting discouraged, and you will find yourself unprepared and unlikely to persevere (Ephesians 6:13). That is why you will need to eventually pursue the practice of second half of life spirituality.

In my last letter to you, I shared with you many personal and psychological signs that individuals show when they practice first half of life spirituality. You asked me if the institutional church practices first half of life spirituality. The answer is yes. In fact, most religious institutions do practice first half of life spirituality which is necessary for our religious development. It is important that we accept and obey the way church structures are designed during the first half of life, but in the second half of life, we may at some point discover that these structures are contributing to keeping us spiritually immature.

I can think of three important signs that could indicate the institutional church practices first half of life spirituality.

Signs of the practice of first half of life spirituality in the Church:

1.  A patriarchal system:

The practice of first half of life spirituality supports a patriarchal system in the Church in which males predominate in the roles of leadership, social privilege, moral authority, and control of all the church property. Men have all the power and control.

For example, one day, by the grace of God, you will be ordained first a transitional deacon and then a priest. In the ordination ceremony of candidates for the priesthood, we notice many signs of the practice of first half of life spirituality. Only males are seated in the sanctuary. Only priests pray over the newly ordained men in the sanctuary, and only the priests exchange with the newly ordained men the Kiss of Peace. The length of the mass is quite long in comparison to a wedding mass. Words and phrases such as "rank" and "advanced to" are noticeable. In viewing an ordination ceremony, it is easy to get the impression that the newly ordained is not being ordained to serve the People of God as much as to serve the "Church" with a male hierarchical connotation. One could get the impression that the newly ordained is joining an exclusive club of males.

The practice of a patriarchal system leads people to believe in a Male God and a Distant God. These images of God are signs that an institutional church is practicing first half of life spirituality.

2. Authority:

Since the male church leaders have all the power and control, they can show signs of using their authority in practicing first half of life spirituality when they emphasize centralized authority rather than practicing the principle of subsidiarity that allows tasks to be performed at a local level. Rules and regulations tend to be looked upon as absolutes. The trust level among the clergy is often low when bishops use their authority seemingly without consultation. Obedience is stressed rather than a Vatican II spirit of collegiality. Extreme vetting is often exercised to stress the leader's authority. Sometimes religious authority figures try to control and determine an individual's spirituality.

I'll give some practical examples that indicate that church leaders use their authority in ways that show signs of the practice of first half of life spirituality.

a. Liturgy:

The General Instruction of the Roman Missal was promulgated in Rome in 2002 and in the United States in 2003. The GIRM gave detailed instructions for celebrating the liturgy. There is a norm about who can open the tabernacle that limits access by laypersons. There is a norm that states"extraordinary ministers of Holy Communion should not approach the altar before the priest has received Communion." The GIRM says that the sacred vessels are to be purified by the priest, the deacon, or an instituted acolyte (a seminarian).

During weekend masses, many sacred vessels may be used so that the people are offered both the precious Body and Blood of Jesus. Laypersons who are designated communion ministers are allowed to handle the sacred vessels during mass for the distribution of the Eucharist and Precious Blood. Since it has been the practice for many years for lay ministers to wash the sacred vessels, some people ask why the change. Most priests want to be available after mass with the parishioners rather than being in the sacristy washing vessels.

The same would seem true with who can open the tabernacle. Common sense would allow both clerics and designated lay ministers to open the tabernacle.

Some bishops who practice first half of life spirituality might send out a guideline from the General Instruction of the Roman Missal (154) that says, "If the celebrant chooses to offer the sign of peace, the priest is not to leave the sanctuary, but is only to exchange the sign of peace with the deacon or other ministers nearest him." Celebrants who practice first half of life spirituality might follow this guideline.

b.  Humanae Vitae:

Pope Paul VI set up a commission to advise him on the matter of birth control. He ignored his commission's report that recommended a change in church teaching, and in 1968, he issued the encyclical, Humanae Vitae, on contraception. All bishops, as a condition for becoming a bishop, have promised they will never question that encyclical.

Fr. Charlie Curran, a brilliant moral theologian who was at Catholic University of America, dissented from Humanae Vitae. Later he was removed from the faculty of the Catholic University of America as a dissident against the Catholic Church's moral teachings.

There is a need for definiteness, principles, and creeds in the Church. However, there is also a need for reflection, deliberation, dialogue, the unfolding of God's spirit, and creative energies.

c. The ordination of women:

On May 22, 1994, Pope John Paul II published a document, Ordinatio Sacerdotalis, in which he said the institutional church has no authority whatsoever to confer priestly ordination on women. He made this announcement without the consensus of the College of Bishops.

Later in November 1995, the Congregation for the Doctrine of the Faith declared that this ruling of the pope was to be regarded as an "infallible" teaching. Rome decreed that Catholics were forbidden to discuss the matter publicly, and bishops were commanded to enforce the ban.

A sign of first half of life spirituality is to demand obedience without questioning.

d. Dominus Jesus:

In June 2000, the Congregation for the Doctrine of the Faith issued the Declaration, Dominus Jesus, which was written for bishops under Cardinal Joseph Ratzinger, later Pope Benedict XVI. Dominus Jesus represents a Vatican attempt to insist that certain church teachings are beyond questioning.

Catholics who practice first half of life spirituality would accept without question this declaration.

Since the church's hierarchical structure encourages people to believe the clergy represents God on earth, authority can easily be misused. The institutional church leaders use of authority supports a belief in a Vindictive God who threatens us with Hell if we do not obey God.

3.  The repression of new Ideas:

The institutional church represses new ideas. Thus, questioning is discouraged. The repression of new ideas naturally flows from a belief in an Exclusive God that leads people to believe that the hierarchy alone is privileged to know the truth. Thus, those who have new ideas are fearful of making their thoughts known when authority figures throughout history have threatened those who presented new ideas with condemnation, burning at the stake, excommunication, or suspension.

a.  Oaths:

I mentioned earlier that during my preparation to become a priest during theology, I had to take an oath against modernism. Pope Pius X, in 1907, decreed that every candidate for priestly ordination had to take an oath against modernism. I recall signing a Latin statement, and I had no idea what I signed! The decree remained in effect until 1967, when it was replaced by the Profession of Faith, updated in 1989.

A sign of the practice of first half of life spirituality is found in those priests who believe that all truth is proclaimed in the Profession of Faith so there is no need to explore new possibilities.

b.  Sr. Carmel McEnroy:

In May 1995, tenured professor Sr. Carmel McEnroy was dismissed from St. Meinrad's School of Theology for signing an open letter to Pope John Paul II asking that discussion continue on the question of ordaining women to the priesthood. Her dismissal shows signs that her superiors were practicing first half of life spirituality.

c. The Creed:

Every Sunday at Mass we recite the Nicene Creed. Some spiritual authors have written extensively on the need to update our cosmology. For example we often refer to heaven as up in the sky and hell below the ground. That is no longer a valid view of reality with a newer cosmology. Church leaders are reluctant to update what we recite in the Creed.

Conclusion:

In another letter, I will explain the different images of God that are found in the practice of first half of life spirituality.

I hope that these three signs of the practice of first half of life spirituality in the institutional church are helpful. These signs are appropriate in helping us to be formed in the practice of first half of life spirituality, but later when people are introduced to the practice of second half of life spirituality, they may question these signs.

Peace,

Uncle Matthew

Letter #4
Wednesday, April 27, 2011

Dear Uncle Matthew,

Thank you for your last letter that outlined three signs that the institutional church practices first half of life spirituality. I was curious about whether or not church institutions practiced first half of life spirituality, but I didn't realize how this practice can prevent spiritual maturity later in life. I guess I thought these three signs were just part of God's design for his Church, but I realize now that human hands are busy at work as well! You are helping me to see what I was unconscious of before our correspondence.

I appreciate all your work in preparing responses to my questions. I am new to the seminary and to a mature understanding of our Catholic religion, so I feel the temptation to just stay grounded in what I am learning here. The material that my professors present is solid. You keep saying that it is important for me when I become a priest not to always stay grounded in what I learn in the seminary, but to gradually try to modify my religion and deepen my spirituality as I mature in age. I presume modification and change will enable me to be more pastoral, a sign of a good shepherd.

We celebrated the Easter Vigil last Saturday evening. That was the first time I attended an Easter Vigil. There were many readings from the Old and New Testament. I wasn't assigned to serve, so I could observe everything. To be honest, I really do not understand the liturgy, so I need the seminary training to appreciate our rich liturgical tradition.

I'm not sure yet what God thinks about my sexual desires. At the age of 25, my sexual desires are strong! Hopefully, our professors here will give us some instructions in that regard. I wonder if our understanding of human sexuality will also have to change in the second half of life. Will first half of life institutions ever be willing to change their long-standing views on human sexuality?

In your first letter to me, you listed various goals that I should strive to achieve in my first half of life. You said that our images of God greatly impact our ability to achieve our goals since they influence our motivation for our actions and inactions. In your last letter to me, you spoke about a Male God, a Distant God, a Vindictive God, and an Exclusive God.

Presently, when I think about God, I have an image of God living up in Heaven. I never thought about my images of God before! Isn't that interesting? Since I am quite careful to observe all the rules in the seminary so as to be approved as a candidate for priesthood, I guess I have an image of God who is concerned about whether or not I observe the rules. My earlier training taught me certain actions were good and certain actions were bad so my image of God is tied up with reward and punishment. It is hard for me to imagine God in any other way.

Could you send me some typical images of God that most people form in their minds during the first half of life? That would be helpful to me.

Thanks.

Joey

Response to Letter #4
Thursday, May 12, 2011

Dear Joey,

Before I plunge in to spiritual matters, I've been absorbed in the news about Osama bin Laden who was killed in Pakistan on May 2 by Navy Seals. Thus, he is no longer a threat to the world-community. He founded al-Qaeda and that organization claimed responsibility for the September 11 attacks on the United States. Hopefully, his death will lessen the chances of terrorism. Time will tell! It is important for us to always integrate world events with the practice of our spirituality.

Handling our sexual desires is a challenge for all of us. Be patient. Avail yourself of your spiritual director at the seminary, and be open and honest with him. Ask him questions. On a one-to-one basis, he may be able to help you if your spiritual director is a wise person in the ways of the body and spirit and if he can carefully balance discipline with self-acceptance. Spiritual direction is an art, and although most people think priests are good spiritual directors, that is not always the case. Spiritual direction requires spiritual discernment and pastoral sensitivity.

I am aware so often as I celebrate liturgies in different parishes of the spiritual hunger that exists. Catholics need to know about the two halves of life spirituality. For example, today, I was in the sacristy before mass, and a lady came in to ask me a question.

She is seventy-two years old. She is going on a cruise this weekend with her son and daughter-in-law, and there will not be a Catholic chaplain to say mass. She was concerned as to whether she should be going on the cruise since she will miss mass. Her question points out that if Catholics never transition to an understanding of second half of life spirituality, they risk retaining a terrible image of a Vengeful God when that image should have been replaced years earlier. Who would want to worship a god that would condemn a person for not attending mass when there was no mass? This example illustrates that many people practice a religion that is based on fear and not love. So much life is not lived because of our false and constraining images of God.

Introduction to some typical images of God that we form during the first half of life:

It is so important for us to be conscious of our images of God. At your request, I will gladly share some different images of God that are quite prevalent during the first half of life. But before I share specific images of God that we hold, let me say a few words about the importance of being aware of our images of God.

Early in life, we begin to form different images of God that are based on how we observe our mom and dad. We think of God as a personal being. We think of God as seeing, listening, and responding to us like our parents. Our images of God change as we grow. All our experiences in life, for good or for ill, can modify our images of God. An image of God doesn't contain God but essentially says, "God is like ...." When you take your sacred scripture courses, you will read that God is like a father, a judge, a potter, a rock, a fortress, a warrior, a friend, and a lawgiver. And these images, full of associations, shape how we feel, think, and act towards God and then towards others around us.

The emphasis on the relationship with members of our family is paramount. Both the parent and the child have to change as they grow or else there will be disastrous results. For example, if a child's dad was cruel, the child will probably acquire an image of a Vindictive God. If a child's mom was compassionate, the child probably will acquire an image of a Compassionate God. Then the child will tend to be compassionate toward others. Compassion is a desired virtue for a good shepherd. As our understanding of life deepens through the years, so too should our images of God change and mature, if our relationship with God is to remain real and vital. Mature images of God enable us to embrace a larger world.

Also an appreciation of the process of "projecting" can help us to understand how our images of God impact us profoundly. Often we "project" on others qualities that are not actually present in them. We may see someone as a hero, but it is our projection that makes that image plausible. We do the same thing with God. As we have different experiences in life, we tend to project on God human qualities. For example, if we are joyful, we may tend to have an image of a Joyful God. If we are unforgiving, we may tend to have an image of an Unforgiving God. The fourteenth century Dominican mystic, Meister Eckhart, said, "All the names we give to God come from an understanding of ourselves." Projections tend to give us images of God in our own image and likeness. So if we want to know God, for what God is in reality, we need to remove our own projections upon God. Our knowledge about projection allows us to understand the ancient texts of Buddhism that say, "God has a million faces."

The New Testament, scholar, theologian, and author Marcus Borg wrote a book entitled The God We Never Knew. In his book he said that our images of God matter because they can make God seem either credible or incredible, plausible or highly improbable. Our concept of God can make God seem distant or near, absent or present. How we see God also directly affects our sense of what the Christian life is all about and our ability to become good shepherds.

Let me give you an example of Marcus J. Borg's insight. The book, Alcoholics Anonymous was written in 1939 primarily by one of Alcoholics Anonymous' founders, Bill W. In the "Big Book,"

Bill wrote a chapter about his life in which he shared that a friend tried to get him to turn his life over to God, but Bill had prejudices about God. Bill said, "The word God still aroused a certain antipathy. When the thought was expressed that there might be a God personal to me, this feeling was intensified. I didn't like the idea. I could go for such conceptions as Creative Intelligence, Universal Mind or Spirit of Nature, but I resisted the thought of a Czar of the Heavens, however loving His sway might be."

Bill's friend then suggested a novel idea when he said, "Why don't you choose your own image of God?" Bill soon realized that he was willing to believe in a Power greater than himself.

Some spiritual writers say we become over time what we believe. I heard Fr. Richard Rohr say, "Your image of God creates you." For example, if we adore and revere a Judgmental God, we may become judgmental ourselves. St. Bernard of Clairvaux, a twelfth century saint and doctor of the Church, said, "What we love we shall grow to resemble." We can deceive ourselves into thinking that our own judgments are but small acts mirroring God. We can think we are acting the way God desires. Or, further still, and perhaps worst of all, if our image of God is remote and cold, indifferent to the human condition, then we too may become callous and insensitive to the needs and sufferings of others. Self righteousness is the result of uncritical thought about how our images of God may not reflect reality.

Likewise, our concept of Church flows from our image of God. Belief in a Judgmental God can influence belief in a judgmental hierarchal church in which authority should come from the "top down." With this image of God, we can think that we are to do what the hierarchal church says since we do not want to be judged by a Judgmental God.

Our images of God should not come from abstractions, but from the images we have of Jesus, testified to in the gospels, who ministered to the marginalized. St. Paul told us that Jesus is the visible image of the invisible God. Thus, especially for you as a seminarian, your images of the Church will change as your images of God change. When we have an image of a Compassionate God, we desire a Church that reflects the compassion and forgiveness of God.

During World War II, Corrie ten Boom, a Dutch Christian, helped along with her father many Jews to escape from the Nazi Holocaust. She said, "God has no grandchildren... God has only sons and daughters." What does that mean to you? It means to me that it is up to each generation to have a personal experience of God. We shouldn't accept as final, complete, or adequate the images of God handed down to us in order for us to be fully human and alive. Each generation has to be converted. Each generation has to be renewed. Each person has to hear the Word and respond personally to that Word. Jesus, in Mark 8:29, asked his disciples the question, "Who do you say that I am?" Perhaps Jesus in asking this question was not only seeking an affirmation of faith, but he was pointing to the deeper question of the character and nature of God.

You have probably heard this story, but it is worth repeating. It is a story of change and transformation, a prolonged wrestling with God, and how we image God. The story shows the influence of human relationships as being essential in the formation of our images of God.

Once upon a time there was a North African Catholic woman named Monica. She had a son who was brilliant, but he showed no interest in Christianity. Monica's husband was a successful business man, but he too had no interest in Christianity. Monica's son's lack of interest in the Church broke her heart. She prayed that one day he might receive the gift of faith. When Monica's husband died, she did not inherit anything which was the custom. She became dependent on her son. She lived in a house with her son, his mistress, and their son.

By the time Monica was an old woman, her son changed. He showed signs of transformation. He began attending mass. He became a friend of the local bishop. Her son's name was Augustine. Monica's whole life was dedicated to helping her son find faith through her prayers, her unconditional love, and her good example. She provided her son many glimpses of God over the years.

Once Augustine embraced the Church, he gave up his mistress and his son. He became a priest and later a bishop. Today we honor him in the Church as St. Augustine, one of the greatest church fathers. We honor his mother as St. Monica.

In my next letter to you, I promise to share some typical images of God that are found when we practice first half of life spirituality.

Peace,

Uncle Matthew

Letter #5
Tuesday, May 31, 2011

Dear Uncle Matthew,

Thank you for your last letter that discussed the importance of being aware of our images of God. I never realized before that our images of God form to a large degree the character of our religion and spirituality. I never knew that our images of God were so important. You are the first person that pointed out to me the important role of projection. I had not heard the story of Saint Monica. I was not yet in the seminary last August when her feast day was celebrated. I guess I have much to learn.

The school year is over. I had a nice Memorial Day weekend at home. While at home, I try to attend daily mass at the parish. Yesterday, at mass, my pastor told us about the history of Memorial Day. During the Civil War, President Lincoln dedicated the Gettysburg Battle Cemetery to honor those who died. Lincoln said, "These dead shall not have died in vain." Echoing these sentiments, Congress made Memorial Day a Federal holiday in 1971 to honor all those veterans living and deceased.

My first year in the seminary went by quickly. My favorite courses were the history of philosophy and ethics because they are so practical. The material in philosophy is so different from my engineering background in college and my work in computer research at the National Security Agency (NSA) because philosophy presumes and encourages plurality of thought whereas science presumes certitude.

I leave next week for my first summer assignment in a parish. I'm a bit apprehensive about my assignment since this will be a new experience for me, and I always find that new experiences stress me. But, I look forward to the opportunity to integrate the knowledge that I accrued during the last academic year with some pastoral insights that I expect will arise in the parish. It should be an experience of the "rubber hitting the road."

I'm eager to continue this conversation with you, and I look forward as you share with me some images of God that we acquire in the first half of life. You are a great help to me.


Peace,

Joey

Response to Letter #5
Friday, June 17, 2011

Dear Joey,

You and I share something in common. Neither one of us attended a Catholic school before entering the seminary.

You now have a chance during the summer to reflect upon what you learned during your first year in the seminary. Enjoy finding God in nature, new friendships, and most of all in your parish assignment.

It is important to keep abreast of what is happening in the Church today. For example, I was sorry to hear about the removal of Bishop William Morris in Australia. Did you hear about that news? Hans Kung and other theologians are urging a peaceful revolution against what they call "Roman absolutism."

I have also been following the story on Fr. Roy Bourgeois, a Maryknoll priest who founded  the School of Americas Watch (SOA WATCH) to protest the training of mainly Latin American military officers by the United States Department of Defense. He claims that some of the graduates of the academy have been involved in actions that violate the rules of the Geneva Conventions. He met recently with his fellow Maryknoll community.

In this letter, I will share with you two typical first half of life images of God, a Distant God and an Exclusive God.

1. A Distant God:

Your grandparents remember the Catholic Church before the Second Vatican Council (1962-1965). The Mass texts, songs, and prayers were in Latin. On special occasions the choir sang songs in Gregorian chant which was foreign to the average person. In churches, a railing separated the people from the sanctuary. The assembly observed what the priest did at the altar. They got the impression that God lived far away from this world and, like Latin, was unknowable. The leaders of the Church in that era taught Catholics to adore a Distant God. They thought God was separate from what God created including themselves. They believed in a sharp and absolute distinction between the sacred and the secular. You mentioned that you think of God as living up in Heaven. This indeed reflects an image of a Distant God.

Mirroring the distant relationship with this remote God, when I was in the seminary before Vatican II, we were likewise not encouraged to develop close friendships with either men or women. The book, The Imitation of Christ by Thomas a Kempis, was a widely read devotional book at that time. Seminarians took very seriously the words in The Imitation of Christ, "Be not familiar with any woman; but recommend all good women in general to God."

The impression given was that the ideal priest had no intimate friendships with men or women; only with a Distant God. You most likely already know that friendships are very important if you are going to be transformed into a person who is fully human and fully alive. We are social beings. We need to be cared for by others and by denying this closeness with others, we become less human.

Reinforcing a sense of separation, silence was stressed in the seminary. In our seminary, we were not allowed to speak after

9:00 PM. We could not visit the rooms of other seminarians. Seminarians took seriously the words in The Imitation of Christ that said, "Withdraw thy heart from the love of visible things, and turn thyself to things invisible." This advocacy of solitude, when embraced by a mature and prepared soul, may indeed be wise counsel. But as a universal ideal for young novices, this advocacy presents potential unintended consequences. Among the consequences are pre-occupation with self. Too much silence can suppress natural and youthful gregariousness.

This promoting of separation, distance, and isolation extended to world events as well. In my seminary, television was limited to one-half hour each night for the evening national news. There was one black and white television for the entire student body. There was one daily newspaper in the library for the entire student body. This attitude of separation promoted much "navel gazing" while the world cried out.

With an image of a Distant God, life on earth was not thought to be holy unless ordained men blessed food, buildings, water, homes, medals, crosses, oils, graves, bread, and wine. The blessings contributed to a dualistic attitude that certain objects were holy and other objects were unholy. A separation was made between holy and unholy, clean and unclean.

With an image of a Distant God, reinforced in these many ways, priests who are my age and older often became unconsciously and uncritically like the God they adored. As a result, many of my peers tend to be distant from people. They have difficulty seeing God in all of creation. They encourage others not to speak in church except at the Kiss of Peace. They find God in church buildings, statues, scapulars, clerical robes, and stained-glass windows. They find God to be present when they are alone in prayer. Being with others is often a distraction for them.

Priests as shepherds who have an image of a Distant God would be greatly limited in their ability to inspire people to experience the presence of God daily in the many circumstances of life. It is not that solitude is bad. At times God does seem remote when we need God the most. Even Jesus retreated to the desert, to a garden, and to silent nights in prayer. But, as with Jesus, the point of solitude is to be energized by closer communion with God so as to return to the community. If there is no balance between solitude and active ministry, the shepherd can seem cool and impersonal. This is in contrast to the ministry of Jesus who consistently revealed God's love to the multitudes.

2. An Exclusive God:

Another image of God is that of an Exclusive God. In the seminary, you are treated as being very special. You are affirmed at home and in the seminary more than the average person your age. This is affirming, but it influences your image of God. Perhaps, by way of compensation for a Distant God, seminarians are offered an image of an Exclusive God, a God who has favorites which naturally includes them.

When I was in the seminary, there was a daily stress on hierarchy which reflects and reinforces a sense of exclusivity. In the chapel, we sat in order according to class ranking. The seminarians closer to ordination sat closer to the altar. There was a stress on titles: "Reverend, Very Reverend, Father, Your Excellency, Your Eminence, Monsignor, Holy Father..." A system or organization in which people are ranked one above the other according to their status and authority is more readily embraced by those who are assured that they are among God's favorites.

Before Vatican II, usually the only women in seminaries were nuns in the kitchen, mostly foreign-born, sixty years old or older. That was all part of the patriarchal nature of the Church. Men ran the Church. Only celibate males were ordained as priests. Women were permitted proximity to those in leadership positions only as servants and as "auxiliary" members of the Church.

We become like the God we adore. And so, as with a Distant God, we become like the Exclusive God. We are subtly taught , and therefore think, that God prefers clerics to lay people. We can easily think that God loves celibates more than married people. We can think that God favors men over women. We can think that God prefers Catholics to Protestants and Christians to non-Christians. This mind set can come to permeate all we think and do.

When Church leaders reflect and endorse an image of an Exclusive God, patriarchy makes sense. It seems natural and good. Yet it is worth questioning whether those church leaders who believe in a patriarchal system are fully equipped to be good shepherds in the complexities of parish life or in the world at large. A patriarchal system diminishes the ability for all church members to think or question because answers to life's many challenges run along pre-ordained channels of authority, often distorting reality. Thus, there is the tendency to find certitude in a higher male authority figure rather than in doing the necessary work to see the world as it is, and to do the hard work of discernment that is at the core of developing one's own conscience. A patriarchal system tends to think that some people are teachers and the rest of the people are students rather than viewing everyone equally as both teacher and student. If we are not open minded as students, we compromise the scope of our understanding and knowledge. If we are not open minded as teachers, we lose the spark of curiosity and the unquenchable thirst for truth.

Many people today have an image of an Exclusive God, expressed in many ways, to the detriment of embracing the full richness of God's creation. Theologians often warn us about clericalism and careerism, both are possible symptoms of holding on to an image of an Exclusive God. Those who hold on to an image of an Exclusive God present to others a very small God that is inadequate and in conflict with a healthy world view.

I hope this helps you, Joey. Let me know what you think. I await your reply.

Peace,

Uncle Matthew

Letter #6
Friday, July 1, 2011

Dear Uncle Matthew,

Thank you for sending me your descriptions of a Distant God and an Exclusive God. I grew up with those images of God, and I still have them. In the seminary, bishops come for visits to meet with their seminarians. They act like they are God's favorites. Even when I am in this parish for a summer assignment, many parishioners treat me better than when I worked during the summers while I was attending Virginia Tech.

My parish assignment is going well, but there are challenges. It is quiet here. I live in a rectory with two priests who are associate pastors. The pastor lives in another house. We do not have meals together. They give money to me each month to buy food. I feel lonely at times since we do not pray together. I guess this is a taste of real life in the priesthood. Already I am discovering that without significant friendships, it is difficult for me to follow the church's rules on chastity.

I did not hear about the firing of Bishop William Morris in Australia, but after you brought it to my attention, I researched him in the library. I found out that in 2006, he released a pastoral letter that discussed the declining number of priests in remote parishes in his diocese. The letter called for the discussion of the ordination of married men and women. He was removed because he challenged the teaching of John Paul II who said that the Church has no authority to confer priestly ordination on women.

What are your impressions of Fr. Roy Bourgeois? I am saddened that he is not allowed to express his beliefs that differ from the leaders in the Church. His actions display, like those of Bishop Morris, opposition to the official church teaching regarding the ordination of women. Rome does not tolerate a different view point.

Can you share with me more images of God that we commonly internalize and form during the first half of life? These early images of God, if I understand you, are the foundation of first half of life spirituality.

Peace,

Joey

Response to Letter #6
Monday, July 18, 2011

Dear Joey,

I'm glad that we talked on the phone about your summer assignment. I am concerned about you since this adjustment to a new experience in life is difficult for you.

You asked my opinion of Fr. Roy Bourgeois. I once met Fr. Roy at a Trappist Monastery in Conyers, GA, where he was living there for a period of time. I view him as a prophetic individual who will eventually be exiled from the Catholic Church. He, like Bishop Morris, have views that are not acceptable to the institutional church, so they must recant or be exiled.

Thank you for sharing with me your struggles with chastity. I know many priests who view the rules of chastity differently from the church's official teaching. I'm not saying that to dissuade you from living a chaste life, but I share this observation with you to lessen any guilt you may be experiencing. In this letter, I'll try to show you that our images of God, formed early in life, have much to do with our understanding of chastity.

Just as you are starting to realize that you have internalized images of God as Distant and Exclusive, you most likely hold images of God as Vengeful and Preoccupied with Sex.

3. A Vengeful God:

Through early parental and grade-school training, most likely you were taught to believe in a Vengeful God that rewards people with Heaven or punishes people by sending them to Hell. For example, in Matthew's gospel there is the story of the final judgment when the Son of Man arrives to judge the nations by separating the sheep from the goats. The goats are condemned to the eternal flames (Matthew 25:31-46). When we practice first half of life spirituality, we assume passages like this are literal words spoken by Jesus.

When we practice first half of life spirituality, we believe that one mortal sin can send us to Hell for all eternity. With this absolute threat hanging over our heads, it is easy for us to relate to God not out of love but out of fear. Thus, many times we keep the Commandments out of fear instead of out of love.

There is a judgmental side of God as seen in Jesus. In the gospels (Matthew 23) we notice that Jesus was critical of the Scribes and Pharisees in his day because they tended to be hypocrites. He even called them "blind guides." Jesus stressed what is inside of a person whereas the Scribes and Pharisees were more concerned with externals. There needs to be a balance. In the journey toward wholeness, the judgmental side of God is only one aspect of God and not the dominant character of God.

Some people during the first half of life derive their image of a Vengeful God from the art-work they see in churches. I remember, Joey, when you were in high school we visited the Shrine of the Immaculate Conception in DC. Remember the mosaic of Jesus in the North apse? Jesus has on a red garment, his hands are raised up, and he has fire coming from his crown. He looks vengeful.

We learn at an early age that Santa Claus gives wonderful gifts but only if children are good in the unseen eyes of an unseen person. In the first half of life, it is easy to assume that God is in this basic sense like Santa Claus. God is "making his list and checking it twice, going to find out who is naughty and nice."

Years ago, there was a newsman by the name of Walter Cronkite (1916 - 2009) who was the anchorman for CBS evening news for nineteen years. I remember in a survey that he was voted as "the most trusted man in America." The survey asked children who they would like to spend a weekend with: Walter Cronkite or God. The children preferred Walter Cronkite.

The choice to be with Walter Cronkite for a weekend shows that the Catholic Church has a lot of work to do so as to convey an image of God as trustworthy and merciful. Priests who celebrate the Eucharist should be mindful in their homilies of presenting God as a God that can be trusted. Trust is essential for any strong relationship. Homilists need to be careful when they stress power and instill fear so that the good news that we believe in a Merciful God who unconditionally loves everyone is not missed.

When you study the New Testament you will notice that changing peoples' image of God was at the core of Jesus' mission. Jesus was always trying to change peoples' images of God.

In the Hebrew Scriptures, we can read that God destroyed whole cities. God at times was angry. God at times appeared to be jealous and vengeful. God loved some people and hated other people. God blessed some people and cursed others. God could love, but then God could withdraw love. The people were fearful of exclusion and banishment.

Jesus advanced and embodied a different image of God. He did not, of course, talk in terms of "image" or state this explicitly, but rather he told parables exemplifying a new vision in the Sermon on the Mount. And most profoundly, he demonstrated, he incarnated, the love of God in his own being and actions. Our faith today believes St. Paul's teaching that Jesus is the visible image of the invisible God.

The English mystic, Julian of Norwich (1342-1416) said, "I saw no kind of vengeance in God. In God is endless friendship, space, life and being… I saw wrath and vengeance only on our part. God forgives that in us."

If we keep an image of a Vengeful God later in the second half of life, we risk being harshly judgmental. We may lack compassion. We may think that God doesn't love sinners the way God loves obedient people. We may feel that we have permission to avoid sinners and write them off as "lost" and unworthy of our time and attention. An image of God as Vengeful can justify capital punishment, a lack of compassion for refugees, war, revenge, and torture. In our late years of life, if we keep this image of God, we will still believe in reward and punishment, strictly and narrowly defined.

### 4.  A God Preoccupied with Sex:

Paradoxically, the images of a Distant and Exclusive God often leads to an image of God who is Preoccupied with Sex. On one hand this doesn't make sense. One would think that a remote God couldn't be concerned with such physical details of earthly life. But there is a different logic at work here. If we seek to become like the image of God we hold, then we too will seek to distance ourselves from physical intimacies, to view them as inferior, as dirty, as wrong. And if we are among the exclusive, then certainly we think that we can have the discipline to live the ideal. During the first half of life, especially during adolescence, our sexual instincts are strong. We experience strong temptations. When I was in the seminary, we were taught that all sexual sins are serious sins, mortal sins, and thus of the gravest nature requiring constant vigilance. Thus, there is a tendency to think that the big sins in life are sexual in nature.

This preoccupation with sex, naturally, within a hierarchical organization, is conveyed with the psychology of the Church to the priests and laity with varied consequences. It is important to understand the psychology of sexuality as it will have a profound influence upon others. A layman told me that during the course of his long life, he had only two bad experiences in the confessional. Both bad experiences dealt with sex. When he was about eight years old, he played doctor with a girl, and later he played doctor with a boy. He went to confession. Whatever the priest said upset him. He ran out of the confessional in tears, full of fear and shame. Later in high school, he went to confession after he nearly masturbated, and the priest drilled him. "Why? When? Where? How?" The priest's questions really upset him. He felt like he was being questioned by a voyeur-judge.

Those who have an image of a God Preoccupied with Sex become preoccupied with sex themselves. They might refer to the virtue of chastity as the singular litmus test of their own holiness to the exclusion of cultivating the many positive virtues of the Christian life; for example, love, humility, devotion, dedication to the truth, and having a passion for social justice.

I read a good book entitled, The Lost Child of Philomena Lee by Martin Sixsmith. The book tells the true story of Philomena who got pregnant as a young women in 1952, and her father sent her to an Abbey at Roscrea in Tipperary, Ireland, to have her child. I hope this book will be made into a movie because the book shows that Philomena's image of a God Preoccupied with Sex contributed to fifty years of suffering guilt over her sin of having sex, and of giving birth, outside of wedlock.

When an image of a God Preoccupied with Sex is held on to, there is also the possibility of not seeing the issues involving peace and justice as being of far greater importance to both the human family and to God.

Those who hold on to an image of God preoccupied with sex can become highly judgmental of others who had been divorced many times. They might think that someone like the late Elizabeth Taylor who had been married eight times could not possibly have been as holy as a virgin.

When we practice first half of life spirituality, it is easy for us to think that all sexual thoughts that lead to sexual sins must be removed. We may attempt to simply use will power to root out all our lustful thoughts. In Matthew's gospel there is the parable of the weeds and the wheat (Matthew 13:24). This parable could describe the spirituality of those who cling to an image of a God Preoccupied with Sex. They will see all their sexual thoughts not as good thoughts but rather as 'weeds' that must be eliminated. Thus, they attempt to pluck out anything sexual instead of learning to integrate their own "wheat and weeds." Further encouragement is given in the Imitation of Christ that might suggest all sexual thoughts to be bad. The Imitation of Christ says, "If every year we rooted out one vice, we should soon become perfect men." Later, we will discuss that the practice of second half of life spirituality offers a different viewpoint.

Many priests who were educated before the Second Vatican Council tend to hold on to an image of a God Preoccupied with Sex. Also, parents, relatives, and The Catechism of the Catholic Church often gave the impression that sins of the flesh are terribly wrong. Many confessions of older men and women indicate a preoccupation with sexual sins.

Today, teenagers do not seem to have an image of a God Preoccupied with Sex. Perhaps this is because modern psychology and our society view sexuality in a more positive way. But seminarians, like you who are being formed in the practice of first half of life spirituality, can be overly concerned with sexual sins. Hopefully in time, you will lose an image of God Preoccupied with Sex and become more aware that while there are serious sexual sins, there are also serious sins of greed, racism, sexism, hypocrisy, and dishonesty.

Those who keep their image of a God Preoccupied with Sex run the risk of being shepherds who live with a lot of unnecessary fear and guilt. Sadly, these shepherds will transmit that fear, shame and guilt to others. As Fr. Richard Rohr often says, "If you do not transform your pain, you will surely transmit it to those around you and even to the next generation."

Peace,

Uncle Matthew

Letter #7
Sunday, July 31, 2011

Dear Uncle Matthew,

Thank you for the over-view of the two images of God that you sent to me; a Vengeful God and a God Pre-occupied with Sex. Once again, these two images of God are the ones I internalized when I grew up. Sharing with me is greatly helping me to become aware of what I never consciously knew about my images of God or about how they influence the way I think and act.

In the seminary, I know I feel guilty over any sins I commit against the virtue of chastity. I have a good friend here, and we have discussed our struggles together. He and I seem to be experiencing the same temptations. Like you said, I, like many other seminarians my age, often judge my ability to be chaste as the determining sign of whether I am called to the priesthood. The image of a Vengeful God certainly follows from an image of God Pre-occupied with Sex.

I am grateful for your letters. You said there were seven images of God that are common during the practice of first half of life spirituality. What are the other three images of God?

Peace,

Joey

Response to Letter #7
Saturday, August 6, 2011

Dear Joey,

I'm glad that my sharing is helping you. I only wish someone had helped me to be aware of my own images of God when I was your age. I never fully knew the importance of our images of God until I attended the Fr. Richard Rohr Conference on "Loving the Two Halves of Life" in January! Since that Conference, my letters to you are helping me to "see" with new eyes what I missed seeing for many years.

When I was completing my second year of theology, a professor told our class that if anyone had a habit of masturbation, he should not come back for third theology. At the time, I was shocked that he could make such a dualistic, black and white, statement. Now, many years later, I see his comment as being totally inappropriate. Each person is different and should be treated with respect. Mercy and compassion are signs of a person who practices second half of life spirituality. Legalism, especially in sexual matters, connotes the practice of first half of life spirituality.

I shall share three more images of God which are common during the practice of first half of life spirituality: a God Demanding Perfection, My God Alone, and a Male God. Remember, Joey, later you will have to make some effort to change or modify all these images of God as you gradually transition into a new way of thinking and acting that is called the practice of second half of life spirituality.

5.  A God Demanding Perfection:

During the first half of life, we tend to believe in a God Demanding Perfection. This image of God is the logical conclusion of the other images of God which I shared with you, particularly images of an Exclusive and Vengeful God. We are taught that we are among the elect, the exclusive, the spiritual elite, but only if we meet the absolute demands of a Vengeful God. An image of God Demanding Perfection gives us the impression that God is not truly sympathetic, much less embracing, of our human condition. The drive for perfection often plays out in the realm of sexuality because our human condition so often expresses our joys and sorrows through our sexuality.

As with the other images of God, when we believe in an image of a God Demanding Perfection, we become like the God we adore. We become judgmental with an eye on perfection as we define it. We can demand perfection in others and in oneself, instead of seeking wholeness, acceptance, fulfillment, and integration.

As a result, a prayer life governed by the notion of perfection can become like that of the Pharisee that Jesus described in the gospel of Luke, Chapter 18. A Pharisee, the supposedly holy man, thanked God that he was not like the tax collector who embezzled money. The Pharisee was proud and boastful. The scribes and Pharisees were held in high regard. They were the religious leaders. They knew what was pleasing to God and what was displeasing to God. The tax collectors were universally hated and treated as outcasts in that society. And yet God could see the humility of the tax collector. The tax collector knew he was sinful. It is easy for us when we hold on to an image of a God Demanding Perfection to pray to God saying, "Thank you, dear God. I am not like these other people who fail to pray, commit sexual sins, abuse alcohol, and smoke marijuana."

These images impact not only our relationship with God but with our ability to form friendships, to love one another, and to embrace and value the full humanity of even those closest to us. If we get stuck with an image of a God Demanding Perfection, we can be disappointed in our parents and reject them because we see their imperfection. We all have met sons who won't talk to their dads and daughters who won't talk to their moms. Growth has to take place to have a different image of God. Giving up a God Demanding Perfection is one of the goals in moving into the practice of second half of life spirituality.

Our culture prizes productivity, riches, and worldly success. Therefore, many people who have an image of a God Demanding Perfection suffer from the addiction of workaholism. Workaholics have to do everything right. They may neglect taking care of even their own needs. They want to please others because they adore a God who demands that they be perfect. They see life in a dualistic way: black/white, right/wrong, good/bad. There is little gray. As I mentioned earlier, dualistic thinking is characteristic of the practice of first half of life spirituality. I know the destructiveness of workaholism because I was a workaholic most of my life.

When we adore a God Demanding Perfection, we can place too much emphasis on ourselves. We can become the center of attention, not God. Our confessions become focused on how bad we are rather than on how good God is. Fr. Richard Rohr says so often, "God does not love us because we are good. God loves us because God is good." I found the book, The Spirituality of Imperfection, Story Telling and the Journey to Wholeness by Ernest Kurtz and Katherine Ketcham to be outstanding in assisting me to find a new way of thinking.

6. My God Alone:

Once we develop an image of a Distant God, we may feel anxious about the need to befriend this remote and demanding God. We are encouraged to spend time making a holy hour alone. It is easy to lose the communal nature of God and relate to God as "My God Alone." Taking the time to pray in solitude is important so as to know yourself. You cannot know yourself through reading more text books. Prayer is an important way to be conscious of who you are, your behavior, and your need for God.

Celibacy encourages us to spend time alone in an effort to be alone with God. That is good if we keep a balance between our prayer time alone and our ministry to others. We must be careful not to be overly concerned with our own moral perfection to the exclusion of ministering to others.

If we continue to relate to an image of My God Alone, our prayers of petition can become selfish when our prayers are exclusively about our needs without including the needs of the community. Likewise, our prayers of thanksgiving can become selfish if we thank God for what we have without a sense of gratitude for what others have been given. A grateful heart thanks God for everything that is good in our life and in the lives of others.

Those who have an image of My God Alone could become like the God they adore. They risk becoming what they believe. They risk becoming self-centered, egocentric, and self-righteous. Egocentricity is the biggest barrier to a deeper spiritual life. Many people who adore an image of My God Alone can be filled with pride and not see it. Church leaders who retain an image of God as My God Alone, in the second half of life, run the risk of being less loving, accepting, and forgiving of others.

7. A Male God:

Permeating all of the images of God I have shared with you is the portrayal of God as male. The effects of this are far-reaching and are so pervasive and natural to us that is it likely that you never considered or questioned the gender of your God.

In our culture as Americans, we have a tendency to put males above females. Often women make salaries less than males while doing the same work. When we were young, we were taught that we live in the greatest country in the world. We were taught that we belong to the Catholic Church, the largest Christian church. When we studied the Bible, we discovered that there is a long history of patriarchy that has continued to this very day. Women are not allowed to be priests in the Catholic Church. We tend to stereotype power and control with males whereas females are stereotyped as compliant, docile, and passive. Many people my age grew up thinking males were superior to females.

However, Jesus spoke of his 'Abba,' an Aramaic word meaning "Daddy." This word connotes intimacy. Jesus speaks of God as a loving parent who embraces and protects God's children. Jesus also used parables that illustrated God as feminine. Jesus treated men and women equally. A group of women were a part of Jesus' ministry. Even in the Hebrew Scriptures, we learn in Isaiah that God is called a mother.

As with the other images of God, the male image of God is internalized in us from many sources derived from historical and cultural conditioning, as I shall illustrate. I am describing, but not endorsing, these influences that led to our belief in a Male God.

Aristotle and St. Thomas Aquinas both wrote about the superiority of men over women. St. Thomas Aquinas wrote about the creation story in the Book of Genesis and emphasized that man should be the head of the whole human race just as God is head of the whole universe.

The Sistine Chapel in Vatican City has some beautiful art work. Michelangelo's classic frescoes on the ceiling certainly display the full range of heavenly, spiritual beings, and famously, the hand of man and the very male hand of God touching in the moment of creation. We have all seen and absorbed this amazing image.

Church doctrine too has reinforced male images from the earliest days. In 325 the Roman Emperor Constantine the Great called the First Council of Nicaea. Christians professed then and throughout history the Nicene Creed. The Creed gives us an image of God, the Doctrine of the Holy Trinity, as Father, Son, and Holy Spirit.

Perhaps most significantly we encounter daily in the life of the Church the patriarchal system. In the liturgy, words like "Father, Lord, and mankind" appear. Thus it is easy, without reflection, to think of God as male. And of course, the priest himself is the visible, physical mouthpiece of male imagery.

If we have an image of God as exclusively male, we are more open to the leadership and advice of men than to women. If we routinely seek the highest authority, the one with the greatest knowledge must be male since God himself is male. We can commit the sin of sexism and not know it. We can think that men are by nature the ideal.

Those who adore a Male God think it is better to have only male priests. Thus, if we exclusively have an image of a Male God as shepherds, we present a God who is incomplete and one-sided. I want to remind you, Joey, that when we practice second half of life spirituality, we are more aware of these historical and cultural influences that shape our image of a Male God.

The practice of second half of life spirituality will encourage you to change or give up your images of a God Demanding Perfection, My God Alone, and a Male God. During the second half of life, you will realize that these earlier images of God will no longer work for you. During the second half of life, your new experiences will make you ask many times the question, "Why?" It is in the questioning that you will gradually discover new images of God so as to form you into a good shepherd who is more loving, more hospitable, more humble, and more fully human and alive like Jesus. It is through your full humanity that you will become a fully alive person radiating the divine.

Peace,

Uncle Matthew

Letter #8
Saturday, August 20, 2011

Dear Uncle Matthew,

I never really thought about my image of God as being male until I received your letter. But, upon reflection, I have always viewed God as male.

In the seminary, I try to do my best so as to become a priest, so I guess I have thought of God as a God Demanding Perfection. I try to be perfect in my appearance, my grades, deportment, and in my moral code of ethics.

Even a belief in My God Alone resonates with me. In the seminary, we are concerned about our spiritual and intellectual growth, so when I pray to God, my prayers are usually centered on my needs rather than the needs of others. Thank you for making me aware of these three images of God. You have greatly helped me to reflect upon them.

My summer assignment continues to go pretty well. I really do not have much in common with the two priests here in the rectory. One priest was born in Haiti. He is young and very nice, but our cultural differences are noticeable. The other priest is older. He is pleasant, but I don't think he has any close friends. I can't quite figure him out. He seems preoccupied with himself, and he is not open to new ideas. As I mentioned earlier, the pastor lives in another rectory. I miss eating with others and praying with others. The pastor does not talk to me except when he is in his church office. He seems to be a workaholic. He seems to put his church work first in his life, which is not bad, but in a way that seems unbalanced. He lacks joy. He has little time to socially relate to his parishioners, his associates, or to me.

I have a couple of questions for you, Uncle Matthew. First, what are the consequences if we do not accomplish the goals of first half of life spirituality? Second, what are the consequences if we do not gradually change these seven images of God that you shared with me?

While I am here in the seminary, my training seems to reinforce these seven images of God. I suppose when I am ordained and have some pastoral experience, I will gradually change.

Peace,

Joey

Response to Letter #8
Sunday, September 4th, 2011

Dear Joey,

Your pastoral experience this summer has helped you to have a taste of the priesthood. In the seminary you have many opportunities for fellowship. But in parishes, a priest often finds himself alone or in a situation where the other priests may be culturally or spiritually different. But that is reality. Facing reality is at the heart of good spiritual direction and genuine discernment. We all tend to deny reality so as to protect our ego. That is why the mystics and many of today's spiritual writers emphasize awareness.

I'm glad you are able to identify with the seven images of God that are common for most of us when we practice first half of life spirituality. We unconsciously have images of God, but we need someone to help us to be aware of these images.

I'll try to answer your two questions. Being aware of and accomplishing the goals of first half of life spirituality are so important. I'll share with you some of the consequences that occur if we fail to accomplish these goals.

Consequences if we fail to accomplish the goals
in the practice of first half of life spirituality:

If we miss achieving some of the tasks when we practice first half of life spirituality, we could end up needing rigid rules and superiority systems later in life. Fundamentalists do this. Without completing the tasks of building a container (foundation, wineskin, false self), learning discipline, acquiring an identity, providing for security needs, and gaining self-acceptance, we risk in the second half of life having relationship problems. Addictions to drugs, pornography, and/or alcohol could be signs that we are living a life of unwarranted liberalism.

When we look at our society today, there is ample evidence that many people never complete the goals found in the practice of first half of life spirituality. Reality programs on television, violent video games, reckless driving, films that glorify crime and sex, and adult entertainment are expressions that indicate that many people in our society have not completed the goals found in the practice of first half of life spirituality.

Consequences if we fail to change our childhood images of God:

You asked me what are the consequences of not growing beyond our early images of God. We all find it easier to simply follow the rules we learned when we were young and to repress new information that disturbs us. I'll try to answer your question by sharing with you several observations.

If we continue to keep the seven images of God that I shared with you in the second half of life without modifications, we run the risk of not being good shepherds. We can lack the necessary qualities that are needed so as to be a mature priest, spouse, parent, grandparent, and friend. The seven images of God that we have during the first half of life may look good, but they hinder us in fulfilling our vocation in life.

Yesterday, I was with a married thirty-nine year-old-man. In the past, he would not go to communion unless he thought he was free of any sin involving thought, word, or deed. I kept telling him to go to communion even if he was not perfect and simply confess later whatever he thought was sinful. I was trying to help him to focus more on God's unconditional love. To my surprise, he did go to communion last Sunday even though he did not consider himself worthy.

One of the consequences of not out-growing our early images of a Vindictive God is that we end up focused too much on our imperfections instead of on a Loving God and Merciful God.

Another consequence of failing to change is that we tend to blame God when tragedies occur. For example, we may blame God for taking a spouse or child. We wonder "Why would God do that?" Some older people pray so fervently for a sick spouse, child, or other relative, and that person doesn't get well. They question "Why doesn't God hear my prayers?"

Another consequence of not changing is the images of God we learned during the first half of life will not work. Thus, we can be smart but not wise. We can look good on the outside but be lacking in spiritual depth. We will most likely be praised by superiors because we will be looked upon as loyal. But eventually those images of God have to be replaced so that we can drink the new wine (Matthew 9:17).

Another consequence of not changing is that we may continue to be the false self. Fr. Richard Rohr founded the Center of Action and Contemplation, in 1987, because he saw the need to integrate both action and contemplation. Fr. Rohr noticed over the years that many social activists were not working from an "energy of love" because they were still living out of their false self with the need to win, the need to be politically correct, and the need to look good. Gradually changing our images of God will enable us to live a more adult spirituality. When our actions flow from what has been termed the true self, we will be motivated by "divine love." The images of God found in the practice of second half of life spirituality better show God as divine love. When our actions flow from the false self, we may contribute to reformation but not transformation. We inspire others to the degree that our actions flow from divine love.

I heard this story. Once upon a time, there was a king who had two sons. The oldest was a rascal and the second son was a very good. The king realized he would die soon and leave his kingdom to the elder son. The king did die, and the elder son inherited the entire kingdom. He treated the people badly. He wasted his time spending money. The people were afraid of him. One day when the new king went hunting, he was accidentally killed so the kingdom went to the younger son.

The younger son wanted to reconcile with the people, so he said he would like to eat a meal from time to time with the representatives of the poor people in their homes. A widowed lady who lived deep in the woods was chosen to be the representative of the people with whom the king would eat supper. The poor woman asked for a week before the meeting with the king. After a week passed, the king did not hear from the woman. He decided to try to find her in the wooded area. He found her very poor home, but she was not there. Again, he never heard from her, so he finally sent out his scouts to find out where she went. He discovered that she, with all the rest of the village, was trying to build a huge castle deep in the woods on a large field. She thought the only way to meet the king was to have a castle for him.

The point of the story is that sometimes we can be like the poor woman who thought she was unworthy to receive her king. We may not think God comes to us in our imperfection. When we have partial and immature images of God, it makes it difficult for us to believe God is with us in our perfection as well as in our imperfection. We may doubt if God really loves us unconditionally. We may doubt if we really need others to become holy and whole. We miss so much of God's love and life.

Tomorrow is Labor Day. This summer went by so quickly. I'll be joining your grandparent's, Bill and Emily, for a cook-out.

Peace,

## Uncle Matthew

Letter #9
Sunday, September 18, 2011

Dear Uncle Matthew,

I'm back in the seminary beginning my second year of philosophy. The first year went by so quickly. One thing I've observed is that although we are from various dioceses, everyone is friendly.

Wednesday the twenty-first is the feast day of St. Matthew, the apostle and evangelist. I'll be praying for you. Your letters indicate that you are very much like St. Matthew. I appreciate that you are helping me to be a disciple of Jesus, and hopefully your influence will greatly contribute to me being a more mature priest upon ordination.

Thank you for your last letter. The consequences of not transitioning to new images of God during the second half of life help me to be more appreciative of your efforts to give me a spiritual roadmap. I will need many new experiences to fully understand the depth of your letters. At present, your letters seem way above my level of experience, but I will keep your letters so that later I will have something valuable to fall back upon for guidance.

It seems logical that my present images of God, the formation program here in the seminary, and the Catechism of the Catholic

Church have much to do with how I view different religious topics. Could you pick out some of the basic beliefs we hold when we practice first half of life spirituality, the beliefs that support and underlie the images of God we are discussing, and briefly summarize how we understand them? I suppose I'm asking for an abbreviated version of the Catechism. I presume that what you share with me will match what I already believe regarding religious topics.

Peace,

Joey

Response to Letter #9
Saturday, October 1, 2011

Dear Joey,

Today is the feast of St. Therese of the Child Jesus. I like the title
we give to her, "Little Flower." I served as a transitional deacon in
the Shrine of the Little Flower in Baltimore. St. Therese died at
the young age of twenty-four. May she bless you on this special
day.

You mentioned on the phone, the clergy sexual abuse crisis. I
read a recent article entitled "Catholic Seminaries: The Inside
Story," by Richard Sipe who made some very good points on
seminary training. He points out that the John-Jay Report states
that the seminaries in this country have not adequately
addressed the issues of emotional maturity and sexual identity.
The Report indicated that this inadequate preparation
contributed to clergy sexual abuse. Sipe concludes that not more
than one in twenty seminarians ordained today is equipped to
hear confessions or counsel penitents. He also concludes that
not one in ten seminarians ordained today is qualified to preach.

Sipe has written several books that are well-worth reading. He is
a former Benedictine monk-priest and he has dealt extensively
with the mental health problems of Roman Catholic priests. I
share this information with you because I pledge to do all I can to
help you in your preparation to become a good priest, a good

shepherd. I believe that you will eventually preach well and be well equipped to hear confessions.

I shall be happy to share with you some typical religious beliefs that we hold when we practice first half of life spirituality. It is necessary for you to have a good foundation regarding these religious topics. Acquiring a good knowledge of Catholic doctrine and our rich tradition is one of the goals in the practice of first half of life spirituality. We want to be whole, complete, integrated, and fully alive. The adoption of a coherent set of creeds helps to serve this purpose. Ideally, the dogmas and creeds we learn early in life help us grow in our love of God, Church, and neighbor. These religious beliefs help to make us credible church members.

I shall share with you in this letter and in my next letter some basic Catholic beliefs we have regarding the following topics: Baptism, Blessings, Devotions, Eucharist, God, Good Friday, Heaven/Hell, Holiness, Holy Thursday, Homosexuality, Jesus, Marriage, Mary, Original Sin, and Pentecost. These beliefs were chosen because they are often points of controversy today. These topics make us realize that our beliefs and traditions are not simple but rather complex. Our beliefs are an attempt to explain world views that later in life may be reinterpreted and relearned very much like our images of God change as we have new experiences in life. The form of presentation used here is simply exposition, not deliberation or argumentation. For a fuller explanation, consult the Catechism of the Catholic Church. I'm just trying to answer your request by sharing with you what an average layperson thinks about these topics, not what a theologian would say.

1. Baptism:

When we practice first half of life spirituality, we think of baptism as a ritual that cleanses us from Original Sin (Adam's sin) and makes us children of God and members of the Church. The Catechism of the Catholic Church teaches that at baptism, "All sins are forgiven, Original Sin and all personal sins, as well as punishment for sin" (#1263). We assume that through baptism we receive God's Spirit.

We believe that throughout history until the coming of Jesus human beings lived in a state of exile from God and that unbaptized people were in some way disconnected from God. We are taught to think of the sacraments as liturgical rituals that literally bring us the sacred. We therefore need baptism not simply as a symbol, or a family community event, but as a necessary act to gain a vital connection to God. We were once taught that Limbo was where deceased unbaptized babies went.

2. Blessings:

When we practice first half of life spirituality, we seek a deacon or priest to bless crucifixes, medals, homes, and even pets. There is a presumption that the object is made holy by the blessing. Many people presume the object was unholy until it was blessed. The prayer used calls down God's gifts and blessings on the object.

3. Devotions:

When we practice first half of life spirituality, we believe that devotions work like magic. Devotions with their promise of indulgences presume that God's intervention can be attained by using a particular formula or ritual. Thus, we might be encouraged to pray rosaries, make novenas, and pray privately the stations of the cross. We think devotions give us privileged access to God. This fits in with an image of an Exclusive God. Devotions enable us to be better loved by an Exclusive God.

4. Eucharist:

When we practice first half of life spirituality, we think that only a priest can produce Jesus on the altar. We perceive the Eucharist as an object rather than an action. There is a tendency to see ourselves more as spectators at Mass watching and listening to the actions being performed on our behalf. The presider carefully reads the words so that the desired transubstantiation can take place. We believe the bread and wine is the literal transformation into the body and blood of Jesus during Mass.

(The first four topics, by the way, have a common trait. They separate the profane from the holy rather than seeing God everywhere.)

5. God:

I described earlier that most people who practice first half of life spirituality believe God is "up there" apart from this world. We use an 'up' and 'down' way of describing heaven and earth. We believe God is a divine male person with a human-like personality. We view God as thinking, feeling, needing to be worshipped, and keeping a record of wrongs much like our image of Santa Claus. We believe God sent his only Son down to us to save us.

6. Good Friday:

When we practice first half of life spirituality, we believe that Jesus died for our sins as a sacrifice. Somehow Jesus offered himself as a sacrificial victim to meet the demands of his Heavenly Father. There is implied or stated specifically that the magnitude of our sins required such a horrific event to compensate and balance a cosmic scale of justice.

7. Heaven/Hell:

When we practice first half of life spirituality, we believe with fear and without questioning that there is a reward/punishment system. This system of divine justice is seen as rendering a verdict on our life, at the time of death, with our eternal destination as either a blissful heaven or a torturous hell. Our image of a Distant God underlies our belief in far-away places called Heaven and Hell. We think that when we die our souls go somewhere either above or below the earth. We tend to think that God exists in heaven. A rigid, dualistic moralism typically follows when we believe we will be judged as fit for either Heaven or Hell, one or the other, forever.

8. Holiness:

When we practice first half of life spirituality, we think that popes, bishops, priests and, religious brothers and nuns are holier than lay persons because of their vows and theological background. We assume that holiness had something to do with apartness. We think God is up there; separate from creation. Religious habits separate "holy people" from ordinary people. We practice a religion so as to become holy. We rely on church leaders to provide for us the means to become holy. We tend to overlook the holiness that can be found in ordinary lay persons or persons outside the Church, since we have an image of an Exclusive God.

9. Holy Thursday:

When we practice first half of life spirituality, we think that at the Last Supper Jesus set up a new religion with its own priesthood. We believe Jesus renounced Judaism when he started a new religion. We believe Jesus instituted the Eucharist and that he bestowed on his male apostles the power to bring his presence through the consecrated bread. We believe in transubstantiation that means something literally happens to the bread and wine so that it turns into the actual body and blood of Jesus. What looks like bread and wine to our human eyes mysteriously undergoes a substantial change beneath the outward appearances.

10. Homosexuality:

When practicing first half of life spirituality, we believe the church's teaching in the Catechism that homosexual acts are intrinsically disordered (#2357). The church teaches that they are contrary to the natural law and under no circumstances can homosexual acts be accepted, much less approved. A Vatican document stressed that men with homosexual orientation are not eligible for a place in seminary or religious life.

(Since this in an important topic in the seminary, can you tell me what is the policy regarding sexuality at your seminary?)

11. Jesus:

Christians generally believe that Jesus is "true God and true man," a human being with a divine "nature" that other human beings do not possess. When practicing first half of life spirituality, we tend to believe that Jesus was radically different from the rest of humanity; unique and singular.

12. Marriage:

The Code of Canon Law says,

"The matrimonial covenant, by which a man and a woman establish between themselves a partnership of the whole of life and which is ordered by its nature toward the good of the spouses and the procreation and education of offspring, has been raised by Christ the Lord to the dignity of a sacrament between the baptized. (c. 1055)

This single citation of canon law excludes the possibility of same-sex marriage.

13. Mary:

When we practice first half of life spirituality, we believe in Mary's literal Immaculate Conception, her virginal conception of Jesus, and her bodily assumption into heaven. We believe that Mary enjoys Queen of Heaven status. She is unique; a feminine counterpart to Jesus.

14. Original Sin:

When we practice first half of life spirituality, we believe that Adam, as a historical event, committed the Original Sin, eating from the tree of knowledge of good and evil. The effects of this transgression have been profound and far reaching. To this day, we are all born with the stain of Original Sin, making us unworthy and separate from God, full of guilt and in need for salvation. We fear God. We believe we need baptism to be restored to a relationship with God. We tend to worry that children will not enjoy the fullness of heavenly life if they die before they are baptized.

15. Pentecost:

When we practice first half of life spirituality, we believe that at Pentecost the Spirit came down externally upon individuals from elsewhere as a first time event. We think of the Spirit as a separate person in God. We think of Pentecost as the birthday of the Church.

I am enjoying this opportunity to summarize our basic beliefs. In my next letter to you, I will share with you some more brief summaries of our beliefs that we hold when we practice first half of life spirituality.

Peace,
Uncle Matthew

Letter #10
Sunday, October 23, 2011

Dear Uncle Matthew,

Thank you for sending me a summary of beliefs underlying the practice of first half of life spirituality. I can tell that I practice first half of life spirituality since what you sent to me seems to be what I believe at this point in my training.

In one of my classes last week, we discussed Catholic fundamentalism. I read in Richard McBrien's Encyclopedia of Catholicism that fundamentalists literally interpret the Bible and also the official teachings of the Church. By that I mean they think it is a one-dimensional factual description of events much like reading a newspaper about a car accident. The Lefebvre schism within the Catholic Church would be an example of a fundamentalist community. They do not generally recognize literary forms other than history. Thus some fundamentalists believe God created the world in six actual days, and they might believe Jonah literally was in the belly of a whale. I can see how their views on scripture and God's actions in history make them think that their basic beliefs contain the full and final truth. Thus, fundamentalists would not be open to changing their beliefs later in life.

You asked about our homosexual policy here. I get the impression that we are following a "don't ask, don't tell" policy.

Most of the men are careful what they say or do.

Last year, I found Ethics to be my most practical and useful course. This year I am enjoying the philosophy courses, especially history of philosophy.

It was good talking to you on the phone. I look forward to your next letter. Please send me some more basic beliefs we hold when we practice first half of life spirituality.

Peace,

Joey

Response to Letter #10
Tuesday, November 1, 2011

Dear Joey,

Today is the feast of All Saints. I've always enjoyed preaching on this special day. The feast makes me aware of all those saintly individuals in my own life who showered me with unconditional love.

I'm glad you appreciated a brief summary of our beliefs, as we understand them, when we practice first half of life spirituality.

I have often been accused of being a relativist. The word "relativism" refers to the doctrine that knowledge, truth, and morality exist in relation to culture, society, and historical context, and are not absolute. In your Ethics course you learned that what is good and bad depends on circumstances. The morality of a terminally ill cancer patient using a narcotic for pain relief is a lot different from a person using a narcotic to have a high. Likewise, killing in self defense can be morally justified. The practice of first half of life spirituality can give someone the false impression that morality is absolute.

I'm going to continue to share some more beliefs that we normally have when we practice first half of life spirituality. I will address Prayer, Resurrection, the Sacrament of Reconciliation, Scripture, Sin, Trinity, and Women's Ordination to the priesthood.

16. Prayer:

We have an image of a Distant God, when we practice first half of life spirituality. We offer God sacrifices and prayers in the expectation that God can change the course of history in direct response to our prayers in our favor. We believe God has a vantage point above the earth, watching, intervening, rewarding, and punishing. Prayer is primarily saying words or thinking thoughts. Since we think of prayer as a specific, conscious, if not formulaic act, we tend to see prayer in a dualistic way: either we are praying or not praying. Thus, we often confess that we forgot our morning and/or evening prayers. We consider prayer part of a merit system, transactional, and almost magical in nature. In the Catechism of the Catholic Church, Part Four offers a long treatise on prayer.

17. Resurrection:

When we practice first half of life spirituality, we exclusively believe the claim that Jesus was physically raised from the dead. We think it is necessary to literally believe the gospels when they indicate that following his Resurrection, Jesus ate food with his friends. The emphasis is on viewing Resurrection as an event in the past. We believe people could touch his wounded body, and that forty days after his Resurrection, he physically ascended from the earth and journeyed somewhere into space to reach God's dwelling place in the sky. We assume the Resurrection stories in the Bible are literally true instead of expressive of a deeper reality.

18. Sacrament of Reconciliation:

Pope Pius X in 1910 made it so that children would receive their first communion at an earlier age, the "age of discretion." This was around the age of seven. Thus, a link was created between confession and communion. Children had to go to confession before making their first communion.

There was a period of time after the Vatican II Council when first communion was given at age seven, and first confession was delayed to a later time. But in 1973, the Congregation for the Liturgy and the Clergy brought back the practice to the rigid order of Pius X in 1910.

When we practice first half of life spirituality, we are taught that we need to confess our sins to a priest to have our sins forgiven. We take seriously the words of Jesus, "Whatever you bind on earth shall be considered bound in heaven; whatever you loose on earth shall be considered loosed in heaven" (Matthew 16:19). We believe these words refer to the Sacrament of Reconciliation and the giving of special papal powers to Peter and his successors. We are taught to tell the priest the number and kind of sins, thinking of the priest as a judge dispensing a penance to make up for our sins. The emphasis is on how bad we were as we seek forgiveness from a Vengeful God.

19. Salvation:

In childhood, most of us thought salvation referred to going to heaven when we die.

The Declaration Dominus Jesus (August 2000) insists that Jesus is the only savior. The Church is the universal sacrament of salvation. It is contrary to the faith to consider the Church as one way of salvation alongside other religions.

The traditional understanding of Jesus' work of salvation is it restored human beings lost access to God. Only Jesus could do that. St. Athanasius thought, in the fourth century, that Adam's sin cut us off from the possibility of eternal life with God. He thought that humankind could not gain entrance into heaven of its own accord. We needed a savior.

20. Scripture:

When we practice first half of life spirituality, we assume the gospels are a direct divine product, literally the Word of God, without any human input. Thus, we assume that everything stated in Scripture must be literally true and there cannot be contradictions or errors of any kind. We presume the Gospels were written as eyewitness accounts, as transcriptions fully and completely the Word of God. If there is a perceived problem with the message or content of scripture, the problem lies with us, the human reader, and not God's revealed truth in scripture written down under the inspiration of the Holy Spirit. A fundamentalist approach to scripture naturally follows.

## 21. Sin:

When we practice first half of life spirituality, we think of sin as a bad deed. We classify sins of commission and sins of omission. Typical stress is given to the sins pertaining to sex, drinking, smoking, gambling, womanizing, and lying. The dualism of good and evil are present. Categories such as mortal sin and venial sin are often employed. A follower of Jesus is regarded as someone who does not commit serious sins.

## 22. Trinity:

It may be argued that the Trinity is the central doctrine in Christian theology. St. Athanasius writing in the fourth century helped to develop our current concepts and rationale about the Trinity. He thought, through a literal reading of scripture, that Adam's sin cut off the possibility of eternal life with God. Only God could restore communion with Himself. So there was a stress on Jesus' divinity so as to save humankind. His writing caused some to think, "If Jesus is the 'image of the Father,' was he really human?" The Council of Nicaea and Chalcedon (fourth and fifth centuries) stated that Jesus had both a divine and a human nature that existed in the one person. It defined and enshrined in the Creed the belief that there are "three persons" in the one God.

We literally believe in the doctrine of the Trinity when we practice first half of life spirituality. Jesus is the incarnation of the Second Person of the Trinity. He is true God and true man. The doctrine of the Trinity simultaneously affirms both the unity of substance and diversity of persons. The Trinity is a mystery, but there is the tendency to see this doctrine as indisputable fact.

23. Women's ordination to the priesthood:

When we practice first half of life spirituality, we believe and accept Pope John Paul II's 1994 apostolic letter, Ordinatio Sacerdotalis, that said, "We declare that the Church has no authority whatsoever to confer priestly ordination on women and that this judgment is to be definitively held by all the Church's faithful." Pope John Paul II said that the priesthood is a special role specially set out by Jesus when he chose twelve men based on a specific reading of scripture and church history. The Church enforces this teaching by only ordaining men to the office of bishop who accept this teaching.

Conclusion:

If you so desire, in a later letter, I will share with you that the above topics are viewed differently when we practice second half of life spirituality that encourages us to question, and if necessary, relearn everything.

Peace,

Uncle Matthew

Letter #11
Sunday, November 13, 2011


Dear Uncle Matthew,

Thank you, Uncle Matthew, for sharing with me a pastoral view of what most lay Catholics who practice first half of life spirituality believe regarding religious topics. You mentioned that in the practice of second half of life spirituality, individuals change their ideas about religious topics. That interests me, but I'm not ready yet for the changes that will later take place.

As I mentioned earlier, my spiritual director this school-year reminds me of you. He is up-to-date, open to new ideas, and he had some pastoral experience in two parishes. When I told him that you were helping me to understand the paradigm of the two halves of life spirituality, he told me about the paradigms of "Cathedral Catholicism" and "Cafeteria Catholicism." He believes these paradigms may be similar to the paradigm of the two halves of life spirituality.

He said that Cathedral Catholicism transfers the act of faith into an act of obedience. The paradigm assumes that one's conviction is not as important as submission. It assumes that average Catholics are incapable of discerning the truth and that church leaders with the proper juridical authority are essential for guaranteeing the truth.

Cafeteria Catholics belong to the Church, but they refuse to violate their conscience or their integrity to do so. The Vatican II Council strengthened their beliefs by its Declaration on Religious Freedom. I can see why my spiritual director thinks that this paradigm seems to fit in with what you have been sharing.

As you know, Uncle Matthew, I am twenty-five years old. I dated several women before entering the seminary. I am still finding it difficult to be chaste. I have done some reading on chastity, but I would appreciate any insights that you could give to me. The formation program here in the seminary seems to be directed mostly to the top two inches of my body. My mind is filled daily with ideas, but my body at times craves for more than just ideas.

Peace,

Joey

Response to Letter #11
Saturday, November 26, 2011

Dear Joey,

On Thursday, I spent Thanksgiving Day with your grandparents,
William, Jr., and Emily. My brother, William, speaks highly of you.
Your parents, Steve and Marie, were also able to be there.
Thanksgiving Day brings back many memories when you and
your brother were able to join us.

I like what your spiritual director said about Cathedral
Catholicism and Cafeteria Catholicism. I once attended a
conference and listened to Dr. Anthony Padovano speak, and he
discussed these two viewpoints on Catholicism. He wrote a
book, Hope Is A Dialogue, which describes what your spiritual
director shared with you. Dr. Padovano has served as a pastor of
an Inclusive Community where Catholics and Protestants
worship together.

Motivation for being chaste:

Let me respond to your remarks about chastity in your last letter.
As a seminarian, your image of God can influence your
motivation for being chaste. When we practice first half of life
spirituality, we tend to have an image of a Vengeful God. You
may be able to stay chaste not so much out of love of God but
out of fear. Also you may be fearful of doing anything sinful that

would jeopardize your goal of becoming a priest.

When we practice second half of life spirituality, we give less emphasis to the sins of the flesh and more emphasis to the sins of the world and the devil. Once you are a priest, you will find some men desire to stay chaste because they consider their chastity as an important indicator of their self worth and integrity. Some men judge themselves, in a dualistic way, as being either good or bad and the determinant is often their ability to live a chaste life.

Church teaching:

When we practice first half of life spirituality, we understand chastity to be a serious obligation. In the Catechism of the Catholic Church, chastity is presented as one of the fruits of the Spirit. (#1832). The Catechism says that chastity means "the successful integration of sexuality within the person and thus the inner unity of man in his bodily and spiritual being" (#2337).

As you know, as Catholics, we take seriously the Sixth Commandment. The Catechism has many pages of text on the Sixth Commandment. We are taught that lust is an inordinate enjoyment of sexual pleasure. Masturbation is an intrinsically and gravely disordered action. We were taught that one act of masturbation could send us to Hell for all eternity. We were taught that it is not possible to commit a venial sexual sin. One sexual slip in thought, word, or deed should be confessed before receiving communion. The Church's teaching can make us fearful of disobeying the law.

The Catechism lists many offenses against chastity: lust, masturbation, fornication, pornography, prostitution, rape, and homosexual acts. We are taught that it is possible to live without masturbating. Why are there laws forbidding sexual acts unless it is possible to obey the laws and live chastely? In this letter, I am confining my remarks to one area of chastity; namely, masturbation, since to cover all the offenses against chastity would be a book in itself. I understand that the topic of masturbation is sensitive, deeply personal, and rarely discussed. But I believe, as your beloved uncle, we can and should be able to discuss all topics of body, mind, and spirit.

An understanding of chastity and its practice is complex. Perhaps the best way I can help you is to share with you the story of a priest friend of mine. I'll change his name and the places where he was assigned to protect his identity. Stories are very good ways to show the blessings and challenges in the pursuit of living a chaste life.

Fr. Tom before Ordination:

A priest-friend of mine, Fr. Tom, told me that while he was a seminarian, he was able to keep the Sixth Commandment with his own will power. He was chaste. He was born in another country and much of his education was abroad. During the eight years when he was a seminarian, fear of God motivated him rather than love of God. He sensed that the Church wanted him to be an asexual person. He repressed his sexual feelings. He thought that he should never dwell on the sexual desires that he experienced. He was afraid of doing anything wrong that might jeopardize becoming a priest.

During the last part of his seminary training in theology, love instead of fear was his motivation for being chaste. He offered up his lustful temptations for a classmate, George, who was having difficulties with his studies. He thought God would let George pass his tests if he gave up any violations of chastity. He had an image of God that allowed him to bargain with God.

Fr. Tom after Ordination:

Shortly after Fr. Tom was ordained, the bishop assigned him to a small town for the summer as the administrator of a parish. That was the first time in his life that Fr. Tom had lived alone. He felt as though he had left a safe harbor and now he was facing turbulent waters for the first time. He grew up with several siblings, and from the time he left home for college until that summer he had always lived with others, eaten meals with others, recreated with others, and prayed with others. Now he lived alone, ate alone, and prayed alone. He lacked a community. He experienced a lot of loneliness and accompanying strong lustful temptations. They went hand in hand. He did not take a day off during those three months. He assumed that he was always on duty since he was the only priest in that rural part of the state. He felt responsible for all the souls in that rural area.

By the end of the summer, he came to the conclusion that he could not keep the church rules on chastity. He was so lonely. He was desirous of sharing his day with someone. He was tempted to seek consolation in unhealthy ways because his loneliness had become so acute, and the related sexual temptations were so strong. Something had to give! He discovered that for him chastity was an impossible ideal to live without a supportive and emotionally intimate community. He was beginning to understand what the Catechism of the Catholic Church says, "The virtue of chastity blossoms in friendship...Chastity is expressed notably in friendship with one's neighbor" (#2347).

The bishop later assigned Fr. Tom to two other assignments, and he found that being chaste was still very difficult. His body craved companionship. He wanted to love another person and feel loved. He asked himself questions like, "Where can I go on a vacation? With whom could I enjoy a vacation? With whom could I enjoy a day off?" There were very few options. Workaholism was his solution. Workaholism only increased his sexual cravings. He still lacked significant friendships and a community in his early assignments.

Ruth, a woman friend:

In one early assignment, Fr. Tom along with two other priests and, Ruth, an unmarried woman who was the Director of Faith Formation in her parish had the opportunity to attend an educational convention together. He and Ruth became good friends on the trip. They enjoyed eating powdered donuts and drinking coffee together in the French Quarter of New Orleans. They had great conversations. Upon returning from the convention, he met with his spiritual director with whom he shared the highlights of the convention. He felt terribly guilty that he wore a leisure suit at the convention. At the urging of his spiritual director, he gave his leisure suit away.

That was Fr. Tom's first experience since he entered the seminary of relating closely with a woman. In the seminary, he was told not to have close female friends. So, being true to the spirit of the practice of first half of life spirituality, he had simply obeyed the rules and never developed deep friendships with men or women.

After the convention, Fr. Tom invited Ruth to go out to dinner a few times. He felt really energized by the conversations and meals. He even went as far to ask Ruth if she wanted to go on a vacation with him. He later retracted the invitation after discussing his actions with his spiritual director. Sadly, out of fear of going against the expectations of church officials, Fr. Tom regressed to his earlier way of thinking by accepting the belief that a priest having a significant friendship with a woman was dangerous and wrong. Therefore, he terminated his relationship with Ruth.

Looking back, Fr. Tom's inner teacher was trying to let him understand an old saying which I will paraphrase: "I sought my soul/identity, but my soul/identity I could not see. I sought my God, but God eluded me. I sought my brother/sister, and I found all three." He needed friendship, intimacy, touch and love. In spiritual direction, he realized once again that celibacy and chastity were nearly impossible for him when he tried to live a life of celibacy alone without significant friendships and a community.

A Jesuit retreat:

Shortly thereafter breaking up with Ruth, Fr. Tom made a thirty-day silent retreat in Grand Coteau, Louisiana at the Jesuit

Spirituality Center. In solitude, he experienced some deep emotions. He desired the company of another person. He desired to touch someone and be touched. He desired intimacy. He walked at night in the Old Jesuit Cemetery, and he talked to the tomb stones! He was so lonely. He realized that he was not prepared to be a participant on a thirty-day silent retreat, but he continued.

At the end of the thirty-day silent retreat, the retreat director asked the retreatants to name an animal that represented their resolution. Despite his earlier realizations of his need for significant friendships, he thought of an ant. He wanted to be like an ant. Ants are programmed to simply do God's will without thinking. He thought the solution for living a chaste life was simply to erase all those lustful sexual desires and just do his work alone without getting too involved with anyone.

The retreat director also asked the retreatants to find a passage in scripture that summarized their resolution. The Biblical passage Fr. Tom selected was, "Seek first his kingship over you, his way of holiness, and all these things will be given you besides" (Matthew 6:33). In Fr. Tom's mind, this passage reinforced his image of My God. He thought if he were simply closer to this Distant God, he could be chaste. He made a resolution not to violate chastity in the future. Fr. Tom still thought it was possible to be like an angel, so that there would be no room for lust. His wise Jesuit spiritual director warned him that will power and good intentions alone would not work. He later discovered that his retreat director was right! He was still assuming that by his own will power and without other people, he could live an ideal life. He did not know at the time that the practice of first half of life spirituality assumes if you live by the law, you will able to be chaste. Fr. Tom, at the end of his retreat, still believed all sexual expressions were wrong for a celibate priest.

Preparation for living a chaste life as a celibate:

Many of us who are priests look back at our journey during the first half of life and wonder why the professors in the seminary did not give us some insights into the mystery and practice of celibacy and the virtue of chastity. As you mentioned in your letter to me, the professors do a good job feeding our brains with information from books, but so little attention is given to helping us to be prepared for a celibate life; especially life without community as a diocesan priest.

Why was so little attention given to living a life of celibacy and chastity? Was it because the faculty was unaware of the transition that takes place into the practice of second half of life spirituality? When we practice first half of life spirituality, our images of a Distant and Vengeful God, our fear of God, our will-power and the church's laws help us to control our emotions. But once we become more aware of our desire to be fully human, which must include intimacy with others, our emotions are more difficult to handle. We discover, like Fr. Tom, that church laws, our own will-power, and images of a Vengeful God and My God Alone won't necessarily keep us chaste.

When we practice first half of life spirituality, there is a tendency not to question the Church's teaching on chastity. We might think in the seminary when we failed to be chaste that we were the only ones with that problem. We can think that we are in need of psychological help. We can think of ourselves as being sinners in need of God's mercy and forgiveness. That inner feeling of failure to some extent can cripple our ability to be good shepherds. We can be shamed by our failures. We can think that if people knew our failures, they would not respect us. We have not reached practicing an adult spirituality that teaches us that it is through our wounds that God enters us.

Looking back, Fr. Tom concluded in his later years that practicing first half of life spirituality in the area of sexuality for so long greatly harmed him. Guilt, shame and feelings of unworthiness took their toll. His own image of a Vengeful God and My God Alone hurt him with his identity. He had great difficulty accepting who he was; a man who desired to become fully human and fully alive with other people; not alone.

Conclusion:

I have often wondered whether some young men are attracted to the priesthood because unconsciously they think priests do live chastely. They think that celibacy could be an easy way for them to solve their own sexual problems since some young men are gay and are troubled by sexual urges. Most young men experience strong sexual urges which are difficult to control around women. They may think that priests have discovered a secret that they want. They may want to be pure, chaste, perfect, and holy. Unconsciously they think there are some men who have achieved these goals. Connecting the ability to keep the laws regarding chastity with priests in the Church certainly can be a motivator for vocations to the priesthood and religious life. Also religious habits (clothing), scapulars, titles, degrees in theology, and holy medals suggest a mystique that is very attractive.

We all have our challenges in life when it comes to living chastely.

Peace,

Uncle Matthew

Letter #12
Thursday, December 8, 2011

Dear Uncle Matthew,

Thank you for your last letter about the virtue of chastity. I
needed that letter. I trust you, so I feel very comfortable sharing
with you some of my deepest thoughts, fears, and temptations.
Yes, masturbation is not a topic most young men want to
discuss, and yet it is a reality that we all face.

I found your story about Father Tom to be very helpful. So far my
training to be chaste as a celibate seems to be focused on
developing more will power, frequenting confession, saying more
prayers, and avoiding, through repression, lustful thoughts and
desires. Your last letter emphasized, instead, the importance of
friendships, intimacy, and living as a vibrant member in the Body
of Christ. Whatever happened to Fr. Tom? Are you still in contact
with him?

Today is the feast of the Immaculate Conception. We do not
have classes. The liturgy this morning was very up-lifting. I
wonder how the bishops expect people to attend a holy day of
obligation on a weekday.

My spiritual director suggested during Advent that I read the
book, A Life-Giving Vision by Fr. John Powell, SJ, who wrote on
the importance of affirmation. Fr. Powell suggests many ways to
increase self-esteem and self-acceptance. He suggests looking

for the good in others. He says to be gentle with oneself. Avoid competing. Be oneself. Think of oneself in positive terms. This book is already proving to be helpful. We all need affirmation. Perhaps affirmation is part of the key to living a healthy celibate life. In the seminary, I have found that the professors do not give the students much affirmation. And yet, I find these guys studying with me to be exceptionally good. My spiritual director said that we cannot give to others what we do not have ourselves.

So far you have given me so much material to ponder. Question: What would a person look like who has reached the developmental goals of first half of life spirituality? First half of life spirituality helps us to develop qualities that are stages along the way pointing to the need for further development. A portrait of some of these positive qualities would help me to better put together many of the insights that you have shared.

I'll leave Saturday for the Christmas break. I'm looking forward to being with mom and dad.


Peace,

Joey

Response to Letter #12
Monday, December 19, 2011

Dear Joey,

Yesterday we celebrated the Fourth Sunday of Advent. This Advent season is going by so quickly. You mentioned that you are home for the Christmas break. Your parents are so glad to see you. I remember when your dad, Steve, was born in 1964. The years are going by so quickly.

Many years ago there were Houses of Affirmation in the United States where priests and religious were sent for healing. These institutions were so named because the root cause of many problems priests and religious face involve a lack of affirmation. Affirmation rather than rigid formation will provide the key to your growth and development. That is why community is so essential and significant friendships with men and women are so critical, if you are to become whole, happy, fully human, and at peace with yourself. I once heard a speaker quote Cardinal Leo Suenens, a leading voice at the Vatican II Council, say, "The greatest good we do to others is not to give them of our wealth but to show them their own." Friendship can do this.

You asked about Fr. Tom . He is now retired. Later, if you wish, I will give you a more detailed update on his unique path to living a chaste life.

The value of institutional opportunities:

During the first half of life, we are supposed to learn the rules. We must begin that way. Organizations such as Boy Scouts, Eagle Scouts, careerists in military service, seminarians like you, and cadets in military academies are good examples of individuals who avail themselves of institutional supports typically needed to nurture and structure good formation. These structures offer great benefits. I attended a military college, so I was blessed with many opportunities to achieve many of the goals in the practice of first half of life spirituality.

Portrait of a person who practices first half of life spirituality:

After completing some or all of the goals found in the practice of first half of life spirituality, individuals display an identity. They know who they are. They accept who they are. Such individuals have clear boundaries. They have some clear goals and objectives. They have made some provision for their security. Their certitude makes them attractive. They have built a foundation that can give them the capacity to become fully alive. But they have not yet identified with the depth of the gospel message. Loyalty and obedience are stressed in military and church formation. But even these virtues must later take a back seat to compassion and mercy. That is why the knowledge and practice of second half of life spirituality must eventually follow if you are to become a fully human person and a good shepherd.

We are tempted to place such individuals on a pedestal, but these individuals are not yet complete. As they grow in age, they will discover that even if they accomplish all the goals in the practice of first half of life spirituality, they will have difficulty coping with the many challenges that will come during the second half of life. Suffering, financial problems, relationship problems, difficulties with raising children, difficulties in one's vocation, facing significant failures in life, serious medical problems, and burdensome addictions all become increasingly difficult to handle without further spiritual growth.

An understanding of second half of life spirituality can better equip us to deal with the mysteries of suffering, crisis, and the loss of significant friends. Practicing second half of life spirituality can make us more complete, more human, wiser, more compassionate, more loving of our neighbor, and more willing to reach out to others in their need.

Our first half of life images of God form us so that we become like the God we adore. When we are limited in our ability to worship a bigger God, we are incomplete. We are not fully human and alive. We cannot fulfill our baptismal call to fully witness to divine life, to forgive others, to unconditionally love others, and to serve others without desiring a reward.

Let me share with you comments about two movies that provide clear portraits of the practice of first half of life spirituality.

Movie: The Remains of the Day:

In 1995, I saw the movie The Remains of the Day. The film was nominated for eight Oscars, including Best Picture. The film stars Anthony Hopkins who takes the role of a butler, Mr. Stevens, in a large wealthy estate, Darlington Hall, in Britain just before World War Two.

Mr. Stevens was loyal, perfectionistic, calm, and efficient. He knew who he was; head butler. He was secure since no one could match his skills. He thought his future was secure because in that period of time good butlers could remain on the property until they died. Mr. Stevens had clear boundaries. He was a master of etiquette. He had no opinions. Mr. Stevens simply accepted without thinking the commands, politics, and opinions of the Lord of Darlington Hall.

The movie shows that Mr. Stevens had developed his mind, but his heart was underdeveloped. He repressed his emotions. He had no interest in peace and justice. He did not have the qualities to be a good shepherd. He couldn't handle love, affection, and teasing. Although Mr. Stevens had some admirable traits that would be considered bench marks in the first half of life, he was not a complete man. He was not a whole person. He was not fully human and fully alive. He needed more qualities to make him a flexible, lovable, joyful, and attractive person.

Sometimes we meet newly ordained priests and we think they are the ideal. Very often bishops will appoint such young men as vocation directors. I was appointed vocations' director after only being ordained for two years. Like Mr. Stevens in the film, these young priests may have achieved many of the goals required in practicing first half of life spirituality. But if we understand that there are two halves to a full spirituality, then we will not place unreal expectations upon them or upon other young people who are in their first half of life. Perhaps we can see traits of responsibility, courage, loyalty, honesty, and self-control, but usually, with reflection, we discover that more wholeness is needed.

Movie: The Browning Version:

I'll share with you another example. Earlier in my life, I saw the movie, The Browning Version. The movie stars Albert Finney who plays the part of Andrew Crocker-Harris, a veteran teacher in Greek and Latin at a British boarding school. Andrew was disliked or ignored by the other teachers. His pupils feared his rigorous discipline. He neglected his young wife both sexually and emotionally.

The film brilliantly shows that at the end of his teaching career, he exemplified so many of first half of life spirituality goals. He had a strong ego, firm boundaries, and an informed conscience. He respected tradition, and he had a well-developed mind. However, Andrew clearly shows that he was not a fully alive person. His coping skills were not working. His tendency to be dualistic became his enemy. As Andrew faced going into retirement, he realized his heart was not yet alive with passion. The film shows the tragic ramifications in marriage when a person fails to progress into the practice of a new spirituality in one's second half of life.

More growth needed:

I hope these two movies helped to give clarity to the necessity for further growth. If you are ordained, people will call you "father." Many people will perceive you as the ideal good shepherd; young, smart, personable, and eager to "save souls." There is the danger that you will think you are "above" the laity because of your status as an ordained priest. This could be manifested in your clerical attire.

A priest-friend of mine attended a Chrism Mass at his Cathedral in the mid-west. The bishop wore a red cassock, a beautiful white-lace alb, an elegant silver chasuble with purple lining, and a new tall miter to match his chasuble. He wore his gold pectoral cross. His hair was perfect. The servers knelt down before him to wash his hands. The servers who handled his miter and crosier wore white gloves. The bishop looked like a very successful and powerful person.

This example illustrates how some of us in the second half of life can be practicing first half of life spirituality, and we don't know it! But some people can see. When my friend shared this story with me, he said it reminded him of Han Christian Andersen's tale, "The Emperor's New Clothes."

With an understanding of the paradigm of the two halves of life spirituality, we realize that a broad set of important life experiences are lacking when we practice first half of life spirituality. Great knowledge may be present, but wisdom is often not yet present. Often we do not find deep levels of compassion or patience when newly ordained priests are with older people. We see an intellectual faith but not a deep faith that comes from the heart. We sense a love based on infatuation rather than genuine unconditional love. We need a further awareness because "we see things as we are, not as they are." Being admired is dangerous because we can think that we see what, in reality, isn't there.

Conclusion:

I once heard the late Fr. Brennan Manning say, "The greatest single cause of atheism in the world today is Christians who acknowledge Jesus with their lips yet deny Him by their lifestyle." I believe that we cannot settle for the spirituality we developed early in life to sustain us until we die. Like all living organisms, we change, evolve, and grow. If our institutions don't do the same, they become irrelevant and eventually become extinct. We need to affect change within the institutions that we love and in turn the institutions should then enable us to affect change in ourselves.

I hope this portrait is of some help to you.

Peace,

Uncle Matthew

# II.  The Journey Turns:
# Doubt, Courage, and Wonder: The Transition
# to Second Half of Life Spirituality

Letter #13
Saturday, January 14, 2012


Dear Uncle Matthew,

My time at home during the Christmas break went well. However,
I did experience loneliness along with the sexual temptations we
discussed earlier. I increasingly see the connection between the
two. Since I am 25 and I am not dating, I missed the daily
companionship of my classmates. My parents were both working
while I was home.

Your last letter to me was helpful. I appreciated the portraits of
persons who practice first half of life spirituality. Also sharing
about the importance of affirmation was helpful. I never thought
about the importance of affirmation, and yet as I now consider it,
I sense its powerful absence here. Without intimate friendships, it
is difficult for me to have my affirmation needs met.

Your letters make me aware that I could easily think when I am
ordained that I am a finished product. I am more aware that I
could become arrogant if I fail to know about and pursue these
new goals you discussed. The title, "Father," can help me to
serve people, or it can make me think that I am better than
others, so I should be served. My education can likewise assist
me in serving others, or my education can mislead me to thinking
I have all the answers, so I do not have to learn from the laity.

Can you give me some help on how and when the transition takes place into the practice of second half of life spirituality? I really like your examples from movies to describe points that you are making.

Thanks, Uncle Matthew.

Peace,

Joey

Response to Letter #13
Saturday, January 28, 2012

Dear Joey,

Happy Birthday! Today is your twenty-sixth birthday! Today is also the feast of St. Thomas Aquinas called the angelic doctor, the author of the Summa Theologica. Perhaps one day you will be able to write words of wisdom to inspire the next generation.

You mentioned loneliness and sexual temptations while you were home for your Christmas break. I'm sure all of us experience loneliness and sexual temptations when we are away from our community and our friends. You will have to learn how to deal with loneliness in a constructive way. Earlier, I shared with you the story of Fr. Tom who discovered as a newly ordained priest the difficulties connected to loneliness, temptation, and practicing chastity. In Alcoholics' Anonymous, loneliness is regarded as one of the triggers to addictive behavior.

I am gratified that you dialogue. You are helping me to re-think my own ministry as a priest. I have made so many mistakes. I have suffered so much needlessly. I have caused others to suffer because I was not sufficiently aware of the practice of second half of life spirituality until last year, a pivotal point for me, when I attended the Richard Rohr Conference on the two halves of life spirituality.

The importance of a solid foundation:

In order to make the transition from the practice of first half to second half of life spirituality, you must have made great progress in completing the goals in first half of life spirituality. Knowing the Ten Commandments is necessary before you can understand the Beatitudes. Knowing the stories in the Bible is necessary before your can appreciate the many literary forms in the Bible. You now have the benefit of a seminary formation program that is preparing you well in the practice of first half of life spirituality. Jesus often told those who listened to him that the time was at hand to repent, to change. As we age, we do need to change as we struggle with the desire for stability, not change.

The transition into the practice of second half of life spirituality:

The transition from the practice of first half of life spirituality to second half of life spirituality comes about over a long period of time. The Parable of the Sower can be found in Matthew 13. Jesus said that seeds are new life; the Word of God. Everyday and in every event of our lives, seeds are planted. Seeds begin to be planted in us when we are young. But usually we are older with more experiences before we understand the meaning behind the seeds that were sown in us earlier in life. New experiences prompt us to think and question old assumptions. It is only later, after the fact, that we realize we are beginning to understand reality differently. Then we are ready to practice second half of life spirituality.

Moving into the practice of second half of life spirituality is not necessarily chronological. Some younger individuals, especially those who have learned lessons from early suffering, practice some goals of second half of life spirituality. Many older individuals are still practicing first half of life spirituality. I see in you, Joey, that you have accomplished many goals found in the practice of second half of life spirituality. The fact that you are questioning is a really good sign that you are willingly transitioning into an adult spirituality.

The transition into different stages of life comes gradually and with much pain. In our early years, we share the opinions, loyalties, and religious faith of our parents. Around our junior year in high school, we begin to detach ourselves from our parents. We make decisions that are independent of and often in contradiction to those of our parents. Already in the teenage years, during this period of transition, we begin to experience new seeds that make us re-think and question.

Rebellion is a critical step in the process adolescents take in growing out of their dependency upon their parents' authority. It is a necessary step for the mental, emotional, and spiritual shift into responsible adulthood.

C. G. Jung called the process of transitioning into a new stage of life "individuation." Just as children must grow up and out of dependency upon parental authority, so too we must continually work to form our conscience so that we no longer give blind obedience to civil or church authorities.

Different ways of seeing reality:

We all observe that people see reality in different ways. Movies sometimes demonstrate that observation as well as our friends who share with us stories about their own experiences in becoming aware of a larger world, a different reality. But most importantly, our own experiences alert us to a bigger world, a plurality of thought, and different viewpoints regarding morality.

Practicing second half of life spirituality invites us to integrate our opposites so as to become whole. When we practice second half of life spirituality, we refuse to separate nature from grace and the profane from the sacred. Teilhard de Chardin said, "By virtue of the creation, and still more, of the Incarnation, nothing here below is profane for those who know how to see."

You said that you enjoy examples from movies, so I shall describe several films that provide interesting observations showing how the transitioning process from the practice of first to second half of life spirituality not only varies with individuals but in some cases never happens.

The movie, Giant:

In 1956, the movie Giant was released. The film starred Rock Hudson who played the role of Bick, the head of a wealthy Texas ranching family.  Elizabeth Taylor played the role of Leslie, a wealthy socialite, who became Bick's wife. James Dean played the role of Jett, a local handyman.

The movie focuses on themes of discrimination (race, class, and gender) over a quarter century from the nineteen twenties until after World War II. The movie realistically shows how difficult it is to change our patterns of behavior and our prejudices. Jett never changed his prejudices involving race and class. Leslie very early in her marriage experienced a local family that was suffering. This experience sowed the seeds that enabled her to lose any prejudice regarding race and class. Bick never changed his prejudices involving race, class, and gender until late in his life when he was confronted by his children and grandchildren.

The movie points out that the transition into the practice of second half of life spiritually may never come about as in the case of Jett, or it can come about early in life when an experience opens one's eyes to a new way of thinking as in the case of Leslie, or the transition may only come about late in life through one's grandchildren as in the case of Bick.

The Film, the Ultimate Gift:

In 2007, I saw the film, The Ultimate Gift that is about a very rich man who died and left his estate to his family members. But to Jason, his grandson, he left the promise of the Ultimate Gift, if Jason could successfully complete twelve separate assignments within a year.

The lawyer who managed the deceased man's estate was

assisted by Miss Hastings, an older woman who was patient and compassionate with Jason.   Without her influence, I doubt if Jason would have ended up accomplishing all the twelve tasks.

Before he accomplished the twelve tasks, he was lazy. He was a spoiled under-achiever who never had to genuinely work. He never knew about or practiced first half of life spirituality. He had no true friends. He could not share with others. He was ungrateful for what he possessed. But after completing the twelve assignments, he was transformed. He showed that he was practicing a spirituality that he formally lacked. He actually showed signs that he was practicing second half of life spirituality that enabled him to value the gifts of work, money, friends, learning, problems, family, laughter, dreams, giving, gratitude, and love.

We can learn two lessons from the Ultimate Gift. First, women play an important role in helping men to integrate their opposites as well as to develop the traits of empathy, compassion, and patience during the second half of life. Second, structures that do not include female leadership run the risk of staying legalistic and self-serving rather than being instruments of patience, compassion, and service to others. Celibate men who are not allowed to marry run the risk of never fully developing their opposites. Engaging in significant friendships with women encourages men to develop the important virtues of patience, empathy, and compassion. The feminine influence is so necessary if men are to become fully alive and fully human.

I have much more to share at another time.

Peace,

Uncle Matthew

Letter #14
Sunday, February 12, 2012

Dear Uncle Matthew,

Thank you for sending me good examples of how and when the transition takes place into the practice of second half of life spirituality. I found your insights from the movies Giant and The Ultimate Gift to be very helpful. You explained the movies very well. I have not seen the movie Giant. I could visualize Bick, Leslie, and Jett who experienced the same situations and yet their responses were so different. This film was like a mirror for me. In the seminary, we all have the same basic experiences, but we each react differently. I guess it shows that the ego is so strong, and it sometimes blinds us to reality.

A few years ago, I saw the movie, The Ultimate Gift. I failed to notice the two spirituality lessons you observed. But upon reflection, I can now appreciate the movie's emphasis on the role of women in the transformation process. With Netflix, I can easily view movies and get the drift of the characters. Wikipedia often provides great movie summaries.

We are having a cold winter up here. We are inside most of the time since it is too cold outside for organized sports. My prayer life is going well. I'm watching my diet, and I walk or jog to keep physically fit.

You said that there was more to come on how and when the transition to the practice of second half of life spirituality takes place. I'm all ears.

Thank you.

Peace,

Joey

Response to Letter #14
Tuesday, February 28, 2012

Dear Joey,

I'm glad that you appreciate what I send to you. I'm so grateful to
Fr. Richard Rohr for making me aware of the two halves of life
spirituality paradigm. Cicero, the great Roman statesman who
died about 50 years before Jesus was born said, "Gratitude is
not only the greatest of virtues, but the parent of all other
virtues."

Transitioning into the practice of second half of life spirituality
(continued):

Remember, transitioning into the practice of second half of life
spirituality is an on-going process that never ends. Throughout
life, new experiences challenge us to see reality differently. In
our retirement years, we still have experiences that challenge us
to see reality differently as I pointed out to you in the movie,
Giant. Bick never changed his prejudices involving race, class,
and gender until late in his life when he was confronted by his
children and grandchildren. No two journeys are ever the same.

Meister Eckhart pointed out that spirituality has more to do with
subtraction than addition. When we practice first half of life
spirituality, we try to attain great spiritual insights and overcome
all our imperfections. It's all about achieving, performing, being

rewarded, and being recognized, yet we do not realize how the ego is in control.

When we practice second half of life spirituality, we try to let go of our own will, our own needs, our preferences, and find our happiness on a deeper level. We gradually realize that so much of what we once thought was so important (a big home, a master's degree, a title, a large bank account, a fancy car, trophies in the den) is really not that important. In the movie, The Ultimate Gift, you saw a transformation in Jason whereby he was willing to share with others.

Since you like examples, I'll share some more movies that show how individuals transition or fail to transition into a new awareness.

The film, The Age of Innocence:

Usually we think of spirituality as something to do with piety, detachment, regimented prayer, and living an other-worldly life. I'm trying to show you that in the practice of second half spirituality to be spiritual means to be animated, fully human, and fully alive. If we believe in an Incarnate God, then everything we do offers us opportunities to witness to God's Spirit alive in us. In the movies I share with you, I'm not defining spirituality in the older dualistic way, but in this newer non-dualistic way of seeing all our interactions as somehow connected to the practice of spirituality.

I'll share with you my thoughts regarding a movie that clearly shows a man who had the opportunity to change and live a totally different life style, a new spirituality, that would have better enabled him to become fully human and more fully alive, but he missed the opportunity.

The film The Age of Innocence is a satire on the culture, morals, and customs of an elite circle of New Yorkers in the late nineteenth century. Newland (Daniel Day-Lewis), a wealthy lawyer, is engaged to marry May (Winona Ryder) from another wealthy family. Newland and May were locked into the rules of conformity, a sign of practicing first half of life spirituality.

May's cousin, the Countess Ellen (Michelle Pfeiffer) returned to New York from Europe after she unwisely married a Polish Count who took her fortune. There was a lot of malicious gossip about the Countess, but Newland began to admire the Countess' unconventional views on New York society. Newland became increasingly disillusioned with his fiancée May. He told the Countess that May was like a curtain with nothing behind it.

The Countess provided Newland many opportunities to leave the world that bound him to a conventional way of living and move instead into a new world of passion and excitement that would have given him a more meaningful existence. But he failed to move into a new way of living. Even later in his life, at the age of fifty-seven, Newland was so bound by his status and the culture that formed him that he could not transition into a new way of thinking and living.

Newland's inability to transition into a life that would bring him greater happiness mirrors how many laypersons realize at age fifty-seven that they are "stuck." Like Newland, they may have had many opportunities to change their way of life, to transition into the practice of second half of life spirituality, but they lacked the courage and a readiness to face the consequences. They found it easier to repress those "temptations" and just stick with what was safe.

What we see in Newland, happens to clerics in the Church. Many priests have left the active ministry and married because they realized at some stage of life that their "temptations" for a fuller life were not bad but good. Other priests dismissed temptations to change and embrace a fuller life. Motivation varies, so discernment of spirits is necessary. But, if God is calling some clerics to make a change and they fail to respond, they pay a price. They miss out, like Newland, because life can offer so much more. We should not judge what others do. Perhaps some priests who have left the active ministry are making a serous mistake. Perhaps others who leave the active ministry see something we fail to see as adults when we continue to practice first half of life spirituality.

The movie, Titanic:

In 1997, the movie Titanic was released. I remember that you told me that you liked that movie which won eleven Academy Awards including Best Picture.

The movie tells the story that in 1912, seventeen-year-old Rose was engaged to an aristocrat named Cal. They were both traveling first class on the Titanic. There was a penniless artist, Jack, who was also traveling on the Titanic. Rose met Jack by accident, and she realized that Jack had qualities she wanted. Jack was a risk-taker, fearless, grateful for life, unattached to anyone or anything, yet relational with many people and very honest. Jack was a young man of integrity. In a short period of time, Rose transitioned from a snobbish-young-women into a person with passion. She experienced dancing and singing and she felt fully human and fully alive. She discovered happiness that could only come by becoming more open to change and being less dualistic in her thinking.

Titanic shows how the influence of a fully alive person can be a powerful instrument in enabling others to transition from the practice of first into second half of life spirituality. We all want to experience the fullness of life. We all want to give and receive love. We all admire and are attracted to individuals who live their full humanity, who are honest, sincere, and willing to take chances. Experiencing individuals who are fully human and alive may be the catalyst that we need to move onto a path that is undefined.  Preaching with words rarely converts anyone. Being fully alive gets people's attention.

Giving up the false self:

The late Trappist monk Fr. Thomas Merton wrote in his book, New Seeds of Contemplation,

"Everyone is shadowed by an illusory person: a false self. This is the man that I want myself to be but who cannot exist, because God does not know anything about him… My false self is the one who wants to exist outside the reach of God's will and God's love; outside of reality and outside of life."

In the above movie examples, we can see that some people are willing to give up their false self, like Rose in Titanic, and move on to discover and display to others their true self that was meant to be fully human and alive. And yet other people hold on to their false self, like Newland in The Age of Innocence. They are fearful of taking a leap of faith, of making that transition that demands major change in their lives.

We are all attracted to individuals who seem joyful, fully alive, relational with many people, and well-rounded. They do not pretend to be without fault. Rarely do "holier than thou" people attract us. We all have met adults who are "nice" people, but we would not want to go on a trip to Disney Land with them. Perhaps these adults are "stuck" still practicing first half of life spirituality.

And yet there are other adults we have met who appear to be imperfect, yet they seem honest and transparent. Those individuals attract us. They seem to have learned that their value is found inside, not in outer appearances. They accept who they are. They have made progress in putting aside their false self and they accept their true self. We all feel comfortable with individuals who live the expression, "What you see is what you get." These men and women show signs of practicing second half of life spirituality.

I once heard the late Franciscan Father Brennan Manning say, "If you want to be a martyr, marry a saint." Too often "saints" in this life cling to their false self. They do not appear real. Such individuals can be terribly difficult with whom to live.

In contrast, let me share a personal story. Recently, a man

named Paul worked on my kitchen sink. He is thirty-eight years old. He told me about his first marriage that ended in a divorce, and now his second marriage is working out so much better. He seems to be willing to give up his false self. He is secure enough to be himself. He wants to be a man faithful to his family and honest and open to spiritual growth. Suffering, set-backs, and failures have helped Paul to be willing to change without shame. His unpretentious authenticity was most refreshing.

Peace,

Uncle Matthew

Letter #15
Sunday, March 11, 2012

Dear Uncle Matthew,

Soon it will be your birthday on the seventeenth, the feast of St. Patrick. Happy Birthday! You are an amazing person. I am so grateful for your knowledge and wisdom.

Thank you for your last letter. I am becoming more aware of the rich value of the spiritual roadmap that you are sharing with me. A spiritual road map challenges me not to practice for the rest of my life the spirituality I now am developing in the seminary. I can see the danger that without a spiritual roadmap, I could spend the rest of my life trying to persuade my parishioners to worship God my way, the "right way." Wow! That scares me. I really appreciate your letters.

I really got a lot out of your examples in the films The Age of Innocence and Titanic. I have seen of these movies, and now I can't wait to watch them again.

I like how you are giving me a new understanding of the word "spirituality." I always thought of spirituality as referring to some form of piety, prayerfulness, self-discipline, and apartness. Your earlier letter that explained to me a Distant God would logically demand a spirituality that consists in novenas, indulgences, and self-discipline to correct sinful faults so as to be loved by God.

Novenas would be an attempt on a person's part to be closer to this Distant God. The way you described spirituality makes it so real and practical; something relevant to everyone, not just to nuns, seminarians, and priests.

You are helping me to see that good shepherds have to be humble if they hope to be open to growth in the spiritual life. At mass today, one of the priests used this analogy regarding humility in his homily. He said that life's suffering and pressures make us what we are, just as the pressure of the earth and length of time make a diamond from charcoal.

In your last letter, you explained very well the importance of transitioning in to an adult spirituality. What happens if we fail to transition into the practice of second half of life spirituality?
Peace,
Joey

Response to Letter #15
Friday, March 30, 2015

Dear Joey,

Recently, I was able to attend a lecture given by Bishop Geoffrey Robinson, a retired bishop from Australia. His talk was entitled, "Confronting Power and Sex in the Church; Changing the Culture." Bishop Thomas Gumbleton from the Archdiocese of Detroit introduced him. His talk was brilliant. I'm quite sure Bishop Robinson and Bishop Gumbleton are both good examples of church leaders who practice second half of life spirituality.

Robinson spoke about the culture of celibacy. He said that celibacy to be healthy has to be embraced with a passionate love for God and for people. He warned that if priests do not discover how to live celibate lives with a sense of loving and being loved, it can lead to problems such as alcoholism, seeking power, intense sexual urges, enhancing one's career, and prejudice against women.

In this letter to you, I'll try to answer your question and explain why it is important to transition into the practice of second half of life spirituality. The following difficulties are all predicated on the completion of the goals found in the practice of first half of life spirituality.

Difficulties we may face when we fail to transition into the practice of second half of life spirituality:

Michael Morwood in his book, Is Jesus God?, indicates that if adult faith is arrested at the conventional stage (first half of life spirituality), it will affect our faith life in the following ways:

1. We literally believe in the myths and the stories that we believed in childhood.

2. We literally interpret symbols. For example we will believe the Eucharist is the actual physical, bodily presence of Jesus.

3. We give uncritical loyalty to external authority.

4. We unquestionably accept dogmas and doctrines.

5. We fear changing what we were taught.

6. We believe hell and heaven are actual places.

7. We insist that our childhood images of God are correct.

I'll suggest some more difficulties that may occur if we fail to transition into the practice of an adult spirituality:

8.  We are prone to shame our children:

When parents fail to transition into the practice of second half of life spirituality, they may insist that their religion is "the only way." They want others to think they have found all the truth. Such parents with children, may unconsciously shame their children if they no longer want to attend Sunday Mass. They may use logic and apologetics to persuade their children and others that they are right. This kind of religion will most likely result in their children fleeing from their religion at a later time rather than wanting to embrace and practice this kind of religion.

9.  We may attack others:

M. Scott Peck says in his book, the People of the Lie, that people are prone to evil when they attack others rather than facing their own failures. When we continue to practice first half of life spirituality as adults, we do risk becoming like the Scribes and Pharisees in Jesus' day. They attacked others and missed being aware of their own failures. When we are prideful and self-righteous, we are unaware of our own limitations, shadow side, and failures. When we condemn other religions and impose our beliefs on others, we are living a lie because humility is missing.

10. We risk turning others away from religion:

The spiritual writers warn us that when we continue to practice first half of life spirituality, but yet we are old enough to practice second half of life spirituality, we risk turning others away from religion. We can appear to others as "too good," perhaps "too innocent." Although we can appear to be believers in all the church's dogmas and follow all the church's rules and regulations (the law), we can appear to have little tolerance with those who are not able to keep the church's rules and regulations (the law). Thus our ability to be good shepherds is diminished. Pride can take over.

The practice of second half of life spirituality teaches us to evangelize by being compassionate and merciful as well as being open to debate and discussion, whereas the practice of first half of life spirituality tends to disallow debate and discussion about many issues that are "defined" as true.

11. Our former ways of solving problems no longer work:

When change is needed in our lives during the second half of life, the ways we deal with situations using the tools we learned in the practice of first half of life spirituality no longer work. Carl Gustav Jung (1875-1961), psychiatrist and psychotherapist said, in Memories Dreams and Reflections, "What is good in the morning of life will be of no help in the evening of life." "What in the morning was true, in the evening will have become a lie."

"What is a normal goal to a young person becomes a neurotic hindrance in old age."

For example, when we practice first half of life spirituality, we may have an image of a Fatherly God up in the sky like our childhood image of Santa Claus. We believe in reward and punishment. When our prayers are not answered the way we wish, we begin to question our image of God. For example a good person may go to church every day, generously tithe, and yet come down with a serious life-threatening illness like cancer. That person faces a crisis. The former belief system did not presume that a Fatherly God would allow such a crisis. The practice of first half of life spirituality no longer works.

12.  We hold on to our "Loyal Soldier," our "Super Ego.":

Fr. Richard Rohr compares the formation of conscience during the first half of life to a "loyal soldier." He says the loyal soldier is similar to the "elder son" in Jesus' parable of the Prodigal Son. The loyal soldier represents the inner voices that remind us of what it right and what is wrong. Our parents, peers, religious leaders, neighbors, and school authorities taught values that were very important. "Hard work pays off. Be truthful! Save energy. Be frugal. Save money for a rainy day. Get ahead in life. Don't touch it or you will go to Hell." The loyal soldier gradually has to change as part of the transition process into the practice of second half of life spirituality. If we fail to modify our loyal soldier during the second half of life, we will determine right and wrong in a dualistic way instead of in a non-dualistic way.

Sigmund Freud called conscience the Super Ego. Problems occur later when the Loyal Soldier or the Super Ego becomes too unwilling to change. What once was black-and-white has to be seen differently during the second half of life. A mature conscience evolves slowly over the years from an awareness of reality that comes through personal life experiences and an awareness of God's inner voice. So often our life experiences show us the complexity of life. These experiences show us that what we thought to be true earlier in life was an illusion. These experiences are stepping stones in the process of seeing reality.

13. We fail to see the gold in our failures and suffering:

We can think in the second half of life that our failures and suffering are all an unnecessary part of the human journey. But, Dr. Carl Jung said, "Where you stumble and fall, there you find pure gold." The mystics taught that losing, failing, sin, and the suffering that comes from these experiences are necessary and even a good part of the human journey. Some of the best good shepherds in the Church have been men and women who experienced great suffering and failure.

For some people, the loss of a job can be the catalyst to move into a new way of thinking, a new spirituality. For some people a humiliation, such as a divorce or addiction, can be what is needed to transition into a better spirituality. The transition into the practice of second half of life spirituality could come about through moral failure. I know one priest who was suspended by his bishop when a sexual accusation became public. The accused priest seems to be more humble after his humiliation.

When we realize we can't keep all the church laws and regulations, we begin to question them. Questioning can lead to truth. For some individuals their moral failures in keeping the Sixth Commandment may lead them to ask many questions regarding the morality of certain actions.

A mid-life crisis can help individuals transition into the practice of second half of life spirituality. In a mid-life crisis, what earlier gave a person joy and happiness no longer does so. Routine sets in. Restlessness is experienced. Addictions may occur which could be signs that new purposefulness is needed in life.

Once again, we see the importance of life experiences that can alter previous illusions about reality. Once we see and hear for ourselves, we are ready to transition into the practice of second half of life spirituality.

I shall stop now. This is quite a lot of material to digest.

Peace,

Uncle Matthew

Letter #16
Thursday, April 12, 2012

Dear Uncle Matthew,

Holy Week was a rich experience for me this year since I know more about the liturgy. Sunday's Easter Vigil celebration was really a wonderful experience with all the readings. The rector gave a wonderful homily about the Risen Jesus being alive in the people that we meet. I have usually celebrated Easter with the thoughts of what happened at the tomb, but the rector said to concentrate on the meaning of Resurrection rather than the details of how it took place.

My studies in this second year of pre-theology are giving me a greater appreciation of the liturgy, philosophy, and the Bible. I am convinced that I am receiving an excellent education. However, in view of your letters, I realize that my formation is almost entirely rooted in the practice of first half of life spirituality. We wear cassocks on special occasions. Some of the seminarians are unfortunately already showing signs of being very clerical. I suspect some of us embrace the celibate life only because it is a requirement to become a priest, rather than because we discern that God is calling us to that charism.

Your insights are very helpful.Thank you. I can see that it often takes a lifetime to gradually transition into the practice of second half of life spirituality, and yet some people do seem to be aware of reality more quickly than others. The Spirit blows where it will! The difficulties we face when we fail to transition into the practice of second half of life spirituality make sense. I liked the "loyal soldier" analogy.

When I was in college, I met so many men in our dorm that were outgoing, funny, studious, and they were loyal friends. I sense that many of my brother seminarians look so good on the outside, but I really don't know them. We all seem to be "on guard" concerning what we say, how we act, and the friendships we make. I do miss that freedom to just be who I am; the wild part of me as well as the socially correct part of me. I sense that I am repressing a lot of anger since I have to be "nice" all the time.

When I was younger, my parents did things at times that confused me because their actions did not fit easily into the Catholic model of behavior. Why is it that these memories, peculiar and seemingly unimportant, stick with me? Was I observing glimpses of the practice of second half of life spirituality?

Peace,

Joey

Response to Letter #16
April 28, 2012

Dear Joey,

Thank you for your last letter. Your inability to be yourself at this phase of training is normal in the seminary, but it is not good. We do mature better when we can be ourselves and learn from our mistakes as well as from our successes.

A number of articles have appeared in the Catholic press concerning the Leadership Council of Women Religious (LCWR). The hierarchy's treatment of the LCWR has many implications when it comes to the practice of first and second half of life spirituality.

Also there are a number of articles in the Catholic press on the United States Department of Health and Human Services controversy regarding contraception. It is important to keep up with the news. In the practice of second half of life spirituality, one goal is to integrate the Bible and tradition with the news of the day.

I am making my letters to you the highest priority in my life. If I can be of any help to make your priesthood better for those you serve and for you personally, it is worth all the time and effort to write to you.

In your last letter, you shared that you are repressing a lot of anger. In the seminary, the expression of anger is not tolerated. It is important to discover why you are angry. Repressed anger can lead to internalized shame which can become toxic. Individuals who repress a lot of anger usually find that at times they are "out of control." I suggest that you pray to God over it so as to understand it and find inner peace. Talk to your spiritual director about this. Tell him what you are feeling. Perhaps he can help you figure out what is being repressed; what is causing your anger.

Earlier in a letter to you, I mentioned Fr. Tom's struggles to be chaste before and after his ordination to the priesthood. When he was ordained at the age of twenty-eight he was functionally a very good priest. He was dedicated to the Church. He was chaste, loyal, disciplined, orderly, and obedient. But, he later realized that he was immature. He was a good man but not a holy man of faith. He tried to be in control. He thought he had all the answers. He was not yet transitioning into the practice of second half of life spirituality. He was supposed to be a good shepherd as a young priest, but he realized that he lacked so many of the necessary qualities to be a good shepherd.

He later discovered that he had a lot of repressed anger that resulted in him being "out of control" in the area of sexuality. He couldn't please his false self that was seeking to please a God Preoccupied with Sex. Whenever we try to please a God Preoccupied with Sex, we take on an impossible goal. As we continually fail to reach that goal, we experience anger. This dynamic occurs whenever our images of God demand inhuman perfection in any areas of life.

Glimpses of the practice of second half of life spirituality:

You asked why you can recall glimpses of your parents' different religious behavior that did not fit the Catholic model. I believe we recall particular experiences of different religious behavior because God plants these seeds in us. I believe these memories are very important to recall because they give us new insights that jar us so as to become aware that there are different ways of thinking, judging, and acting.

You also wondered if these experiences were glimpses of the practice of second half of life spirituality. Yes, very often these experiences are the seeds that alert us to the practice of second half of life spirituality. I'll share with you some examples of individuals who saw glimpses of the practice of second half of life spirituality when they were young, but they did not understand at the time the significance of these glimpses.

I ran into an old friend, Fr. Joe, while at the Conference on the Two Halves of Life last year. He shared with me some little seeds that were planted early in his life that gave him glimpses of the practice of second half of life spirituality, but he was unaware at the time of their significance. At the Conference, he realized that these experiences helped him later to transition into the practice of second half of life spirituality.

When Fr. Joe was about twelve years old, he recalled that his mother gave him permission to join the YMCA because this Protestant organization taught young boys how to swim. At the time, a priest told his mother he could not belong to that Protestant organization. But since the Y taught swimming, his mother let him join. Later in life, Fr. Joe realized that his mother broke a church rule because the rule did not make any sense to her. She listened to her own inner authority.

Fr. Joe's mother smoked cigarettes when he was young. She told Joe the cigarettes were in a drawer if he ever wanted to experiment. Likewise, Joe knew where his parents kept liquor for guests. When he grew up, he and his siblings were offered spiked eggnog at Christmas and wine on festive occasions. The attitude of his parents helped him to see rules more as guidelines rather than absolutes. Because his parents trusted him to make good decisions, he was never tempted to abuse cigarettes or alcohol.

When Fr. Joe was an early teen, his aunt and uncle visited. Their visit was during the holy season of Lent. Fr. Joe's parents bought food for a special dinner when their guests arrived on a Friday.

When the meal was served, his aunt and uncle said they couldn't eat the meat his parents had prepared since it was Friday. Fr. Joe's parents were very upset since they did not have a lot of money. The lesson Fr. Joe learned was hospitality should override legalism. His aunt and uncle should have appreciated what his parents prepared and overlooked his parents' mistake rather than being legalistic about a day of fast and abstinence.

I had some significant experiences early in my own life that sowed seeds for my later transition into the practice of second half of life spirituality. My own experiences earlier in my life have proven the proverbial saying, "You learn more from things that happen to you in real life than you will from hearing about or studying things that happen to other people" to be true.

When I completed my junior year in a public high school, the principal announced that in the fall the school would be integrated. Since I had never known a person of color or gone to school with any African Americans, I was fearful of this new experience.

In the fall when I went back to school, I met an African American girl named Gail in a writing club after school. She was extremely bright, very friendly, and quite attractive. To my surprise, I soon found out that there were some new classmates that I liked and others I did not like. My image of an Exclusive God that loved people like me more than people not like me was challenged.

One day in the boys' locker room, I noticed an African American boy next to me who did not have underwear. I was shocked. I never knew that some kids might be so poor as not to have underwear. My image of My God was challenged. Seeing this boy made me realize that I should be more concerned about others instead of just my own needs.

In my senior year, I admired our senior class president, Henry. He was handsome, a star quarter-back on the football team, personable, smart, and humorous. He was a Protestant. I could tell that although Henry may not have been Catholic, he was psychologically healthy, robust, talented, and on the way to being a fully human and fully alive person. My gut intuitions did make me question why I was taught in my faith formation program to feel sorry for those kids who were not Catholic and did not have our sacraments.

During my senior year of high school, seeds were planted that helped me to see reality in a new way. I was still learning the basics of practicing first half of life spirituality that encouraged me to see reality in a dualistic way, but the seeds were planted that would help me later to be more compassionate, more sensitive, less dualistic, and less judgmental of others. God was planting seeds that already made me question my unconscious images of God with newer images of God. I was thinking that maybe God is unconditionally loving, far more inclusive than what I thought, and somehow instead of being far away, God was closer to me in the kids in school.

I learned from going to a public high school that included students of different races, religions, and creeds that this is reality! We are all different yet one. Seeds were planted that helped me later to understand the practice of second half of life spirituality that stresses our interdependence.

When I was twenty-four years old, I returned to my college seminary after Christmas vacation. At the bus station, I met a college student named Charlie who was returning to the University of Pennsylvania. We sat together on the bus and talked about many things. He was so gifted. He was not practicing any religion. I was deeply attracted to him. I saw in him many traits I did not have. I wanted some of his traits. He was friendly, positive, self-disciplined, healthy, and self-confident. He could accept himself as he was. The trip was an "epiphany experience" for me. Perhaps I sensed that he was accomplishing some of the goals in the practice of first half of life spirituality as well as some of the goals in the practice of second half of life spirituality even though at the time I did not have knowledge about this paradigm of the two halves of life spirituality.

The twenty-one hours of time with Charlie on the bus had a profound influence upon me because seeds were planted that helped me later to understand the words of the second century Saint Irenaeus who said, "The glory of God is a person fully alive." I sensed that his wholeness made him holy. Up to that point, I thought holiness had to do with simply worshipping my images of God. Charlie was showing me that holiness could also be found in a fully human person who uses his talents wisely to relate well with others and be fully alive.

I realize now that when I was your age, my practice of first half of life spirituality had left me with an inability to see beyond what I was told to be true. My heart was telling me Charlie was holy, good and radiant with something special. I shared the experience with my spiritual director, a priest, upon returning to the seminary. I asked him if Charlie could avoid mortal sin as a non-Catholic. The priest told me with sadness that Charlie would fall into mortal sin since he did not have the sacraments. My religion was telling me that Charlie was doomed for Hell unless he changed.

Already at the age of twenty-four, these early experiences of seeing glimpses of the practice of second half of life spirituality were urging me to question. But I did not have a spiritual roadmap. I did not have a broad overview of the spiritual journey. I did not have anyone to show me a new path that embraced an adult spirituality. I also lacked a wise and good shepherd to guide me.

Peace,

Uncle Matthew

Letter #17
Saturday, May 12, 2012

Dear Uncle Matthew,

This academic year went by so quickly. In the fall I shall begin first theology. These two years of pre-theology were good. I now have a better foundation to prepare for theological studies, and I have a better grasp of the practice of first half of life spirituality.

The bishop assigned me to a different parish this summer. I'll let you know about the assignment after I arrive.

I liked your last letter very much. The glimpses of the practice of second half of life spirituality that Fr. Joe and you both experienced helped both of you to begin questioning at an early age. You are helping me to realize that personal experiences are so important in life to teach us about reality. So often in the seminary, we rely on books to teach us instead of being urged to dig deep into our own experiences so as to discover the truth.

I am beginning to journal about my own remembrance of seeds that were planted earlier in my own life. My two years of work experience at the National Security Agency (NSA) give me some insights that I am writing down. Also my four years in college afforded me many insights about people, situations, religion, and spirituality. Up until now, it never crossed my mind to map my own spiritual journey. I want to write down reflections, like you

did, about those individuals who were "stepping stones" in my
own spiritual journey.

Your story about Charlie also was so insightful. When you
became aware that Charlie was fully human and fully alive, you
were struck as though by lightening that his ability to celebrate
life was a sign of holiness. Here in the seminary, I find that we
get along better with the faculty if we are not too human; not too
fully alive. The quiet ones who are smart seem to succeed better
than the extroverted ones who speak up.

Let me hear more. Thank you.

Peace,

Joey

Response to Letter #17
Monday, May 28, 2012

Dear Joey

Today is Memorial Day. It is a day for me to remember the bravery of all those individuals who died while serving in the armed forces.

In my last letter to you, I shared some glimpses of the practice of second half of life spirituality that stimulated Father Joe and me to question our early images of God that we assumed were true. I shall share some more experiences that provided the seeds for transitioning later into the practice of second half of life spirituality.

Glimpses of the practice of second half of life spirituality (con't):

Fr. Louis:

During my years in the seminary, I was confused at times when well-educated priests seemed to say things that did not make good common sense to me. I did question remarks that were made, but only in my mind, not in my actions. I gave up my inner authority and usually accepted what my professors told me to be true. Looking back, I can see that some of my professors really were poor shepherds. I realized much later that some of my professors who were practicing first half of life spirituality were doing me a disservice. But, I also realized later that they were simply conveying to us in class what they had learned as students.

For example, one day in a philosophy class I asked my priest-professor, Fr. Louis, if a lay-person could be holier than a priest. His answer was, "No." He said, "A priest has the Sacrament of Holy Orders, so a priest is holier than a lay-person." I doubted his correctness, but I still felt intimidated by his answer. I kept my opinion to myself. The atmosphere in the seminary when I was studying did not encourage students to disagree with the professors.

Father Lorenzo:

During my theological preparation for the priesthood, I met an older pastor, Father Lorenzo, who was going to be transferred to another parish. He wanted to get rid of some of his possessions. I helped him pack his belongings, and he told me I could look at his books and take whatever I wanted. I immediately grabbed up a few spiritual classics. I took Abbot Marmion's book, Christ the Life of the Soul and Edward Leen's book, In the Likeness of Christ. I did not realize then that these books were classics for first half of life spirituality.

At the time I could not understand why Fr. Lorenzo would give away such classic works. Many years later, I realized that he was practicing second half of life spirituality. He was replacing his books that stressed primarily the practice of first half of life spirituality with books that better helped him to understand and practice second half of life spirituality. He was a good shepherd to me, but I was too young to appreciate his wisdom. He made me think. Why would he give away such good books?

Now that I am aware of the paradigm of first and second half of life spirituality, I have often thought about his willingness to change, to be open to reform, to repent, and to be open to new ideas. His witness to me of his willingness to continue to grow has served as a paradigm of what we all have to do.

Father Marvin:

Shortly after being ordained a priest, the pastor in the parish where I resided suddenly died. The bishop replaced him with Father Marvin who earlier was my vocations' director. He was progressive in his thinking. In fact to this day, I refer to some of the reflections he had published on the Sunday liturgies. He was a mentor for me as well as for so many other young men. He was a born leader. People respected him. He stressed the issues of peace and justice. His vision of a Vatican II Church with active participation inspired me. He took a leadership role in integrating an Afro-American parish and school with a predominately Caucasian parish and school. He was willing to maintain his integrity as he faced strong opposition, and he persevered. He had deep values and strong boundaries, and he stuck to them. I did not know at the time that he was practicing second half of life spirituality, but I could tell that he was a good shepherd. He made me think. How can he be so courageous? How did he become a man of such integrity? How can I become more like him?

Jonathan:

In my third year of priesthood, I met a college student named Jonathan. He was barefoot. He wore a wrinkled green shirt and old faded blue jeans. His hair was quite long, parted down the middle and tied in the back. He had recently dropped out of college. We took a walk together. I asked him, "Do others misjudge you?" He said, "Yes, in fact they do." His way of dressing and acting embarrassed his parents. Some of his peers came to him for drugs, but he did not smoke marijuana or use any drugs. Some of his relatives thought he was a failure for dropping out of college. His father, a retired colonel, was disappointed in him because he was a pacifist. He was not practicing the religion in which he was baptized, so some of his friends thought he was irreligious.

But as I walked with him and talked to him, I had the strong impression that he was on the way to becoming fully human and fully alive. He told me he spent long periods of time in contemplative prayer. He fasted. He read about the eastern religions. He didn't eat meat. His lifestyle was simple. He had few clothes. He had no car. He was growing his own food. He had many friends. I sensed that he was a holy young man with a deep spirituality. I could tell he was very intimate with God. I was humbled because I could tell he was far holier than I.

Jonathan was an important stepping stone in the process of transitioning into the practice of second half of life spirituality. It would take me many years before I could appreciate this chance meeting with him as another "epiphany experience." Meeting Jonathan forced me to think. I had to re-evaluate what I had learned about an Exclusive God. His holiness went beyond the boundaries that I learned in the practice of first half of life spirituality. He made me aware that God must be bigger than what I had been taught. Walking with him resonated with words from Proverbs, "Walk with the wise, and you will become wise." St. Augustine discovered in the fifth century, "Many belong to the Church who do not belong to God, but many belong to God who do not belong to the Church."

Jonathan made me re-think that holiness comes when a person works to be holy. I was into a "capitalist spirituality." When practicing first half of life spirituality, it is easy to think, "More is better." In my earlier years in the seminary, I made novenas. I counted my rosaries and the times I privately prayed the stations of the cross. I spent a lot of time alone in the chapel. I thought saying more prayers was making me holy. I thought my prayers made it possible for me to bargain with God. I would say, "God if you do this for me, I will offer up six rosaries." Meeting Jonathan made me re-think about my image of My God Alone whom I thought I could manipulate.

Meeting the two college age young men, Charlie attending the University of Pennsylvania and Jonathan a college drop-out, made me realize some holy people do not say many prayers, but they love their neighbor. Jesus said, "By this shall all men know that you are my disciples, that you love one another as I have loved you" (John 13:35).

An openness to new paradigms:

After Easter, our first readings at mass were from the Acts of the Apostles. The members of the early church shared their possessions in common and worked to form a community that embraced both the Jews and the Gentiles. Your experiences and my experiences in life remind us of the challenges today to duplicate what the early Christians modeled for us. With adult images of God, we are better able to be open to new paradigms.

When we practice first half of life spirituality, we are suspicious of those who embrace other religions and even those who live in other countries. We can seek to build walls to divide rather than bridges to unite. We can forget about the common good and think only of our good. We can be judgmental of those who don't practice any religion. So as a result, we can be poor shepherds.

Conclusion:

I'm so glad that you are going to write down some of your own reflections on individuals and situations that were stepping stones in your own spiritual journey. Memories that provided us glimpses of the practice of second half of life spirituality make us grateful for and aware of those men and women who challenged us earlier in life to re-think, re-learn, change, convert, and question.

The goal for us when we practice second half of life spirituality is to become good shepherds who love and serve all God's children.

Peace,

Uncle Matthew

# III.  The Journey Forward:
# The Emergence and Impact of Second Half
# of Life Spirituality

Letter #18
Friday, June 8, 2012


Dear Uncle Matthew,

Thank you for your last letter. I especially liked your story about Jonathan. I can see that meeting him shortly after you were ordained really helped you to become aware of your unconscious images of God. By "unconscious images of God" I am pointing to the fact that although we are not aware of it, we have images of God that shape our experiences of reality so becoming conscious of our images of God is very important

I have always thought that holiness is connected to devotions, external signs of piety, and manifested in those who attend mass frequently. You were lucky enough to attend a public high school, so you were fortunate to meet students that qualified or even contradicted what you were being taught in faith formation. Your unconscious images of God were challenged. So, for you, the questioning began early in your life.

Yesterday, I arrived at my parish assignment which officially begins on Monday. The parish is in the inner–city, so this assignment should give me an opportunity to meet people from many nationalities and different backgrounds. The pastor told me that there are many homeless individuals who come to the rectory daily, and so it is fortunate that we have a Society of St. Vincent de Paul on church property to assist them. The pastor appears to be in his early sixties. He is the only priest assigned to this parish of about 600 families.

To further our dialogue, can you give me some examples of how our images of God change as we have new experiences in life and transition into the practice of second half of life spirituality?

Peace,

Joey

Response to Letter #18
Wednesday, June 27, 2012

Dear Joey,

Thank you for calling me last week. I'm sorry it took me so long
to respond to your last letter. I had to gather information from my
journal to share with you.

I'm glad that you like your summer assignment although as you
hinted, it is difficult for you to be yourself when you are living in a
"fish bowl." On top of that, you are aware that you will be
evaluated at the end of your summer assignment.

I know you are aware that all your new experiences are so
important. This makes me think of Mark Twain who said, "Travel
is fatal to prejudice, bigotry, and narrow-mindedness, and many
of our people need it sorely on these accounts."

When I was a seminarian, all my summer assignments were at a
summer camp where we provided religious education for boys
and girls who lived in the rural part of the state. Many of the boys
and girls were from poor families. The seminarians were joined
by ten female counselors, ten nuns, and several lay college
students. Unlike your current experience, we were basically able
to be ourselves during those camp assignments. The camp
director, a priest, often looked the other way so as to give us
some freedom which was healthy. We instructed the kids in the

morning with a faith formation program, and in the afternoons we organized swimming, boating, games, and other sports. The kids loved to come to summer camp, so they were easy to manage. I enjoyed working on the dock with my classmate Fred where we taught the kids how to crab.

I have noticed in this diocese that when seminarians are assigned to parishes for the summer, they can unconsciously try to be "little priests" which is not healthy if they are to have normal relational experiences. In this diocese, the seminarians who assemble for their annual retreat during the summer are pictured wearing black pants, white shirts, and black ties which could be a sign that they are being instilled with seeds of clericalism early in their formation. I urge you to be aware of these subtle temptations.

Introduction to our images of God in the practice of second half of life spirituality:

As we shared in the last two letters, our images of God can change if we are consciously open to change. New images of God both enable and reflect the transition process into the practice of second half of life spirituality.

Earlier in a letter to you, I shared some thoughts about the importance of our images of God. Before I share some new images of God, I'll review some basic information about images of God.

Early encounters with behavior, not in accord with the traditional Catholic way of acting, such as joining the YMCA, flexibility during Lent, experimenting with cigarettes and wine, and befriending people like Charlie and Jonathan, can result in questioning and eventually changing our images of God. Our images of God that come from our new experiences essentially are saying, "Wait! God is more than that! Look at this!" As our experiences in life become more varied, our images of God may become more enriched. As life's lessons, often accompanied by suffering, yield hard-won worldly wisdom, so too our understanding of God is given new qualities. When transitioning into the practice of second half of life spirituality, we discover that God is no longer the simple, remote, bearded old man on a heavenly throne.

Images of God, just like words about God, do not contain God. They point to God. They suggest and approximate. They may evoke but they are not themselves God. And so our faith, lived, guided, and informed, in part, through the images of God we hold, is a process, and yes, a struggle. Though not easy, this is good. For change, growth, and struggle all go together.

We use anthropomorphisms when we form images of God. That means we see God, who is not human, in terms of human or personal characteristics. Thus, we have images of God as a father, male, vindictive, judgmental, fully human, a mother, a potter, a warrior, a friend, a lover, and a lawgiver. St. Thomas Aquinas commented that the highest form of knowledge about God is the knowledge of God "as the unknown."

Paradoxes force us to grow. As we have new experiences we begin to think, "I could be wrong." We doubt. As we grow, evolve, change, and observe, we accept the fact that we do not believe the same things that we did four years ago. We should be glad of this. We experience leaps of faith when we trust in the unknown. Our faith helps us to believe that God is with us, for us, and sustains us as we strive for a more authentic life.

For most of us, the process is like taking two steps forward and then one step backwards. There is a Zen proverb that says, "When the pupil is ready, the teacher will appear." For many priests, our images of God began to change after leaving the safe harbor of seminary formation. The teacher appears through new experiences. The form of instruction varies, as suggested above, but a common element is an encounter with change. Change is an essential part of life whether it is a new career assignment, a new friend, a new city, a new awareness of oneself.

1. An Incarnate God:

You asked me for some examples that show that our images of God change as we have new experiences in life. I'll share how I discovered an Incarnate God. My first assignment was to teach religion in a Catholic high school in the fall of 1968. As the school year progressed in an atmosphere of young and eager students, I had a strong sensation of having just returned to the world after a ten year absence. It was as if I was waking up! The seminary had nurtured me in some ways, but had isolated and blinded him in other ways. Up until that moment, I had held an image of a Distant God. During that first year of teaching, confronted daily by the buoyant, tumultuous reality of a classroom of high school students, I began to experience an image of an Incarnate God.

I was forced to question my image of a Distant God that seemed adequate within the narrow confines of the seminary. Yet outside the seminary, the world was full of change, conflict, dreams being killed, and ideas being born. During the year when I was ordained, in 1968, 16,000 young American soldiers died in Viet Nam. In March, President Johnson announced that he would not seek again the office of president. In April, Martin Luther King, Jr., was assassinated. Students took over Columbia University. In June, Robert Kennedy was assassinated. The Vatican II Council's documents were beginning to turn the Church upside down.

I discovered that the students I taught were not finding God by being quiet and spending time saying their prayers in a church building. The students were personally gripped by the moral conflicts of Vietnam and engaged in the civil rights' movement. They were interested in the Friday night football games. They were enthusiastically communicating with one another, and they were sexually experimenting in an attempt to discover their identity.

I found most of the students to be good, wholesome, well balanced, and lovable. God seemed to be feeding them spiritually through their daily activities. I thought I was a good person, but I realized that I was not too exciting to be with at a party! So, I felt challenged. If I was to be a good shepherd to these kids, certainly I had to be able to relate, understand, and speak their language. I gradually realized that the root cause of my inability to adapt at becoming a good teacher was my image of God. I worshipped a Distant God whereas the students were worshipping an Incarnate God that was part of their daily lives.

I began to change, not by giving up basic principles or beliefs, but rather by looking for God's presence in new ways and in new places. I made an effort to hear God in the "secular" music and see God's presence in the Friday night football games. I thought to myself, "After all, wasn't the nature of the Holy Trinity communication between the Father, Son, and Holy Spirit?" I tried to communicate better, being more receptive to new experiences and ways of seeing. I tried to develop some friendships not on the basis of authority, but on the foundation of receptivity and respect. The students were showing me something that I would not understand until years later when a good friend told me, "Matthew, you are as near to God as you are to your closest friend."

A few years ago, I attended a homecoming football game at Virginia Tech with several friends. I noticed that nine of the ten players on the football team were African-American. I reflected that in an earlier day this would have caused much discussion, if not controversy. Yet, happily, the students at the game seemed to be color blind. The student body seemed to accept all races as we sat in the stands, surrounded by a feeling of excitement and goodwill. The football game against Wake Forest seemed to be like a liturgy. There was rich pageantry. There was "full active participation" in the game. By way of contrast, when I came back to my parish, I noticed at a youth mass that so many young people were lethargic and uninspired.

Today, most young people seem to unconsciously believe in an Incarnate God that allows them to experience God not only in a church building but in tailgate parties and at football games. As I changed, I became more like the God I was trying to adore. I had new reverence and respect for all of life, seeing God's actions and presence not only in the Bible and in a church building, but alive in today's world in the most ordinary and common of places.

One of the most prominent poets of the Victorian era was Elizabeth Barrett Browning (1806-1861). In her work, Aurora Leigh, she expressed poetically the notion of God's presence in our daily lives, but only for those with eyes to see!

> "Earth is crammed with heaven
> And every common bush is afire with God.
> But only he who sees, takes off his shoes.
> The rest sit 'round plucking blackberries."

Mechthild of Magdeburg, a medieval mystic, said, "The day of my spiritual awakening was the day I saw all things in God and God in all things."

Fr. Richard Rohr says,"God is everywhere." I recall Fr. Richard Rohr saying, "Any attempt by any religion to say God is here and not there is pure heresy."

Julian of Norwich said, "The fullness of joy is to behold God in everything."

During the practice of first half of life spirituality, we usually think of "incarnation" as referring only to Jesus taking flesh. We think of Jesus as being sent down by the Father to redress the wrong that human beings had done and to win back God's friendship. When I gradually began to have an image of an Incarnate God, I was beginning to see incarnation as a metaphor for all human life rather than a term applied uniquely to Jesus. I read in a book where Fr. Richard Rohr asks "When did the incarnation begin?" He answered his question by saying, "It began 14.5 billion years ago..."

I heard Fr. Richard Rohr say on a CD, "This world became the hiding and revealing place of God. It was henceforth the physical, the animal, the elements, sexuality, embodiment, and the material universe that are the hiding places and the revealing places of God."

I believe that an image of an Incarnate God has helped me to be a better shepherd and a better teacher. I began to embrace a new way of seeing. I am better able to lead others to appreciate the Incarnate God all around them. Jesus did say, "For where two or three have gathered in my name, there I am in the midst of them" (Matthew 18:20). I now am better able to believe the words, "Even though I walk through a valley dark as death, I fear no evil, for you are with me" (Psalm 23).

I hope this is helpful to you. For me and for others, changing from a belief in an image of a Distant God to an image of an Incarnate God is very important if we are to be good shepherds to the people we meet in life.

Peace,

Uncle Matthew

Letter #19
Sunday, July 8, 2012

Dear Uncle Matthew,

Your sharing of the quotes about an Incarnate God really opened my mind. I've never heard of God spoken about in that way. Every time we pray the Our Father, we say, "Our Father who art in heaven..." I guess over the years, I have always unconsciously believed that God is distant and remote, and to now conceive of Him as nearby excites me.

Your story about your first year of teaching very well described your evident awareness of a different image of God; an Incarnate God. Your insights at the Virginia Tech football game struck me as presenting a paradox. You observed that the fans were excited and fully participated in the game, but in stark contrast, at a youth mass so many of those attending were lethargic and uninspired. And yet church leaders who believe in an image of a Distant God give the impression that attending a football game is a secular event while attending mass is a holy event! We shall know by the fruits, right?

I have always thought of Jesus' birth as an event that marked the incarnation; the first time God became one with us. And yet maybe that is not the full story. You presented another view of the word "incarnation" that gives me much food for thought.

Wednesday, Independence Day, July 4, was quiet here. I watched the fireworks in the park. I find it so easy to get caught up in the beer and good food at the picnics on Independence Day, and I forget what and why we are celebrating.

Earlier you shared with me an image of an Exclusive God. Does that image of God also change?

Thank you for all the time you are giving me to help in my formation for the priesthood. With each letter you send me, I realize I have so much to learn over many years ahead.

Peace,

Joey

Response to Letter #19
Tuesday, July 24, 2012

Dear Joey,

Thank you for your last letter. You asked if our early image of an Exclusive God changes. Yes, as you grow with new experiences in life you will hopefully transition from a belief in an image of an Exclusive God into a belief in an image of an Inclusive God. New experiences can leave us confused. We cannot understand what is happening. At times we are suddenly touched by a new experience that turns our lives up side down.

When I met Charlie on a bus while I was a seminarian, and when I met Jonathan, a college drop-out from the University of Georgia shortly after my ordination, these two experiences confronted me with an image of an Inclusive God who greatly loved and favored these two men.

2. An Inclusive God:

Kathryn Kuhlman:

Early in my priesthood, I heard about Kathryn Kuhlman (1907-1976), a Methodist faith healer and evangelist. Intrigued, I drove to Atlanta, Georgia, to attend one of her services. Katherine Kuhlman was sixty-three years old at the time. I went with another priest who was also curious, but skeptical, regarding her reputation as a healer. We waited outside of the Civic Center for the doors to open. A crowd gathered, and when the doors opened, everyone rushed in. My priest-friend and I could only find two seats together in the last row of the balcony.

Kathryn, dressed in a beautiful white gown, came out to begin the service. She was tall and thin. Her first words were, "God is love." I began to cry uncontrollably when I heard those words. I knew I was receiving the Gift of Tears. I could feel the presence of God working through her in that service where many people experienced some kind of healing.

I realized that God was much larger than what I had ever imagined. I never thought God would bless a Methodist faith healer and evangelist with so many spiritual gifts. This experience of an Inclusive God helped me to be open to the possibility that great holiness can be found in non-Catholics.

Dialoguing with Mormon Missionaries:

In 1979, when I was a young pastor, two Mormon missionaries (they called themselves "elders") knocked on the door of the rectory. They wanted to share with me their beliefs in the Church of Jesus Christ of Latter-day Saints. Impressed with their fervor, I invited them in and we discussed our religious beliefs. At the time I was the diocesan vocations' director, and I was fascinated by what I might learn for my own ministry, so I invited them to return the following week. We ended up dialoguing over many weeks about our religious beliefs. I soon realized that while there were substantial, even fundamental differences, there were also important points of convergence in their beliefs to the Catholic, Protestant, and Orthodox churches.

Beyond the theology, I was very impressed with their dedication, simple life-style, sincerity, and willingness to devote two years of their lives to evangelize. I admired their self-discipline, and I learned the importance of ministering in pairs. They protected, supported, encouraged, and affirmed one another.

Over the course of two years, I attended one of their religious services. I played basketball with them in their gym. Since the rectory employed a wonderful cook who prepared meals for the three priests living in the rectory, I often invited the six missionaries in the area to join us for meals. I studied their belief system. I asked many questions. Through it all, the Catholic books critiquing the Mormon religion helped me to better appreciate their religion and my own faith as well. I felt more secure in this knowledge.

Meeting with these two young missionaries helped me to perceive God's love for them because I experienced in my own heart as well a great love and respect for them. I thought to myself, if a single human being can love them and admire them, God must likewise love them and bless them for their devotion, no matter the external form of expression or how misguided some of their beliefs may be. Meeting with these two young Mormon missionaries was an important stepping stone that helped me immensely to believe in an Inclusive God.

Over the years, I lost track of one of the young men who later became a doctor and moved to Canada with his wife and children. The other missionary is now married and is the father of six children. He and his wife live in Utah where he has become an active leader in the Mormon Church. For thirty-five years, we have exchanged Christmas cards. He wrote in his last Christmas card that he was a better person because he had met me. I can truthfully say that I too am a better person because I met, and knew, those two fine missionaries working in the service of their church.

Promise Keepers:

Fifteen years after meeting the Mormon elders, I became involved with a mens' ministry called Promise Keepers. Every Saturday morning I would go to a Protestant Church and listen to a layperson give a talk during a prayer service. That is when I again discovered an image of an Inclusive God. I couldn't believe my ears how ordinary non-ordained men could speak about God in a way that indicated that God had anointed them.

Since I was a pastor, I also invited the men in the local Promise Keepers ministry to my church and we had a prayer service when I or someone else preached. Some of my parishioners joined the movement, but other parishioners where not too supportive of my new interest.

In the Catholic Church we only allow priests and deacons to preach during mass. That policy can give the impression to the assembly that a lay person is neither worthy nor capable of preaching about God. Even at funerals, lay people are invited to give eulogies only before Mass or after communion. If a member of the non-Catholic clergy comes to a funeral and wishes to say a few words, the time offered is only after communion. While I didn't agree with all the promises, practices and statements of faith in the Promise Keeper movement, I did find that they helped me to have an image of an Inclusive God.

The Georgia Dome:

The highlight of my participation in Promise Keepers came when I attended a Promise Keepers' Conference in Atlanta, Georgia, at the Georgia Dome in 1996. Forty-thousand pastors were present. It was the largest gathering of pastors ever recorded in history. I went with three pastors from the local First Alliance Church. One of the pastors, Larry, whom I just met, would hardly speak to me on the way there. I found that strange for reasons unknown to me.

But something happened between Pastor Larry and me when on the way to the Georgia Dome. We started talking to one another. It was though a light went on within both of us. As we dialogued, we both began to be aware of our fears, prejudices, and labels of one another. We could see goodness in one another. Only through the recognition of our own limitations could we begin to see the goodness in one another.

At one session at the Conference, there was a reconciliation service when I confessed to Pastor Rick, another First Alliance pastor, and he confessed to me. Tears were streaming down our faces. At communion, they offered bread and grape juice to the forty-thousand present. Tears of joy were coming down our faces. I knew God was present in that service, in the assembly, the Word, and in the bread and grape juice.

Pastor Larry and I became the best of friends, and after the Conference, I invited him to my church to give a reflection at the Sunday Masses, and he invited me to his church to give a reflection at their Sunday service. To this day, Pastor Rick and I exchange Christmas cards. I strongly experienced an Inclusive God through the Promise Keepers ministry and Pastors Larry and Rick.

After we returned home from the Conference, I would join three pastors at the First Alliance Church for prayers once a week. I had no problem confessing my sins to them and being accountable to them. I begged for their prayers. Their counsel, wisdom, love, and affirmation were tremendous blessings.

Different forms of worship:

A few years ago, I became sick and unable to celebrate mass during my convalescence. I decided to use this opportunity to explore the many ways humans seek and find God in the world. I attended various services in different Christian churches. I discovered that God was powerfully present in both men and women who led the services.

I concluded that if we open ourselves to receive God's Word, this Inclusive God appears. It really doesn't matter where it occurs or how. The important thing is for the worshipper to desire and expect to be blessed with access to God.

Consequences of not believing in an Inclusive God:

We become like the images we have of God. That is why, Joey, if you are to become a good shepherd, it is important for you to gradually believe in an image of an Inclusive God who loves all people equally. Otherwise, if the people to whom you minister perceive that you are presenting to them an Exclusive God who loves people like them more than others, then you will be encouraging your parishioners to hold on to their prejudices because ignorance feeds prejudice. We can only really love those whom we know.

When we adore an Inclusive God, we discover that God is much larger than what we previously thought. This new image of God enables us to believe that God can use celibate men, married men, and women as church leaders. We realize that holiness is not necessarily coupled with institutional religion. God can give spiritual gifts to whomever God pleases in any house of worship. This is a joyful discovery.

As with all groups of people in all walks of life, the reality is that there are many priests and bishops who do not accept or embrace an image of an Inclusive God. This is, to my way of thinking, regrettable and a basic impediment to being a good shepherd. When priests and bishops are stuck in the practice of first half of life spirituality, it could limit their ability to witness to God's unlimited love and grace.

Our images of God determine who we are, how we act, and who we become. When we worship an image of an Inclusive God, we more likely can lead people to see glimpses of God in the most unusual of places. This is glorious to behold! Praise be!

Peace,

Uncle Matthew

Letter #20
Sunday, August 12, 2012


Dear Uncle Matthew,

Soon I will be leaving my summer assignment. I met so many people this summer from various economic and religious backgrounds. The experience was very enriching, and Pastor Jack was very kind to me. He spent a lot of his time with me. I hope that when I am ordained, the bishop will assign me to his parish. He is compassionate and wholesome. He seems to always be on duty as though he were married to his church-work. I admire his pastoral work, but I wonder if his workaholism is a toxic manifestation of one danger of a life of celibacy. I wonder if some celibates try to find meaning in life through the mechanics of their work rather than through an authentic deep personal relationship with God and with significant people.

Your many examples about a belief in an Inclusive God were very helpful. True stories about how you discovered a new way of viewing reality help me. So often in the seminary the knowledge we acquire is very abstract. You are providing me with pastoral examples that emphasize the importance of being aware of the meaning found in new experiences and in a consciousness of the role of the Gifts of the Holy Spirit. I am so grateful.

What other images of God should I be aware of in the practice of second half of life spirituality? I find it so interesting that you are able to present different ways of imagining God. I never heard anyone speak about our different images of God and how these images can and should change as we grow into an adulthood spirituality.

Peace,

Joey

Response to Letter #20
Friday, August 31, 2012

Dear Joey,

When I was a pastor, the bishop assigned several seminarians to my parish during the summer months. One of the seminarians was Peter who now is a wonderful pastor in a large suburban parish. He was willing to grow intellectually and spiritually while he was a seminarian, and he still has a thirst for new knowledge and a willingness to change. We have spent many vacations together over the years. We both enjoy the mountains. His companionship shows me that age is not a barrier to friendship. The big barriers to friendship are failures to communicate and an unwillingness to change. So I applaud your positive relationship with Pastor Jack.

There are many ways of consciously thinking about God. Many years ago, I read Joseph Campbell's book The Hero with a Thousand Faces. He observed that underlying many of the stories and myths central to cultures throughout the world, there was a common theme, or archetype, that he called "the Hero." In a similar way, if we have eyes to see, we can discern throughout our culture the human effort to express, to see, to draw close to the presence of God. These many "faces" of God come in many surprising forms and, so it seems to me, are sometimes profound and sometimes merely the product of human projection. But taken together they represent the human longing for the divine.

Exploring new images of God is an attempt to let God be a big God, not a small God.

I'll share with you my thoughts on two more images of God, a Just God and a Merciful and Compassionate God. These stories are reminders that an awareness of these new images of God came about through new experiences in life and an awareness of the life of the Spirit within.

## 3. A Just God

During the 1969-1970 school-year, I taught religion in a Catholic high school, and I had an experience that challenged me to re-examine my primary image of a God Preoccupied with Sex. In the process, I discovered a new image of God; a Just God.

It was announced that in the fall of 1970, the public schools would be integrated in the state where I lived and served. The principal of the Catholic high school announced that he would accept white transfer students, even those going into their senior year from the public schools, during the summer of 1970 before the integration was to take place. I thought the principal's decision to accept many of the best white students from the public schools at that critical time of integration would terribly hurt the public schools. More importantly, I thought the motive for students to transfer to a predominately white school would be racism, and I thought that this action by the principal was an effort to subvert integration. There were very few Black students at the Catholic high school.

I could not agree with the moral underpinning of the principal's decision, so before the end of the school year, with the permission of my bishop, I submitted a letter of resignation to my principal. I said that I would not return in the fall. My resignation was done in secret because I was told to do it quietly. The students were not told that I would not return. The faculty was not told. No one knew why I didn't return in the fall. The institutional church wanted to protect her institutions. In hindsight, I regretted remaining fully silent.

I gradually became conscious that at its core, racism is a failure to acknowledge the basic humanity of all God's children. Racism is a profound sin, at the root of much of the world's sufferings, and as such needed to be resisted. I became conscious of an image of a Just God that was more concerned about the sin of racism than with other sins, usually sexual or legalistic in nature, that I had previously obsessed about and based my spirituality upon.

As I began to adore a Just God who detested the sin of racism, I began to see that racism was far more serious than I had ever known. I had to relearn many things. In the late 60's, the civil rights' movement was in full swing with broad public sympathy for its general aims of basic social justice. I came to realize that the civil rights' challenge was not only personal and spiritual, but it challenged institutions that supported systems of inequality and injustice. With this insight, and motivated by a greater love, I came to see the world around me differently. I became more aware of systems that supported inequality and injustice.

I became aware both within and without that old ways die hard. I lamented that although I could see a new image of God as a Just God, the image of God Preoccupied with Sex was still in my head exercising significant control over my life. My "loyal soldier" was still at work. My conscience still was dualistic when it came to sex. I was only beginning to enter the practice of second half of life spirituality in the area of human sexuality. I was still holding on to an image a God Preoccupied with Sex and that image of God continued to hamper my efforts and best intentions. Thus while I was growing as a shepherd who was aware of the call to social justice, I was still hindered from the fullness of my ministry because I was still clinging to an image of a God Preoccupied with Sex.

4. A Merciful and Compassionate God:

When we practice first half of life spirituality, we often hold an image of a Vengeful God. In our Catholic culture, this image of

God often takes root early. We may be taught that if we commit a serious sin, God will send us to Hell for all eternity. Vengeful, indeed! And with this notion of God engrained in our minds, we become likewise quick to judge others by rigid rules and norms. Our expectations of others are high and uncompromising. We have little tolerance for imperfections in others, and in ourselves. We can be especially judgmental of priests who don't meet our idealized (and unrealistic) expectations. Our judgmentalism is not softened or balanced, in spite of the love and mercy that defined the life of Jesus.

Over the years, I preached many times on the Feast of Christ the King, the last Sunday in the liturgical year. I would always wrestle with the question, What kind of king was Jesus? I concluded that he was not what we ordinarily think of as a king. He did not advocate having a large army; in fact he had no army. His early followers were not the wealthy ruling class, those who typically benefit from a king's rule, but they were the poor, the simple, the outcasts, the sinners. Jesus was not a king who was most interested in making the lives of the rich better, but rather he wanted to feed the hungry. He did not see his mission as teaching the healthy, but as healing the sick. He was not a king who wished to be served, but rather he was a servant who washed the feet of others. What a strange and wonderful king! He didn't hold grudges or seek vengeance, but rather he forgave others readily and generously, even the thieves on the Cross. He didn't make money so as to separate himself from others, but rather he laid down his life for others, knowing that when we give we truly receive.

I concluded that if we were to find one virtue that marked Jesus as a King, we would say it was his mercy and compassion. The temptations, the struggles, the many conflicts endured during his ministry, transformed him to be the merciful, gentle, and compassionate person we see portrayed in the gospels. Jesus endured great suffering, and it transformed him into a merciful, gentle, and compassionate person.

I admire greatly those who are compassionate. Perhaps this is because I saw this trait in my father, William. I would like to share with you, Joey, how my father taught me about compassion without ever saying to me anything about being a compassionate person.

When my father retired, he and my mother, Regina, spent many years playing golf. Later, when my mother was in her late seventies, she had a massive stroke that left her blind in her left eye and paralyzed on her left side. She was in a nursing home for eighteen months before she died. It was by watching my father during those eighteen months that I saw firsthand the reality of mercy and compassion here on earth, and thus the probability of a Merciful and Compassionate God, the source of all goodness.

During those eighteen months, my father would arrive at the nursing home at 7:30 in the morning so that he could wash my mom and prepare her, with dignity, for the day. He would spend all day with her except for a brief time away for his meals. He would feed her when her meals came. He held her hand until she fell asleep each night. Then he would leave. During those months, I witnessed my father's incredible love, mercy, and compassion for my mother. He didn't play golf or indulge in any frivolous behavior, but instead visited his beloved wife seven days a week. She was his devotion.

My parents had always loved going to a near-by lake. Before my mother died, despite being blind in one eye and being paralyzed on her left side, she asked my father to take her down to the lake to see and feel once again nature's beauty. My father had to smuggle her out of the nursing home to his car. He managed to get her in his car, and he took her over to the lake. When they returned, he couldn't get her out of the car. He was very weak, so when he struggled to remove her from his car, she ended up falling on top of him in the driveway. I said, "Dad, what did you do then?" He said, "We just smiled at each other."

I share this story with you because there is a deep lesson here that speaks to the issue of compassion, and its hard counterpart, vengeance. I believe that my father, who died a year later, would have never become the gentle and compassionate man that I so well remember had it not been for my mother's stroke. Sickness, suffering, and pain were the means whereby God molded my father into a gentle, merciful, compassionate, and beautiful man; someone I will never forget as an exemplar of virtue and role model for my own life.

This experience of seeing my father transformed by God into an agent of compassion, combined with the realization that Jesus as a king mirrored a God of mercy, served to change my image of the divine from a Vindictive God to a Merciful and Compassionate God.

As a result, I began to appreciate other people more, as I become less judgmental. I eagerly embrace the words Jesus spoke, "Be compassionate as your heavenly Father is compassionate." And I better understood a quote by Abraham Heschel, "When I was young, I admired clever people. As I grew old, I came to admire kind people."

When we witness compassion and show mercy to others, we are truly good shepherds because we help others to know and believe in a God of Mercy and Compassion. Conversely, when we are cold, stern, judgmental, legalistic, hypocritical, and vindictive, we make it hard for others to let go of their Vindictive God. Our duty, our vocation, makes the choice clear, let us love one another.

In 2000, Pope John Paul II canonized Sr. Faustina on Divine Mercy Sunday, a universal feast day in the Catholic Church. Rev. George W. Kosicki wrote a book entitled Tell My Priests that shares what our Lord said through St. Faustina to priests about their ministry. Saint Faustina said in her Diary, "I understand that the greatest attribute is love and mercy. It unites the creature with the Creator. This immense love and abyss of mercy are made known in the Incarnation of the Word and in the Redemption [of humanity], and is here that I saw this as the greatest of all God's attributes."

Peace,

Uncle Matthew

Letter #21
Saturday, September 15, 2012


Dear Uncle Matthew,

I am beginning my courses in first theology. This university has a different atmosphere. I think it is because the student body is larger. We are from many different dioceses, whereas the college seminary was smaller and the seminarians were mostly from the same diocese. I have enjoyed meeting new men who have different personality types, political views, and varying degrees of faith formation. We are also closer to our eventual ministry. My courses are interesting. We will study the Old Testament in depth this year.

Thank you for your last letter in which you described images of a Just God and a God of Mercy and Compassion. I especially liked the story about your parents. What a blessing to have a dad who is merciful and compassionate.

This discussion of yours really got me focused on the larger issues of peace and justice instead of the relatively small matters connected to sexual behavior. I realize as we mature we should be focused on the bigger issues in life. I have thought about a Merciful and Compassionate God when I have listened to different homilies during my life. But most of the time, I have carried images of a God Preoccupied with Sex and a Vengeful God without being conscious of other alternatives.

All these new images of God certainly make me think and become aware of different ways of viewing God.

You mentioned that there are many more images of God that we can discover when we practice second half of life spirituality. Would you share them with me?

Peace,

Joey

Response to Letter #21
Saturday, September 29, 2012

Dear Joey,

I'm glad you are settled in your new seminary. Your formation
there will have a lot to do with the kind of priest you will become
in four years.

I can still remember when I entered first theology. I was assigned
to room 411-A. The seminary was crowded with seminarians. I
had a roommate during my first two years of theology. We had
bunk beds, no air conditioning, and almost no closet space. In
those days, we wore cassocks all the time, so there was no need
for too many items of clothing. The few washers and dryers were
in the basement. It was difficult to wash and dry my clothes since
my room was on the fourth floor.

My retirement is so wonderful! I finally have the time to learn and
re-learn from the experiences when I was your age. I have the
opportunity to avail myself of so many good books. I am so
grateful to have this amazing chapter in my life. It gives me great
joy to have the time to share with you, my beloved nephew,
these reflections that hopefully will benefit you in your formation
so that you become a good shepherd who truly serves others.

There are more images of God that we discover when we
practice second half of life spirituality. Our images of God have a

lot to do with our projections. When we are young, ideally our parents and church leaders expect us and enable us to be good, smart, religious, chaste, and honest. If we fail to develop these virtues, our parents correct us, possibly punish us, and we are told we must confess our sins to a priest. We assume if our parents and church leaders have these expectations about virtues and sin, then God must likewise have these expectations. We project onto God the behavior and expectations that adults have for us. Thus, we end up with many early images of God: A Vengeful God, a Distant God, a God Demanding Perfection, A God Preoccupied with Sex, My God Alone, and an Exclusive God.

Later in life, we ideally still desire to be good, religious, smart, chaste, honest, and to avoid sin. We realize that it is God's desire that we manifest and live out these virtues so that we become fully human and fully alive; the fruit of living as members of the Body of Christ. With new experiences, we don't necessarily eliminate our earlier images of God, but rather we seek a balance whereby we also have images of God as a Just God, an Incarnate God, an Inclusive God, and a Merciful and Compassionate God.

I have two more images of God to share with you in this letter: Our God and a Male/Female God.

5. Our God

Gradually, as we become conscious that our individual self is not the center of the universe, and as we become embedded in family, church, school, friendships, community, and people of different ethnic and religious backgrounds, we experience an image of Our God. All of these social groups remind us that God loves all people. At times this may seem scary, but when we become conscious of the limitations of My God Alone, we are freer to discover a bigger God. There are times in prayer when we continue to focus on My God Alone no matter what our age since we always want to adore God. As we spiritually mature, we focus more on others, not just on ourselves. We become more conscious that we do not live life on earth just to follow the rules so as to assure that we will get to Heaven, but we live on earth with our brothers and sisters in Christ so as to share eternal life here. Jesus said, "Unless a grain of wheat falls into the earth and dies, it remains alone; but if it dies, it bears much fruit" (John 12:24).

I'll share with you how I discovered an image of Our God. When I was in my thirties, the bishop assigned me to not only be the principal of a Catholic high school, but he also appointed me as diocesan vocations' director. To promote vocations, a vocation team came up with the idea of forming a community with eight college students (four men and four women). I lived with the community that also included a transitional deacon and a religious sister during the summer. The motive behind the project was to offer an experience of the value and joy of community life so as to encourage collegians to think about church vocations.

The bishop gave permission for the newly formed community to live in a closed-down Catholic Church building with an abandoned school and rectory in the inner city. We ministered as a community of eleven in the inner city for six weeks. We visited nursing homes. We helped in food pantries, participated in summer programs for children, experienced community prayer, and we shared life together. We lived very simply that summer with no television set, and we had very little furniture. We did our own cooking and cleaning. We had the luxury to simply share time with one another, to recreate after serving in our ministries, to laugh and sing, and to entertain visitors.

I noticed that through this community experience my image of God changed from My God Alone into an image of Our God. In the seminary, we were never encouraged to develop friendships. We were encouraged to be independent. I believed in an Exclusive God. Celibacy made it difficult for me to share intimately with others. Up to this point in my life, I was unaware of the necessity of living a life of interdependence. I thought my holiness was supposed to be achieved in my perfection rather than achieved through serving the needs of the community and discovering Jesus in the faces of all people. So this new experience enlightened me to the blessings and transforming effects of sharing my life with others. The experiences of vulnerability, honesty, openness, and interdependence were great blessing for me that summer.

I was never the same after that summer. I discovered the value of praying with others, sharing a bedroom with a charismatic transitional deacon, praying on a deep level with others, feasting daily on the Eucharist, and simply depending upon others. Discovering the need to be interdependent is a sign of second half of life spirituality. That summer experience made me aware that without a community, I could be caught up in egocentricity. Within a community, I could better live celibacy, find happiness, and become fully human and fully alive.

In the two years of running the program, two men later became priests, one woman became a nun, and one man who entered the marital state continues to serve as a lay minister in a diocesan Catholic pastoral center.

Our images of God determine who we are and how we act. Likewise, how we act in the world shapes our images of God. As long as we hold on to an image of My God Alone, we can be highly egotistical. We can be overly concerned about our own needs, comforts, and spiritual welfare to the neglect of fully living as a member of the Body of Christ.

As our image of My God Alone becomes more an image of Our God, we became more naturally concerned about the welfare of other people, not only those in our community who may think and act like us, but also people of a different color, people who practice different religions, and people who practice no religion. Worshipping Our God enables us and encourages us to be good shepherds who truly love all our neighbors, not only those in our country, but those who live throughout the world.

6. A Male/Female God:

We can become aware of a new way of thinking when someone asks us a question that disrupts our habitual ideas and assumptions. For example, one day when I was a pastor, a parishioner named Sandra, who was a student at Boston College and home during the Christmas break, asked me if I thought God was male. Since I was trained in a patriarchal church, I said that I did assume God was male. After dialoguing with Sandra, I realized that I had never given it much thought, and I became more conscious about the language I used in describing God.

As I reflected on the matter, I realized that since human language about God is always metaphorical, describing God in male terms was only half the picture. To speak more fully and therefore more truthfully, feminine qualities and images of God were also needed. Thanks to Sandra, I realized that God is not literally a father, so if God is like a father, then God is also like a mother.

Before you were born, Joey, we had a wonderful pope, John Paul I, for only a short time. On a Sunday in April of 1978, in his Angelus address, he said,"God is our Father; even more he is our mother." In the Bible there is the passage, "Can a mother forget her infant, be without tenderness for the child of her womb? Even should she forget, I will never forget you" (Isaiah 49:15).

Through these and other similar experiences, I became more aware that in the formal liturgy, God is referred to exclusively as male. So now, in order to provide a more complete image of God, I sometimes refer to God as "Father," but I also use other titles such as "Merciful God," "Forgiving God," and "Loving God." These phrases not only have a more balanced, nurturing way of impacting the assembly, they also serve to remind me that I have outgrown my image of God as always male. And since our image of God reflects back upon our image of ourselves, rightfully so, I sometimes change the word "mankind" to "humankind" when it appears in liturgical texts.

I once attended a Pax Christi Retreat. The female leader of a small group was asked to begin with the prayer, the Our Father. She said that she couldn't use traditional language. I realized her hurt went deep. Conceiving God as "father" brought back negative memories involving her own father. She began the prayer with "Divine Creator," and the effect on the whole group was healing and enriching.

Some people who practice second half of life spirituality think that the most sexist institution in the life of Western civilization is the Church that continues to hold before the world an image of God as exclusively masculine.

An image of a Male God suggests that only a man is capable of reflecting and symbolizing God, a stance that affirms patriarchy. The ordination of women as priests and bishops has only been legally possible in most church denominations in recent years. "Faith of Our Fathers" is sung in some liturgies. I spoke to one woman who told me that she believes when churches present the ideal woman as a virgin and demand that all ordained men be celibate, the result is guilt, inadequacy, and the diminishment of the sacredness of human sexuality. Despite marriage being a sacrament, it is not elevated as is the life of a virgin or celibate.

As I have said several times, we become like the images we have of God. As we deepen our relationship with God, others, and self, we come to realize that we have taken literally what was meant to be a metaphor. Once we understand this, we are able to see women as equal to men in their value and their essential role in God's creation. A Male/Female image of God makes some people question the church's practice of patriarchy.

Those who practice first half of life spirituality seem to present a God that we can define. Those who practice second half of life spirituality presume God cannot be defined because God is mystery. As good shepherds in the Church, our images of a Male God or a Male/Female God influence the affirmation or non-affirmation we give to women and to the assembly since an image of a Male God is associated with power, authority, and judgment. Theologians wrestle with the question, "What is God like?"

Conclusion:

Letting go of our fears is difficult. Letting go of our images of a Distant God, an Exclusive God, a Vengeful God, a God Preoccupied with Sex, a God Demanding Perfection, My God Alone, and a Male God is scary to some. Exclusivity in general tends to presume control and certitude. Inclusivity tends to connote mystery, trust, and faith. The practice of second half of life spirituality is all about letting go of control.

I realize, Joey, as I write to you, that until I attended Richard Rohr's Conference on "Loving the Two Halves of Life," I was unaware of the significance of these experiences I am sharing with you. I knew at the time they were changing my way of seeing God, but my world view was too small to understand the importance of those changes. Also by sharing these experiences, I am realizing that books and conferences can be so helpful in providing us with a wider world view so that we can become aware of the opportunities to learn, re-learn, and change in our every day experiences.

Finally, author and motivational speaker, Wayne Dyer said, "If you change the way you look at things, the things you look at change."

Peace,

Uncle Matthew

Letter #22
Sunday, October 14, 2012

Dear Uncle Matthew,

Thank you for your last letter. I have never been conscious that I primarily have an image of My God Alone rather than Our God. This is a big issue. This makes me question whether God is a personal God or a God of all. You are making me realize that God is both. God loves each of us like God loves each sparrow that falls to the ground. Balance is needed. Most of my private prayers are about me. I pray to pass exams. I pray for good health. I pray penances when I confess my sins. I pray for perseverance so that I will be ordained. So for all practical purposes, I do primarily worship an image of My God Alone!

Sharing about changing your images of God opens up many questions. Without thinking about it, I always thought of God as male. Naturally, patriarchy makes sense with a Male God. I have not talked to women about their images of God. I wonder if an image of a Male God makes women feel inferior to men? I wonder if a person of color who has only been given an image of a White God feels inferior? I wonder if a gay man who has only heard about an image of a Straight God feels inferior?

The weather here is very nice. I love the change of seasons. The fall colors always uplift me.

Earlier, you sent me some goals of first half of life spirituality which I am striving to achieve. What goals should I be aware of as I hopefully transition into the practice of second half of life spirituality? I'm quite certain they are different just as our images of God should change as we age.

I have shared some of your letters with a classmate. He can't believe that we have never heard about the topics you are sharing with me. I am grateful!

Peace,

Joey

Response to Letter #22
Saturday, October 27, 2012

Dear Joey,

I was uplifted by the recent special supplement in the National Catholic Reporter on the Second Vatican Council 1962-1965. I was in the seminary during those important years. I hope you can acquire a copy of that supplement so that you are familiar with our church's rich heritage. The Spirit of God was alive and moving during the Council.

You brought up good questions regarding our images of God that do not match who we are. It is true that most of us have an image of a White God and a Heterosexual God. My hunch is a person of color and a person in the LGBTQ community suffer when they learn of images of God that do not reflect who they are. Catholicism gives the impression that only heterosexual persons and heterosexual love share in divine life. When we practice first half of life spirituality, we are unaware that there are other images of God including a Black God and a Gay God. The practice of second half of life spirituality makes us aware that there are many images of God because we are all God's children; God's creation. God loves all of us. Therefore all of God's creation is holy. Isn't it interesting how our images of God are so important? Aren't our images of God formed by our human experiences? Our understanding of God is not about God but our understanding of God.

There are many goals to pursue, to be aware of, and to be open to during the practice of second half of life spirituality. These goals cannot be presented in a neat format because the Spirit works differently in each person. I am sharing with you my way of giving consciousness to the life of the Spirit. I will share five goals in this letter, and I will share more goals in letters to come. In the second half of life, as witnessed throughout the scriptures and in my own life of the Spirit, I believe we are meant to mature into the practice of an adult spirituality. St. Paul said, "When I was a child, I used to talk as a child, think as a child, reason as a child; when I became a man, I put aside childish things" (1 Corinthians 13).

"Spirituality:"

When I use the word "spirituality," I am referring to a life of the Spirit that produces a wholeness and completion that is grounded in images of God that affirm the goodness of life on earth and the importance of the Body of Christ here on earth. I am discovering as I age that a deep spirituality is found in individuals who seem to be fully human and fully alive because they have learned to live as vibrant members of the Body of Christ. Spirituality is distinct from religion that is more focused on following the leadership of an external authority.

Spirituality is a process of transformation that can take place within organized religion or separate from organized religion. Organized religion usually greatly assists us in developing first half of life spirituality because organized religion provides goals along with the means to reach those goals.

The practice of second half of life spirituality challenges us to go farther in the transformation process so that we rely on the Holy Spirit and our experiences. Blessings are experienced when we are more fully conscious of the power of unconditional love, the ability to forgive, the ability to genuinely affirm, the freedom to live our true self, and the willingness to accept ourselves and others.

I'll now share with you five goals that you should be aware of as you transition into the practice of second half of life spirituality. These five goals are: (1) ask questions, (2) develop an interest in the deeper mysteries of life, (3) accept past failures, (4) identify your shame, and (5) purify your motivation. I have written about twenty-two goals in my journal. These goals are helping me to have a better awareness of reality.

1. Ask questions:

One goal found in the practice of second half of life spirituality is to question everything. The psychiatrist, M. Scott Peck says in his book, The Road Less Traveled, "The path to holiness is in questioning everything." Peck goes on to say, "We must rebel against and reject the religion of our parents, for inevitably their world view will be narrower than that of which we are capable if we take full advantage of our personal experience, including our adult experience, and the experience of an additional generation of human history. There is no such thing as a good hand-me-down religion."

Isn't that a great insight? I would add, however, in many situations, the rejection may be temporary. Later, many who rejected their religious upbringing found value and returned to their religion in a new way. They made their religion their own.

2. Develop an interest in the deeper mysteries in life:

Another goal in the practice of second half of life spirituality is to become more interested in the deeper mysteries in life such as wisdom, suffering, inner peace, beauty, joy, and happiness. You will find that you will later doubt many beliefs that you now accept as true without question. When you develop an interest in the deeper mysteries of life, you will attempt to answer for yourself what matters most in life.

  a. Suffering:

I'll attempt to share a few thoughts about three deeper mysteries in life: suffering, beauty, and happiness. When we practice first half of life spirituality, we tend to look upon our suffering as a personal curse. We may easily think when we suffer, "Poor me." Bound by egocentricity, we may feel too ashamed to share with others our suffering, and that only makes our suffering worse. We feel alone. Hurricanes, earthquakes, and floods can cause us to easily lose our trust in God. Usually in the first half of life, the spiritual framework that holds us together is weak. There may be a tendency to think if we tithe, worship God every Sunday, and avoid serious sin, God will spare us from suffering. But when we pray, pay, and obey and still experience great suffering, we come to realize that our practice of first half of life spirituality is not working. So in our pain, we may begin to open ourselves to change and to new growth.

Viktor Frankl, the famous Austrian psychiatrist and neurologist once said in his book, Man's Search for Meaning, "When we are no longer able to change a situation, we are challenged to change ourselves."

The mature person in the second half of life knows that life is a series of continuing defeats. Fear and lethargy are familiar to us during our lifetime. Questioning, failing, and making mistakes are all vitally important parts of our learning process.

The fourteenth century anchoress and mystic Julian of Norwich said, "You will have pain and affliction, trouble and strain, and doubt. But you shall not be overcome, and all shall be well. Yet, all shall be well, and all will be well, and thou shall see thyself that all manner of things shall be well."

As we grow in wisdom, we better understand the mystery of suffering while at the same time being content to know that we never will be able to answer all of our questions. We see suffering in a larger context that helps us not to solve our problems at hand, but to outgrow them. Suffering involves not only mystery, but suffering challenges us to deepen our faith and our deep dependence upon God and other people. Personal suffering motivates us to be more compassionate when others suffer. We gradually realize that our suffering enables us to see things in a better perspective. We realize we are not alone but part of the "Body of Christ." The phrase, "Body of Christ" takes on new meaning. We realize that everyone suffers. Everyone carries a Cross. Everyone needs affirmation, prayer, compassion, understanding, and empathy. Suffering is part of the process of transformation, the ultimate goal of second half of life spirituality.

b. Beauty:

When we practice first half of life spirituality our understanding of beauty is more focused on externals. Tattoos, coloring one's hair, wearing the right clothes, and being seen in the right places are typically youthful attempts to appear attractive, beautiful, desirable, and in tune with the expectations of others.

When we practice second half of life spirituality, our view of beauty becomes more focused on internal qualities. Joey, you were only eleven years old when Mother Teresa of Calcutta died in 1997. People intuited that she had a beauty that was not coming from externals. She exuded beauty from the inside; a manifestation of the life of the Spirit.

c. Happiness:

The achievement of goals in the practice of second half of life spirituality can enable us to discover more joy, greater inner peace, greater acceptance of others, more compassion, and patience for others. How is this achieved? When we practice first half of life, we wrongly assume that more is better. We assume more possessions, more titles, more money, more degrees, larger homes, and newer cars will bring us happiness.

When we practice second half of life spirituality, we discover that less is better. The mystics refer to the wisdom of subtraction rather than addition. We discover that what we want in our innermost being is not found by obtaining more external possessions but through inner qualities. Jesus, St. Francis of Assisi, and so many other saints owned few or no material possessions. We admire them because they were able to clearly show us that real joy, happiness, success, attractiveness, and holiness come from inside us. Their joy was marked by a freedom of being free of fear, and they became unattached to material possessions, titles, and their status in society.

3. Accept past failures:

Another goal in the practice of second half of life spirituality is not to be ashamed of our past failures but to see these failures as important stepping stones in the spiritual growth process. We realize that some of our actions and desires that we were ashamed to admit to anyone were all part of a mysterious process of struggling to become a whole person. Failing and making mistakes are the inroads to knowledge and understanding. As Dalai Lama XIV said, "When you lose, don't lose the lesson."

I have met men who committed felonies when they were young. Once I knew the circumstances, I felt a deep compassion. They did the best they could in an imperfect world. As an image of a Merciful and Compassionate God replaces your image of a Vindictive God, you will perform a vital ministry when you radiate God's love and compassion to those who are fearful that their past wrongs will be exposed. As we mature, we come to realize the mystery of our own internal complexity.

4. Identify shame:

Another goal in the practice of second half of life spirituality is to identify our shame. John Bradshaw, counselor, theologian, management consultant and public speaker, wrote the book, Healing the Shame That Binds You. At the age of forty-five, he realized that the core demon in his life was shame. He discovered that he had been bound by shame all his life. He realized that shame is one of the major destructive forces in all human life, and to name the shame allows one to have power over it.

The practice of second half of life spirituality provides the opportunity to name the shame in our lives because we have had more experiences, we ask questions, and we are more open to change. Healthy shame about specific behavior helps us to be humble, but shame becomes toxic when we believe we are flawed and defective as a human being. Bradshaw says, "Toxic shame is the root of all addiction." He says that since personal relationships set up our toxic shame, we need to form non-shaming relationships to heal our shame. When we compare ourselves to the "perfect" male or female, we inflame sexual shame. Shame can lead to serious addictions to alcohol, drugs, and pornography.

5. Purify motivation:

During the practice of second half of life spirituality another goal is to purify our motivation underlying our actions. Jesus' condemnation of hypocrisy has new resonance for us. We not only try to obey the rules, but we are willing to examine and purify our motivation, our intentionality, for our good actions. Second half of life spirituality invites us to go even beyond the Commandments and to practice the Beatitudes which are attitudes, invisible to others, that help us to imitate Christ. We gradually attempt to replace fear with love. We replace being motivated by what people will say to what God desires. The whole notion of intentionality is fundamental to a mature practice of spirituality. It is difficult because we are somewhat molded, determined, and influenced by the morality we have been exposed to.

By way of analogy, the liturgical season of Lent is a holy period of time each year when we can examine our motivation. Jesus said to give alms, fast, and pray in secret. And yet when we perform religious actions publicly, we risk being motivated to enhance our public image. We want others to see us as good and moral. In the practice of second half of life spirituality, we begin to ask, "Why do I do this? Am I doing this good work for

God or for my own benefit?"

On a personal note, in my retirement years I have examined the motives that guided me while serving as an active priest. My motives, admittedly, were mixed. It is indeed hard to serve only one master. At times, my motive for working hard was to please my bishops. I was motivated to keep the church and civil laws so as to appear good. I was motivated to make my parents proud of my successes. I was motivated to do good so that the parishioners would like me. My fear of giving scandal often motivated me to avoid sin more than my love of God.

I was often like the priest in the story of the Good Samaritan. My duties came first even if members of my family would have appreciated a visit. It is so humbling to realize how strong self-deception can be. And yet, though humbling and painful in ways, this honest self-scrutiny of our short-comings gifts us with a deep conviction and firm image of an Unconditionally Loving and Patient God. As we grow older, we realize over and over again "everything belongs"as Father Richard Rohr shared in his book with that title.

Peace,

Uncle Matthew

Letter #23
Tuesday, November 13, 2012

Dear Uncle Matthew,

Thank you for sharing with me five of the many goals found in the practice of second half of life spirituality. I can see the benefit of spiritual direction. If the director and the directees are knowledgeable about the goals in the practice of second half of life spirituality, then, like a coach and an athlete, they have achievable goals.

In your last letter to me, you mentioned when we practice second half of life spirituality and experience serious suffering, we can better persevere. I have met many older individuals who experienced great suffering, and they gave up on life and even God when their prayers were not answered. They ceased to smile. They lost their joy. I'm sure they were never introduced to the practice of second half of life spirituality.

Today is the feast of St. Frances Xavier Cabrini, better known as Mother Cabrini. I thought about what you wrote to me, and it seems that she was practicing second half of life spirituality that enabled her to persevere under the worst conditions. In his homily, Father Jack told us that Mother Cabrini founded the Missionary Sisters of the Sacred Heart. The pope urged her to come to the United States from Italy to minister to Italian immigrants. There were 50,000 Italian immigrants living in the New York area, and most of them lived in poverty, and they were not going to church. When she came to the United States, the Archbishop of New York did not welcome her. He thought the work was too difficult for a woman, but she stayed and worked without any support from the Archdiocese. She and her nuns stayed in terrible conditions where someone had to stay awake at night to keep the rats off the sisters.

Despite many setbacks and much suffering, Mother Cabrini founded fifty schools, hospitals, and orphanages in the United States, in Central and South America, in Italy, and in Canada. She died in 1917. What an amazing example she is to all of us of her ability to handle terrible suffering!

I hope you are doing well. What are some more goals in the practice of second half of life spirituality?

Peace,

Joey

Response to Letter #23
Sunday, November 25, 2012

Dear Joey,

I spent Thanksgiving Day with your parents. They prepared a wonderful meal, and we shared an uplifting conversation. We indeed have much for which to be thankful.

I was saddened by the recent conflict between Israel and Gaza. We need to pray for a peaceful solution to this terrible situation. A study of the situation shows that ignorance of the paradigm of first and second half of life spirituality is very much rooted in that conflict. Peace can only be achieved through dialogue, respect, and reconciliation.

I'm glad that you are already applying some of the goals of second half of life spirituality. Yes, in second half of life spirituality we can develop a different attitude about suffering. St. Frances Xavier Cabrini had a positive attitude towards her suffering which transformed her into a saint.

In an earlier letter to you, I referred to author and sociologist, Richard Sipe. Earlier this month, he published an article, "Frequently Asked Questions." Enclosed is a copy of that four-page article. He stirs the water and shares many insights. I think it would be wise to read this article. It is your life. Know what you are getting into as a cleric in the Catholic Church.

Sipe thinks that the Church's basic teaching on sexuality is simply wrong. He disagrees with the church's position that homosexuality is an intrinsic disorder. He also disagrees with the Church's teachings on masturbation and birth control. He disagrees with the Church's exclusion of women from the priesthood. He also says that mandatory celibacy is untenable because no one can impose a charism.

I'm not judging Sipe to be necessarily correct. Each of us has to discern the truth. I would assert that he is asking important and crucial questions that pertain to the Church today, a sure sign of second half of life spirituality. Sipe may be too radical for you. I'm sure his questions and answers would be met with displeasure by most of your professors.

In my last letter, I shared with your five goals in the practice of second half of life spirituality: (1) ask questions, (2) develop an interest in the deeper mysteries of life, (3) accept past failures, (4) identity your shame, and (5) purify your motivation. I will share with you three more goals in the practice of second half of life spirituality: (6) re-examine your foundation, (7) move beyond the Law, and (8) avoid the trap of perfectionism.

6. Re-examine your foundation:

The central goal of first half of life spirituality is to build a strong foundation. In the second half of life, we need to re-examine our foundation, "wine skin," "container," so as to discover what needs to change. Through this process, we hopefully discover that our false self, which we build up over the years, is immature, egocentric, based on fear, and often self-deceptive. We increasingly realize that our false self has become constrictive, restraining the fullness of life that is seeking to emerge. So we begin, intentionally or not, often prompted by suffering to varying degrees, to reevaluate our goals, motives, objectives, success achieved thus far, and as touchstone, our degree of happiness. Articles like the one by Richard Sipe force us to examine the false self to see if our basic philosophy, our understanding of issues, is correct or incorrect.

Perhaps suddenly, more likely through many twists and turns, we come to realize that we need to replace our false self so as to hold the "new wine," a new philosophy of life, our emerging true self. This process of change has many dimensions that allow us to see into the heart. This process of change asks big questions about whether we are living with integrity, truly happy, fully alive, unconditionally loving others, and forgiving. We reach out to God, in prayer, in longing, and by doing so we question and examine our images of God.

Perhaps our images of God need to change, to grow. You asked some interesting questions in an earlier letter about a black man's image of a White God and a gay man's image of a Straight God. We look to see if our ladder to success is leaning against the correct wall. We realize that God writes straight with crooked lines. We appreciate mystery in others and in ourselves. We learn to appreciate and reflect upon paradoxes.

For example, as I mentioned earlier, we have all met some individuals who were not practicing any religion, and yet they ended up more charitable than some religious people. There is a spiritual principle, a paradox, in second half of life spirituality, "We must go down to go up." I mentioned earlier to you that Franciscan priest, Richard Rohr, brilliantly works with this paradox in his book about the two halves of life, Falling Upward- A Spirituality for the Two Halves of Life.

In short, in the first half of life, we build the false self that eventually must die so that the true self emerges. Jesus said, "Unless the grain of wheat falls to the ground and dies, it remains a grain of wheat; but if it dies, it produces much fruit" (John 12:24).

Thomas Merton said in his book New Seeds of Contemplation, "All sin starts from the assumption that my false self, the self that exists only in my own egocentric desires, is the fundamental reality of life to which everything else in the universe is ordered."

7. Move beyond the Law:

During first half of life spirituality, we try to obey the rules that our parents, church leaders, and civil leaders taught us. These codes and rules are good and necessary in character formation, and they provide the essential foundation to reach the higher goals found in second half of life spirituality.

When we practice second half of life spirituality, we come to realize that we have to go beyond simply keeping the church laws and working within fixed structures because the law doesn't provide adequate answers to the problems of life, and often the law fails to mold us into individuals who are fully human and fully alive. We must learn to follow God's law written on our hearts. We increasingly ask the question, "What would Jesus do?" ("WWJD")

Jesus, guided by love and motivated by compassion, broke the laws of the Sabbath in order to serve a higher law. Jesus said, "The sabbath was made for man, not man for the sabbath" (Mark 2:27). Jesus preached a message that was often outside the structure of the organized religion of his day. Yes, the sabbath and temple are important, but never more so than the human beings and the love of God they claim to serve.

Often, older Catholics confess that they missed mass while on vacation. Common sense would say that on a long trip there will be times when the Sunday obligation can be fulfilled in another way rather than seeking out a church in a new environment so as to simply keep a church law. Some Catholics feel guilty when they missed mass while they were sick, so they confess it, as if they sinned. Common sense would say they should let go of a rigid, formalized following of the rules, and simply stay home when they are sick.

St. Teresa of Avila once said, "When one reaches the highest degree of human maturity, one has only one question left: How can I be helpful?" As priests, we can easily succumb to the temptation to substitute obedience to human laws for the greater reality of service to God, even union with God, that comes when we are helpful to our neighbor (the corporal works of mercy). Once we realize the message of the Beatitudes, we realize that keeping the Ten Commandments are not the standard for holiness but actually the lowest common denominator.

8. Avoid perfectionism:

The scribes and Pharisees, as portrayed in the gospels, sought to be perfect through their works. They were motivated to do everything correctly rather than being motivated by their love of God.

Author, Dr. Ann Wilson Schaef says in her book, When Society Becomes an Addict, "Those who treat addictions consider perfectionism to be a major stumbling block for recovery." She contends that we all suffer from some form of addiction, rather it be to drugs, alcohol, sex, sleep, shopping, gambling, food, the Internet, pornography, status, winning, power, and pleasure. The list is endless! Self-deception is common and almost unavoidable when we first try to give up an addiction. We can be easily motivated by self-righteousness rather than our love of God.

Under the right spiritual director or guidance, accountability can be helpful in fostering humility. Avoiding accountability can worsen perfectionism which is an unattainable goal that can lead to depression, discouragement, as well as procrastination and indecision. Franciscan priest, Richard Rohr says in his book Falling Upward, "The demand for the perfect is the greatest enemy of the good." Perfection is a mathematical concept. Goodness is a human concept. Pursuing perfection usually prevents the realization of goodness in others, the world at large, and in ourselves. Those who practice second half of life spirituality gradually develop images of a Compassionate God; a God who accepts imperfection.

As you can tell, there are many goals to strive for when we

desire to practice second half of life spirituality. In my next letter, I will share some more goals.

Peace,

Uncle Matthew

Attachment: Copy of Sipe's article

Letter #24
Sunday, December 9, 2012

Dear Uncle Matthew,

Today at the liturgy, we celebrated the Second Sunday of Advent. To prepare for Christmas, I have been using your reflections on the goals found in the practice of second half of life spirituality. I am praying that I will be open to change now and in the future. I do want to move beyond the Law and avoid perfectionism. Your last letter helped me to realize that I often try to be perfect so as to escape my guilt when I fail to be chaste.

I liked what you said about re-examining my container; my foundation. At one time, I planned on becoming an engineer. I wanted to get married, have children, and obtain a good-paying job. Now I am challenged to understand and integrate what the call to priesthood means to my identity. Now I must ask what are my gifts, weaknesses, true motives, and how does this fit in to my true self. Separating the false self from the true self is a challenge!

My dad often inspires me because he puts people first in his life. He goes beyond what he is expected to do so as to help others. What a wonderful virtue! Also my dad has good common sense. He doesn't agonize over things that don't really matter. My dad once gave me a book by Richard Carlson, Don't Sweat the Small Stuff...and it's all small stuff. My dad seems to be able to practice the message in that wonderful book.

Soon I will be taking my exams before the Christmas break.

Please continue to share with me more goals that I should be aware of so that I will be encouraged to gradually transition into the practice of second half of life spirituality.

Peace,

Joey

Response to Letter #24
Wednesday, December 19, 2012

Dear Joey,

Thank you for your phone call last night. As you leave today for your Christmas break, I hope you have a safe trip home. Call me before Christmas.

Wasn't that terrible about the Sandy Hook Elementary School shooting last Thursday? The perpetrator first killed his mother, and then he shot twenty innocent children and six adult staff members. Terrible incidents like this show that there are many individuals who have never heard about or achieved the goals of first half of life spirituality (boundaries, a conscience, self-awareness, identity, respect for life, etc.) They lack the most basic foundation of humanity, and they fail to develop an inner moral compass. The practice of first half of life spirituality is necessary for compassionate functioning.

I'll be spending a quiet Christmas here at home. As part of my own Advent preparation, I'm sharing with you these thoughts on the goals of second half of life spirituality. My sharing reminds me of my own need to be open to new ways of thinking and acting; the essence of an adult spirituality.

In my two previous letters, I have shared eight goals in the practice of second half of life spirituality: (1) ask questions, (2) develop an interest in the deeper mysteries of life (3) accept past failures, (4) identify your shame, (5) purify your motivation, (6) re-examine the container, (7) move beyond the law, and (8) avoid perfectionism. I'll share with you three more goals found in the practice of second half of life spirituality: (9) discover the will of God, (10) develop a new understanding of the Bible, and (11) develop a deeper understanding of liturgical practices.

9.  Discover the will of God:

During the first half of life, we assumed that we were incapable of knowing the will of God alone, so we needed a few select individuals to show us the will of God. Organized religion makes known the "experts" who will tell us the will of God. In our early formation of conscience, we thought that simply doing what the pastor or bishop said would guarantee us that we were doing the will of God. We appreciated bishops who vetted speakers. Vetting assured us that we were hearing only what God would want us to hear.

When we practice second half of life spirituality, we question our belief system and we gradually work to form our conscience in an effort to discern more directly and personally the will of God. This increasing awareness of our "inner moral compass" and our personal ethics that may differ from external authority often arises through conflicts where traditional moral codes offer no simple solution. In these times, turning to prayer and guidance from God leads to a greater sense of God's living presence within our own lives. We must be quiet and listen to the Spirit speaking to us so that we can make decisions on our own. Although we seek the opinions of others, we assume that we are capable of discovering the will of God.

In John's gospel, we have the words "...and you will know the truth, and the truth will set you free" (John 8:32). When we are willing to do inner work, we take in a wider range of experiences and understandings so as to make informed judgments regarding the morality of our actions. Those who practice second half of life spirituality assume that they must follow their conscience even if their actions go against a church authority figure or a church teaching.

10. Develop a new understanding of the Bible:

You have been studying the Old Testament. I'm sure that you are aware that in first half of life spirituality, we try to avoid the conflicts, dilemmas, paradoxes, and contradictions that are found in the Bible. There is a tendency to see the Bible as a simple answer book to today's problems, and so we often read the scriptures uncritically, looking for confirmation rather than challenge.

When we practice second half of life spirituality, we realize the importance of Lectio Divina which means we are willing to wrestle with the text. We begin to realize that the Bible is like a mirror that reflects back to us our lives.

When we practice second half of life spirituality, we become aware that the Bible is made up of many literary forms. We no longer assume the Bible gives us a literal presentation of history. In fact, we recognize that much of the Bible is not historical fact, but rather a narrative expressing God's truth outside of and beyond time. We make an effort to learn about the origin of the gospels. This deepens rather than dissipates our reverence for the books in the Bible since they become more real and alive. We note with interest that the gospels were written at different periods of time and for different audiences. We realize the importance of viewing the gospels through the lens of Jewish eyes since the gospels were born from a Jewish culture and context.

In the practice of second half of life spirituality, we discover the literary form of "midrash" which contains commentaries and interpretations of passages in the Bible. Through this approach, we appreciate the many other literary forms in the Bible: metaphor, biography, paradox, analogy, history, fiction, hyperbole, autobiography, and poetry. We appreciate the many paradoxes in the Bible that Jesus and the sacred authors used to convey mystery. We come to realize that Jesus had the ability to reconcile paradoxes by reframing the questions he was facing and often looking at deeper issues at hand by thinking non-dualistically. For example, the biggest paradox surrounding Jesus was the nature of his humanity and divinity. Paradox, once frightening to us, becomes a point of revelation.

11. Develop a deeper understanding of liturgical practices:

When we practice second half of life spirituality, we begin to appreciate a deeper understanding of our traditional liturgical practices. The Advent wreath symbolizes the light of Christ coming into the world. We can ask how we are light to the world. Often churches have Christmas trees with tags for giving gifts to children. This reminds us of sharing with our neighbor, even the stranger.

Even though we are in Advent, I think it is important to look at the Lenten regulations on fasting and abstinence. The emphasis is mainly on individualism; the body. Some form of self denial is emphasized. The rules for fasting and abstinence are printed in church bulletins. Abstinence from meat is to be observed on Ash Wednesday and all the Fridays of Lent, including Good Friday.

When we were young, we were encouraged to give up candy or refrain from going to a movie in a theatre. There is also an emphasis on receiving the Sacrament of Reconciliation during Lent. In some dioceses, the bishop requires that all parishes offer additional opportunities weekly for confessions during Lent. The Church considers individual confession to be the way for persons aware of serious sin to be reconciled with God and the Church. Bishops often remind the faithful that the precept to confess grave sins and receive Holy Communion must be done at least once during the Easter Season.

The Lenten regulations are a good example of first half of life spirituality which are necessary to build a foundation, a container, the "wine skin," the false self. The practice during Lent of prayer, fasting, and almsgiving are valuable disciplines also in the practice of second half of life spirituality. In many church congregations in this country, the majority of the attendees at Mass are in their second half of life. A goal in second half of life spirituality is to challenge believers to go beyond the quest for personal sanctification through the mortification of the body and instead do something in the area of social justice so as to serve the Body of Christ.

At my age, I realize my unawareness, arrogance, and self-righteousness over the years in the way I observed Lent. I observed all the rituals, said my prayers, but largely missed the point that I should have changed my life style so that I could better share my bread with the hungry, my clothing with the naked, and provided shelter for the homeless.

Often when we practice first half of life spirituality, we unconsciously take at face value liturgical practices that focus on individual piety; the means to be holier like Jesus and the saints. Alternatively, in the practice of second half of life spirituality, we become more concerned with the material and spiritual welfare of all the members of the Body of Christ. Therefore, issues like poverty, homelessness, universal heath care, domestic violence, gun control, drug addiction, racism, terrorism, and unemployment take on a greater importance to us, and we wish these issues to be better stressed in our liturgical practices, especially in the homilies that flow from the rich liturgical readings.

Peace,

Uncle Matthew

Letter #25
Monday, January 21, 2013


Dear Uncle Matthew,

Today is a holiday in honor of Dr. Martin Luther King, Jr. Fr. Jack
was the homilist today at mass. He said that 250,000 people
were present at the Lincoln Memorial on the Mall in 1963 for
King's "I have a dream" speech. Father Jack said Dr. King
inspired people all over the world because people could see in
him glimpses of God's integrity, wisdom, and unconditional love.
He told us that Dr. King was the youngest person ever to receive
the Nobel Peace Prize in 1964 at the age of thirty-five. As you
know, tragically, he was assassinated at the age of thirty-nine.

Fr. Jack's homily really inspired me. Dr. KIng's "I have a dream"
speech gave us all a vision of society that has moved beyond the
duality of racism. I'm sure Dr. King was able to live out many of
the goals you shared with me regarding the practice of both first
and second half of life spirituality.

The eleven goals of second half of life spirituality that you have
shared with me are already helping me to have a vision of where
I would like to be in the future. I can see that doing the will of
God is not only a personal struggle but also a struggle with
church leaders. I must learn to trust not only in church teaching
but also in my own "inner moral compass." In our Ethics class,
we were taught the importance of the sensus fidelium (the sense

of the faithful). Determining what most people believe is an important part in the process of discovering my own inner moral compass.

I have now been exposed to the different literary forms in the Bible in my Old Testament course. Midrash has changed my whole perspective on reading the Bible because it has opened up the meaning of the Bible in wonderful ways by showing me its complexity. Fr. Ray Brown in his book, An Introduction to the New Testament, says that midrash is an ancient commentary on the Hebrew Scriptures, attached to the text. Midrash can be used to teach lessons.

I hope during Lent to be more aware of the needs of others rather than simply giving up something to make myself holier, thinner, or more pure.

I'm looking forward to hearing from you. Please share more goals of second half of life spirituality.

Peace,
Joey

Response to Letter #25
Thursday, January 31, 2013

Dear Joey,

I hope you had a good birthday celebration on Monday, the feast of St. Thomas Aquinas. You are now twenty-seven years old! I offered my mass for you. I thought about the wonderful gift you are to me and your friends.

Prophets are needed in every age. Certainly Martin Luther King, Jr., was a prophet in my lifetime. I'm glad the homilist made the student body aware of this wonderful contemporary prophet. When King gave his famous speech at the Lincoln Memorial, I was home alone while visiting my parents, and I watched the speech on my parent's black and white television set. I remember when Dr. King was assassinated in 1968. His death challenged all of us in this country to be aware of the challenges that hinder equality for all. Racism was deeply rooted then, as it still is today.

Dr. Martin Luther King, Jr., is an important example of the next goal that I shall share with you. The goals that I am sharing with you are not inclusive of all the goals. Each one of us can probably think of some additional goals. We are not working with certitude but mystery.

12.  Develop a prophetic dimension:

When we practice second half of life spirituality, we become aware of the importance of a prophetic dimension, as exemplified so well by Dr. King. A prophetic voice alerts us to the many issues involving social justice. A prophetic voice sensitizes us to the suffering that is occurring in many parts of the world. Hopefully, we embody a spirituality from which naturally flows a prophetic dimension. The Church and society need men and women who have a prophetic vision.

When the practice of first half of life spirituality dominates, there is a tendency for church leaders not to desire to hear, acknowledge, or permit any critique of religion. Prophets point out the injustices that exist in the world, in civil and church leaders, and in religious institutions. When the prophetic voice is ignored, religion often becomes self-maintaining, self-serving, and self-perpetuating. Very often bishops do provide a prophetic dimension. For example, some bishops have pointed out that the prison system in our country needs attention. The United States has five percent of the world's population and nearly twenty-five percent of the world's prisoners. It is estimated that one in three African-Americans will spend time in prison during his or her lifetime. Our system of incarceration helps to create a class of citizens who have little hope of ever advancing beyond their dreadful way of life.

Church leaders point out to us that we must serve the poor and the marginalized. Most people are aware that an interest, appreciation, and implementation of social justice issues are indications of the fruits of second half of life spirituality.

13. Practice collegiality:

Often we find that those in leadership positions who practice first half of life spirituality tend to centralize and micromanage authority. They fail to be collegial and seek consensus. They fail to assume that everyone's opinion is valuable. Egocentricity leads many leaders to give greater importance to their opinions rather than also seeking the opinions of others.

When we practice second half of life spirituality, we become aware of the importance of leading in a collegial way. As our appreciation of the gifts found in all humanity increases, we become willing to delegate, to seek consensus, to practice subsidiarity and collaboration. These traits were encouraged in the Second Vatican Council documents.

14. Think non-dualistically:

When we practice first half of life spirituality, we tend to see reality in a dualistic way. You mentioned to me that an engineering background helped you acquire a scientific mind whereby you could quickly evaluate reality as good/bad, dark/light, right/wrong, positive/negative, up/down, left/right, and beautiful/ugly.

When we are practicing an adult spirituality, we move out of a dualistic mind-set into a harmonizing and integrating mind-set. We attempt to see the "gray" in life. This has both a cognitive and moral dimension to it. We realize how unfair and distorting it is to think we see reality when we use labels to describe people. For example someone might ask, "Who is John over there?" A response might be, "John is divorced, and he recently declared bankruptcy." In that response, we do a disservice to John since he is so much more.

When we practice second half of life spirituality, we begin to appreciate that John, along with ourselves, is a mystery. We are aware that we can see some characteristics of other people and of ourselves, but all of us are far more complex than what the eye can see or the mind can comprehend. When we begin to see reality in a non-dualistic manner, we discover our own patterns of self-deception. Then we realize that in the past we falsely judged individuals who turned out to be totally different from what we thought. We realize that reality and truth are multi-layered and that appearances often conceal more than they reveal. Ambiguity pulls us deeper into life. We come to accept that deeper, more expansive truths often reside where we least expect them, and in contrast to our initial judgments. For example, within our pain often lies our healing. Within the mud lies the gold. Good shepherds must learn to tolerate ambiguity so as to better serve others. An appreciation of ambiguity and inconsistency assist us greatly in understanding human nature. Even Mother Teresa, an acknowledged saint in her time, harbored grave doubts about her religion, faith, and self.

As we begin to think in a non-dualistic way, we increasingly become aware of our ignorance and hence our culpability. Socrates was identified by the Delphic oracle as the wisest person in Greece. He came to understand that his wisdom was grounded in his awareness that he knew that he did not know. The authorities did not like this being pointed out to them. They said he was corrupting the youth of his day. He lost his life in the cause of questioning.

The practice of second half of life spirituality allows us to say, "There, but by the grace of God..." We can pray the prayer, "Lord, have mercy on me a sinner," and mean it. Humility about oneself leads to humility about judging others.

When I was studying in the seminary, I recall one of the priests saying that the secular and the spiritual are two sides of a coin. There is no ultimate separation between them. If you want to be spiritual, you have to live fully in this world. I heard Fr. Richard Rohr say that there is only one reality. And how could it be otherwise, unless you are a dualist? Any distinction between natural and supernatural, sacred and profane is a limited, relative one.

In the practice of first half of life spirituality, some parishes emphasize perpetual adoration. While there are wonderful spiritual benefits to this devotion, some parishioners get the impression that Jesus is in the tabernacle, but not outside the physical church.

The practice of second half of life spirituality tries to remove dualisms such as this. Of course Jesus is present in the tabernacle, but this should serve as a reminder that Jesus is also present outside the church building too. We cannot comprehend everything being holy and sacred until we can appreciate the Eucharist as holy and sacred. But if we do not see the connection between the Eucharist and the rest of life, there is that danger of seeing a divided reality. We end up seeing the common, ordinary, and mundane as separate entities from the holy.

I heard Fr. Richard Rohr on a CD say to think non-dualistically, we must be willing to experience situations that challenge us. He suggested going to a Protestant church or going to a bar. I am not suggesting that you do this while in the seminary, but I think you get his point.

15. Be willing to engage in constructive dialogue:

When we practice second half of life spirituality, we increasingly desire dialogue in a constructive manner with those who hold different opinions. Differences of opinion show up in politics, religion, and in each person's philosophy of life.

People can sense whether or not we are open to constructive criticism or whether we are not capable of receiving criticism. Some clerics and lay persons resort to anonymous letters and petitions to higher superiors because they know from experience that their church leader, pastor, or bishop is either unwilling or incapable of dialogue.

Unfortunately on the political scene, we see on television so much negative advertising. Politicians try to discredit their opponents. They use "ad hominem" logic. Building bridges with one's opponents and attempting to understand issues leads to resolution. Simply attacking others and arrogantly judging who is right and who is wrong only leads to more division, conflict, and even warfare.

An attitude of dialogue is foreign to an attitude of condemnation and marginalization. The practice of second half of life spirituality encourages an attitude of mercy, compassion, and understanding rather than bullying and condemning other people.

There are still more goals in the practice of second half of life spirituality. As you can tell, it does take a life time to take on an attitude of openness to change. Jesus talked about change; conversion. Being open to new ways of thinking is more difficult as we advance in age. Please stay young of heart.

Peace,

Uncle Matthew

Letter #26
Monday, February 11, 2013

Dear Uncle Matthew,

Thank you for your last letter that shared some more goals or indications that a person is pursuing an adult spirituality. I liked the way you described these goals as indications of a more mature spirituality than what we enjoyed in our youth. I appreciate all your effort to help me to have a roadmap for the spiritual journey. I'm sure if I follow your insights, I'll be a good shepherd in whatever vocation I embrace in my life.

Yesterday, Pope Benedict XVI resigned. All of us were surprised. I think that his resignation took a lot of courage on his part. He seems to be aware of his failing health.

A pope, like any leader, must face terrible stress. The press reported that in 2009, authorities investigated the Vatican Bank for possible money-laundering. I presume that scandal is one example of the stress the pope must have endured.

Today is the Feast of Our Lady of Lourdes. St. Bernadette Soubirous reminds us that God can favor anyone with extraordinary blessings; something you constantly remind me of in your stories.

I am beginning to better understand your point that the goal of my seminary training should not just be to receive more information but to help me to be transformed into a good shepherd. I want to develop a flexible mind so as to avoid being rigid. Your last letter encouraged me to become non-dualistic in my thinking. I am convinced that prayer and suffering will eventually help me to see deeper realities and to shift away from my shallow, dualistic thinking.

In the seminary I am finding that I am very egocentric. I guess that is part of my false self. At least I am aware that further growth is necessary.

Please share with me the last seven goals of second half of life spirituality.

Peace,

Joey

Response to Letter #26
Monday, February 18, 2013

Dear Joey,

Today is George Washington's birthday. We now refer to it as Presidents' Day so as to honor not only George Washington and Abraham Lincoln but all the presidents. Our president certainly needs our prayers.

In my last four letters to you, I shared with you indications that I call goals that can be seen in the practice of second half of life spirituality. I will now share with you the last seven goals of the practice of second half of life spirituality that I have written in my journal: (16) be open to seeing reality differently, (17) place less emphasis on competition, (18) be more grateful, (19) live the Sermon on the Mount, (20) be courageous, (21) be less judgmental, and (22) be less self-righteous.

I could go on and on, but after this letter, you will get the idea that the spiritual journey does not end after the seminary. The beauty of a spiritual roadmap is that we see everything in perspective. I'm simply trying to give you a long-range perspective of the spiritual life. The point of these goals is to help you enter mystery where you will discover God. These goals will also help you to discover your true self; who you are before God.

16.  Be open to seeing reality differently:

When we practice second half of life spirituality, we expect to view the world differently as well as act differently than when we practiced first half of life spirituality. For example, we can worship in different surroundings. If we attend a non-Catholic worship service, we are flexible enough to believe that God is there too. We learn to tolerate a very conservative homily or a homily that stirs us to think in a new way. We believe God is everywhere. We believe that everything is holy. We give up our ego preferences. We give up attempting to control situations. We realize that a degree in theology or using religious symbols (the sign of cross, holy water, candles, kneeling, cassocks) are not enough to transform us.

When we practice second half of life spirituality, we begin to see with the heart. One of the most revered classics of nineteenth century literature is the book, The Little Prince by Antoine de Saint-Exupery. In the book, a fox gives advice to the little prince. One famous quote is, "One sees clearly only with the heart. What is essential is invisible to the eye." As the virtue of wisdom increases, we begin to perceive reality in a new way. The senses are helpful and necessary, but something else takes place that allows us to know things without depending entirely upon the senses. We become better at seeing the wolf in sheep's clothing. We become better at discerning the will of God for our lives. We become more open, even expectant, to seeing glimpses of the divine in those who are least among us.

Father Joseph F. Girzone wrote a wonderful book entitled, The Homeless Bishop. He points out, using fiction, that those who practice an adult spirituality can appreciate the goodness of homeless people. The absence of external coverings or trappings may more easily reveal an inner beauty to those who are merciful and compassionate.

In the Book of Psalms, we have the phrase, "Taste and see that God is good." When we practice second half of life spirituality, the Spirit living within us eagerly welcomes many different experiences as a means to grow in wisdom.

When we practice second half of life spirituality, the Spirit enlightens us to understand that it is a false idea to think that there are some individuals who learned the Catechism of the Catholic Church in the eighth grade and then kept the rules until death, thereby winning salvation. When we were young and heard about the lives of the saints, we got the impression that they continually progressed in holiness. Jesus taught us that keeping the law does not necessarily lead to love of God or love of neighbor. We realize that some individuals who appear to have it all together, like a military academy graduate or a newly ordained priest, may actually be infantile in their spiritual journey. Jesus' message was more like taking three steps forward and two steps backwards. In giving spiritual direction, we learn that everyone is on more of a spiral path to holiness and transformation rather than on a linear path.

17. Place less emphasis on competition:

When we practice second half of life spirituality, the Spirit within encourages collaboration. In the first half of life, all of us typically are very competitive. We judge ourselves by our worldly successes. We all want to be part of a winning football team. In the seminary there is competition regarding grades, and in the priesthood there is competition among pastors regarding pastoral concerns.

Gradually when we practice second half of life spirituality, we become aware that we don't have to be part of a winning sport's team or part of a successful business to be happy. The Spirit enlightens us to be aware that our failures and defeats earlier in life were stepping stones to greater wisdom. Our standards of what is success and failure change. Being number one as the world judges is no longer important. I enjoy teasing some friends of mine who seem to live or die depending on their football team's victories or defeats. I like to say, "It's all passing. Tomorrow no one will care." Of course that elicits some anger and hopefully some laughter as well.

18. Be more grateful:

When we practice second half of life spirituality, the Spirit enlightens us to God's love for us. As our images of God change and God become larger, we are over-whelmed by God's mercy, unconditional love, forgiveness, and patience. These new images of God gradually urge us to increase our gratitude. As a result, we become willing to share our possessions with others. We become sensitized to the homeless, the marginal, the outcasts, and the broken-hearted. Spiritual writers teach us that gratitude is synonymous with holiness. Gratitude not only defines sanctity, it also defines maturity in the spiritual life. A good shepherd is grateful to God for everything. Gratitude is shown in the way we reverence all people, irrespective of color, creed, nationality, or country of origin. The mystics teach us that it becomes very difficult for us to commit serious sins when our hearts are filled with gratitude.

19. Live the Sermon on the Mount:

When we strive to practice second half of life spirituality, the Spirit urges us to appreciate and live the message found in the Sermon on the Mount that includes the Beatitudes. We willingly make the transition from simply following a religion based on the Ten Commandments to a new path of deeper spirituality based on the Beatitudes. We begin to see the difference between simply practicing a religion and becoming a spiritual person.

For instance, when we embrace a deeper spirituality, we are challenged in radical ways. For example, in the Beatitudes, Jesus says, "...I say to you, love your enemies, and pray for those who persecute you..." (Matthew 5:43-44). This is a profoundly difficult task. During his ministry, Jesus spoke about forgiveness, in one form or another, more than any other subject. When we practice a deeper spirituality, we must learn to forgive. We gradually learn to forgive others and ourselves by being patient and showing compassion.

The seminary formation program teaches you to teach, correct, inform, judge, and administer. Thus, it is difficult to change gears. We were trained to think we have the right answers. It is difficult to be humble and verbalize that our "enemy," the person who annoys us, or disappoints us, or argues with us may have a point.

20. Be courageous:

One of the goals found in first half of life spirituality is to develop survival mechanisms which means to enhance our assets: physical, social, spiritual, and mental. When we practice second half of life spirituality, we are better able to courageously stand up for truth regardless of the impact it will have on the very things we pursued in the first half of life. Courage flows from a deep relationship with the Spirit of God living in us.

We can become more courageous when we are willing to do "soul work" which means we seek help in spiritual direction, therapy, prayer, counseling, and in honest and intimate friendships. Priests who serve in parishes can never please everyone. Priests in parishes may not reach their Catholic Faith Appeal. Priests in parishes are expected to do more than they are capable of doing. Courage enables them to recognize the absurdity of the goal to please everyone. Courage enables them not to take on an addiction that relieves their pain. Some priests are addicted to alcohol and/or some sexual outlet. Is it because they have not developed a courageous spirit that enables them to comprehend with the help of the Spirit, the truth?

21. Be less judgmental:

The scribes and Pharisees were typically harsh and terribly judgmental. They were always ready to condemn anyone who transgressed the laws or who were morally inferior to themselves. They even ended up plotting to condemn Jesus. Their rigid adherence to rules, conformity, and expectations of proper behavior prevented them from seeing new and greater realities.

If we continue to practice first half of life spirituality in the second half of life, we risk, like the religious authorities of Jesus' day, becoming very judgmental. Some church leaders are tempted and tend to become highly judgmental as they age, especially after they have accepted titles such as "monsignor," "most reverend," "very reverend," and "your eminence."

When we practice second half of life spirituality, the Spirit makes us aware of our own addictions and our sins of commission and omission. Knowing who we are helps us to refrain from being judgmental of others. We increasingly are able to see the human reality before us. We learn to accept, embrace, and truly love others, rather than be angry that life and the world are not perfect, as we judge the perfect to be.

22. Be less self-righteous:

The scribes and Pharisees were self-righteous. They thought they were much better than everyone else. For example in the parable of the Pharisee and the Tax Collector (Luke 18), Jesus warned them of their self righteousness. This should not surprise us, since judgmentalism and self-righteousness are two sides of one coin.

Some church leaders who continue to practice first half of life spirituality in the second half of life can easily tend to become self-righteous. Indeed, we often support this attitude by excessive deference to church leaders and the use of institutional props that insulate our church leaders from criticism. Some clerics preach against abortion and same-sex marriage, issues that they are not connected with personally. All those parishioners who have not experienced these two topics feel superior and self-righteous too.

In one of my early assignments as a parochial vicar, there was a retired priest who included in his preaching the horrors of abortion in nearly all his Sunday homilies even though the congregation was mostly older Catholics. I got the impression that he enjoyed the admiration that many parishioners gave him because he was against something. It is an easy way to score points, but with little or no benefit to others.

When we practice second half of life spirituality, the Spirit urges us to humbly connect our words to issues that appropriately meet the congregations' concerns. Also there is an attempt never to shame anyone but rather to examine the root causes of human failures that involve poverty, ignorance, and human frailty.

When we practice second half of life spirituality, we desire to be for something, love of our wonderful God and the glorious world of God's creation instead of simply preaching against something. We seek to build up rather than tear down. We seek to build bridges and not walls.

Conclusion:

When we practice second half of life spirituality, we increasingly realize that we gain knowledge in the first half of life and hopefully wisdom in the second half of life. As someone said, "In youth we learn. In age we understand."

Father Thomas Merton, the well-known Trappist monk who lived in a monastery in Gethsemani Kentucky, pointed out that we spend our whole life climbing the ladder of success. But with the virtue of wisdom, we become aware in the second half of life that our ladder was leaning against the wrong wall. He wrote this famous and beautiful second half of life prayer in his book, Thoughts in Solitude.

"My Lord God, I have no idea where I am going. I do not see the road ahead of me. I cannot know for certain where it will end. Nor do I really know myself, and the fact that I think I am following your will does not mean that I am actually doing so. But I believe that the desire to please you does in fact please you. And I hope I have that desire in all that I am doing. I hope that I will never do anything apart from that desire. And I know that if I do this you will lead me by the right road, though I may know nothing about it. Therefore I will trust you always though I may seem to be lost and in the shadow of death. I will not fear, for you are ever with me, and you will never leave me to face my perils alone."

Peace,

Uncle Matthew

Letter #27
Saturday, March 2, 2013


Dear Uncle Matthew,

Your last five letters have been most helpful to me. Your explanation of the goals, or the manifestation of the Spirit's work in the practice of second half of life spirituality, provides me with a standard to strive for as I mature in age and acquire more life experiences. Your letters are helping me to realize that the goals of the spiritual journey result in not so much what we do but rather in who we become. The goal of the spiritual journey seems to me to boil down to living our entire life in a deep loving relationship with God. This relationship with God brings about a transformation whereby we love God, our neighbor, and self, and thus we become fully human and fully alive.

However, at this stage of my development, I feel a tension. Part of me wants a more loving relationship with God, but part of me wants to experience many pleasures that are not compatible with a celibate life. At times, I doubt if I can give up all the pleasures I desire.

My spiritual director is helping me to be aware of the tension that I am experiencing. Here in the seminary, faith seems to be a function of the mind; an act of believing as opposed to doubting. But my spiritual director keeps telling me that faith is located in the heart. Faith is not so much a matter of believing doctrines and reciting creeds but rather an attitude toward life. He encourages me to live courageously each day with the faith to believe that I have the graces to live the life I so desire. He said that Abraham, the patriarch of the Hebrew nation, was a man of faith because he courageously journeyed into the unknown each day.

Earlier, you shared with me glimpses of second half of life spirituality which we might see, but not understand, early in life. Now that I know something about the goals of an adult spirituality, can you give some practical examples of applying the goals to real life situations?

Peace,

Joey

Response to Letter #27
Sunday, March 17, 2013

Dear Joey,

Of course, you heard the big news that Pope Francis is our new pope. He is the first Jesuit pope, the first pope from the Americas, and the first pope from the Southern Hemisphere. He is noted for his humility and his emphasis on God's mercy. He is choosing to live in the guesthouse rather than the papal apartments. I'm so excited.

Today I turn eighty years old! I do not know where the time went! I can still recall so well when I was in first theology in the seminary. There were over one hundred seminarians in my class! Those were the days when vocations to the priesthood were plentiful.

Practical examples of the practice of
second half of life spirituality:

You asked me to give you some practical examples to encourage you to be mindful of the blessings that can come about when we practice second half of life spirituality. There are many practical examples of second half of life spirituality that can be observed in Bible stories, films, people we meet, and in ourselves. I'll share with you in this letter three practical examples that illustrate a positive change in behavior when different goals in an adult spirituality are practiced. I hope that these examples will be helpful.

1. Bob believes in a new image of God:

There is the well-known idiom, "Experience is the best teacher." I'll share with you an experience Bob had when he changed his attitude toward other religions. He previously was dualistic in his thinking, but a new experience helped him to see that his previous attitude of being judgmental had denied him new opportunities to find God.

Bob is an eighty-four year-old Catholic man who told me that each summer he visited some Methodist relatives in Mississippi. Each time he visited, he would borrow a car and go to a Catholic Church for mass alone on Sunday. He found the local Catholic Church to be cold and unfriendly.

Each year he would be invited to go with the others to the small Methodist Church in the woods. On one visit, he decided to accept their invitation. He thought that he would pray to "his God" in the Methodist Church. He was pleased to find that the people in that Methodist Church were very friendly, and he experienced an atmosphere of warmth, hospitality, caring, and welcoming. He realized for the first time that his God and their God were the same.

Bob's tiny step of experiencing God's presence in another religious community was a stepping stone to a deeper awareness of truths that the Spirit reveals to us in the practice of second half of life spirituality. Bob not only realized he had been too judgmental, but he also changed his image of an Exclusive God to an image of an Inclusive God. Through his own experience, Bob realized that God is alive and operative in other religions too.

2. Fr. Raymond changes his motivation:

I'll share with you a story about Father Raymond who purified his motivation. He is a former classmate of mine. He is several years older than I. He studied for an archdiocese, and we attended the same seminary for studies in theology. He was very bright, and after his ordination to the priesthood, he had a very successful church career.

During his years of active ministry he served as a principal of a Catholic high school. He served as pastor of two of the largest parishes in his archdiocese. He was on numerous archdiocesan committees, and he was named a monsignor.

Raymond told me that for many years his false self was embellished because he received public respect, and extraordinary affirmation from his parishioners who projected upon him idealized qualities that may have had little bearing on his unique and individual reality. He unconsciously thought that his success in life was dependent upon his ability to preach good homilies, raise large sums of money for the bishop's annual faith appeal, and to avoid formal sin.

Now Raymond is retired. When he first retired at seventy, his health was good so he continued to "help out" in his former parish. He led retreats. He gave talks on many topics. He was involved in Emmaus.

A new pastor was appointed, and this new pastor did not want Raymond to be taking such an active role in the parish. Raymond began to experience a crisis. He began to question his ideas on success. He began to feel that he was no longer needed or wanted. His identity was in crisis since he no longer was able to relate to the world as a monsignor. He had to change because he could not change the situation.

Raymond and I happened to be on a retreat together last summer, and we shared our priestly journeys with one another. That is when I learned what I am sharing with you. Raymond was questioning his motivation, one of the goals of second half of life spirituality. He realized that his success in the priesthood had little to do with the gospel and the love of God. He was painfully realizing that his success in the priesthood was all too often "worldly" and it encouraged him to live his false self.

Raymond now realizes that his true self is at his core, his basic and unchangeable identity in God. Now he is trying to live in the love and mercy of God through the discovery that his true self is the "treasure hidden in the field." His true self is the "pearl of great price." Now that he is more aware of his motivation, he seems to be on the path of transformation as a man of integrity. He told me that now he proclaims the gospel message in a new and courageous way rather than delivering homilies that would not upset anyone in his parish. He is attempting to live daily as a compassionate and merciful person rather than living as a priest who is seeking a career that brings him praise and affirmation.

In New Seeds of Contemplation, Fr. Thomas Merton says,

"God alone can make me who I am, or rather who I will be when at last I fully begin to be. But unless I desire this identity and work to find it with Him and in Him, the work will never be done."

3. Henry overcomes his toxic shame:

One of the goals of second half of life spirituality is to identify our shame. I met a young man named Henry who suffered from toxic shame. He thought that because he was gay, he was flawed and defective. HIs shame led to an addiction. His false self denied that awareness. He felt ashamed and angry because of his sexual feelings. The Church, to put it mildly, doesn't look too kindly on gays. So a young gay man, like Henry, will likely try to maintain a false self to cover up his toxic shame.

Henry began to realize that his false self was demanding so much energy to maintain, all at the cost of not being his authentic self, his true self. I put him in contact with a good spiritual director with whom he shared his concerns. His spiritual director helped him to understand the shame that was binding him. Gradually, Henry was able to transition to an acceptance and eventually a positive embrace of his true self. He discovered what Carl Gustav Jung said many years ago, "The acceptance of oneself is the essence of the whole moral problem and the epitome of a whole outlook on life."

Conclusion:

Acceptance of one's true self, because it is ultimately grounded in God's reality, is necessary for transformation into a more mature, loving, and relational self. We see reality to the degree that we can know and accept our true self. I believe it was the German theologian, Paul Tillich (1886-1965) who defined grace as accepting the fact that we are accepted, despite the fact that we are unacceptable.

When we practice second half of life spirituality, we begin to realize that God's acceptance is not based on adhering to the Law. We realize that trying to be legally perfect, to be acceptable, is doomed to failure. By discovering and following the promptings of one's true self, we reduce the conflicts and toxic shame that can cause addictions, depression, self doubt, loneliness, and egotistical perfectionism. When we practice second half of life spirituality, the Spirit may enable us to no longer be depressed, lonely, egotistical, and addicted to something or someone.

You mentioned in your letter that you realize that the ultimate goal of the spiritual journey is to be transformed into union with God. The Spirit makes that goal clear and tells us how to do it in our own unique way. As the false self gradually loses its power over us, the obstacles to divine union diminish. Fully living as a member of the Body of Christ demands that we attempt to love our neighbor, forgive our neighbor, and show compassion for our neighbor. The practice of second half of life spirituality witnesses these virtues; the fruits of transformation; union with God. When we serve others without seeking a reward, we also witness to others the practice of second half of life spirituality because we bring the light of Christ into the world.

Peace,

Uncle Matthew

Letter #28
Saturday, March 23, 2013


Dear Uncle Matthew,

Tomorrow is Palm Sunday. I'm learning so much about the liturgical cycle in the Church. I read an article on Palm Sunday and the author asked the question, "Why did Jesus die?" since this week we will focus on the death by crucifixion of Jesus. Most people would answer the question by saying that Jesus died for our sins. The author said, "What God, but a Vengeful God, would require the death of God's beloved son to die for our sins." The article agrees with what you wrote about how, through the Spirit's promptings, and our cooperation, we replace our image of a Vengeful God with an image of a Merciful and Compassionate God.

We are all happy here about the election of Pope Francis. I love his smile and his reputation of being merciful.

The three practical examples of applying the goals of second half of life spirituality to real life situations was very helpful. You clearly showed me the importance of being aware of the goals of second half of life spirituality. Once a person is aware of some of the goals of second half of life spirituality, change comes about. Your examples showed me that Bob changed his image of God, Fr. Raymond purified his motivation, and Henry discovered his toxic shame. The result was new life for all three men. Change occurred for the better. I never took a psychology course so the material about the true and false self was difficult for me to understand. Until you shared in your letters, I didn't know about Fr. Thomas Merton and Fr. Richard Rohr. I know you are simplifying much of their material for me to comprehend.

I would appreciate a few more practical examples that illustrate the change that can occur once a person is aware of the goals of second half of life spirituality and is willing to apply them to real life situations. I especially like your examples from movies. Your examples are giving me a pastoral view of reality as well as encouraging me to eventually embrace an adult spirituality.

Peace,

Joey

Response to Letter #28
Monday, April 1, 2013

Dear Joey,

Yesterday was Easter Sunday. I celebrated a mass in the parish where I retired. I enjoyed celebrating the good news of the gospel with the people.

You mentioned the question, "Why did Jesus die?" I'm glad you are paying attention to good questions that jar our traditional ways of thinking.

I read a thirteen page essay, "Joseph's Son: Was Jesus Married," by Anthony Padovano in the March/April issue of CORPUS. Padovano asks many questions in the essay such as "Was Jesus married? Did Jesus have children? How does celibacy play a role in the answers to these questions?" Questions make us think. Questions cause us to reinforce our earlier beliefs or to see reality differently.

You mentioned in an earlier letter that you are experiencing a tension between a desire to be in union with God and a desire for the pleasures of this world. I experience the same tension, even though I am eighty! The wrestling match continues! This tension we both experience is another good example of how the false self dies with great difficulty. It takes great faith to move forward each day with a belief that God is with us and we can become our true self.

I'll share with you three more practical examples that illustrate a positive change in behavior when different goals in an adult spirituality are practiced.

Practical examples of the practice of second half of life spirituality (con't.):

4. A Christmas Carol:

In 1843, Charles Dickens, an English writer, published A Christmas Carol. In this well-known story, Ebenezer Scrooge, a cold, stingy, greedy, and miserly old man who was living out of his false self, was visited on Christmas Eve by his former business partner, Jacob Marley, now in ghostly form. He now is in chains and suffering the torments of Hell. Marley tries to warn Ebenezer that he too will end up that way unless he changes.

Then the Ghost of Christmas Past arrives and shows Ebenezer what he was like when he was young: kinder, innocent, and in love with his fiancée, Belle. The Ghost points out to Ebenezer how his false self developed. Scrooge had come to love money more than Belle or anything else.

Next, Ebenezer was visited by the Ghost of Christmas Present. He sees clearly the hunger and suffering of little children and the homelessness in the city of London. This Ghost begins to stir Scrooge's conscience, sensitizing him to the stark reality around and near him.

Finally, Ebenezer was visited by the Ghost of Christmas to Come. He sees what will happen to him when he dies. He becomes aware that if unchanged, his life is a failure. He missed the whole point of life which is to become charitable, joyful, and a vibrant member of a community. In sum, his missed becoming fully human and fully alive.

Charles Dickens in his novel was showing us that we must

examine and eventually change the container, the "wine skin," the false self to find purpose and happiness in this life. Ebenezer is a good example of what life can be like if we stay in our false self and fail to live our true self. Once Ebenezer became aware through the ghostly visits that his false self had molded him into a miserable, miserly, and insensitive person, he was willing to let go of his false self, his container, and embrace his true self, a new container with fresh "wine." And so the novel ends with a vivid and happy scene. The people loved him. He discovered the joy, love, sensitivity, and charitableness that he had lost. Living as one's true self is the essence of second half of life spirituality.

Most of us are not visited by ghosts to help us change our views of reality, but with eyes to see and ears to hear we all are afforded many experiences that challenge us to see reality differently.

5. Social justice issues:

We show signs of practicing second half of life spirituality when we question our attitudes and beliefs. We become willing to go beyond the Law. We search for the will of God. We become aware that we are too judgmental and desire to become less judgmental. We become aware that we are too self-righteous, and we desire to change and become less self righteous. We become aware that our compassion motivates us to be interested in peace and justice in the community, even the world at large, rather than just staying focused on our own spiritual growth. For example, we may take an interest in the Society of St. Vincent de Paul. We may be willing to go to a third-world country such as Haiti to see how the people live. We are concerned about the minimum wage, a fair tax system, food stamps for the poor, and universal health care. Our circle of compassion enlarges when we practice second half of life spirituality.

The root causes of crime:

In the practice of first half of life spirituality, there is an emphasis on judgment and punishment. We support incarcerating more Americans who commit crimes. We support building more prisons.

When we practice second half of life spirituality, we develop an interest in the root causes for incarceration. In the past four decades, the prison population has quadrupled in the United States. There are 2.2 million in prison, or one of every hundred adults. Those who practice second half of life spirituality are concerned that the worse the treatment meted out to prisoners, the more recidivism there is. Too often the prison system fails to treat prisoners as human beings. Compassion increases when there is awareness that most criminality is rooted in economic and social inequality. We show the practice of second half of life spirituality when we believe that there should be alternatives for incarceration for those who suffer from addictions and mental illness.

The elderly who are financially burdened:

When we are open to seeing reality differently, our compassion alerts us to the plight of so many who are financially unable to retire. We are willing to engage in constructive dialogue. This is a complex issue. There is the issue of financial responsibility. Some people failed to be responsible so they were not prepared to retire. But many people suffer from circumstances that are out of their control. They are not at fault. There are more than seventy-million baby boomers, those born in the early sixties through the early eighties, heading towards retirement. Many of those individuals who will be retiring have skimpy reserves. The incomes for those in the top fifth of income are well prepared for retirement. But householders in the bottom fifth of income do not have the reserves to retire. To the degree that we become less judgmental of others and we develop a prophetic dimension, we change so that we can better practice the Golden Rule (Matthew 7:12).

Peace in the middle east:

When we begin to practice second half of life spirituality, we feel and express empathy and compassion for all those individuals caught up in the disputes in the middle east. We desire to pray for an end to the festering conflict between the Palestinians and Israel. The practice of second half of life spirituality eliminates partisanship and focuses on the welfare of all the people involved.

Immigration reform:

When we begin to practice second half of life spirituality, we vote to support immigration reform. To the degree that we have grown in compassion and increased our respect for all life, we tend to be more concerned about those who come to our country at great risk to themselves, especially children. Many Central American children from the countries of El Salvador, Guatemala, and Honduras have arrived after arduous travel to the United States border. Many people are trying to leave these countries because of violent gangs who run entire towns and murder and rape at will. They force families and businesses to pay protection money. So many people are left with the stark choice to flee or to die. Some children who flee are as young as four. Some people think the training of Honduran officers in this country has added to the economic problems in Honduras. United Nations figures show that Honduras is the murder capital of the world.

6.   Pastoral sensitivity:

Pastors exemplify second half of life spirituality when their compassion motivates them to be more pastoral. This may mean that they have to go beyond the Law. They must be courageous. They must avoid perfectionism. They must be willing to understand that compassion and mercy are the core of loving our neighbor. They are wiling to engage in dialogue and think non-dualistically.

A Sunday wedding:

I know a priest who told me about a wedding ceremony that he celebrated on a Sunday afternoon. One day a young Presbyterian man called the church office to inquire about marrying a woman on a Sunday. The priest showed pastoral sensitivity by asking him to come by so as to discuss the request. Normally, diocesan guidelines discourage Sunday weddings. The priest found out that the young man was from the middle-east and his family worked seven days a week at their service station. The only day the family could slip away for a short time was on Sundays. Once the priest knew the circumstances, he willingly scheduled the wedding ceremony. The young man mentioned that when he called two other church offices, he was simply told "we do not perform weddings on Sunday." There was no invitation to discuss his situation. This example reminds me of the story when the Pharisees criticized Jesus and his disciples for picking heads of grain on the sabbath. Jesus responded by saying, "The sabbath was made for man, not man for the sabbath" (Mark 2:27).

A wedding that included Rover:

Another priest told me about a wedding ceremony that he performed that included the bride and groom's dog, Rover. A short time before the wedding ceremony, the bride, who was not Catholic, said she had a request. She wanted their dog, Rover, to be in the wedding ceremony dressed in a tuxedo with the rings pinned on his suit. She wanted him to come down the aisle in the entrance procession. The priest realized that if he said, "No," she would probably walk out and say, "you can forget our wedding!" So the priest agreed to let Rover be in the wedding party. It all turned out well. Rover was better behaved than some of those who attended the wedding.

After a couple of years, Rover died and the young woman called the priest and asked for a "church service." The priest agreed and set a time for the couple to bring in their dead dog. The priest had the music director play a couple of songs and he made up some prayers. The couple was crying, and the priest gave them great comfort.

As it turned out, every year the young woman sends the priest a beautiful Christmas card with a long letter. The priest touched her with his kindness and sensitivity. Rover was like a child to them. Not too many priests would do what this priest did, but again the practice of second half of life spirituality emphasizes the welfare of the people involved more than worrying about what people will think. Priests exemplify second half of life spirituality when they are not caught up in trivial legalisms but rather minister in a manner that address the deeper issues that help people.

Conclusion:

I hope these practical examples of the practice of second half of life spirituality were helpful to you.

Before I end this letter, I have another observation. Since most people are unfamiliar with the paradigm of two halves of life spirituality, they assume that when a priest preaches on social justice topics, like the ones I mentioned above (the root causes of crime, the plight of the financially burdened, peace in the middle east, and immigration reform), he is preaching just politics. Those who dismiss issues that they claim to be political may unconsciously be avoiding difficult truths about social justice. The paradigm of the two halves of life spirituality stresses that all social issues are spiritual in nature since there is no longer the dualism of the secular and holy. Adults should be exposed to challenges that call them to believe in a bigger God who loves all people. Second half of life spirituality challenges us to feed the hungry, clothe the naked, and give water to the thirsty, so that we live as vibrant members of the Body of Christ.

I am trying to show you by these examples that a transformation takes place whereby the religion, the spirituality, of our youth (the old wineskin along with its old wine) is gradually replaced by a new religion, a new spirituality (the new wineskin along with new wine) as we move into adulthood.

Peace,

Uncle Matthew

Encl.: Padovano's essay from CORPUS

Letter #29
Sunday, April 14, 2013

Dear Uncle Matthew,

The practical example from A Christmas Carol helped me to better understand the difference between the practice of first and second half of life spirituality as well as to become more aware of the link with the false and true self. I'll try to remember when I eventually preach to use movies and current events to illustrate a point. As the English idiom says, "A picture is worth a thousand words."

The examples about social justice issues hit me hard. So many times in my lifetime I have not heard homilies on social justice issues. Also the two examples of pastoral sensitivity struck me as beautiful stories that illustrate that people are more important than just keeping the Law. You are making the practice of second half of life spirituality attractive, but I can see that it takes the virtue of courage to practice this adult spirituality.

Since we have been corresponding, I have taken a greater interest in the ways a person's spirituality influences others. For example, my spiritual director is very much like you. He questions. He is open to new ideas. He smiles. He respects me despite my failings. He is patient and merciful. By way of contrast, the rector seems to be quite different. He comes across to us as stern, the keeper of the laws and rules of the seminary.

If a seminarian seeks consolation, he probably goes to my spiritual director rather than to the rector. Compassion and empathy seem to be the signs that a person is practicing second half of life spirituality.

You probably have some ideas about the influence a person's spirituality has on others. Can you share your thoughts with me? Thank you.

Peace,

Joey

Response to Letter #29
Monday, April 29, 2013

Dear Joey,

We are so often unaware in the present moment of our own
actions. We often act without thinking. And yet our actions
influence others, and our actions are framed by the way we see
the world, other people, and ourselves. In politics, the way we
see the world, our philosophy of life, and our spirituality shape
our social policies and the institutions in which we participate. All
our political views are formed by our spirituality and therefore
they affect our morality. We convey our spirituality to others not
only in what we say, and how we act, but even in the way we
appear (our clothing, gestures, tattoos, hair color, and facial
expressions).

You made the distinction between your spiritual director and
rector. It is interesting that you picked up on the traits of
compassion and empathy. The presence or absence of these
two virtues has a great influence on others.

I'll gladly share with you how a person's spirituality or lack
thereof, has an influence on other people. I'm glad you are
interested in these topics; signs of second half of life spirituality.

1. The Boston Marathon bombing:

Let's be current. The Boston Marathon bombing earlier this month was so senseless. Three people were killed and two hundred and sixty-four were injured. During an initial interrogation in the hospital, Dzhokhar Tsarnaev said that he and his older brother were motivated by extremist Islamist beliefs and the wars in Iraq and Afghanistan. Dzhokhar and his brother failed to develop the essential goals of first half of life spirituality. They failed to develop good boundaries. They failed to develop an informed conscience so as to know what was right and what was wrong. They failed to know who they are. Regardless of what religion a person adheres to, no religion condones such terrorism. We can question what kind of spirituality these two brothers have. Certainly, Dzhokhar's violent actions will have a profound negative influence on everyone who participated in the Boston Marathon. We can learn from tragic situations like this that a person's spirituality does affect others.

2.  The influence of our images of God:

Our images of God, as we discussed in great detail earlier, greatly influence our spirituality and thus our view of life, morality, and influence upon others.

3.  The influence of the popes:

For the past thirty-five years, the popes in the Catholic Church have had a huge influence on all Catholics. We often look to the pope to provide us with a model of what it means to be a Christian.

Pope John Paul II reigned from 1978 to 2005. Some Catholics call him Saint John Paul the Great. He was one of the most travelled world leaders in history, visiting one hundred and twenty-nine countries during his pontificate. He selected his bishops based on their adherence to orthodox teachings.

Pope Benedict XVI served as pope from 2005 until his resignation in 2013. He found his certitude in church doctrines. Earlier in his career as head of the Congregation for the Doctrine of the Faith, he censored many theologians who questioned orthodox doctrines. Earlier, I mentioned the Declaration, Dominus Jesus that was published by the Congregation for the Doctrine of the Faith. The document discourages questioning church dogmas. He elevated the Tridentine Mass to a more prominent position. He and Pope John Paul II had the reputations of being theologically conservative, and they advocated a return to basic Christian values.

Yesterday, I saw a picture of Pope Francis washing the feet of some young males and females. Pope Francis is a different kind of pope from Pope John Paul II and Pope Benedict XVI. Pope Francis is influencing people in a different way since he practices a different spirituality. Pope Francis' manner of speaking is scary for those who believe the pope should be giving them absolute answers and perfect certitude about everything.   Pope Francis said the Church is a home for all, not a small chapel that can only hold a small group of select people. Pope Benedict XVI seemed to prefer a smaller and doctrinally purer Church. When the pope envisions the Church as a home for all, he is presuming respect for peoples' differences. Respecting different cultures, religions, and philosophies are signs of a more inclusive spirituality.

4. The influence of a prayerful seminarian:

I remember in the seminary my classmate George who was in the chapel every night from 10:00-10:30 praying. I observed him praying each night for four years. He knelt in the same spot in the chapel. Without any words spoken, his spirituality, his faithfulness to God inspired me and I'm sure other seminarians. His willingness to pray each night influenced me because his example encouraged me to also make a visit to the chapel to pray.

My friend George provided me with an important paradigm early in my life. He taught me that individuals who are good, prayerful, and virtuous can do so much to influence those around them. They do not have to be famous, just faithful to God, to influence the transformation of others who know them. This example reminded me of the story of the poor widow who put in two small coins in the temple (Mark 12:41-44). The small, charitable, sincere acts that we perform often affect others the most!

I hope these examples affirmed your observation that our spirituality can have a profound influence upon others.

Peace,

Uncle Matthew

Letter #30
Saturday, May 11, 2013

Dear Uncle Matthew,

Thank you for affirming my observation that our spirituality influences other people in a profound way. Your insights about the influence of the recent popes were very helpful. From what you have said about the two halves of life paradigm, it seems Popes John Paul II and Benedict XVI practiced first half of life spirituality, which doesn't surprise me, because they spoke about our beliefs in black and white terms.

I've noticed that those seminarians who are eventually ordained tend to agree with everything they are taught. It seems to me that this is both good and bad. It is good because it gives them a starting point for their ministry. It could be bad if later in life they do not realize that the Holy Spirit will be prompting them, and everyone else, to be open to new realities and to modify their religious beliefs and deepen their spirituality so as to savor the "new wine."

I have observed that the formation program sorts out those who do not fit into the box of first half of life spirituality. Many men who leave have an open-mindedness to the Spirit of God that is not appreciated by those in charge. This has an effect on the future of the institutional church which is weighed in favor of ordaining more conservative men as priests who are rule-followers.

My prayer life needs some attention. My spiritual director wisely told me that my prayer life is supposed to transform me so that I become less judgmental of others, less self-righteous, and more compassionate so that I serve others. I still think of prayer as saying words and thinking holy thoughts. I need to remember that prayer is an awareness of God's presence in others and in myself. I do need to listen more to the prompting of the Holy Spirit. My spiritual director said prayer is not for God's benefit, but for mine. I shouldn't be trying to change God's mind but trying instead to change my own mind and will. He said, for example, that over-coming an addiction to alcohol is only achieved if our experience of God is more powerful than the desire to drink. Do you have any thoughts to share with me on prayer?

In our classes we occasionally talk about topics that are relevant in society today such as health care, poverty, immigration, and global warming. I've noticed that the political opinions of my classmates greatly vary on these topics. Earlier in letters to me, you shared that our beliefs in church doctrines change when we move into the practice of second half of life spirituality. I was wondering how our spirituality affects our political opinions on social issues. I assume that just as our spirituality is expressed in our words and actions in daily life, so too our spirituality influences our political views.

I look forward to your next letter.

Peace,

Joey

Response to Letter #30
Sunday, May 26, 2013

Dear Joey,

You have already left the seminary for your summer assignment. In the fall, you will begin your second year of theological studies. The time is going by so quickly. I do agree with what you observe about the men who are being ordained. Most of them are likely to practice first half of life spirituality since the seminary is basically a first half of life spirituality institution. This fact diminishes the likelihood that priests will be able to help adult parishioners become aware of the practice of second half of life spirituality.

You asked if I had any comments on prayer. I would refer you to James Finley's book, Merton's Palace of Nowhere, A Search for God through Awareness of the True Self. I have found Finley's book to be easy to read and very insightful. In his book, he shares many of Father Thomas Merton's thoughts about prayer. Merton viewed prayer as a response to the Father's call to be like his Son through the power of the Holy Spirit. I'm sure your ideas about prayer will continually change as you are exposed to new situations over the coming years. I very much like the insights on prayer that your spiritual director shared with you.

I recently read the book, Don't Think of an Elephant by George Lakoff. He helped me to understand why people vote in political elections the way they do. His book is a masterpiece. I'm sharing many of his ideas with you and formatting them into the paradigm of the two halves of life spirituality. Though not a perfect application of his theories, I hope this helps you to see why people have such radically different opinions on the four important topics you mentioned.

Let me begin by providing you with general descriptions rather than critical assessments regarding two divergent political viewpoints that express the practice of first and second half of life spirituality. As you begin reading my notes, consider that political views can be critiqued on the basis of life experiences, reason, interpretation of scripture, tradition, theology, and an understanding of history. In the conclusion of my notes, I will share with you my own critical reflections on these two viewpoints. As you read these descriptions, please consider as well what images of God underlie these two different viewpoints since our spirituality is the way we allow our images of God to guide our actions.

Your observations and questioning are good regarding the influence of our spirituality on our political views. I'll be happy to share with you my thoughts on what underlies and informs different viewpoints regarding the four political issues of (1) health care, (2) poverty, (3) immigration, and (4) global warming.

Our spirituality influences our political views:

1. Political views on health care:

Whether we practice first or second half of life spirituality, we hold underlying values, assumptions, and beliefs. In all four of these political topics, it is important to discover these different underlying values, assumptions, and beliefs. By getting to the bottom of things, Joey, you can decide for yourself which viewpoint is valid and moral.

Before I get into specifics, I'll give a thumbnail sketch of the three psychosocial stages in life because these stages of life affect our spirituality which in turn affects our political views. When we are young, we are dependent upon our parents for food, shelter, education, and clothing. Later, in the teen years through adulthood, we live in an independent stage of life whereby we increasingly seek our independence so as to accomplish the goals found in the practice of first half of life spirituality. We establish our identity, acquire an education, strive to be successful, develop a strong ego, acquire financial resources, and provide for security. We realize we must stand on our own two feet to survive. During this developmental stage of life, we view ourselves as fundamentally separate from other people. We presume we are essentially independent of others. Finally, in the interdependent stage of psychosocial development, we live in a balanced way, a holistic way, whereby we are neither wholly dependent or independent. We see the reality of, and value of, being both dependent upon others and at other times independent of others. We are both.

When we practice first half of life spirituality, we assume our underlying identity is that of a solitary being. We live predominately in an independent stage of life. We think we are responsible only for the care of ourselves, and we don't have an inherent responsibility for the care of others. We prefer that charity, freely given, be the sole means of helping the needy rather than through the assistance of governmental organizations. We do not want public taxes to pay for the health care of others. We feel as though it is better to refuse material help to others in order to force them to help themselves. In order to justify this, we may simply espouse the proverb, "It is better to teach others to fish rather than to give them fish to eat." We would be likely to view the Affordable Care Act as an unwanted governmental over-reach that should be repealed.

Normally, it is later in life when the Holy Spirit, through suffering and difficult experiences, enlightens us to the reality, profound importance, and desirability of interdependence. This awareness of our interdependence helps us to transition into the practice of second half of life spirituality when we question, move beyond the law, discover the will of God, think non-dualistically, see reality differently, and try to live the Sermon on the Mount. This changing sense of identity has profound ramifications for our political views.

When we practice second half of life spirituality, we presume the goodness of both personal responsibility and empathy for others. We believe that God calls us to live in an interdependent stage of life (neither wholly dependent or independent) whereby we know we are not essentially separate from others. We develop strong personal relationships that create and reflect empathy for others. We not only believe in the doctrine of the Body of Christ, but we increasingly experience its profound reality. This awareness informs our conviction that society has a responsibility to aid those in real material need, and that our government should be a major instrument in achieving this objective with the support of public taxes. We support the Affordable Care Act for theological, moral, and practical reasons.

2. Political views on poverty:

As with the issue of health care, there are many people whose views on poverty are based on the underlying assumptions that they are essentially independent and separate from other people. This objectification of others, the opposite of putting yourself in someone else's shoes, makes it easy to condemn. And so the poor are judged to have failed in their personal responsibility. The poor are poor because of their moral failings. It is believed that people are poor because they lack the discipline to prosper, so they get what they deserve.

In addition, many people with this mindset embrace the underlying assumption that some people are superior to others. Slavery is the most extreme example reflecting this belief system. Even though we do not have legalized slavery today in America, the attitude of dehumanizing others is nonetheless manifested in different ways. Some believe that society actually needs superiors and inferiors in order for society to function. Some people (the poor) need to serve other people (the rich). Those people holding this viewpoint are not upset with the vast gap between the rich and the poor, but in fact view it as a natural, even moral, expression of worthiness.

Further, a belief in the basic independence from others leads to an easy embrace of free markets where people pursue their own individual profits, as well as theories of free trade, capitalism, and competition, (if it doesn't hurt their self-interests!). They believe regulation is bad since it gets in the way of the pursuit of their profits. Owners and investors most likely would not support unions and pensions unless they somehow contribute to their personal profit.

Other people who practice second half of life spirituality presume a philosophy of life, a moral code, based on the idea that they are members of the Body of Christ. This means that they deeply believe that they are not essentially independent of and separate from other people, but that we are all brothers and sisters in Christ.

They deny the assumption that some people are essentially inferior to others who are destined to serve the rich. Thus, they are empathetic with those who have not had a fair chance to achieve the American dream because of poverty.

They embrace the underlying belief that the government has an obligation to provide programs to help the poor with the support of public taxes. They support affirmative action programs and policies that level the playing field for those who tend to suffer from discrimination, especially in relation to employment or education.

They support unions and pensions, and they consider these to be justice issues. They believe that the decline of unions has meant a decline in most people being able to fairly share in our nation's wealth.

3. Political views on immigration:

The United States is a country with many documented and undocumented immigrants along with refugees who fled from brutal oppression or from terrible poverty.

As with the issues of health care and poverty, there are many people with a viewpoint on immigration based on the underlying assumptions that they are essentially independent and separate from other people. Thus, believing they are fundamentally separate from the immigrants, they easily lack empathy for them. This objectification can lead to dehumanization. Thus, undocumented immigrants can be seen simply as criminals deserving jail and deportation.

They also assume that some people are inherently superior to others, making it easy to discriminate against undocumented immigrants because of their color and language. They have little empathy for the poverty the immigrants endure, nor do they take into account the conditions they face in their native countries.

As with the issues of health care and poverty, those who practice second half of life spirituality presume a philosophy of life, a moral code, based on the reality that they are members of the Body of Christ. They believe God loves all of us equally, so they do not believe that some people are superior to other people in essential terms. They therefore have natural empathy for immigrants and refugees. They are painfully aware of human trafficking and the death squads in Guatemala, Honduras, and parts of Mexico where children are murdered and kidnapped. They respect refugees as human beings who should be assisted without judgment.

4. Political views on global warming:

Those who practice first half of life spirituality are prone to deny global warming. They view the Earth with its water, fish, flora, and animals as radically separate from humankind. Their spirituality does not teach them the sacredness, the presence of God, in Mother Earth, so they are not aware of how morally wrong it is to fail to be good stewards of the earth's resources. Egocentricity blinds them to the moral implications of contributing to the destruction of Mother Earth. They fail to be aware of the dire conditions that some nations face today with the effects of climate change. In the pursuit of their own interests, they even use scare tactics to claim that addressing global warming is too expensive, would ruin the economy, cause the loss of jobs, and increase energy dependency on foreign countries.

Those who practice second half of life spirituality believe that Mother Earth is not separate from God. They view Mother Earth as precious, a gift that God gives us to enjoy, honor, use wisely as good stewards, and protect. They view global warming as the greatest moral issue facing the world today because of its profound effect on all of life today and of all generations to come. They consider the unbridled accumulation of wealth by the wealthy a close runner-up.

Accordingly, they support governmental efforts to prevent global warming. They are willing to discuss the impact of population growth, production of food, consumption, creative solutions, disasters such as hurricanes and tornadoes, and the diminishment of our natural resources. They recognize that we all are in this together and the solution will require a joint effort.

Conclusion:

As you can tell, I find profoundly inadequate the viewpoints of those who practice first half of life spirituality on all four of these topics. I find it inconsistent and unjustifiable for a person to hold such positions and yet claim to be a follower of Jesus because it goes against what he preached and demonstrated in his life. The heart of Jesus' ministry was a profound empathy for the suffering of all people. I find it wrong to deny affordable health care to everyone since we are all God's children. I find it wrong to deny helping the poor and hungry with public tax money since private charities cannot adequately do the task. I find it wrong to dehumanize immigrants since we are all God's children. I find it sinful to deny the over-whelming scientific evidence of global warming because we are destroying God's creation, Mother Earth, with untold suffering to come.

In one of my early letters to you, I mentioned that egocentricity is detrimental to the spiritual life. When we continue to practice first half of life spirituality as adults, we risk staying egocentric. We risk thinking only about our own financial security, possessions, health insurance, family, neighborhood, and country. As brothers and sisters in Christ, God calls us to live the Beatitudes so that we are also concerned about other peoples' incomes, health care, family situations, neighborhoods, and countries.

Duplicity is present when we say we believe in Jesus and then deny his basic warnings concerning wealth. Jesus said, "How hard it is for those who have wealth to enter the kingdom of God" (Mark 10:23). Jesus viewed wealth as a gift from God to be used to assist others. When we fail to share with our neighbor, we can easily become self-justified, hypocritical, and dishonest without awareness. We may believe in the church doctrines pertaining to the Body of Christ, but practically speaking, when we fail to love our neighbor, we show that we are duplicitous; more concerned about our own salvation, blessings, wealth, possessions, indulgences, and reception of the sacraments.

Earlier, I mentioned that our images of God change when we practice second half of life spirituality. As you know, I believe our images of God greatly influence our political views.

Consider, for example, when we practice first half of life spirituality, we believe in an image of a Distant God. It is easy for us to assume that God is separate from other people, so, by analogy and imitation, we separate ourselves from other people. We can also think God is separate from Mother Earth, so we can separate ourselves from Mother Earth. When we practice second half of life spirituality, we believe in an image of an Incarnate God. We become aware of the divine presence in all people, in ourselves, and in Mother Earth.

When we practice first half of life spirituality, we believe in an image of an Exclusive God. By analogy and imitation, we then think that some people are superior to other people. The poor are meant to serve the wealthy. God loves and favors the rich more than the poor, citizens more than immigrants, the healthy more than the unhealthy, those who have health insurance more than those who lack health insurance. When we practice second half of life spirituality and believe in an image of an Inclusive God, we realize that everyone is favored by God who has no favorites. In God's eyes, we are all equal and precious!

When we practice first half of life spirituality, we believe in an image of a Vengeful God. By analogy and imitation, we can think people get what they deserve in life. We think that certain people deserve being poor, homeless, refugees, or sick. This belief goes back to the Old Testament when people believed God punished people for their sins, so they suffered. In the Book of Job, the sacred author reveals that God does not punish people by making them suffer for their sins in this life. When we practice second half of life spirituality, we believe in an image of a Compassionate God. We become aware that God is love. God doesn't punish certain people with bad health or a life of poverty. God loves all of us alike; saint and sinner, healthy and unhealthy, rich and poor, educated and uneducated.

When we consider our political views in light of our spirituality, we realize, Joey, that most of us who claim to practice second half of life spirituality have a long way to go. Practicing second half of life spirituality manifests its fruits in those who, with the Spirit's leading, have gradually imitated Christ, undergone a spiritual transformation, and are now more fully human and fully alive. Notice, these fruits of the Spirit are God-given. We can respond to God's promptings, but we cannot earn them.

Earlier, in a letter to you, I mentioned that those who practice first half of life spirituality don't understand those who practice second half of life spirituality and visa versa. Perhaps that is why you notice at the seminary such divergent opinions and misunderstandings among your classmates on these four important issues. Let's discuss this more in the future.

Peace,

Uncle Matthew

Letter #31
Friday, June 7, 2013

Dear Uncle Matthew,

Thank you for your last letter in which you well described how our spirituality influences our political views. I find it amazing how some laypersons can go to church every day and yet seem insensitive to the needs of the poor, the immigrants, those without health care, and the very future of our planet.

My summer assignment is going well. I visit the hospitals, interact with the youth in the parish, serve at all the masses as sacristan, and sometimes I serve as a lector and/or a Eucharistic minister. I am getting a real feel for what goes on in the life of a priest. We are near the beaches, so there are many visitors here.

The pastor is good to me. The one associate pastor is older than the pastor. I sense that there is some friction present. Based on what you have shared in your letters, it seems to me that the pastor practices second half of life spirituality but the older associate pastor practices first half of life spirituality. They do not seem to be "on the same page" in their ministry. They do not seem to even be friends, just co-workers, who want to keep the institution going. I'm sure if I can pick up on their differences, the parishioners can also tell that they are not friendly with one another.

This is my third summer assignment to a parish. Each summer assignment is different. In my first summer assignment and in this summer assignment, I have observed that when two priests are assigned to ministry together in a parish, their ministry is often unproductive because the priests practice different spiritualities. Bishops often assign priests to serve in parishes without appreciating the practice of different spiritualities. I can see why an awareness of a spiritual roadmap is so important so that the priests can better understand each other; the first step required for friendship and good ministry. I wish in the seminary we had a course that would introduce us to the different spiritualities so that future conflicts could be reduced, friendships could better develop, and happiness would increase.

I was wondering how our spirituality affects our views on morality. Could you share some of your insights with me?

Peace,

Joey

Response to Letter #31
Wednesday, June 26, 2013

Dear Joey,

Thank you for sharing about your summer assignment. When I was your age, I did not know the difference between religion and spirituality let alone anything about the practice of first and second half of life spirituality, so when I saw priests who were not "on the same page," I reflexively sided with the more conservative priest. I thought since he was more traditional, and more orthodox, he must be the "correct" one to follow.

Often priests who practice first half of life spirituality tend to be literalists. They tend to read the Bible as though it were a history book without understanding the deep truths being presented. They never go beyond the law; the written liturgical guidelines. They never go beyond what the Catechism or Rome has spoken on a particular issue.

I did try to go beyond the law on many occasions and for many years in my active ministry, but I never really felt validated until I attended the Fr. Richard Rohr Conference in January, 2011. Now I can at least better understand what is going on when it comes to the morality of actions.

In recent letters, I shared that our spirituality influences other people and our political views. At your request, I will share some thoughts about the connection between morality and spirituality. Our spirituality influences our morality, the distinction between right and wrong or good and bad behavior. I'll begin with some introductory remarks, and then I'll refer to a couple of topics that are current and controversial; abortion and contraception. I will try to portray the mindset, underlying thinking, regarding the practice of first and second half of life spirituality with respect to these topics.

Our spirituality influences our morality:

Introductory remarks:

I would like to note up front that I am not a moral theologian. I am not trying to present systematic moral theology, but rather I am attempting to show how the formation of conscience varies. I am not making a judgment about what is ultimately correct morality. My motive, instead, is to facilitate dialogue and promote understanding.

Morality differs in the practice of first and second half of life spirituality. When we practice first half of life spirituality, we presume that morality comes in the form of rules or commandments which are taught to us by others. We believe in a God of reward and punishment. To act morally is simply to be obedient to those in authority: parents, teachers, civil leaders, military leaders, and church leaders.

When we practice second half of life spirituality, our images of God evolve. We no longer have an image of God as distant and vengeful. We no longer believe in an image of a God who loves us with requirements and conditions. We better appreciate mystery. We no longer view God as simply, crudely, rewarding and punishing us.

When we practice second half of life spirituality, we become more interested in a bigger and more complex world. We no longer see morality in a dualistic way, the way we were taught when we were young. We appreciate a plurality of views. We discover our own inner moral compass which is meant to lead us in making good moral decisions. We realize the presence of and the important role of the Holy Spirit within us. We realize the deeper dimensions of conflict that makes us aware of our duties to others, church, country, and self. For example, in the case of abortion, we not only ask and follow what the church teaches, but we also weigh the many factors involved in that particular situation. We draw upon our own experiences, seek God's will, and we trust that God is with us in the discernment process.

Parishioners ask priests many questions pertaining to moral issues. Parishioners want to know what is right and what is wrong. These questions are often difficult to address, if a good shepherd, a church leader wants to build bridges of understanding within the church community, and not simply exercise institutional authority. At times we find ourselves in simple agreement with others. At other times we find ourselves at odds with others. The practice of second half of life spirituality emphasizes respect for the moral challenges and discernment of others.

1. Abortion:

The late Jesuit priest, Fr. Anthony DeMello once said in his book, Awareness, "The day you teach the child the name of a bird, the child will never see that bird again." Once the child knows the bird is a sparrow, the child never sees the uniqueness of each sparrow again. The child will say, "Oh, sparrows. I've seen sparrows. I'm bored by sparrows." We do tend to categorize, which is useful to do in terms of how we acquire knowledge. When we grow older, categorizing can be flawed.

This illustration applies not only to birds but to humans as well. We tend to see and judge others through our concepts. We forget every person is unique. Labels can be helpful from the point of view of efficient communication, but labels can be terribly misleading too, particularly when it comes to moral judgments and stereotyping. For example, when we practice first half of life spirituality, there is a tendency to judge that all "pro-choice" people thoughtlessly support abortion. When we practice second half of life spirituality, we realize that it is unfair to presume too much about another person. Life is far more complex.

A few years ago, I signed up in Milwaukee for an all-day workshop entitled, "Understanding Abortion." I thought of myself as a pro-life priest. We were not allowed to use name tags. We were not allowed to give our occupations. We were not allowed to say whether we were pro-life or pro-choice. There were two facilitators for a limited group of about twenty participants.

I discovered at the end of the day that no one supported abortion as a positive good. Those who were pro-choice were stressing a woman's right to decide moral issues and there are many factors that can determine an unwanted pregnancy. Varying degrees of forced sexual behavior, ignorance, unavailability of contraceptives, premature sexual experiences, social pressure, and alcohol and drug use during dating can be contributing factors to unwanted pregnancies. Those who were pro-choice were not advocating abortion as a simple solution to life's difficulties. They were rather being compassionate towards the women involved rather than judgmental. They were recognizing the many forms of conflict and struggle in life, of competing moral goods, and the complex ways that evil may directly, and indirectly, enter the world.

Those who were pro-life stressed that all life is equal in its right to exist, so no person has the moral authority to make choices between life and death. Some were "absolutists" in the sense that there are no exceptions. Every life is vulnerable. Several people broadened the pro-life position to include other social issues: capital punishment, modern warfare, poverty, and euthanasia. I realized the issue of abortion was far more complex than what I thought. There were not just two positions on the issue of abortion, but many options were shared between those who emphasized the rights of the unborn and those who emphasized the rights of women.

I realized how sad it is that we tend to label people. We miss the many-hued reality behind the labels. We should not assume that those who disagree with us are amoral but instead they practice a different spirituality so they ask different questions and make different conclusions.

I am not saying that being pro-choice is a sign of the practice of second half of life spirituality. I am simply trying to show the influences that contribute to individuals forming and exercising their conscience. While those who practice first half of life spirituality tend to live by church law, the Catechism of the Catholic Church, and the Ten Commandments, those who practice second half of life spirituality generally take in more information before making a decision as to the morality of an action. They attempt to put themselves in the other's shoes. They try to understand rather than cast stones. They listen not only to the official teachings of the hierarchy, but they also listen to the opinions of the theologians and the laity. They presume that everyone is both a student and a teacher. They question the notion of "absolutes" in making moral decisions; a sign of dualistic thinking, and instead they wrestle with their conflicts and the competing values involved.

For example, if a doctor tells a woman that she is carrying a child with Down Syndrome, the mother may question her ability to be a good mother for a child with special needs. She may question her financial and emotional resources. She may question if having the child will make it impossible to earn a livelihood and possibly end her marriage.

The Catechism of the Catholic Church (#2272) says, "A person who procures a completed abortion incurs excommunication by the very commission of the offense." As you can see the Church's teaching on abortion is clearly black and white.

Both conservatives and liberals agree that there are too many abortions. In a better world, there would be no call for abortion. However, we live in an imperfect world. We have rape, sexual harassment, abusive sexism, and contraception is unavailable for hundreds of millions of women. Pregnancies may occur when unmarried teens have "illicit" sex. Many older women want to delay child-rearing to pursue a career. Some people believe that if the woman gets pregnant out of wedlock, she should be punished by bearing the child.

Film, Juno:

I suggest that you view the film Juno in order to illuminate this difficult subject. The film is about Juno, a sixteen year old high school student who discovers she has become pregnant. The film shows the subsequent events that put the pressures of adult life on her. The film Juno uses characters who show characteristics of the practice of both first and second half of life spirituality. Initially, Juno considered an abortion. At the abortion clinic, she was alienated by the staff's authoritarian attitude. She then decided to give the baby up for adoption. During the pregnancy, she realized the love that existed between her and the baby's father, Paulie. Later, she gave birth to a baby boy, and she was joined by Paulie. The film shows that the formation of conscience is complex, on-going, and influenced by many experiences.

Dr. Daniel C. Maguire wrote a book entitled Sacred Choices-the Right to Contraception and Abortion in Ten World Religions in which he makes the case that many world religions support the moral and human right to an abortion when necessary. About 200,000 women die every year from unsafe and illegal abortions.

Those who practice second half of life spirituality say that the best way to end abortions is to promote education, eliminate poverty, provide universal health care, provide more day-care centers, and make contraceptives available.

Many who are "pro-life" are against prenatal care and postnatal care if they are the responsibilities of taxpayers. They tend to believe that health care is the responsibility of parents. Those who are truly "pro-life" do support prenatal care, postnatal care, and health insurance for poor children.

There is an organization in the US called Catholics for Choice that states that a Catholic acting in good conscience and for sound theological reasons might support women's access to legal abortion in certain circumstances. Catholics for Choice also says that the bishops do not represent lay Catholic opinion (sensus fidelium) in public policy debates about abortion.

2. Contraception:

Many sincere Catholic couples try to follow the church's directives and not use contraceptives. Most couples find it impossible to be responsible parents if they cannot space their children factoring in their economic status, emotional welfare, health issues, and age.

Humanae Vitae:

On July 29, 1968, Pope Paul VI published his "birth control encyclical," Humanae Vitae. His decision regarding the prohibition of all forms of artificial contraception was at odds with his Commission that voted seventy-five out of ninety in favor of changing the church's teaching and allowing contraception for married couples.

Fr. Charles Curran at the Catholic University of America led the opposition to the encyclical. He and ten others at Catholic University believed that Catholics could responsibly decide to use birth control if it were for the good of their marriage. The late Fr. Bernard Haring, a renowned Catholic moral theologian, also signed a statement disagreeing with the encyclical. Ultimately six hundred theologians signed. Current polls indicate that more than ninety percent of Roman Catholics ignore the encyclical.

Pope Paul VI meant for Humanae Vitae to settle the issue of contraception. But it seems the issue has, in practice, been settled by the voice and actions of the Catholic people. And so we see that a controversial issue like contraception can be viewed from the practice of first and second half of life spirituality. The clergy, as good shepherds, face the challenge of being faithful to church teaching but yet being respectful of an individual's conscience.

I am not saying that using contraceptives is a sign of the practice of second half of life spirituality. I am simply observing that those who practice second half of life spirituality take in more information not only from the hierarchy but also information from theologians, the opinions of the laity, and scientific information which enables them to make sound and reasonable judgments alongside their conscience. Most fundamentally, they examine their own life experiences. They are willing to embrace mystery and complexity.

For example, the practice of second half of life spirituality takes into account that the issues facing the world have changed over the last two thousand years. Human birthrate has begun to threaten the viability and even survival of the whole ecosystem. Today, a population explosion is occurring in the third world, where poverty, ignorance, and traditional religious teaching combine to produce a high number of births. Under these conditions, the value of life becomes a more complex issue.

In 1996, the Irish author Frank McCourt wrote Angela's Ashes. This book very well shows what can happen if a married person sticks with the practice of first half of life spirituality and fails to be led by the Spirit and transition into the practice of second half of life spirituality. In this memoir, he shares about his impoverished childhood and his struggles with poverty. He shows that poverty in his family led to the diminishment of life. McCourt's parents were taught that the sex act was sinful unless it was used for reproduction. Thus, no matter how desperate life was, his Irish Catholic parents would not think of disobeying the pope. The book very well indicates that the practice of first half of life morality is largely based on rules, encyclicals, and one's obedience to church authority figures.

Health coverage including contraception:

I hope you are taking the time to keeping up with the news about health coverage that includes contraception. A big controversy began last year when the Secretary of the United States Department of Health and Human Services announced that most employers, including Catholic employers, would be required to offer their employees health coverage that included sterilization, abortion-inducing drugs, and contraception. Almost all health insurers would be required to include these "services" in the health policies they wrote.

The United States bishops and other Catholic leaders said that the Administration had violated the First Amendment by denying to Catholics their nation's first and most fundamental freedom, that of religious liberty. The First Amendment says the government may not establish or define religion or impede its free exercise. The First Amendment says the state has no competency to adjudicate on matters religious.

Catholic advocates for women and the poor argued that it was an issue of women's health.

Fortnight for Freedom:

We now have the Fortnight for Freedom which began last year when at least one hundred bishops who headed dioceses issued letters condemning the Health and Human Services rules, and many bishops had their letter read at weekend Masses. The United States bishops placed at the center of their arguments the concept of "conscience" saying that the United States Department of Health and Human Services' mandate would force Catholics to go against their own consciences.

Last year in February, President Obama announced a compromise solution by which religious institutions would be exempt from paying the objectionable premiums, but women would not be denied contraceptive coverage. The cost would be provided by the insurance companies. The US Conference of Catholic Bishops rejected the president's "accommodation" as insufficient.

Many people who practice second half of life spirituality see this issue differently not as an issue of religious liberty but of women's health. They argue that the issue of conscience cuts both ways. Religious groups have no legitimate mandate to impose their religious convictions, as employer to employee, in a pluralistic society.

Those who practice second half of life spirituality ask, "What about the role of conscience? Does the Fortnight for Freedom campaign take into account the consciences of otherwise faithful Catholic women and couples who feel that it may be more responsible to use contraceptives to plan and provide for their families?" Some would say, "No." The Fortnight for Freedom does not take into account the consciences of faithful Catholic women.

Many people who practice second half of life spirituality presume that women should have access to contraception. They like to see their Church defend their religious liberty but not try to impose their faith on others, especially when it comes to restrictions on intimate matters like human sexuality.

Those who practice second half of life spirituality ask, "Is birth control contrary to the teachings of the Catholic Church as expressed in Pope Paul VI's encyclical, Humanae Vitae?" As critics point out, so many sexually active American Catholic women practice birth control, and many Catholics think a "good Catholic" can reject the bishops' teaching on birth control. Theological experts tell us what the bishops have taught over the centuries, but this does not tell us whether these teachings have divine authority. In our democratic society, the ultimate arbiter of religious authority is the conscience of the individual believer.

The majority of women do not see providing contraceptives as part of health care as a moral issue. Instead they see it as a long-awaited opportunity to make better decisions regarding child-bearing based on their financial, medical, and individual situations. It is also because they have more advanced knowledge, scientific, psychological, social, and emotional, that informs their mind and conscience.

I am "stirring the pot" once again with you, Joey, to make you question. Many people today, think including contraception in health insurance coverage is not an issue of religious liberty. You told me that in your moral theology course in the seminary, you already studied the two issues of abortion and contraception. I am just trying to show you another way that some people view the morality of these two important and complex issues.

Peace,

Uncle Matthew

Letter #32
Thursday, July 4, 2013

Dear Uncle Matthew,

At mass this morning, the pastor gave a good homily on this civil holiday that commemorates the adoption of the Declaration of Independence that took place in 1776. The Declaration of Independence contains these essential words,

"We hold these truths to be self-evident that all men are created equal, that they are endowed by their Creator with certain unalienable rights, that among these are life, liberty, and the pursuit of happiness."

Nearly ninety years later in 1863, when President Abraham Lincoln dedicated the Civil War Cemetery at Gettysburg, he cited the Declaration of Independence, stating that our nation was dedicated to the proposition, "All men are created equal." He said that slavery could not be reconciled with the Declaration of Independence.

When I heard the pastor's homily, it reminded me of the story you shared with me last August when you discovered a Just God when you became aware of the sin of racism and followed your conscience by resigning from your teaching position at the Catholic high school. That experience not only introduced you to an image of a Just God, but it also helped you to diminish your earlier image of a God Preoccupied with Sex. I am becoming aware that it takes great courage to apply the Declaration of Independence to different peace and justice situations so as to ensure that all people are treated equally.

Thank you for sharing how our spirituality affects our views on morality. The examples of abortion and contraception helped me to see the complexity of these two issues. We studied these topics in our first year moral theology course, but we did not view the topics from different viewpoints. The impression given in class is that there is only one valid viewpoint.

I look forward to hearing from you about the morality involved in other pastoral issues.

Peace,

Joey

Response to Letter #32
Saturday, July 13, 2013

Dear Joey,

Keep up the good work that you are doing in the parish. I appreciated your last phone call. I'm glad that what I shared with you about abortion and contraception was helpful. Most people never have the opportunity to study different viewpoints and the competing values that underlie these two important issues. As such, they fail to develop an informed conscience and remain polarized and hostile toward their fellow human beings who hold divergent viewpoints. They often end up unnecessarily later in life with a guilty conscience when their actions are contrary to the church's official teachings. Leaders in the Church very often fail to inform people that they have an internal moral compass in spite of the fact that it is at the heart of the New Testament message. Our individual conscience is indeed an unavoidable fact of life! Some actions are easy for us to discern as being right or wrong such as killing another person or stealing. But other actions such as abortion and contraception are complex and therefore not easy for us to discern as being clearly right or wrong.

In my last letter to you, I described how our spirituality affects our morality regarding abortion and contraception. Since this dialogue we are having seems to be fruitful, I'll share with you three more topics that illustrate how our spirituality affects our morality regarding divorce, fasting, and the obligation to pray the Liturgy of the Hours. As you know, from our family history and your own personal life, these issues are not abstract.

3. Divorce:

Last April, I mentioned in a phone conversation with you that when Fr. Joe was in middle school, his aunt obtained a divorce and remarried outside the Catholic Church. Fr. Joe remembered her tears, guilt, shame, and confusion. The civil marriage left Fr. Joe's aunt terrified that she would go to Hell. She visited Fr. Joe once when he was in college, and when she got off the plane, on her coat was a piece of paper that said, "In case of an accident, call a priest." Joe's aunt practiced first half of life spirituality, so she simply accepted as true without question her understanding of the church's teaching on divorce and re-marriage. Thus, in many ways, Fr. Joe's aunt ceased to live as a vibrant life-giving person. She was paralyzed by her guilt and fear. She never was encouraged to develop her inner moral compass. Sadly, the church's teaching on divorce profoundly affected her ability to love because of her fear. This is the opposite (or antithesis) of "Perfect love drives out fear" (1 John 4:18).

Later, in third theology, you will study the history of the sacraments, providing perspective while raising important questions. For three centuries in the church, the dissolution of marriage by mutual consent of the spouses was allowed. Until the 11th century divorce and remarriage were permitted under certain circumstances including adultery, desertion, and a spouse entering religious life. After the 12th century, divorce was forbidden. The Church declared marriages indissoluble except upon the death of one of the spouses.

The Council of Trent (1545–1563) declared that marriage was a sacrament in the Catholic Church. For the first time, the bishops insisted that all Catholics be married in the presence of a priest and two witnesses or the marriage would be invalid. This view that all Catholic marriages are under the control of the Church still exists today.

Today we follow the church's teaching that once two baptized Christians enter into a valid marriage and have sexual intercourse, a bond is created between them. No power on earth can break that bond. If they try to marry again to rebuild their lives, they will be living in adultery and cut off from the sacraments.

The Church has recognized that the faithful in daily life reject absolute indissolubility. Therefore annulments, as a concession to this actual practice, are made possible in the Church. Divorce recognizes that a marriage existed, but that it has died. An annulment, in contrast, says that no sacramental marriage bond ever existed. However, there are many Roman Catholic dioceses throughout the world with no tribunals to process annulments. Although the annulment process was recognized in the twelfth century, its popularity did not dawn until well after the Code of Canon Law in 1917.

Many people who practice first half of life spirituality view the scriptures as literalists and see the scriptures as moral imperatives. They believe that the scriptures apply to all people, at all times, in all cultures. They believe those who marry must abide by the rules found in scripture under pain of sin. Other people who practice second half of life spirituality view the scriptural depictions that marriage is a permanent relationship as an ideal, but not an imperative. Of higher importance to them are the virtues of love, truthfulness, and obedience to conscience.

When we practice first half of life spirituality, we accept the analogy of human marriage as being comparable to Christ's love for his Church. Therefore, marriage should never end. Further, in a patriarchal system, marriage is understood as a dominant-subordinate relationship. Morality in earlier periods of time was typically based on, and favored, the dominant male. But today there is the increasing realization that women are no longer, or at least should not be, in a dominant-subordinate relationship. There is a mutuality of the sexes and within this relationship of equality there is greater freedom to acknowledge the reality of the quality, truthfulness, and strength of the relationship.

Those who practice second half of life spirituality believe that the love in a marriage can, for many reasons, come to an end. Many marriages stay together, but the love is gone. There is no real bond. Children and close friends can tell that the marriage is a sham. Then the question arises, "What should the couple do?" Some couples, following their conscience, decide to live their lives outside, or beyond, the literal laws, realizing the laws have become contrary to the fullness of life. They seek to reclaim the joy of true love. These individuals want to try again to reach the ideal where there is mutual growth in spirituality and mutual help in keeping the Commandments. They desire to receive the Eucharist and be part of the faith community. Most people do not feel called to a life of celibacy after a failed marriage.

Many couples are unable to find Church leaders who practice second half of life spirituality who could help them to resolve the conflict they experience between their conscience and the church's stand on the permanency of marriage. Thus they leave the institutional Church. How does this serve God and God's love on earth?

Some priests who practice second half of life spirituality help couples by respecting the conscience, the moral compass, of the couple. Currently, the church law says that without an annulment, divorced Catholics who remarried outside the Church are not allowed to receive the Eucharist. After explaining the church's teaching on divorce and remarriage and the annulment process, they help the couple by explaining to them Epikeia which means setting aside the law in favor of good sense. Epikeia might be translated, "The law doesn't make sense in this case, so use your good sense." The mercy of God supersedes the law.

These priests help couples by using the "internal forum." They explain a pastoral solution that some couples might need if they are old and no longer capable of doing the necessary work to obtain an annulment. In some cases the key parties involved in the previous marriage are deceased or their whereabouts are unknown. There are other couples who in good conscience cannot relive the hurts of the past that the annulment process would require. The "internal forum" solution then allows the couple to receive the sacraments if they believe, before God, that their previous marriage was never sacramental; never capable of being a permanent bond. Oddly, Joey, in my own ten years of preparation to become a priest, I never heard a professor speak about the "internal forum" solution.

The internal forum can be exercised in or outside the framework of sacramental confession.There are limitations to the internal forum. The use of the internal forum doesn't validate a second marriage while the spouse of the first marriage is still alive. The use of the internal forum cannot be used as permission for a previously married person whose spouse is still living to remarry in the Catholic Church. The internal forum does not allow a priest to perform any kind of public or private ceremony that has the appearance of an official marriage ceremony or validation. A priest has to be loyal to the Catholic Church's proclamation of indissolubility of marriage and avoid scandal in the Catholic community. Yet the internal forum, in particular cases, can prove to be of great value to those seeking to reclaim love in a marital relationship.

4. Fasting:

The Catholic Church has precepts that are of an obligatory character. The Catechism of the Catholic Church indicates (#2041) the precepts are meant "to guarantee to the faithful the indispensable minimum in the spirit in prayer and moral effort, in the growth in love of God and neighbor."

The first precept-"You shall attend Mass on Sundays and holy days of obligation."

The second precept-"You shall confess your sins at least once a year."

The third precept-"You shall humbly receive the Eucharist at least during the Easter season."

The fourth precept-"You shall keep holy the holy days of obligation."

The fifth precept-"You shall observe the prescribed days of fasting and abstinence." The Catechism (#1387, #1388) states that days of fasting help to "acquire mastery over our instincts and freedom of heart."

Parishioners often ask about fasting and abstinence during Lent and they confess when they have failed to comply with a day of fasting. I recall when I was in grade school my family was going to attend Mass on Christmas Day. On Christmas Eve, we were up shortly past midnight opening presents. My father took a small bite of pound cake that would be served on Christmas Day. Then he remembered the fast. He told my mother, brother, and me that he couldn't receive communion on Christmas Day. At that time, fasting from food and water was to commence at midnight.

Those who practiced first half of life spirituality would have supported my father's decision. Those who practiced second half of life spirituality would have said that when one factors in the motivation involved in an action, something changes. Common sense says that unintentionally breaking a rule is a lot different from breaking a rule with full knowledge and willfulness. Those who practice second half of life spirituality go beyond the literal law and reach for the heart.

Those who practice second half of life spirituality also try to be aware of the essence of fasting when considering its practice. There is a phrase, "Mind fasting and spirit feasting" pointing to the temptation of hypocrisy. Perhaps at times it would be better to fast from lustful thoughts and greedy habits, actually embracing an inner poverty, rather than simply fasting from food. At other times it would be better to "fast" from habitual work routines and to instead passionately work for peace and justice.

Isaiah 58:5-7 says,

"Is not this the kind of fasting I have chosen: to loose the chains of injustice and untie the cords of the yoke, to set the oppressed free and break every yoke? Is it not to share your food with the hungry and to provide the poor wanderer with shelter, when you see the naked, to clothe him, and not to turn away from your own flesh and blood?"

5. The Liturgy of the Hours:

When I was ordained a transitional deacon, I assumed the responsibility of praying daily the Liturgy of the Hours. Canon Law explicitly establishes that obligation. We were taught in the seminary that when praying alone, we had to move our lips so as to make some kind of sound. No snacking allowed! (As if we need to be told this.) The Church has celebrated this form of liturgical prayer since ancient times. Together with the Eucharist, it remains today the principal form of daily prayer throughout the Church.

When I was a transitional deacon working at a summer camp, I tried one night to pray the Liturgy of the Hours while reading the texts under an outdoor street light. We had worked long hours during the day with the children. The camp director, a priest, saw me under the outdoor light, and he told me not to worry if I didn't finish the Liturgy of the Hours. I could tell that his advice made sense. He had a different image of God. He used common sense. He practiced second half of life spirituality. This priest later got permission from the bishop for the priests in the diocese to choose various forms of prayer rather than the obligation to daily pray the Liturgy of the Hours. The bishop allowed priests to spend time doing spiritual reading, preparing a homily, saying the rosary, praying contemplatively, etc.

Religious priests and sisters very often live in community, so they pray together the Liturgy of the Hours that can be a meaningful form of prayer. However, most diocesan priests live alone, and many do not find this form of prayer to be meaningful. Those who practice first half of life spirituality see this obligation as a law to be obeyed under penalty of sin. Those who practice second half of life spirituality believe in the value of prayer, but they feel comfortable selecting a form of prayer that is more meaningful.

I hope these reflections help you to understand how one's spirituality affects one's morality in the pastoral issues of divorce, fasting, and the Liturgy of the Hours. Literalism, rigidity, and legalism can neglect the important role of the Holy Spirit. Follow the rules while in the seminary, but know that there are other ways of thinking and acting in pastoral situations. Hopefully, your grasp of reality will continue to make you more compassionate when individuals you meet do things differently than what you are trained to expect.

Peace,

Uncle Matthew

Letter #33
Tuesday, July 23, 2013

Dear Uncle Matthew,

Thank you for sharing with me those most important insights into how and why different people think differently about divorce, fasting, and the obligation under sin to pray the Liturgy of the Hours. I have several college friends who have already obtained divorces. Two of these good friends are Catholic, and they have no intention of going through a lengthy and expensive process to obtain an annulment because they do not want to relive so many unhappy times as they now make new lives for themselves. I wonder if I will be taught anything about Epikeia and the internal forum? I hope so.

I liked your ideas about fasting. I had never thought about fasting, not just from food, but from lustful thoughts and greedy habits, feasting instead on the Life of the Holy Spirit. I could fast, with God's loving help, from negative thinking, excessive worry, and judging others.

Since I am not obligated to say the Liturgy of the Hours yet, I haven't had the experiences that you had of rushing before midnight to fulfill an obligation. That sounds onerous and I appreciate the wisdom of your camp counselor. I am becoming aware that our concept of what constitutes prayer is so important. Isn't prayer more than just reading texts in the Liturgy of the Hours? Also I am becoming aware that our images of God determine our prayer life. I personally am finding my prayer life is becoming real.

I've got a couple of other big questions. What about the morality of same-sex marriage and teacher contract clauses? These questions are prompted by personal encounters with those for whom these questions are not mere abstractions. I met several gay men in college who were talking about their futures. There is a large Catholic high school in the parish where I am assigned this summer, and a teacher there was telling me about morality causes in her contract.

Peace,

Joey

Response to Letter #33
Wednesday, July 31, 2013

Dear Joey,

Today is the feast of St. Ignatius of Loyola who was born in Spain in the year 1491. He was the youngest of thirteen children. He was a soldier, and while he was recovering after being wounded in battle, he read the lives of the saints. After recovering, he went to the Shrine of Montserrat where, after an all night vigil, he exchanged his rich clothes for those of a beggar. He laid his sword and dagger on the altar of Our Lady, and he became a soldier for Christ. St. Ignatius later became a priest, and he founded a new religious order, the Jesuits. During his lifetime the members of his order went from ten members to a thousand members. He wrote the Spiritual Exercises, a book that is still used on directed retreats. As you know, Pope Francis is a Jesuit.

I made a thirty day Retreat once at a Jesuit house of studies in Grand Coteau, LA. The Spiritual Exercises helped me to meditate on some challenging mysteries. When I retired, I had a chance to visit the Shrine of Montserrat that is located near Barcelona, Spain. These personal experiences made St. Ignatius more real to me.

In my last two letters, I shared with you that the practice of second half of life spirituality influences morality regarding the topics of abortion, contraception, divorce, fasting, and the liturgy of the hours. At your request I'll share with you that the practice of second half of life spirituality affects the morality of marriage equality and teacher contract clauses. I offer these thoughts not as systematic moral theology, but as practical and pastoral reflections so that you are more aware of the plurality of thought.

6. Marriage equality:

Notice that I prefer not to use the language of "same sex marriage" but "marriage equality" that communicates commitment and a loving bond of protection and responsibility between devoted couples. Our focus should be on love, not biology, and our language should reflect this.

Jesus lived in a world where marriage was primarily an economic and social contract. Jews considered marriage a commandment that was intended to benefit not only the immediate family but also the wider community by ensuring stability and economic prosperity.

Some early Christian writers suggested that Jesus, whom they regarded as the ultimate moral authority, had raised marriage to the dignity of a sacrament because Jesus performed his first public miracle at a wedding. The Catholic Church did not make marriage a sacrament until the 13th century, and only began to enforce strict religious conformity in marriage in the 16th century.

Those who practice first half of life spirituality presume a moral person is someone who simply obeys legitimate authority. They assume that the authority they obey is infallibly and morally correct, and that it is God's will when it is found in church encyclicals (such as Humanae Vitae), church councils (such as Vatican II), and in the Catechism of the Catholic Church.

The Catholic Church and her Catholic bishops have traditionally supported marriage between a man and woman for many historical and social reasons. This advocacy has taken place not only within the realm of the Church, but as a matter of public policy as well in many countries. Accepting or participating in marriage equality therefore goes against the reflexive practice of first half of life spirituality because marriage equality conflicts with the doctrines of church authorities.

Let me give you a brief secular history. In 1996, President Bill Clinton signed the Defense of Marriage Act. The law barred the Federal Government from recognizing same-sex marriages approved by states. Section 3 of the DOMA says a marriage is between a man and a woman. At the time, a majority of American people agreed with the intent of DOMA.

Later in 2011, President Clinton called for an overturn of this bill because he had come to believe that it denied same-sex couples "equal liberty" guaranteed by the Fifth Amendment. Although same-sex couples were then married in some states and in the District of Columbia, they were, because of DOMA, denied the benefits of more than a thousand federal statutes and programs available to other married couples. For example, some same-sex couples couldn't file their taxes jointly, take unpaid leave to care for a sick or injured spouse, or receive equal family health and pension benefits as federal civilian employees. President Clinton believed that DOMA not only provided an excuse for discrimination, but it was, in itself, discriminatory and should be overturned.

In June of this year the Supreme Court in a 5-4 vote declared that DOMA was unconstitutional.

The topic of marriage equality brings up many points for discussion. Many people who practice second half of life spirituality believe that civil and church leaders should focus on the consciences of those people who accept, embrace, and are direct partners and participants in marriage equality. It is easy and simplistic to understand human beings based on the pre-scientific idea that life was created perfectly only to fall into Original Sin. This mythic worldview, based on Adam and Eve, is used by some to justify a range of beliefs and attitudes about life on earth, including hostility towards homosexual love. In contrast, those who practice second half of life spirituality take joy in the mental rigors of embracing and integrating the discovery of science with their faith in God. This leads them to celebrate the fullness of God's creation and the many manifestations of God's love. And so the practice of first and second half of life spirituality engage one another and evolve as part of God's plan.

For example, in the past, homosexuality was diagnosed as a mental illness, but after the publications of the Kinsey reports in 1948 and 1953, and much public and professional debate, the American Psychiatric Association officially removed it in 1973 from The Diagnostic and Statistical Manual of Mental Disorders. We now recognize that homosexuality is a natural part of life and reality among many higher mammals and other life forms. No reputable scientist today supports the idea that anyone simply chooses his or her sexual orientation.

Despite scientific evidence to the contrary, those who practice first half of life spirituality are more accepting of the literalism that marriage is between a man and woman and cannot be between two members of the same sex. They believe that homosexuality is a curse and thus unacceptable in the eyes of God. A gay marriage is looked upon as an attack on the values of traditional marriage.

Those who practice second half of life spirituality tend to see marriage in a non-legalistic way, and thus are more embracing of those who believe marriage can be between any two individuals who are willing to commit themselves to a permanent relationship grounded in love that will enhance the lives of both. They accept the conscience of those who wish to enter into same-sex marriage. The stories of many same-sex couples show that there are many benefits for the couples and for the wider community when same-sex unions are allowed and acknowledged. Most homosexuals do not feel called by God to live celibate lives. They wish, like heterosexuals, to enjoy the companionship and intimacy that come in a permanent bond.

Those who practice second half of life spirituality say that the Church does have the responsibility and authority to teach in the name of Jesus, but that the Church, historically, has not always been correct or judicious in exercising this authority. Worldly interests, the lust for power first and foremost, have too often clouded our discernment of God's love and will.

I'm sure in the years to come, more states will allow marriage equality and the Supreme Court will have more to say on this subject. Dialogue is needed. Respect for others who think differently is needed. Understanding, appreciating, and practicing what it means to live in a pluralistic society is needed. Blessed are the peacemakers.

7. Morality clauses in teacher contracts:

Another aspect of how the practice of first and second half of life spirituality clash regarding human sexuality is that of morality clauses in teacher contracts. The point is not that Catholic schools have the right to have teachers agree to morality clauses in their teacher contracts. The disagreement centers on whether or not the teachings that teachers must sign are correct. For example, some Church employees in this country were fired, resigned, refused to renew restrictive contracts, or had job offers rescinded over LGBT-related employment disputers. Some laypeople believe that the actions of some church leaders regarding morality clauses in their teacher contracts is morally unjustified.

Those who practice first half of life spirituality would be respectful of and observant of the clauses. A hallmark of the practice of first half of life spirituality is to defer to established authority.

Those who practice second half of life spirituality question morality clauses that they argue are unjust in their application. For example, is it just to fire a woman who is pregnant out of wedlock when no such penalty is applied to the man involved? What about a teacher who enters into a same-sex civil marriage?

Are such clauses in teacher contracts regarding same sex marriage unjust? St. Augustine, knowing the distinction between moral law and civil law, said that an unjust law is no law at all. St. Thomas Aquinas likewise endorsed that stance.

Different administrators handle things differently. Administrators who practice second half of life spirituality realize they must rely upon their own conscience even if they are in disagreement with a particular morality clause in a teacher contract. They may discern that the teacher in question is serving well in the school, to the benefit of many, despite an infraction of a morality clause that may be unjust.

Wisdom and dialogue are needed because when Catholic school students, teachers, and parents sense dishonesty and hypocrisy, seeds are planted that prompt them to question their images of God, the Church, faith, and respect for those in leadership positions.

Conclusion:

My last few letters to you have been about the morality, from the practice of second half of life spirituality, of (1) abortion, (2) contraception, (3) divorce, (4) fasting, (5) the Liturgy of the Hours, (6) marriage equality, and (7) morality clauses in teacher contracts. I hope this is helpful.

Jean Paul Sartre, one of the leading figures in twentieth century French philosophy, said, "Evil is the product of the ability of humans to make abstract that which is concrete."

Let's keep our feet on the ground.

I'm will send you with this letter a long article on Fr. Roy Bourgeois. He is an example of a priest who has tremendous courage to follow his convictions. I'm quite sure he has an image of a Courageous God; an image of God that I would like to share with you.

Peace,

Uncle Matthew

Enclosure: Article on Roy Bourgeois

Letter #34
Thursday, August 1, 2013


Dear Uncle Matthew,

Thank you for sending me the 47-page article, My Journey from
Silence to Solidarity. He must be a very talented man to have
been nominated for the Nobel Peace Prize. I was saddened that
Fr. Bourgeois was dismissed from both the Maryknoll Fathers
and the priesthood because of his participation in Lexington,
Kentucky, in August 2008, in what the Catholic Church viewed as
an invalid ordination to the priesthood of a woman. Earlier you
described some of the goals in the practice of second half of life
spirituality which included: moving beyond the law, discovering
the will of God, developing a prophetic dimension, and being
courageous. What will happen to him now that he is seventy-five
years old?

I agree with you that Roy Bourgeois is certainly a brave priest
who acted on behalf of those who believe in the ordination of
women. When I was in college, I heard about his leadership role
in the annual protests at the School of the Americas Watch (SOA
Watch) in Fort Benning, GA.

This article increased my awareness that there are individuals
who believe so strongly about peace and justice issues that they
are willing to courageously sacrifice everything to share their
beliefs with others so as to contribute to a better Church. The

article also makes me aware that when we practice second half of life spirituality, the Holy Spirit may urge us to act on our convictions despite the cost. Faith seems to be a willingness to follow the Spirit's lead to act on our convictions without arriving at certitude.

One professor gave us Pope Francis' new encyclical, Lumen Fidei, The Light of Faith. I shall read it and hopefully learn more about the church's tradition of bringing the great gift of Jesus to others.

You mentioned earlier that there are more images of God that are discovered in the practice of second half of life spirituality. You mentioned that you think Fr. Roy has an image of a Courageous God. Could you share with me an image of a Courageous God?

Peace,

Joey

Response to Letter #34
Saturday, August 24, 2013

Dear Joey,

Today we are celebrating the feast of St. Bartholomew the
Apostle. Some scholars identify Bartholomew with Nathaniel in
today's Gospel. Philip was excited about Jesus, but Nathaniel
said, "Can anything good come out of Nazareth?" Jesus saw
Nathaniel coming toward him and said of him, "Here is a true
Israelite. There is no duplicity in him."

Jesus was aware that St. Bartholomew was not deceitful. He
was straightforward. He did not say one thing to one person and
something else to another person. What people saw was what
they got. His virtue of being genuine, without pretense, is
certainly a virtue we all want to imitate. The practice of second
half of life spirituality helps make it possible to be authentic.

In your letter to me, you shared about Roy Bourgeois who was
brave to courageously act on his convictions. The practice of
second half of life spirituality invites us to pray for wisdom to be
aware of important issues and to possess the courage to act.

In earlier letters to you, I shared six images of God that we can
acquire when we practice second half of life spirituality: (1) an
Incarnate God, (2) an Inclusive God, (3) a Just God, (4) a

Merciful and Compassionate God, (5) Our God, and (6) a Male/Female God.

I mentioned in my last letter that Fr. Roy Bourgeois seems to have an image of a Courageous God; an image that embraces the qualities of an Incarnate God, an Inclusive God, a Just God, and a Merciful and Compassionate God. I believe that giving you examples is the best way to convey this image of God. When we observe great courage in others, we admire that virtue, and we believe that virtue is showing us a glimpse of a Courageous God.

I shall share with you some examples of individuals who not only became aware of what they perceived to be truthful, but they likewise were courageous to act upon their perceptions. Once a person is led by the Spirit to live out of second half of life spirituality, issues regarding peace and justice, poverty, and charity increasingly pull upon a person's conscience, prompting and demanding action.

#7    A Courageous God:

(1)  Dr. Daniel C. Maguire:

Daniel C. Maguire is a professor of Christian Ethics at Marquette University. He had a son, Danny, who at the age of two was diagnosed with a congenital disease that progressively deprived him of his mental and physical capabilities. One day Danny, who was ten at the time, and his dad were walking in a park and Danny said, "Daddy, look!" Danny saw some birds and ducks on a nearby lagoon. His dad, Daniel, drove past this site on his daily trip to Marquette University, yet he was only barely aware of the ducks and birds there. That incident in his life seems to have motivated Daniel Maguire in his writings to call out to his listeners to "look" at the broad underlying issues that we face.

Daniel Maguire taught me moral theology in the seminary. He was, without a doubt, the best professor I had in my ten years of preparation to become a priest. Even before Daniel was married and was the father of two sons, he made his students aware of so much that could have been missed or taken for granted.

Later in 2007, I attended a Pax Christi Florida retreat led by Daniel Maguire. He was brilliant. He made all of us aware of so many issues regarding justice and peace. He was on fire with his message. We all got the impression that we were listening to a prophet who has been rejected by the hierarchy.

Daniel Maguire challenges us, through his books and articles, to look, to be aware of the deeper issues and concerns. He is filled with courage. He has looked deep inside himself which takes great courage. He proclaims what he believes to be the truth in the face of great opposition. He doesn't play it safe to please people. Wow! Rarely do we find in our lifetime anyone so courageous! Rarely do we find anyone with so much integrity! Rarely do we find anyone who has witnessed so well to us the gift of generativity! His books and articles will influence generations to come. When I think of Daniel Maguire's courage, it makes me think of how Jesus was transformed into the visible image of the invisible God (Colossians 1:15) through a life of courage and integrity.

(2.) Sister Theresa Kane, RSM:

In October 1979, Pope John Paul II visited the United States. While he was at the National Shrine of the Immaculate Conception in Washington DC, Sr. Theresa Kane, the president of the LCWR (Leadership Conference of Women Religious) welcomed him. In her welcoming speech, she asked for equality and ordination on behalf of Catholic women everywhere. What great courage that took! Her words were not welcomed by the pope and Vatican officials.

Sister Theresa Kane is a professor at the age of seventy-five at Mercy College in New York. She still continues the fight for feminist equality in religion. When asked if she would repeat the address again, she said she would because she believes so strongly in equality in the Church and in society. The LCWR gave Kane the Outstanding Leadership Award in 2004.

(3.) School Board:

When I was assigned as principal of a high school, I was only thirty-two years old. I had to hire a math teacher shortly before the school-year began. I interviewed a very nice young lady who was a single mom with a young daughter. The young lady had very fine credentials. I sat in on her classroom, and I found her to be a good teacher. The students liked her. She was generous with her time.

The School Board subsequently found out that the new teacher was a single mom and wanted me to get rid of her. The Board thought that she would give a bad example for the students. I disagreed with the Board's request. I sensed that it was an attack on a good woman who was trying her best to be a good mother and a good teacher. I knew about civil laws that protect teachers, so I courageously stood up for this teacher and said, "If you get rid of her, she could file a law-suit against the school for discrimination." The School Board backed down when I threatened them with a possible law suit.

Do you see, Joey, what is happening? If I had been practicing first half of life spirituality, I would have probably backed down and obeyed the School Board. First half of life spirituality is characterized by obedience, conformity, tradition, and status quo. I was just beginning to practice second half of life spirituality, so I was able to find the courage to stand up for this woman's rights. I was willing to make my own decisions, defy convention, and put into practice the images I was developing of a Compassionate and Courageous God.

Conversion experiences help us to think less about ourselves and more about others. We are less concerned about taking risks and making sacrifices if our actions will lead us to be more compassionate and just for others. During this process of taking risks, we discover in the recesses of our heart a remarkable courage that enables us to do things that we previously were fearful of doing.

In my second year as principal, I got into another disagreement with the School Board. This was a serious conflict that the student body was aware of, and the controversy got into the local news press. The school over the years had given scholarships to African-American students who were financially in need. The pastor of a predominantly African-American parish would simply determine who he wanted to attend the Catholic high school, and we would accept the students with no tuition. The School Board wanted to eliminate the money for these scholarships in the budget. The School Board was thinking about future finances, and to save money, eliminating scholarships to African American students was a "solution."

I prayed that I would know what to do. I believed the School Board's actions were unjust. I came up with the idea of "contributed services." I figured out what it would cost the school to replace the priests and nuns on the faculty with lay teachers. The difference in salaries I labeled "contributed services." As I prepared my strategy to go against the School Board's recommendation, I became more aware of an image of a God of Justice, a God very concerned about moral values.

In preparation for a "show down" with the School Board, seven of the nine lay teachers along with the two priests and three nuns on the faculty agreed to resign at the end of the school year unless the School Board backed down. There was a special meeting of the School Board and they voted again, and they backed down. The scholarship fund was safe for predominately African American lower income students. A willingness to stand up for others is a good sign that a person is courageously witnessing an adult spirituality. My courage had a positive effect on the students because they became aware of an important justice issue as well as the integrity and courage of their principal.

As you can see, my examples are ordinary experiences, just like the nature of a mature adult spirituality that takes you to the very heart of things. We become less concerned about our own safety and we are willing to serve others with an amazing courage that we discover in the presence of the divine within. Examples of an awareness of the Spirit's promoting to courageously act can be found in the lives of teachers, principals of schools, writers, parents, pastors, students, and nuns.

M. Scott Peck said, "Courage is not the absence of fear; it is the making of action in spite of fear, the moving out against the resistance engendered by fear into the unknown and into the future."

Martin Luther King, Jr., said, "Our lives begin to end the day we become silent about things that matter."

Peace,

Uncle Matthew

Letter #35
Saturday, September 14, 2013


Dear Uncle Matthew,

I am now back in the seminary ready to begin my studies in second theology. I am looking forward to studying the New Testament, especially the synoptic gospels, because I want to find out how to reconcile different accounts of Jesus.

Your last letter was very helpful with the examples of courageous action taken by those who live with an image of a Courageous God. I especially appreciated your own experiences with the School Board when you were the principal of a Catholic high school. I recall you saying several times that we become like the God we adore. If the Holy Spirit leads us to embrace an image of a Courageous God, then we may become aware of our baptismal call to be courageous. I liked your quotes from M. Scott Peck and Martin Luther King, Jr. I find it confusing how the institutional Church condemns people like Roy Bourgeois who display so much courage. I get the impression that such treatment of those who think outside the box says a lot about the practice of first or second half of life spirituality.

My new spiritual director seems to be more like you, Uncle Matthew. He is up-to-date, positive, and was previously an associate pastor in a parish. We were talking about the topic of detachment the other day, and he gave me a good insight. He told me to think of detachment not so much as detaching myself from things but rather detaching myself from myself in order to see God in all things. Seeing all creation as good and permeated with God is much more positive than an older way I was taught to detach myself from things and people as though they were evil. My ego still desires things that are both good and bad for me. The challenge is to detach myself from my ego so that the Spirit of God can allow my true self to permeate my life. My spiritual director also stresses prayer as a time to listen to the presence of God.

Today is the feast of the Exultation of the Cross. The homilist asked the question, "How can suffering, a 'cross' in life, actually bring us new life?" He showed us the emblem for the American Medical Association that depicts two serpents wrapped around a pole. The emblem reminds us that if we want good health, we have to take bitter medicine. For example, vaccinations, such as flu shots, introduce into our bodies harmful elements that stimulate the body to produce anti-bodies. The homilist then referred to St. Francis of Assisi who taught us that sometimes we need to embrace a cross, something very difficult, to grow spiritually. For example, St. Francis one day was riding on a horse and he came upon a leper. He usually rejected lepers. On this occasion, he felt moved by God to kiss the leper. By kissing the leper instead of rejecting him, he was embracing a "cross." As a result, he grew spiritually in profound ways that shaped his subsequent ministry. He was able from that moment on to see all people as sisters and brothers in Christ.

I look forward to hearing more stories about courageous individuals who acted on their convictions, despite the cost. Bring it on!

Peace,

Joey

Response to Letter #35
Sunday, September 29, 2013

Dear Joey,

Pope Francis has only been pope for six months, but already he is sending shock waves through the Catholic Church. He is courageous! He said that the Church has grown obsessed with the topics of abortion, gay marriage, and contraception, and he has chosen not to talk about these moral issues so as to have a new balance so as to better serve the poor and marginalized.

Pope Francis has a vision of a Church that is inclusive; "a home for all." In July, he was so courageous on an airplane returning to Rome from Rio de Janeiro, when he said, "Who am I to judge?" when asked about gays and lesbians. The new issue of America Magazine has the exclusive interview with Pope Francis. I hope you will read it.

Your new spiritual director sounds like a rich blessing. Thanks for sharing about the feast of the Exultation of the Cross. People who attend mass are not looking for the history of a feast day, but rather they seek to take something practical home with them that will make their lives better. The homilist seemed to have been very pastoral rather than purely academic.

An image of a Courageous God (Continued):

I'll share with you a couple more stories about men and women who were willing to courageously follow the Spirit's lead and act since courage is such an important virtue. I'm giving you examples, in my last letter and in this letter, that courageously following one's conscience leads to action that may be unacceptable to the higher authorities in the Church.

(4.) Sister Christine Vladimiroff, OSB:

In 2001, Sister Christine Vladimiroff, OSB refused to follow a Vatican order that she prohibit, as superior, Sister Joan Chittister from speaking at a conference advocating the ordination of women. After a long period of reflection and discernment, she wrote a letter to the Vatican explaining that she could not, in good conscience, prohibit Sr. Chittister from going to a Conference and speaking her mind. She read to the community the letter she had written to the Vatican, and all 121 active nuns in the community, through individual choice, signed the letter.

Afterwards, the Vatican appeared to soften its stance. Perhaps this one decision of Sister Christine's deep faith in a Courageous God was the inspiration the religious women needed in her community to join in courageously signing the letter.

Those who practice second half of life spirituality are not afraid to courageously challenge others whereas in the first half of life spirituality, the ego prefers to "play it safe." An awareness of an image of a Courageous God changes lives because people act on what they believe to be true.

(5.) Father Helmut Schuller

During this summer, Fr. Helmut Schuller from Austria has been traveling around the United States to fifteen cities. He is the leader of the organization, Call to Disobedience, that was founded in 2006. He and the priests in his group are concerned about the priest shortage, and they support equality and open dialogue in the Catholic Church. Pope Benedict criticized this movement describing the members as heretics and schismatics.

Call to Disobedience favors the ordination of women, a married and non-celibate priesthood, and allowance for the Eucharist to be given to remarried divorcees and non-Catholics.

I share this example with you because Fr. Helmut apparently is practicing second half of life spirituality, and he senses a compulsion to courageously act on his beliefs; be they right or wrong.

Conclusion:

Being missionaries in today's Church can take many avenues. There are so many opportunities to courageously work for justice and peace. Love motivates us to share, forgive, console, and be sensitive to the issues of today.

Peace,

Uncle Matthew

Letter #36
Monday, October 7, 2013

Dear Uncle Matthew,

Thank you for your last letter. I got a lot out of your examples of men and women who were courageous in acting upon their convictions.

Today my spiritual director was the celebrant at mass when we celebrated the Feast of Our Lady of the Rosary. Father told us that this feast had its origins in the sixteenth century when the Christian armies of Europe won a number of victories over the Muslim Turks. In thanksgiving for the victory of the Christian navies at Lepanto, Greece, on October 7, 1571, Pope Pius V declared October 7 the Feast of Our Lady of Victory since, in Rome, people were saying the rosary as the battle was being fought. Later, in 1573, Pope Gregory XIII changed the name to the Feast of Our Lady of the Rosary.

As I sat in the chapel, I felt uncomfortable realizing my views on world events and theology are changing. I could see the dualism in a belief that the Church has expounded for centuries that God would bless the Christians and curse the Muslims in a military battle. From what you have shared with me, Uncle Matthew, I now believe that God is love, so God can only love all those involved in warfare.

I had never thought about an image of a Courageous God, but you are making me once again aware that our images of God are so important because they greatly influence our attitudes and actions. Jesus is the best example of someone who showed his tremendous courage in his preaching and in his willingness to suffer and die for us.

Recently, I read an interview where Pope Francis was quoted as assailing the bureaucracy of the Catholic Church, saying it is overly clerical and insular, interested in temporal power and often led by narcissists. The pope has great courage.

Do you have any other images of God that you could share with me when we practice second half of life spirituality? I hope so!

Peace,

Joey

Response to Letter #36
Wednesday, October 23, 2013

Dear Joey,

Thank you for sharing the new insights that you experienced during the Feast of Our Lady of the Rosary. This was an important moment in your life when you realized that the Spirit of God was awakening you to a new mind-set. Be ready for more of this!

#8 An Empathetic God:

I think it is time now to share with you my thoughts about an Empathetic God. In our last two letters, we have looked at the importance of courage which is the foundation of something even greater; empathy. I now want to share with you a story that exemplifies courage lived out. This image of an Empathetic God is difficult to describe because it encompasses and contains the images of a Just God, a Merciful and Compassionate God, and a Courageous God. This image of an Empathetic God connotes that God is deeply affected by human suffering to the point of tears, as demonstrated by Jesus' tears when Lazarus died (John:11). Empathy is the extreme expression of courage when a person willingly suffers, bears the pains of the world, and enters into the suffering of others. When we think of a bleeding heart, we think of someone who feels sorry for everything and everyone and gives in to emotions quickly. This is a simplistic and misleading depiction. Tears can make a person look weak while they may as well show great strength of character. Men and women who imitate Jesus have the courage to act with unconditional love. St. Paul said, "and now these three remain: faith, hope and love. But the greatest of these is love" (1 Corinthians 13:13).

Now let me tell you my discovery of an Empathetic God.

A number of years ago, I went through a remarkable conversion, when to my surprise, I gradually discovered the power of an Empathetic God over a two year period of transformation. I shared my story with a friend of mine, William Coleman, and he changed the names and places so as not to identify me. He included my story, without my permission, in a small book. I'll share some of the author's account with you.

I was a pastor who tried to practice what the Church teaches about economic justice, but I discovered resistance from many lay persons, members of my own staff, my family, and eventually my bishop. My attempt to practice second half of life spirituality describes in the story below the cost of empathetic discipleship.

I had a very good relationship with my bishop who had appointed me to serve in many positions. My primary responsibility at the time of my discovery of an Empathetic God was to serve as the pastor of a large urban parish with an elementary school. I practiced collaborative ministry; a Vatican II approach.

It all began, that is the emergence of an Empathetic God, when I heard of the Catholic Church's work in Haiti. My curiosity was aroused, so I decided to investigate one of the organizations that helped the poor, Food for the Poor. I identified the leader, Ferdinand Mahfood, and I invited him to the parish to preach at all the Sunday masses and take up a second collection to feed the hungry in Haiti. The idea was generous, but routine. I was going through the routine of every-day life as a busy pastor. I expected a normal acceptance.

I was surprised when Mr. Mahfood replied that he did not usually go to parishes to preach unless the inviting pastor was first willing to spend a few days in Haiti to observe the poor and see what the Church was doing there. I thought Mr. Mahfood had presented an unorthodox proposition, but a reasonable one, so soon enough I was traveling to Haiti to immerse myself in the one-week program that Mr. Mahfood had developed.

I had never been to a third-world country. As I flew into Haiti's capital, Port-au-Prince, it looked so beautiful from above with it's surrounding mountains and water. But on the ground, leaving the airport for the hotel, I confronted a depth of poverty that I had never seen before. I had prepared myself to see human want and need, but I never imagined the reality of men and women struggling for their very survival, sorting through garbage heaps for food, or the sight of little children with stomachs distended by malnutrition, and infants whose teeth looked too large for their faces, shrunken by a lack of food.

One night during the visit, Mr. Mahfood and our group were eating supper in a pleasant restaurant, the kind that tourists frequented. The waiter had seated us next to an attractively decorated window overlooking the crowded street. As we ate our meal, a group of small children began to gather outside to watch us eat. The children were obviously hungry and the sight of food on our plates showed their distress if not their desperation. They seemed to hope that somehow, in some way, they might get some of that food to ease their great hunger. Their little faces were mournful and desperate as they pressed against the window.

I was troubled. I thought to myself, "I'm eating here, self-satisfied, while these little children, my brothers and sister in Christ, are hungry." I was unable to finish my meal. My stomach was in knots. I realized how naive I was about hunger and poverty. Many thoughts passed through my mind. I asked, "Have I deluded myself over the years? Have I tried to be a successful pastor, as the world judges success, rather than proclaiming the gospel? Was I the rich man in Luke's gospel story and these children are the poor man, Lazarus, sitting at the rich man's gate? What will Jesus say to me at the end of time? Was sending them the money from a second collection really aimed at feeding the hungry or was it simply a gesture to reaffirm us of our goodness?" That night and in the days that followed, the picture of the children looking through the window haunted me.

When I boarded the plane to return to the United States, I realized I would never be the same. The visit to Haiti was a major conversion experience. My vision for the future came together, and I discerned that it was in accord with the gospels. I experienced not only empathy to the point of tears for the poor, the hungry, and the disadvantaged in Haiti, but I felt this incredible urge to be part of the solution. My tears helped me to be aware of the movement of the Spirit in my heart.

I discovered a new image of God that wanted me to give up my false gods so I would be an authentic person, fully committed to those members of the Body of Christ who were suffering. I discovered a God that wanted me to keep first and foremost the First Commandment, "I the Lord am your God; you shall not have other gods besides me." For me this meant I could no longer worship the gods of ambition, position, and worldly acclamation.

When I returned to the parish, I could not show my slides of Haiti to parishioners without welling up with tears. I, along with some parishioners, began going into the inner city to help at the homeless shelter. We served food and handed out clothing and spent nights there.

One night at the homeless shelter, a poor man truly gifted me with another experience of an Empathetic God that wanted me to not only feel sorry for the poor, the homeless, and the hungry in the city, but to be more a part of the solution. This is what happened. There was clothing on a table and a poor man took only one pair of socks. I said to him, "Why not take two pairs?" The poor man said, "There may not be enough for someone else." Those words would forever be engraved on my heart. I began to see my false gods (success, acclamation, pleasing superiors, climbing the ladder), and I began to fall in love with a God who was calling me to a deeper level of courage and empathy as a priest. I began to understand a powerful insight of St. Vincent de Paul, "The poor convert us."

As long as I kept my devotion to an Empathetic God private and limited to the homeless shelter, there would be no problem. The trouble began when I began to challenge the accepted ideas of where we put our money. I challenged the parishioners to act in ways in accord to an Empathetic God. I discovered that the many parishioners did not want to be challenged on how they were spending their money. I was raising the question, "Is building more church buildings the best way to serve God when the poor are desperate?"

For several years, the parish had been planning an expansion drive to acquire land to build a new church building, a new rectory, improve the parish school, and perhaps add a gymnasium. More and more, over the years, the makeup of the parish had changed, and there were many well-to-do parishioners. The building plans were mixed with notions of providing the best environment for worship and supposedly the resulting glorification of God. When I met with the Parish Council, they could tell I had changed. I did my best to explain what had happened to me and how profoundly my old way of thinking had changed. Many meetings followed, and it become clear that I could no longer support an ambitious building drive because I did not judge a need yet for an ambitious building drive. Without my support, there could never be the money needed to build the new buildings, so a group went to the bishop and asked him to clear the impasse.

During this time, the bishop held a fund drive to renovate the diocesan Cathedral. I was upset about this drive. I could not understand why hundreds of thousands of dollars would be spent to reinforce steeples on the Cathedral when millions of people in the world were on the brink of starvation. Later, when I saw in the newspaper that the new Cathedral organ would cost

$270,000, I was again troubled. There were so many poor and homeless people living in the shadows of the Cathedral at that time. All the parishes in the diocese would be taxed to pay for the renovations to the Cathedral. I felt as though I was looking in a mirror. The bishop was placing the emphasis on a building, and I realized I would be doing the same thing if I proceeded with the parish's building fund. I wondered how I could place so much emphasis on buildings knowing that the poor would be neglected. I asked, "Shouldn't the poor have a higher priority?"

My questioning indicated that I was transitioning between the practice of first and second half of life spirituality. I was in that gray area when I was becoming aware of issues involving peace and justice, but in a new and acute way. My images of God were expanding. I was unclear as to what action I should take, but I felt this powerful urge to be part of the solution. I often looked at a quote by Mahatma Gandhi, "Recall the face of the poorest and most helpless person you have seen and ask yourself if the next step you contemplate is going to be of any use to that person."

For some people, especially those who have lived a sheltered life, travel facilitates the transition into the practice of second half of life spirituality. Earlier in a letter to you, I quoted Mark Twain who once said, "Travel dispels ignorance." We are motivated to move into the practice of second half of life spirituality when we take trips to third world countries. The experiences of helping out in the inner city at a shelter can open our eyes to reality. But the big surprise comes when we realize that many others do not see what we see. Then we are forced to question, "Am I right or wrong? Why do I set myself up for failure? Why couldn't I just do what I am told instead of following my conscience?"

Several months after my return from Haiti, I reached the point where I had to follow my conscience, so I wrote,

"As pastor, I cannot ask the parish for additional hundreds of thousands of dollars for buildings when I compare our needs to the needs of the poor in the world. I have been trying to educate myself about the plight of the poor by extensive reading over the last few years. I realize more and more that our affluent way of life is crushing the poor economically and well as spiritually. Thousands die daily because of hunger and malnutrition; and this tragedy is a sign to all of us that the will of God is not being followed. I realize more and more that it is not so much an issue of what we will give to the poor (Ethiopia, Haiti), but rather the question is when will we stop taking from the poor by our consumerism and rich life-style?"

The bishop listened to different opinions and later decided that I should build the church buildings. The bishop told me if I did what he was asking me to do, I would be doing God's will. I rejected that argument as self-serving. When I refused to go against my conscience, the bishop said, "You are Father Matthew from now on." Up until that time, the bishop and I had been on a first-name basis because I always did what he asked me to do without hesitation. The bishop asked me if I would like to resign as pastor. I told the bishop I would not resign, but I would not object to being transferred to a new assignment. I would not violate my conscience by being complicit in the bishop's plans to expend great resources on buildings in the face of great human need.

The practice of first half of life spirituality would have allowed me to do what the bishop wanted regardless of the demands of my conscience. Once I experienced an image of an Empathetic God, my practice of second half of life spirituality enlightened me to the deeper and more difficult moral choices I was facing. I was awakened to the underlying reality of the priority of love and empathy which took priority over the construction of more church buildings. This story is similar to Jesus' conflicts with authority figures. Jesus' priorities were love and empathy. For example Jesus said, "The sabbath was made for man, not man for the sabbath" (Mark 2:27).

Later the bishop sent a letter to all the parishioners and said that it was his conviction that both goals (building parish buildings and helping the poor) could be pursued simultaneously. He also said he would replace me as pastor. The bishop came up with a non-dualistic solution that, if grounded in reality, would be considered the practice of second half of life spirituality. Under a new pastor, a large amount of money later went into building all the buildings that the people desired. Only God (and the bishop) knows if a fundamental option for the poor was implemented or forgotten.

Albert Einstein once said, "No problem can be solved from the same level of consciousness that created it." When individuals move into the practice of second half of life spirituality, they understand his words. They can reach a point where they discover that their ecclesiastical model is outdated and ill-suited for their faith development. Problems will be solved and conflicts will be resolved only when people are willing to change.

Some spiritual writers call it a "desert experience" when we go through a period of time that is terribly difficult. Discovering an image of an Empathetic God enlightens us to the value of legitimate suffering. We grow. We change. We see reality. We develop a vision. We find meaning in life. New images of God pull us away from our false gods. New images of God gift us with more courage and tears, as they draw us into a deeper love of God which replaces our fear of God.

This true story points out that my own transformation was not a one-time experience but a gradual and continuing process. When I flew into Haiti, from the air, all was well. But on the ground, reality set in. So it is true for us. We can so easily miss seeing reality until we have new experiences of pain and suffering when the Holy Spirit touches our hearts and changes our way of thinking. It was as though I was on a journey without a map. I was on the "road less traveled." I was blessed with a desire to spend time in prayer more than any other time in my life. I had to pray for discernment. I had to be clear about my vision. I had to be as sure as possible that my conscience was true to God. I had to pray to be sure God was calling me to risk everything so as to be more responsive to the tragic situation of hunger, poverty, and homelessness.

Earlier in several letters to you, I mentioned some of the goals in second half of life spirituality. One goal is to develop our conscience so as to discover the truth. An informed conscience takes in many factors. St. Thomas Aquinas is paraphrased as insisting, "Even the dictate of an erroneous conscience must be followed and that to act against such a dictate is immoral."

The bishop and I followed our conscience. Perhaps that is all that we could have done at the time. In my estimation, the bishop's conscience was formed by his thinking in terms of hierarchal categories, the real world of building big buildings to enhance the institutional church's growth. I awakened to a new set of values, so I acted from a more moral and gospel way of thinking.

The practice of first half of life spirituality is characterized by dualisms. So the questions by those living from this perspective would be, "Who won? Was I right or was the bishop right?" The practice of second half of spirituality would ask different questions: "Did the bishop follow his conscience? Did I follow my conscience?" Those who practice second half of life spirituality discover and appreciate mystery, uncertainty, and ambiguity.

I learned on the night in Haiti when the little children stood at the window and watched me eat that my priesthood was a universal calling. God called me to serve all of God's people, not merely the people in one parish or in a particular diocese. Good Catholic theology insists that our baptism calls all people to serve not only the members of their own families but every child of God. If serving the poor means confrontations with the rich and powerful, is that any different from the life Jesus himself had lived? Following the imperatives of the Empathetic God may lead to suffering, marginalization, and defeat as the world judges it. Jesus' life attests to this gospel reality. So it has been and so it will be.

Peace,

Uncle Matthew

Letter #37
Monday, November 11, 2013


Dear Uncle Matthew,

Thank you for your last letter that shared your discovery of an Empathetic God. Your empathy for the poor in Haiti motivated you to change the entire focus of your life, a sure sign of the practice of second half of life spirituality. I never heard this story from my parents or your brother. I am honored that you shared this painful but important chapter in your life.

Today is Veterans Day, a day to honor military veterans; that is, persons who served in the United States Armed Forces. Coincidentally, today we celebrated at mass the feast of St. Martin of Tours who was born in the fourth century. In the homily, the celebrant said that Martin was forced into the Roman army against his will when he was in the process of becoming a Christian. After becoming a Christian, he refused any further military service as a matter of conscience, and he was imprisoned and later discharged. During this period of his life, according to a legendary episode, on a bitter cold day he had a profound experience when he met a poor man who was almost naked. Martin cut his cloak in two with a sword and gave the beggar half and he wrapped himself in the other half. That night he had a dream and Jesus was in the cloak that he had given to the poor man.

Some people believe that St. Martin was a conscientious objector. The celebrant made a good point when he said that the celebration of Veterans' Day and the Feast of Saint Martin on the same day remind us that opposing opinions regarding service in the military and conscientious objection are helpful in the continuing process of reform both in the Church and in oneself.

What other images of God can emerge with the practice of second half of life spirituality?

Peace,

Joey

Response to Letter #37
Monday, November 25, 2013

Dear Joey,

I'm glad my story about discovering an Empathetic God was helpful to you. This is the first time I am sharing what happened in that nine-year assignment as pastor of a large suburban parish. After the bishop removed me from being pastor of that parish, I requested the opportunity to begin a new Catholic Worker House and minister to the very poor so as to live out my new awareness of an Empathetic God. The bishop told me that was impossible because of the shortage of priests in the diocese. In response, I asked and grudgingly received permission to enter a monastery where I would rekindle my own spirit. There the abbot selected me to be on the retreat team, and I was trained to be a spiritual director. In the monastery, my desire to help those who were poor was fulfilled when the abbot assigned me to spiritually direct many visitors who were spiritually broken, poor, addicted, and suffering.

#9   A God of Grace:

I'll share with you another image of God, A God of Grace, that assisted me in practicing second half of life spirituality. We can experience a God of Grace when we suffer with the love and safety of a community.

Personal suffering is difficult for everyone. The spiritual writers tell us that during periods of great personal suffering, we can become conscious of an eternal truth that grace, the activity of God's love, works for us constantly. Grace is something we do not have to work to earn. At times, we just have to surrender to God and receive God's love.

Eric Butterworth, a spiritual icon in the Unity Movement, said God is in us like the ocean is in a wave. There is no possible way in which the wave can be separated from the ocean, and there is no way in which we can be separated from God. When we practice second half of life spirituality, we get rid of the idea, prevalent in the Book of Job, that suffering is a sign of God's punishment or that God gives grace to some and withholds grace from others. Grace and love are the same thing since God is love. Let me explain.

Before the Holy Spirit enlightened me to an awareness of a God of Grace, I felt as though I had to work to receive God's grace. I tried to be in control of my life by being orderly and methodical. I allotted time for this and that with very little time to spare. I obeyed the laws of the Church. I frequented the sacraments. At the age of forty-nine, I was in great physical shape. My life was predictable. I didn't know that the practice of second half of life spirituality is about letting go, surrendering to God, and letting God lead us. I was unaware that God still works in us and showers God's love on us even when we can do nothing except surrender to God.

A hike:

I took a hike in the Rocky Mountains with two companions. We climbed to the top of a mountain that had an elevation of 12,500 feet. We just started down the mountain when I stumbled on a loose rock and fell on my left side and dislocated my left shoulder. It took many hours of agonizing hiking to get back to the car and then to the emergency room of the hospital. Once there, they relocated my arm and discovered that my left arm was paralyzed with a brachial plexus injury. A neurologist said he might have to amputate my arm! The neurologist said that a dangling arm might get caught in an elevator door. How is that for bedside manners? I was stunned. The thought of losing my arm was mind-boggling. The day had begun with a spectacular mountain hike and had ended with the threat of losing my arm. That was the beginning of a journey that blessed me with the awareness of a God of Grace that emerges with suffering and the blessings of a loving community.

Physical therapy:

For months I was in physical therapy, and I endured terrible chronic nerve pain in my left arm. I wore a TENS unit that sent small electrical currents to my arm to alleviate the pain, but the pain exceeded the unit's ability to help. The doctor prescribed strong pain medications. I had six Stellate Ganglion Block operations, but after each operation, the terrible nerve pain returned. Going to bed at night was a nightmare. Fighting the pain at times took all my energy and concentration. I gradually learned how to surrender to God since I could no longer be in control, and to my surprise, I experienced a deep inner peace in my helplessness.

The doctor was successful when he did the seventh Stellate Ganglion Block. I was relieved of my terrible pain. The physical therapy continued, and gradually the therapy played an important part in bring about feeling in my fingers and wrist.

Part of the process of surrendering to God was being dependent upon others for daily prayer for my hand. Each night several friends in the monastery would place their warm hands on my hand and pray for a healing. Also a good friend worked each day on my hand so as to give me additional physical therapy. One day, my female therapist told me, only after I was recovering some feeling in the fingers of my hand, that I was her third patient with a brachial plexus injury in the shoulder. The other two men had fallen off their horses and both men had committed suicide because their pain had overwhelmed them. At the moment I felt an over-whelming gratitude for God's grace.

I became aware that God's grace was present when I surrendered and gratefully received physical therapy, the prayers of a community, the blessing of friendships, the comfort of words, and the touch of friends. This profound lesson of the importance of community remains with me to this day. My suffering led to an awareness of how God works in our human suffering through surrender and community. I realized that being alone in my suffering was not an option. My ability to surrender was possible with the support of a loving community.

Letting go:

There are times in our lives when we may have a physical problem that results in great pain and suffering such as rheumatoid arthritis, cancer, an addiction to alcohol, heart disease, AIDS, or any of the countless afflictions of human life. We feel, and we are, out of control. It is then, and only then, for most of us, that we are open and ready to encounter the Holy Spirit and discover a new image of God; a God of Grace

When we practice first half of life spirituality, we try to control our environment both within and without. When we practice second half of life spirituality, we recognize the falsehood of trying to be in control and eventually we give up control. As we age, we discover more and more that we need others if we are going to be whole. We are on the deepest level interdependent. We can no longer be, or pretend to be, independent. When we become interdependent, we can come to appreciate a God of Grace.

This episode in my own life helped me to brace myself for many situations in the future that would bid me to let go and trust God.

Living as a vibrant member of the Body of Christ:

A willingness to surrender to God is a strong sign of the practice of second half of life spirituality because it shows deep faith and trust in God. It takes humility to surrender to God through other people. The twelve step programs are all about surrendering to a higher-power. Surrendering to God means that we willingly live as a member of the Body of Christ. We can realize that our particular suffering has become a great blessing; true gold, because we become aware of a bigger God who continually sheds God's love in us whether we do something or simply surrender. Perhaps a person who is a stroke victim in a nursing home may be doing more to build up the Kingdom of God than at any other time in his/her life! Jesus on the Cross reminds us that suffering is not a sign of God's punishment but an opportunity to be transformed into the likeness of Christ. Although we may no longer have our physical strength, or we suffer an addiction, or we lack certitude when we courageously act so as to follow our conscience, or we lack affirmation from others, we have discovered a new image of God that is like finding "the treasure hidden in a field" (Matthew 13:44).

The first beatitude is, "Blessed are the poor in spirit, for theirs is the kingdom of God" (Matthew 5:3).

Conclusion:

I was blessed to become aware of a God of Grace. However, once I recovered the use of my left arm and hand, I gradually forgot to fully trust God and surrender myself totally to God. The lesson I learned was that we are never converted once and for all. The ego is so strong and yields only grudgingly. We need multiple experiences to teach us the eternal truths of life. Growing old usually provides experiences of helplessness. If we believe in a God of Grace, we can be at peace and still find happiness in our dependence upon others. We can be at peace when we must give up the privilege of driving a car. We can be at peace when we are in an assisted living facility. We can be at peace if we suffer a paralyzing stroke. If we never become aware of new images of a bigger God, we may end up bitter and angry when we are in a state of helplessness. We do not realize that we are simply in a chapter of our life cycle that is normal, and God is still with us and desires to do great things through us.

Peace,

Uncle Matthew

Letter #38
Thursday, December 12, 2013


Dear Uncle Matthew,

Thank you for sharing your beautiful and incredible story about how you arrived at an awareness of a God of Grace. I sensed your terrible pain when you shared that your physical therapist told you that two of her patients eventually committed suicide after incurring brachial plexus injuries.

This reminds me of Steve, a friend of mine in college, who lost a leg in a terrible car accident. I watched him live in the stages of anger and bargaining with God. Finally, in his despair, he rejected the help his friends offered and he isolated himself. He was unable to experience safety, consolation, love, and support. His despair deepened. He eventually committed suicide. Your story about becoming aware of a God of Grace and Steve's tragic inability to open himself to the same God supports your insights that we can become aware of a God of Grace in our human suffering when we are willing to surrender to God by finding God's presence in the hands, prayers, words, and touch of those in our community. I have never suffered with any serious injuries, so I have yet to experience how to surrender with a deep trust in God's love being ever-present. I hope, if I do have to endure a serious suffering, that I pass the test by humbly seeking the love and consolation of a community. After all, as you keep saying, we are the Body of Christ.

I have a long journey into the spiritual life ahead of me. I can see that it is a life-long process of growth. Your honesty in sharing with me your long path in discovering an adult spirituality is so helpful.

Our exams are coming up after which I will be visiting my mom and dad. My brother Paul will be home from his senior year in college. We always get along well together although we are five years apart in age. I'll call you on Christmas Day.

Last week, Nelson Mandela died. Before I entered the seminary, I watched the film, Invictus, the one where Matt Damon played the role of a rugby player on a national team. Nelson Mandela, in his first term as South African President, enlisted the national rugby team to help unite the apartheid-torn country. Nelson Mandela inspired me greatly. Surely he was a man who experienced a God of Grace. He suffered greatly and humbly surrendered with a deep love for his nation (his community) which filled him with hope and not despair while he was in jail for twenty-seven years.

I look forward to hearing about any other images of God that we may become aware of when we practice second half of life spirituality.

Peace,

Joey

Response to Letter #38
Sunday, December 29, 2013

Dear Joey,

Your telephone call on Christmas Day was special. Bill, Emily, and I were so excited to talk to you, your parents, and Paul.

In previous letters to you, I have presented nine images of God that, with the Holy Spirit, may infuse our lives when we practice second half of life spirituality: an Incarnate God, an Inclusive God, a Just God, a Merciful and Compassionate God, Our God, a Male/Female God, a Courageous God, an Empathetic God, and a God of Grace.

I would like to share with you another image of God, a Forgiving God. Notice that as we move into the practice of second half of life spirituality, our understanding of God becomes more lovable, larger, more abundant, and expansive. We are receptive to a larger reality when we are less fearful. How beautiful it is, as our understanding of God enlarges, our own lives get bigger. There are many more images of a bigger God that can emerge as we open ourselves both to the Holy Spirit and to a wide range of life experiences.

The practice of second half of life spirituality offers us new images of God that can help us to experience more directly and meaningfully what is perhaps the fundamental Christian message; God is with us, and God is for us. We come to experience that humanity and the divine exist in the same time and place, always and forever. We gradually become aware that the gospel is truly revolutionary in upending many societal norms that serve the false gods of power, respectability, and, of course, money. We become aware, haltingly but steadily, that the gospel isn't about being perfect so that God will love us. Rather, the gospel is about giving one's heart in devotion and acting out of the awareness that God is with us even in our sickness, sinfulness, and brokenness. This truth sets us free to love and free to serve.

As I mentioned earlier to you, Joey, there is no correlation between age and the practice of second half of life spirituality, but as we grow older, the demands and ambitions of youth recede and we can become more aware of the many opportunities to experience new images of God. Then God becomes less abstract and more real and immediate.

"Repent:"

Before we can believe that God is always with us, we need to be aware of our need for God. All of us suffer from some kind of addiction and/or some destructive behavior no matter how veiled and subtle these may be. We need to acknowledge our addictions and wrong-doings, as taught in twelve step programs such as AA, so as to be liberated from shame and guilt or their twins, pride and self-righteousness. Jesus began his ministry by saying, "Repent, and believe in the gospel" (Mark 1:15). (Literally, "turn away from" or "to turn around") That means that practicing an adult spirituality presumes a willingness to change our thinking and to try to see things in a new way. This may seem obvious or easy, but truly changing requires humility and courage, not always found.

#10   A Forgiving God:

New images of God come from human experiences that invite us to see and hear God in a new way. Even though sometimes we are blessed with an insight into a new image of God, we may discover that it will take more experiences for us to truly understand and appreciate this insight. For example, we may need many experiences of both being forgiven and having the opportunity to forgive others to be aware of a Forgiving God.

We live in a culture permeated by violence that involves property disputes, fistfights, gun violence, and a criminal system of punishment that emphasizes justice instead of mercy and rehabilitation. Gandhi said, "An eye for an eye and a tooth for a tooth leaves the world blind and toothless."

We need divine help to truly forgive someone. Jesus recognized this, including in the Lord's Prayer the petition, "Forgive us our sins as we forgive those who sin against us."

If we increasingly become aware of a Forgiving God, we can be inspired and enabled to forgive others. We need divine help to let go of our demands for perfection and our high expectations of others and of ourselves. So often our expectations are virtually impossible to meet. We need divine help to accept that all of us are fallible. We need divine help to move on and stress the essential goodness of others and ourselves.

Tim:

In an earlier letter to you, I mentioned that I was the principal of a Catholic high school. On a beautiful October day, a student came to me at lunchtime and told me that a student named Tim was selling marijuana in the parking lot. I went out to the parking lot and found Tim, and I brought him to my office. I asked him if he had been selling marijuana, and he at first denied it. Eventually, after prolonged discussion, he admitted he had been selling drugs, and he had hidden a bag of marijuana in his pants. Tim pulled the bag out and gave it to me. I read to him the school policy in the handbook stating that a student bringing drugs on the campus faced automatic expulsion. I told Tim that I had to expel him. My heart was saddened.

As we approached the office door, Tim said, "If I give up doing drugs and finish out my junior year in a public school, may I come back in my senior year and graduate with my class?" I was impressed with his honesty and his apparent willingness to change. I sensed that he was sincere.

In chapter 11 of John's Gospel, we have the story of Lazarus being raised from the dead. Jesus went to a dark cave and called him out. I guessed that Tim's drug use had put him in a dark cave, and he was eager for someone to say, "Come out into the world of Light." I agreed to his request with the condition that while he was in the public school, we would have frequent talks to assure me that he was free of his drug habit.

Tim did return in his senior year, and he graduated with his class. I felt in some way that I had helped in "untying" Tim. He was a different person once he came out of his cave of darkness and lived in the light.

I knew I needed forgiveness for my sins, so I could forgive Tim. I was gradually becoming like the image of a Forgiving God since we become like the images of the God that we reverence. If we have an image of a Vindictive God who acts like a prosecuting attorney, then we find it difficult to forgive. If we have an image of a Forgiving God who acts like a defense attorney, then we are more able to forgive; a sign that we are practicing second half of life spirituality. When we can forgive others, we are good shepherds.

The bishop:

In an earlier letter to you, I mentioned that I discovered an Empathetic God that led to a serious conflict with my bishop over a building project. I mentioned that there is more to his story, so this seems to be a good time to share.

Several years after I entered the monastery and took simple vows, I became aware that I was still holding on to some anger and hostility toward my former bishop. This was understandable because the conflict had cost me greatly emotionally and financially. I experienced a deep longing and a hunger for reconciliation. I became aware that my longing for reconciliation was rooted in my desire to be like the Forgiving God I was trying to adore. I realized that the bishop and I had acted out of integrity and followed our conscience.

When I had an opportunity to be in the same locale as the bishop, I took the initiative to call him. By now he was retired. The bishop invited me to come see him and spend the night in his home. I could tell by the friendly conversation that the bishop also wanted to be reconciled. During our visit, the bishop treated me to supper. We drank wine together as we dialogued long into the evening. The bishop was very friendly, and we discussed the many wonderful years when we had worked together. However, the bishop never brought up the subject of the building project that led to our conflict. I realized that the main topic did not have to be brought up since it didn't matter at the moment who was right and who was wrong. The important thing was we both wanted to be reconciled. The reconciliation that took place was a rich blessing for both of us. Even without any absolution given, we experienced God's presence. We realized we were both human beings with a love for each other and for the Church. Loving one another was more important than proving who was right and who was wrong. Later, the bishop called me on Christmas Day to wish me a Merry Christmas, and he asked how I was doing.

Jesus' teaching:

In Matthew's gospel, Jesus gave us an image of a Forgiving God when he said to his disciples, "If your brother sins against you, go and tell him his fault between you and him alone. If he listens to you, you have won over your brother. If he does not listen take one or two others along with you, so that every fact may be established on the testimony of two or three witnesses" (Matthew 18:15-17).

Jesus reminds us that we should strive to resolve any situation in which there is a breach of personal relationship between another member of the Christian community and us. Thus, if we feel that someone has wronged us, we should act in a conciliatory manner at the first opportunity. We should not simply brood over it. We should attempt to settle a difference face-to-face. If a private meeting fails to resolve something, then we should take it to some wise person. The goal is not retaliation but reconciliation; to bring back together those who have missed the mark.

Later in Matthew's gospel, Peter said, "Lord, when my brother wrongs me, how often must I forgive him? Seven times?" Jesus replied, "Not seven times, I say, seventy times seven times" (Matthew 18:21-22).

Since Jesus is the visible image of the invisible God, we can assume Jesus' many instructions about forgiveness were reflections based on his awareness of a Forgiving God.

The practice of second half of life spirituality makes us aware that forgiveness and attempts at reconciliation are of supreme importance no matter who is at fault. After all, we believe that we are blessed with divine life. A willingness to forgive and show compassion are litmus tests of God's presence.

The Sacrament of Reconciliation:

Family arguments are common. But we all know how wonderful it is when we can go to bed at night and know that we are not holding a grudge against anyone. When we have a willingness to forgive and forget, we will be able to sleep soundly with no guilt or fear.

The worse thing we can do to others who genuinely ask for forgiveness is to fail to forgive them. When we fail to forgive those who are willing to admit that they sinned and are sorry, we misuse power. That is why in the Sacrament of Reconciliation, priests who practice second half of life spirituality will always find a way to give absolution no matter how imperfect the confession might be. To deny absolution or to make it difficult for a penitent to confess his or her sins is a negation of the reality of a Forgiving God.

Julian of Norwich said, "My own sin will not hinder the working of God's goodness." We all are sinful. As I mentioned in my last letter, when we practice first half of life spirituality we can easily presume that a serious sin prevents God's grace from being operative in us. When we practice second half of life spirituality, we presume that God is so much bigger than our personal sinfulness. God continues to work in us even when we make bad choices. The experiences of many of us show that even clerics who are not living a life of integrity are sometimes able to preach and teach in ways that convert others.

Book-The Railway Man:

In 1998, I read an autobiographical book by Eric Lomax, The Railway Man. This true story tells about the torture of a British Army officer, Eric Lomax, at a Japanese prisoner-of-war camp during World War II. He was forced in captivity to help build the Burma Railway for the Japanese military. For many years after the war, Lomax suffered from traumatic stress disorder. He had nightmares and flash-backs of the horrible torture, including water boarding, he underwent. He harbored a desire to seek revenge and kill his enemy.

Thirty-five years after the war, Lomax learned that the Japanese soldier, Nagase, who tortured him, was alive. Nagase had turned the former torture camp in Thailand into a war museum that was dedicated to reconciliation. Lomax returned to Southeast Asia to confront his demons. He met Nagase with a well prepared plan for revenge by smashing Nagase's arm and cutting his throat. Out of guilt, Nagase did not resist. Nagase revealed how he had been brainwashed as a young man to think Japan was right in going to war. Lomax finally freed Nagase and they were reconciled. They realized that they both were no longer the same young men that they were during the war.

Suddenly all the depression, anger, hatred, desire for revenge, and suffering that Lomax was carrying was taken away. His enemy, Nagase, was also released of all his guilt, suffering, and sorrow for his sinfulness and ignorance during the war. The story exemplifies so very well that a willingness to forgive can awaken us to a Forgiving God who heals by changing our hearts.

Conclusion:

If we hold on to an image of a Vindictive God, we risk being judgmental, vindictive, and tormented by depression. We can easily think that violence is the solution and the means for creating justice and peace, internally and externally.

We do become like the image of God that we honor in our heart. If we believe in a Forgiving God, we probably will use our opportunities well to be reconciled with others. We will be slow to judge others. We will believe that love, mercy, and forgiveness triumph over hatred, revenge, and even torture.

You mentioned that Nelson Mandela inspired you. His death earlier this month made the world aware that forgiveness and reconciliation can change the course of history for a whole nation. He forgave his captors after twenty-seven years in captivity saying, "Resentment is like drinking poison and then hoping it will kill your enemies." His willingness to forgive was a clear sign of his practice of second half of life spirituality. May we benefit from his example to willingly forgive others and ourselves.

Peace,

Uncle Matthew

# IV.  Living the Journey:
# The Practice of Second Half of Life
# Spirituality

Letter #39
Sunday, January 12, 2014

Dear Uncle Matthew,

Thank you for sharing with me an image of a Forgiving God. I'm glad that you and your former bishop were reconciled before the bishop died. As we shared on the phone, this story is a reminder to all of us not to wait until tomorrow to do what we can do today. It makes sense that if God is love, God must be all-Forgiving. If we come to believe in a Forgiving God, then to be a genuine follower of Jesus, we must forgive others.

Today is the feast of Jesus' baptism. The homilist at mass told us that after Jesus' baptism, he walked the face of the earth and became like the ideal servant. He became fully human and fully alive with God's Spirit. Jesus brought forth justice. He opened the eyes of the blind and released those bound by sin. He brought light to those living in darkness.

The homilist told us that once we are baptized, God expects us to live life fully. God expects us to bring forth justice, to help those without faith to see, to forgive others so they will be released from their prisons of shame, resentment, and fear. God expects us to bring the light of love, joy, and peace to others. The homilist said that humility is needed to accomplish these ideals in life. He offered a great message that sounded like a message you would share.

Being home over the Christmas holidays with my mother, father, and Paul was so good. Of course some people I met at church tried to put me on a pedestal. You have helped me to be aware of the dangers of separating myself from others. I'm glad your time after Christmas gave you more time to think, write, and help others.

Since the homilist mentioned the importance of humility, do you have any reflections on that topic that you will share with me?

Peace,

Joey

Response to Letter #39
Friday, January 31, 2014


Dear Joey,

I am glad that you liked my story about my discovery of a
Forgiving God. Suffering, major conflicts with others, new
exciting experiences, and prayer provide us with rich
opportunities to discover new images of God.

Did you see the article about Pope Francis who is calling for a
change in the culture of seminaries? He said that priests who are
taught only to toe the line will become "little monsters." This was
a swipe at clericalism. That is why it is so important to keep up
with our culture. You are in the seminary to change, to be
transformed, so as to have a new heart. I was pleased that you
shared in your last letter that you were aware of the tendency
some people have to "elevate" you. Stay humble!

Today is the feast of St. John Bosco who was born in 1815, in
NW Italy. He became a priest, and he was the founder of the
Society of St. Francis de Sales, the Salesians. After his
ordination, he began a lifelong devotion to vocational training for
boys and young men. He opened workshops to train them as
shoemakers, tailors, printers, bookbinders, and ironworkers.

I have met several Salesians, and I have been impressed with
them. I have a prayer card that was printed by the Salesian

Missions that reads:

On, God, when I have food,
Help me to remember the hungry;
When I work, help me
To remember the jobless;
When I have a warm home,
Help me to remember the homeless;
When I am without pain,
Help me to remember those who suffer;
And remembering, help me
To destroy my complacency
And bestir my compassion.
Make me concerned enough
To help, by word and deed,
Those who cry out
For what we take for granted.

Samuel F. Pugh

The prayer seems to be sharing the important lessons that we need to be conscious of the needs that others have and be grateful for what we have. The prayer is an example of the practice of second half of life spirituality that attempts to sensitize us to the needs of others rather than remaining focused on our own perfection.

The importance of humility:

I will gladly share some thoughts on the importance of humility with you. I agree with the homily that you mentioned. Humility is basic in both the practice of first and second half of life spirituality.

Today's gospel was from Matthew 18:1-5: "Whoever humbles himself like this child is the greatest in the kingdom of heaven. And whoever receives one child such as this in my name receives me."

In society during Jesus' life, a child had no standing or status. A child was a "nobody." And yet Jesus indicated that the least or most insignificant people in society are the greatest. Father Joseph Girzone so well shared in a fictional literary form in his two book, Joshua and The Homeless Bishop, that insignificant humble people can make a terrific difference.

Why do you think that Jesus suggested that we must be humble to follow him? Perhaps, it is because when we are childlike, we have a better chance of knowing ourselves. The mystics tell us that we cannot know God if we do not know ourselves first. We know we need others. We are made to love and not hate. If only we can be humble and simply be open to new ways of seeing reality. I am convinced that when we are open to new images of God, we have a golden opportunity to change our perception of reality which affects the way we socialize, vote, pray, and think.

The spiritual writers tell us that we cannot be humble by merely deciding to do so. If we try, we will depend upon our ego which will fail us. The same is true of an alcoholic trying to be sober. Alcoholics who simply depend upon their ego will fail in their quest for sobriety. We need God. We need other people. Being humble helps us to become more conscious of our pride and our ego that can operate in a selfish or unselfish manner.

I mentioned that early in our lives seeds are planted that show us different ways of viewing reality. As Catholics, we were introduced to the practice of first half of life spirituality that taught us that our religion is the one true religion. We even sensed that we should feel sorry for those Protestants who do not have our sacraments.

When we are child-like and practice second half of life spirituality, we view reality differently. We rely upon common sense, and we view many things that are sometimes missed by those who may have doctorate degrees, but yet practice first half of life spirituality. Therefore, it often comes as a shock when Catholics later discover that non-Catholics, even non-Christians, also share in the Gifts of the Holy Spirit.

Those who practice second half of life spirituality appreciate the gifts and talents of all those who preach and live out the gospel. It takes a leap of faith, a profound humility, a willingness to change, to believe that someone outside of our group can be loved by God and blessed by God as we presume we are. Earlier, I shared with you that by being humble enough to attend a healing service conducted by a Methodist, Katherine Kuhlman, and by participating in a predominately Protestant movement, Promise Keepers, with pastors of the First Alliance Church, I discovered an Inclusive God.

Unfortunately, it is difficult to grow in humility because your academic preparation can tempt you to think that your education and celibacy have given you advantages over the laity. Upon ordination, you can think you are the teacher, the bearer of truth, and miss the humility needed to realize that you need to continue to be taught by your parishioners, Protestant and Jewish friends, and non-Christians to become a whole person.

A map of the spiritual journey can help you to see the full picture so that you stay humble knowing that you have much more to learn and you will need many more experiences to become God-centered, fully human, and fully alive.

In my next letter to you, I'll share with you how we discover new images of God.

Peace,

Uncle Matthew

Letter #40
February 10, 2014

Dear Uncle Matthew,

I did see the article about Pope Francis' warning that if seminarians are taught only to toe the line, they will become "little monsters." From what you have shared with me, I can see that unless church leaders keep growing spiritually, they can risk being "little monsters" to their parishioners. This is a fate I will seek to avoid!

Your excellent description of the need for humility made me realize my own need for that virtue. I am tempted to be arrogant when I think God loves me more than lay persons my age since I am on my way to becoming a priest. I am tempted, often, to consider myself morally superior, just because I have studied philosophy and theology. It does not mean that I understand these truths, as valuable as they are, that can only be learned through living them out.

You are a good spiritual teacher because you listen to new ideas. You listened at the Richard Rohr Conference on the two halves of life. You are encouraging me to question. You tell stories that help me to understand new ways of looking at reality. I am so grateful for you in my life. I told my spiritual director about you, and he agrees you are an excellent spiritual teacher.

Today is the feast of St. Scholastica who was born in Italy, in 480, of wealthy parents. I didn't know that her twin brother was the famous St. Benedict. The homilist told us that they established religious communities within a few miles of each other. Once a year, they visited each other in a farmhouse because Scholastica was not permitted inside her brother's monastery. When they met, we are told, they spent the time discussing spiritual matters.

The last time they met, St. Scholastica sensed it would be their last time together, so she urged him to spend more time with her. He refused because to spend a night outside of the monastery would break his Monastic Rule. She prayed, and a severe thunderstorm developed, forcing him to remain, enabling them to talk all night.

When Benedict was back in his monastery, a few days later he saw the soul of his sister rising heavenward in the form of a white dove. Benedict then announced the death of his sister to the monks (which was later confirmed by a messenger). He recovered her body, and then he buried her in the tomb he had prepared for her.

What interested me the most about St. Scholastica was not the miracles but how God worked through her. On the surface she lived a fairly ordinary life in most respects. No great human achievements are recorded of her. She was humble. She relied upon God to hear her prayers.

This makes me think of Jesus. Yes, we focus on his divinity, but we should not forget he lived an ordinary life. Although his birth was extraordinary, we are told that he was a carpenter and a layman with no formal education. The last three years of his life, he was a traveling preacher and healer. He had no official status, no formal role in the power structures, and yet his life of thirty-three years has changed the world.

A lesson I am learning is that truly humble people, although they are saintly to us, believe they, in themselves, to be in essence fallible, ordinary people. They are unaware they have a deep spirituality.

You said in your last letter that you will share with me how we discover new images of God. Please share!

Peace,

Joey

Response to Letter #40
February 21, 2014

Dear Joey,

You mentioned that St. Benedict did not want to break a monastery rule by spending the night outside of the monastery. That is a good example of the practice of first half of life spirituality. When we follow all the rules we may miss hearing the Holy Spirit encouraging us to break the rules for a higher good.

How we discover new images of God

I mentioned in my last letter to you that I wanted to share with you how we discover new images of God. In an earlier letter, I shared with you that experiencing Katherine Kuhlman's Methodist healing service, dialoguing with Mormon missionaries, and friendship with Promise Keepers of all denominations were the means whereby I discovered a new image of God; an Inclusive God.

When we practice first half of life spirituality, we learn about God through what our parents, clergy, teachers, and society at large tell us about God. We know about God through what we learn about the life of Jesus. We are taught to look for glimpses of the qualities of God in the lives of the saints who were remarkably courageous, merciful, just, empathetic, and forgiving. We learn about God in the historical characters, such as Peter and Paul, recounted in the Bible. All these opportunities to know God are important, yet they are not the end of the journey. As I explained to you in earlier letters, most of us in the first half of life are constrained by images of God as (1) distant, (2) exclusive, (3) vengeful, (4) preoccupied with sex, (5) demanding perfection, and (6) exclusively male.

When we practice second half of life spirituality, we look beyond the normal teachers and discover through life experiences new images of God. We discover glimpses of God, qualities of God, new images of God, in today's world, in everyone, and in every thing. We conclude that the sacred is present everywhere and in all times. We become aware that new images of God are often discovered in surprising ways that strike us as epiphanies. If we only look to find God in holy places and in saintly people, we risk missing seeing God in everyday life. Every day, every moment, God may appear to us in disguises through which we can discover the God who is (1) incarnate, (2) inclusive, (3) just, (4) merciful, (5) courageous, (6) empathetic, etc.

The great Greek philosopher, Heraclitus, who was active around 500 BCE, said, "Unless you expect the unexpected, you will never find truth." Let me give some illustrations of how we become aware of new images, qualities, and glimpses of God in ordinary situations.

Movies:

Watching movies may be occasions when we become aware of new images of God in characters whom we would least expect.

In the film, Gone with the Wind, the two stars, of course, were Rhett Butler and Scarlet O'Hara. But there was a woman in the film, Belle Watling, a prostitute who owned a brothel. She, paradoxically, was the one Rhett found to be wise, compassionate, and sensitive to his needs and the needs of others. Rhett was seeing in her a glimpse, quality, an image of a Merciful and Compassionate God.

In the film, Titanic, Rose, a wealthy young passenger, was engaged to Cal, a well-to-do elitist snob. Early in the ship's ocean voyage, Rose met another passenger, a young man named Jack Dawson. He had no money and little formal education. And yet Jack was the one who had real character, integrity and courage, not Cal who was so privileged. Rose was seeing in Jack a glimpse, quality, and image of a Courageous God.

Elad:

In ordinary everyday experiences, we need to be conscious of God's presence found in disguises. I'll share with you an epiphany experience I had that made me conscious of an Inclusive God. The "disguise" was a hitchhiker named Elad who radiated God's inclusive love for all children of the one true God.

About twenty years ago, I drove my car to Apalachicola, Florida, to meet, Jacob, my good friend with whom I was going to enjoy a few days of vacation. On the way to Apalachicola, located in the Florida Panhandle, I drove through many rural counties seeing few cars. Ahead on the right side of the road, I saw a man hitchhiking. Even in those earlier more innocent days, I never picked up hitchhikers, but just as I went by, I glanced at the man and a ray sunlight hit his face in such a way that I sensed that he was a good man. He had a beautiful smile. His teeth were white. His skin was dark in color. He had a black beard. His hair was thick and black. I turned the car around and stopped my car as I pulled up beside him. I asked him where he was going. He said, "to the Pacific."

I told him I could take him as far as Apalachicola. So we traveled for a couple of hours in the car together. He had a strong body odor. He shared his life story with me. He was twenty-eight years old. He was born and raised in Israel. His name was Elad, and he had been on the road for two months in this country. He told me, "the goal is the journey, not the destination." As he hitchhiked, he told me that he blessed cars that would not stop to pick him up. He had a deep interest in Christianity.

He shared with me that he was taking time in this chapter of his life to travel, to meet new people, to learn about our culture, and to learn about the meaning of life. He was a law student in Israel. He had also attended an International University in England. When I told him I was a priest, he shared his continuing journey to find God. He had been to India several times looking into the eastern religions. He dated a girl who was a Christian from New Zealand, but she was not a practicing Christian. He even took some courses on the New Testament. He was looking for proof that there really was the compassionate Jesus he read about in the New Testament. His Jewish tradition somehow was not meeting all his needs and answering all his questions, so he was willing to take some time to ask questions and search.

We stopped for lunch in a small town in the Panhandle, and while Elad was in the restroom, the waitress wanted to know who he was and why he was with me. I could tell that he was unacceptable in this small town.

What happened to me was unforgettable. Though I of course knew that I was speaking presently with a young man, named Elad, at the same time I had a profound and undeniable sense that I was catching a glimpse, in a most uncanny and mysterious way, of Jesus himself. I clearly saw Jesus in this man who reminded me of Jesus' love for all God's children. His ascetical look, his physical features which made him look like the archetypal Jesus, his Jewish background, all contributed to a bonding that took place between us. Together we discussed how we were brothers with the same God. Here we were, a wandering Jew (literally!), and a Catholic priest talking about the deepest questions of life, and we had never met before. I felt as though, on some elementary level, I had known him all my life. I sensed that I was living out the Emmaus story in Luke's gospel.

When we arrived at a cabin near Apalachicola, my friend Jacob welcomed us both. After short introductions, Jacob suggested that we all take a walk on a nearby beach. Jacob soon recognized Elad's many gifts, so we all talked at great length together. As late afternoon was approaching, and apparently his departure was imminent, Elad suggested that we conclude our time together with a ritual. Elad took a coconut out of his backpack. Together we drank from it on the beach. Then he broke the coconut into small parts, and he gave us coconut flesh to eat. I had tears in my eyes when the obvious parallels to the Last Supper became manifest. We even fed some of the coconut flesh to the many seagulls that began to circle about. Following the ritual of celebration, we hugged, we prayed, and then Elad went on his way seeking another opportunity to discover God and our culture.

Meeting Elad was an experience that made me aware, in this traveling Jew, of an Inclusive God who blesses Jews as well as Gentiles with virtues that are extraordinary. He made me realize that saints like Francis of Assisi are surprisingly still among us giving us glimpses of God's inclusivity for all God's children.

In my next letter to you, I will share with you two more images of God; an Unconditionally Loving God and a Patient God.

Peace,

Uncle Matthew

Letter #41
Wednesday, March 5, 2014


Dear Uncle Matthew,

I liked your story about Elad who gave you a glimpse of an Inclusive God who loves all God's children. Do you think you will ever hear from him? I also liked your use of movies to point out that glimpses of God can appear in disguises in the least likely of characters. Thank you! I see I've got a lot of Netflix watching when visiting with mom and dad! All these new images of God and the stories you have shared in the practice of second half of life spirituality have opened my mind and excited me about discovering them in my own life.

Today is Ash Wednesday. Pope Francis said yesterday, "Lent is a good time for sacrificing. Let us deny ourselves something every day to help others." I suppose he means we should practice the corporal works of mercy: feeding the hungry, giving drink to the thirsty, clothing the naked, sheltering the homeless, visiting the sick, and burying the dead. Pope Francis said recently, "The ministers of the church must be, above all, ministers of mercy." Those words really hit me hard and got me thinking.

It is so easy in the seminary to simply learn knowledge contained in books and shared in lecture halls, while missing the real life opportunities to minister to those in immediate need. However, my education should provide me with valuable tools for doing spiritual works of mercy, teaching the ignorant, counseling the doubtful, forgiving offenses, and comforting the sorrowful.

The corporal works of mercy and the spiritual works of mercy help us to turn our whole heart over to God. Pope Francis seems to be saying exactly what you have been telling me; namely, the practice of second half of life spirituality is focused more on helping others than it is on the pursuit of one's own perfection or simply adhering to the letter of the law.

I look forward to hearing about images of an Unconditionally Loving God and a Patient God.

Peace,

Joey

Response to Letter #41,
Wednesday, March 19, 2014


Dear Joey,

Today is the Feast of St. Joseph. I was baptized on this day. I always try to ritualize the day of my baptism since I do believe that the Sacrament of Baptism is even more important than the Sacrament of Holy Orders. My baptism makes me aware of my true identity, a child of God. Over the years, we can very easily forget our true identity. We need to be reminded over and over again that we are children of God.

I'm glad you liked the story about Elad. My friend, Jacob, told me that Elad was taking a big risk hitchhiking in the rural areas of NW Florida. I hope he made it to the Pacific coast, but I doubt if I will ever hear from him. Brief friendships remind us of the gratitude we need to have when we are awakened to new glimpses of God in very ordinary situations.

Last November, Pope Francis released his encyclical letter, Evangelii Gaudium, The Joy of the Gospel. In writing this encyclical letter, we can tell that Pope Francis was inspired by Jesus' poverty and concern for the dispossessed during his earthly ministry. In his encyclical, Pope Francis calls for a "Church which is poor and for the poor." The poor "have much to teach us." He writes, "We are called to find Christ in them, to lend our voices to their causes, but also to be their friends, to listen to them, to speak for them, and to embrace the mysterious wisdom which God wishes to share with us through them."

Let me share with you, Joey, two more images of God; an Unconditionally Loving God and a Patient God.

#11  An Unconditionally Loving God:

(1.). Jesus:

Jesus is the exemplar of Unconditional Love. Throughout the gospels we have a record of his words and actions that indicate his unconditional love for all those he encountered. That means we are to love the young and the old, the rich and the poor, the Republicans and the Democrats, the good and the bad. That is seemingly an impossible task!

How can we love everyone? How can we love people who are so different from ourselves? The answer is found in continually being aware of an Unconditionally Loving God who loves all of us and then serving as an instrument of this love in our lives.

(2.). Maurice:

My first experience when I discovered an image of an Unconditionally Loving God took place a year after I was ordained a priest. It was the month of June and I was on hospital duty one night when a nurse called the rectory from the local hospital and said, "Please come to the emergency room. A young man was in a bad automobile accident."

When I arrived at the emergency room, I discovered the patient's name was Maurice. Earlier that day, I had gone to the same hospital to visit the sick, and Maurice and I got on the elevator in the lobby. He had graduated a year earlier from the local Catholic high school where I was teaching. He and I went up to the fourth floor. He visited his grandmother, and I visited some sick parishioners. After I made the sick calls, I went to the elevator, and there was Maurice. On the first floor, the elevator doors opened. We stepped out, and again exchanged pleasantries and went our separate ways.

That night, the doctor and I watched Maurice die in the emergency room at 11:59 PM. This was the first time that I was actually present when someone took their last breath. As I watched him struggling to breathe, I could see his gift of life fading.

As Maurice was dying, I was deeply conscious of my own deep love for Maurice even though I had just met him in passing earlier that day. If I could experience this deep love for Maurice in his brokenness, and I hardly knew him, what about the God who created him?

Today, I have a picture of Maurice on my prayer table to remind me he opened my eyes to believe in an Unconditionally Loving God.

(3.). AIDS

Later in my priesthood, I served as diocesan vocations' director. One of the seminarians was named Jack who was outgoing, cheerful, and charismatic, but he was not academically achieving up to his potential. He risked being expelled, so the bishop granted me permission to let him live in my rectory and attend a local college so as to build up his grade point-average.

Jack attended the local college. We discovered that he was undisciplined and his grades continued to be poor. After nine months of living in the rectory, the two priests with me agreed that we needed to dismiss him as a candidate for the priesthood. The bishop agreed with our discernment, so I had to tell Jack to leave. He vented all his anger on me when he left. He considered me his enemy, and his mistreatment of me made him seem like my enemy.

I had to make a decision to love my enemy or carry anger in my heart. I choose to love Jack. To express my love, I sent Jack birthday cards and Christmas cards for many years to his hometown address, but I never heard from him until one winter night, ten year later. He called to tell me that he was dying. He had contracted AIDS while serving in the military. He wanted me to be the presider at his funeral in his hometown.

Before Jack died, I spoke to him and his partner several times on the telephone. Jack told me that a conservative religious group had told him that if he wanted to be saved, he had to repent of his sins and give up his partner. Jack did repent of his sins. I suggested that he not separate himself from his partner who was taking care of his most basic needs, feeding him, bathing him, and comforting him. Jack did live a chaste life until he died at the age of thirty-four.

The night before Jack's funeral, I had a powerful dream in which Jack was embraced by an Unconditionally Loving God. I had no doubt that God loved Jack and accepted him as he was. This dream was an important stepping stone in helping me to believe in an Unconditionally Loving God.

At the funeral, Jack's dad would not enter the church. He remained outside. His angry brother sat in the front row with his arms folded. Jack's own family members were embarrassed by his death from AIDS since the family was well-known in this small southern town. They had not forgiven Jack, so they were unhappy, confused, angry, and unable to love him.

After the funeral, I cried and cried. My tears were indications of my own unconditional love for Jack. I remembered his humor, goodness, and interests in so many things other than studying. He had helped me in many ways to be a better person, a better priest. I felt so sorry that his own family members missed seeing what I saw, a good young man who tragically contracted a horrible virus.

Jack's death was an important experience that helped me to discover that a willingness to love our enemy is the key to inner peace and happiness. I also realized the importance of giving up images of a Vengeful God and a God Demanding Perfection. These images allow us to hold on to grudges, anger, and a desire for punishment because we feel justified when we think God does the same. When we believe in an Unconditionally Loving God, we realize God can only love.

(4.) Eric:

When returning from Jack's funeral, I met a college student named Eric at the airport. We were assigned to sit together on the flight. Eric was twenty-one years old in his third year of college. He shared his story with me since I was wearing my clerical clothing. He no longer attended the Catholic Church, although he was a baptized Catholic. He had never received the sacraments of First Reconciliation or Confirmation. He said that he wore all the right clothes so as to "have the girls." He told me, without regret or shame, that he had been intimate with more than a dozen women.

But in the course of the conversation, something happened. He shared with me that his heart was restless and that he was unhappy. I had noticed that his eyes lacked the glow of a happy person. St. Augustine said in his Confessions, "You have made us for yourself, O Lord, and our heart is restless until it rests in you." I realized that Eric was becoming aware that God loved him and blessed him with extraordinary gifts. God had planted in his heart a desire to be in union with Him. With a contrite heart, he shared with me his desire to change. He wanted to become a model for others. He said he was a believer in social justice. He believed in helping the poor. He realized he had too many material possessions.

I share this story with you because as he shared with me, I could sense that he was becoming aware of who he was, a child of God, a man created to love. As I listened to his story of an admittedly checkered past, I felt as though I was looking into his soul and thus able to see his awareness of God's unconditional love for him. I have often thanked God for that experience that helped me once again to believe in an Unconditionally Loving God. What are the odds of being assigned to sit together on that flight?

(5.). Tommy:

Let me share with you one more story about Tommy. His mother, Veronica, awakened me to an image of an Unconditionally Loving God. I was in a Sport's Bar on a Sunday afternoon with a friend and a young man named Tommy was there with some friends. I said hello to Tommy as he was leaving the restaurant. I knew his family, and I knew that he no longer attended Mass. I heard a couple of days later that he had accidentally over-dosed at his girl friend's apartment on Oxycodone.

Tommy was in a coma in the intensive care unit of the hospital where I visited him several times. When I last saw Tommy alive, shortly before he died, he was in a private room. As I was leaving the room, I looked at Tommy for the last time when I saw something that convinced me that Tommy was deeply loved by an Unconditionally Loving God. His mother, Veronica, was stroking his head as she cradled him in her arms. Although he never came out of his coma, he seemed aware and desirous of her touch. Veronica exuded unconditional love for her son. I was struck by their resemblance to Michelangelo's famous sculpture of the Pieta which beautifully reveals the intense love of Jesus' mother, Mary, as she cradles her son after his crucifixion. Tommy's face appeared to me to be the face of Jesus and Veronica strikingly appeared to be Mary. I still well up in tears thinking about that glimpse I had of Tommy who died shortly thereafter at the age of twenty-two.

In my parish, we once had a mission conducted by Matt, Dennis, and Sheila Linn, and I remember that one of them said, "God loves us at least as much as the person who loves us the most." But I didn't understand the importance of that insight until I met Veronica and her son, Tommy. Also every year on the Sunday after Easter, we celebrate Divine Mercy Sunday. St. Faustina, a Polish nun and mystic, said that the last hour of a person's life abounds with God's mercy and love. She said that if a dying person opens even slightly the door of his heart, God's merciful grace comes in and grants that person final grace.

The funeral liturgy was sad because we were losing a wonderful young man with great possibilities. I shall always be grateful for the rich opportunity to see Veronica's unconditional love for her son. Tommy's last hour on earth gave me a glimpse of God's Unconditional Love coming into the door of Tommy's heart. Through Veronica, I knew that Tommy was with his Unconditionally Loving God.

#12. A Patient God:

Joey, I have one more image of God that usually comes to us only when we grow older and are blessed with more time to think and reflect on life. We realize that God is so patient with us. Any one of us, with some reflection, can recall many times when we forgot God, and yet God loved us and gifted us even during times of our forgetfulness.

When we practice first half of life spirituality, we are taught that a mortal sin takes away grace. When we do something seriously wrong, we are told that God abandons us. If our parents caught us in a sexual act while we were adolescents, we were most likely shamed, embarrassed, and punished rather than corrected in a nurturing way. We easily thought if our parents were so upset, so must God be upset with us and ready to punish us.

Self-acceptance is a gradual process. Accepting the fact that we act in good and bad ways takes a certain degree of humility. Many of our struggles are rooted in the fact that we are embodied, sexual beings full of desires, wants, and fears. When we practice first half of life spirituality, we dualistically think we must be all good with no traces of evil. We want to be perfect, God-like. Only with time do we realize that we must accept ourselves as we are, not as we wish we were. An awareness of a Patient God can be the key to self-acceptance.

Marjoe:

Many years ago, I watched the documentary film, Marjoe. It won the 1972 Academy Award for Best Documentary Feature. Marjoe was a talented child preacher, and his parents earned large sums of money off of him. When Marjoe grew older, his ministry became solely a means of earning a living. He was no longer a believer in God. And yet the videos from genuine revival meetings showed that God was still working through Marjoe. God was patient with Marjoe.

The film Marjoe serves as a paradigm. If we become aware that God can work though someone who is not a believer and be patient with someone who uses religion for one's own gain, we can come to believe that God is patient with us when we continually miss the mark by our sins. As we begin to believe in God that we can love instead of fear, we are actually less prone to sin. Fear motivates us only for a short time to do good deeds and avoid evil. Love motivates us to the inner core of who we are.

The second largest grouping of Christians in this country is former Catholics. When we practice first half of life spirituality, there is a tendency to believe that those who left the Church have "hurt God" when they stopped practicing their faith. When we practice second half of life spirituality, we believe that God is patient and that people are doing the best they can. We can't judge. We too must be patient when our loved ones do not act the way we would wish. We never know what God is doing through another person, whether that person is a regular church attendee or not.

As I mentioned above, self-knowledge is linked to discovering an image of a Patient God. To the extent that we are aware of our own sinfulness, we can be patient with others. Thus, paradoxically, our sins can be the means God uses to reveal to us an image of a Patient God.

Conclusion on newer images of God:

I have tried to share with you in my letters twelve images of God that you may experience and come to know when you practice second half of life spirituality. Most of these images of God reflect human qualities that are expanded beyond normal human capacities. We are taught to know God through these images. For example traditionally we were taught that God is Omnipotent whereas humans do not know all things. We were taught that God is Omniscient whereas humans are bound by space and natural laws. We were taught that God is immortal whereas human life is finite.

But even if you have personal experiences that validate these images of God, you need to be mindful of what the mystics of every religious tradition have warned against; simply idolatry, but more generally thinking that any image of God fully captures the fullness and reality of God. As human beings, we need images of God to relate to God, but we should humbly remember that the images are not the same as the fullness of the reality behind it. Mysticism assumes that we are capable of discovering God in the depths of our own being. One person's image of God may not be the image of God for another person. This counters idolatry.

The mystics remind us that when we try to describe God, we are entering into mystery. The mystics stress contemplative prayer through which they believe all of us can meet God.

There is the danger that our images of God do not really reveal God, but our own yearnings. Sometimes our images of God that we held on to for so long die. For example an image of a Distant God seems to diminish with the practice second half of life spirituality.

The mystics are not dualistic so they stress both going deep inside to find God and also going out of ourselves to find God. When we practice second half of life spirituality, we take seriously the words in 1 John, "... God is love." God is encountered in all that we love. Friends, children, sunrises, dogs, and cats can all become epiphanies that reveal glimpses of God. Matthew Fox in his book Christian Mystics sums it up beautifully by saying "all love is a taste of the Divine…"

Twenty-five hundred years ago the Indian sage Siddhartha Gautama said, "Don't believe anything on the authority of your guru or priest. What you yourself feel is true, what you experience and see for yourself, what is helpful to you and others, in this alone believe, and with this alone align your behavior."

The assumption of perennial wisdom is that no god is God and that all the images we have of God fall short of the reality of God that can't be named.

In writing to you, I have noticed that all twelve images of God I have shared with you were originally encountered through experiences of prayer, suffering, and love that triggered a new awareness within.

1.  I discovered an image of an Incarnate God when I taught in my first high school assignment and became aware that my world-view was too narrow.

2.  I discovered an image of an Inclusive God when I heard Katherine Kuhlman preach, when I observed Basil's deep spirituality, when I joined the Promise Keepers, and when I met Elad, a wondering Jew.

3.  I discovered an image of a Just God when I was confronted with a situation in my high school assignment that forced me to face the evil of racism.

4.  I discovered an image of a Merciful and Compassionate God when I became aware of the compassion my dad had for my mother.

5.  I discovered an image of Our God when I became aware of

the new life that comes with love and prayer in a community environment.

6. I discovered an image of a Male/Female God when Sandra questioned.

7. I discovered an image of a Courageous God when I became aware of the many men and women in my own life who acted so courageously in following their conscience.

8. I discovered an image of an Empathetic God when I visited Haiti where the poor converted me.

9. I discovered an image of a God of Grace when I suffered a terrible injury while mountain climbing.

10. I discovered an image of a Forgiving God when Tim, a student, challenged me to forgive him and when I became aware of my deep longing for reconciliation with my former bishop.

11. I discovered an Unconditionally Loving God when I watched Maurice die, in a dream before Jack's funeral, Eric's discovery of who he was, and Veronica's unconditional love for her son Tommy.

12. I became aware of a Patient God through the documentary film, Marjoe, and in my old age when I became conscious of God's patience with me.

Meister Eckhart was the most famous and perhaps greatest German Dominican spiritual master. According to him, detachment means letting go of our images of God. According to the mystics, our images of God should continually change throughout life and lead us to an awareness of God as mystery. Eckhart said, "In letting go of God, we let God be God."

Peace,

Uncle Matthew

Letter #42
Wednesday, March 26, 2014

Dear Uncle Matthew,

In your last letter, I found the two images of an Unconditionally Loving God and a Patient God to be very helpful in examining my own life. At times I am impatient. I need to pray over these images of God since I still am holding onto images of a Conditionally Loving God and an Impatient God that I learned from my boyhood. I was very impressed how you were able to trace an awareness of these new images of God had their origin in personal experiences of love, suffering, conflict, and prayer. Your insight gives credence to the principle that suffering and conflict offer us not only trials but potential blessings.

Your letter made me aware that practicing first half of life spirituality when I am in my second half of life could make me a poor shepherd. For example, The Imitation of Christ, which advocates first half of life spirituality, tells us to avoid sinful people. The Pharisees followed this spirituality by avoiding sinners. They missed opportunities to be personally transformed and to minister effectively as good shepherds to the very people who needed it the most. They closed off themselves from experiences involving love, conflict, and suffering in contrast to Jesus who was involved in love, conflict, and suffering.

My Lenten practices are going well. My primary focus this Lent is simply to be open to change. I still tend to view reality in a rigid binary way that locks me into a position of seeing half the truth. Reflecting on your letters helps me to be aware of the process of becoming a more flexible person.

May I ask you a big question? I've been thinking a lot about Jesus. How does all this material relate to him? I presume, according to the paradigm of the two halves of life, he practiced second half of life spirituality when he reached adulthood. Can you elaborate your thoughts about Jesus' spirituality?

Peace,

Joey

Response to Letter #42
Sunday, April 6, 2014

Dear Joey,

Today is the Fifth Sunday of Lent. The beautiful story in today's Gospel (John 11:1-45) is about Jesus raising Lazarus from the dead. When we hear gospel stories each Sunday, it is so easy to listen to the stories and only hear them as historical events or orthodox lessons. But we must keep reminding ourselves that the Bible is the living Word of God. The challenge is to become aware of how the gospels, although in a different time and place, are now lived out in our own lives.

In an earlier letter to you, I mentioned that I was willing to give Tim, who was being expelled for selling marijuana, a second chance. Although this act was not as dramatic as Jesus with Lazarus, in a real sense Tim experienced being "raised from the dead." The story is a good example of the good news that we celebrate when the gospel is applied as the living Word of God.

Your question about Jesus' spirituality is a big one indeed! But yes, I shall be happy to share with you some thoughts about Jesus' spirituality based on the paradigm of the two halves of life spirituality.  From the commencement of his public ministry, Jesus seems to have practiced second half of life spirituality. I will share with you three areas of Jesus' life that indicate he practiced second half of life spirituality. First, the way Jesus directly ministered to others. Second, what Jesus taught. Third, who Jesus was as a person.

Jesus practiced second half of life spirituality:

1. The way Jesus directly ministered to others:

a. Jesus ministered beyond the Law:

The religion of Jesus' time was based on the Law, the Torah, the first five books of the Hebrew Scriptures. The law was not only the Ten Commandments but also many other rules and regulations found in the ritual purity and cleanliness codes. Jesus ministered in a way so as to give new life and understanding to the Law as indicated in his words, "The Sabbath was made for humankind, and not humankind for the Sabbath" (Mark 2:27). Jesus' ministry was based on an understanding that we do not live to serve the Law as an end in itself. Jesus felt justified breaking the Law whenever it would harm people. He saw that legalisms should not blind us to the bigger imperatives of love and compassion. Jesus said, "Do not think I have come to abolish the law or the prophets. I have come not to abolish but to fulfill" (Matthew 5:17). What mattered most to Jesus was eliminating the unnecessary suffering of others.

b. Jesus' deep inner convictions motivated him:

Central to Jesus' ministry was his profound strength of inner conviction. Jesus was not a priest but a layman. Jesus could and did minister to others without being controlled by the religious and civil authorities in his day. Jesus' strength of conviction sprang from his inner authority and direct awareness of God's indwelling presence.

c. Jesus ministered in a counter-cultural way:

We all know the desire to conform and to be accepted is a powerful human instinct. Just look at the fans at a home-coming football game! Remarkably, Jesus was not afraid to be counter-cultural and to receive the wrath of established leaders. Jesus did not minister in a way that made him like the religious leaders in his time. He felt free and courageous to preach and teach in a way that was at times counter to his day's institutional Judaism. He had a mature spirituality that enabled him to be self-confident and loyal to God regardless of the personal risks and cost to him. Jesus disassociated himself from ego-based rituals and sacrifices. Jesus saw that these shallow practices fed the false self. He urged us instead to love one another and to practice compassionate service to any and all.

We notice in history that prophets were not accepted by the power structures while they ministered to others. To the degree that we minister in a counter-cultural way, we probably won't be acceptable to many of the leaders in institutional religion. Ministering in a counter-cultural way makes it difficult for us, when we practice second half of life spirituality, to fit into many religious groups that are often built on a foundation that encourages only the practice of first half of life spirituality.

2. What Jesus taught:

a. Jesus witnessed what he taught:

In the Sermon on the Mount, Jesus not only preached this way of life, but he lived out the message that he preached. He practiced the Beatitudes that profoundly and poetically express the essence of second half of life spirituality. The Beatitudes call us to be peacemakers, merciful to others, meek, and poor in spirit.

Jesus practiced what he preached when he said, "Do to others whatever you would have them do to you" (Matthew 7:12). Jesus treated others the way he would have liked to have been treated. For example, Jesus washed the feet of his disciples. Jesus could always see the good in others. In the story of Zacchaeus the tax collector, Jesus called him down from a sycamore tree and told him that he would stay in his house. Jesus forgave others as was shown when he met the woman caught in adultery. The Sermon on the Mount was subversive to almost everything the religious leaders took for granted. He spoke of loving one's enemy, turning the other cheek, blessing those who curse us, and forgiving others seventy times seven times. Jesus said it is not the rich who are blessed or fortunate, but the poor.

b. Jesus encouraged questioning:

A willingness to wrestle with mystery is a sign of the practice of second half of life spirituality. I read in John Dear's book, The Questions of Jesus, that Jesus was asked in the four gospels 183 questions, but he directly answered just three of them. He did not answer people in the same terms of framing the question itself. He knew that to do so would typically reinforce prejudices or lock people into the rigid practice of first half of life spirituality. So, he often responded to a question with another question, or a story, metaphor, or a simple act. In these ways, he made people wrestle with the non-dualistic world of mystery and uncertainty.

c. The parables:

Jesus specifically used parables instead of straight logical discourse because he recognized they were effective to bring about true inner transformation on the part of his listeners. The parables he used illustrate truths about second half of life spirituality.

For example, in Chapter 15 of Luke's gospel, Jesus tells the story of the Prodigal Son. The elder son was loyal, obedient, and he felt entitled. He thought he was better than his younger brother. He was stuck in his practice of first half of life spirituality. He could not rejoice that his younger brother had returned to his father.

The younger brother was transitioning into the practice of second half of life spirituality. He was becoming aware of who he was. He was ready to change, to repent, and to seek forgiveness. He realized that his goals and objectives up to that point in his life had been selfish and had not worked. He was humble in his brokenness. Notice, Joey, how suffering and conflict were the catalysts for transformation in the younger brother. Suffering was like a new birth contributing to a new image of God when he met his dad who welcomed him home.

The parable of the Rich Young Man (Matthew 19) is not simply about giving up material possessions, but it is an invitation to move into the practice of second half of life spirituality by giving up one's ego possessions. The rich young man's obedience up to this point has been for self-gratification. Jesus was asking the rich young man to leave it all. Give so that he would get nothing back. Get rid of his quid pro quo thinking. Give up his sense of being better than others.

3. Jesus as a person:

a. Jesus lived his true self:

Jesus discovered his true self and he lived his true self. One of Jesus' image for the true self is clear vision and healthy eyes. This image brings the focus on one's own moral and spiritual health and not on judgment and competition with others. Jesus said,

"Remove the wooden beam from your eye first, then you will see clearly..." (Luke 6:42). "The lamp of your body is the eye. When your eye is sound, then your whole body is filled with light, but when it is bad, then your body is in darkness" (Luke 11:34).

Jesus was conscious of his fears, insecurities, and anxieties. Therefore when Satan, the trickster, tempted him in the desert, he refused to identify with false images of himself. He did not follow his ego, his false self, but rather his heart, his true self, his inner moral compass, which was telling him what to do and what to avoid.

Jesus showed signs of living his true self when he was moved with compassion for those in need of food, healing, and faith in the goodness of God, and he responded to those needs. His

Sermon on the Mount described a way of life that is built on living one's true self.

b. Jesus was a non-dualistic thinker:

Jesus lived in a world where most people were practicing first half of life spirituality which divided and separated individuals based on externals. Lepers lived with lepers. The rich associated with those who were rich. The educated associated with those who were educated. The religious leaders associated with the other religious leaders. Power and wealth were the easy basis of division.

In contrast, Jesus welcomed strangers, sinners, and those spiritually and physically wounded. He was a carpenter by trade, and yet he selected fishermen for his close friends. He practiced a deep spirituality, but he could relate to those who practiced a religion based on strictly obeying laws. He could show compassion to lepers although he was healthy. He could speak with ease to women although the law at times did not allow for males to speak to unknown women.

For Jesus, the way of seeing and living reflected God's ways on earth; "Your Heavenly Father makes his sun rise on the bad and the good, and causes rain to fall on the just and the unjust" (Matthew 5:45).

c. Jesus, a revolutionary:

To the religious leaders in his time, the historical Jesus looked dangerous, heretical, unorthodox, and even sinful because he associated with sinners. Various authors have described Jesus as a revolutionary, not a reformer. He was not patching up an old garment, but he was interested in a social revolution, supplanting Roman power with the love of God, based on a deep spiritual conversion.

d. Jesus' attributes:

In sum, Jesus manifested distinguishing attributes that indicate that he practiced second half of life spirituality. He was secure with few material possessions. He faced his problems instead of avoiding them. He could delay gratification. He knew himself by taking time to reflect upon his life's meaning and direction. He could relate to children as well as adults. Somehow every moment of Jesus' life was lived with a sense of purpose. He could accept failure. He had an understanding of and appreciation for the deeper mysteries of life. He avoided perfectionism. He preached with integrity. He was not dependent upon the affirmation of those who heard him speak. He could laugh as well as cry. He could associate with sinners, women, and those who were "holy." Courage enabled him to be fully human and fully alive.

Conclusion:

In his book, YES, AND, Fr. Richard Rohr says, "Jesus is the microcosm; Christ is the macrocosm." The Risen Jesus has become the Christ. This movement from the historical Jesus to the Christ is the path that we are called to follow. Jesus reached a holistic state of maturity, the Christ, the ideal, through his practice of second half of life spirituality.

Peace,

Uncle Matthew

Letter #43
Easter Sunday, April 20, 2014


Dear Uncle Matthew,

Thank you for your last letter that described Jesus' practice of
second half of life spirituality. I have never heard anyone present
Jesus in that fashion. The paradigm of the two halves of life
spirituality is brilliant. It opens up so many new insights. I'm
grateful to you, Uncle Matthew, for helping me to know and to
make real the historical Jesus.

Now I can see that the practice of first half of life spirituality
generally starts and ends with a literal reading of the scriptures.
The practice of second half of life spirituality is helping me to
understand and embrace the Bible that was written by humans,
inspired in different ways, over many centuries, affecting the way
Jesus is presented. In first half of life spirituality we don't
approach the scriptures as historical documents bound by the
culture, history, and religion of their day. You are helping me to
be conscious that the sacred authors wrote in many different
ways using various literary forms.

Last night at the Easter Vigil Mass and at today's Mass, I
appreciated the wonderful liturgy, but I kept trying to be aware of
Jesus' practice of second half of life spirituality expressed in his
virtues of unconditional love, compassion, mercy, and
forgiveness. I saw, like never before, that Jesus reflected in his

life clear and unmistakable images of God that we can discover in the practice of second half of life spirituality. He became like the God he adored.

I guess, Uncle Matthew, I get discouraged when I realize I can't seem to "get it together," and thus I am unlike Jesus in so many ways. There is a big gap between the person that I am now at the age of twenty-eight and the person whom I would like to be.

In earlier letters to you, I mentioned my difficulties living a chaste life. Certainly it has been slightly easier in the seminary to be chaste than it was in high school, college, and while living alone. Now, I have the most difficulty living chastely while I am in an unstructured environment such as while I am away at home, on a vacation, or when I am on a summer assignment.

In one letter to me, you shared about Fr. Tom who had learned some valuable insights about chastity. I need your help. Could you help me with some examples of individuals you know who have some insights in regard to living a chaste life? Thank you.

Peace,

Joey

Response to Letter #43
April 30, 2014

Dear Joey,

The topic of human sexuality, and chastity in particular, is complex. Rather than just quickly giving you some examples of some priests I know who have made different choices regarding living a chaste life, I would first like to give you some background. When I was studying in the seminary, we never explored directly this topic. I hope this background material will be helpful to you. Much of what I will share comes from my journal.

Introduction:

Joey, as a condition for ordination to the priesthood in the Roman Catholic Church, you must be celibate and strive to live perfect and perpetual chastity. Later in life, often as we age, we view our commitment to chastity differently than during our earlier years. Many priests realize that the sexual rules and beliefs they held during the first half of life have now become inadequate, immature, and incompatible with being fully human and fully alive. This changed perspective may develop slowly, or come suddenly, in bursts of insight, born of struggle.

I will try to share with you, Joey, a number of ideas regarding sexuality, beginning with some early Church history.

Church history:

As you know, synods and councils in the Church have occurred over the centuries that promulgated directives for the local and universal Church. In the fourth century at the Synod of Elvira in Spain, the bishops promulgated a requirement for celibacy for all clerics in Spain, married or not. At the same Synod, several canons related only to the behavior of women, such as Canon 67: "A woman who is baptized or is a catechumen must not associate with hairdressers or men with long hair..."

In the list of canonized saints, it is priests and martyrs that head the list, along with virgins and widows. It is difficult to find a married person with an ordinary marital life who has entered the ranks.

At the First Lateran Council (1123), canon 21 was promulgated, stating that, clerics in major orders could not marry, and marriages already contracted must be dissolved. The text reads,

"We absolutely forbid priests, deacons, subdeacons, and monks to have concubines or to contract marriage. We decree in accordance with the definitions of the sacred canons, that marriages already contracted by such persons must be dissolved, and that the persons be condemned to do penance."

With these decisions, emphasis was given to the belief at the time that celibacy was a "higher" way of life than marriage. In contrast to this view point, the practice of second half of life spirituality emphasizes the holiness of human sexuality, the goodness of creation, and the avoidance of the heresy of angelism; a theological concept which regards human beings as essentially angelic.

The Church's teaching:

As I pointed out to you earlier, the church's teachings are absolutist and dualistic on matters of sexuality. The Church teaches us that all sexual sins are considered to be serious and grave. Sexual moral doctrine is often stated in terms of right/wrong, good/bad, black/white. The church's doctrines are explicit about the full range of topics that it lumps together under the category of human sexuality: abortion, contraception, homosexuality, pre-marital sex, and masturbation. This black and white understanding of sexuality leaves very little room for dialogue, discernment, nuance, understanding, and wisdom.

Celibacy and chastity:

It is important to understand the difference between celibacy and chastity. Celibacy is generally understood as a state of non-marriage and abstinence from sexual activity. Celibacy can be a positive way of life that promotes holiness for exceptional persons who have integrated their sexuality often within a supportive community of fellow celibates. The Church lists many saints who were celibate whom we admire for their holiness.

Chastity according to the Catechism of the Catholic Church (#2337) "means the successful integration of sexuality within the person and thus the inner unity of man [woman] in his [her] bodily and spiritual being." The virtue of chastity involves the integrity of the person. All baptized persons are called to chastity.

During our earlier years of life, integrating our sexuality is a major concern. We discover that it is not by repression and denial that we will achieve the integration of our sexuality but through learning to accept who we are and being given the freedom to have various personal experiences. Through these reflections and experiences we develop a mature capacity for discernment as to how to live and express our sexuality.

The integration of our sexuality is made more difficult because the Catechism of the Catholic Church conflates and confuses a broad range of sexual acts that are lumped together. The Catechism lists several offenses against chastity: lust, masturbation, fornication, pornography, prostitution, rape, and homosexual acts. Successful integration demands mature discernment. Yet the effect of the Catechism is to make this mature discernment all the more difficult through wholesale rejection of any and all aspects of our sexuality outside of the narrow constraints of reproductive intercourse within marriage.

Concerning masturbation, the Catechism of the Catholic Church (#2352) says, "Both the Magisterium of the Church, in the course of a constant tradition, and the moral sense of the faithful have been in no doubt and have firmly maintained that masturbation is an intrinsically and gravely disordered action."

The practice of first half of life spirituality:

If someone is practicing first half of life spirituality, sexuality may seem to be separate from spirituality, even opposed to it. Sex is often viewed in a way that diminishes its potential holiness, or worse, presents it as exclusively in the realm of temptation and vice. Church teaching has often reinforced this view point. Some scholars believe that St. Paul was antagonistic to emotions in general and erotic ones in particular. Some people say that St. Paul tended to see anger, sexual desires, and erotic yearnings as evil. As is well known, his writings have had a profound effect on the development and direction of church teaching throughout history.

When practicing first half of life spirituality, we try to be in control by obeying all the rules. We tend to repress our emotions in accord with St. Paul's teachings. We believe in Original Sin with its connotations of sexual transmission. We equate nearly all expressions of human sexuality with sin creating untold conflicts and suffering for the many. When we fail to keep the church rules regarding chastity, we will experience depression, guilt, and a sense of failure. Integration of our sexuality is difficult because there is a tendency to be fearful of sex rather than to have a healthy interest in it. Secrecy and shame predominate rather than openness and honesty.

The practice of second half of life spirituality:

When we practice second half of life spirituality, we view our passions and sensual longing as gifts from God; as a life-force that is inseparable from the goodness of creation itself. If we remain open to the fullness of reality, then we are more open to information that comes from a full range of sources of human knowledge and understanding. This would include comparative religions, religious studies, the medical profession, the experiences of friends, and the insights of modern theologians, biology, sociology, psychology, physics, and spirituality. Also, our openness allows us to not necessarily stick with only Catholic opinions on the topic of human sexuality. We feel comfortable inquiring what people in other denominations are saying. This process is part of the ongoing formation of an informed conscience.

Some people begin to realize that the Church has set forth sexual norms of behavior that were developed in the ancient world, through late antiquity, to medieval times. They begin to question if at one time it was good to practice certain sexual norms, but whether it is good to practice these norms today.

In practicing second half of life spirituality, we desire first and foremost union with God and to live our lives as instruments of God's love. We desire toward these ends deep transformation. We realize that we can't be perfect. Nor do we want to be! We realize we are human! We realize that our goal, not perfection, is to "Be merciful, just as your Father is merciful" (Luke 6:36). We look to Jesus' parables for insights. Remember, Joey, in the Parable of the Pharisee and the Tax Collector, God was closer to the Tax Collector who was far from perfect and not the Pharisee who obeyed all the rules. We begin to understand what Fr. Richard Rohr meant when he said, "It is all about willingness not worthiness" that keeps us in union with God.

Statistics and psychological insights:

It is important to realize, Joey, that masturbation is not an isolated or rare practice, but rather is nearly universal among males. Alfred C. Kinsey, writing in 1948, in his book, Sexual

Behavior in the Human Male, said the highest incidence for masturbation among single males (in the population taken as a whole) lies between 16-20 years of age. Kinsey also said for most males of every social level, masturbation provides the chief source of sexual outlet in early adolescence.

Kinsey pointed out that millions of boys have lived in continual mental conflict over masturbation. For that matter, some young men, especially seminarians, still do. Many boys pass through a periodic succession of attempts to stop the habit, inevitable failures in those attempts, and consequent periods of remorse, the making of new resolutions, and a new start on the whole cycle. Kinsey remarked that it is difficult to imagine anything better calculated to do permanent damage to the personality of an individual.

Kinsey writes that one's attitude toward and practice of masturbation is significantly influenced by a person's religious background. In his study, he considered the religious practices and beliefs of Jews, Protestants, and Catholics and how they related to sexual behavior. Those who are less concerned about their religion masturbate more than those who are religiously active. From what I have observed, Joey, those who are religiously active feel more guilt after masturbating than those who are less concerned about their religion. He says that through most of its past history, the Protestant church as well as both Jewish and Catholic communities have been severe in their condemnation of what they call "self-abuse."

Psychologists tell us that experimentation is central to identity formation particularly as it relates to one's sexuality. Through masturbation, one can explore sexual needs and fantasies and establish a basic self-knowledge about one's sexual identity. Exploration can help a person understand their sexual longings, who and how they love, and where along the spectrum of heterosexuality or homosexuality they lie. Perhaps most importantly, masturbation can foster a sense of acceptance, even celebration of oneself, befriending rather than alienating a vital part of one's being. Stated humorously, some human behaviorists say that it is important to discover that we don't want an enemy living in our pants!

Images of God:

Joey, think about how our understanding of chastity applies to our discussion of images of God. A change in our images of God influences our views on the practice of chastity.

For example, if when practicing first half of life spirituality we have an image of a Distant God, we probably connect that with an image of a Judgmental God. If when practicing second half of life spirituality we have an image of an Incarnate God, we probably have an image of an Unconditionally Loving God. As God becomes more incarnate and less distant, through the blessings and goodness of the physical world, our image of God becomes less judgmental.

If when practicing first half of life spirituality we have an image of an Exclusive God, we believe that if we keep the rules of chastity, we will be closer to God; more special in God's eyes. We tend to measure our spiritual growth by our worthiness that we believe comes from living chastely.

If when practicing first half of life spirituality we have an image of God Preoccupied with Sex, it greatly affects our sexual behavior. We become preoccupied with sex like the image of the God we adore.

Insights:

So what are some observable insights when we reflect upon the complex topic of human sexuality from the viewpoint of second half of life spirituality?

1. Many priests who are my friends realized later in life that their celibate commitment was made under great pressure. The only way they could respond to a calling to priesthood was to accept the celibate state of life. Many older priests question whether or

not they ever received the charism of celibacy. They now believe that celibacy should never have been imposed when a candidate to the priesthood sensed a calling to the marital state.

2.  Celibacy can be an individual charism that is extraordinary. However, it does not mean that it is superior to an integrated sexual life. Celibacy from all that I have seen over the years, is, for most people, not healthy and much less possible.

3.  Many priests who are my friends realize now that the church's teaching on human sexuality is outdated, absolutist, dualistic, and largely not followed by the clergy or the laity. For example, they question whether it is spiritually and biologically sound to say that a celibate, in order to be strictly chaste, should not and must not ever masturbate. Is that a realistic or even desirable ideal?

4.  Many teens have no desire to attend mass or serve in the sanctuary because they are not living chaste lives. They are integrating and experimenting with their sexuality, so they don't feel comfortable in a Church that judges them to be in serious sin.

5.  All of us find it difficult to be chaste according to church teaching. It is made all the more difficult because of modern entertainment that constantly presents to us images of immodesty and unfaithfulness. We need God's help to live chaste lives. To live a life of chastity by just obeying all the church's rules and developing stronger will-power is impossible for most people.

6. As you know in today's developed world, there is an extended period of time between the onset of puberty and marriage. For environmental and dietary reasons, puberty is occurring at an earlier age, but for cultural reasons, marriage is generally being postponed to a later age. Principle among the reasons for delaying marriage is the increased time required to complete an education. For an increasing number of persons, it is common to pursue full-time education well into one's early or mid-twenties,

the very time period when sexual impulses are at a high intensity. The question arises as to whether cultural and moral norms can continue to insist that the only proper sexual outlet is inside marriage. This situation seems to create a basic and profound conflict for men and women with their core biological reality.

I have much more to share with you, Joey, on this important topic, but at a later time.

Peace,

Uncle Matthew

Letter #44
Sunday, May 11, 2014

Dear Uncle Matthew,

I very much appreciate all the work that went into your last letter to me regarding human sexuality. I liked Alfred Kinsey's insights on masturbation, a topic that is taboo in the seminary. I seem to be one of those young men Kinsey talks about who is in "mental conflict" over this "problem."

It was helpful the way you linked our images of God to our expression of human sexuality. You are making me aware that the practice of second half of life spirituality could change our morality regarding sexual actions.

I liked the six insights that you shared with me.

Insight #1 came as a surprise. I had heard that upon ordination to the priesthood, a candidate automatically receives the charism of celibacy if not already received. If what I heard is true, that never made any sense to me. How can the Church claim that God grants charisms based on our earthly actions? Seems a bit arrogant! To view the calling to priesthood as necessarily including this special charism seems to affirm a belief in an Exclusive God rather than an Inclusive God.

Insight #3 does not surprise me. Although I am still a young adult, my experiences so far do not support the church's teaching on masturbation that it is "an intrinsically and gravely disordered action." Church teaching says not to masturbate, but I am not so sure, as even my doctor says occasional masturbation has healthy physical and psychological effects. I trust my doctor in most matters related to my body.

My experiences do validate insight #4. Most of my friends in high school and college never went to Sunday mass partially because they were experimenting with women and partying.

And I wholly agree with insight #5. In my efforts to be chaste in the seminary, will power alone is often not enough.

As always, your letters give me much upon which to reflect, and much moral support for the path of integrity.

Today is Mothers' Day. I called my mother earlier. She and my father are doing well. Have you spoken with them lately? Paul also called mom.

Our exams begin tomorrow. I will leave here on May 18 for some vacation time before my summer assignment.

Please continue with the over-view that you are giving me on chastity.

Peace,

Joey

Response to Letter #44
Saturday, May 24, 2014

Dear Joey,

I'm glad that you are open to discussing human sexuality and that you are aware of this sacred part of you. Later, you will discover new challenges when you publicly promise to live a celibate and chaste life as a priest.

I did not forget that in a letter to me last month you mentioned that when you are away from the seminary, your sexual urges increase. We all have a sexual appetites not unlike our hunger for food and our thirst for drink. This is normal. Most of us find that our sexual urges are stronger at different times, and in different places, and in different circumstances.

I believe the more important question, once we assume the naturalness and goodness of human sexuality, is to ask, "How can I best respond to my sexual urges?"

Sexuality is an integral part of life:

Let's begin with the assumption that sex is an integral part of life. Former monk-priest and sociologist Richard Sipe in his book, Living the Celibate Life, says the sexual drive, with its feelings, desires, and responses, is a fundamental part of being human. Each person has to assume personal responsibility in the struggle to be chaste. Neither I nor anyone else can show you, Joey, what will be your personal way of being chaste. To progress in living a chaste life, you have to continually work to discover your identity and complex nature, determining how to accept, embrace, and express your true self.

A documentary movie illustrates this reality:

Previously, I mentioned how movies may show a slice of reality that includes human sexuality. Movies show us that we humans make many different choices in expressing our sexuality. Movies allow us to vicariously see, experience, and reflect on human sexuality.

For example, in January, at the Sundance Film Festival, the film, Boyhood was shown. The reviews are good and it will be released in July in theaters across the country. I read that the movie traces the growth of a boy, Mason, during the course of a period of time from 2002-2013. Mason grew up in Texas with divorced parents. The movie traces his development from the age of six to eighteen. By his fifteenth birthday, Mason had experimented with marijuana and alcohol. In his senior year of high school, he was caught sleeping with his girlfriend. In his freshmen year of college, he experimented with drugs. The movie is likely to receive some Academy Award nominations.

This movie and other similar movies about adolescents very well show that the church's ideal of being chaste is not an ideal shared by many young people today. This has clear relevance for your ministry.

Sexuality and the danger of repression:

When we practice first half of life spirituality, we are told to simply repress our sexual appetite. We simply accept without question an outside authority. In your case, the church authorities will tell you not to masturbate. They say it is absolutely wrong.

When we transition into the practice of second half of life

spirituality, we begin to ask questions. We wonder if it really is wrong to masturbate. We listen to the Spirit inside of us. We ask, "What is the Spirit saying?" Some celibates who practice second half of life spirituality may question whether the repression of their sexual nature actually serves to heighten sexual appetites in the most unexpected and unwanted ways, including the widespread phenomenon of the viewing of pornography. Episcopal Bishop John S. Spong says in his book Why Christianity Must Change or Die:

"Any repression of our humanity can never be a doorway into life. The repression of sexual energy, for example, which marked traditional ethics for so long, did not lead to the fullness of life. It only created a backlash of an uninhibited exercise of sexual energy, which was also destructive to our essential humanity... When the value of human sexuality is repressed, it returns as pornography."

Sexuality and the danger of isolation:

I have discovered, Joey, that the call, or command, for priests to be celibate is part of a system that often serves to socially isolate the individual priest. Everything from clerical dress, to living arrangements, to honorary titles, to solitary prayer disciplines can serve to set apart, to alienate, the singular priest from deep impassioned relationships with fellow human beings that make possible healthy chastity. This alienation from others, a result of social and institutional structures, often goes hand in hand with alienation from oneself, a result of trying to deny and resist vital elements of one's being. This outward and inward isolation may increasingly be felt as an anxiety and conflict that are preventing the priest from fully pursuing the abundance of life that Jesus promised when he said in John's gospel, "I came so that they might have life and have it more abundantly."

Sexuality and the importance of integration:

Psychologists today believe that the ability to be chaste, and to be so in a healthy manner, has much to do with the formation of one's whole personality. Remember, the Catechism wisely said that chastity means the "successful integration of sexuality within the person." Many priests who were ordained before the Vatican II Council went through a seminary formation program that was closed, legalistic, rigid, and suppressive. These men were given little to no room for curiosity, developmental experiences, and experimentation in the area of human sexuality. They had to repress many thoughts, behaviors, and words that were not allowed and which were presented as matters of greatest importance upon which, literally, the fate of their souls rested. Fear of sex, rather than a healthy interest in it, predominated. Secrecy and shame were present rather than openness and honesty.

As a consequence, many of these seminarians were prone to developing an intense and massive "shadow." The shadow in psychological parlance is the opposite of the "persona." The persona is what we allow people to see. The word "persona" means "mask." It is the face we present to the world. Naturally, we want people to see our good qualities whereas the shadow is that part of our personality that we don't want people to see; the unwanted side of our personality. The shadow has energy patterns that are repressed but not destroyed. Without integrating our shadow, we cannot be whole. Integrating the shadow means to be conscious, accepting, and willing to acknowledge it as a part of self. Somehow we have to subordinate our shadow to our larger personality so that it doesn't control us.

As a seminarian, you are expected to be loving, forgiving, and sexually chaste. In trying to conform to this ideal, you are rejecting the part of yourself that gets angry, is vindictive, and has uncontrolled sexual urges. When we can integrate the shadow, it is easier to be chaste. A larger shadow increases the difficulty for being chaste whereby molehills become mountains.

I don't want to presume I can answer all your questions so I suggest that you attempt to do some journaling. Write down your questions and attempt to give your own answers. Rely on your insights. Believe God is within you to help you to discern with the help of the Spirit's gifts of Knowledge and Wisdom.

The blessings of workshops:

I want to suggest that workshops can be helpful to you in the future to deal with your sexuality. Earlier in my own life, Joey, I attended some workshops that helped me to understand that different individuals form different sexual identities and practices as part of their process of forming their conscience.

As for example, I attended a Fr. Richard Rohr men's retreat in Glorieta, New Mexico where Richard conducted a male initiation rite to help the participants to become aware of and integrate an adult spirituality. The initiation rite, beautifully constructed and performed, enabled all of us to appreciate the sacredness of human sexuality. The rite helped to replace whatever toxic shame and guilt we may have been carrying with a deeper appreciation and gratitude for our bodies, our sexuality, and the gift of genuine community.

As another example, I attended a Vincent Bilotta Workshop in Attleboro, MA. This workshop was mainly for priests, but several participants were laymen. Once more, I discovered that all the men who shared their sexual histories struggled with questions and conflicts about how to be true to themselves and God as embodied and sexual beings. After I heard the stories of these men, I felt a great love for them and the integrity they brought to their struggles. They were willing to be open, honest, and vulnerable seeking the truth in all things. Their sexual orientation seemed of secondary importance relative to these virtues. I learned that having a soul friend is vital for genuine spiritual growth. Spiritual directors tell us that trusted friends are often necessary to help us discover our shadow-side and our true self.

Conclusion:

It is my observation, in nearly fifty years as a priest, that the vast majority of seminarians and priests are struggling with sexual issues that could be fruitfully explored and engaged at professional conferences, retreats, and workshops. Yet, many priests claim that rarely do diocesan-sponsored retreats or convocations deal with human sexuality. Perhaps one reason for few if any diocesan-sponsored workshops on sexuality stems from the vetting process in many dioceses. Speakers who are vetted by bishops are fearful of saying anything that would not be acceptable to those who practice first half of life spirituality. As a result the topic of human sexuality is typically neglected, serving to further repress a very large issue within the hearts and minds of priests.

Although a full understanding of human sexuality cannot be taught, insights from books and articles can be helpful to you, Joey, in the process of living a chaste life. We are helped so much when we read about men and women who were models of chaste living. Richard Sipe has offered many suggestions in his books on how to live a celibate and chaste life. In his book, Living the Celibate Life, he says, "In my experience there are ten elements that support celibacy: work, prayer, community, service, proper attention to physical needs, balance, security, order, learning, and beauty."

I hope, Joey, this background material on sexuality and chastity is helpful before I give you real life examples. I still want to share more background material with you at another time.

Peace,

Uncle Matthew

Letter #45
Sunday, June 8, 2014

Dear Uncle Matthew,

I look forward to seeing the film Boyhood this summer. From what you said, Mason's growth in the documentary resonates with my observations in many of my peers.

You mentioned the dangers of isolation and repression and the goal of integrating the shadow. I find it difficult not to repress the shadow side of my personality at times since I am being judged each year as to whether I am a fit candidate for the priesthood. I experience at times secrecy and shame that increases my anxiety and indicates I have soul work to do to integrate my shadow in a healthy way.

The new questions you raised give me some anxiety, but I guess you are sharing reality with me. I hope someday to attend workshops on human sexuality.

After exams, I went home. Mom, dad, and I attended Paul's graduation from college that brought back many memories of when I graduated six years earlier. He also graduated with a degree in electrical engineering. He was offered a position with the National Security Agency, and he accepted. Paul and I are leaving tomorrow for the Smoky Mountains for a week. We will camp in the Elkmont Campground and hike together. I'm looking forward to the time with him. Although we are five years apart in age, we have always been close. My summer assignment begins June 23.

We went to our local parish for mass today to celebrate Pentecost Sunday. The pastor gave a good pastoral homily. He pointed out that we all know individuals in this parish who are suffering from serious health problems. Many of them are able to persevere along the road of recovery. Some of them have had major operations and yet they were able to bounce back. He said that what we are seeing is the blessings of community and an outpouring of the Holy Spirit. The Holy Spirit, working through us as members of a community of believers, gives us courage, patience, and fortitude.

Our pastor seems to be compassionate and kind; marks of the practice of second half of life spirituality. Please continue to share with me more about human sexuality and chastity. I am so grateful.

Peace,

Joey

Response to Letter #45
Saturday, June 21st, 2014

Dear Joey,

Earlier this month, I read in the New York Times that Pope Francis fired the entire board of the Vatican's Financial Information Authority. This board supervises everything from the Vatican Bank to the real estate of the Holy See. The pope seems adamant about transparency and accountability.

Summer begins today. Your summer assignment begins on Monday. I'm glad you were able to attend Paul's graduation and then to go camping with him.

Since you are both very close, have you ever thought of sharing with him your thoughts on chastity and human sexuality? Sometimes, when we realize that our closest friends struggle with the same issues, we get valuable insights. In the seminary, some seminarians share in a confidential way their problems with their spiritual director, but he cannot share his problems with them. Most seminaries discourage seminarians from sharing their sexuality with other seminarians. Unfortunately, refraining from dialogue can isolate you and lead to further repression of your emotions. You can easily think that you are alone in your struggles. Isolation is destructive, but dialoguing rewards us with an awareness of reality. We are the Body of Christ. Dialogue, openness, and honesty allow the Holy Spirit to work. Don't ever forget, "We are as sick as our secrets."

Warnings:

The purpose of this background material, Joey, is to warn you that the path of celibacy is extremely difficult, and I believe quite dangerous. I am so proud of you as you study for the priesthood, but at the same time as your uncle, I want you to be well prepared for the priestly vocation. I want to reiterate that I am not attempting to teach morality or doctrine in my letters to you. I am only trying to help you, by presenting the following warnings, to be aware of the bigger picture so that you make mature decisions.

1.   You should try to be aware of the sources of your guilt and shame that produce anxiety.

Awareness is the beginning of transformation. The minor order ceremonies (lector and acolyte) use rituals that include albs, special prayers, holy water, candles, stoles, cassocks, and oils. These special church rites separate you from ordinary men. Do these church rites only increase the mystique that some men, with the help of holy signs and symbols, are empowered to do something that most men cannot do? When any ideal is so difficult to reach and it is embraced with sacred signs and symbols, failure in reaching the ideal can produce terrible guilt and shame.

The Catholic Church's teachings on chastity and celibacy can make you feel guilty that you have a sex drive. You can easily get the impression that the Catholic Church wants you to be asexual, a denial of who you are; a denial of your dignity as a man. Normal men your age have a healthy sex drive and they are tempted to experience sexual gratification in many ways: actual genital contact with a male or female, masturbation, pornography, voyeurism, etc. If you violate your commitment to chastity as a celibate, instead of feeling shamed, you should question why the ideal of living as a celibate isn't working. Difficulties being celibate are opportunities to re-evaluate your ability to live a celibate life.

You most likely will not ask the following questions while you are a seminarian, but later, if you are ordained a priest, you should ask: Why can't priests today be married? Why and when did the rules for celibacy in the Catholic Church come about? Why is masturbation wrong? In short, questioning will help you to pray for the Gifts of the Holy Spirit (wisdom, understanding, fortitude, knowledge), and it is likely that you will re-learn much of what you were taught in your first half of life with the development of your own inner authority.

2.   You must continually deal with the tension between your desire to live a chaste life and your sexual longings.

To deny the tension is to invite problems. Many seminarians and priests deny their sex drive. Many priests have left the priesthood when the needs of their humanity forcefully broke into their consciousness. Many celibates who practice second half of life spirituality believe that they were inadequately trained in human sexuality. I share these four warnings to make you more conscious of your human sexual needs and the church's rules on living as a celibate. Sociologist, A. W. Richard Sipe, wrote an article on Catholic seminarians, and he said,

"Celibacy is neither well taught nor well observed by Catholic clergy... The clerical culture is elitist, narcissistic, and the seminaries are dysfunctional...Priests coming out of Roman Catholic seminaries are dangerous to others and to themselves."

3.   You must remember that your path of celibacy is a life-long commitment.

Only by keeping the life-long commitment in mind can you enter into it seriously. I am retired so I know about the strong emotions that celibates experience, sometimes regret, sometimes gratitude, as they move into old age. Some retired priests, once they have had a lot of time to reflect upon their busy lives, identify with what the prophet Jeremiah said, "You duped me, O

Lord, and I let myself be duped…" Other retired priests are filled with gratitude and they wish they had many more years to enjoy their celibate priesthood.

When a priest retires, he is no longer engaged in his full-time priestly ministry. He has to face living life alone in a new way. No longer is he sought out on a daily basis as a spiritual father. He has to give up power and control which, in many ways, is just as difficult as giving up expressions of sexual longings. He notices men his age in restaurants with their wives. He notices men his age in the mall holding hands with their wives. Loneliness beckons, or threatens. Most retired priests find that living alone, eating alone, and watching television alone can be extremely difficult.

4. One of the big obstacles to a life of chastity is the use of the Internet for the consumption of pornography which is a fast-growing addiction.

Pornography is only a few keystrokes away. Pornography is defined in the dictionary as "printed or visual material containing the explicit description or display of sexual organs or activity, intended to stimulate erotic rather than aesthetic or emotional feelings." The Catechism of the Catholic Church says (#2354) "pornography offends against chastity…pornography is a grave offense. Civil authorities should prevent the production and distribution of pornographic materials."

Some leading experts in neuroscience claim that viewing pornography is similar to a drug addiction because it can release dopamine which is similar in nature to morphine. Pornography on the Internet can lead to a chemical dependency commonly experienced with drugs, alcohol, and tobacco. Pornography mimics sexual intimacy and thus fakes the body to release many chemicals that the body can become addicted to.

Pornography not only objectifies the women or men viewed on the Internet, but it creates impossible standards and expectations for real men and women. Pornography can breed narcissism, alienation, and depression since the more a viewer of pornography looks outward to fulfill his/her expectations, the expectations will be unmet. It can lead to violence in sex especially among the young. Viewing pornography, no matter at what age, can easily lead to concupiscence, and thus be destructive for the viewer. Temperance is needed.

Nudity:

I want to add a comment. I do not believe that all nudity is necessarily pornography. In the world of art, nudity appreciates God's creation not lustfully and exploitively, whereas pornography involves lust and exploitation. In practicing first half of life spirituality, there is a tendency to equate looking at nudity with looking at pornography. Thus, false guilt can occur. Of course we must factor into any situation the age and circumstances of the viewer. The object being viewed may be harmless, but the viewer may or not be mature enough to view it. Thus, the viewing of nudity presumes a maturity that equips a person to distinguish art from pornography.

In practicing second half of life spirituality, we treat the human body with respect, admiration, and awe! God created all human beings in body, mind, soul, and spirit. The practice of second half of life spirituality invites us to get rid of the absolute dualisms of right-wrong, good-bad, body-spirit, to see mystery and beauty in places that formally were "forbidden." Beautiful bodies, both male and female, can be seen as manifestations of God's great beauty and love. Art work often contains nudity. One only has to look at the art work in the Vatican Museum to appreciate art that contains nudity. Spiritually healthy individuals can appreciate mystery before them. Some plays and films show nudity. These expressions of art can likewise be seen as holy moments to contemplate the beauty of God's creation.

The practicing of second half of life spirituality encourages us to look at nudity in others and ourselves and see aesthetic beauty and appreciate emotional feelings that are sexually natural and good.

Conclusion:

I've said a lot, Joey. I'm interested in your feed-back. I promise in my next letter to you to respond to your earlier request that I share with you different choices priests have made in living a celibate life.

Peace,

Uncle Matthew

Letter #46
Monday, June 30, 2014

Dear Uncle Matthew,

For the last week, I've been at my summer assignment where I'm assigned to a pastor who is living alone in this parish of twelve hundred parishioners; a mixture of Caucasians, African Americans, Filipinos, Haitians, and Polish Americans. I think the pastor is over-worked. He seems well-read, and he is very gracious to me with his time and thoughtfulness. He treats me with great respect. He is good at delegation and collaboration with his staff.

The bishop is closing parishes in this diocese, so my pastor has been asked to absorb the parishioners from a neighboring parish. The bishop wants my pastor to offer a mass in the parish, soon to be closed, only on special occasions until the church building is sold.

I get the impression that the real reason for consolidating parishes is because of the shortage of priests. The people are the ones who get a raw deal because the parishioners desire to stay in their local churches. I'm afraid many people will leave the institutional church. There are so many married men in this parish who are well-educated and filled with the Spirit who would be outstanding priests.

I like your idea of opening up to my brother Paul about my struggles with chastity. He is more introverted than I, but dialogue could work. We have never discussed anything that personal before. I'll be with him later this summer at home, so I'll see what happens.

I have a good friend in the seminary named Bill who is in my class. As I mentioned before to you, we have shared some of our struggles together. He is my age, and he also worked after college before entering the seminary. I agree with you that I need to stay not only open and honest with my spiritual director but also with someone my own age. Uncle Matthew, you radiate mercy, forgiveness, and compassion. That is why I feel comfortable sharing so deeply with you. I know you will love me even as you know more about the fullness of who I am, shadow and all.

This parish is promoting the Fortnight for Freedom from June 24-July 4. Yesterday's bulletin article stressed that marriage is between a man and woman and that efforts to redefine marriage are harming religious liberty. In letters to me earlier, you shared how one's practice of spirituality affects our belief in marriage equality. I have no idea what the pastor thinks on this topic, but I know pastors are sent bulletin articles that promote the church's position on this topic. The Fortnight for Freedom has got me thinking about the nature of human love.

I read that the Presbyterian Church voted on the nineteenth of this month to change its constitution's definition of marriage from a "man and woman" to "two people," and to allow its ministers to perform same-sex marriages where it is legal. At least, Uncle Matthew, I am asking more questions.

I liked the four warnings in your last letter. We do not hear about the lives of retired priests, so you made me aware of their situations and what this may mean for my own life. Also I liked your quote from Richard Sipe since I do believe we live in an elitist atmosphere in the seminary. I have experienced, like most young men my age, the crazy addictiveness that comes with viewing pornography. There are so many opportunities on i-phones, i-pads, and computers to view just about anything.

I can't adequately express to you, Uncle, how grateful I am that you are spending all this time to help me acquire a spiritual road map so that I will be a good shepherd.

My bishop mentioned this summer that I may be ordained in May 2016, if everything continues to go well.

Now that you have shared with me a wonderful background on human sexuality, could you share with me how different priests, once they have been ordained for a number of years and are out in the world, handle their sexual drive?

Peace,

Joey

Response to Letter #46
Tuesday, July 8, 2014

Dear Joey,

Thank you for being so honest with me. You are an unusual young man to be so willing to listen to and share with your uncle. You are a blessing for me. Keep asking good questions.

At your request, I'll share with you sketches of three imaginary priests that have made different choices in regard to living chaste lives. I use the word "imaginary" meaning the three sketches are composites of individuals I have met over the years just as my sketch of Fr. Tom in an earlier letter was a composite of several priests.

Fr. Stan:

Fr. Stan is a diocesan priest in his mid 50's. He thinks that God is always watching him to see if he is doing something sexually wrong. He tries not to masturbate. He believes that perfect chastity is the determinant of his success as a celibate priest. He uses will-power to refrain from masturbating, and he just tries harder if he fails to control his body. He is accountable to another priest, and he often avails himself of the Sacrament of Reconciliation. He believes the teaching in the Catechism that masturbation is a serious sin. He represses many of his sexual thoughts and desires by living in a way that he thinks is modest so as to control his sex appetite. He avoids viewing any sites on the Internet that he thinks are dangerous. He often practices some of the devotions that are characteristic of the practice of first half of life spirituality such as blessing himself with holy water when he is tempted or reciting familiar prayers that he was taught earlier in life.

Fr. Stan represents those priests who continue to practice first half of life spirituality during their second half of life. Their motivation for being chaste is largely based on fear stemming from their images of a Vindictive God, a God Preoccupied with Sex, and a God Demanding Perfection.

Fr. Raymond:

Fr. Raymond is a religious order priest in his early sixties, and he is having good periods of success at being chaste. His motivation to be chaste is his desire to turn his life over to God. He practices the Alcoholic Anonymous phrase, "Let go and let God." He has reached a degree of spirituality that enables him to love God and other people more than himself. He acknowledges his sexual feelings, but he wants to be chaste by integrating his sexual appetite into positive avenues of expression so as to express his gratitude to God for his vocation, friends, health, and deep faith in God. He believes that it is difficult for him to sin to the degree that he is grateful to God for all his blessings.

Fr. Raymond belongs to a twelve–step program, and he has a spiritual director to assist him in his quest for sobriety. He even joined an organization called Reclaim Sexual Health to control his sex drive. He wants to witness to others the positive fruits of a chaste life. He knows that repression is not the way to be chaste but rather an awareness of the need for community wherein his can have some close friends, male and female

Over the years, Fr. Raymond has changed his images of God to a Forgiving God, a Merciful God, an Incarnate God, and an Unconditionally Loving God. He no longer believes in a God Preoccupied with Sex.

Fr. Raymond represents those priests who are practicing second half of life spirituality.

Fr. Tom:

Fr. Tom is now in his late 70's. He was a classmate of mine in the seminary and I shared his story of trying to live a chaste life in an earlier letter to you. I mentioned that during his theological studies, he was motivated by his love for a classmate named George to be chaste and thus not masturbate. He realized that his love for his classmate helped him to be more concerned about someone else rather than himself. However, at that stage of development, he used repression of his sexual desires as a way to be chaste.

His images of God have changed over the years. He has dropped his earlier image of a God Preoccupied with Sex. He has acquired images of a Just God, and an Unconditionally Loving God.

Fr. Tom looked at the medical and psychological studies, along with the experiences of others, and his own sexual history, and concluded that occasional masturbation is a positive good for him. He does not find that giving up masturbation is an ideal worth pursuing. His experiences have shown that masturbation allows him to experience the intense goodness of his body which helps him in becoming a fully human and fully alive person. Fr. Tom is aware of the dangers of repression, so for him simply giving himself permission to masturbate is a more honest approach to recognizing and honoring his body.

Fr. Tom no longer believes that any institution has the right to require that all men be celibate if called to the priesthood. He believes that there are many individuals such as Mahatma Gandhi who experienced a special call to be celibate, but they embraced a celibate life-style based on their inner-authority according to their own development and personal context rather than being forced to do so by an institution.

Fr. Tom is accountable to his spiritual director. He has shifted his attention from the quest for spiritual perfection to that of meeting the needs of other people. He doesn't feel guilty about sexual actions that once weighed on him earlier in life. He now realizes that most of his earlier confessions were more about his own narcissism rather than about his failures to love his neighbor. Fr. Tom over the years shifted his focus of concern to issues involving climate change, universal health insurance, world hunger, domestic violence, immigration, poverty, the threats of terrorism, and the problems ordinary people in his parish. He believes that his own prejudices and his lack of compassion are more important to confess than an occasional act of enjoying some form of sexual pleasure.

Fr. Tom is still devoted, as he was as a young priest, to do the necessary inner work to remove obstacles to his spiritual growth. Fr. Tom seems to be very happy and fulfilled, and he seems to be a good shepherd to those who know him. He is expressing his human sexuality based on his conscience rather than on traditional moral norms. He practices second half of life spirituality. I am not judging Fr. Tom' choices as being right or wrong, good or bad. I'm only trying to point out that there are different spiritualities that priests follow in living a chaste and celibate life.

Integrating our sexuality:

Fathers Stan and Raymond desired not to masturbate as an important part of their spirituality, whereas Fr. Tom concluded that occasional masturbation, if so motivated, and so discerned, could well be a positive good for him. For Fr. Tom, masturbation diminished in its significance in any punitive sense and became inseparable from his overall relationship to his body, his embodiment. Fr. Tom embraced the Catechism's definition of chastity as "the successful integration of sexuality within the person." As you can see, Joey, the three different priests relate quite differently to their sexual urges.

Why does unwanted sexual behavior occur? I'll share a few insights that may be helpful to you in the process of learning how to integrate your sexuality whereby you will become whole.

Five insights:

a. In twelve-step programs, there is the principle that people are more inclined to do what they want to avoid if they are hungry, angry, lonely, and/or tired. Perhaps Fathers Stan and Raymond failed to keep their sexual goals when these conditions occurred in their lives.

b. Fathers Stan and Raymond may not have made friends with their shadow side. A lack of integration with one's shadow can lead to unwanted sexual behavior. Repression is not a long-term solution to handling one's sexual energy.

c. Masturbation often occurs to relieve stress. Perhaps Fathers Stan and Raymond have not yet learned how to handle their stress in a creative way.

d. Fathers Stan and Raymond may be suffering from a lack of affirmation. Receiving affirmation is a necessity. The ability to genuinely affirm others is also a necessary part of life. An inability to affirm others as well as not receiving adequate affirmation can lead to unwanted sexual behavior.

e. Fathers Stan and Raymond may realize that their seminary formation did not adequately address issues of emotional maturity and sexual identity. If the two priests continue to be unable to meet their sexual goals regarding chastity, they may conclude that Fr. Tom has a chosen a better spirituality that has transformed him into a beautiful, fully human, and fully alive person.

Personal failures:

Our personal failures in life can make us aware of wonderful truths. There is an old saying that God writes straight with crooked lines. I've observed over the years, that some celibate priests who fail at times to be chaste are less judgmental and more compassionate. Their failures opened the door for a change in their images of God.

The late Jesuit priest, Rev. John Powell, said in his book, A Life-Giving Vision, that ninety-five percent of suffering grows out of a wrong or distorted way of looking at reality. That is why it is important to continually grow in to a spirituality that is based on reality. If during the second half of life you keep the images of God you learned in the first half of life, you will miss seeing reality.

Projection:

People tend to project their ideals for a priest, seminarian, or member of a religious community. Parishioners might see us as innocent, naive, always available, pure, and without any vices. We realize early in our formation that our superiors encourage us to stay, as they define it, pure and innocent. They may encourage seminarians to all dress in clerical attire. Recently at an ordination, I noticed that all our seminarians wore cassocks which tend to emasculate them. It is important to know that already people are projecting their image of a priest upon you which, if you are not aware of this, can cause you to repress your sexual urges so as to meet their ideals, instead of you integrating them for your own well-being. Know thyself!

Within our human nature there is something operative that we may call the law of opposites. William Miller in his book, Make Friends with Your Shadow explains it this way: "The more we strive for something bright, the more its dark counterpart is constellated unconsciously. The more innocence and goodness get reinforced into the persona, the more their opposites build up in the shadow."

Clerics fear that their human weaknesses, their shadow side, will be exposed. As celibates, we are shamed when our sexual sins become public because both the Church and society set high standards for us. However, when the sexual sins of ordinary people, civic leaders, and Hollywood movie stars are disclosed, society tends to be more forgiving and accepting.

Those who practice second half of life spirituality ask good questions: "Why can some people be honest and share how they grew from their mistakes in life, whereas celibates are fearful of being honest in sharing their mistakes for fear of rejection?" "How can we make friends with our shadow in our society and in our Church when so many people project their own lofty ideas of celibacy and chastity upon us?"

When we unconsciously use projection, we can do so much harm when we assume good and bad qualities in others that do not exist. Perhaps if priests and seminarians were not placed upon pedestals, they would not try to maintain a persona of perfectionism, as they are currently encouraged to do, and could instead better serve their community.

A Sioux Indian medicine man:

Perhaps parish members are not yet ready to drop ideal projections, but in some cultures we do see this happening. I was reading about a Sioux Indian holy man, who obviously practiced second half of life spirituality, in John Sanford's book, Evil, the Shadow Side of Reality. A Sioux medicine man, Lame Deer, wrote that he had to experience getting drunk, poverty, sickness, and jail. He had to be both God and the devil. He had to be in the middle of the turmoil, not shielding himself from it. The holy medicine man acts like himself. He writes that by way of contrast, white people pay a preacher to be good, to behave, and to act responsibly.

Conclusion:

When practicing second half of life spirituality, the good news is that we serve an Unconditionally Loving God, a creator who loves us regardless of which of the three choices we make regarding living a life of chastity, when we are true to our deep conscience, the voice of the Spirit within. Our loving God, who created us, knows that we are trying to be honest, sincere, and desirous of being the best shepherds possible for the people. Here on earth, an indicator of our capacity to so serve, is the degree to which we are fully human and fully alive, made possible through the gradual integration of our sexuality.

Joey, I hope this is helpful.

Peace,

Uncle Matthew

Letter #47
Friday, July 18, 2014


Dear Uncle Matthew,

The brief sketch of the three priests that you described in your last letter helped me to be aware that priests form their conscience differently, and thus they act accordingly. I have viewed all priests as though they all practiced first half of life spirituality, so I never thought about different motivations and goals that occur in the practice of second half of life spirituality. I have so much to learn.

I also liked your explanations of why unwanted sexual behavior occurs. Handling loneliness is a factor in my life. I wish we had some psychology courses in the seminary to help us better understand terms like persona, shadow, anima, animus, archetypes, ego, false self, and true self. You use these terms so easily in a way that gives great clarity. I wish to develop a similar aptitude.

The sharing about projection and the Sioux Indian medicine man was enlightening. We so often project impossible demands upon others, and we shame celibates when they fail to live up to their vows of perpetual chastity.

As I mentioned earlier, we had our Fortnight for Religious Freedom that has supporters as well as dissenters in the parish.

Also I can see how the Supreme Court's June 30 ruling in the Hobby Lobby case has supporters and opponents. I realize now that when we practice first half of life spirituality, there is a tendency to accept without question church pronouncements and Supreme Court decisions. But when we practice second half of life spirituality, we feel both the responsibility and freedom to question the motivation and power dynamics behind certain pronouncements and decisions.

I read in the newspaper on Tuesday that the Church of England voted on Monday to allow women to serve as bishops. Is this a sign of things to come?

The pastor and I continue to work well together. He is not as busy in the summer, so he does have more time to talk to me and occasionally we will have a meal together. I wish my assignment here was longer so that I could learn more about the people in the parish. I leave here on August 4.

Pease continue to share with me your thoughts on human sexuality.

Peace,

Joey

Response to Letter #47
Saturday, July 26, 2014

Dear Joey,

I have been following the Hobby Lobby case that is testing whether the federal government can require corporations to provide, through employee health plans, contraception services that the management finds objectionable on religious grounds. Since we live in a pluralistic society, and appeals to religious convictions are a two-edged sword, I personally disagreed with the 5-4 decision. Also I have reservations about some of the local Fortnight for Religious Freedom bulletin articles as they cross the line, as I see it, of the wise separation of church and state.

I have a lot more to share on human sexuality. Most of this material is from my journals wherein over the years I have collected the opinions of many authors and theologians.

The "lost part":

In Luke 15:1-16:13, we find Jesus' parables of the lost sheep, the lost coin, and the lost son. These passages can be used to help us to form images of an Inclusive God. Everyone is important and precious. God loves the Christian, Muslim, and the atheist. These stories can also provoke us to examine ourselves and to consider what we have lost in ourselves and in our lives.

We are given the promise of great rejoicing when what was once lost is now found.

Applying the parables to us, what is our "lost part?" Through prayer, reflection, and life experiences, we discover our lost parts; parts of our personality that were unconscious such as deep anger, excessive greed, all-consuming lust, and terrible jealousy as well as positive attributes such as talents we never developed, creativities we repressed, and sexual longing we never admitted. The lost part is hidden behind the mask we wore when living as the false self. When we acknowledge these lost parts, and when others are able to join us, we can rejoice, forgive, and show compassion.

In the area of sexuality, those who practice second half of life spirituality believe that there should be a way whereby celibates who publicly violate the Sixth Commandment and repent can grow spiritually from their sin rather than being shamed, shunned, or even dismissed from their vocation. Those who advocate for this relative leniency are not referring to transgressions such as pedophilia, where serious psychological problems are likely to exist, civil law has been broken, and others have been profoundly harmed.

A retired priest-friend of mine, Fr. Brown, was telling me about some priests who had discovered their "lost parts" when they acknowledged their addictions to drugs and alcohol. The bishop treated the priests with compassion and he sent them away for treatment. One priest with a drug problem was sent back after treatment to the parish from which he came and because both the bishop and priest were open and honest, the people gave their returning pastor a standing ovation welcoming him back. However, Joey, we rarely hear about such compassion for clerics who struggle with some kind of sex addiction.

Rob Lowe's story:

Rob Lowe is a film, television, and theater actor and producer. He has a wife and two sons. I read his autobiography, Stories I

Only Tell My Friends. It struck me that his story provides an important insight for clerics in their quest to live a chaste life.

Lowe is not afraid to share his wild sexual excesses that marked the nineteen eighties when he was part of the "Brat Pack." He tells about his first love when he was only fifteen. He shares about his mother's three divorces and his limited experience with fathering. He shares that he videotaped so many of his life experiences. He even shared in his book his sexual encounter in Atlanta in 1988 when he was twenty-one years old and videotaped a sexual encounter with two girls, and one of the girls was only sixteen. The negative publicity from that encounter caused him to heavily drink. Later, he had to seek treatment for alcohol addiction.

I just finished Rob Lowe's second book, Love Life. He shares how as a young man he explored all he could about love, relationships, and sex. At nineteen, Hugh Hefner invited him to the Playboy Mansion. He writes:

"The temptations and situations that present themselves daily to a teen movie star proved too irresistible for me to experience the daily lessons that your first serious relationship should teach you. Jealousy, boredom, commitment, honesty, vulnerability and all the other often-times uncomfortable feelings that come with truly being present for your romantic partner, I was able to disassociate from. If I felt any sort of malaise, instead of learning that all feelings (even bad ones) pass if given time, I made myself feel better by sampling the sexual circus that was always waiting just outside the door."

He shares how during his second half of life, he changed when he married his wife, and his two sons were born. Then he began the best chapter of his life.

As I read these two books, I felt a deep compassion for Hollywood actors like Rob Lowe who are exposed to so many temptations. Unless the goals of first half of life spirituality are known and met, individuals in the second half of life can drift when they do not learn to form boundaries. I also felt envious of Rob Lowe because he could share his life with great honesty. He was not ashamed to share that he had done many things he regrets, but now that he has been married twenty-two years, he has gained sobriety and he is learning to be a good father. Rob Lowe had made friends with his shadow. As William Miller says in his book, Make Friends with Your Shadow, "He achieved good not apart from evil, but through it; even in spite of it." Reading his two autobiographies made me realize that we can't judge others. We all form our conscience differently and at different ages based on our upbringing, religious influences, heredity, and the friends we meet.

Some signs of both first and second half of life spirituality seem to be present in Rob Lowe. He now knows who he is. He is aware of his strengths and weaknesses.  He has found his community, his stability in his wife and children. His wife knew that he longed to be better than he had been. She saw in him the potential to be more than he was, both as an actor and as a man. She supported his efforts to quit drinking and get sober. Rob Lowe's life shows the mystery involved in transitioning into second half of life spirituality. The steps are not mathematically able to be defined. There will always be two steps forward and one step backwards.

Celibates can learn lessons in Rob Lowe's two autobiographies. Celibates need accountability. Celibates need to make friends with their shadow. Celibates need friends who believe they can be better. Celibates need friends with whom they can be honest. Celibates need a community setting that allows them to be who they are. Celibates are encouraged to move into the practice of second half of life spirituality when they have friends who give them glimpses of a Patient and Forgiving God. Our images of God determine how we judge others and how we judge ourselves.

Suggestions for living a chaste life:

Living a chaste life is a challenge. Whether a person practices first or second half of life spirituality, the practice of chastity requires prayer, reflection, self-discipline, and, importantly, self-acceptance. I will share with you four suggestions that help me to live a chaste life, and I recommend them to you. You might find them helpful.

1. Make friends with your shadow:

When we practice first half of life spirituality, we tend to repress our shadow; those parts of ourselves that we cannot accept and we do not want others to see. Most seminarians and priests are not trained to understand and integrate into consciousness their shadow side which, not surprisingly, involves their sexuality.

When we practice second half of life spirituality, we try to make friends with our shadow by accepting those thoughts and desires that don't fit our image of ourselves (that is our false self which tends to see ourselves as pure, honest, perfectionistic, and even angel-like, devoid of human sexuality). We try to be honest with ourselves before God with a loving and accepting disposition. The process of integrating the shadow seems at first to be a defeat for the ego, but when we make friends with our shadow, we are no longer nervous and fearful, but through God's grace, we experience joy, peacefulness, and gentleness. We can serve God better.

When we integrate the shadow, we come to accept that there is more to us than the public role we play in the Church. The church's ideal sexual norms make it difficult for many priests to make friends with their shadow whereby they can become fully human and fully alive. The result is that countless seminarians and priests become depressed and discouraged when they cannot please their superiors, their parishioners, and they cannot even accept the fullness of their own identity. This in turn leads many priests to be tempted to seek relief both from external and internal conflict in the arena of human sexuality. Priests have been universally trained to think that acting out is a cardinal sin without having the benefit of an integrative approach. Thus, when they act out sexually, there is usually great shame and guilt, compounding all of the other problems in an ongoing cycle. The result is that there are unhealthy and unhappy priests who impact the life of the parish in which they serve.

2. Learn to appreciate the importance of affirmation:

As you can see, living a life of chastity and celibacy in our Church and contemporary society is terribly difficult, perhaps destructive for some. Many parishioners are very affirming of the priests and their human struggles, but other parishioners relate to the priests as they relate to their image of God. Parishioners can and often do project their image of God onto the priest. When priests sense that some parishioners are displaying negativity towards them, it is reflexively easy for them to doubt their self worth.

Celibate priests, like all humans, desire to be accepted and affirmed. The need for affirmation often takes precedence over taking basic care of one's body. In marriage, ideally, a spouse affirms his/her partner. A priest has no one intimately present to affirm him, so he is trained to rely on his bishop, his fellow priests, a few close friends, and the parishioners for affirmation. For me, I never received adequate affirmation from bishops, fellow priests, or parishioners because most of my relationships were superficial. I recommend that when possible, you seek to supplement your relationships outside of your normal relationships in the Church in recreational, educational, and service groups so as to increase your opportunities to affirm and be affirmed.

When I was in the seminary for ten years, I hardly saw any women. Even on summer breaks, close friendships with women were discouraged. Now I realize this part of our formation was so unfair. To receive the affirmation we seek and to become fully human and fully alive, we need friendships with men and women. We miss so much affirmation in life if we only have male friends. I am trying, Joey, to learn how to communicate, love, and appreciate females. For many years, I have had dinner with a wonderful married couple on a weekly basis, and as a result, I find I am happier and more affirmed.

3.  Continue to avail yourself of spiritual direction:

Older priests who practice second half of life spirituality should have great compassion for their younger brother priests who are trying to be holy through perfectionism and rigid, willful, discipline. Older priests realize that the younger priests' daily path is like walking unaware through a minefield. Some dioceses encourage support programs such as Jesu Caritas to build up fraternity among the priests. Some younger priests are wise enough to seek out older priests for spiritual direction.

In AA, there is a phrase, "We are as sick as our secrets." Wise individuals are willing to share their secrets, and their secrets benefit everyone. When we practice first half of life spirituality, there is that tendency to think that novenas, religious rituals, scapulars, rosaries, frequenting the Sacrament of Reconciliation, and making better resolutions are the keys to progressing spiritually. When we practice second half of life spirituality, we become aware that God works through other people. We are willing to share our joys and sorrows with others, and we discover that spiritual progress occurs when we are willing to be accountable to someone.

Thomas Merton, the late Trappist monk at the Abbey of Gethsemani, was honest and open about his journey in life as a celibate priest. In his journals, he shared that he fell in love with a young nurse. Few priests have ever exposed themselves to the degree of Merton in the struggle to be celibate and chaste. His honest struggles and perseverance in the face of conflicts remains a great help to those of us striving to be celibate and chaste.

Rev. Henri J. M. Nouwen is regarded as a very popular spiritual writer for priests, religious, and laypersons. He died in 1996. He is regarded as a man of integrity. At age fifty-four, he admitted that he was still struggling with the same problems he had on the day of his ordination. He admitted being restless, nervous, and impulse-driven. He opened himself to a particular friendship with a young man. His secret journal was later published. His story reveals, like that of Merton, the difficulties that he faced in living a chaste life.

4.  Appreciate and develop your hidden gifts:

The task of making friends with your shadow involves suffering. However, the process of integration, becoming aware of one's identity, not only involves suffering but also joy. All of us have unconsciously repressed our gifts and talents. When we practice second half of life spirituality, we take seriously our belief that we are children of God; sharers of divine life. We begin to realize that to be fully human and fully alive, God expects us to develop our hidden talents whereby we may discover the ability to sing, paint, dance, play racquetball, play a musical instrument, or even cook a meal. For men in our society, many of these activities are considered feminine, but as men, we need to appreciate and develop our hidden gifts.

When I studied electrical engineering in college before entering the seminary, the courses were mainly math and science and did not include humanity courses such as physical fitness, theology, music and art appreciation, cooking, or even a philosophy course that could have helped us to know who we are. Later as a young priest, my spiritual director advised me to jog, play racquetball, and even yell and scream to release tension. He advised me to take up a musical instrument and to learn to paint. I did take up acrylic painting and later I took organ lessons. I urge you, Joey, even in the seminary, to appreciate and develop your hidden gifts.

When we appreciate and develop our hidden talents, we are more in control of our emotions that impact our ability to live a chaste life. When we are not seeking to be wholistic, we experience inner emotional turmoil.

New questions:

In the future you will have many new experiences. With these new experiences will emerge new questions. Your success, inner peace, and happiness will depend upon how you answer these questions.

1. "Why can't priests marry?" You will most likely experience at seminary reunions that some of the men who left the active priesthood to get married seem to be much healthier, in a spiritual sense, than those who remained as celibate priests.

2. The presence of wholesome married men resurfaces the lingering question, "Would the intimate love of another human being impede or help one's love of God in devoted service as a priest, if this is the calling that one carefully discerns?"

3. If you practice second half of life spirituality, you may increasingly wonder whether maintaining your views on human sexuality, learned while you practiced first half of life spirituality, keep you in a constrictive box that likewise constrains your gifts to the world. Canon 277 reads,

"Clerics are obliged to observe perfect and perpetual continence for the sake of the kingdom of heaven and therefore are bound to celibacy which is a special gift of God by which sacred ministers can adhere more easily to Christ with an undivided heart and are able to dedicate themselves more freely to the service of God and humanity."

Conclusion:

The late French author, Francois Mauriac (1885-1970) wrote, "We are all molded and remolded by those who have loved us, and though that love may pass, we remain, none-the-less, their work...No love, no friendship can ever cross the path of our destiny without leaving some mark upon it forever."

These words can help us to be patient with others and ourselves. It takes many years to be molded by the friends we meet during our journey in life. During our whole life, there will be a struggle to define, clarify, and achieve our goals and objectives in regard to living a chaste life. Certainly your friends play a major role in so far as their ability to inspire you, motivate you, and assist you in seeing reality.

Peace,

Uncle Matthew

Letter # 48
Thursday, August 14, 2014


Dear Uncle Matthew,

You mentioned in your last letter, that you not only disagreed with the Hobby Lobby decision but with some aspects of the Fortnight for Freedom. I too have some reservations, but I am not equipped to understand the big picture. Can you further explain your disagreements?

I liked the sharing about the "lost part." It takes a lot of humility to share that the "lost part" is something sexual. I liked the way you shared with me Rob Lowe's autobiography. I wonder why we can't be as open and honest once we enter the seminary. I'm beginning to realize the many challenges of living a celibate life. The four suggestions were very insightful regarding living a chaste life. I agree that accountability is so important if I am going to be able to live a chaste life.

Following your suggestion, Paul and I did discuss our sexuality together. He was not at all embarrassed to share. We both have been through similar experiences. We were amazed at how similar we are. We embraced each other after our dialogue. We are closer now than ever before.

Today we celebrated the Mass for the Feast of St. Maximilian Kolbe. The celebrant gave an excellent homily quoting from

John's gospel, "This is my commandment: love one another as I love you. No one has greater love than this, to lay down one's life for one's friends."

I didn't realize that with the Nazi invasion and occupation in Poland, priests were added to the millions of Jews that were rounded up and sent to prison camps. Maximilian, a priest, was sent to a prison camp in Auschwitz, Poland. Several million people were exterminated there. I find it amazing that when Pope John Paul II canonized Maximilian as a saint and martyr in 1982, in St. Peter's Square, 200,000 were there for the ceremony including a man who owed his life to St. Maximilian who sacrificed his life for him while in prison.

I'll be back at the seminary on the 18th when I will begin Third Theology!

Uncle Matthew, earlier you shared with me a portrait of a person who completed many of the goals in the practice of first half of life spirituality. Can you share with me a portrait of a person who is practicing second half of life spirituality?

Peace,

Joey

Response to Letter #48
Wednesday, August 27, 2014


Dear Joey,

I applaud your initiative to converse with your brother Paul on the topic of human sexuality. The dialogue will help you in your quest for self-knowledge which leads, with God's help, to self-acceptance. We can accept ourselves to the extent that those closest to us know us and accept us for who we truly are. Remember, self acceptance was one of the goals I presented in the practice of first half of life spirituality. For all of us, this goal is never fully realized in this life-time.  Self knowledge and self acceptance are an on-going journey.

As I mentioned earlier, Alcoholic's Anonymous wisely states, "We are as sick as our secrets." Once you discover that most people your age think and act similarly in the area of sexuality, your own secrets dissipate or become less shameful. Indeed, one day they may be your gifts!

In your last letter, you asked why I disagreed with the Hobby Lobby Supreme Court decision. In addition to what I earlier shared with you, I agree with those who think that the Hobby Lobby verdict granted First Amendment freedom of religion rights to corporations as though they were persons.

You also asked why I disagreed with some of the Fortnight for

Freedom articles that I read in one parish's church bulletins. In addition to what I shared with you earlier, first, the Church tends to focus primarily on reproductive issues, such as contraception and abortion, which to me is unbalanced when we look at the many other issues facing the world such as war, justice, disease, poverty, climate change, and hunger. Jesus seemed to be focused on the latter issues, condemning, according to scripture, only infidelity in the realm of sexuality. Second, I think that some articles strongly suggest that parishioners should vote Republican, which seems to me needlessly partisan, since President Obama in his Health Plan allows contraceptives to be available as a part of medical coverage. Third, the articles fail to point out that most moral theologians agree that women do have the right to form their conscience and follow their conscience even if it is in disagreement with church teaching. Fourth, I question whether anyone's freedom of religion is taken away if contraceptives are part of a health care plan.

The canonized saints:

When we practice first half of life spirituality, we tend to place on a pedestal  those saints who were hermits, martyrs, celibates, and men and women who spend long periods of time in deep prayer and contemplation. We assume that the celibate saints never violated their vows of chastity. We assume they are distant from us as is our image of a Distant God. But once we begin to practice second half of life spirituality, we question if the biographies describing the saints are always literally true. We question if the stories are often embellished so as to illustrate a lesson much like the scriptures include fictional stories to teach powerful lessons.  We painfully realize that we can't imitate many of these saints, and really we shouldn't. We need instead to recognize our own divinity and no longer feel we must imitate the life of someone else. Your goal, Joey, is to be authentic, and to be the best person you can be with your gifts and talents expressed authentically.

Portrait of a person who practices second half of life spirituality:

I'll try to provide a portrait for you of a person who is practicing second half of life spirituality. It is important to keep in mind that no one completes fully all the goals found in the practice of first and second half of life spirituality. All of us may have certain traits that demonstrate our practice of first and second half of life spirituality, but we also have traits that show our under-developed side and our "shadow side." We all experience the power of sin. We are all mis-led by the ego. We all have difficulty knowing and living the true self. We all have a "lost part." We all experience some degree of egocentricity. The journey is never complete. This is not to be lamented, but rather is at the heart of the very meaning of life.

Behavior reflects our image of God:

Earlier in my letters to you, I presented short stories about different individuals who discovered images of God that are more associated with the practice of second half of life spirituality. The common theme of all the stories was that once we acquire new images of God, this new awareness may change our behavior in ways that illustrate second half of life spirituality.

For example, once we acquire an image of an Incarnate God, our new awareness helps us to appreciate the holy in the ordinary as well as in the extraordinary.

Once we experience an image of an Inclusive God, our new awareness helps us to appreciate the giftedness of all those around us; the forgotten and exalted; the poor and rich, the young and old. We become aware and appreciative that God is found in unlikely disguises.

Let me share a few traits that illustrate some essential characteristics when we practice second half of life spirituality. Many years ago, I read Doctor Wayne Dyer's book, Your Erroneous Zones. The last chapter of the book is entitled, "Portrait of a person who has eliminated all erroneous zones." What I share with you is greatly influenced by his insights.

1. We witness the Fruits of the Spirit:

One sign that individuals are practicing second half of life spirituality is they know that the divine lives within them. Thus, they believe that the Gifts and Fruits of the Holy Spirit are the essence of their spirituality.

Many years ago, I read Eric Butterworth's book, Discover the Power within You. In his prologue, Butterworth shares a beautiful Hindu legend which I will abbreviate.

According to an old Hindu legend there was once a time when people abused their divinity so Brahma, the Hindu creator god, decided to take it away and hide it where people would never find it.

The lesser gods were called together to discern where to hide the divinity. Some suggested burying man's divinity deep in the earth. Some suggested sinking his divinity in the deepest ocean. Some suggested taking it to the top of the highest mountain and hiding it there. Brahma rejected all this suggestions. The lesser gods gave up and concluded that there was no place on land or sea where man will not eventually reach.

Then Brahma suggested hiding it deep in man himself because he will not think about looking for it there. Ever since then, man has been going up and down, climbing, digging, exploring, and searching for something that is already in himself.

Two thousand years ago a man named Jesus found it and shared its secret, but in the movement that sprang up in His name, the divinity of man has been the best kept secret of the ages.

When we practice second half of life spirituality, we witness, in ourselves and in others, the presence of the Holy Spirit. St. Paul said, "The fruit of the Spirit is love, joy, peace, patient endurance, kindness, generosity and faith, mildness and chastity" (Galatians 5:22). In your last letter, you mentioned St. Maximilian Kolbe who was motivated by love to give his life so another man could live.

2.  We become fully human and fully alive:

When we practice second half of life spirituality, we are more fully human and fully alive. Jesus said, "I have come that they may have life and have it to the full" (John 10:10).

We become good shepherds when we know our divine nature and when we use all of our human faculties, powers, and talents. We see a beautiful world. We experience wonder, awe, compassion, and tenderness. This makes me think of Socrates (permit me with some artistic license here) who said the examined life is very much worth living indeed! The unexamined life is not worth living implies that the examined life is what makes life worth living. We need to do inner work to know and understand ourselves in order to give life meaning.

3.  We are healthy and whole:

When we practice first half of life spirituality, we tend to think dualistically. We think that our success, and the over-coming of our self-destructive behaviors, is simply a matter of personality development focused on external factors regarding how we adapt to the external world.

When we practice second half of life spirituality, we experience the world more holistically so we think that the means of our spiritual growth are found internally in terms of quality of character, moral values, and in general living the life of the Spirit. Spirituality pertains to our inner experience of how we think and feel and choose to live in relation to our interior, and how this translates into our behavior and conduct in the world.

Retired Bishop John Shelby Spong in his book Jesus for the Non-Religious says, "Being a Christian is not to be a religious human being; it is to be a whole human being. Jesus is a portrait of that wholeness and that is why he is for me, in his complete humanity, the ultimate expression of God."

Those who willingly try to practice second half of life spirituality strive to honor their humanity so that they will increasingly move toward wholeness; a sign that they are sharing in divinity.

4. We live a life of integrity:

Erik Erikson (1902-1990) described eight stages of human development. He saw growth as a lifelong process. Erikson called the final stage of growth the age of integrity or the age of wisdom. When we are men and women of integrity, we do not seek honors as ends in themselves. We are true to our baptismal promises. In previous letters to you, I shared many practical examples of men and women who exemplified integrity.

5. We are givers:

In life, we make the basic choice of whether in sum we will be givers or takers. We make that choice every day. In the practice of first half of life spirituality, we tend to compete with others. We may tend to be takers rather than givers. We accumulate many material things and we work to earn more and more money.

In the practice of second half of life spirituality, we are attracted increasingly to a life of simplicity. This is so because we find joy in being able to focus on important realities before us which leads to empathy. Ideally, we are more generous. We forget ourselves when we love others. Paradoxically, when we are takers and spend money on ourselves, our happiness doesn't increase. But when we are givers and place our focus on the needs of others, our happiness increases. As our grip on things loosens, our heart may likewise open to both give and receive the fullness of life.

I know a retired couple who take their grandchildren each year on a trip to a far-away place. They are generous so that their grandchildren will be able to see the world and thus become more mature at an earlier age. This couple could just spend their money on themselves, but they support an orphanage in South

America along with being very generous with their time, talent, and treasure in their local parish. They volunteer time with the Society of St. Vincent de Paul. Their generosity as givers inspires many of their friends to think about their own lives during the retirement years.

6. We can forgive others:

On May 13, 1981, Mehmet Ali Agca attempted to kill Pope John Paul II. The pope was left seriously injured with one bullet passing through his abdomen and another narrowly missing his heart. On December 27, 1983, Pope John Paul II visited Agca in prison and forgave him. This act is a vivid example of how forgiveness liberates all those involved.

The book, Unbroken:

Last year, I read the 2010 non-fiction book, Unbroken, by Laura Hillenbrand. Soon it will be released as a film. The book is a true story about Louis Zamperini, an Olympic track star who later was in the Air Force during World War II. He was bombardier, and his B-24 bomber crashed in the Pacific. He and two of his crew-mates survived on a raft for forty-seven days, only to be captured by the Japanese and placed in a POW camp where he and other prisoners were nearly starved and beaten to death with fists, sticks, and belt buckles.

At the end of the war, Louis and the other prisoners in the camp were set free to return to the United States.  He suffered constant nightmares and inner turmoil with frequent memories of a sadistic Japanese guard beating and demeaning him. He suffered from post-traumatic stress disorder (PTSD). Many of the POWs held by the Japanese showed a disturbingly high rate of suicide, unemployment, depression, and other mental illnesses after their arrival home.

It was at a Billy Graham tent revival that Louis turned his life around. Louis threw away his booze, girlie magazines, and cigarettes. Louis came to a profound peacefulness that never left him. He became free of the self-destructive, self-centered behaviors that had so dominated him and replaced them with a capacity for empathy and care for others. Louis forgave his wartime captors and met with many of them in Japan in acts of reconciliation. His willingness to forgive his enemy is a witness of one of the highest goals found in the practice of second half of life spirituality. Within the act of forgiveness is the profound capacity to recognize and accept the complexity and mystery of God's will on Earth. Forgiveness entails the radical renunciation of the world's desire for revenge, replacing it with God's message of mercy and love.

7. We can laugh:

Healthy individuals know how to laugh. I believe it was Wayne Dyer who said, "Laughter is the sunshine of the soul, and without it, nothing can live or grow."

Alice and Gene were once parishioners of mine. In the last few years of Alice's life, she would call me almost every day. She was in her late eighties, and every time she called she would share some story relating to her grandchildren or great grandchildren. On many occasions the stories were sad, but Alice could always laugh at life. She had so many of her own medical problems, but her focus of energy was on loving others. Her ability to laugh and create laughter inspired me while she was alive and even today when I think about her.

8. We accept ourselves:

When we are whole and at peace with ourselves, we can accept ourselves and live without complaint. We know that our self-worth is located within. We are honest. We do not blame. We have a high energy level precisely because we don't waste time and attention facing useless and old battles, whether within or without. We seem to require less sleep. We are not afraid to fail. There is no room for self-pity.

Occasionally, on Youtube or the national news, a person who

inspires others will be featured and more often than not what inspires most are the living out of the eight qualities described above. One extreme example is Nick Nujicic, an Australian Christian evangelist and motivational speaker who was born without arms or legs. He gives talks to young people so as to help them to be grateful for the gifts they have. It is common to want more luxuries and a better life. Yet what inspires us is when we meet individuals who can accept themselves as they are with their human limitations.

9.  We choose to be happy:

Children at Disney World are in awe of the characters: Cinderella, Winnie the Pooh, Eeyore, Pluto, Goofy, Tigger, and Mickey and Minnie Mouse. The world of fantasy is real for them. Children see the colors, the people, the rides, and the atmosphere and they respond with excitement. They are happy because they can let go and simply enjoy the present moment.

As we age, it is easy to think our happiness comes with an absence of problems, but we all face problems in life. The practice of second half of life spirituality introduces us to new images of God that convince us that God is with us. God is ever-present. God is lovable. God is not remote but touchable. When we practice second half of life spirituality, we believe that with God's help we can face our problems with confidence and choose a path that leads to happiness.

Spirituality is all about how we choose to handle our sadness, pain, and suffering. We are not overwhelmed by suffering, but rather we make a choice to retain those child-like qualities that help us live in the present moment rather than being caught up in fearfulness regarding the past and future. Thus we choose to be happy.

We are tempted through our exposure to advertisements to think that more money, power, and status will bring greater happiness. Society tempts us to believe that it is better to stay as takers rather than givers. Healthy and whole individuals see through the illusions that they face. We learn from children that happiness, a sign of being healthy and whole, is a result of a good attitude rather than an accumulation of more goods. The late author, Fr. John Powell SJ wisely entitled one of his books, "Happiness is an inside job."

Peace,

Uncle Matthew

Letter #49
Sunday, September 13, 2014

Dear Uncle Matthew,

Thank you for your last letter that shared a portrait of a person who practices second half of life spirituality. I liked your first point that ties in the Fruits of the Spirit with those who practice second half of life spirituality. I naturally enjoy being with those who are joyful, kind, and generous, while I'm turned off by those who are judgmental, angry, stubborn, and stingy. I can see how dangerous it may be for a priest to be seventy-five years old and think he is so holy and yet not manifest genuine effects of the Spirit.

Now that you brought it to my attention, I never could identify with many of the canonized saints who seemed "distant" and not the kind of friends I would want to hang out with. Perhaps writers sometimes project on saints their images of God. If they believe in a Distant God, they will portray the saint as distant and removed from earthly matters. I appreciated the profound insight, "We can't imitate the lives of many of the saints, and we shouldn't."

In an earlier letter when you shared with me a portrait of those who practice first half of life spirituality, you presented individuals who looked good on the outside, but were still quite far from being fully human and fully alive. Eagle Scouts, newly ordained priests with the title "Father," cadets in military schools may often look so good, but they lack depth that can only occur with further growth. Strange how even though I am no longer a child, I view the clergy with their titles and their special clothing with the presumption that they are the holy ones. I often ignore the truths revealed by my own inner authority. Clericalism presumes that the ordained church leaders have authority and power over their lay followers.

The academic year is starting out well. We lost a few classmates over the summer. My pastor in my summer assignment gave me a very good evaluation. I worry about him. He is a good man, but I think the leaders in the institutional church are unconsciously abusing him so as to keep the church's status quo without realizing they are assigning him to do too much.

I read an article in this week's NCR entitled, "Church on track to become a shrinking cult." The article quoted surveys that suggest that young Catholics are increasingly turned off by the attitudes and actions of some American bishops who fail to address the child abuse scandal, who harshly oppose civil gay marriage, who are clueless about the opposition to the church's teaching on contraception, and who refuse to consider women priests.

Please continue to share with me your thoughts on a portrait of a person who practices second half of life spirituality. I'm hungry for it!

Peace,

Joey

Response to Letter #49
Sunday, September 21, 2014


Dear Joey,

Today the Church celebrates the feast day of St. Matthew, my
patron saint, although the Sunday liturgy takes precedence.
Matthew was a tax collector. He worked for the occupying
Roman forces. Many who knew him, especially the religious
leaders, scorned him. And yet Jesus called him to be one of the
twelve apostles. Why was he selected? I think it was because
Matthew knew he was a sinner and therefore was open to the
good news. Remember, Jesus did said, "I came not to call the
righteous but sinners" (Luke 5:32).

In Jesus' day, as portrayed in the gospels, so many religious
leaders were more concerned with the preservation of their own
holiness than with helping others. They were like doctors who
refuse to visit the sick lest they should incur some infection.
Essentially their religion was selfish; ego-centered, not other-
centered. And when they were focused on others, they were
more likely to point out their sins and faults rather than offer
encouragement. They failed to show others the Fruits of the Holy
Spirit (joy, love, peace, kindness, etc.) because their selfishness
made them barren. They stressed outward orthodoxy rather than
offering compassion. We must be constantly careful to avoid the
trappings of clericalism so that we don't practice our priesthood
like the Pharisees in Jesus' day.

I liked your insight that writers may project on to saints their images of God. If we have an image of a Distant God, we may think that the canonized saints were not engaged in the important issues of their day, but they were solely preoccupied in the world to come. So many parishioners are focused on their devotions and miss opportunities to be engaged in the issues of today regarding peace and justice, the work of the living God.

If we have an image of an Exclusive God, we may think that the saints were almost supernatural and not living human beings. Could that be why there are so few canonized married saints?

If we have an image of a God Demanding Perfection, we may think that the most important quality of the canonized saints was their willfulness to be perfect rather than their willingness to let go and let God use them to do God's will.

Let me now share with you further thoughts on a portrait of a person who practices second half of life spirituality.

Portrait of a person who practices
second half of life spirituality (con't):

10. We appreciate and develop strong friendships:

The ability to appreciate and develop strong enduring friendships is an important sign of maturity and wholeness. Strong friendships can help weaken, even dismantle egocentricity, whereas the lack of friendships can feed the ego and a self-centered life.

Hopefully, we discover the connection between our images of God and our ability to develop strong friendships. When we believe in an Incarnate God rather than a Distant God, friendships become more inviting. An image of a Distant God discourages intimate friendships.

Perhaps we come to realize that our lack of trust in God and other people has its roots in a distrust of our parents from many decades before. Indeed, the early concepts and images we have of our parents largely determine our first half of life images of God. If we are fortunate, new life experiences challenge us to reflect upon these early influences and if trust was absent before, we may begin to change our sense of trustworthiness of others in general, and God specifically.

The Catholic Church is a hierarchical structure. Clericalism makes friendships between lay Catholics and clerics difficult to develop since there is an assumption, just as in the military, that friendships between persons in different levels of authority and rank reduces discipline and compromises the command structure. Once a man is given the title "father," "monsignor," or "bishop," it creates a barrier for lay persons to simply call him by his first name.

Today, many children grow up in homes where a divorce or separation has taken place. Let me make an observation about families. Sometimes a divorce is necessary for the good of the family. A marriage in which there is hatred and a lack of integrity can damage the children. I have noticed over the years, that the relationship that boys have with their dads is sometimes damaged by the divorce. For example, if a mom is divorced, she may say negative things about her former husband in front of the children. Or perhaps the boy may be resentful of the father simply because of his absence. As a result, the boys may find it difficult to love, respect, or trust their dad. There seems to be a connection with a boy's ability to form a bond of love and trust with his dad and a boy's ability to love and trust God. Usually when a boy develops a healthy friendship with his dad, it better enables him to gradually develop an image of an Unconditionally loving God. Very often we notice in families where there was a bitter divorce, the children no longer desire to attend church. Likewise, if a divorced father speaks poorly of his former wife in front of his daughters, he can damage their ability to trust their mom and to discover an image of an Unconditionally Loving God.

11.   We strive to have an informed conscience:

When we practice second half of life spirituality, we will make a regular practice of praying, studying, dialoguing with others, and reflecting so as to be aware of reality and our role as a responsible person. This awareness is at the heart of the informed conscience. Keep in mind, however, that an essential part of developing an informed conscience is to follow its voice wherever it might lead.

Michael Morwood in his book, In Memory of Jesus, has a chapter that develops an imaginary conversation between Jesus and his prison guard the night before he died. In this dialogue Jesus said, "I decided I would make a statement with my death. I would stand up and be counted, and people would know I was ready to die for what I believed and preached. So I came to Jerusalem." Jesus followed his conscience even to the point of knowing it would lead him to the Cross.

The great Swiss psychiatrist C. G. Jung once said, "Man's worst sin is unconsciousness, but it is indulged in with the greatest piety, even among those who should serve mankind as teachers and examples."

The positive corollary here is that consciousness, and particularly the development of conscience, affords a possible pathway to virtue.

12. We are sensitive to the needs of others:

When I was studying moral theology in the seminary, Daniel Maguire said that one of the primary goals of the spiritual life is to be sensitive to the needs of others and to respond to those needs. He used the analogy of a tooth that was sensitive to cold or hot liquids. Just as a tooth aches when touched by hot or cold liquids, so too our heart should be touched by the needs of others.

Meister Eckhart, a member of the Dominican order and one of

the most notable preachers and thinkers of his time, summed it up beautifully when he said, "What happens to another, whether it is joy or sorrow, happens to me." We can spot those who practice second half of life spiritually when we observe that they respond quickly to the needs of others. They attract us as being good shepherds. We desire to follow them and become like them.

13. We are authentic:

The courage to be authentic is another attribute found in those who practice second half of life spirituality. We all have met people who appear to be quite simply who they truly are. They do not pretend to be someone else. This is most refreshing!

When we practice second half of life spirituality, we no longer feel compelled to protect our roles, titles, possessions, and status symbols. We do not have to prove we are morally better, holier, or smarter than others. We realize God is to be honored and praised as the giver of our talents. We realize we came into the world naked, and we will go out of this life naked.

I know a man by the name of Randy who is now forty years old. Since knowing him as a teenager, he reminded me of the saying, "What you see is what you get." Randy doesn't pretend he is other than what others can readily see. He answers honestly the questions of others that reveal both his virtues and vices. He has very little in the way of material possessions, but his honesty, truthfulness, goodness, wholeness, and sensitivity to the needs of others gives him an authentic quality that is remarkable. He radiates a peacefulness and goodness that makes him very attractive.

Joey, one of your distant cousins, Steve, recently lost a close friend to heart disease. To honor his deceased friend, Steve had a tattoo placed on his body as a sign of gratitude for this person in his life. That took courage. Most of us would wonder, "What will people say if I do this?" Your cousin only tried to be authentic in his love for his friend.

Just as hair pieces and face lifts hide our true self, so too most of us are not fully authentic. We hide our shadow side. We present our false self for others to admire. We name drop. We brag about who we know and where we have been. How refreshing it is to find and know a person who is truly authentic. They are the good shepherds we would like to better know and follow because their motives are transparent and not aimed at exploitation. They are the best church leaders we know, love, and revere because they do not fall into the trappings of clericalism by making believe they are superior to us.

14. We avoid workaholism:

When we practice second half of life spirituality, we realize that workaholism is dangerous even though it appears to be so good. It denies opportunities for growth in the areas of wisdom, compassion, and tenderness.

Retired priests are financially rewarded and affirmed when they volunteer to celebrate masses and perform other liturgical functions. This furthers the habit of workaholism. The illusion being promoted is that one's worth is tied up in one's ability to be productive for the sake of the on-going operation of the institutional church. It takes courage to resist the affirmation "we need you, Father, to say these masses for us." Perhaps instead of incessant busyness, God is calling retired priests to "walk the talk." Instead of telling others what to do, or speaking to a crowd, perhaps God is giving retired priests the opportunity to do hands-on-ministry. That means really spending time with the sick, showing compassion for the weak and vulnerable, and wisely helping in some way those that are marginalized. Workaholism can give us an excuse for not wrestling with the urgent issues in our lives. Workaholism makes it difficult to avoid the trappings of clericalism. Spending time in some form of prayer, recreation, art, music, or other form of creative activity can encourage us to be open to God's work so as to discover those "lost parts," the underdeveloped areas of our integrity, honesty, authenticity, forgiveness, and wholeness.

15. We unconditionally love others:

Jesus died not as a perfect man who achieved all his goals in life, but rather he died, by worldly standards, as a failure. Most importantly from one perspective, he was a man who unconditionally loved others even at the expense of his own life.

Those who practice second half of life spirituality believe that when we unconditionally love someone, we at times may have to bend or even break a rule in the service of a higher law that supersedes a rule. Most likely those who believe in an image of an Unconditionally Loving God can bend and break a rule at times when they follow their conscience, but those who believe in an image of a Vindictive God cannot.

Conclusion:

In closing, Joey, I hope this portrait of a person who practices second half of life spirituality has been helpful to you. As you continue to journey on your own path in life, you will be able to describe in your own words a portrait of a person who practices second half of life spirituality.

Peace,

Uncle Matthew

Letter #50
Thursday, October 2, 2014

Dear Uncle Matthew,

Thank you for having shared with me your portrait of a person who practices second half of life spirituality. I like your emphasis on developing strong friendships and being authentic. In the seminary, sadly, we are not encouraged to develop strong friendships. Perhaps there is a fear of homosexuality on the part of the administration. I think that the church's fear of human sexuality, rather than helping, actually contributes to the difficulty for us to be chaste and celibate. Also it is difficult for seminarians to be authentic when we are constantly being judged as to whether we are suitable candidates for the priesthood. The ego is tempted to only show the false self to others, to secure its advantages and not to serve others in truth.

I saw a DVD recently entitled, The Fault In Our Stars. A young man, Gus, had bone cancer and a young woman, Hazel, had thyroid cancer. They met each other at a support group meeting for young people with cancer. Gus radiated qualities found in the practice of second half of life spirituality in so many ways. In a nut shell, he was able to celebrate life despite his suffering and he could accept his mortality. Gus's suffering enabled him to become less egocentric and more focused on serving other people. He was not fearful of developing a strong relationship with Hazel. He was authentic. As a result, he could see the face of God in Hazel, and Hazel became less egocentric in her gradual transformation through Gus' love and affirmation. She gradually could see the face of God in Gus. I recommend this film to you, Uncle Matthew. I learned through the film that when we develop strong friendship and are authentic, we have a rich opportunity to be an instrument of transformation. The Fruits of the Spirit are alive!

Today is the feast of the Holy Guardian Angels. The celebrant today gave a good homily. He shared that in his own life certain people briefly crossed his path and, in a mysterious way, they showed him glimpses of divine love. He wondered if he were seeing angels in disguise. He humbly admitted that many times in his own life he ignored his guardian angel's urges to avoid foolish and harmful mistakes and to resist even the temptations of evil.

Uncle Matthew, I am beginning to see some religious topics differently now. Earlier you sent to me a couple of letters that contained a summary of beliefs held during the practice of first half of life spirituality. Could you update me on how these beliefs are viewed when we practice second half of life spirituality? Thank you ahead of time.

Peace,

Joey

Response to Letter #50
Sunday, October 19, 2014

Dear Joey,

Today Pope Francis beatified Pope Paul VI who died in 1978, well before you were born. He was the pope that published the encyclical letter, Humanae Vitae, in 1968 on birth control.

Thank you for sharing some of your thoughts about angels and guardian angels. I wonder how our understanding of angels and archangels is influenced by our images of God. If we believe in an image of a Distant and Exclusive God, do we then assume that angels help us be to be aware of the divine presence only in special people and places? How would our belief in angels and guardian angels change if we see reality through the lens of an Incarnate and Inclusive God who dwells in each one of us? These question have no final answer, but asking and seeking can lead you forward on your journey.

Did your professors say anything about the recent Synod? I read in the NCR that the Synod wants to carry out its pastoral practice "with the tenderness of a mother and the clarity of a teacher." There was a positive tone away from condemnation of unconventional family situations and toward understanding, mercy, and openness.

During the second half of life, many Catholics begin to ask

questions and challenge in both small and big ways some of the beliefs they held during the first half of life. Usually through the years as we have new experiences our world view evolves and changes. This is completely normal; a sign of vigor.

I'll share with you how the practice of second half of life spirituality may alter and transform our views that we hold when we practice first half of life spirituality.

THE WEEK magazine each week shares different view points on the news. The purpose of different viewpoints is to allow readers to make their own judgments. Each one of us must seek new ways to understand reality. New experiences help truth to emerge. I am not making any categorical demands that you change, and I am not making any claims of universal truth. It is your journey, Joey. Many people do not deny what they learned earlier in life, but they simply shift the emphasis or integrate earlier views into larger frameworks. My purpose is not to articulate my own viewpoints or argue for a particular position. Observing different viewpoints is part of the paradigm of the two halves of life that offers a framework for presenting the complexities of reality in an understandable form.

Let me share with you some contemporary books that helped me to understand different viewpoints. Since we all are in different stages of development, some of these books may be helpful to some people but unhelpful to others. Several books by Michael Morwood, an Australian theologian, have helped me to understand how individuals view reality when they practice second half of life spirituality. These books include: It's Time-Challenges to the Doctrine of the Faith, From Sand to Solid Ground; Questions of Faith for Modern Catholics, Is Jesus God-Finding Our Faith, and In Memory of Jesus.

The many books by Retired Bishop John Shelby Spong, especially his book, Why Christianity Must Change or Die-a Bishop Speaks to Believers in Exile, also helped me to understand the thoughts of those who practice second half of life spirituality.

The meditations and books by Fr. Richard Rohr, especially his book, YES, AND Daily Meditations, also offer viewpoints found in the practice of second half of life spirituality.

In sharing with you, I will often use "we" to describe the understanding that can be found among those who practice second half of life spirituality. However, I do not want to give the impression, which would be characteristic of a dualistic paradigm, that everyone who practices first half of life spirituality thinks the same way and everyone who practices second half of life spirituality thinks the same way. Of course there is a mixture of ideas regardless of classification on any issue.

1. Baptism:

As we mature in life, we experience great love for others and unconditional love others have for us. These experiences lead us to a belief in an Unconditionally Loving God. As we believe more and more in an Unconditionally loving God, we realize the inconsistence of our past beliefs that we were born with Original Sin, as we were earlier taught to understand Original Sin. We question the idea that people will lose salvation if they are not baptized. St. Augustine taught that human sin goes back to Adam and has literally been transmitted, unbroken down to our day through sexual intercourse. Doesn't this idea call into question the holiness of marriage and human sexuality?

Most people who practice second half of life spirituality disbelieved in limbo many years before April 2007, when the Vatican agreed that infants could go to Heaven without being baptized to remove Original Sin, and thus they could enjoy the beatific vision.

Matthew Fox, in his critically acclaimed book Original Blessing, provides alternative images of God, Original Sin, and humankind. Fox's images of God seem more in tune with the images that emerge and prevail in the practice of second half of life spirituality. As our images of God change, baptism is thought of as a ritual not to cleanse us from Original Sin, but for the family and community to recognize both the newly baptized and those present as members of the Body of Christ. Baptism calls us to be who we are meant to be with the support of the community. Fr. Richard Rohr in his book, YES..AND..., views baptism as a public ritual that gives "permission to be the image and likeness of God that you already are." Baptisms are often celebrated in the midst of the community so as to emphasize that those who are newly baptized are making a public commitment to live in union with God.

2. Blessings:

When we practice second half of life spirituality, we are less likely to ask a priest or deacon to bless a rosary, home, car, religious medal, or pet because we presume that the object is already holy. We no longer see the need to have a Distant God come "down" to bless the object because we believe that an Incarnate God is already present in the object. If we seek a blessing, the purpose is not to change the object but to make us more aware of and appreciative of God's presence which was and is already there. Priests and bishops who practice second half of life spirituality will encourage lay persons to bless children and even homes to help them realize that anyone can pray a blessing so as to increase awareness that God's Spirit is alive today everywhere.

3. Devotions:

When we practice second half of life spirituality, we place less emphasis on devotions that promise indulgences and place more attention on ministering to the sick, bereaved, lonely, and poor. The act of caring for others becomes a higher form of devotion.

Being a sensitive and forgiving spouse requires a spirituality that is other-centered. Being a good parent requires a spirituality that is other-centered. Being concerned about the plight of homelessness in one's surroundings somehow overshadows one's preoccupation with devotions aimed at the benefit of oneself. Devotions become less important or not important at all, and peace and justice issues become the heart of our spirituality. Helping the Society of St. Vincent de Paul a few hours a week may take priority over participating in a weekly hour of perpetual adoration. The form that our acts of devotion takes will change as the object of our devotion matures and deepens, moving beyond and outside of oneself.

4. Eucharist:

Let me share with you some entries in my journal from many articles and books, especially from Michael Morwood's book, From Sand to Solid Ground.   In the early centuries of the Church, the Eucharistic celebration gave the assembly a deep conviction and awareness of being the "Body of Christ." The Eucharistic celebrations made them aware of who they were. When these early Christians said, "Amen" to the words, "Body of Christ," they were expressing the felt reality that they were the Body of Christ for one another. The presiders at the liturgies were the appointed leaders in the community. The people did not come together to pray as spectators but as active members of one body.

Constantine in the fourth century was the first Roman emperor to convert to Christianity. More people joined the Christian religion. As the Church became aligned with political power, the leaders of the Church increased their own power and control. Their theology was influenced by the structure of the Roman empire.

Gradually, a dualism emerged mirroring the division in society between ruler and ruled, priest and laity. By the middle ages, there was a growing sense of separation between the human and divine, between the every day and the sacred. Combined with the doctrine of Original Sin, as humans felt more remote from their God and the presence of the sacred, a theology of unworthiness flourished. The focus became human sin and failure, instead of God's blessing and human service. People questioned how their bodies could be sacred or considered part of God's good creation. A shift occurred in the church's core message, from "God-with-us; the God to be loved," to that of "God far from us; the God to be feared." As this message was internalized, many people stopped going to communion because they felt unworthy of actually being a living part of the Body of Christ.

Within this structural and liturgical setting, the Blessed Sacrament was increasingly reserved for adoration and processions. Genuflecting to the tabernacle reinforced the concept that the sacred was found primarily there, rather than in and among the people. Gradually the assembly thought of the sacred as present only in the consecrated bread and wine rather than seeing themselves as the "Body of Christ." Thus the laity became passive, separate, and even alienated.

Garry Wills in his book, Why Priests?, says, "The host, as a separate object of worship, outside and apart from the Mass, had become the whole point of the faith."

The Eucharist thus became an object, a "thing" rather than a shared celebration and affirmation. The Eucharist was no longer a sacred time of heightened awareness of the presence of God within and among God's people themselves, but instead God was seen located in the Eucharist that was adored and present in a tabernacle or a monstrance.

Today, some priests and bishops exemplify this theology of the host as being a discrete and singular focus of God by holding up for a prolonged period of time during the consecration part of the mass the Body and Blood. The host becomes in this way a totem.

In contrast, other priests and bishops give emphasis through their actions that the host represents the immanent presence of Christ among all participants who form the Body of Christ. The host in this way makes us aware that God is among us. We are the Body of Christ.

The Second Vatican Council tried to make us aware once again that we are the "People of God." The liturgy was to remind us that we come as a "body," not as separate individuals. Taking communion in the hand, participating in the offertory procession, offering the Prayers of the Faithful were all attempts to make us aware that the presence of God is not only "out there" and "in" the host, but also within and among us. Those who practice second half of life spirituality believe in the sacredness of the consecrated bread and wine, but there is a greater emphasis on recapturing the early tradition in the Church that the Eucharist is something we participate in. We are to live in a way that demonstrates who we really are, the People of God, the living Body of Christ.

Those who practice first half of life spirituality tend to remain caught up in a piety focused on the Eucharist as a thing to be adored. Both those in first and second half of life spirituality genuflect before the tabernacle. We are encouraged to bow just before receiving the Eucharist. These gestures are signs of reverence for the sacramental presence of Christ in the Eucharist and in the tabernacle. Those who practice second half of life spirituality believe the Eucharist encourages us to respect and reverence ourselves, our neighbor, and in all things around us. They desire to live as the Body of Christ rather than just to adore the sacred in a particular place. God permeates all of creation. We cannot comprehend everything being holy and sacred, so we have to start somewhere. The Eucharist is just such a place where we begin to recognize that the holy and sacred are present everywhere and in all times. Fr. Richard Rohr says in his book, YES, AND..., "If you can comprehend the sacred in one moment, know it is in all moments too."

Michael Morwood in his book, It's Time, says that the Passover Meal was permeated with the power of symbols. For instance, Jesus beautifully summarized his life of service for others when he washed the feet of his disciples. Further, Morwood says that the breaking of bread and the giving of wine can be understood as Jesus saying, "This is what it is like to be me, someone blessed and broken and given." The Eucharistic celebration reminds us that we do God's will when we, like Jesus, see ourselves as blessed and are willing to be broken and given to others.

5. God:

In earlier letters to you, I outlined some images commonly held of God when we practice first half of life spirituality. As we have more experiences in life, we question our earlier images of God. Jesus spoke about children and nature. Jesus used images familiar with the people to help them have vivid, real, and healthy images of God. Parents see wonderful positive traits in their children that help them catch glimpses of God, the Spirit of the Resurrected Christ, alive today. These positive traits (innocence, docility, transparency, honesty) help parents to practice these virtues.

We may, if blessed, and if open, gradually outgrow many of our images of God such as belief in a Distant God, an Exclusive God, a Vengeful God, a God Preoccupied with Sex, a God Demanding Perfection, My God Alone, and a Male God. Our human experiences as parents, grandparents, church leaders, friends, co-workers, even as strangers all contribute to changing our images of God.

We may gradually embrace images such as an Incarnate God, an Inclusive God, a Just God, a Merciful and Compassionate God, Our God, a Male/Female God, a Courageous God, an Empathetic God, a God of Grace, a Forgiving God, an Unconditionally Loving God, and a Patient God. When this happens, we increasingly understand the words in scripture, "Whoever does not love does not know God, because God is Love" (1 John 4:8).

As our images of God change, we tend to fear God less and love God more. God is no longer a Vengeful Judge. Our admiration of Jesus and our desire to imitate his virtues enlighten us to see in Him, what we see in God.

When we contemplate the marvels of nature, we experience the presence of God everyday and everywhere. When we experience in our own everyday lives acts of extraordinary kindness and rich compassion, we experience God's Spirit, the Spirit of the Resurrected Christ, in a direct and immediate way. We gradually realize that when we are generous, forgiving, and compassionate, we are witnessing the presence of God's Spirit in ourselves.

We firmly believe in the second half of life that our personal experiences are the means whereby we can discover new images of God that are quite different from those images that we learned in the first half of life.

Conclusion:

I hope this material is of some help to you, Joey. Please keep in mind that every person is at a different place on their life's journey. As a good shepherd, you must be able to put yourself in their shoes as you minister to them. Be open to new ideas.

Peace,

Uncle Matthew

Letter #51
Sunday, November 2, 2014


Dear Uncle Matthew,

Your reflections on the way some people change their religious
beliefs made me think deeply about my own religious beliefs. It is
so easy for me to just accept what I am taught without question.
My Catholic upbringing and current schooling reinforce this
tendency. I find in the seminary that the atmosphere lacks the joy
and excitement that comes when there is open discussion on
controversial topics. The atmosphere of discouraging
questioning contributes to my tendency to think dualistically, but I
am making some progress in thinking holistically and embracing
mystery. I find that being aware of new ideas is the key to being
open to change.

I liked what you said about the Eucharist. Our theological studies
on the sacraments presented the Eucharist through the dualistic
lens of the sacred and the secular. My professor said that only
the priests can confect the Eucharist. What do you think about
this, Uncle Matthew?

Today is All Souls' Day. I remembered at Mass your mom and
dad even though they died before I was born, and I know them
only through family stories and photos.

One of our professors took several days to teach us about the

Synod. I found it hopeful in some ways but disappointing that no women were there to vote. In this day and age, not allowing women to vote is like an "elephant in the living room," demanding attention and the addressing of grievances. The Church has a long way to go to be acceptable to those who believe in the equality of women. The bishops reaffirmed their objection to same-sex marriage, but they did not use the "intrinsically disordered" language of the past. That's progress, although slow. The Synod will meet again in 2015. There was a call to welcome and accept gay people, unmarried couples, and those Catholics who are in divorce situations.

Please continue to share with me your insights on how our beliefs may change when we practice second half of life spirituality.

Peace,

Joey

Response to Letter #51
Sunday, November 16, 2014

Dear Joey,

Today is the Thirty-third Sunday in Ordinary Time. In the gospel, Jesus spoke about using our talents wisely. In my homily, I shared Shel Silverstein's story of the Giving Tree. I know you recall that beautiful story about an apple tree that loved a boy from the time he was a child until he was an old man. The tree offered the boy everything it had—apples, branches and trunk—and the tree was happy.

The story about the Giving Tree reminds us that the God we adore each Sunday loves us so much and continually gives to us everything we have. God is like the Giving Tree. When we give to others, share with others, show compassion to others, we are happy, and we are like God who created us to be like the Giving Tree.

You asked me if only priests can confect the Eucharist. Today, some church leaders are caught up in the notion of the "real presence" and how it works and who has it and who does not have it. This springs from first half of life thinking that tries to define mystery. Those who practice second half of life spirituality know that mystery can't be defined. Their focus is on the People of God as the "Body of Christ." They ask, "Isn't our shared commitment to live as members of the Body of Christ more important than doctrinal issues that involve us?" They ask, "If God is everywhere, then isn't God also present in the communion services in other Christian church denominations?" Why would God offer a splendid feast to members in one denomination and jelly sandwiches to members of another denomination if we all are God's children? Would parents deny one of their children good food, and yet give splendid food to another child in their family? "Who is God?" becomes the question that we both ask and answer through our practice of and belief in the Eucharist. What are our images of God? Once we change or modify our images of God, our theology changes regarding the Eucharist.

Many people who practice second half of life spirituality deny that only a priest has the power to bring God's presence to the people. They cite the fact that Jesus never ordained anyone. For over one hundred years following the death of Jesus, there was no such thing as ordained priests to perform priestly rituals for a church. This history raises profound questions such as: "Do we believe that we are a priestly people who can do what Jesus did?" "Why do we need a separate cast of ordained priests when we are all priests?" And relatedly, "Did Jesus ever intend to found a church outside of the Jewish community in his day?"

In my previous letter to you, I shared that our beliefs may change when we practice second half of life spirituality. I emphasized that by presenting these changes in our beliefs, I was not necessarily agreeing with all that I am sharing with you. I simply want you to be aware of different viewpoints so that you can respectfully appreciate and dialogue with more people.

I discussed (1) baptism, (2) blessings, (3) devotions, (4) Eucharist, and (5) God. At your request, I will continue to share how our viewpoints may change regarding (6) Good Friday, (7) Heaven and Hell, (8) holiness, (9) Holy Thursday, (10) homosexuality, (11) Jesus, (12) marriage, (13) Mary, (14) and Original Sin. I'm sharing this material from my journal where I have written down many reflections of others on these topics.

6. Good Friday:

St. Paul taught that the world was essentially sinful because of Adam's sin. St. Paul believed that Jesus had to die for our sins so that God would forgive us. This understanding of Jesus' death on the Cross is understood as the "ransom theory."

When we practice second half of life spirituality, we question whether Jesus ever believed he had to die in order to win God's forgiveness or for God to impart forgiveness upon the world. We gradually dismiss an image of God as Vengeful; requiring the death of his Son. We see Jesus' death on a Cross as a consequence of what he stood for as a man of integrity, courage, and faithfulness in a world where the political and religious powers could not tolerate this. The Spirit that gave Jesus the ability to die while loving and forgiving is the same Spirit we share or at least hope to share as followers of Jesus.

Good Friday gives us an image of Jesus as broken, self-giving, and forgiving; a Suffering Servant. Jesus' death gives us courage and faith that in our own suffering the same Spirit that gave Jesus the strength he needed is with us.

7. Heaven and Hell:

When we practice second half of life spirituality, we come to realize more fully the infinite love of God as we experience human love for our partners, children, grandchildren, friends, and even strangers. As our human love broadens, we come to realize first hand God's love of all. When we experience such great love for others, we begin to question whether God sends people to Hell for eternal punishment. We would never want our children to suffer eternal damnation, no matter what our children may have done.

Our experiences show us that the person who loves us the most on earth would never put us into Hell or fail to forgive us. I believe I heard Fr. Richard Rohr say that God loves us at least as much as the person who loves us the most on earth. In regard to the Bible, Fr. Richard Rohr says in his book, YES, AND...,

"If you see God operating at a lesser level than the best person you know, then that text is not authentic revelation....Literalism is the lowest and most narrow hermeneutic for understanding conversation in general and sacred texts in particular."

When we practice second half of life spirituality, we lose interest in supporting, or trying to live within a system of rewards and punishments. Retired Bishop John Shelby Spong says in his book, Why Christianity Must Change or Die,

"I do assert that one prepares for eternity not by being religious and keeping the rules, but by living fully, loving wastefully, and daring to be all that each of us has the capacity to be."

Fr. Ronald Rolheiser says in his book, Forgotten Among the Lilies,

"It is easy to go to hell in this life. It is not so easy, however, to stay there for eternity. Why? .... God's love can, as we see in Christ's death and resurrection, descend into hell and embrace and bring to peace tortured and paranoid hearts."

Fr. Richard Rohr says in his book, Falling Upward, that Pope John Paul II said that heaven and hell were primarily eternal states of consciousness more than geographical places of later reward and punishment.

Most people practice first half of life spirituality that clings to a belief in winners and losers because that is the way our society works. In schools, work places, sports, and even in religion, we are accustomed to winners and losers; the haves and the have-nots.

As we assume an adult spirituality, we begin to discard the dualisms of winners and losers, and we begin to believe that love makes it possible to overcome these dualisms.

8.  Holiness:

One of the principle documents of the Vatican II Council was
Lumen Gentium; The Dogmatic Constitution on the Church. The
first words, Lumen Gentium, in the document mean in Latin,
"Light of the nations." The document was promulgated by Pope
Paul VI in November 1964. The fifth chapter in this document is
about the universal call to holiness. All Christians are called to
the fullness of Christian life and to the perfection of charity.

Those who practice second half of life spirituality believe the
good news that there is only one vocation to which all baptized
individuals are called; the vocation to holiness which takes place
in and through the experiences in our daily lives.

When we practice second half of life spirituality, we try to avoid
the dualisms that create a separation between the holy and the
unholy. We realize that we are already holy because we were
born as spiritual beings. We emphasize becoming more human;
a manifestation of our divinity. We emphasize who we already
are.

Contemplative prayer helps in that awareness process. Once we
realize that holiness is not necessarily apartness, we can better
appreciate the wisdom in this insight Fr. Richard Rohr shares in
his book, YES, AND...,"There were only unholy hearts and
minds for Jesus, but not inherently holy or unholy places,
actions, or people."

Once we assume that God is present everywhere and in
everyone, we can believe that all people are holy, and capable
of, and called to, sanctification. This belief gives us a greater
respect for all life. We avoid the dualisms of thinking Christians
are holier than non-Christians or that believers in God are holier
than atheists. Who can judge the heart of others?

Thomas Merton in his book, New Seeds of Contemplation, said,

"It is true to say for me sanctity consists in being myself and for you sanctity consists in being yourself and that, in the last analysis, your sanctity will never be mine and mine will never be yours, except in the communism of charity and grace."

Holiness is manifested when we serve others and when we are patient and compassionate with others and ourselves. Jesus warned us to beware of false prophets. He said that there are both false and true prophets, but the difference could be recognized by the quality of their deeds, their fruits, "By their fruits you will know them" (Matthew 7:16).

9. Holy Thursday

On the night before Jesus died, as was regular Jewish custom, he had a Passover meal with those closest to him. Jesus was, from the scriptural accounts, not intending to start a new religion nor to form a new  priesthood. At the Last Supper, Jesus was asking his disciples to commit themselves to carrying on his ministry so that there would be a better and more compassionate humanity. As Michael Morwood says in his book, It's Time, the bread symbolically expressed what it is like to be Jesus; to be blessed, broken, and given.

Rob Bell, Jr., an American author and pastor says in his book, What We Talk About When We Talk About God, that when Jesus took bread and wine and said that these ordinary foods were his body and blood, he was treating them as sacred. For Jesus, all bread and wine were holy and sacred because all of life is holy and sacred. Joey, this makes me think of our discussion on the Eucharist when we said through a ritual consecration and prayer our awareness of God's presence is heightened. God's presence, and our awareness of it, is the essence of holiness.

10. Homosexuality:

When we practice second half of life spirituality, we consider the Church's basic teachings on human sexuality to be incompatible with the gospel and thus harmful and fallacious. We see beyond and beneath rigid and literal proof-texts, and we seek God's will in scripture, tradition, and, importantly, in the revelations of life experiences. When in humility we accept mystery as the heart of God's message, we believe love is the primary litmus test of sexual expression, and human relationships in general.

We consider homosexuality not a "chosen life style," but a God-given orientation for some, as heterosexuality is for the many. Some church scholars say that Aelred of Rievaulx (1109-1167) was a gay saint. He is the patron saint of friendship. His treatise on "Spiritual Friendship" is still considered to be one of the best theological statements on the connection between human love and spiritual love.

It is widely acknowledged that many good priests are gay and celibate. We question, "Why is the Church against homosexuality when so many church leaders are gay?" A hidden cost of this perceived hypocrisy is a diminishment of respect for broader church authority on other issues.

Michael Morwood says in his book, From Sand to Solid Ground, that the condemnation in Genesis 19 has as much to do with an abuse of hospitality as it has to do with particular sexual activity. He further suggests that people should have respect for the divine presence in all people as well as respecting people's rights to express love according to their particular sexual orientation.

Retired Bishop John Spong in his forward to Daniel A. Helminiak's book What the Bible Really Says About Homosexuality says when people take the Bible literally, they can justify their own prejudices. Dr. Helminiak in his book has a whole chapter on the Sin of Sodom in Genesis 19. He also understands the sin of Sodom as a sin of inhospitality.

11. Jesus:

Joey, to attempt to say something about Jesus in a short letter is almost impossible. But let me say this. When we practice second half of life spirituality, we contemplate more the human side of

Jesus. We marvel at how a boy, then a young man, became so God-filled, and so powerfully inspiring to so many. When we see Jesus as more like us, it challenges us to be more like him. Books could be written on this topic, but this will have to suffice for now.

12. Marriage:

The Catholic Church holds that marriage is a life-long covenant between a man and a woman and only a man and a woman.

When we practice second half of life spirituality, we are more tolerant with those who do not fully accept all of the official teachings of the Catholic Church. This fact is relevant to our thinking about marriage. We tend to be less judgmental because we have experienced over the years our own virtues as well as vices. We see how different experiences lead to different understandings. There is a willingness to listen, to be open to new ideas, and to see reality more as gray rather than in the dualism of black or white. There is also a belief in the sensus fidelium; a belief in "the sense of the faithful" and an appreciation of the beliefs of all the people.

We see that throughout the Christian faith, not to mention secular society, institutional reforms reflecting these changing perspectives.  For example, same-sex marriage or marriage equality has been affirmed by the United Church of Christ, the Unitarian Universalist Association of Congregations, and the Reform and Conservative movements in Judaism.  Elsewhere, in May next year, the government of Ireland will hold a referendum asking if voters want to add to their Constitution such that, "Marriage may be contracted in accordance with the law by two persons without distinction to their sex." Ireland is 72% Catholic. Further, the Supreme Court, with relevant cases moving through the appellate courts, will eventually issue a ruling whether to legalize same-sex marriage across the United States. The justices may rule that states cannot deny gay men and lesbians the same marriage rights enjoyed by opposite sex couples.

You mentioned earlier in June of this year, the Presbyterian Church voted at its general assembly to change its constitution's definition of marriage from "a man and a woman" to "two people," and to allow its ministers to perform same-sex marriages where it is legal.

When we practice second half of life spirituality, we are likely to disagree with bishops who warn diocesan employees that any action in support of now-legal same-sex marriage could cost them their jobs. The issue becomes that of freedom of conscience.

## 13. Mary

When we practice second half of life spirituality, we begin to question our understanding of Mary's immaculate conception, her virginal conception of Jesus, and her bodily assumption into heaven. The problem is that we think that mythical stories are actually historical and literal. Thus, we tend to make false conclusions and beliefs. It can support negation of the body and sexuality. We also find ourselves needlessly defending miraculous stories as literal historic events instead of expressions of deep spiritual truths. During the practice of second half of life spirituality, we are able to avoid the excesses of Marian devotion, while at the same time seeing her relevance more deeply in our lives.

Michael Morwood in his book, It's Time, says,

"Mary can still be held as a model of the Church community, not because she was immaculately conceived, but because she can be viewed as a woman who mirrors the struggle we all experience in shifting from a faith perspective we never thought we would question to a faith deeply committed to the dream of Jesus."

## 14. Original Sin

By the time we reach the second half of life, we have had many experiences that may challenge or confirm what we were taught earlier secondhand. For many, bringing children into the world, more than anything else, initiates profound questioning about human nature. What is Original Sin? If this dogma is true, is my child defective from birth? How could my child be considered born in sin when my baby appears to be so purely innocent? Many holding what they believe to be a miracle in their arms conclude that children are not born in sin. Their hearts tell them that they do not need to have the stain of Original Sin taken away because it was never there. They do not believe that children are fallen creatures who will loose salvation if they are not baptized.

The impact of Original Sin has been profound. Author, educator and counselor John Bradshaw says in his book, Homecoming,

"The doctrine of Original Sin has been a major source for many repressive and cruel child-rearing practices. However, there is no clinical evidence to support any kind of innate depravity in children."

Instead of this abstract theology of Original Sin, there is another way of looking at the moral nature of our children. The nineteenth century naturalist Charles Darwin wrote On the Origin of Species in 1859. After decades of natural observation and rational reflection, he believed we emerged from an evolutionary past and we are still being formed. Many conclude, based on their own lives and modern science, that we never were "perfect." Thus, the former ways of teaching the Adam and Eve story are called into question.

Fr. Thomas Merton offers an understanding of Original Sin that is acceptable to some people in the second half of life because it is more spiritual and psychological in nature. He says in New Seeds of Contemplation,

"To say I was born in sin is to say I came into the world with a false self. I was born in a mask. I came into existence under a sign of contradiction, being someone that I was never intended to be and therefore a denial of what I am supposed to be."

Joey, I hope these reflections help. As you can see, the range of beliefs held by faithful Christians is broad, and deep, and embracing of the many truths of our shared existence. In my next letter, I will share some more viewpoints found in the practice of second half of life spirituality.

Peace,

Uncle Matthew

Letter #52
Monday, December 8, 2014

Dear Uncle Matthew,

Today we celebrated the feast of the Immaculate Conception. You mentioned earlier Michael Morwood's book, It's Time. I picked up a copy at the book store, and I was drawn to Chapter Thirteen, "The Unreality of Doctrine; Mary, the Mother of Jesus." I found that chapter very interesting, and it made me think hard about today's feast. It made me wonder about the deep spiritual truths expressed in the Mary story, and why we do what we do as a church.

Your letters are wonderful. Thank you! The viewpoints on different religious topics held by those who practice second half of life spirituality are very helpful to me. I especially liked the provocative, yet sensible, viewpoints on original sin and homosexuality. In college, I had a good friend who was (and is) gay. Although I am straight, I admired him in so many ways, particularly his character and absolute trustworthiness. He had so many sterling qualities, many of which I didn't have. I found that the issue of sexual orientation receded in importance the better I got to know him, simply, as a fellow human being that had become a good friend. I believe that shaming individuals because of their sexual orientation is unjust and something that Jesus would never have done. The gospels tell us he was focused on more important matters (love!).

Unfortunately, here in the seminary, we are not exposed to the ideas you are presenting. I'm grateful that you are muddying the waters for me. I'm forced to think every time I read your letters. I realize that you don't necessarily embrace all the viewpoints you share. Rather,  you are illustrating how different life experiences, from different places in society, lead to many different paths to God. I am grateful that your letters force me to think rather than just accepting without reflection church dogmas. I believe this abundance of ideas reflects the glory of God.

I'm interested in you sharing some more viewpoints from the perspective of second half of life spirituality. Will you please do so?!

Peace,

Joey

Response to Letter #52
Sunday, December 21, 2014

Dear Joey,

I'm glad the viewpoints of noted second half of life theologians, clerics, and lay persons are helping you. I wish someone had shared this material with me much earlier in life because it would have allowed me to be a more flexible and mature pastor open to new ideas and God's mysteries. I didn't take the time until I retired to research these various viewpoints. I envy academics who have the time and resources to study various issues from different viewpoints because they seem to fear less and contribute more to a true understanding of reality.

I realize that yesterday you left the seminary for your Christmas break. This letter will be waiting when you return. I'll call you after Christmas.

Today is the Fourth Sunday of Advent. In my homily I summarized the film, It's a Wonderful Life. James Stewart played George Bailey who learned to trust the angel, Clarence. In my homily, I offered the idea that the angel represented George Bailey's inner self, his true self. The overall message is that a deep faith in God is not found in our acceptance of dogmas but in our everyday trust in God. George Bailey inspired others because he was a good man who derived his goodness from living as his true self.

We need to constantly thank God for those individuals in our lives who inspire us so as to be more receptive to the peace, joy, and love that is central to the feast of Christmas.

I'll share some more topics that can be understood from the viewpoint of second half of life spirituality.

15. Pentecost

Most of what follows, Joey, is material from Michael Morwood's book, Is Jesus God?

The Jewish religion had its own feast of Pentecost fifty days after Passover commemorating the giving of the Torah at Mount Sinai. The feast also celebrated the annual harvest and the bringing of the first fruits to the Temple.

Some scholars believe that the early Christian preaching and writing about Pentecost may be best understood as adapting the Jewish celebration about the giving of the Torah to fit the emerging Christology to proclaim a new beginning. This new beginning was identified with the giving of the Spirit from God that the disciples experienced in a profoundly transformative way. While believing that there was a new giving of the Spirit at Pentecost, some scholars do not view Pentecost as the time when Jesus' disciples received the gifts of the Spirit not formerly possessed. They believe that God's Spirit had never been absent from any aspect of creation.

After Jesus' death, his disciples increasingly realized that they shared the Holy Spirit that Jesus had been filled with and lived out of. They were challenged by that awareness, as are we, to witness to the Spirit in their lives as courageously as Jesus. So today, from this perspective, Pentecost is a time to affirm that we all are, or may increasingly become, temples of the Holy Spirit. Pentecost is not about begging God to send the Holy Spirit but rather a time to be grateful that we already share in God's Spirit.

## 16. Prayer

When we practice second half of life spirituality, we begin to see that much of our prayer life has been based, whether we realize it or not, on the idea that it is God who needs our prayers. The truth is that it is we who need to pray because it is we who need God. Indeed, we are increasingly drawn to prayer because it heightens our awareness of God's transforming presence and thus satisfies our thirst for this presence. We want to pray because it puts us in touch with the joyful and liberating truth that we are to revere and respect all human life. Prayer can foster a realization that we are earthly temples, wondrously imperfect, of the Holy Spirit.

We come to realize that all our actions may be seen as prayer rather than prayer being an exclusive act, as something we are either doing or not doing. Prayer is a stance, a way of living in the presence of an Incarnate God.The replacement of an image of a Distant God with an Incarnate God ends the practice of praying to a heavenly God that watches, rewards, and punishes us from on high afar. Praying becomes more personal, more immediate, more real. The loving God is always present here and now.

Garry Wills says in his book, Why Priests?, "The true aim of prayer is to make the believer acknowledge that the will of God is better than one's own will." And he adds that prayer not only leads to acknowledging God's will, but to the joyful transformation of one's own will so that it truly aligns with God's intent. Prayer is not as concerned with a legalistic concept but with a personal relationship with God. Prayer helps us to remember that we are created in God's image. Prayer stresses the humanity of Jesus. Thus there is an avoidance of relating to Jesus as a remote god-figure on a heavenly throne but rather as someone who is a friend and a companion that truly understands us, our burdens, and our longings.

Retired Bishop John Shelby Spong relates that when we have an image of a Distant God (in the practice of first half of life spirituality,) we assume that prayer is a withdrawal from this world so as to concentrate on this Distant God. With this mindset, we seek to pray in a way that is separate from others in a more isolated way. We may seek to make private retreats, take pilgrimages to far-away Marian shrines, spend an hour in an adoration chapel, and pursue quiet days in search for union with God. These activities in themselves may be good indeed. Yet if not part of a broader understanding of prayer that includes emersion in the community, these activities may become egocentric and counter-productive to mature spirituality.

For years Bishop Spong spent the first two hours of the morning in his study for his prayer time. Then as Bishop Spong evolved (in the practice of second half of life spirituality), he came to see the two hours in the morning not as his discrete "prayer time" but rather as his "holy time", a time to renew his commitment and preparation to being a prayerful person the rest of the day. In his book, Why Christianity Must Change or Die, he says that prayer is "a process of being open to all that life can be and then of acting to bring the fullness to pass." In short, he believes that prayer can never be separated from acting prayerfully.

17. Resurrection

Pope Benedict XVI demanded that Catholic theologians not engage this topic but rather give public submission of intellect to a literal belief in a bodily resurrection. And yet, St. Paul in his writings never referred to a bodily resurrection. He was not concerned with how the resurrection happened. His focus was on its effects.

Some people who practice second half of life spirituality do not believe that God literally raised Jesus from death three days after he died. They do not believe that the stories of an empty tomb and ascension into heaven are to be taken literally. Nor are these literal beliefs necessary for their faith. Michael Morwood has written many books that reflect ideas found in the practice of second half of life spirituality. He says in his book, Is Jesus God?, "Jesus' dead body did not come back to life again and resume human existence as Jesus had experienced it before death..."

When we practice second half of life spirituality, we are not concerned about the "how" of the Resurrection. We believe the Resurrection is a mystery with significance for life here on Earth and beyond. We believe in Jesus' Resurrection, but we see Jesus' Resurrection as a new way of living and existing that is open to all. We believe Jesus' Resurrection is proof that life does not end in death but continues on. Jesus' Resurrection proves that love triumphs over sin and death.

Fr. Ronald Rolheiser, in his book The Holy Longing, speaks about the Paschal Mystery and does so by differentiating between terminal death and paschal death. Terminal death ends life. Paschal death represents the ending of one kind of life and the opening of a person to a deeper and richer form of life. It is a death that is in fact a birth. Fr. Rolheiser distinguishes as well two kinds of life: resuscitated life and resurrected life. Resuscitated life is when one is merely restored to one's former life. Resurrected life, on the other hand, is not a simple restoration of one's old life but the reception of a radically new life. Jesus both taught and illustrated the Paschal Mystery.

Pastor Rob Bell, in his book What We Talk About When We Talk About God, says, "Jesus faced the worst that can happen to a person and came out alive on the other side, alive in a new way." Those who practice second half of life spirituality believe that God had always raised human beings into the mystery of eternal life beyond this present mode of existence.

Those who practice second half of life spirituality believe that the Resurrection teaches that not only was the presence of the divine alive in Jesus, but now the Resurrected Christ is alive in us and also in our neighbor. We now have the power to love and forgive just like Jesus. Being non-dualistic, we believe that the divine and human are not separate, but rather our bodies are the means in which the divine lives in us. Religion should be helping us to expand our consciousness so that we might see things that we previously missed, namely the presence of Christ in ourselves, others, and in all the things we see!

We believe that if we face our sufferings and our shadow side with trust, accountability, and integrity, then we too will come out of it alive in a new way. Easter proclaims to us the validity of a Forgiving God, an Unconditionally Loving God, an Empathetic God, a God of Grace, and a Patient God. Easter proclaims that Jesus is alive and that God is with us!

18. Sacrament of Reconciliation:

When we practice second half of life spirituality, we observe that most parishioners at Advent and Lenten Reconciliation Services are middle-aged or older. And yet the liturgical format is usually structured for youth and young adults. Therefore, so many older people practice confession the same way they did when they were children. "I missed mass once, but I was sick. I forgot to say my morning prayers. I was impatient while driving. I said twelve bad words...."

In Reconciliation Services where the majority of attendees are middle-aged and older, those who practice second half of life spirituality believe that the presider should try to help the attendees look more deeply into their lives for what is missing and what still may be done so that they could be whole. When a person is complete and whole, there is joy and peace.

So often the Reconciliation Services emphasize how bad we are. The long examination of conscience makes everyone feel like losers. Some people wonder if it would be better if the Reconciliation Services placed the emphasis on God's infinite mercy and forgiveness?

The practice of first half of life spirituality tends to judge, correct, admonish, and even humiliate others. The practice of second half of life spirituality tries to affirm, praise, induce gratitude, and instill true forgiveness. Second half of life spirituality attempts to promote an Unconditionally Loving God instead of a Vengeful

God to be feared.

There is a useful tool for spiritual discernment, the Enneagram, that identifies nine compulsions and nine corresponding virtues. Reconciliation Services for adults could be a time to examine one's virtues and compulsions in this context. The nine compulsions are often called the nine Passions and they include the Seven Capital Sins. The celebrant of the Penance Service could invite those present to think about their anger, pride, deceit, envy, greed, fear, gluttony, lust, and laziness. He would explain each passion with some examples. Then the celebrant would explain the virtues (the Fruits of the Spirit): patience, humility, honesty, harmony, objectivity, courage, sober joy, innocence, and action. The compulsions point to what is missing from our lives if we are to be whole, while the virtues are good indicators of spiritual health.

Confession should be about naming the darkness and pain that lies within, and through this conscious naming, before a fellow human being, we realize liberation and freedom. Confession should rob the darkness of its power so that we experience a transformation into becoming more holistic. Confession should be permeated with the light of Christ. When we are honest with someone who is accepting and loving, we see our shadow side with compassion. Honesty allows us to be less divided so that we have a chance at integrating our missing pieces. Reconciliation reminds us that we need each other. We need friends and community so as to live whole, integrated lives, with nothing hidden.

Today those who practice second half of life spirituality want to hear less about who has the authority to forgive and more about the need, even the duty, for all of us to forgive. Many people today believe that they can tell their sins to a friend, in person or on the telephone, or share their sins at a Twelve-step meeting, and the sins are forgiven. They believe reconciliation with God takes place. They believe that God is so much bigger than what they imagined when they practiced first half of life spirituality. They believe that Jesus, a layman, an unordained Rabbi, was always ready to forgive the sinner and so should we!

Pope Francis said, "The confessional is not a torture chamber." Today fewer people celebrate the Sacrament of Reconciliation on a regular basis. Despite many efforts to make people aware of the Sacrament of Reconciliation, the people have voted with their feet. The dark past of the confessional is fading away.

Peace,

Uncle Matthew

Letter #53
Monday, January 12, 2015

Dear Uncle Matthew,

I enjoyed our  conversation on the phone Christmas Day. The holidays overall were so up-lifting. Mom and Dad were so very loving and affirming of me and Paul during our stay at their home. I mentioned to them that I am still discerning my vocation in life. They told me that they only want me to be happy in life, regardless of the vocation I choose. I returned to the seminary last Thursday, grateful yet sad to leave my family.

Thank you for sharing with me further insights into religious topics from the viewpoint of second half of life spirituality. The sharing on Pentecost was enlightening. It makes sense, when we believe in an Unconditionally Loving God, that God's Spirit was, is, and never will be absent from any aspect of creation.

I like what you said about prayer, especially the insight from Bishop Spong when he said prayer is best understood not only as a discrete act but as an entire disposition towards life. His notion of prayer as deliberate, mindful living, is quite different from the typical understanding of prayer as a specific act where I am either praying or not praying at any given time. This conventional understanding of prayer strikes me as dualistic and needlessly constraining.

I liked the quote from Pope Francis, "The confessional is not a torture chamber." Here at the seminary, it is hard to be fully honest in confession when we know we are being scrutinized and judged under a microscope. I liked the way you described an adult spirituality in the celebration of the Sacrament of Reconciliation. In the seminary, we celebrate the sacrament occasionally in a group setting in the traditional way that you described. But the stress here is on individual confession. My experience with individual confession has been that I am being taught, even encouraged, to become painfully aware of how bad I am and how ungrateful I am, rather than as a time to better appreciate God's forgiveness and unconditional love for me. I find that, after confession, I feel diminished through self recrimination, not enlarged through God's sustaining love.

Please continue to stir the pot so that I am forced once again to become aware that people have different viewpoints regarding the same religious topics. I believe in the end, this will make me a better shepherd.

Peace,

Joey

Response to Letter #53
Thursday, January 29, 2015

Dear Joey,

I hope you had a wonderful birthday yesterday on the Feast of St. Thomas Aquinas. You are a remarkable young man. I truly enjoy this rare dialogue that we share with one another.

I'm glad you are still discerning your life's vocation. You made an abrupt change when you left your job at the NSA after only working there for two years. I realize the importance of your sudden conversion experience when you saw an etching in one of your high school catechisms of a young man at a crossroads in his life. New life experiences can bring about a sudden awareness of one's call in life.

A practical way to discern your life's vocation, a question that cuts through a lot of abstraction and well-meaning religiosity, is to ask yourself if you can live a life of chastity within the framework of celibacy. Very few men can remain celibate and chaste, as the Church defines chastity, and still become fully human and fully alive. I have, however, met some celibates, although rare, who appear to be happy, fulfilled, and fully human. Truly, many are called but few are chosen!

Last Friday Pope Francis repeated his view that it should be easier for divorced Catholics to get an annulment and at no charge. That was good news.

And now, as you asked, I'll share further how key religious topics may be viewed through the practice of second half of life spirituality.

19. Salvation:

Michael Morwood in his book, Tomorrow's Catholic, states that salvation is, first and foremost, being set free, here and now, from images, ideas, and practices that enslave us to a distant overseer God.

Retired Bishop John Shelby Spong in his book This Hebrew, Lord, says that salvation is not an escape from life, but it is being full of life, and fully in life. Salvation means God's creation is to be loved. The world is to be entered into. Life is to be lived. And we are to know that we are loved.

Marcus J. Borg, in his book Convictions describes salvation as transformation. Salvation is about this life, not the next. Liberation from bondage is a metaphor for salvation. Salvation is a return from exile which is the central metaphor in the story of the prodigal son who returns so as to be reconnected with his father (God).

20. Scripture:

Joey, I won't share too much in this area since you are taking Biblical studies in third theology. I already shared a lot of information with you about revelation, inspiration, and inerrancy as they relate to scripture.

By now you realize the Bible is not simply the literal, unmediated word of God. Scriptural texts come to us through the inspired human hand, expressing and relating how different people understood their experiences of God. The scriptures reflect a specific cultural setting, inescapably shaped by the beliefs of that time and place. Oral tradition, often for centuries, preceded any writing of the actual texts themselves. The texts were added to and edited over time, particularly the older Hebrew Scriptures. None of this understanding of the human and historical nature of the texts need diminish the power of scripture, but can instead make its truths deeply, undeniably real for the reader with clear eyes.

When we practice second half of life spirituality, our curiosity and thirst for the truth often lead us to explore the origins of the gospels. We seek to first view the gospels through the lens of ancient Jewish eyes since the text emerged from within the context of ancient Jewish culture.

Also our clarity of thought and devotional passions may be enhanced when we come to appreciate the many literary forms in the Bible: metaphor, paradox, analogy, history, fiction, parable, midrash, hyperbole, autobiography, and poetry. It is also important as not to confuse things and unwittingly promote error, to appreciate the many paradoxes in the Bible that Jesus and the sacred authors used to convey mystery. Paradox, once frightening to us, becomes a point of revelation.

An excellent resource to study these issues is the Pontifical Biblical Commission's book, The Interpretation of the Bible in the Church. I find the works of Marcus J. Borg to be very instructive in complementing The Interpretation of the Bible in the Church. Borg seems to view the scriptures through the lens of someone who is practicing second half of life spirituality. He retired in 2007 as Hundere Distinguished Professor of Religion and Culture at Oregon State University. He is the author of many outstanding books, including my favorites, Reading the Bible Again for the First Time, The God We Never Knew, and JESUS.

I also find the works of Retired Bishop John Shelby Spong to be outstanding, especially his works, The Sins of Scripture, Rescuing the Bible from Fundamentalism, Reclaiming the Bible for a Non-Religious World, and Why Christianity Must Change or Die. Spong writes with a simple style that is very easy to follow.

I do not suggest that you feel compelled to read any of these books while you are in the seminary, unless you find the Spirit irresistibly leading you their way. Rather, I am simply planting seeds that may bloom later if you desire to explore another way of understanding the scriptures.

21. Sin:

When we practice second half of life spirituality, we view sin not only as a specific action, something specific that we may do, but also as a state of being in which we are divided and discontent, feuding with ourselves, others, and even God. We need to understand our underlying spiritual state as both the cause and the solution to our sinful actions. For example, we may be addicted to alcohol, so when we are intoxicated, we are likely to act in sinful ways. Or more subtly, greed, anger, and lust may all be hidden beneath the veneer of civility, only to be discerned through resulting sinful acts and associated harm.

So, may our spiritual state be in itself a sin? I believe yes and no. If we are ignorant of our spiritual state as the cause of our sinful actions, it is not a sin. We have, however, the responsibility to attempt to be aware of our spiritual state and to do something about it though God's helping Spirit. We see, for example, Jesus' condemnation of those who were self-righteous with no interest in taking responsibility for their spiritual state. Our specific acts of sin can help us to understand our underlying spiritual state, to sense our vulnerabilities involving security, love, and affirmation. Sinful actions can help us to discover that we want to be other than who we are. Sinful actions can make us aware that we must address truthfully our spiritual state. And so if we continue to ignore our spiritual state beneath our sinful ways, then we may indeed be blamed for failing to get to the bottom of things.

Of course, there are many forces in contemporary life that encourage, or even cause the distortions of our spirit. The advertising industry tries to convince us that if we use their product we will feel better, look better, be better. We are encouraged to think that if we could just overcome our insecurities through the use of products, we would finally feel better.

Fr. Rohr, in his book Falling Upward, quotes St. Gregory of Nyssa who said in the fourth century, "Sin happens whenever we refuse to keep growing." The spiritual writers agree that the ego, the false self, hates change more than anything else.

When we practice first half of life spirituality, reinforced by messages from the institutional church, we consider sins of the flesh to be our worst sins, producing the greatest shame and guilt. In contrast, Fr. Richard Rohr says that sins of the flesh are usually best seen as sins of weakness, and that it is our sins of the spirit that are far worse. They proceed from a cold heart, a superior and separate false self. The sins of the spirit include greed, arrogance, pride, and ambition.

When we practice second half of life spirituality, we look for the root causes of our sinfulness. We try to be more aware of who we are. We are more in touch with the Seven Capital Sins. We are willing and able to name the root causes of our sinfulness: for example, "I am lazy. I am lustful. I am greedy. I am selfish, etc." We are able to do this, to endure the discomfort of self-scrutiny, because of our trust and faith in the forgiveness and all-healing love of God.

22. Trinity:

When we practice second half of life spirituality, there is no need to view the Trinity as a fact to be proven or defended, but it is rather a profound truth discerned and lived through by faith alone. The doctrine of the Trinity represents humanity's attempt to make the mystery of God, the many faces of the divine, understandable and approachable. The Trinity, in short, provides us with images of the living God. We come to understand that our images of God ought not be taken as literal, empirical descriptions of God. And we know this in our hearts that this is not a bad thing! When we realize that we are dealing with mystery, we become less rigid. When we realize we are trying to define the indefinable, we no longer seek the false security of absolutes. We allow instead the embrace of the infinite God.

The image of God as Trinity helps us to realize that God is somehow, in many ways, in communion with us. In a mysterious way, God is relationship itself. To be in communion with one another, as members of the Body of Christ, is one way for us to embody and experience the life of the Trinity.

What about Jesus, the Son? Scripture scholars remind us that Jesus never spoke of the Trinity. The closest he came to that is the passage, a binary formulation, "The Father and I are one" (John 10:30). Yet, Michael Morwood says in his book, From Sand to Solid Ground, that even this statement appears to have originated generations after Jesus died. These words were put on Jesus' lips to express the beliefs of later generations. In sum, these words do not "prove" that Jesus saw himself as part of a Trinity of Persons in God, and even less prove that Jesus knew he was the incarnation of one of them.

But to those practicing second half of life spirituality, this is all rather beside the point, as the truthfulness of the Trinity is experienced directly through the many relationships of life. When we gaze into the eyes of a beloved, we gain a glimpse of God's love for humanity. In our relationships with others, we long for glimpses of God found in our desires for oneness, honesty, goodness, and beauty. We experience in relationships the fire that embodies divinity. Our passions pull us to union with others as Dag Hammarskjold said, "The lusts of the flesh reveal the loneliness of the soul." Saint Augustine said, "You have made us for yourself, Lord, and our hearts are restless until they rest in you!" When our heart moves us to compassionate action, we experience the living Spirit.

23. The ordination of women to the priesthood:

Pope John Paul II supported a document that said, "Women will never be priests in the Roman Catholic Church because Jesus did not choose any woman to be his disciples."

Some people who practice second half of life spirituality think that things may not be so straightforward. They tend to agree with Richard Sipe, a writer and speaker as well as a consultant on sexual abuse, who said in an interview entitled "Frequently Asked Questions,"

"Excluding women from the priesthood is based on a bad cultural habit and destructive tradition of degrading women and keeping them from equality and power. That stance has a long history and must be faced just as the practice of slavery was. There are no solid theological reasons for keeping women out of ministry."

Fr. Michael H. Crosby, in his book, Celibacy, says,

"I know no scholar of reputation in the academy of scripture scholars who has defended the scriptural argumentation of the Holy Father about women and the priesthood."

As you know, Joey, the Church's stance on these issues is quite strict. In 2007 Pope Benedict XVI warned all Catholic persons or groups that attempted the ordination of women that they would incur automatic excommunication.

Many people in the Church today are hopeful of change in the Church's policy regarding the ordination of women to the priesthood. In November 2012, the Vatican excommunicated and dismissed Roy Bourgeois from the priesthood because of his activities regarding the ordination of women to the priesthood. The Sisters of Mercy of the Americas, one of the largest groups of Catholic sisters in the western hemisphere, were saddened and disturbed by the Vatican's actions toward Bourgeois. The Sisters viewed Bourgeois' actions positively, as advocating for justice in both the Church and society, nationally and globally.

Elizabeth A. Johnson, the distinguished professor of theology at Fordham University, offered in an article published last year in CORPUS REPORTS some statistics from the United Nations. Johnson says that sexism is rampant on a global scale and the

Church reflects this inequality in all of its aspects. Her reflections seem to support Richard Sipe's comparison, in certain basic aspects, of slavery to the non-ordination of women to the priesthood. Johnson says,

"Women, who form half of the world's population, work three-fourths of the world's working hours and receive one-tenth of the world's salary. They own one percent of the world's land; form two-thirds of illiterate adults; and together with their dependent children form three-fourths of the world's starving people."

Conclusion:

Joey, I hope these examples of evolving perspectives are helpful to you. Perhaps these reflections will help you consider other doctrinal topics, such as the infallibility of popes and the claim that there is but one true Church.

By understanding the process of developing a different spirituality in the second half of life, you can better grasp how easily misunderstandings arise over controversial subjects. As I mentioned earlier, those who practice first or second half of life spirituality see reality differently. Unless there is openness to new ideas and a willingness to listen while dialoguing, conflicts will take place. Fear and even violence will surface. Obedience demands mutual listening. Unless there is an openness to new ideas, there will be a tendency to quickly judge and condemnation will occur.

People typically do not like change, and do not like challenge, yet in any viable organization there will always be plurality of thought. Democracies thrive when there is the freedom to speak and write one's thoughts. Is the Catholic Church inclusive enough to not only allow but also encourage the expression of different ideas so as to better understand reality?

I thought of this analogy. When we are young, we believe in Santa Claus. We learn from that experience that we have to be good in order to receive presents. Later, we discover there is no actual Santa Claus, but the spirit of Santa stays with us the rest of our life. In a way, Santa Claus was an early good shepherd figure for us.

When we are young, we believe in the Easter Bunny. We learn that there is great joy connected to the Easter Bunny, brightly colored Easter eggs, a basket of delicious candy, new clothing, beautiful spring flowers, pretty music at church, and happy faces. In a way, the Easter Bunny is a good shepherd figure for us too. Later in life, we discover that there is no actual Easter Bunny, but the spirit of Easter stays with us the rest of our life.

When we are young, hopefully we are given the experience of being with our parents in some church setting. Then we begin to believe that God is like a good shepherd. We are taught that the church's leaders are like good shepherds who lead us on the path to Heaven. We gradually learn the value of generosity, forgiveness, truthfulness, and the value of keeping the Commandments. But most importantly, we learn the purpose of life is to love God and to love our neighbor.

When we are young, we think most of what we hear in church is literally true. For example, we think that the Assumption of Mary, the virginity of Mary, the Resurrection of a resuscitated cadaver, the Ascension, and the stories in the Bible are literally true. When we start questioning, we realize much of what we thought to be true couldn't be so. But, the experience helped us to have a foundation, a belief in something upon which we could derive the spirit of what we were taught. In my opinion the transition we must make in religion is found in the paradigm of the practice of first and second half of life spirituality.

We need good shepherds in the Church. But we discover that our good shepherds are not perfect. Some are hypocritical. Some are very sinful. A difficult part of life is to give up expecting perfect good shepherds who are church leaders, politicians, parents, teachers, and spouses. The reality is we must learn from the good in life, but we must also avoid the evil in life, if we are going to be good shepherds to one another.

Many people who practice second half of life spirituality think it is absurd when the church leaders demand obedience, without questioning, to beliefs that no longer make any sense. It is similar to parents telling their adult children they must believe in a literal Santa or a literal Easter Bunny. Different kinds of good shepherds are valuable to us at special times in life, but they may no longer be always needed when we become adults.

In 1947, Karl Barth said, "Ecclesia semper reformanda est." ("The church is always to be reformed.") Karl Barth was a Swiss Reformed theologian who is often regarded as the greatest Protestant theologian of the twentieth century. He believed that the Church must continually re-examine herself in order to maintain its integrity of doctrine and practice. The phrase was also used by Hans Kung, a Swiss priest, theologian, and author in the Roman Catholic Church and other ecclesiastical reformers who were inspired by the spirit of the Vatican II Council. God's Spirit continues to blow where it will.

Peace,

Uncle Matthew

# V.  The Journey and the Church: Challenges and Choices, Spirituality and Institution

Letter #54
Saturday, February 14, 2015


Dear Uncle Matthew,

Thank you for sharing with me your reflections on those essential religious topics. The ideas shared, particularly about salvation, sin, and the trinity, were profound and transformative for me.

Also, the many reflections offered regarding scripture were immensely helpful. Thank you. I increasingly am determined to avoid the deadening literalism that so many preachers convey and impress upon their congregations.

The ordination of women is indeed a controversial topic, but no one mentions that subject here. I loved your final quote by Barth. I agree that just as we each individually need to be open to change if we are to be open to God's spirit, so too must any institution be open to change if it is to remain vital and viable. When I worked at the National Security Agency, I saw that the practical and empirically minded engineers were also always open to change. They continually sought new and better ways to build giant computers. Openness was the way of discovery and adherence to truthfulness.

I read in the newspaper that the Archbishop of Miami, Thomas Wenski, warned archdiocesan employees that any action in support of Florida's now-legal same-sex marriage could cost them their jobs. What about the issue of freedom of conscience? The Church stresses the Fortnight for Religious Freedom that should include following one's conscience. Unfortunately, the following of one's conscience is underplayed from the Church's recent Fortnight for Religious Freedom program. We studied the Vatican II document, Dignitatis Humanae, the Declaration on Religious Freedom, which stresses in a balanced way not only the principle of religious freedom but also freedom of conscience.

I'm most curious to know why some priests are hesitant to practice second half of life spirituality. From all I can see, your openness to second half of life spirituality is helping you to grow in wisdom and love. Do you have any ideas why some of your priest-friends are not open to a new spirituality?

I am also wondering, based on your pastoral experience, what you consider to be some of the challenges facing the institutional church today? I am, after all, committing my life to its service. You alluded to some of these challenges in your previous letters, but I would appreciate some explicit comments. Thanks!

Peace,

Joey

P.S.

Ash Wednesday is next week. This school year is going by so quickly.

Response to Letter #54
Friday, February 27, 2015

Dear Joey,

Did you see the recent NCR article by Jack Ruhl about the serious flaws in diocesan financial management? He points out how priests in the United States are disproportionately older and that many are certain to retire within just a few years. The article says that most diocesan pension plans are significantly underfunded. I am fortunate in this diocese that we have a fairly good pension plan for retired priests.

Since you asked me, yes, I will be happy to share with you some reasons why I believe some of my priest-friends avoid the practice second half of life spirituality. And yes, let me share with you as well some of the challenges the institutional church faces today.

Why do priests often avoid practicing second half of life spirituality?

Let's look at four reasons why priests may resist the transformation that occurs in one's thinking, and the practice of one ministry, when embracing second half of life spirituality.

1.   Some priests are reluctant to practice second half of life

spirituality because they realize they depend upon the Church for their daily bread. If they practice second half of life spirituality, their livelihood may be threatened. Many priests, in order to survive, attempt to believe that things are really not so bad. They reconcile any pangs of conscience with appeals to material necessity.

2.  Relatedly, some priests are reluctant to practice second half of life spirituality because they want to avoid the suffering they believe it would entail. By avoiding the fears inherent in making changes, priests believe they will be able to lessen their suffering. Indeed, when we face a broader and deeper reality, our first experience is often suffering. When we face the shadow side of the Church and take some action to make things better, we often suffer. After I saw the poverty and hunger in Haiti, I tried to make things better, but I suffered. Despite suffering when I worked for peace and justice in the Church, I grew in courage and wisdom. My suffering blessed me with the ability to "connect the dots" which is a sign of wisdom. I was blessed with perhaps the greatest of spiritual consolations, a clear conscience. I was at peace both with myself and God. You see, Joey, the truth is that those who seek to avoid suffering at all costs are the very persons who can never escape suffering because its source lies within.

3.  Some priests continue to practice first half of life spirituality not because they are consciously avoiding suffering, but simply because they are distracted. When priests are "on duty" twenty-four hours a day, numbness and a lack of awareness can set in. Many priests who are pastoring several parishes that have been merged together fall into workaholics. Distraction is a powerful barrier that hides the truth. When priests are kept continuously busy with parish responsibilities, diocesan committee meetings, and with raising money for the bishop's faith appeal, it is likely that they will miss seeing the depths of reality about their own lives and the life of the Church. They will fail to understand complex and urgent issues of peace and justice. The status quo prevails, and they try to be obedient and responsible to the church leaders in performing their many duties. Rarely, when

chronically distracted, are we capable of serving as prophetic leaders.

4.      Finally, some priests continue to practice first half of life spirituality because they do not want to be branded as disloyal. They desire to happily celebrate their jubilee (fifty years as a priest). They fear the disapproval of their bishops, friends, peers and family members, and even their parishioners. The moral courage required to clearly and resolutely speak one's truth in the face of powerful opposition is rare. The Bible, in many ways, and through many persons, tells this story.

Joey, all this is so important because whether we practice first or second half of life spirituality, our spirituality will determine the kind of shepherd we will be. Our spirituality will also determine how we understand and engage the challenges facing the Church. If you become a priest of the Church, you will be responsible for not only being aware of the challenges but also doing what is within your power to being about some positive change.

Twelve challenges facing the institutional church:


Though the challenges, and the corresponding opportunities facing the universal church are countless, let me identify twelve for your consideration. Some of these twelve are topical, while most may be considered perpetual. I am sharing these twelve challenges that I have written about in my journal to assist you to stay in touch with the ideas shared by the People of God. I agree with some of the ideas I share with you, but I disagree with other ideas. Once again, my purpose in journaling is to help to better respect others, to increase my awareness of and my faith in the on-going revelations of an Incarnate God, and to assist in discovering an adult spirituality.

1.  Self-idolatry and the lust for power

2.  Denying the church's shadow side

3. Engaging human sexuality

4. Vetting, free thinking, and the formation of conscience

5. Dissent from church teaching

6. Clergy assignments

7. Clergy retreats and educational opportunities

8. The Annual Faith Appeal

9. The welfare of active clergy

10. Priests and sexual misconduct

11. The welfare of retired clergy

12. Fraternal correction

1. Self-idolatry and the lust for power:

While there are many present challenges in the universal church, the most profound and pervasive, the one underlying all others, is the urge toward self-idolatry and the accompanying thirst for power.

The practice of first half of life spirituality is prone to idealization, so it often denies the imperfection and the potential for evil in the institutional church. On the other hand, the practice of second half of life spirituality is dedicated to reality so it accepts whatever imperfection and evil one may find in the Church. Pope Francis is not afraid to turn the light of the gospel on the Church!

Pope Francis has warned against what he calls the culture of "clericalism" in which holiness is seen as largely reserved for the ordained in the Church. Clericalism is tied to a top-down model of authority in the Church that results, as history attests, in the abuse of power. Thus, correction of the hierarchy is more difficult, often impossible, when the laity has little or no power. Careerism, the lack of accountability and transparency, as well as all exclusionary practices that appear inclusive when no such intention exists, feeds the urge for self-idolatry.

Profound lessons can be learned when we attempt to see clearly and understand fairly the imperfections and capacity for evil in the Church. Evil made real in specific, individual acts, becomes systemic when members of the Church or citizens of a society do not stand up and fight the injustice and sinfulness that have enabled the evil.

One way of exploring the church's culpability is to consider the Capital Sins: gluttony, greed, lust, pride, envy, sloth and wrath. Considering the manifestations of the Capital Sins in the Church, as well as in ourselves, provides us with many opportunities to grow spiritually. Reality is truth, sometimes bitter truth. But if God underlies reality, and that which is false is ultimately unreal, then we should not fear this examination of difficult truths. Practicing second half of life spirituality encourages us to face reality and to thus deal squarely with the issues at hand.

I think you know, Joey, that I have been sharing all this material so as to help you to have a "spiritual road map" to assist you in seeing reality so that you best discern your vocation in life. Seminarians who study in first half of life spirituality institutions are often presented a narrow view of the Church and the world. A limited and constrained view may be comforting in the short-term, but is likely to have negative and far-reaching consequences in the long-term.

M. Scott Peck, in his book, The Road Less Traveled, writes that the temptation "to avoid problems and the emotional suffering inherent in them is the primary basis of all human mental illness." Conversely, when we can see reality as it is, we have a better chance to use our mind to formulate good questions, conceive creative answers, and, as a result, make better choices in life. When adapted to reality, we are more likely to be an effective and positive force for good in the world, precisely because we are then living and acting in the world God created, and not some fantasy of our own making. In this way, knowing the truth sets us free and actually enhances faith development in ourselves and others.

In sum, those who practice second half of life spirituality believe that we cannot effectively work to build a better Church unless we clearly understand its actual problems and how love and justice provide the needed remedies. I believe it was St. Augustine who spoke to this dynamic when he said we can only love what we understand, just as we can understand only what we love.

2. Denying the church's shadow side:

The hierarchy has a history of denying the shadow side of the Church, just like you and I deny our shadow. The term "the shadow," as a psychological concept, refers to that part of our personality, usually unconscious, that our ego fears and seeks to avoid. In developing a conscious personality, we all embody in ourselves an idealized image of what we want to be like. Those qualities of ours that are not in accord with the person we want to be are rejected and repressed and constitute the "shadow side." Individuals as well as institutions have a "shadow side." We usually think of the shadow in negative terms, but the shadow contains many vital qualities that can add to our life and strength if we can relate to them, and express them, in a conscious, disciplined, and civil manner.

In our culture, the shadow side of large institutions is most often exposed through external investigative reporting: mass media-television, movies, published books, and, of course, online reporting. One recent example was the PBS show the Secrets of the Vatican; aired on February 25, 2014 (it can still be viewed on the internet.) The documentary made widely known many of the challenges facing Pope Francis as he works to transform and heal elements of the hierarchy's shadow side.

Published books have also done a great deal in recent years to bring to light grievous problems within the Church. American investigative reporter Jason Berry has written two books (Lead Us Not into Temptation and Vows of Silence) that give extensive accounts of the sexual abuse of children by priests. In his books, Berry exposes the sexual abuses of the late Fr. Marcial Maciel, a Mexican priest who founded the Legion of Christ in 1959 and the Regnum Christi movement. Berry later wrote a book, Render to Rome, that critically examined the church's handling of its finances. Apparently after examining the Vatican Bank, he concluded that Italian clerics showed favoritism to relatives, friends, and friends of friends, all to the detriment of the church's integrity and mission.

Films too can have a broad impact on our awareness of the shadow side of the Church. In 1994, Miramax films released the movie, The Priest. Miramax is an American entertainment company known for distributing independent and foreign films. The film was about a young, newly ordained conservative priest who was struggling with his homosexuality. The film was challenging for some. EWTN, a network that is embedded in the practice of first half of life spirituality, urged viewers not to see the film and to boycott Miramax. The film not only conveys a glimpse of the "shadow side" of the hierarchy, but it strikingly portrays the bishop's failure in his role as a "good shepherd." EWTN's attempt to prevent church members from seeing the film illustrates how those who practice first half of life spirituality often avoid acknowledging the reality of the church's imperfection and even discourage freedom of thought.

Since the practice of first half of life spirituality tends to deny the "shadow side" of the hierarchy, officials in the Church often accuse the media of being prejudiced against the Church when evil is revealed. On the other hand, the practice of second half of life spirituality accepts as real the "shadow side" of the hierarchy and the positive effect of confronting it and transforming it. Many people place priests, bishops, cardinals, and especially the pope on an illusory pedestal. Yet, those seeking the truth of things readily accept that whenever there is a group of people, no matter who they are, there will always be a mixture of good and evil. There is no perfect person, church, or society. Exposure of the shadow side brings us closer to this all-important reality.

We are fortunate that Pope Francis is leading us in a direction of seeking truth and correcting abuses. By turning the light of the Gospel on the Church, he is putting into practice what he asks of others. Pope Francis is confronting the sexual abuse of children, the ramifications of the sexual abuses of the Legion of Christ founder, Fr. Marcial Maciel, the alleged corruption at the Vatican Bank, and the alleged corruption and the blackmailing of homosexual clergy by individuals outside the Church that was exposed in Vatileaks in May 2012. He has his hands full.

3. Engaging human sexuality:

For many church leaders, one of the greatest challenges is constructively engaging the topic of sexuality. In the Frontline presentation, Secrets of the Vatican, someone said,"Don't ask, don't tell" has long been a tradition in the Catholic Church. But given the wide-spread sexual dysfunction within the priesthood, most notably in the many pedophilia scandals, we would do well to ask, "What psychological difficulties occur both for priests and parishioners, when priests repress in shame their sexuality in general and their gender preference in particular?"

Some Catholics have left the Church because homosexual persons face discrimination within the Church. Last month, the Vatican released a document entitled "Concerning the Criteria for the Discernment of Vocations..." that states, "The Church, while profoundly respecting the person in question, cannot admit to the seminary or the priesthood those who practice homosexuality, present deep-seated homosexual tendencies, or support the so called 'gay culture.'"

In the Synod of 2014, a significant number of prelates could not decide whether gays and lesbians have gifts to offer to the Church. Bishop Johan Bonny of Antwerp, Belgium, has called for ecclesiastical recognition of gay relationships, according to an interview published last December in a Belgium newspaper. The bishop said, "The Church urgently needs to connect with contemporary society, showing more respect for homosexuality, divorced people, and modern kinds of relationships."

Gays now have the legal right to marry in many states and in many other countries. Our society and many of its religious institutions are becoming more and more accepting of men and women who have different gender preferences. Many people wonder why the Catholic Church can't learn something from a society that accepts without condemnation a plurality of viewpoints concerning sexual issues. The practice of second half of life spirituality tends not to view reality dualistically, so there is less of a tendency to categorize individuals as gay or straight but rather to see individuals on a continuum that lends itself to mystery. Further, when sexuality is placed in the context of love, rather than biology alone, it further calls into question a superficial and simplistic morality.

Conclusion:

The challenges that church leaders face are numerous. It is up to you, Joey, to ask questions as your interests and understanding develop.   Many people believe that the institutional church is dying because of the failure of her leaders to name and face the challenges of today. It will be up to your generation to embrace with courage the full reality of God's creation and the challenges it provides.

A way forward:

To end on a positive note, what are some possible solutions to these challenges? One solution or at least a start is simply to dialogue.   Resolutions come about through dialogue. By dialoguing about the theological differences between those priests and bishops who practice first and second half of life spirituality, there is a better chance for some resolution.

I know a priest who I think handled the sexual abuse scandal in a positive way. He didn't try to provide simple answers, but simply addressed the crisis in his parish by holding open discussions. Once parishioners were given the opportunity to express their feelings in a safe church environment, healing took place. Open dialogue, respectfully listening to others, and direct engagement of the challenges facing the Church is advocated by those who practice second half of life spirituality. Good shepherds provide such leadership. A failure to address the challenges and crises in the Church creates more problems since problems rarely, if ever, simply resolve themselves.

Dialogue, relearning, getting rid of myths, and offering information about the practice of second half of life spirituality can prevent the departure of believers that is occurring world-wide in all church denominations. When people hear the truth and are given some hope that the wrong-doing is not being hidden from them, they will more likely want to be part of the solution rather than simply leaving a church.

Peace,

Uncle Matthew

Letter #55
Wednesday, March 11, 2015


Dear Uncle Matthew,

Thank you for sharing those keen insights into why priests are reluctant to practice second half of life spirituality. Although I am not yet a priest, I can already see in the seminary my tendency to bond with my classmates, which is good, but with the accompanying temptation to be accepted, affirmed, and valued by my superiors. The end result is I can see why it would be difficult to practice second half of life spirituality if it means not conforming with the group.

Your presentation on three of the challenges that the institutional church faces was far-reaching and profound. In the seminary, I have not heard any professor address the three challenges you outlined. I never thought about the urge of self-idolatry, even though its symptoms surround me every day. Among my seminary classmates, many appear to embrace clericalism. Some tend to see the vocation of priesthood as superior to lay marriage. Some enjoy wearing cassocks that set them apart, and in their minds, above the laity. This mentality strikes me as profoundly dualistic, and contrary to the life and teachings of Jesus.

As I mentioned, I have never taken a psychology course, nor have I heard of Jason Barry's books, nor have I seen the PBS show, the Secrets of the Vatican, but I could follow your description of the Church's denial of the shadow side.

And then, of course, there is the issue of our sexuality. The topic of sexuality has not been widely discussed except in Canon Law where we focused exclusively on what the Church considers to be sexual offenses. When I was in college and while working at the NSA, many of my friends disagreed with the church's teachings on human sexuality. Through these experiences, I was left with the feeling that the topic is so rich and wondrous and problematic that my education on the matter had just begun.

I appreciate your willingness to share with me an additional nine challenges the Church faces today. Before you describe these challenges, would you clarify what you meant in your last letter when you stated that Christianity risks dying because of a failure by church leaders to clearly name and address the challenges of today. This assertion is both frightening and motivating. I believe these challenges are connected to two questions. Why do some people, both lay and cleric, choose to leave the institutional church? Why do some people, both lay and cleric, choose to stay in the institutional church even if they can see the challenges and weakness in the institutional church?

I wish all my classmates could see what you are sending me, but I am smart enough to know that if I shared your letters, I would possibly be labeled as a trouble-maker. My vocation to the priesthood would be in jeopardy, and the good that I hope to do would forever remain undone.

Peace,

Joey

Response to Letter #55
Tuesday, March 24, 2015

Dear Joey,

I had a wonderful birthday last Tuesday. Thank you for the birthday card. I was invited over to your grandfather Bill's home. He and Emily prepared a fine meal to celebrate, and the meal was topped off with a fine birthday cake. I am now 82 years old. How time does fly!

In my last letter to you, I shared with you three broad challenges that the Church faces today, and I identified nine other challenges which I will outline for you, but let me first address the two important questions that are on your mind.

Question 1. Why do some people, both lay and cleric, choose to leave the institutional church?

Over the years, I have observed many parishioners who have left the institutional church, whether slowly or suddenly. Let me share with you based on their own accounts and my own observations some of the reasons why they left. As you will see, the common theme is that when challenges are not faced and scandals are not properly handled, people will leave the Church as surely as day follows night. Fortunately, Pope Francis seems open to debate and discussion in the institutional church, raising the possibility that available solutions will be recognized and employed.

1. Sexual scandals in the Church:

In my last letter to you, I mentioned that one of the core challenges in the Church is to face the shadow side of the institution, and that this often involves issues surrounding human sexuality. Countless numbers of Catholics have left the institutional church, here in the United States and throughout the world, because of the many sexual scandals that regularly appear in the press. The laity has been repeatedly shocked and outraged. Some bishops are accused of "covering up" and enabling, sometimes over periods of many years. Millions of dollars have been paid in settlements. Some dioceses have declared bankruptcy. Stories circulate that the victims were not only abused initially but were often treated without due respect when they met with their bishops to report the violations. Many people were disappointed that our popes have not done more to show their concern for this terrible manifestation of evil and to take forceful corrective action. They ask,"if this is not evil, what is?"

Even when church leadership faults the perpetrator and accepts responsibility, the Church as a whole has generally failed to ask the deeper questions about the context in which the sexual violations occur. Though sexual sins are not unique to the Catholic Church, our organizational structures and traditions do create specific conditions that we ought to examine. For example, is mandatory celibacy working in today's church? What was the priest's living situation? How are vocations discerned? What about the formation process? How do we think about chastity? Why did the priest seek out this or that person? These are all important questions we need to explore.

2. Contraception:

Some Catholics, for decades now, have left the Church because of the Church's position on contraception. The decision not to allow artificial contraception was made by Pope Paul VI in 1968 against the recommendation of his own Commission that studied the issue. To many of today's practicing Catholics, the Church's position seems to be out of touch with the daily experience of married life, what it takes to be a responsible parent, and the positive nature of marital sexual relations. Many Catholics were disappointed, given his legacy, that Pope Francis beatified him in October, 2014.

3. Civil divorces:

Some Catholics have left the Church because they were once married in the Catholic Church, but subsequently obtained a civil divorce and then remarried civilly. They were told that their unions were "irregular" and that they could no longer receive the Eucharist. Thus, not surprisingly, they felt rejected and betrayed, following a lifetime of devotion to the Church.

Many people, who are remarried without a priest-witness after a civil divorce, believe, in spite of what the Church might say, that their relationship is sacramental. They feel as though the hierarchy treats them like lost sheep even though they believe that God has witnessed and blessed their new marriage. Pope Francis addressed this issue in the Synod meeting of 2014, and he will continue to address this issue in the Synod meeting later this year.

4. Priests who resign from active ministry:

It is not uncommon that Catholic priests who leave the active ministry and get married would still like to minister as priests, either full-time or part-time, but they are not allowed to do so. Relatedly, to many people the Church's policies seem to be particularly absurd when many parishes have been closed due to a shortage of celibate priests! The situation is so dire that Bishops are seeking candidates for the priesthood from other countries. As a result, some people get frustrated at the most basic level because they literally cannot understand what their foreign-born priest is saying. It is hard to receive the Word when you cannot understand the words! Even some married

Protestant ministers have been welcomed into the Catholic Church and are ordained as priests. As a result of all this, inactive priests often experience a deep sense of rejection and consider the Church's policy to be profoundly inconsistent, unfair, and punitive in nature.

5. Model of the parish:

Relatedly, some Catholics leave their Church because, due to a shortage of priests, their local parish is closed or merged with others, dissolving established communities built up over decades. The result is that local churches have become more impersonal.

The late Avery Cardinal Dulles in his book, Models of the Church, outlines five different approaches, types, or models of the Church. He describes how as the clergy decreases in number and increases in age, the Church takes on a more institutional-business model rather than a pastoral-servant model. The ideal would be for the good shepherd in the parish to know not only the names of the parishioners but something about their inner and outer lives as well. With the merger of smaller parishes into larger parishes, that becomes an increasing impossibility.

6. "Sheep:"

The Church often uses the beautiful metaphor of the shepherd with his sheep. When properly understood, it provides parishioners with a sense of loving support, responsibility, and compassion. Balance in using this metaphor is important because at times we act as sheep and at times we act as shepherds. For example, when a priest goes to a parishioner's home for a meal, he assumes the role of a sheep being fed by a shepherd. At other times, the priest acts as a shepherd when he celebrates mass and shares his homily with the people.

The notion of a bishop or pastor being a shepherd with "sheep" offends many laypersons when they sense that the church leader is using his responsibility at a shepherd in a paternalistic way with hierarchical overtones. This abuse of the metaphor can hurt those individuals who simply follow willy-nilly without accessing their moral compass and assuming responsibility for their actions. Priests, nuns and lay people want to be considered as adults.

A good example of some nuns feeling as though they were treated like stupid sheep occurred in April 2012, when the Congregation of the Doctrine of the Faith began investigating the Leadership Conference of Women Religious (LCWR) in the United States. This group represented more than three-quarters of American's 57,000 women religious. Critics of the nuns said the Leadership Conference has allowed some nuns to defy Vatican teaching on the issues of abortion, gay rights, and the ordination of women as priests. The women religious criticized the Vatican's investigation saying that it was paternalistic and based on unsubstantial accusations. The Vatican appointed Seattle Archbishop J. Peter Sartain to oversee a program of reform for LCWR. The investigation has contributed to nationwide protests of support for the women religious. Some women and men left the Church because they asked, "Why is the Vatican criticizing the United States nuns?" Hopefully, Joey, Pope Francis will call an end to this investigation soon.

Sometimes church leaders shepherd by judging those who have left the Catholic Church as lost sheep. Those who practice second half of life spirituality ask, Who can judge? Many who left the institutional church may have actually discovered an adult spirituality.

In a family, the parent/child dynamic was never meant to be permanent. In the Church's hierarchal structure, the shepherd/sheep model is permanent and it should not be. In the Synod of 2014 the bishops saw themselves as parents and the laity as children. Those who practice second half of life spirituality desire that the hierarchy treat them as adults.

7. Lack of affirmation:

Some priests, nuns, and lay persons are tempted to leave the Church when they feel that they are being taken for granted. For example, in some dioceses, the bishop announces the transfer of priests on a very short notice when there is a crisis. Other dioceses plan assignments months in advance. The priest being transferred is often told to move rather than asked if the new assignment would be at least acceptable, if not outright desirable to him. He may be given little time to respond to accepting the new assignment and he is not given the chance to dialogue with the leaders in the new parish to see if the assignment would work. The priest being transferred may not be consulted in regard to the associate priest who will serve with him. All of this creates a strong feeling of being treated impersonally.

A pastoral church leader, a good shepherd, would realize that it takes time to change mailing addresses, notify people, and reschedule weddings, vacations, and appointments. It takes time to say goodbyes. It is difficult to lose friends and to leave as a member of the church community. For anyone, including priests, to transition to a new community can be disruptive. Time is needed to know new working colleagues, parishioners, new schedules, and the new area. This insensitivity on the part of some church leaders goes against the Church's proclamation of respecting life. It is unconscionable to believe that priests are so inhuman so as not to need such consideration. Living in a rectory with someone with dramatically different life experiences, a different theology, different habits, and perhaps a different nationality may cause problems. Conversely, affirmation can occur when the bishop allows the priests involved to discuss ministering together first before assignments are made.

8. The non-ordination of women to the priesthood:

The Roman Catholic Church, to state the obvious, ordains only men to the priesthood. This tradition was reaffirmed in 1976 by the Congregation for the Doctrine of the Faith and in 1994 by Pope John Paul II. In 2007, the Vatican issued a decree saying the attempted ordination of women would result in automatic excommunication for the woman and the cleric trying to ordain her. This was codified in canon law in 2010 when the attempted ordination of women was added to the Church's list of grave crimes. Some priests and lay persons have left the institutional church or the active ministry because women are prohibited from serving in ordained ministries. They consider that the non-ordination of women is unjust and not consistent with the gospel. They believe that God's gifts can be distributed to anyone. The non-ordination of women seems patriarchal.

As an example, John J. Shea, OSA, is a former Augustinian priest who was solemnly professed for over fifty years. He wrote Cardinal O'Malley to inquire why women are not ordained priests in the Catholic Church. Shea said he wanted a theological explanation of this teaching. St. Anselm said, "Faith seeking understanding." Shea wanted help in understanding the church's teaching. Before sending his letter, Shea stepped aside from active ministry as a priest until women are ordained.

9.  The institutional church caters to those who practice first half of life spirituality:

Some Catholics have left the institutional Church because they sense that the Church too often caters to those who remain inside its safe dogmas and structures. Vetting is sometimes used to exclude thoughts, ideas, and thinkers that would challenge orthodoxy. Vetting can be misused to retain control. It has been used so that the faithful will be safe and secure out of fear that their faith will be offended. In other words, one gets the impression that the institutional church is designed for those who continually practice first half of life spirituality.

Once individuals begin practicing second half of life spirituality, they are likely to feel disconnected and experience that they are perceived as a threat by the church leadership in places where the church leadership practices first half of life spirituality.

Martin Luther King, Jr., once said, "If today's church does not recapture the sacrificial spirit of the early church, it will lose its authenticity, forfeit the loyalty of millions, and be dismissed as an irrelevant social club with no meaning for the twentieth century. I meet young people whose disappointment with the church has turned into outright disgust."

Those who practice second half life spirituality notice that their churches seem to protect the status quo, so they look outside their church for the living spirit.

Joey, the reasons go on and on why Catholics, lay and clerical, leave the Church. Perhaps Pope Francis will help to rededicate us to reforming the Church's policies regarding some of the above issues.

Question 2: Why do some people, lay and cleric, choose to stay in the institutional church?

In your second question, Joey, you wanted to know why some people, lay and cleric, choose to stay in the Church even though they know the challenges and weakness in the church structure.

1. Salvation:

Some Catholics really believe that under penalty of serious sin they have a divine obligation to attend mass so as to keep holy the Lord's Day. They believe that salvation requires them to participate in the sacraments of the Church: baptism, Eucharist, reconciliation, marriage, and the sacrament of the sick. They are grateful for their religious upbringing and they strive to be loyal to the hierarchy. They feel that they have an obligation to accept as well as to obey official church teachings. This kind of reasoning does motivate some people to stay in the Church.

2. Proclamation of Jesus:

Some Catholics stay in the Church because they realize that despite the many imperfections and even sin, the institutional church still proclaims Jesus. The Church proclaims Jesus' story and his presence with us today. The Church gives us great hope that despite our own suffering, God's graces of unconditional love and forgiveness will triumph. We need to hear good news weekly that God is with us. We need the witness of the men, women, and children who worship weekly and have faith enough to accept imperfection. They know it is unreal to demand perfection of any group or individual in this life. They are not deterred when they experience both the "weeds and the wheat." They know that spiritual desolation and consolation are part of the journey. They are proud of the Church's world-wide ministry and the impact for good the Church has in the area of social justice. They are proud when the pope makes pastoral visits to countries.

3. Rich tradition:

Some Catholics stay in the Church because of the rich tradition that the Church offers. The writings of both liberal and conservative theologians are at our finger tips. The Church provides us with invaluable devotional works. For example, the writings of the deceased Cistercian monk, Fr. Thomas Merton who died in 1968, inspire us even today. His many books show his wisdom and deep spirituality even though he lived in an imperfect situation in his Monastery at Gethsemani, Kentucky. In former days, those who read books by Anthony Padovano or Garry Wills might be considered disloyal to the institutional church. Today, in the institutional church, we have come a long ways. We do have the freedom to read and write as we continue our journey as seekers of the truth and seekers who are desirous to share more fully in divine life.

4. Hope for the future:

Some Catholics stay in the Church because of their hope for a better Church in the future. Many Catholics admire and are encouraged by the papacy of Pope Francis so they have hope for the future. This attitude is expressed in Anthony T. Padovano's book, Hope is a Dialogue, that was written in 1998. The purpose of his book was to assist in dialogue so that hope for the future could emerge in an institutional church that welcomes and accepts those who practice first and second half of life spirituality.

Conclusion:

I hope that this material, Joey, provides you with a pastoral model of lovingly accepting people where they are rather than judging them as being right or wrong. I am praying that, if you are ordained a priest, you will be a good listener, a man of compassion, and a person who is patient with others as well as yourself.

Peace,

Uncle Matthew

Letter #56
Monday, April 6, 2015


Dear Uncle Matthew,

The Easter celebrations at the Saturday Vigil and yesterday morning were beautiful. I was a lector at the Vigil mass, and I was one of the servers yesterday. When I am a lector in the sanctuary, I am aware of my responsibility to proclaim the Word of God well and with integrity. Unfortunately, the rector's homily was highly academic. I doubt if many lay persons went home with anything practical to help them.

In contrast, you are greatly helping me! Our discussion on the shadow side of the Church is on my mind every day. I realize that any large organization has a shadow side, but I guess I'm still naïve when it comes to our beloved Catholic Church. Your reflections about the nine reasons why some people choose to leave the institutional church were so thought-provoking. I also liked the way you described reasons why some people choose to stay in the institutional church, even if they are aware of the shadow side of the Church. This goes to show you that it is not always easy to discern the inner motives of peoples' big life decisions.

In a recent Old Testament class, we studied that, when the Babylonians invaded Israel, Jerusalem was devastated, the temple was destroyed, and the Jewish people were exiled to

Babylon (597-539 BCE). Our professor, who is what I would call a free thinker, made the comment "Some people believe we are living in 'exile' today." What do you think he meant by that remark?

Also you got me thinking about the pros and cons of vetting since earlier you listed vetting (number four of your list of challenges). A friend of mine was telling me that in his diocese, all guest speakers coming into the diocese must be approved by the bishop before a pastor can allow them to speak at a mission, retreat, or seminar in the parish. Hearing this from my friend surprises and bothers me on some level. Will you share with me further reflections on vetting?

Peace,

Joey

Response to Letter #56
Monday, April 20, 2015

Dear Joey,

I hope you can read the outstanding article in the April 10th edition of America Magazine entitled, "Open House, How Pope Francis Sees the Church." Cardinal Walter Kasper wrote the article. He portrays Pope Francis' image of the Church as the People of God, with a corresponding aversion to all forms of clericalism. What a breath of fresh air!

In my last letter to you, I mentioned the investigation into the LCWR (Leadership Conference of Women Religious). It was announced in the Vatican last Thursday that the controversial three-year program of Vatican oversight of the LCWR has unexpectedly come to an early end. That too is good news and hopefully an indication of good things to come.

"Exile:"

You asked what your professor meant when he said, "Some people believe we are living in exile today." That is a provocative and fascinating thing to say, and I can only speculate as to his meaning. As I pondered his words, I brushed up on the topic of exile in Marcus Borg's book, JESUS and in Spong's book, Why Christianity Must Change or Die. I'll try to condense what I read as a way of addressing your question.

In Hebrew Scriptures, in the Book of Kings, you can read about the Babylonian Captivity in the sixth century BCE. When the Jews in Jerusalem were defeated and sent into exile, their physical images of God (the temple, the tabernacle, etc.) were destroyed. Prior to their military defeat and humiliation, they had believed in an Exclusive God who was on their side. They had believed they, and they alone, were God's chosen people, but now they faced the painful contradiction of being defeated by their earthly enemy. They had believed that God lived in Jerusalem, dwelling in their temple. But now, in exile, they were forced to re-evaluate their belief that God was only in Jerusalem. Their captivity and exile, though deeply painful, gave them new experiences that enabled and forced a re-learning of their images of God and a re-birth of their religious beliefs and convictions.

Perhaps sharing the mind-set of your professor, Marcus Borg says that exile is a powerful metaphor for the human condition. Exile is central to the story of Adam and Eve. Exile is a condition of estrangement from one's true and ultimate home. The metaphor of exile is central as well to the parable of the Prodigal Son, a story of exile and return. The longing for, and finding of one's true home, may be seen as nothing less as the central story of the entire Biblical narrative. I find myself at peace with a thought from Saint Augustine: "Because God has made us for Himself, our hearts are restless until they rest in Him."

Perhaps your professor is referring to something more specific, to a condition of exile today that exists in the Church. This sense of exile arrives when some church leaders enforce the practice of first half of life spirituality for all the people in their dioceses, thus frustrating those who want to, or are called to, change their relationship with God through the practice of an adult spirituality. This always involves a corresponding change in one's images of God.

For instance, many people today no longer believe that God takes sides when countries engage in warfare. Many people do not believe that God controls the weather, nor prevents hurricanes and earthquakes from occurring. Some people doubt that God, here on earth, punishes evil and rewards goodness. Many people no longer believe in a Distant God who capriciously intervenes in life on earth, in a simplistic and magical way, to accomplish the divine will. Those who practice second half of life spirituality have no desire to return to this former way of thinking.

It is a paradox that those who claim to be orthodox leaders can actually deter their people from knowing the fullness of their rich tradition. Our own traditions speak of how God's will is often conveyed through prophetic voices that challenge established authority. The Hebrew prophets spoke of the need for change and spiritual rebirth. However, the priests in the Hebrew Scriptures, defending their own authority and power, often killed the prophets and their message of reform. Tragically, the Biblical story does seem to eternally recur.

I can see, Joey, how the condition of exile relates to your second question regarding the practice of vetting. We should recognize that change has always been present in the Church. And why should it not be, if God's Spirit is alive? To deny speakers advocating for change goes against Jesus' call for repentance, or metanoia (a Greek word meaning to turn around or to change one's mind). Jesus' first words of his ministry were "Repent for the kingdom of heaven is near" (Matthew 4:17). If we do not change our images of God that were formed when we were children, we risk that the living God will effectively die in us. Religion will lose value for many people unless their religion is capable of changing as they themselves change throughout life.

Consider how the Exile in the Hebrew Scriptures was a painful blessing in disguise. By analogy, it is my hope that the current sense of exile by many within the church will ultimately be seen as a blessing in disguise. The denial of the full implementation of the Vatican II spirit is motivating many people to leave the institutional church and perhaps this, in God's mysterious way, will lead to rejuvenation. Thomas Moore's book, a Religion of One's Own, a Guide to Creating a Personal Spirituality in a

Secular World, makes sense if we understand the exile that some people face today in the Church.

In response to your letter, I will share with you the pros and cons of vetting, a fourth challenge that I believe the institutional church faces.

4. Vetting, free thinking, and the formation of conscience:

When bishops exercise their authority through the lens of first half of life spirituality, there is often disagreement and conflict when pastors must request permission to allow those who come from outside the diocese to speak. No one disagrees that church leaders have a responsibility to teach what is right from wrong and how to live the Christian life both by word and example. However, when these responsibilities express themselves in and through excessive control, then the parishioners' formation of conscience and free thinking can be stifled. A proper balance needs to be sought and attained.

Vetting can be useful:

There are many times when vetting can be a useful practice for a community. For example, state child welfare officials carefully vet foster parents. This protects innocent children. Another example is that employees routinely vet prospective employees.

In the institutional church, vetting can be good. Pastors and principals must be careful who they hire to work and volunteer in Catholic parishes and schools to assure all their parishioners that everything is being done specifically to protect both the children and elderly from various forms of physical harassment and abuse.

There are those times when a pastor or principal needs the advice of a higher church source for help in the vetting process in the hiring and firing of personnel. Thus, bishops can provide a wonderful service to parishes and schools by providing a vetting system to assist pastors and principals.

Excessive vetting can be harmful:

Some bishops who practice first half of life spirituality claim that they have the right and obligation to vet all speakers coming into their dioceses to hold speaking events on church property. It is not clear to me whether these bishops give adequate consideration to the harm they may be causing. Not surprisingly, some people who practice second half of life spirituality claim that these bishops are failing to facilitate the formation of conscience and mature understanding on the part of their parishioners.

This practice extends beyond parishes and reaches the vetting practices within our school systems. Some members of school boards try to remove books that challenge their antiquarian way of thinking. For example, some members of school boards try to impose a creationist dogma as science so as to literally interpret the Bible. The result of this is that extremists gain disproportionate influence within our schools. The effect of this can be harmful to students but also to the community as a whole, with some people being labeled as unpatriotic and disloyal because they disagree with those doing the vetting.

Why do some bishops practice excessive vetting?

The framework of first and second half of life spirituality can provide insights as to why some church leaders practice excessive vetting. Anthony Padovano in his book, Hope is a Dialogue, gives a description of the "Roman System" which can help us to understand the practice of excessive vetting and its relationship to first half of life spirituality.

Padovano describes the Roman System as centralized, legalistic, clericalized, male, and celibate. The System as a self-protecting entity is dogmatic and infallible. The System determines who will become a bishop. Chosen by the System, the new bishops generally reflect the System and benefit from the System and they work to perpetuate the System. As a result, many bishops have difficulty being collegial, delegating authority, listening to different opinions, and being open to change. The System encourages the very tendencies that will keep us in the practice of first half of life spirituality.

A good question to ask is "What are some of the effects of excessive and narrow vetting?"

Some effects of excessive vetting:

a.   Excessive vetting makes it more difficult to develop an informed conscience:

Those individuals who practice second half of life spirituality claim that one effect of excessive vetting is that the laity has difficulty developing an "informed conscience" when all the speakers in a diocese are vetted by a bishop motivated by control rather than the exploration of new ideas and dialogue. The vetting process presents the laity with speakers who are obedient to orthodoxy and obedient to the local bishop. We form our conscience not only from church teaching, but also from social ethics, family tradition, and the moral law inscribed in our hearts. Sometimes ideas heard validate and confirm the directives of our conscience. For example, we may have been taught that homosexuals are objectively disordered, but if we hear a speaker say that God creates both heterosexual and homosexual people, it could validate what we knew in our heart to be true. As parishioners struggle with life decisions, we are doing them a disservice by not exposing them to different ideas so that they can be in touch with the complexity of moral discernment.

Fr. Philip S. Kaufman in his book, Why You Can Disagree and Remain a Faithful Catholic, makes the case that denying Catholics their right to mature reflection may be considered immoral. He says that the laity needs to develop an informed conscience to make good decisions regarding contraception, homosexuality, same-sex marriage, physician-assisted suicide, the possibility of remarriage after a broken marriage, and abortion.

The denial of permission to be a speaker typically occurs when the vetting process identifies the proposed speaker either dissented from official church teaching or was disobedient to the institution's officials. Individuals who have had some association with Call to Action or Voice of the Faithful are almost always vetted negatively. Those Catholics who say that the Church has irrational sexual moral norms, a lightening rod issue for sure, are almost always vetted negatively as well. Some bishops and archbishops seek to extend their control over the lives and thoughts of clerics and laity by forbidding them from attending certain events that have been negatively vetted even though they are held in non-Catholic church locations.

Conclusion:

In my next letter to you, I will continue to share some effects of excessive vetting that can lead to the diminishment of faith, or the loss of faith, when individuals are not encouraged to search for new ways to describe reality through the different stages of their lives. As you will see, there are reasons to believe that the "defenders of the faith" and their practice of excessive vetting, rather than strengthening the mission of the Church today, are actually contributing to its diminishment.

Peace,

Uncle Matthew

Letter #57
Monday, May 4, 2015

Dear Uncle Matthew,

Today, the rector spoke to our third-year theology class to inform us about the upcoming diaconate ordinations. As you know, each diocese celebrates the ordinations to the transitional diaconate at different times. My vocations' director was here over the weekend, and he said the bishop has given me a green light based on his reports about me from the seminary. I'm a bit nervous about making a life-long commitment. The date for the ordination is set for Saturday, August 22.

Thank you for your last letter. I have never before thought of the Babylonian Captivity as a basic metaphor for the human condition. The way you described it to me was so simple to comprehend.

Your discussion of vetting was eye-opening. I never realized how troubling excessive vetting can be in some dioceses. You have made me aware that I there is a lot of vetting here in the seminary regarding who teaches us, what they teach us, the rules we follow, and even restrictions while off campus. I found it brilliant the way you connected excessive vetting to difficulties in forming one's conscience.

You mentioned Call to Action and Voice of the Faithful in articles found in the National Catholic Reporter. I know almost nothing about these two organizations since we do not get the National Catholic Reporter in the seminary library.

When we last talked on the phone, you said that you have a lot more material in your journal on excessive vetting. Please share! I am curious to know more.

Peace,

Joey

Response to Letter #57
Sunday, May 17, 2015

Dear Joey,

Thank you for telling me about your scheduled diaconate on August 22. I'll be there! As for any nervousness, it is normal when making a big decision, but keep an eye on your heart and soul.

Today we celebrated the feast of the Ascension. I did some research on this feast. Some theologians think the Ascension did not literally happen. Some theologians think the Ascension teaches us that Jesus was greater than Elijah and he is the new Elijah. As for me, I view it as a mystery, a devotional passage, that keeps me aware that like Jesus I was created to be with God forever.

In my previous letter, I shared that excessive vetting can make it difficult to develop an informed conscience. Let me share more reasons now why some people believe that excessive vetting can be harmful.

b. Excessive vetting promotes an "exile" atmosphere:

Earlier, I mentioned the Vatican's investigation of the Leadership Conference of Women Religious (LCWR). At one point, the Prefect of the Vatican's Congregation for the Doctrine of the

Faith ordered that speakers at the group's annual conference had to be approved by Seattle Archbishop J. Peter Sartain, before the Conference agendas and speakers were finalized.

Some of the sisters, those committed to a rich exchange of ideas, considered this action to be an abuse of authority. They said that the selection of speakers should be the prerogative of the LCWR. Sister Nancy Schreck, a Franciscan sister and a past president of the LCWR, last fall told the members, "The experience [of excessive vetting] is like that of the biblical 'Exile' in which we have been so changed that we are no longer at home in the culture and church in which we find ourselves."

As I mentioned in my last letter, the investigation of the LCWR ended last month, but the report issued gives no details for what processes might be used in the future to review LCWR speakers or writers.

In summary, Joey, many people who are trying to practice second half of life spirituality want to stop believing in archaic dogmas, ordination requirements that deny women, trappings of royalty, and unquestioned obedience to authority.

c. Excessive vetting reduces the Vatican II spirit:

I shared in my last letter how the Roman System and its practice of excessive vetting contributes to church leaders finding it difficult to be collegial, to be willing to listen to new opinions, or being open to change. Excessive vetting also reduces the Second Vatican Council's spirit of collaboration and subsidiarity. Excessive vetting can also violate the rights of parishioners as found in the documents of the Second Vatican Council, especially the Declaration on Religious Liberty. Adults want to take seriously the Second Vatican Council's principle that the Church is the People of God, not just the hierarchy.

d. Excessive vetting diminishes trust and promotes fear:

Excessive vetting conveys a lack of trust in the professionalism of local pastoral leaders. In the practice of second half of life spirituality, one presumes that principals of Catholic schools, pastors, leaders of organizations like the LCWR, and the chairs of lay organizations can be trusted to make good decisions regarding the choice of speakers. Overruling their judgments should occur only in extraordinary circumstances.

When adult leaders are treated like children, it ultimately promotes a climate of fear. Many pastoral leaders, for good reason, are afraid of making mistakes regarding vetting. Creativity is thus lost in an atmosphere of fear.

Consider how fear begets fear. Those doing the vetting are rejecting what they cannot control. They are condemning what they do not understand. In the final analysis, excessive vetting relates to the fear of losing control and power.

e. Excessive vetting discourages questioning and encourages dualistic thinking:

As we move through adulthood, all of us will face paradoxes, disappointments, setbacks, suffering, and doubt. These experiences force us to ask questions and to doubt some of our belief systems analogous to the way the prophets in the Hebrew Scriptures, when feeling internal dissension, critiqued the religious systems in which they were living. In the second half of life, critiquing institutions, other people, and oneself is a normal and necessary development in the formation of one's conscience and the development of a mature belief system. When we are free to choose to listen to a speaker who challenges simplistic ideas but provides broader understandings, we can develop a deeper faith. We change our opinions and see our prejudices when we are presented with new experiences that force debate and a re-evaluation of our positions. It also forces us to realize what we do believe and to discredit false claims.

One specific effect of excessive vetting is that it causes us to hear the same types of messages over and over simply reinforcing the beliefs we learned when we were children. As adults, we need to realize that there is no perfect mom or dad, child or spouse. There is no perfect religious institution. Reality is not black and white. When ready, we need to hear differing opinions concerning religious matters. Prayer, suffering, love and even sin can open us up to God. To assume that the experiences in life are dualistic: black and white, good or bad, right or wrong in the second half of life prevents us from seeing reality and growing spiritually from the mysteries of life.

f. Excessive vetting denies people the thrill of hearing new ideas:

Many Catholics over the years have attended the national Call to Action Conferences held every year in November. Participants often find these conferences to be immensely enriching. So many challenging topics are presented through dynamic speakers that make everyone reflect and scrutinize the adequacy of their thinking. Change (metanoia) is possible, even probable! There is an excitement in the air. The liturgies are different from those that most people have experienced because they are inclusive with male and female leaders; lay and cleric. Everyone feels as though they are actively participating. I bring this up because, by way of contrast, it shows how excessive vetting results too often in excessive dullness, making rare the thrill of discovery.

Nearly all Catholics want to respect their bishops, but at the same time they desire to spiritually grow through the stimulus of new ideas. When church leaders practice excessive vetting, it tends to stifle and thwart the Spirit of God in those who are practicing second half of life spirituality, if they choose to stay in the institutional church.

Joey, there are many nationally known speakers who are widely regarded as wisdom figures (as persons who practice second half of life spirituality). They stir the pot. They muddy the waters. They make us think. They stretch our imaginations. They provide spiritual roadmaps. In sum, they greatly contribute to our faith development.

Some authors in this category are Fr. Andrew Greeley who passed in 2013, Fr. Richard McBrien who passed in January, and Robert McClory who passed just last month. These writers have inspired many of us to think, to change, to repent, and to love and embrace a bigger God.

Some nationally known speakers who are currently banned from speaking on Catholic property are: Eugene Kennedy, John Dear, Charlie Curran, Joan Chittister, Edwina Gateley, Anthony Padovano, John Shelby Spong, Matthew Fox, Tom Fox, Richard Rohr, Sister Nancy Schreck, Michael Crosby, and Michael Morwood.

Sister Jeannine Gramick, who was censured earlier for her opposition to Catholic Church teaching on homosexuality and marriage, was not allowed to speak yesterday at a Catholic Church in Charlotte after she had been invited as the keynote speaker at a public program entitled "Including LGBT People and Their Families in Faith Communities: A Conference Open to All." Does banning these wisdom figures really contribute to the spiritual growth of the Church and its individual members? Those who practice second half of life spirituality believe that these speakers offer us opportunities to hear new ideas that can deepen our faith and enlarge our self awareness, guided by the belief, "Perfect love casts out fear" (1 John 4: 18).

g. Excessive vetting is suspicious of Voice of the Faithful (VOTF):

VOTF meets in many dioceses, but some bishops treat this organization with suspicion, if not outright resistance. VOTF is a lay organization formed in Boston in 2002 in response to the sexual abuse crisis. VOTF tries to build bridges of trust between the laity and the hierarchy. The organization does not seek to change church dogma. VOTF goals are: to support victims/survivors of clergy sexual abuse, support priests of integrity, and support structural change within the Church. VOTF quotes Canon Law (212.3) that states,

"The laity has the right, indeed at times, the duty, in keeping with their knowledge, competence, and position to manifest to the sacred pastors their views on matters which concern the good of the Church."

Some bishops do not respect VOTF, hence bridges of trust have little chance of being built. Dialogue fails. The dualisms of "right-wrong" and "good-bad" prevail, reflecting the polarization and conflicts associated with first half of life spirituality.

h. Excessive vetting contributes to serious pastoral consequences:

Priests tend to imitate the style of leadership that they experience through their bishops and pope. If a bishop practices first half of life spirituality, it is likely that the seminarians, deacons, and priests in his diocese will unconsciously tend to emulate his conduct.

For example, a woman told me she pre-planned her funeral at her local parish. She requested a particular song to be played at her funeral. Her pastor, who was greatly influenced by his bishop, told her that the song she selected was "secular." He said that her selection had to be in the church hymnal so that it would fall under the category of a "sacred" song. Such hurtful and needless silliness!

The practice of first half of life spirituality demonstrated in this story reflects a strict dualism of sacred and secular, whereas the practice of second half of life spirituality sees beneath the simplistic surface in the search for spiritual, soulful truth.

Conclusion:

In conclusion, broadly speaking, vetting can be helpful or harmful. Yet in today's Catholic Church, all too often an excessive use of vetting reflects an unhealthy exercise of power and control to the point of absurdity. Good shepherds attempt to keep a sensitive balance regarding vetting so as to enable their people to grow mentally, morally, and spirituality, rather than to deny them opportunities to mature through their own faith journey.

Peace,

Uncle Matthew

Letter #58
Sunday, May 31, 2015

Dear Uncle Matthew,

I'll be home until June 15 when my summer assignment begins. Paul is also home now for a few days. He likes his job with IBM, and he is dating a beautiful woman named Pamela. Our paths are different indeed.

Earlier, you suggested that I should actively discern whether or not I am able to live a healthy celibate life. At times I am discouraged in this regard. There are moments when I want so much to be with a woman and perhaps have children. I don't know if I can live as long as you as a celibate and be happy and fulfilled. Does it become easier over time? Do thoughts of loving another, as a man, ever go away or at least fade into the background? As you can see, I am still discerning my vocation, and praying about it daily.

The in-depth sharing about excessive vetting was very helpful for me to understand some subtleties of power and control. I admire you so much for delving into these common practices that many priests never question. I was unaware of the extent and seriousness of excessive vetting in the Church until you shared your thoughts with me. I will henceforth be on the lookout.

One of our professors recently told us about men and women,

Catholic, who have dissented from some of the teachings of the Church. He cited Roy Bourgeois whom you mentioned earlier as the founder of the human rights group, School of the Americas Watch (SOA Watch). Our professor said Bourgeois was dismissed from Maryknoll and the priesthood because of his participation in 2008 in an invalid ordination of a woman. I'm not sure, but based on classroom discussion, my fellow seminarians appear to support the non-ordination of women to the priesthood.

Can you share with me something about dissent from church teaching? In an earlier letter, you cited dissent as the fifth challenge that the Church faces today. I want to know more.

Peace,

Joey

Response to Letter #58
Saturday, June 13, 2015

Dear Joey,

Today is the Feast Day of St. Anthony of Padua, a thirteenth century saint. When I was young in high school, I prayed to him for the virtue of purity. There is a beautiful statue of him in the Franciscan Monastery in Washington, D. C., where, as a youth, I attended mass with my family. Perhaps, when the time is right, you yourself will see that beautiful statue one day and think of me and our dialogues, and the passage of time.

I have shared with you four challenges facing the institutional church today: (1) the urge of self-idolatry, (2) the denial of the church's shadow side, (3) human sexuality, and (4) excessive vetting. At your request, I'll now share with you some thoughts on dissent from church teaching, the fifth of twelve challenges that many people believe the institutional church faces today.

5. Dissent from church teaching:

In your last letter to me, you mentioned that your professor told your class that Roy Bourgeois was suspended, silenced, laicized, excommunicated, and banned from church ministry because he dissented from a church teaching. In the practice of first half of life spirituality, dissent is not usually considered a complimentary word. Authority, if it focuses on self-preservation, by its very definition does not favor dissent. In the case of our beloved church, anything that challenges the present way of thinking regrettably seems to be viewed as a form of dissent.

Yet, when we practice second half of life spirituality, dissent is seen as an important means of providing new insights, correcting past errors, and enriching the Church. Through this welcoming and curious mind-set, we try to judge less. We begin with the assumption that individuals are doing the best they can. We accept that those who dissent may be enriching the Church by opening new pathways and building new bridges that foster awareness and vitality. We believe it is better to think, act, and risk making a mistake, knowing that in this way we grow, rather than not to think, act, and thus not err, but to remain stagnant.

The Roman Catholic Church, like every other institution, has a right to uphold and fight for its moral beliefs in the public life of a nation. However, some say that church leaders act inconsistently today thereby weakening their claims for moral authority and positive impact on the world. For example, church leaders rarely oppose lawmakers who vote for higher military appropriations or tax breaks for the very wealthy. This calls into question our commitment to peace and social justice. Instead, the hierarchy seems to focus on opposing health insurance that provides contraception and abortions for women and international-aid programs that emphasize condoms and gay rights, thereby focusing on issues that may promote divisiveness, judgmentalism, and even hostility towards others.

Some parishioners are asking why the Catholic laity doesn't have the right to dissent when they do not agree with their bishops' opposition to married priests, women priests, death by choice, contraception, divorce followed by remarriage without a priest, and legalized abortion. This suppression of dissent on this wide range of issues could well be why many are leaving the Church today. Of course, it is important to know church doctrine as an important part of forming one's conscience. But those who practice second half of life spirituality say that it is also important to respect the fact that at times people will dissent from some church teachings. Dissent has shown in the past that this is how the institutional church receives God's living Spirit, thereby discerning unfolding truth. And if the formation of conscience is central to the Christian life, and it is, than dissent, the expression of conscience, must be essential as well.

The role of conscience:

The Vatican II Council affirmed the importance of conscience in the Pastoral Constitution of the Church in the Modern World (16) saying,

"Conscience is the most intimate center and sanctuary of a person, in which he or she is alone with God whose voice echoes within them. In a marvelous manner conscience makes known that law which is fulfilled by love of God and of neighbor."

Pope John Paul II, in his 1993 encyclical letter, Veritatis Splendor, said, "The judgment of conscience also has an imperative character: man must act in accordance with it."

Some people who practice second half of life spirituality ask, "Shouldn't the Catholic Church be a place where we can disagree with certain doctrinal teachings without being shamed, laicized, or excommunicated?" Some people ask, "Shouldn't the Catholic Church respect, love, and accept as children of God those who not only think within the box but also those who think outside the box? More directly, didn't Jesus himself think outside of the box in his day?" Dissent by clerics and the laity has always been a part of Catholic tradition and it has served a positive role throughout our long history.

I will share with you examples of some dissenters to illustrate my point. In some situations, the hierarchal church later accepted some dissenters as truth-speakers who greatly enabled the institutional church to be more aware of truth. Some dissenters I will mention are still alive and although their views are not in conformity with the Church's current teaching, they stimulate questioning, dialogue, and an opportunity for growth in knowledge and faith.

Examples of individuals who have dissented from church teaching:

1. Father John C. Murray, SJ:

In 1954, his writing on religious liberty led to a conflict with Cardinal Ottaviani, Pro-Secretary of the Vatican Holy Office. The Vatican demanded that Murray end both writing on religious freedom and publishing his two latest articles on the issue.

In 1963, he was invited to the Vatican II Council, and his writings were largely responsible for the Vatican II document, Declaration on Religious Freedom. It was through his dissent that discussion occurred, minds were changed, and truth was revealed.

2. Robert McClory:

In 2000, Robert McClory, who just died a few weeks ago on Good Friday at the age of eighty-two, wrote a book entitled, Faithful Dissenters, Stories of Men and Women Who Loved and Changed the Church. Robert McClory wrote this book not to encourage dissent as a general practice but to point out that sometimes dissent can be a means of providing new insights that enrich the Church.

He tells stories about Galileo Galilei, John Henry Newman, Mary Ward, Catherine of Siena, Hildegard of Bingen, Yves Congar, and John Courtney Murray. McClory shares how these individuals, although they suffered for their dissent in their life time, later were seen as providing valuable knowledge and insights.

3. Father Philip Kaufman, OSB:

In 1995, the late Benedictine priest, Philip S. Kaufman, in an effort to engage disaffected Catholics, wrote a book entitled, Why You Can Disagree and Remain a Faithful Catholic. In his book, Fr. Kaufman wrote about many topics: conscience, birth control, infallibility, divorce and remarriage, abortion, and democracy in the Church. Fr. Kaufman stressed that everyone is obliged to follow a sincerely informed conscience.

Although Father Kaufman presented contrary opinions to church teaching, he was never reprimanded by the Vatican since he was writing to foster an awareness that followers of Jesus have many different viewpoints.

4. Cardinal Yves Congar, OP:

Father Yves Congar was a French friar, a Dominican Catholic priest and theologian. Congar was an early advocate of the ecumenical movement. He promoted the concept of a "collegial" papacy and criticized the Roman Curia. He also promoted the role of the laity in the Church.

The Vatican restricted his writings from 1947-1956, and he was prevented from teaching or publishing during the pontificate of Pope Pius XII (1939-1958).

In 1960, Pope John XXIII invited him to serve on the preparatory theological commission of Vatican II. During the proceedings, he became known as a theological expert and has since been described as the single most formative influence on the Second Vatican Council. Pope John Paul II named him a cardinal of the Catholic Church in November 1994. He died in June 1995.

5. Sr. Jeannine Gramick, S.L.:

In my last letter to you, I mentioned that Sister Jeannine Gramick, SL, is a Roman Catholic religious sister. She is a leading advocate for lesbian, gay, bisexual, and transgender rights. She was the cofounder of New Ways Ministry. In 1999, the Congregation for the Doctrine of the Faith charged her with grave doctrinal error and prohibited her from any pastoral work with homosexual persons.

In 2000, her religious congregation, the School Sisters of Notre Dame, told her to cease speaking publicly on the topic of homosexuality. Sister Jeannine responded by saying, "I choose not to collaborate in my own oppression by restricting a basic human right to speak." Sister Jeannine then transferred to the Sisters of Loretto that supports her ministry of education and advocacy on behalf of the LGBT community.

In my last letter to you, I mentioned that in April, Sister Jeannine was banned from speaking in the Diocese of Charlotte by Bishop Peter Jugis. A Diocese spokesman stated: "We are not going to have someone who opposes Catholic teaching to be teaching in a Catholic diocese."

I share this example of dissent with you for two reasons. First, it provides a good recent example of what some would consider to be excessive vetting, and second, it illustrates how following one's conscience, as the Pastoral Constitution of the Church in the Modern World teaches, may affect one's ministry.

6. Rev. Helmut Schuller:

In an earlier letter, I mentioned the Austrian priest, Helmut Schuller. The Vatican stripped him in 2012 of his title, "Monsignor." He stressed a "graduated obedience," first to God, then to one's conscience, and finally to church order.

In Boston, Cardinal Sean O'Malley barred him from speaking on Catholic property. Schuller said, "There are bishops in this country who have forbidden that I can speak to people like you. It is not sad that I should be forbidden to speak. What is sad is that you should be forbidden to listen."

7. Rev. John Dear, SJ:

Rev. John Dear, SJ, graduated magna cum laude from Duke University and is the author of thirty books. He has been arrested seventy-five times for his acts of nonviolent civil disobedience. He works for peace and justice and has protested against the most heinous instruments of war, nuclear weapons.

In January 2014, he took a leave from the Jesuits after thirty-two years with them. He said that his Jesuit superiors had tried over the decades to stop his work for peace.

Those who practice second half of life spirituality question why there is not room for him in the institutional church where he can make us aware of these important issues through his committed work for peace and justice.

8. Rev. William Brennan, S.J.:

I read an article in the March 23 edition of the National Catholic Reporter about Fr. William Brennan, SJ. At the age of ninety-two, in 2012, he celebrated a mass at Fort Benning during a protest known as the School of Americas, where a woman, Rev. Janice Sevre-Duszynska, who was ordained through the Association of Roman Catholic Women Priests, con-celebrated. He was punished by his Jesuit superiors who prohibited him from practicing his priestly faculties, speaking to the media, attending public worship, and leaving Milwaukee without permission from his Jesuit superiors.

Seven months after Father William Brennan's death at the age of 94, a video was released in which he pleaded for equality of women in administrative and spiritual functions. Fr. Brennan wanted this video released after his death so as to honor his vows of obedience to the Jesuits and to be obedient to his conscience.

Conclusion:

I have presented the above examples to heighten your awareness about the reality of what has happened and is happening in the Church. Clerics who dissent are not tolerated in the institutional church and are suppressed and silenced in multiple ways. In Matthew Fox's book, The Pope's War, he lists ninety-three names of silenced, expelled, banished theologians, and pastoral leaders when Cardinal Ratzinger was Prefect of the Congregation for the Doctrine of the Faith.

Those who practice second half of life spirituality agree that the pulpit is not the place to publicly dissent from church teachings, but they wonder "Why can't a religious leader write or share an opinion that might help us to become aware of the presence of the Spirit?" We can reject as well as accept what we hear, read, or learn in any way. Both our intellect and our conscience need to be well informed. In the final analysis, it will be our experiences in life that temper both. When dissent is looked at through the long lens of history, and has a chorus of contemporary voices in our very own day, many believe that it is an unmistakable sign of God's living Spirit.

Jesus provided a lesson in this regard, as he expanded his ministry to the Gentiles (Mark 7:24-8:10). He listened prayerfully to new information, dialogued with others who had opposing views, and respected others as they were.

When we remain open to the possibility that those who dissent from church teachings may actually be helping us to increase our dedication to the Risen Christ, we are following the example of Jesus. In this way, we are demonstrating that we are willing to expand our own ministry to those who think differently, and to embrace the Spirit at work with us, so that we may reaffirm what we already believe or see something to which we have been previously blind.

Peace,

Uncle Matthew

Letter #59
Sunday, June 28, 2015

Dear Uncle Matthew,

Thank you for your last letter regarding dissent from church teaching. I realize that most of us have fairly closed-minds, perhaps we are even hostile to different opinions regarding controversial issues when we practice first half of life spirituality. I am not familiar with most of the dissenters that you mentioned: John C. Murray, Yves Congar, Charles Curran, Jeannine Gramick, John Dear, and William Brennan. I remember you spoke so highly of Fr. Philip Kaufman OSB who wrote Why You Can Disagree and Remain a Faithful Catholic. I recall that you heard Robert McClory, the author of Faithful Dissenters, speak at a conference. I haven't read either book yet, but I hope to read these books after I am ordained.

I recall that back in January, we celebrated a mass honoring Saint Anthony the Abbot, the father of all monks. In the homily, one of the professors shared with us a parable Abbot Anthony related to a younger monk whom he was counseling. The parable suggested that the time is coming when people will be insane, and when they see someone who is sane, they will attack that person saying: "You are insane because you are not like us." When I read your last letter, I thought of this parable in connection with how clerics are often punished when they dissent from official church teaching.

Here in the seminary, as I mentioned before, it is best not to refer to controversial names or ask too many questions. I think that the atmosphere here is permeated with fear. We are trained to be loyal and obedient, unconsciously fearing the rejection and isolation that would accompany being labeled as disloyal.

Last Friday, the Supreme Court legalized same-sex marriage across the United States. The justices ruled that states cannot deny gay men and lesbians the same marriage rights enjoyed by opposite-sex couples. I read that almost two dozen countries allow gay marriage. Isn't it ironic that the Supreme Court is standing up for freedom of conscience whereas the Fortnight for Freedom Campaign seems to be trying to impose the church's sexual values on all members of society?

My summer assignment is the best one I've experienced so far. I'm with a pastor who believes in the Spirit of the Vatican II Council. He is kind, compassionate, and he spends time with me. He is an alumnus of this seminary, and he, like me, worked for several years for the government after he graduated from college. He has a very high level of integrity. His love for all people, especially the poor, makes him popular. He preaches bravely on social justice issues. He shared with me his appreciation of Pope Francis' new encyclical, Laudato Si, On Care for our Common Home because my pastor is very concerned about climate change.

Earlier in a letter to me, you mentioned twelve challenges that the institutional church faces today. On Friday night my pastor took me out to dinner, and I asked him about diocesan clergy assignments, priestly retreats, and the annual faith appeal. My pastor told me a sad story regarding a newly appointed parochial vicar from another country whom the bishop assigned to a parish without first consulting the pastor. To me that shows an abuse of authority when a bishop is that insensitive to the lives of the priests in his diocese. Didn't Cardinal Bernardin challenge us to have a pro-life position, a "seamless garment," on all pro-life issues from "womb to tomb?"

My pastor also shared with me the diocesan policy on clergy retreats. He said that he feels curtailed in choosing a retreat since the bishop selects the directors of the retreats.

Finally, my pastor shared his thoughts about the annual faith appeal. Once again, he has not met the required assessment for the appeal, but his focus on gospel values enables him to keep financial matters in perspective.

I would like you to share with me your reflections on these three topics which I believe you called challenges 6, 7, and 8. Please know that I greatly appreciate all the time you give me through your devoted letter writing.

Peace,

Joey

Response to Letter #59
Saturday, July 11, 2015

Dear Joey,

In our church bulletin this weekend, there is an article from the President of the Catholic Bishops' Conference that asserts that recognizing same-sex marriage is a tragic error that harms the common good. I presume that his statement is backed by the hierarchal church's teaching that marriage is the union of one man and one woman. Catholic teaching is confirmed by divine Revelation and sacred scripture.

By way of contrast, Justice Anthony Kennedy said every American had a constitutional right to marry and form a family. To deny same-sex couples that right, he wrote, deprives them of the "equal dignity" they deserve. We know that the Justices have different opinions on controversial issues, but they can respectfully accept each other's opinion and dialogue among themselves. I think they are giving us an important lesson regarding tolerance of dissent and respectful dialogue. We live in a changing society. We must also listen to the wisdom of the people so as not to be out of touch with reality.

On another subject, did you read in the recent issue of the NCR the editorial entitled, "Time to end pattern of deceit, denial?" The editorial points out that for thirty years some church leaders badly mishandled sex abuse cases. The editorial considers this to be their betrayal, at a sacramental level, of the community they were charged to serve. In the same issue, Fr. Tom Doyle in an essay shares a sad truth about the deceit and corruption that existed in chancery offices as thousands of priests who abused children were protected by their bishops.

By way of contrast, there was also a good article in America entitled, "Pastors, Not Princes." The article shares the healthy role of a bishop under Pope Francis. It is an invitation that no bishop or priest let himself be robbed the joy of being a shepherd.

I want to let you know, even though I am older than you, that our correspondence is helping me to review, relearn, and clarify my own understanding of what it means to be a good shepherd. This process in our dialogue about spiritual matters makes me wish that I had a spiritual road map when I was your age so that I could have made better choices in my own life. But, thank God, it's never too late!

Let me continue, as you suggested, to share with you some reflections on (6) clergy assignments, (7) clergy retreats and educational opportunities, and (8) the Annual Faith Appeal. Conflicts occur in the Church when some bishops practice first half of life spirituality and some priests practice second half of life spirituality. Part of the solution to resolving conflicts is to be aware of these two spiritualities and to be convinced that respectful dialogue is an important means to alleviate conflicts.

6. Clergy assignments:

Newly appointed bishops:

At times, a priest is appointed to become bishop without ever having been a pastor. A newly appointed bishop may come from another part of the country, so he doesn't know the culture of the people, and the people do not know him. At times a priest who is a member of a religious order is appointed to head a diocese with diocesan priests.

Over the last several decades, different approaches have been pursued by the Vatican to appoint bishops. Archbishop Jean Jadot was the apostolic delegate to the United States from 1973-1980. He appointed pastoral bishops. He was one of the leading Vatican II Council progressives in the US. Following Jadot was Archbishop Pio Laghi, the papal delegate, and he usually appointed new bishops who were conservative and sent them to states and parts of the country never visited by the new bishops. He died in Rome in 2009 at the age of 86.

Newly appointed parochial vicars, pastors, and administrators:

Some Catholics get upset and even leave the institutional church because the laity has no real input in the selection of church leadership. The laity may invest an immense amount of time, money, and heartfelt effort in support of their local parish, and yet have no effective voice, none, in choosing the church's leadership.

Some laypersons get discouraged when they sense that some priests are selected to be administrators or pastors in their parish when they are not, in fact, suitable for the parish to which they are assigned. For example, sometimes the bishop will replace a pastor who practices second half of life spirituality and is noted for his pastoral sensitivity with a new pastor who practices first half of life spirituality and lacks pastoral sensitivity.

Many clerics lack an understanding of the pastoral needs and concerns of the laity. Clericalism separates the local priests from their parishioners.  Clericalism is very much alive when people are exposed to a misuse of authority, preaching on first half of life images of God, and permeating it all, is an unhealthy sexuality.

The sad story your pastor shared with you sounds like situations I have observed over the years when a bishop occasionally will assign a parochial vicar (assistant pastor) to a parish without first respectfully dialoguing with the pastor.

Sometimes administrators are appointed to a parish without regard for the parish's traditions, liturgical customs, past emphasis on collegiality, and creativity in ministry. The new administrator could make the tragic mistake of using his authority to force all his parishioners into the practice of his own spirituality. Such administrators think they are preserving the tradition, but in their single-minded blindness they cause much harm.

For example, some new parochial vicars, pastors, or administrators might start wearing a cassock when that had never been a tradition in the parish. They may refuse to bless children after communion although that had been a tradition in the parish. They may preach too much on a few select topics and accentuate the depravity of humankind. They may make too many liturgical changes quickly whereby the people erroneously get the impression that the former pastor was "incorrect." By trying to "restore" tradition, they are in fact destroying it.

Seasoned pastors:

Seasoned pastors wisely try to know their new parishioners and the local traditions before making changes. They respect the former leadership in a parish. Hence, when they are assigned to a parish, they begin their ministry with an appreciation for continuity. This is not only a matter of style but substance. They know that if the parishioners trust them, then the people will later be open to some changes. More importantly, seasoned pastors recognize that they have much more to learn when embarking upon a new assignment, even if the lessons learned are received and known only in the quiet recesses of the heart.

Seasoned pastors who practice second half of life spirituality know that each aspect of worship, the homily, hospitality, participation, and the bulletin can all be used to create and nurture an adult spirituality. The Eucharistic celebration, as the primary source and expression of faith, is brought to a deeper level of faith. Pope Francis' The Joy of the Gospel, Evangelii

Gaudium (#135), his 2013 apostolic exhortation on the Church's primary mission of evangelization, said, "The homily is the touchstone for judging a pastor's closeness and ability to communicate to his people... The homily can be a constant source of renewal and growth."

Foreign-born clergy:

Many dioceses, like your diocese, because of a lack of domestic vocations, recruit foreign-born men to study for the priesthood. When these men are ordained, they bring with them a different culture, a different understanding of Church, and a different understanding of priesthood. This adds an additional layer of complexity and challenges for both the clergy and parishioners. These priests need local mentoring from the outset so that parishioners do not reject their particular understanding and practice of Catholicism.

Those who practice second half of life spirituality welcome foreign-born priests because they believe that these priests provide valuable opportunities for the assembly to hear and see reality differently. Being exposed to a new culture, new interpretations of doctrine, and a new understanding of the gospels can lead to greater growth in faith. However, special care needs to be given to their assignments so that their pastors welcome them and accept them as valuable assets to the parish. When pastors accept foreign-born priests and respectfully work with them, the people will do the same. We proclaim that we are "catholic," an adjective that means "universal." A priest from a foreign country provides an opportunity to test this implicit claim.

7. Clergy retreats and educational opportunities:

Introduction:

I mentioned in a previous letter to you that Canon Law (c.276) requires priests to make a retreat each year. Retreats and workshops are important for priests as a time of priestly fraternity as well as an opportunity to foster an awareness of and an appreciation for different spiritualities, including what we call first and second half of life spirituality. Continuing education, retreats, and workshops should be opportunities for priests to discover new means to grow in wholeness and find greater fulfillment in their ministry.

Retreats:

I believe I understand what your pastor meant when he mentioned to you that he feels curtailed in choosing what he would like for a retreat experience. When a bishop is not comfortable allowing his priests to be introduced to different spiritualities, either because of his adherence to orthodoxy or his lack of awareness of different spiritualities, there is that temptation to just provide retreats that are grounded in the practice of first half of life spirituality.

For example, I heard about a bishop who told his incardinated priests that the money allotted to them each year for their annual retreat was to be used within the diocese at the Catholic Retreat Center. The bishop provided several retreat opportunities from which the priests could choose. In this manner, the bishop used financial pressure to effectively control the retreat experience for the priests. Those who practice second half of life spirituality view such a restrictive policy as too controlling on the part of a bishop.

By way of contrast, bishops who are more open to different spiritualities allow their priests to use their retreat money to attend a diocesan retreat or to choose a retreat of their choice, even if it is conducted outside the diocese.

Educational opportunities:

Not only can a bishop be too controlling of retreat opportunities, but even local educational opportunities may be banned. In one diocese, a group of Catholic laypersons, who probably practice second half of life spirituality, sent out an invitation regarding a workshop entitled, "The Future of the Laity in the Church." The workshop was to be held in a non-Catholic church. Later, the Chancellor of the diocese sent out a memo forbidding Catholics, both lay and clerics, from attending the workshop.

One priest, a classmate of mine in that particular diocese, met with the Chancellor to share his concerns about the ban. The Chancellor was very nice, but my classmate quickly realized that the Chancellor was viewing the workshop from the viewpoint of the practice of first half of life spirituality. The Chancellor viewed the bishop as the guardian of orthodoxy who had to protect the people. The Chancellor believed that it was wrong to have Catholic laypersons hosting speakers who were not in full agreement with certain strictly orthodox teachings of the hierarchal church.

These two examples of retreat and educational opportunities illustrate that church leaders who do not know about the richness of practicing second half of life spirituality can unintentionally keep clerics and laypersons spiritually immature by limiting their exposure to new ideas that stimulate questioning, re-learning, and growth in faith.

8. The Annual Faith Appeal:

Introduction:

Pastors and administrators in parishes are given strict instructions to raise money for different causes. One such cause is the Annual Faith Appeal. Pastors who practice first half of life spirituality usually do not question the "appeal." To them, the bishop represents the unquestioned voice and authority of the institutional church. Many Catholics are highly devoted to the institutional church, so they are more likely to ask "How much should I give?" instead of "Should I give?"

With the practice of second half of life spirituality, it becomes more likely that both lay and clerics begin to question the true nature of the "appeal" and the moral issues involved in deciding whether to give, and if so, how much.

The practice of first half of life spirituality:

No one disagrees that bishops need funds to operate a diocese. Many bishops typically assess the parishes annually a sum of money to be paid to the chancery in support of the diocese. Sometimes the assessments can be as high as twenty-five percent of the parish's annual offertory income. Some bishops require parishes that do not meet their assessment to take out an interest-bearing loan with the diocese.

The quantity of money often becomes the major focus of the appeal rather than the spiritual motivation behind the giving and the proportional sacrifices born by the individuals. (Remember the story of the poor widow's contribution to the treasury, Mark 12: 41-44.) For the duration of the Faith Appeal drive, great attention in the pulpit, bulletins, and elsewhere is focused on financial giving in support of the institution. Pastors, unconsciously perhaps, are less likely to preach prophetic messages of social justice when they need money from wealthy parishioners to reach their assessment. Remember, Jesus said, "For where your treasure is, there also will your heart be" (Matthew 6:21).

Pastors can be tempted to use in their appeal the Proverb found in 22:9, "He who is generous will be blessed," in a way that seems like a "quid pro quo" (one thing in return for another). The pressure on pastors to raise their assessment is considerable.

Many pastors that never reach their assessment goals are made to feel like "losers." They feel as though they let down their bishop. They feel as though they were not "convincing" in their appeal. They can take the defeat personally.

It probably is easier for pastors who practice first half of life spirituality to meet their quotas than priests who practice second half of life spirituality since they are more committed to a church structure that is regimented, and they are more willing to promote the financial demands of the bishop over other concerns. Parishioners may be pressured in ways that result in significant costs of which priests are unaware.

The practice of second half of life spirituality:

It seems that your pastor believes that the Annual Faith Appeal can lead to the avoidance of preaching on the important issues involving peace and justice so that the appeal will not be hurt. Also in the minds of many parishioners, when the appeal is stressed every week in the liturgy and in the bulletin, religion comes to be viewed as a means of raising money to keep the institutional church alive instead of the exercise of its primary mission of transforming people into men and women who live out the gospel message.

Bishops, who practice second half of life spirituality, when given the task, raise money differently. They make it a point to express their gratitude for the money raised in the appeal. They assume the parishes did their best even if their assessments were not met. They attempt to show that they value people more than money and that the money raised will serve the people. If the amount collected does not match the assessments, then the bishops adjust their budgets accordingly.

I know of one diocese where the bishop, now deceased, assessed parishes annually for the appeal. The bishop did not require parishes to take out an interest-bearing loan if they did not meet their assessment goal. The bishop's gratitude and affirmation gave credence to his "appeal." To the surprise of many, parishes in this diocese often collected more money each year than their assessments.

When people are treated with respect, people are more generous and joyful in giving. They are living proof that to truly give is to truly receive. People want bishops who are good shepherds who affirm them and trust they are doing the best they can. With this method of conducting an "appeal," there is less likely going to be a status quo mentality in the parish and the gospel issues of social justice will still be preached.

It sounds like your pastor who has not met his assessment is honest about it, and he probably promotes the gospel more than the appeal. Your pastor sounds as though he respects the consciences of his parishioners concerning sacrificial giving, and he avoids taking his failure to meet his assessment personally. I'm glad to hear that!

In parishes where the practice of second half of life spirituality is preached, very often there are strong out-reach ministries. Thus parishioners give more money to the local church organizations that they are familiar with such as the Society of St. Vincent de Paul, the Homeless Coalition, the Women's Sodality, and the Knights of Columbus.

Pastors who practice second half of life spirituality know that maintaining their integrity is an absolute goal, so they will promote the gospel message more than simply promoting fund-raising. These pastors know that they must be true to their conscience in the context of their primary ministry of evangelization.

I hope my reflections on clergy assignments, priestly retreats, and the annual faith appeal helped you to understand the complexity of these issues from the standpoint of the practice of first and second half of life spirituality.

Peace,

Uncle Matthew

Letter #60
Sunday, July 26, 2015

Dear Uncle Matthew,

Thank you for answering my questions regarding three more challenges the institutional church faces: clergy assignments, clergy retreats and workshops, and the Annual Faith Appeal. What you said confirms my experiences as a seminarian during my five summer assignments. The challenges are daunting, and I pray that I may play a part in their resolution.

Earlier you mentioned that the first challenge the institutional church faces is the urge for self idolatry. I sense that the urge for self idolatry appears when some church leaders manifest their addiction to power, fund-raising, and control.

Earlier, you shared with me that the ninth challenge facing the institutional church is the welfare of the active clergy. Could you share with me your thoughts on that topic?

Also, I saw Fr. Tom Doyle's article in the NCR entitled "Time to end pattern of deceit and denial." Could you also share with me your thoughts on the tenth challenge the institutional church faces: priests and sexual misconduct?

Uncle Matthew, I signed the papers requesting that I be ordained a transitional deacon next month. I am still unsettled about my vocation in life, but my spiritual director says that this is normal. He said that entering marriage is similar to entering a faith journey, and so is entering the priesthood. We do not know what the future will bring. And so, I trust in God. My bishop accepted my letter of request for diaconate, and he assured me that he is praying for me.

My pastor on this assignment has been extremely helpful in the discernment process as have you in your many letters. Like you, my pastor is honest with me. He tells me the truth as he sees it. He told me to follow my desires. I discern now that I desire foremost to be a spiritual doctor, a good shepherd, and a servant to God's people. I wish this were sufficient, and yet against my will, I also desire to have a wife and raise children. I can only pray that with time God's Spirit of Love will transform this apparent irreconcilable conflict into unexpected blessings.

Peace,

Joey

Response to Letter #60
Sunday, August 9, 2015

Dear Joey,

I am happy that your vocational desires enabled you to sign the necessary papers for ordination as a transitional deacon. You are very talented; a rich gift to the Church. You are blessed to have the support, love, and affirmation of Paul, your parents, and your friends regardless of whatever decisions you make in life. If a strong desire is to be a spiritual doctor, go for it. Time will tell if your desires change.

We have so much for which to be grateful in the Church. We have a rich tradition. We cherish the Bible. We have some wonderful leaders in the Church, including your bishop. The priesthood needs men like you who love God. I am so proud to be a priest. I pray that our letters will be an encouragement to persevere when you are discouraged by the demands you will face later in your ministry. This spiritual roadmap should provide you some help.

On the phone you said that you feel that you are losing your masculinity. You identified two reasons why this is happening: wearing a cassock and refraining from developing intimate friendships with women.

Many years ago in my seminary formation, we were led to

believe, through many practices and subtle messages, that being asexual was the goal for living as a healthy celibate. In other words, we thought that having no sexual feelings or desires was achievable and desirable. Wearing a cassock seemed to desexualize us. I found out later, like so many other priests, that trying to become asexual is ultimately destructive because it denies our basic humanity. The practice of second half of life spirituality invites celibates to celebrate their identity as male or female; not to repress it. Learning to integrate our human sexuality is key to becoming fully human and fully alive.

I'm glad your summer assignment is going well. Fr. Steve seems to be a good man and a fine mentor for you. You are fortunate that he spends time with you, shares with you highlights of his day, prays with you, eats with you, and even has a glass of wine with you at night. That is great! In many rectories there is very little dialogue and community among the priests.

At your request, I will now share with you some ideas on challenges nine and ten that the institutional church faces: clergy welfare and priests and sexual misconduct.

9.   The welfare of active clergy:

Bishops who practice first half of life spirituality:

How one approaches the issue of the welfare of active clergy depends in large part upon whether one practices first or second half of life spirituality. Those church leaders who practice first half of life spirituality emphasize discipline, rules, order, and obedience. Unfortunately, some church leaders are too egocentric, preoccupied with their own comforts, to apply these disciplines wisely. Their focus is more on keeping up appearances rather than addressing the real issues. These bishops are poor shepherds unfocused on the welfare of active clergy. We all have read about church leaders who have lavish homes and enjoy many perks. But these bishops may not be aware of how some priests live in conditions that are not conducive for their emotional, physical, and spiritual welfare.

These bishops can make it a priority when they come for the Sacrament of Confirmation to correct their priests making sure that they use the correct rubrics and follow the correct liturgical principles rather than address their living conditions.

Later, I will share with you my thoughts about the welfare of priests in retirement, but when a bishop practices first half of life spirituality, some retired priests complain that they are no longer on the diocesan mailing list. They are no longer allowed to vote for members of the Presbyterial Council. They no longer receive the minutes of the Presbyterial Council. They no longer are given financial support for an annual retreat. They are not invited to the bishop's home once a year along with active priests. They do not receive an increase in salary every year, like active priests, as part of their pension plan. The effect of this is financial stress in a way that seems punitive to some. They question why their welfare isn't also important.

Bishops who practice second half of life spirituality:

In many dioceses, the bishops who practice second half of life spirituality are good shepherds as demonstrated by their sincere and consistent interest in the welfare of all their priests. They are attentive to the emotional, physical, and spiritual needs of their priests. As good shepherds, they are "other-centered," and not "ego-centered."

A good sign that a bishop is practicing second half of life spirituality can be found in the way he conducts the annual priests' convocation. He is collegial and practices his belief in the principle of subsidiarity. He specifically engages in issues at the priests' convocation relevant to the priests, such as intimacy, friendship, human sexuality, loneliness, morale, prayer, holistic health, and stress. He shares his vision for the future of the diocese, and welcomes feed-back and even criticism. He strongly recommends and affirms support-groups for his priests.

Further, some bishops give out their cell phone number to their priests. This must seem like a small matter, but it demonstrates concern, accessibility, and collegial humility. Some bishops personally call sick priests to inquire about their well-being. Some bishops publicly affirm their pastors on occasions when they celebrate the Sacrament of Confirmation in parishes. These are all signs of the love and affirmation that priests and parishioners naturally desire from their bishops as a manifestation of God's love here on earth.

Bishops such as these want to keep retired priests informed about the state of the diocese. They encourage retired priests to vote in the election of Presbyterial Council members, and they send out the minutes to retired priests. They offer retired priests money for an annual retreat. They invite retired priests to a meal once a year. They provide an annual increase of money in the pension plan, similar to the increase active priests receive so as to keep up with inflation. In sum, the bishop wants retired priests to continue to feel part of the church's ministry.

Soon after his election in 2013, Pope Francis suspended the granting of the honorary title of monsignor except to members of the Holy See's diplomatic service. Often in dioceses where honorary titles were granted, it caused divisiveness. Inevitably some priests feel slighted if they are not honored. A good shepherd desires unity and equality and attempts to affirm all of his priests. As I see it, this development is supportive of second half of life spirituality.

10.  Priests and sexual misconduct:

Sexual misconduct means any unwelcome behavior of a sexual nature that is committed without consent or by force, intimidation, coercion, or manipulation. Sexual misconduct is a sin. In some cases, sexual misconduct is a crime that should be dealt with by the proper authorities. A priest who is guilty of sexual misconduct must assume responsibility for his actions.

I suspect that the stresses and strains of living a celibate life with little or no support must be one of the underlying causes of sexual misconduct in the priesthood. I once attended a workshop presented by the House of Affirmation, and the leaders of the workshop stressed that the underlying reason that so many priests are guilty of violating their celibacy is because of a lack of affirmation. When affirmation is missing in the life of a priest, it contributes to alcoholism, drug addiction, and sexual misconduct.

The issue of sexual misconduct has so many dimensions and is of such profound consequence that I cannot attempt to address all of it right now. So let me speak to an aspect often ignored, justice tempered with mercy that needs to be shown to priests who are accused of sexual misconduct. I say this fully recognizing that the church's principle responsibility is the compassion, justice, and reforming actions that need to be demonstrated to the victims of sexual abuse. Much has been written from this perspective, as it should be, but in my letter to you let me now say something about how the Church treats implicated priests.

You may want to read the Dallas Charter and the John Jay Study that emerged from the sex abuse scandal. Let's speak more broadly to sexuality in the priesthood.

Areas of concern:

The Dallas Charter has been amended over the years, but I'll try to point out some difficulties in tempering justice with mercy. For starters, not all violations of priestly celibacy are equal. However, whatever the crime or failing in sexual matters, justice tempered with mercy within the family of the Church has to be exercised. It is unconscionable to think otherwise.

I shall share with you five areas of concern involving a priest accused of sexual misconduct: (1) the reputation of the accused priest, (2) the possibility of shaming the accused priest, (3) his need for a civil and canon lawyer, (4) the possibility of depression, (5) and laicization.

1.    The permanent reputation of an accused priest, prior to

investigation and determination, is put at grave risk. It is a criminal offense to slander, libel, or defame someone. However, anyone who gets angry with a priest can falsely accuse him and have him suspended, regardless of the ultimate veracity of the charge. Once the bishop has been notified of an accusation, a public announcement is made in all the parishes in which the accused priest has served that explicitly identifies the priest and the nature of the accusation. The investigation to determine the validity of the accusation and the culpability of the alleged offender may then take months or years to complete, with the reputation of the accused in tatters. When children are concerned, our hope is that the law and the Church will protect the children at the expense of harming a priest's reputation even if eventually proven to be not guilty.

The Charter does state that the Church must take every step to restore the good name of the priest when an accusation is proven to be unfounded. However, most of us wonder if that can ever be effective. The loss of one's public reputation often occurs even though Canon 220 says, "No one is permitted to damage unlawfully the good reputation which another person enjoys or to violate the right of another person to protect his or her privacy."

2.     The shaming of an accused priest is a real possibility. Accused priests may be shamed by their bishops, their brother priests, and parishioners, yet often all the circumstances are unknown. The accusation could even be false. The accused priest may be told to live somewhere without communicating to others in the locale. Sometimes a bishop will reduce a priest's salary while he is suspended. Sometimes a bishop will not want the accused priest to attend priestly functions such as a diocesan retreat, the Chrism Mass, or the priests' convocation.

3.   When a priest is accused of sexual misconduct, it is in his best interest to hire both a civil lawyer and a canon lawyer. As is well known, hiring a lawyer is typically very expensive. Some bishops fail to offer the accused priest financial help so he can hire an attorney. The accused priest has to depend on his friends to financially assist him, if he chooses to retain the professional

legal help of a canon lawyer and a civil lawyer.

4.   When a priest is accused of sexual misconduct, he may become depressed or even suicidal. Let me tell you a story. When I was forty years old, a religious order priest would occasionally visit his sister in my parish. I would invite him to celebrate Mass during his visits. He was in his early sixties at the time. I learned that the priest had been accused of sexual misconduct that allegedly occurred decades before at an altar server outing when the alleged victim was a minor. The priest wrote a letter to his sister and told her that he was innocent. Shortly afterwards, the priest took his own life. Later, the accuser retracted his accusation. How tragic!

5.   When a priest is accused of sexual misconduct that violates his celibacy and is found guilty of some offense, the Charter allows a bishop to request laicization of the priest or deacon from the clerical state without the consent of the priest or deacon. If the Congregation for Clergy grants the bishop's appeal, the decree might say that the decision cannot be appealed. There is no recourse. The priest may be given a month to leave a rectory. The bishop may offer him a small financial settlement to start his new life. His medical insurance may cease in a month. A priest who is laicized will be banned from ever teaching theology in institutes of higher studies. He may not teach religion in institutes of lower-level studies. He may not give a homily. He may not be involved in any office involving the direction of pastoral activity or parochial administration. The area of concern is how the bishop can temper justice with mercy in handling this painful and difficult situation.

First and second half of life spirituality:

Earlier, I shared with you some images of God that are commonly embraced while practicing first half of life spirituality: A Distant God, a God Preoccupied with Sex, and a Vindictive God. As we discussed before, our world views and behavior reflect the images we hold of God. "We become the god we adore."

For example, if a bishop believes in an image of a Distant God, he may fail to see God's incarnate presence in both the perpetrator as well as in the victim.

Or, If a bishop believes in an image of God Preoccupied with Sex, he may judge sexual misconduct as though it is the worst of sins.

And, if a bishop believes in a Vindictive God, he may act like a Vindictive bishop. Therefore, the priest accused of sexual misconduct who meets with the bishop may tell his friends that the interview with his bishop was severe, impersonal, and legalistic. He may say that he felt as though he met with an aloof CEO of a large corporation when he noticed at the chancery office surveillance cameras, codes for entry into the building, security gates for parking the cars of the employees, locked doors for entry past the foyer, and someone who escorted him to the bishop's office.

Regardless of the practice of first or second half of life spirituality, a bishop needs discernment so as to handle well each situation involving the sexual behavior of an accused priest. A bishop who hides a genuine crime of a priest's sexual behavior gives scandal to the faithful. But likewise a bishop who fails to render justice with mercy gives scandal to the faithful. How a bishop treats those priests accused of sexual misconduct should be in tune with Pope Francis' Jubilee Year of Mercy (December 8, 2015-November 20, 2016).

We hope that our bishops will be like the loving father (the Christ figure) in the Parable of the Prodigal Son who faced the challenge of tempering justice with mercy. The wayward priest is like the younger son. Forgetting who he was, he inappropriately acted out and then, upon discovering and confession, he "came to himself." I believe it was St. Thomas Aquinas who said, "We choose apparent good, no one willingly does evil." He saw his shadow side and seeks to return home and to his True Self. Now great growth is possible for him. He is ready, now that childish illusions are behind him, to enter the practice of second half of life spirituality.

Most of us in the institutional church tend to be like the elder son in the story. We, who are largely practicing first half of life spirituality, have little compassion for a priest who is caught breaking the rules, when we have not. Like the older son, we demand justice, wanting to crush the sinner with power and shame for his sexual misbehavior. We do not want to share with the sinner God's mercy.

Let me share with you two examples of the difficulties bishops face in tempering justice with mercy in accordance with God's love.

The film: The Priest:

In an earlier letter to you, I mentioned the 1994 British film, The Priest. The film described two priests, Fr. Matthew and Fr. Greg who ministered together in Liverpool, England. Fr. Matthew was a seasoned priest who supported liberation theology. He had an on-going sexual relationship with his housekeeper. Fr. Greg arrived as a young associate. He was rigidly conservative. He could not accept Fr. Matthew's blatant relationship with the housekeeper. Yet, Fr. Greg experienced loneliness. He wrestled with his homosexual feelings.

One night Fr. Greg went to a local bar frequented by gays, and he met a man by the name of Graham. In his loneliness Fr. Greg acted out sexually in a car with Graham, and the police caught them. The incident was a front-page story in the local newspaper. Fr. Greg's bishop had no compassion for him. The bishop sent him to a rural parish to live with a pastor who was disapproving and unforgiving of Fr. Greg. Later, Fr. Matthew was the one who was the hero in the film because he accepted Fr. Greg with love and compassion, with salutary effects for all. The contrast between the bishop's lack of mercy and compassion and Fr. Matthew's mercy and compassion was like night and day.

We can learn many lessons from this film. If we practice first half of life spirituality as we enter middle age and beyond, we may become terribly judgmental. We can become like the Pharisees. This becomes a very real issue when we have responsibility and authority over others.

And yet, the practice of second half of life spiritually also comes with a price; the loss of one's innocence. Fr. Matthew was practicing second half of life spirituality as demonstrated by his compassion. He was a wounded healer. He could see beyond the rules and his vows. He avoided clericalism and isolation so he could touch the hearts of ordinary people who, like him, were struggling.

Fr. Greg's "fall" marked his entrance into an adult spirituality. Before his "fall," he refused the Eucharist to a man that he judged to be in sin. Fr. Greg at the time was only part of a person; not yet whole. The film ended without showing what kind of priest Fr. Greg became after his "fall," but to viewers, this one at least, the offer of God's mercy, and the need for it by all, was the big takeaway.

Father Albert Cutie:

Father Albert Cutie was ordained as a Catholic priest for the Archdiocese of Miami in 1995. He was the first priest to host a secular talk show on both radio and television. In May 2009, photographs of him embracing a woman on a beach were published. He admitted he was in love with the woman. This revelation about his friendship with a woman led to his leaving the Roman Catholic Church and embracing the Episcopal Church.

Fr. Cutie wrote a book entitled, Dilemma, a Priest's Struggle with Faith and Love. In his autobiography, he said that mandatory celibacy was the only theological difference that led him to leave the Roman Catholic Church for the Episcopal Church.

Fr. Cutie claims that when he met with his archbishop on May 6, 2009, the archbishop's disposition was clear to him. "He was not even remotely interested in knowing any details about my personal situation. His main concern was to protect and defend the image of the institution he represented, and maybe even his own image as the local leader of that institution."

Fr. Cutie says he was cut off from his position in the parish, at the radio station, and he lost his salary and benefits. His medical insurance was canceled within two weeks. He writes in his book that the archbishop referred to him as the prodigal son, yet he didn't put the parable into practice. The entire conversation with the archbishop lasted nineteen minutes. Fr. Cutie says, "I most needed an understanding father figure and I received quite the opposite treatment." Fr. Cutie felt abandoned by the Church and was left to sink or swim upon his own resources alone.

Fr. Cutie writes about the obligation of celibacy for the priesthood. He shares, "One of the real scandals nobody wants to see in the church: good people, mostly good men, who are so lonely on the inside that they are often driven to satisfy basic human emotional and physical needs in all the wrong ways."

Fr. Cutie's book reaffirms the need for all of us to have a deep spirituality, a spiritual roadmap, if we hope to become good shepherds who can temper justice with mercy for oneself and others.

Fr. Richard Rohr in his book YES...AND describes Catholic tradition that teaches that there are three sources of evil, the world, the flesh, and the devil. There is the tendency when we practice first half of life spirituality to focus on the sins of the flesh. There is a tendency to become an insensitive leader who enforces without mercy the correction of those who violate the sins of the flesh. Those who practice second half of life spirituality warn us that those leaders who correct offenders can ironically become like the devil, the third source of evil, because while they appear so virtuous, they are missing the great command to love their neighbor.

Fr. Cutie's story and the stories of many others who have been punished for their sins of the flesh indicate the need for follow-up if a priest has been suspended or laicized. After spending years of preparation and service in the priesthood, if a priest's ministry suddenly ends, there should be an outreach on the part of a bishop to ensure that the priest is not shamed by being wholly excluded from the life of the Church. Counseling should be offered and additional financial help if necessary, during his period of transition to his new diminished status. Justice should not exclude mercy.

Archbishop Weakland:

There are many people who believe that there is a sixth area of concern regarding the Dallas Charter; the inequitable application of justice. The Dallas Charter has a double standard for the treatment of priests in comparison to bishops who have been accused of sexual misconduct. The Dallas Charter explicitly doesn't apply to bishops. Under canon law, only the pope has authority over bishops, archbishops, and cardinals. The Bishops Conference does not have the authority to set norms for their own bishops. Just as there is zero tolerance for the sexual abuse of minors by priests, there should be, if justice is to be equally served, zero tolerance for bishops who abuse children or cover up the abuse of a child by a priest or deacon. Bishops accused of sexual misconduct have the benefits of diocesan financial support to hire an attorney, medical benefits, and they can still perform ecclesiastical ministry.

Archbishop Rembert Weakland, OSB, is an American prelate of the Catholic Church. He served as the Archbishop of Milwaukee from 1977-2002. He is the author of the book, A Pilgrim in a Pilgrim Church: Memoirs of a Catholic Archbishop. He retired in 2002 at the mandatory retirement age of seventy-five when it was revealed that he paid $450,000 to settle a sexual assault claim that a former Marquette University student made against him. The alleged assault happened more than two decades earlier.

Weakland says in his autobiography that he became aware of

his homosexual orientation when he was a teenager and repressed it until he became an archbishop. He had relationships with several men because he experienced a deep loneliness. He disagrees with the church's teaching on homosexuality as being "objectively disordered." He is probably the first bishop to voluntarily come out of the closet. Unlike some priests who have been laicized for violating the Sixth Commandment, Archbishop Weakland has his title in retirement, and he can still celebrate mass.

I once was present when he celebrated mass after his retirement, and I was deeply moved by his presence. I could tell that he was merciful, compassionate, and non-judgmental; a rich blessing to all of us who celebrated the liturgy with him.

Conclusion:

Fr. Richard Rohr says, "We grow spiritually much more by doing it wrong than by doing it right." He goes on to say in his wonderful book, Falling Upwards, "A perfect person ends up being one who can consciously forgive and include imperfection rather than one who thinks he is totally above and beyond imperfection."

When a brother priest is accused of a sexual violation of celibacy, hopefully his brother priests will not abandon him but will exhibit mercy as the institution applies its justice. The accused priest soon discovers his real friends, those who truly love him, expecting nothing in return except the joy of loving their friend. If a priest is accused of a serious sexual infraction or an insignificant one, hopefully his brother priests will give him emotional, prayerful, and practical support (including financial if needed). The accused priest needs his brother priests to show him "unconditional love" that reflects an adult image of an Unconditionally Loving God.

We can ask, "Are our demands, although true and good, unrealistic when we expect local, state, and federal government officials, along with the leaders of the institutional church to render justice tempered with mercy?" Reality, as difficult as it is to accept, indicates that there always will be injustice, sin, and a lack of mercy in any institution that hopes to survive. However, the practice of second half of life spirituality can contribute greatly to the rendering of justice with mercy, and it is natural for us to hope and expect that the universal church should never cease aspiring to this ideal.

Peace,

Uncle Matthew

Letter #61
Tuesday, August 25, 2015

Dear Uncle Matthew,

I'm so grateful that you were able to join my family last Saturday. When the bishop ordained me as a transitional deacon, it was great to have you concelebrate with the bishop. This was the first time I have been with you in person in such a long time, but of course with all our letter writing, I feel like you are close to me all the time.

During the ordination mass, I experienced many mixed emotions such as joy, freedom, and gratitude as well as sadness, loss, and a strange sense of guilt. I have always been a pleaser personality-type, so I try to please my bishop, vocations' director, parents, you, and some close friends, and I was aware of this during the ceremony. I am blessed that my parents, Paul, and you do not place any pressure on me.

As I mentioned earlier, my summer assignment was really positive. In an atmosphere of affirmation, honesty, and integrity on the part of the pastor, I grew immensely. If I could be like my pastor, I would be both a good priest and a compassionate shepherd. I now have this real-life image in mind to emulate.

Thank you for sharing challenges nine and ten that the Church faces regarding clergy welfare and priests and sexual misconduct. I'm not aware of any sexual misconduct among the priests I know, but that of course doesn't mean that secrets don't exist. The Dallas Charter is new to me, so I am grateful that you pointed it out to me as a resource. I'm quite sure we will study the Charter in class. The five areas of concern that you outlined make me realize how difficult it is to render justice with mercy.

Please share with me your reflections on the last two challenges that you have listed that the institutional church faces: #11 the welfare of priests in retirement and #12 fraternal correction. I can't wait to hear your thoughts.

Peace,

Joey

Response to Letter #61
Saturday, September 5, 2015

Dear Joey,

In the September 5 edition of our diocesan newspaper, there was an article entitled, "Fewer priests for more Catholics." Since 1965 there has been a thirty-five percent decrease in the number of priests whereas the number of Catholics has increased sixty-four percent.

Soon Pope Francis will be coming to Cuba and then to the United States. He wants to build good relations with Cuba. He backs immigration reform. He calls for aggressive climate change action. He supports the Iran nuclear deal. What a breath of fresh air!

I'll be happy to share with you some reflections on the last two of the twelve challenges that I believe the institutional church faces today: the welfare of priests in retirement, and fraternal correction. When challenges are not addressed, conflicts occur as surely as night follows day.

11. The welfare of priests in retirement:

Introduction:

In every diocese there are retired priests. Most bishops expect their priests to stay active in ministry until they are seventy or until their health fails. In a few dioceses, the bishops expect their priests to stay active in their ministry until seventy-five. Many priests do not retire at seventy because they simply cannot afford to retire. If priests minister beyond the retirement age, they receive money, but a more important motivation for many is that by continuing in a priestly role, they find continued purpose in life.

You are so young, Joey, to be asking questions about the welfare of retired priests! When I was your age, I rarely thought about retirement, as if it would never happen to me. But then again, it is I, your Great Uncle, no spring chicken, that brought up the subject!

Retirement demands maturity if one is to retain one's dignity and spiritual health. Retirement is a major transition in life. During periods of transition, it is terribly important to establish new goals in life as a way of remaining open to the Spirit, otherwise, life becomes a repetition of mere existence centered on trivial things. Conversely, with new goals in life, these goals enable one to give and receive in fullness until one's last breath. Rediscovering how to cope with loneliness, friendship, intimacy, health problems, and sexuality are serious challenges because the retired priest is no longer caught up in a whirlwind of pastoral activity. He has more time to think and be alone. I like this quote that was in the film, The Shoes of the Fisherman, when a priest said, "Without some kind of loving, a person withers like a grape on a dying vine." When a priest retires, he must be so careful not to get isolated from the Body of Christ if he is going to stay on a healthy path.

The plight of many retired priests:

I have met some priests in their retirement years who say they are unaffirmed, leaving them feeling like that withering grape. They say that the institutional church "used" them when they were young, making the feeling of abandonment by the institutional church even more bitter. They feel like they were "cheap labor." The sad truth is that the institutional church talks about the "dignity of human beings" but often neglects the retired diocesan priests who gave their lives to the institutional church only to realize in their retirement years that in many dioceses there are no retirement homes, assisted living facilities, or nursing homes available for them. The retired priest is expected to have saved enough money to provide for his retirement needs, but most retired priests worked for small salaries during their active years, so they had no way to save large sums of money for long-term independent living, assisted living, memory care, or full nursing care.

Some retired priests discover that there is no cost of living increase in their pension plan that is already inadequate, especially if they live for many years. Many retired priests must resort to living in a rectory, if they can find one that will accept them. This arrangement is not good because bishops transfer pastors, and the new pastor may not have room for a retired priest in the rectory. He may not know the retired priest, except by name. He may want to use the quarters for another purpose. Also, living in a rectory encourages the retired priest to remain "a cleric" whereby he sees his value in what he can continue to do rather than in the person he is trying to become. He risks never growing up to embrace an adult spirituality. He may never savor the "sage stage of life." If he has never transitioned into the practice of second half of life spirituality, he runs the risk of being encouraged by his circumstances to continue practicing first half of life spirituality. It might be even more difficult for someone who has progressed to the practice of second half of life spirituality.

When I was a newly ordained a priest, I was assigned to a rectory where there was a retired priest, the former pastor, in residence. My memories of him are melancholic. He conveyed sadness. He didn't appear to read anything inspiring, theologically stimulating, or even the significant news of the day. He was moody and often critical of the changes made by the new pastor. I cannot recall him ever complimenting the new pastor or those of us living in the rectory. I learned early in my priesthood that those retired priests who are lonely and unaffirmed have difficulty affirming others and being happy themselves.

Looking back, I now realize that this retired pastor's miserly pension left him with no options except to live in a rectory. I now believe that being stuck in the practice of first half of life spirituality never provided him with the joy, peace, love, and acceptance of himself that the practice of second half of life spirituality could bring. He died as an unhappy old man before learning how to be fully human and fully alive. We will never know whether his failure to grow was due in part to the failure of the bishop to provide him with viable options for his retirement.

Sadly, I did not understand his plight until many years later. I was practicing first half of life spirituality when I was ordained and so I lacked the perspective that would have provided me with some understanding of his situation. I was judgmental and lacked sufficient compassion so as to reach out to him. I lacked an adult spirituality and a spiritual roadmap to help me understand and engage him.

I can truthfully say in my own retirement, I am very happy because I have set goals in my life that excite me to live each day as a fully alive person. I was blessed with wonderful parents, William and Regina, who left your grandfather, William, Jr., and me with inheritances. Thus, I have the advantage of having my diocesan pension and Social Security along with money from my inheritance. Presently, I can live in dignity because of an inheritance, not from the low monthly Social Security check and the inadequate pension I receive from the institutional church.

Diocesan pension plans:

I realize the subject of pension plans is quite removed from elevated talk about spirituality, but it is brutally important to the earthly welfare of retired priests. So let me address the topic.

As I mentioned earlier to you, Jack Ruhl in an article in the National Catholic Reporter in February reported that thousands of Catholic diocesan priests are expected to retire within the next few years. Questions are being raised concerning diocesan priest pension plans. Some say the pension plans are underfunded, some seriously. When diocesan pension plans are severely underfunded, the bishop may not be able to meet the financial obligation as his priests and lay employees retire.

The Department of Labor does not require churches to disclose the details about their pension plans, and dioceses are not required to disclose any pension funding information to enrollees. There are one hundred and ninety-four dioceses and thirty-two archdioceses in the United States. Of the one hundred and two dioceses that provide some level of financial information, Ruhl indicates that only sixty-one dioceses have pension information that is publicly available.

By way of contrast, I visit on a regular basis Aunt Muriel who, as you know,  is living in a large retirement home with 420 apartments. She will turn 91 on her next birthday. She is a strikingly beautiful person who relates well to others. She is out-going, interesting to be with, and interested in others. She travels with her relatives to Disney World. She still dances, drinks wine, and she has a wonderful network of friends. She can afford to live a wholesome life-style because of her pension and the pension of her late husband. I've learned from Aunt Muriel that some companies are more just in their pension plans than some church pension plans. Even the less generous 401 K plans of many companies offer the chance for a more financially secure future. I believe pension plans are a justice issue, not a charity issue. Also I believe that providing an adequate pension plan is a respect life issue as well!

Retirement is a time to acquire a new vision in life:

Retired priests need to be given the opportunity to retire with dignity so that with reflection, prayer, and discernment, they can grow in a new understanding of the Cosmic Christ. They need affirmation from their bishops to encourage them to value their retirement as a great opportunity to acquire a new vision in life.

Retirement is the special time to become aware of the deeper values in life rather than the all too often shallow values of popular culture. Retirement is a time to see beyond those who are idealized by our commercial culture. Retirement is a time to see beyond those who are wrinkle-free with beautiful skin. Retired priests need the opportunity to get in touch with their natural empathy and compassion for those afflicted with poor health. Retired priests can grow in compassion when they meet and have the opportunity to spend time with those who have hearing and vision impediments. Retirement is a special time to discover our purpose at this stage of life which may include being a new kind of witness, a mentor, a wisdom figure, and even a sage for those in our own family. One of my very best lay friends, Bill, who is retired in Connecticut, told me that he believes his ultimate purpose in life is to be a loving and affirming person for his wife and three children.

Retirement is a time to embrace one's life with integrity:

Erik Erikson was a twentieth century developmental psychologist who developed a personality theory based on eight stages of development. Each stage involved a decisive conflict which must be successfully navigated if one is to continue to grow and evolve. For instance, the very first stage of life is centered on the core issue of trust vs. mistrust. His eighth stage (and last) of development deals with integrity versus despair. Generally, a person is not likely to reach this stage until sixty-five or older. This is the period of time to access what accomplishments one has realized, and what failures have occurred, while upholding one's integrity. Despair could set in if a priest realizes that his accomplishments were not motivated by charity and love and if he was not wholly truthful with himself and God. In contrast, a sense of integrity would prevail if there is clear-eyed and broad acceptance of the fullness of one's life, all of the complexities, messiness, ups and downs, joys and tears.

Retirement is a time for reconciliation:

Retired priests can look back on their ministry and pray for those whom they offended or injured in any way, and ask for forgiveness in spirit or in person. For example, I wrote a letter to two priests with whom I ministered many years ago and I asked for forgiveness for harming our friendship. Although they never responded, this simple act was healing and liberating to me. Retirement offers the time to take seriously the wisdom found in twelve step programs that emphasizes the need to admit our wrongs and make amends.

After all, death is approaching, so with prayer and reflection, retirement provides a golden period of time for reconciliation. Retirement offers us an opportunity to be aware that our ministry will be judged by our service to others, our love of neighbor, our degree of compassion, and our willingness to live a life of reconciliation.

Delaying priests' retirement:

Recently, I was with a priest who is sixty-nine years old. He wanted to retire at seventy, but his bishop wanted him to work until he will be seventy-five. This priest was trained to be obedient, so he accepted his bishop's request even though he had the money from a good military pension plan to retire.

I felt sorry for him because I think he is missing a rare opportunity in retirement to not only reflect on his life and to deepen his spirituality, but also to engage in the work of the Risen Christ in any way the Spirit moves him. Instead, he will be caught up for the next five years in keeping the institutional church alive. I believe he will miss a once in a life-time opportunity to better become a sage, a person of greater wisdom, a man of integrity, a more compassionate person, and a forgiving person. This lost opportunity will not only cost him, but all those who might have known him as a different man in a different context. During the retirement years, our value is measured by our presence that magnifies the Risen Christ.

I wonder sometimes if bishops who raised the retirement age to seventy-five for their priests are principally motivated by a desire to keep the institution alive by having the necessary staff rather than respecting and protecting the natural dignity of their priests. So often the "good guys" are taken advantage of like the one I mentioned above. Those priests who now are at the age of retirement were trained to be strictly obedient to their bishops, as if obedience to their human supervisors is the most important virtue. The principles of second half of life spirituality hold that obedience is not the greatest of all virtues, but rather the higher virtues are integrity, generativity, openness to the Holy Spirit, forgiveness, patience, compassion, mercy, and unconditionally loving and accepting others as they are without judgment. Retirement should be the period when we learn and relearn as a student and lover of life. It should be a precious opportunity to reflect upon, and act upon, our potential generativity. Foremost is the question, "What can we pass on to the next generation?" And surely this is the time when a retired priest can risk practicing second half of life spirituality if he has not done so before.

Retirement is a time to grieve:

Many retired priests need walkers so that they can walk without falling. Some retired priests have hearing problems, so they wear hearing aids. Some retired priests experience vision problems, so they cannot drive at night. Some priests have to give up driving their car because of a combination of factors in old age.

Joey, I am now eighty-two years old. With my heart problems and some abdominal problems that occurred after surgeries, I can no longer travel by air or even travel very far in a car. I can no longer visit Disney World, enjoy cruises, and visit friends in other states. I can no longer attend Chrism masses and long funeral celebrations. I am no longer able to "help out" in parishes. I find that I can no longer enjoy a former hobby of acrylic painting. I can no longer play a guitar or piano like I once enjoyed. These new shrinking boundaries that curtail my activities are difficult to face. That is another reason why priests in retirement should be given the dignity of living comfortably so as to be transformed by their natural sufferings into holier men rather than transmitting the pain of their suffering to others.

Retired priests' retreats:

I have attended three retired-priests' retreats at my own expense. My diocese does not offer any money for the retired priests to make an annual retreat. Some bishops create retreats for the active priests and the retired priests. This practice of dividing the priests into two groups is divisive and ultimately demeaning to the retired priests. This not only relegates the retired priests to secondary status but denies the active priests the presence of their elders. This is an unhealthy dynamic for all members of the presbyterate.

I have found the three retreats that I attended to be good opportunities to see what happens to priests in their last chapter of life, "the evening of life." Most of the priests I met had serious physical health problems. Some priests had lost the joy of their youth. Most retired priests seemed to be still practicing first half of life spirituality. They are good men who appear to be trying harder to be perfect so that God will love them instead of allowing God's love, already present, to perfectly transform them. They eagerly look for their bishop to affirm them, and they feel downcast when this is missing. They share thoughts about their everyday work, current assignments where they "help out" in parishes, as well as past tangible successes, but few share the wisdom one would expect from those who have decades of church leadership immersed in the lives of their parishioners. It does not need to be this way!

What can be done?

What can be done to change this discouraging scenario? How can we change the circumstances of their lives to help retired priests to find joy, dignity, and excitement in their retirement years? What can be done to help many of these men to create and find a new purpose in life? How can retired priests become fully human and fully alive, and to witness this for all to see? I can think of a few suggestions that may be helpful to bishops in addressing some of these challenges. Perhaps you, Joey, will one day be in a position to help these ideas to become a reality!

1. In some dioceses the bishop could provide a more adequate and more realistic pension plan with cost of living increases similar to Social Security. When there are no adjustments for inflation over the years, retired priests get less real purchasing power from their pension plan over the years. Compassionate bishops realize that the small pensions that retired priests receive are not adequate to provide them with the means to live a long life with dignity. Therefore, compassionate bishops work to correct that injustice.

2. Priests who are vowed members of a religious order or congregation are provided with medical care until they die. Incardinated diocesan priests should be provided with the promise of similar medical care, if needed. If not part of the diocesan pension plan already, a medical plan needs to spell out places where a priest can go for short periods of rehabilitation care, long periods of assisted living, memory loss, or nursing-home care. The expenses would be paid for by the diocese as part of the pension plan. In some dioceses they have a Shepherds Fund or a Retired Priests' Fund and the amount collected is distributed to the retired priests to help them. As I see it, while we still inhabit this earthly body, medical care is a fundamental element of practicing compassion and protecting the dignity of those who serve the Church.

3. Some retired priests who choose to live alone may need personal medical attention. Most of us have friends who will gladly help us with most of our immediate, practical needs, but it would be a sign of great respect and affirmation if a bishop would appoint a priest or some other person on a full-time basis to assist, if necessary, priests who are seriously ill and confined to their home. If necessary, this appointed person could visit the sick priests, be familiar with their prescriptions, arrange for support services, and keep the bishop informed. This appointed person could also compassionately support a priest who is recovering from surgery and has particular needs. The bishop cannot do these tasks, but just as there is a full-time vocations'

director who works to recruit potential candidates, so too there should be someone appointed to care for the retired priests. Wouldn't it be a great opportunity for a younger priest to be appointed to this position? Think of the dynamic and possibilities! Since I retired, I realize I never knew how difficult it is after surgery to have someone bring in meals, shop for groceries, and take me to doctors. When I was young and healthy, I never knew. Now I do know the plight of many diocesan priests, and I believe it is incumbent as an institution to heed Christ's call to care for the sick.

4. The diocese could develop additional practices and traditions to affirm the retired priests for their years of service. As a current example, at the Chrism Mass, those priests who are celebrating twenty five or fifty years of service are thanked and congratulated. We should see more of this! A yearly invitation to dinner or lunch with the bishop for instance would be another way to affirm retired priests. In contrast, some bishops exclude retired priests from the annual dinner for active priests at their residences. When a bishop ignores the retired priests who gave their lives to the Church, it hurts deeply not only the retired priests but the integrity of the institution.

5. A program could be provided to prepare priests for retirement. For most priests, dealing with Social Security, pension plans, and medical benefits is very complex, and professional help would be a significant benefit.

6. In sum, our guiding principle on these matters should be that caring for retired priests is considered an issue not only a matter of charity but also of justice. Jesus said, "I say to you, there is no one who has given up house or wife or brothers or parents or children for the sake of the kingdom of God who will not receive back an overabundant return in this present age and eternal life in the age to come" (Luke 18: 29-30).

12. Fraternal Correction:

Introduction:

Joey, you also asked me to share my reflections on fraternal correction, the last of the twelve challenges that I listed earlier. Occasionally bishops are suspected, by lay and clergy, of abusing their power. For example, there may be a strong suspicion that a bishop covered up the sexual abuse of a minor by not reporting it to the public authorities. Or, a priest may claim that he has been abused or bullied by a particular bishop, but he refrains from speaking up for fear of reprisal. What can be done when priests, individually or collectively, determine that their bishop needs fraternal correction?

The Association of US Catholic Priests:

It is the awareness of the existence of different spiritualities and the fact that these different spiritualities were not receiving sufficient attention or respect that led a group of priests to form the Association of US Catholic Priests. This organization attempts to nourish the hearts, minds, and souls of priests, regardless of their different spiritualities, so that prayerful dialogue can occur in the institutional church. I've been a member of this organization since 2013. As an example of their ideals, a resolution passed by members in the 2014 Assembly of the AUSCP in St. Louis, that reads: "To foster individual AUSCP member dialogue with their respective bishops across the country."

Genuine dialogue, where mutual interests and perspectives are shared and explored, is the best solution and the normal procedure to handle conflict. Dialoguing with the local bishop is, or at least should be, basic for a healthy church organization. Doesn't charity require that we meet with the bishop first, seeking just and fair redress, when there are grievances? Jesus said, "If your brother should commit some wrong against you, go and point out his fault, but keep it between the two of you. If he listens to you, you have won your brother over. If he does not listen, summon another, so that every case may stand on the word of two or three witnesses. If he ignores them, refer to the church. If he ignores even the church, then treat him as you would a Gentile or a tax collector" (Matthew 18:15-17).

Apostolic Nuncio (Delegate):

If for some reason meaningful dialogue with the local bishop cannot occur or doesn't occur, should a group of priests contact the Apostolic Nuncio? There is the expectation that the Apostolic Nuncio would be interested in the local situation and formally acknowledge the complaint and follow up with an investigation of the situation.

Most likely, priests who practice first half of life spirituality are more deferential to authority and would likely refrain from signing any letter of complaint to the Apostolic Delegate because they would be fearful of the risks involved. Priests who practice second half of life spirituality might take the risk, despite their fear, if they were certain their actions were motivated by truth, justice, and integrity.

I know of some priests in a diocese who did sign a letter to the Apostolic Delegate asking for an investigation of their bishop. The news media found out about their letter and reported the conflict. To his credit, the bishop called all of the diocesan priests together to discuss the letter of complaint and the conflict that had developed. I believe that misunderstandings in the Church are rooted in an inability for those who practice first and second half of life spirituality to understand one another.

In closing, the willingness to engage the Apostolic Delegate rests on the belief that the system will work justly and fairly. This assumption is not shared by all, especially by those who practice second half of life spirituality and are familiar with the Roman System.

Conclusion:

Becoming a good shepherd with the ability to listen to and respond to the welfare of retired priests is a continual process of growth. Likewise, learning how to give and receive fraternal correction involves humility that takes many years to acquire.

I hope this helps. I congratulate you on being interested in these two topics that you may not have to face for many years to come.

Peace,

Uncle Matthew

# VI.  The Journey Onward for Individuals and the Church:
# Present, future, hope and caution

Letter #62
Saturday, September 19, 2015


Dear Uncle Matthew,

I found your last few letters discussing twelve key challenges facing the Church to be very helpful. From even my limited experiences in the seminary and my five summer assignments, I have found that when challenges are not addressed, conflicts occur. The information that you have shared is helping me to realize the importance of recognizing and embracing the practice of different spiritualities by different people, the ignorance of which is often the root cause of our conflicts.

This issue speaks directly to the Church's recent history and present challenges. During the Post-Vatican II period until the pontificate of Pope Francis, bishops were appointed that tended to practice first half of life spirituality. Strict orthodoxy to church teaching and deference to institutional authority were the litmus tests for being appointed to a higher position in the Church. In contrast, Pope Francis seems to be looking for pastoral leaders. Pastoral sensitivity, always placing a human being first, is a sign of the practice of second half of life spirituality and integral to the definition of a good shepherd. This makes me hopeful.

Pope Francis arrives in Washington, D. C., next Tuesday. I am looking forward to listening to the welcoming ceremony at the White House on Wednesday and viewing his visit to the Capital on Thursday.

When I read over your remarks about retired priests, I thought about a religious brother. He is assigned full-time to take care of the brothers and priests who are retired and living at the congregation's retirement headquarters in Columbus. Your suggestions would be beneficial to individuals and to the Church as a whole.

I was wondering, Uncle, as I continue to seek clarification in my own thinking, if you could summarize the paradigm of the two halves of life spirituality. In a nutshell, how are these two spiritualities different? We have dialogued about them since 2011, and I believe I understand and have internalized much of what you shared. But can you boil it down one more time for me and put it into simple form? That would help me to better understand and benefit from the roadmap of spirituality that you are sharing with me. Many thanks ahead of time.

Peace,

Joey

Response to Letter #62
Wednesday, September 30, 2015

Dear Joey,

I was proud to be a priest, a most welcome feeling, while Pope Francis was visiting this country. The pope's speech to Congress was brilliant when he referred to four Americans: Abraham Lincoln, Martin Luther King, Jr., Dorothy Day, and Thomas Merton. These four individuals espoused a common spirit by hard work and sacrifice, grounded in love and service to others, whereby we can build a better tomorrow. Pope Francis' visit and positive message fills my own heart with hope.

At your request, I will try to summarize what I have read, learned, and thought about the two halves of life spiritual paradigm. I gladly undertake this challenge, Joey, because it is my fervent hope that you live a life of great joy and abundant ministry, and that this spiritual roadmap that we have discussed for so long will help guide you on your spiritual journey.

Introduction:

Earlier, I quoted the late Jesuit priest, Anthony DeMello, who said, "Spirituality means waking up." I have been writing these letters to you with the intention of nudging you to be awake to the paradigm of the two halves of life spirituality because I believe on both a personal and communal level this paradigm can be a rich blessing. Let me try to explain this paradigm.

First, we all have a world view, a framework, a spiritual container, a set of assumptions that help us to understand the world around us, our identity, our purpose in life, and at the beginning and end of all, our images of God. Our specific world view comes mainly from the influence of our parents, teachers, religion, culture, historical time frame, and our particular place in society (education, socio-economic status, race, etc.). Our world view is largely unconscious, and it greatly determines what we see and what we don't see. We are inescapably biased in our world view. In the paradigm of the two halves of life spirituality, when we are young, our world view ideally informs and expresses itself in the healthy practice of first half of life spirituality.

Second, as we age, new experiences reveal the inadequacy of our overly simplistic world view. We recognize our biases. This causes us to question, doubt, examine, test, relearn, and even reject some of our former ways of thinking. We realize that what we thought was giving us a true and full picture of reality was not in fact giving us a view of reality the way it is. If we cling to the old way of seeing for too long, we find ourselves excluding and denying the fullness of God's creation. But as we open ourselves to a bigger world, we start to focus less on proving ourselves to be right to others and more to being right with our own self in relation to God. This stage of transformation is a sign of transitioning from the practice of first to second half of life spirituality. We begin to put away childish things (1 Corinthians 13: 11).

Third, through trust, we open ourselves to this change. Through questioning, doubting, re-learning, and the firm formation of one's own conscience, we liberate ourselves from an excessive dependence on the judgments and strictures of others. In this way, we enter into the practice of second half of life spirituality. We come to know ourselves as adults and no longer practice a religion that was adequate for us when we were young, but is not suitable in meeting the full demands of adult life. This new spirituality is the basis of living a life of integrity and leads into love of neighbor. We have been calling this new way of thinking and acting the practice of second half of life spirituality.

A summary of the practice of first half of life spirituality:

Most historic religions are grounded upon and are perpetuated by the teaching and practice of first half of life spirituality. Each religion begins with its own set of tribalistic goals and objectives whereby members acquire an identity, an informed conscience, and a purpose in life. Our Catholic Church is no different in this regard.

During the early stages of life, we internalize specific images of God as conveyed by our parents, teachers, church leaders, friends, and culture at large. Too often, either subtly or explicitly, the Church promotes images of God as distant, exclusive, vengeful, preoccupied with sex, demanding of perfection, and patriarchal in nature.

Our spirituality informs and determines our views on a full range of religious topics that shape our daily lives and give meaning to life itself. Further, our spirituality is not only derived from the Church but profoundly affects our relationship to that Church. For Catholics, this means that the pope, bishops, and priests are the primary mediators between God and us. We believe that priests alone have Eucharistic power. We believe that priests alone can forgive sins. We believe that priests alone can handle holy things, and we cannot. We think that priests wear special clothes because they are in fact special. We believe that monsignors, bishops, and the pope, climbing the hierarchal ladder, are even more elevated and set apart from the rest of us.

This portrayal of religious professionals as distinct from, and superior to the laity, has been encouraged not only by the hierarchy of the Church, but also by the world view and daily practices of the laity. For example, since the nuns and priests have taken vows of celibacy, we are told that they have special graces that enable them to do what most humans are incapable of doing. In this way, celibacy and charisms are presented as inexorably intertwined. Lose one, lose the other. This concept of mandatory celibacy gives bishops in the Latin Rite immense power and control over the priests who work for them.

Formal religions teach us to follow the rules with both carrot and stick. Obedience is the chief virtue. For us, there is a stress on the absence of sin rather than living a full life. There is a focus on the fear of the devil rather than on the love of the Creator. We are taught to recite the Creed, learn the Catholic Catechism, and attend church each Sunday. We obey the Commandments, revering and imitating holy men and women who are the appointed church leaders, while worshipping a God that is wholly "other." Conformity is the primary goal. Religion, spirituality, in the first half of life, is in practice, centered largely on oneself. Religion's goal, at its core, is to ease the fear of death by promising a place in heaven. It is, too often, transitional in nature, self-serving of both the individual and the institution. It is an arrangement where the religious institution receives obedience in this life by claiming authority over the next. In this way, however, the goodness of God's creation and the meaning of this life here and now are diminished, if not denied, until awakened by the Holy Spirit or a prophetic human voice.

Transitioning into the practice of second half of life spirituality:

For the institutional church to be relevant today, it is essential that lay persons and church leaders alike transition from the practice of first to second half of life spirituality. And yet, this is not always the case. Sometimes church leaders, practicing first half of life spirituality, make it difficult for the laity to engage in the urgent issues and questions being raised in the world of today. Since this thirst for truth and understanding cannot be denied, this disconnect between leaders and laity leads to pervasive tension, misunderstandings, conflicts, and wounds, as evidenced by chronic dropouts from the institutional church.

As we have new experiences in life, challenges, surprises, and mysteries, we realize that our world view is naturally changing because we are taking into account the fullness of these experiences. As our world view changes, so does our moral framework, political views, capacity for love, and perhaps, most importantly, our actions that impact others in the world at large. For example, I shared with you in detail that our views on human sexuality often evolve as we discover not only the pervasive power of the sex drive, but also the range of its root motivations from simple lust to profound love. We learn that the sex drive impels us to do its bidding, come what may. In short, we learn that the sex drive is a beautiful God-given gift.

But as it is, we too often allow ourselves, encouraged by the hierarchy, to become fixated on the validity of programs such as the Fortnight of Freedom and Supreme Court decisions like the Hobby Lobby case. And yet, the Spirit blows where it wills, so there are persons, perhaps many, who become aware of the many challenges facing the Church today, and act so as to be part of the solution. In this context, we must decide for our well-being and according to conscience, whether to become more embedded in practicing first half of life spirituality or trust and risk moving into the unknown practice of second half of life spirituality. If we do trust and courageously act, we become more empathetic toward those, cleric and lay, who no longer practice their religion in the institutional church. Instead of referring to them as "drop outs," we refer to them as "Nones," the fastest growing religious demographic in the United States.

As we transition into an adult spirituality, we begin to question our earlier belief that the stories in the Bible, from Adam and Eve to Revelation, are to be understood as being literally true. We come to see that a dogmatic reading of scripture constricts the fullness of God's reality and distorts our relationship to the truth. Relatedly, we begin to question our uncritical loyalty to external authority which we find increasingly in conflict with the wider world into which we are growing. For many, the issue of birth control is a case in point leading many couples to question the wisdom of established external authority. Or, as another example, if parents have a gay son or daughter, they may question the official church teaching, which is laden with judgmentalism, regarding gays, lesbians, and transgender individuals.

Or closer to home, as we experiment with our human sexuality, we are likely to question those teachings that do not match our experiences. As our spirits and minds open, the full range of our youthful images of God are increasingly questioned, modified, doubted, and even rejected. Sometimes this happens consciously with much struggle. Other times this transformation occurs without conscious effort, like a single act of nature. For example, with the birth of a child, we may vividly experience the presence of an Incarnate God that makes us call into question our image of a Distant God. In this way, we begin to question the dogmas and doctrines of the Church if they become remote or even in conflict with our life-giving experiences.

A summary of second half of life spirituality:

The paradigm of the two halves of life spirituality reminds us that our religious formation and the pursuit of holiness is in fact a life-long process. The Vatican II Council reminded us that the call to holiness is not just for a select group of people with religious titles but for all of us, for we are all, equally, children of God.

Second half of life spirituality encourages us to pursue new goals in life, authentic to who we are in obedience to conscience. These new goals have a profound influence on the whole of our morality, individual and public, social and political, fundamentally changing the way we engage and influence the people we encounter.

This new adult spirituality introduces us to many new images of God that challenge us to modify or discard our earlier images of God. This is often difficult and painful, but also the means of spiritual rebirth and the source of the greatest of joys. Our images of God are so important because, as the twentieth century teacher and academic Leo Rosten said, "We see things as we are, not as they are." Or, alternatively, Thomas Merton once said, "Our idea of God tells us more about ourselves than about Him." And so, the greatest of life's questions and answers are to be found in the way we see God. And so, if we can let go of fear, and be open to the wide world around us and within us, we may come to know an Incarnate God rather than a Distant God. We come to celebrate an Inclusive God instead of an Exclusive God. We find strength in a Just God instead of a God Preoccupied with Sex. We find solace in a Merciful God rather than a Vindictive God. And we come to embrace a God who is both masculine and feminine instead of simply a Male God.

We discover that we may need to change our viewpoints on many religious topics sometimes in the details, and sometimes in the fundamentals. I have shared with you different viewpoints on many religious topics viewed through the lens of both first and second half of life spirituality. For example, we have discussed prayer, a vital and central part of any person's life no matter how prayer is understood by them. When we practice first half of life spirituality, we are taught to go to church on Sunday to pray. We are taught when we are young to say our morning and evening prayers. We are taught to say grace before and after meals. When I was a seminarian practicing first half of life spirituality, I was told not to fall into "heresy of action." In other words, I was told not to work all day to help others but then forget to spend time with God in prayer. I was told to have a quiet day, to make a pilgrimage, and make a yearly retreat so as to get away to be with God. As an immediate consequence of not praying, we were taught that our soul was in jeopardy and we would likely fall into sin. Many of us felt guilty if we failed to say our prayers (the Divine Office, make an hour of silent prayer, attend daily mass, etc.) We said a lot of intercessory prayers. Grounding this view of prayer was an image of God external to earthly life, as someone absent and out of contact with us if we failed to pray.

Looking back, I see the good intentions of that kind of religious formation, and yet, it is an expression of first half of life spirituality that has its limitations. If we are honest with ourselves, prayer seemed to be self-serving and based on the idea that God somehow needed our prayers, rather than we needing God.

Earlier, I shared thoughts about how our understanding of prayer changes when we practice second half of life spirituality. I used the example of Bishop John Spong who for years thought that his prayer time comprised the first two hours of morning that he spent studying the scriptures, journaling, and other spiritual practices. But now, older and wiser, he considers those first two hours to be his preparation time, essential yes, but his real prayer time is the rest of the day when he tries to live in a way where he is open to all that life can be. He tries to deeply enter into the pain or joy of another person. Spong writes, "Prayer is what I am doing when I live...passionately, and wondrously, and invite others to do so with me or even because of me." He continues,"Praying can never be separated from acting." Prayer is no longer one activity separate from others, but a way of seeing and being that influences all our actions. With this changed view of prayer, God is no longer seen as distant. God is seen as ever-present in the world around and within us.

With a new understanding of prayer and our relationship with God, the practice of second half of life spirituality awakens us to the inadequacy and contradiction of attending church every Sunday while ignoring the suffering and injustices in the world around us. For example, have our hearts hardened over the plight of immigrants fleeing to our country seeking safety and freedom? And do we realize the laughable hypocrisy of having "In God we trust" on our coins while failing to be courteous in our church parking lots? And do we realize how scandalous it is when we pray at daily mass and then neglect to be courteous to a cashier at a grocery store or a waiter in a restaurant?

Gandhi chose to practice Hinduism over Christianity. Why? Because, in significant part, he saw how poorly he was treated and how much he felt judged by the Christians he knew. Gandhi is reported to have said, "I like your Christ. I do not like your Christians. Your Christians are so unlike your Christ." Hopefully, Joey, the practice of second half of life spirituality alerts us to the full meaning of prayer which we need to embrace if we are to become who we are, not to simply give God our time and attention in a self-serving manner.

I confess I have a long ways to go to be a man of prayer. We all do. The life of prayer is nothing less than the life-long journey of increasingly allowing God to act through us in compassion, forgiveness, and unconditional love for our neighbor.

The effects of living prayerfully though a second half of life spirituality are many. For example, while practicing first half of life spirituality we tend to see reality in a dualistic way. In contrast, second half of life spirituality encourages us to see reality non-dualistically so as to be aware of and more appreciative of mystery.

More broadly, the practice of second half of life spirituality may bless us with special gifts and virtues beyond those of simply fulfilling our external, daily, earthly duties. For example, blessings include becoming better witnesses to the Gifts of the Holy Spirit, accepting with confidence and courage ourselves as we are, knowing how to choose to be happy, having an informed conscience, being more sensitive and compassionate to the needs of others, and living authentic lives. This adult spirituality greatly enables us to become fully human, whole, fully alive, unconditionally loving, forgiving of others, and empathetic. We are more appreciative of God's call to value ourselves on the basis of who we are rather than on what we do.

Further, beyond these gifts, the practice of second half of life spirituality helps us to see through the darkness and walk through the valley. We are better able to face suffering, the loss of a loved one, major illnesses, and relationship problems because our faith is now better grounded in reality. We no longer blame God when tragedy occurs or when our prayers are seemingly unanswered. The love of God replaces the fear of God so we end up doing the right thing for the right reason.

Conclusion:

Most homilies preached in churches reflect first half of life spirituality. Perhaps many adult Catholics that are now referred to as "Nones" would return to the pews if they heard homilies pertaining to the blessings that are present in the practice of second half of life spirituality.

If we are to become mature followers of Jesus, the goals in both first and second half of life spirituality need to be understood, encouraged, and pursued. I now know that to continue practicing first half of life spirituality at my age would be crippling!

At a later time, if you are interested in how my ignorance about the paradigm of the two halves of life spirituality harmed me in earlier days, I would be glad to share with you. Perhaps through sharing, you may avoid similar pitfalls along the way.

Peace,

Uncle Matthew

Letter #63
Thursday, October 15, 2015


Dear Uncle Matthew,

Your summary of the paradigm of the two halves of life spirituality greatly helps me to see the value of a spiritual roadmap because it motivates me to ask more questions and be aware of the need for deeper consciousness. Thank you. Your summary was clear and thought provoking, and through it I hope to become a more pastoral priest. My dialogue with you over these formative years is all the more valuable because I doubt if I will hear about this paradigm or a spiritual roadmap in my seminary studies. My formation program is grounded in the practice of first half of life spirituality with few hints that a secondary way even exists and beckons us.

One specific note, you helped me in a most important way by sharing Bishop Spong's understanding of prayer. I had never thought about formal prayer as primarily a "preparation time" and the essence of real prayer as "living a prayerful life." Now I try to be conscious of praying by being mindful of God's presence throughout the day.

The Church teaches the obligation to attend church on Sundays and holy days of obligation under pain of grave sin. Spong's ideas on prayer have a direct implication to attending mass on Sundays. Do you think some people apply Spong's principle of "preparation time" and "living a prayerful life" to attending church on Sundays? At times, they may think there are more fruitful ways to prepare themselves to live a prayerful life.

Sometimes I am tempted to resist what you share with me because I must admit I enjoy many privileges here in the seminary. I am treated like a young prince! And yet my heart tells me that this wonderful education in theology separates us from the cares of the world. I am hopeful that, if I am ordained a priest, I will serve well the people because I now know about a spiritual roadmap to guide me in the years to come.

Although outwardly the faculty treats me like I am special, inwardly I am humbled as I continue to face many challenges and conflicts; for example, living a celibate life. I feel that the church authorities judge my worthiness to be here in the seminary by my ability to stay chaste and obedient. After much reflection, I disagree with the present church discipline that all men who are called to the priesthood must forgo marriage and be celibate. If celibacy is a charism (and I believe it is), how can the institutional church mandate it? Further, I do not agree with the church's rules excluding married men and women from the priesthood. I keep this dissent to myself, but I believe that before my life is over, changes will occur. I wonder what my role will be?

I am wrestling with many other questions besides my daily struggle to live a chaste life. For example, what is my purpose in life, not just generally, but specifically? Is God truly calling me to become a priest or should I have continued as an electrical engineer? Which path is God calling me towards?

I'm also beginning to question something as basic as why we have priests. I know this question may sound a bit surprising coming from someone approaching ordination! We are now studying the Sacrament of Baptism and the Sacrament of Holy Orders. But consider that there were no priests at the Last Supper. Paul wrote in 1 Corinthians, around the year fifty-five, about a husband, Aquila, and his wife, Prisca, who acted like church leaders (priests). It was only later after Constantine died in 337 AD that priesthood became more institutionalized. Baptism invites all of us to be a priestly and prophetic people so why are the baptized not able to celebrate all the sacraments when the community requires or seeks them?

On a positive note, my doubts and questions are helping me grow in faith and humility because my questions constantly keep me aware that I need a deep spiritual relationship with God to know and do God's will. Perhaps this awareness hints at what Spong meant by his deeper understanding of prayer.

I wonder, Uncle Matthew, if I am ordained, will I be able to fit into the prevailing practice of first half of life spirituality now that I know so much about the practice of second half of life spirituality?

In general, your letters are helping me to better see and accept reality. I cannot change the rules of the Catholic Church. My challenge will be to best serve God and be true to myself in the context of meeting the expectations of my bishop and living out the rules as they are now. I do want to become a priest so as to promote the good news of the gospel and serve as a doctor of the soul. I admire so many of my classmates who are truly good men. I admire you, Uncle Matthew, for your integrity, honesty, and willingness to help me become aware of a truer, clearer, and larger vision of reality.

You mentioned in your last letter that you were handicapped earlier in life by being ignorant of the paradigm of the two halves of life spirituality. Would you mind sharing with me how you were handicapped earlier in your priesthood without a spiritual roadmap and an understanding of the two halves of life spirituality? I realize that sharing on this question would be very personal on your part. I suspect that many priests your age were also handicapped.

Peace,

Joey

Response to Letter #63
Saturday, October 31, 2015

Dear Joey,

You mentioned your on-going struggle with being chaste. All men attempting to live chaste celibate lives have struggles. There was a good article in the October 9 edition of Commonweal written by Fr. Donald Cozzens entitled, "Sins, Mortal and Otherwise." Cozzens says he struggled to be chaste when he was young. He addressed this issue by way of an analogy. He explores the church's teaching that all forms of artificial birth control are intrinsically evil and therefore mortally sinful and how this conflicts with many persons direct experiences. According to Cozzens, such teachings threaten the credibility of the Catholic Church's teaching and authority. This article gives me hope that people, through their many experiences in life, have a wider world view that urges them to think for themselves rather than obeying without question church rules and regulations that seem contrary to their mature reflections and promptings of conscience. This certainly pertains to priests and their views on chastity and celibacy.

This issue of independent thought and sources of authority has far reaching implications. When I was young, I believed it was a mortal sin to eat meat on Fridays during Lent. And priests were taught that they could commit a mortal sin for failing to fulfill the daily obligation to pray the Divine Office. Even in the minds of many Catholics today, missing mass on a Sunday could be a mortal sin. With the blessings of a spiritual roadmap, we come to realize that we can and must learn to think for ourselves and conform to external authority but only when it requires no violation of reason or conscience. The practice of second half of life spirituality believes that church authorities can no longer expect people, under pain of mortal sin, to comply with all official church teachings when the teachings go against their experiences in life and their conscience.

So, thank you for sharing with me some of your questions regarding a life of celibacy. You are asking very good questions. Continue to discuss your spiritual journey with those whom you trust. I have always suggested to you that if you have a classmate whom you trust, discuss your questions with him so as to get a different perspective rather than just asking the opinion of someone with a vested interest in you conforming to the hierarchical church. You already discovered that sharing with your brother Paul was helpful to both of you.

Your question regarding attending mass on Sunday as "preparation time" for "living a prayerful life" is a profound question. I had not thought about that application of Spong's understanding of prayer. I would say, "What Would Jesus Do" in any particular situation to best "prepare" to "live a prayerful life" of unconditional love. Jesus himself was criticized for not observing the Sabbath as the Law prescribed, precisely because he prioritized human need and the command of love. "The sabbath was made for man, not man for the sabbath" (Mark 2:27). I believe we should do the same.

Thomas Moore in his book, A Religion of One's Own, writes that individuals can fashion a religion of their own whether they are inside or outside a formal religious practice. To me this means forming a personal worldview that involves the nature of creation and the purpose of human life. For some Catholics, this means not adhering to any particular religion but adopting perennial wisdom so as to become more spiritually interdependent. He writes that the creation of a religion is not an optional step but a necessary step in one's spiritual journey to develop a rich inner life and a larger world view. Your questions and doubts show that you are doing that! I admire your courage to question and doubt. I rarely ever questioned what I was taught when I studied theology. A spiritual roadmap is enabling you to have an awareness of the cost of your commitment to live as a chaste celibate priest. A spiritual roadmap is helping you to make a realistic and mature decision regarding your vocation in life.

I was saddened to read that the gay Jesuit priest, John McNeill, the patron to gay and lesbian Catholics, died last month. He helped so many gay, lesbian, bisexual, and transgender individuals to accept their own sexuality and to defend themselves against what they viewed to be misguided church teaching.

I realize now in writing to you that a constrained, unhealthy spirituality produces unhealthy shepherds in the Church. I failed many times to be a good shepherd because I was ignorant of the goals of second half of life spirituality. I was unclear about my real purpose in life. My world view was too narrow. I was unclear about my own identity. Retired Bishop John S. Spong in his book This Hebrew Lord says, "To be in Christ is not to be religious, but to come alive. It is to discover the fullness of living. It is to turn on to life. It is to know the power of love. It is to experience freedom from our self-centered bondage. It is to be made whole; to be affirmed." Aren't his remarks insightful? In self acceptance we find freedom, and in freedom we find love.

When I studied In the seminary, in many ways, my formation kept me like a child. Now I realize I am not called to remain a child but to grow in to an adult human being, to become a person who is fully alive and fully human.

I will try to fulfill your request and share four ways I was handicapped without a spiritual roadmap. If I had discovered the paradigm of the two halves of life spirituality earlier in life, enabling me to engage and integrate life's complexities and mysteries, I would have been blessed with a healthier spirituality.

Regrettably, I was unaware of how handicapped I was until I attended Richard Rohr's Conference on "Loving the two Halves of Life" in 2011. But what a wonderful journey it has been since!

How I was handicapped without a spiritual roadmap:

1.   I idolized the Catholic Church:

First, for nearly all of my priesthood, I put the Catholic Church first instead of God, family, friends, not to mention my own health. I was, in the clinical sense, codependent on the institutional church. I spent my whole priesthood building up the institutional church and pleasing its leaders rather than making my first priority the transformation of the world by bringing the People of God the good news of the gospel.

There are many symptoms of codependence. Pia Mellody, a nationally recognized authority on codependence in her book Facing Codependence, What It Is, Where It Comes From, and How It Sabotages Our Lives, describes five core symptoms of codependence:

1) Difficulty experiencing appropriate levels of self-esteem.
2) Difficulty setting functional boundaries.
3) Difficulty owning our own reality.
4) Difficulty acknowledging and meeting our own needs and wants and being interdependent with others.
5) Difficulty experiencing and expressing our reality moderately.

The problem with all of this is that idols and falsehoods become established as reality.

When seeking to prove my worthiness to others and myself, I worked when I should have taken time off to rest and recuperate spiritually. My present medical problems are a result of stress from the years of being on duty twenty-four seven. When I was a young priest, I believed my superior when he told me that I was responsible for all the souls in the parish, day and night, even those who were non-Catholic. That is quite a burden for any human being.

In my first three years as a priest, I never took a day off, and no one encouraged me to do so. I missed almost all the weddings and funerals of my relatives because I was busy serving the parish and school where I was assigned. I thought it was a virtue to totally serve the Church so as to keep her functioning, strong, and attractive. I failed to realize that through my workaholism, I was becoming none of these myself.

Through my compulsive need to please, I missed one of the primary qualities of becoming fully human and fully alive. I fixated on the ideal while missing what is most real. I thought I was truly loving my neighbor through various acts, and sometimes I was, but often my interactions were transactional and somewhat forced. And while spreading myself thin among the many, I missed unconditionally loving my parents, siblings, cousins, and close friends because I didn't give them the time they needed or the attention they deserved. In this way, I thus failed to live life fully because I didn't have to trust others, be vulnerable to others, and be intimate with others. Consequently, I was more like a church robot rather than a warm fully alive human being.

We were trained to be this way in the seminary. We were discouraged from having close friends. For example, I thought saints were men and women who were super human, almost a different order of being, courageous, intellectually superior, celibate, asexual, chaste, detached from other people, impervious to pain, dutiful, and totally obedient to the Church and to God. Yes, by trying to be humble, I was actually being prideful.

Alas, if I had possession of a spiritual roadmap earlier in life and known about the two halves of life paradigm it would have helped me to realize that it was not wrong to miss my church duties and functions if there were a more compelling call to love and serve the people most in need. For example, when I was newly ordained, I was stationed at an inner-city parish. On a Saturday afternoon, the rectory phone rang and a man wanted me to buy bus tickets for him and his girl friend who were stranded. I was assigned to hear confessions at 3:00, and I was worried that I would be a few minutes late, if I went through the process of buying them tickets. Since I was an assistant pastor, I explained this to the pastor who told me I couldn't help the couple because I might miss being in the confessional for a few minutes. For reasons still unclear to me, courage and compassion prevailed. I disobeyed my pastor and went to help the couple, and I still managed to get back in time to hear the confessions. I share this because this was the mentality I was exposed to when I was newly ordained. Except for a few experiences, like the one I just shared, I obeyed without question my superiors who led me to believe that church needs came first. I suspect now that I violated the First Commandment for many years of my priesthood since, for all practical purposes, I made the Catholic Church my god, and therefore superior to the People of God.

In talking to former priests and nuns who were members of religious communities, many of these individuals were unconsciously trained to do what I did, to practice a subtle idolatry, effectively making the Catholic Church their god.

2.   I lived with a repressive concept of sexuality:

Another way that I was handicapped by not having a spiritual road map was that I was taught to have a constrained, repressive, and destructive concept of sexuality. In the seminary, the Sacrament of Reconciliation was available in the mornings before mass. Somehow, I internalized messages from the Catechism, teachers, priests, and even my parents, that anything sexually pleasurable, outside of marriage, was seriously sinful. Sexuality needed to be repressed, controlled, and contained. It was like a beast in the basement to be feared rather than being understood as a vital part of God's good creation

As part of this aversion to celebrating the goodness of creation and the goodness of the human body, I got the impression that my goal in life was to become an asexual person. In practical situations, I fixated on my chastity at the expense of being focused on my neighbor's well-being. As a result of a warped view of sexuality, it took me many years to appreciate the sacredness and beauty of the human body, and to appreciate a healthy sexuality as part of the human experience. Toxic shame of my own body and its instincts became a daily reality.

In the seminary we sang hymns in Gregorian chant. Somehow, I connected the soft music, the incense, the Latin language, the high-pitched tone with who and what I was supposed to be, angelic! The music reinforced my images of God as Distant, Demanding of Perfection, and a God Preoccupied with Sex. I thought being angelic meant being apart from other people and devoid of sexual feelings and actions. Thus, I missed out on so much of the richness and goodness of life amidst God's physical creation. No doubt, high on the list of blessings foregone by anyone succumbing to the temptation of being angelic is the positive embrace of oneself as an embodied sexual being.

There is a quote that I like because I believe it offers a rich nugget of wisdom. The quote is from William Blake, the English poet and mystic, who said, "The road of excess leads to the palace of wisdom." Yes, there are hazards we ought to avoid, but chief among them is the failure to fully live and love. The Church's emphasis on repression of our sexuality has a good intent but has many unintended consequences.

For example, when I entered the seminary, I thought I had selected a safe vocation in life that would keep me chaste. In the quest to become holy, I didn't realize it at the time that unconsciously I was giving up my freedom to know myself as I truly am. I thought that the questions and problems of human sexuality could be contained and spiritually satisfied in the seminary setting. But the reality was I engaged in denial of my human sexuality and human sexuality in general. The seminary rules and church rules sought to reinforce this viewpoint. We were not allowed to visit students in other rooms. We wore cassocks. We had private shower stalls. We were not allowed to foster close friendships with either males or females. We were also fearful of sexually sinning because being ordained presumed the ability to be totally chaste. The point of all this was to minimize our opportunities to sexually sin, and to encourage the repression of our sexual feelings such that our self identity became that of an asexual angelic person. This is not the basis of genuine virtue.

Now I realize, with the help of a spiritual roadmap, that I need to be conscious of and to befriend my sexuality in order to become whole and to live from my true self. One of the goals in the practice of second half of life spirituality is to become fully alive and fully human. This is not only for our own well being, but because if we don't become conscious of who we are, we risk becoming self-righteous and judgmental of others. But when we integrate and embrace our human sexuality, we have a richer capacity to be merciful and compassionate towards others because we know who we are, and thus we also know our other brothers and sisters in Christ.

I paid a price by being encouraged in the seminary to repress my sexuality. Eventually I experienced unmanageable behavior. Some people describe unmanageable behavior like a water bed. When a person sits in one spot, the water goes down but pops up in another spot. It is interesting to note the wisdom in the Alcoholics' Anonymous steps. The first of twelve steps reads,"We admitted that we were powerless over alcohol, that our lives had become unmanageable."

I have met some wonderful people in my life, especially during those times when I provided spiritual direction. I discovered that the honest and repentant directees, the ones who had risked living life fully, the ones who had many sexual sins to admit, the ones who now wanted to change, were very conscious of the nature of their sexuality because they had the freedom to act out and had learned a great deal from their errors. They were blessed as William Blake seems to suggest with a wisdom that was rooted in their own experiences. So many people I have met don't realize how very blessed they are! They are humble. They are the "little ones."    And though some still judge themselves, thinking they are among the "last," I see that in their honesty and humility they are among those that Jesus spoke about as entering first in the Kingdom of Heaven. Their freedom to sin, if humble and repentant, actually led them to great wisdom and the fullness of life.

3. I denied my inner authority:

A third way I was handicapped by not having an adequate spiritual roadmap was my habit of giving away my inner authority, not to God from where it came, but to superiors in the institutional church.

In the seminary, I always received high grades for deportment. I was docile, polite, kind, helpful, friendly, obedient, rule-abiding, and a pleaser. I rarely asked questions. By being a nice person, I avoided any real emotional contact and intimacy. The seminary training with the emphasis on external authority contributed to my fears as a flawed human being in need of forgiveness from the very institution that set the standards for right and wrong. My habitual guilt, lack of self-confidence, and perceived sinfulness allowed the church authorities to have great control over me. I gave up my freedom to think and rely on my own inner authority because I was fearful of the dangers and responsibilities inherent in that freedom.

As a pastor, this personality trait of giving away my inner authority helped me to work in a collegial way with both the staff and parish organizations. As you have observed, bishops are pleased with docile seminarians and priests who don't question their authority. I now understand that docile priests who give up their inner authority practice first half of life spirituality because that is how they were trained in their formation program.

The cost of denying my own inner authority was significant. By failing to listen to my own experiences of God, I was prevented many times from living out the gospel message. What the institutional church taught on various topics was what I followed instead of asking questions, listening to the Spirit, forming an informed conscience, and deeply reflecting on the important issues that people were addressing. For many years, I failed to allow my own experiences of God to change my earlier acquired images of God. The result was I was a good priest, yet without the zest and passion of original expression. I admire those saints like Francis of Assisi who maintained respect for the institutional church's authority while honoring their own inner experiences of God.

In the seminary, I assumed that the institutional church had all the answers. Thus, I was obedient, but my ability to be a man of faith was hindered. My inner emotional growth and development were blocked. I didn't realize that people-pleasing was self-destructive. I thought that the seminary program of formation had passed down to me all of the certitude that I needed. The church's moral teachings and canon law seemed to have the correct answers to every moral situation. When I was in denial of my own inner authority, I was incapable of saying, "No" to my bishop. I accepted too many additional diocesan assignments. I was out of touch with my inner authority that was saying, "I can't realistically assume any more responsibilities now."

I was fearful of making a mistake, so I was slow in developing my creative talents. I realize that one of the best ways to learn is to make mistakes. It is a very powerful teaching tool especially for gifted students who have little tolerance for themselves or others who get it wrong. But it is also valuable for very compliant, ardent, bright and able students too, who see themselves as unacceptable failures. When we are fearful of making mistakes, we can unconsciously come to think that by being docile and simply obeying our bishop without questioning we will advance in the church's hierarchy. Under these circumstances, we can lose an awareness of our prophetic call that comes with baptism and ordination to the priesthood. We can fail to be good shepherds because we tend to act without filtering our motives and actions through a mature adult conscience. We can adhere to tradition without examining whether change is needed or whether the teaching is outmoded and doesn't make any common sense to most people.

The fact that the Catholic Church is a hierarchical and a patriarchal structure makes it easy for church leaders to presume, assume, and proclaim superiority to lay Catholics. Some bishops assume superiority over their clergy. Some bishops have been accused of "bullying" clergy. Lay Catholics, deacons, and priests can easily deny their inner authority in favor of the certitude that the institutional church promises.

Often in church news, we hear about "prelates" in the Church. The word "prelate" means a church leader, such as a bishop or abbot, of superior rank. This hierarchical relationship exists among the laity and priests as well. Lay persons, even though perhaps holier than some prelates, will give up their inner authority and presume the prelates are holier and wiser because they are formally designated as professional religious.

Over the years, I have met some very holy lay persons, and yet I often missed seeing their holiness at the time since they did not fit the stereotype of the male church leader. But the problem goes beyond how I perceive others. It saddens me to think of how many people do not realize how good they are, and of how my own presumed superiority contributed to their diminished self image. I'm speaking from personal experience. When my parents died, it finally dawned on me that they were holier than any church leader I had ever met. While my parents were alive, I denied my inner authority that was telling me that they were saintly. I regret not telling them this while they were still with me here on earth.

As a result of not being in touch with our inner authority, we can be good leaders in the institutional Church but miss being good shepherds who proclaim the gospel and who are aware of God's gifts in all the persons in our midst.

To this point, I recommend reading Discover the Power Within You by Eric Butterworth, an author who was considered by some to be a "twentieth-century Emerson." In the book, he shares a legend which I will simplify for you. Regrettably, it took me many years to understand this legend and to apply its teachings to myself.

According to an old Hindu legend, there was once a time when humans were gods, but they abused their divinity. Brahma, the chief god, took away man's divinity and wanted to hide it so humans would never find it. He consulted his lesser gods, and after they suggested many ideas, Brahma decided to hide man's divinity deeply within humans. Brahma thought they would never think to look for it there.

For most of my life I looked outside of myself seeking union with the divine in the sacraments, in the hierarchy's authority, and in my religion. I didn't understand what St. Paul said many years ago to Timothy, "I remind you to rekindle the gift of God that is within you" (2 Timothy 1:6). I failed to grasp Jesus' words, "The kingdom of God is among you" (Luke 17: 21). Some Bibles say, "The kingdom of God is within you."

4. I tried to be perfect:

A fourth way that I was handicapped by a lack of a spiritual roadmap was a chronic urge toward perfectionism. In an earlier letter, I mentioned that one of the goals of second half of life spirituality is to no longer strive to be perfectionistic, but rather to be whole, true, real, and loving.

My own problems with striving to be perfect go back to my literal and simplistic understanding of the Book of Genesis in the Bible. I thought that there once was a perfect world in which Adam and Eve lived. I thought that I was born imperfect because of Adam's sin, so my goal in life was to become perfect without sin. I thought I was baptized so as to have a Savior who could make me perfect. That construct helped me to give blind acceptance to the atonement theory that asserts we are born imperfect and need a Savior to be perfect and to save us.

The practice of second half of life spirituality rejects the idea that we are born stained and corrupt and need to be made perfect so that Jesus will then live in us and save us. Instead, we embrace the conviction that the Risen Jesus is already within us. We should name our sins and try to grow spiritually, but we must remember the Easter message that Jesus is not in a tomb. The Risen Jesus is already with us.

The movie, East of Eden:

Do you recall watching East of Eden together? Remember the movie was based on John Steinbeck's novel? I particularly liked the way it characterized thoroughly first and second half of life spirituality. The film is, in essence, a retelling of the story of Cain and Abel.

The movie portrays Cal, a wayward young man (James Dean) who vies for the affection of his deeply religious father who favors his older brother Aron because he seems on the surface to be perfect, since he was obedient to authority figures. Aron and his dad shared the belief that obedience was a hallmark of perfection. The "deeply religious father" applied the Bible to all matters of life to the exclusion of all else. The father's literal interpretation of the Bible turns off Cal because he could sense his father's hypocrisy, he loved the Bible, but couldn't love him.

Perhaps the father and Aron were stuck in first half of life spirituality. They looked good on the outside, but unconditional love, compassion, and forgiveness were missing in their lives. Cal, the "wayward son," though judged by his father, none the less displayed compassion for him at the end of his life. He was able to truly forgive his father. And for those who follow Jesus, compassion and forgiveness are more important than strict obedience, quoting the Bible, compulsory attendance at religious services, and the simple adherence to rules without understanding their purpose.

For most of us who were formed to practice first half of life spirituality, we remain fixated on achieving our own perfection. Year after year, with the help of the sacraments and spiritual directors, we tried to purge our vices, one after another, in pursuit of narcissistic perfectionism. And as we judge ourselves without end, so we judge others as well, leading to a glaring self-righteousness. And to complete the circle, even when we sought forgiveness and healing in the Sacrament of Reconciliation, we focused more on our own unworthiness instead of God's mercy and compassion.

In an earlier letter, I described how I discovered an image of an Empathetic God when I visited Haiti. In many ways, up to that point in my life, my spirituality was like the man in the story of the Rich Young Man (Mt 19: 16-22). I was trying to be perfect. Jesus called the young man to live a new way of life. Once I discovered an Empathetic God, I knew I was called to change and to lead in a new way as a good shepherd.

Conclusion:

I find it sad that some of us in our senior years are focused on our physical failings that are impossible to avoid, and entirely beyond our fault. Many people my age are focused on tummy-tucks and face lifts. But it is equally sad when individuals my age remain more focused on achieving an illusory perfection of their inner selves than they are on the suffering and needs of others. If we enter our later years still practicing first half of life spirituality, we risk mirroring in our own lives the images of God that we hold as Distant, Exclusive, Vengeful, Perfectionistic, and of course a Male God. As stated earlier, we become like the God we adore, even when we believe in these exclusionary images of God. In this way, we risk being self-righteous, judgmental, perfectionistic, perhaps scrupulous, selfish, and aloof from the suffering of others. During Lent, we may worry more about accidentally eating meat on Friday than we do about the plight of hundreds of thousands of refugees with little or nothing to eat at all.

I was handicapped, Joey, in these four ways by not having a spiritual roadmap that enabled understanding the two halves of life spirituality. Now I realize that my own happiness depends upon my frame of reference, my basic vision, my world view, and my self acceptance. Most importantly, I now realize my images of

God must be allowed to grow with life itself for these images are the means by which I may approach the reality of the divine itself. That is why I am so happy to be able to share with you these letters that at least give you a different frame of reference and a newer basic vision while you are still young.

Peace,

Uncle Matthew

Letter #64
Sunday, November 15, 2015

Dear Uncle Matthew,

Thank you for sharing how you were handicapped in four ways
without a spiritual roadmap. Although you may deny it, I know
you to be a humble man. No priest in the seminary, including my
spiritual director, has shared so openly about the difficulties of
living a celibate life in the priesthood. This gives me strength.
Also, I liked the way you analyzed the movie, East of Eden, to
illustrate the dangers of perfectionism. I remember the movie
well.

You are making me aware that without a spiritual roadmap, I
could make a commitment to a life of celibacy without having a
clue about the challenges I will face and the price I will be
expected to pay. But, with the map, I can discern a purpose and
an unfolding journey.

I see a parallel to marriage. Young people entering marriage are
largely unaware of the many challenges they will face and the
price they will be expected to pay. I have great compassion for
married men and women who discover later in life that they were
never made aware of, nor did they achieve, the necessary
building blocks for a life-long commitment. I can see why
parishes require pre-marital preparation for couples. To

responsibly embrace major commitments in life, good preparation, realistic questioning, and extensive planning must occur. Otherwise, commitments and hearts may be broken.

I read that Pope Francis closed the Synod in Rome (October 4-25) with a warning against a spirituality that ignores people's struggles. This reminds me of a comment of yours in your last letter. There does seem to be some movement from legalism to mercy when it comes to the Eucharist. I read that Pope Francis is making it simpler and less expensive to get an annulment. He stresses the importance of the Church and its leaders showing mercy. This to me is more in accord with the life of Jesus.

My five summer assignments have given me many opportunities to be aware of the everyday lives of numerous priests. I have observed priests under stress to raise money for the Annual Faith Appeal. I have observed the pressure that priests experience when they try to appease their rich donors by avoiding controversial topics both in and out of the pulpit. I observed that some priests lack the training to be good administrators, so they fail to pay their employees fair salaries. I have noticed that some priests do not do a good day's work, whereas other priests work too hard at great cost to their health. Some priests take care of their bodies, and other priests fully neglect to exercise and watch their diets. I have met two retired priests over the past five summers, and both priests complained that the bishop spent so much time and effort recruiting young men for the priesthood, but that he neglected to show gratitude and affirmation for retired priests.

I read in the National Catholic Reporter that the Catholic Church has incurred nearly $4 billion in costs related to the priest sex abuse crisis during the past 65 years. That is shocking! Obviously, many priests need significant help in living a celibate life, or perhaps they should pursue another path in life altogether. Relatedly, I also read in the NCR an article, "Ordination of Married Men Would Cause Other Major Changes within the Church," by Sister Joan Chittister. She said that the question of the theology of ordination to the priesthood isn't going to go away. From all that I see, I agree.

I know a young man named Joseph who is twenty years old. He is a trainer at the gym where I work out. He is not a Catholic, but he belongs to an evangelical church where he plays the drums and sings during worship. In spite of our probable theological differences, I believe that he is a holy young man because he is more holistic, mature, and authentic than most young men his age. He shares with me thoughts about his girl friend, and he shares with me his goals for the future. Do you think there is a connection between exuding joy and radiating wholeness and being on a path of holiness? You seem to have indicated that connection earlier when you shared with me the stories about meeting Charlie on a bus when you returned to your college seminary in Albany, and when you took a walk with Jonathan at a monastery shortly after your ordination. Certainly, joy is a spiritual fruit that bears witness.

I do miss my former girl friend who married in May after waiting a year when I entered the seminary. Her husband went to the same college I attended, and he was a year ahead of me in his engineering studies. We still occasionally talk by phone. (I typically call her.) The phone calls often leave me feeling melancholic. She was the love of my life.

Embracing celibacy as a life-long commitment is still a daunting prospect for me, especially when I consider celibacy's frequent connection to egocentricity. I've been with some priests over the last few years who seem to be terribly egocentric, thinking it is all about themselves. Other priests, like my pastor last summer, inspire me because their celibacy has afforded them opportunities to have many spiritual intimate friendships, and they live their true self which has brought them joy and wholeness. They are truly good shepherds. As you often tell me, new experiences can bless us with new insights, new questions, and a desire to change. We just have to be aware of the graces that are present every moment of every day.

In closing, would you mind sharing with me your thoughts on the future of the Catholic Church in light of all that you have shared?

Peace,

Joey

Response to Letter #64
Sunday, November 29, 2015

Dear Joey,

Since we last corresponded, I suffered a minor stroke. I was in the hospital for a couple of nights. The doctor said it was a warning since stroke victims are more likely to have more strokes in the future. Both my parents suffered from heart disease. I am now taking Plavix, a blood thinner. For now, all is well. And though frightening in some ways, I count the stroke as a blessing, reminding me of the preciousness of every moment and the fragility of all earthly life.

Thank you for sharing with me your observations about Joseph, the trainer. Yes, I believe that those individuals who are joyful, wholistic, alive, and willing to dialogue with others are exhibiting signs of holiness. Saint Paul described the Fruits of the Spirit as love, joy, peace, patience, kindness, goodness, gentleness, and faith itself (Galatians 5:22). You and I have had experiences validating the belief that the presence of the Risen Christ can be found in any person regardless of their age, religion, sexuality, nationality, creed, and skin color. The Spirit blows where it will.

When we practice first half of life spirituality, we judge holiness more by external signs, a person's religion, church attendance, title, attire, and language. But when we practice second half of life spirituality, we look for the inner signs found in the Fruits of the Spirit. I like to think every day we preach a sermon, to the world and to all whom we encounter, by the language we use, through the little things like the way we say hello and goodbye, the way we drive our cars, through our expressions of gratitude, our readiness to forgive, our willingness to be vulnerable and interdependent, and above all by meeting the needs of others with mercy and compassion.

I'm so glad you're finding this spiritual roadmap on the two halves of life helpful as you continue to discern God's call. A spiritual road map keeps us aware of the necessity to continually change, something Jesus urged us to do many times in many ways. No one has lost the capacity to change while still alive. The map and the journey it implies reminds us of that truth.

I just finished reading Jimmy Carter's new book, A Call To Action, Women, Religion, Violence and Power. I admire him so much. He and Rosalynn have been married sixty-eight years and throughout his long life of public service, he has never lost his basic goodness and devotion to living a life of integrity.

Earlier this month, a Call to Action Conference was held in Milwaukee. Sister Joan Chittister gave a keynote presentation entitled, "Love Radically, Live Faithfully." She asked the simple but profound question, "What is your role and mine, if we are to live the Gospel faithfully and radically?" Her talk focused on the role of public intellectuals who have an interest in and commitment to the great questions of life. As I read over the text of her address, I realized her talk was brilliant and challenging. Regrettably, I realized as I read the text that I have failed during most of my priesthood to love radically. Fear motivated me to play it safe by simply obeying rather than questioning. How foolish of me! As I think about it, many of our letters have engaged some of the great questions of life. And what could be more important?

For now, let me respond directly to your question in your last letter regarding the future of the Catholic Church.

Reflections on the Catholic Church's future:

Despite being hopeful overall, I have grave doubts about the future of the Church. I'll share with you in this letter two hopeful signs regarding the Church's future. I can discuss the reasons for grave doubts later, if you wish.

The first hopeful sign is that change is taking place in the hierarchy. Pope Francis is the leading spokesperson for this change in the Church. And what better ally can there be? There is a new book entitled The Great Reformer, Francis and the Making of a Radical Pope. I want to read it. Have you heard about it?

The second hopeful sign is the fact that the laity is demanding change in the Church. This in turn supports change in the hierarchy. There is the possibility that a virtuous cycle is under way.

First, change is taking place in the hierarchy.

Pope Francis recently encouraged employees of the Vatican to reflect upon ten resolutions for the upcoming new year. The first resolution is "Take care of your spiritual life, your relationship with God, because this is the backbone of everything we do and everything we are." I believe that our correspondence is helping both of us to strengthen our spiritual backbones, and in this way to serve God and others more faithfully.

Pope Francis is doing much to reform and invigorate the Catholic Church. Fr. Drew Christiansen, S. J., a former editor in chief of America Magazine, said in an article last May that, "Openness to dissenters and critics, welcome for sinners and outreach to people on the margins of society are becoming the defining pattern of Catholic life." May it be so!

Before the Vatican II Council, the Church was described as a pyramid structure with the hierarchy at the top and the laity at the bottom. The Vatican II Council revitalized this model of the Church using a circle with the hierarchy and laity mutually working together to bring about the message of Jesus.

In an earlier letter, I mentioned that Pope Francis married twenty couples at the Vatican in September, 2014. The event was symbolically important because it demonstrated the practice of second half of life spirituality. Some couples had lived together. One couple had a child out of wedlock. Hence, some couples had obviously enjoyed sex before marriage. These actions are considered sinful by the Church. By officiating at the marriages, Pope Francis witnessed to the world his belief in a Merciful, Forgiving, and Unconditionally Loving God. In his homily to the couples, Pope Francis stressed forgiveness for past sins and the importance of present love. This event signaled that the pope is trying to change the Church to be more open and inclusive. His model of shepherding enables people to trust and believe in a Forgiving and Merciful God. May we do the same.

Pope Francis appears to have great inner freedom. He is not bound by traditions and customs that are not an essential part of the gospels. He courageously thinks outside of life-stifling boxes. The world was favorably impressed with the pope when in June 2014, he met with President Shimon Peres of Israel and the Palestinian President Mahmoud Abbas in the Vatican Garden. He is hoping to open conversation with the Chinese leadership and bridge the sixty-three year old divide between the Vatican and China. All these actions reflect a desire to overcome dualisms that divide the world.

Pope Francis' leadership at the Extraordinary General Synod Assembly of Bishops that was held in Octobers 2014 and 2015 helped to kindle a sense of God's mercy and love. The Synods stressed the issues of sexuality, marriage, and family life. Although the process of engaging in dialogue was imperfect, there was an attempt to bring about dialogue in the Church on important family issues. In the final draft report of the 2014 Synod, Pope Francis included explicit mention of the gifts of homosexuals. He asked if the Church was willing to welcome them into the Church. As a positive sign, nearly two-thirds (62%) of the bishops voted Yes, indicating that many of them have a latent capacity for mercy, understanding, and openness to change.

Second, the laity is demanding change in the Church.

In an earlier letter to you, I outlined a number of reasons why Catholics have left the institutional church. Some practicing Catholics look upon the exodus of so many baptized Catholics as a tragedy. They worry about the salvation of those who have left the Church. I have a different reaction. I am hopeful because many people who have left the Church are aware of something that many devout Catholics cannot see or understand. Did they leave the Church because they realized the inadequacy of the information and skills they learned when surrounded by the practice of first half of life spirituality? Could the large number of "fallen-away" Catholics simply be a sign to us that many people are disillusioned by the Church's failure to speak to the current times? Perhaps they found the joy they wanted but they couldn't find it within the confines of the Church and believed it to be a natural human right. Perhaps the institutional church became irrelevant to them. Perhaps they were turned off by the hypocrisy they observed. Perhaps they attended liturgies where they could not understand what the priests were saying. Perhaps they were preached to by priests who espoused pre-Vatican homilies. Perhaps they could not always name precisely what was wrong, but their numbers send a powerful message to us that something is indeed wrong. People all over the world are changing their world view, their framework, and the change is springing from both the younger and older generation.

In an earlier letter to you, I mentioned some of the goals that guide the practice of second half of life spirituality. The first goal, really a discipline, is to rigorously ask questions. So, let me pose some questions to you, questions I have heard from others that suggest a hunger for change. Questions may start a dialogue, or they may be ignored. But if rational answers are not given to people's questions, and if change doesn't occur to make the

Church more relevant, then many people will continue to leave the institutional church. The questions of many people both within the Church, which is more important, but also those outside that make me hopeful about the church's future because the questioning indicates that God's Spirit of renewal is alive and well. And this is as it should be for change must continually take place in all living organisms including the Church. As Bob Dylan said, "He who's not being born is busy dying."

Questions:

Here are the questions, drawn from diverse conversations and from one book in particular, Bishop Spong's Why the Church Must Change or Die? Don't be fooled by the simplicity of some of the questions. Within their mundane nature lie profound issues.

1.   Why are the chairs in the sanctuary larger, more ornate, and of better quality than the seats provided for the parishioners?

2.   Why does the announcer before mass tell the people to prepare for "the holy sacrifice of the mass?" Doesn't this expression reflect St. Augustine's atonement theory to the exclusion of all other theologies?

3.   Why did the English version of the mass change in July, 2010? The bishops of the United States accepted from Rome this new English version of the mass, derived from a strict translation from the Latin, and the strict translation suggests a Distant God and diminishes our pastoral understanding of the worship service.

4.   Why does the laity kneel in most churches during the Eucharistic Prayer while the presider stands? What does that say about the Body of Christ and the community of believers?

5.  Why do prelates sit on thrones and have servers kneel before them to wash their hands? Why do prelates dress up with miters that connote the worship of a king when we are actually worshipping a broken, wounded, loving man who showed us an

image of the Incarnate God, not a God who sits on a heavenly throne?

6. Garry Wills' book, Why Priests?-A Failed Tradition, motivates people to ask searching questions such as: Why can only priests confer some of the sacraments? Why does it take a degree in theology to share the Body and Blood of Christ, that is to provide the Eucharist? Why can't the laity be part of the selective process for their own priests and bishops? Why does the hierarchy still circle the church wagons so that they can protect the way we have always done things instead of listening to the promptings of the Holy Spirit?

7. How can an understanding of second half of life spirituality be promoted in parishes? How can books and educational media on second half of life spirituality be accepted and embraced in parishes? How can priests, nuns, deacons, and lay leaders be enabled and empowered to understand the two halves of life paradigm so that they can teach others?

8. Did all of Jesus' miracles literally and historically occur as written in the Bible's many, sometimes conflicting, stories?

9. Is the church's teaching correct that there are infallible popes and inerrant scriptures? And why is infallibility and inerrancy considered so important?

10. Is there really only one true Church?

11. We deny women ordination to the priesthood based on the questionable idea that Jesus was intentionally giving us an institutional model for priesthood. If Jesus did not create an institutional priesthood, why can't the Church today ordain women? And further, should we allow any cultural norms of two thousand years ago dictate to what we do today?

12. Has the Church embraced the role of science in our modern day? Spong treats this subject in his book Why Christianity Must Change or Die when he says that Nicolaus Copernicus (1473-

1573) and Galileo Galilei (1564-1642) helped us mature beyond the Biblical view of the physical universe by demonstrating that the earth is not the center of the physical universe. This issue of science impacts many issues of significance in today's Church.

13. When we practice first half of life spirituality, we believe that there was an historic fall from a life of perfection in the Garden. We believe that there was a need for a rescuing act of redemption or payment for ransom. Conversely, Charles Darwin (1809-1882) in his work, The Origin of Species, taught us that God's creation is not finished but in fact is continually evolving. Creation continues. Thus, Darwin's work encourages us to re-think the Genesis story and to ask, "Was there ever a perfect place where humankind lived?

14. How can the LGBTQ Catholic community be reconciled to the Church? Or more to the point, how can the Church be reconciled to them?

15. Why is the church hierarchy so opposed to same sex marriage, the use of condoms to fight AIDS, and the acceptance of homosexuality in general when so many members of the hierarchy are reportedly gay themselves? Must we accept hypocrisy on top of inhumanity?

16. Why do some prelates in the Church live in splendor similar to emperors in the Roman Empire when Jesus, our model, was a poor man?

17. Why does the Church require mandatory celibacy for its priests in the Latin Rite when the problems created by this practice are so overwhelming large, falling numbers of vocations, sex scandals, and a disproportionate number of homosexuals in the priesthood? (Just to be clear, the problem is not homosexuality but the disproportionality.)

18. Why do bishops reportedly "throw under the bus" priests accused of sexual abuse when, if bishops are accused, they have a different standard to protect them? How can parishioners

understand the justification for this practice?

19. Why doesn't the hierarchy affirm that the fundamental option of feeding the hungry is a higher priority than the construction of redundant discretionary buildings?

20. Why doesn't the hierarchy strongly affirm and support members of the Church who protest the government's stock piling of nuclear weapons? Or, on inaction on global warming? etc.

Conclusion:

I can think of a few more reasons why I am hopeful for the future of the institutional church, but let's wait until another letter. For now, perhaps you could ponder a few of these questions we have discussed.

Peace,

Uncle Matthew

PS    I almost forgot, today we celebrate the First Sunday of Advent. This year has gone by so quickly!

PSS    Don't think my recent stroke will slow down my letter writing. I'm eagerly awaiting your reply.

Letter #65
Sunday, December 13, 2015

Dear Uncle Matthew,

I am so sorry to hear about your recent stroke. You are in my prayers. I don't want anything to happen to you. On the phone, you said that you were doing much better, and that there is no noticeable damage to your body. Is there anything I may do? Please don't hesitate to ask.

I'm going to take you at your word in not slowing down in your letter writing. Thank you for sharing with me your thoughts on the future of the Church. I am grateful that you are taking all this time to provide me with a spiritual roadmap. By praying, reflecting, and reading in your retirement years, you are reflecting upon many questions that you obviously never had the time to study when you were a full-time pastor. I appreciate the list of questions that people are asking because the questions are seeds to challenge me now and in the years to come, and I have as you suggested been pondering these questions.

When I go into the chapel for daily mass, my mind is filled with questions. I ask "Why this and why that?" I'm also more analytical instead of simply assuming everything I hear is literally true. Your questions are helping me to question everything. I am aware that my earlier knowledge of chemistry, physics, biology, and astronomy is changing with the discovery of new information. I must be open to new insights in religion and spirituality too since our understanding changes and evolves with new life experiences. My willingness to be open to changes will depend upon my prayer life, spiritual reading, attendance at conferences, journaling, and most of all staying open to the Gifts of the Holy Spirit.

I was disappointed to read that the Church of Jesus Christ of Latter-Day Saints issued a new policy that states the children of same-sex couples can't be baptized until they move out of their parents' homes. This is wrong on so many levels, denying the validity of love between same sex partners, shaming a child for that which he/she is blameless, and creating a division within families. How can this be godly?

On the other hand, a sign of hope. I was greatly uplifted by Pope Francis' six-day trip to Africa when he called for Christians and Muslims to be "brothers and sisters." This is the kind of language and imagery we so need.

The December fifth-agreement among 195 countries, creating a blueprint aimed at limiting global warming, was good news. I read an article that said this agreement is the last best chance we have to slow down global warming before profound dangers arise. I'm amazed that some politicians don't accept the science of climate change (or at least they say they don't). I understand that some people who think dualistically think of climate change as a "secular" issue. But you have taught me that when we think holistically, we will view climate change as a spiritual issue as well as a physical one, for every person as well as every thing in creation is holy.

Last week, I saw the movie Spotlight that certainly made me think and question! I hope it wins Best Picture in the Academy Awards. The movie was about the sex abuse crisis in the Archdiocese of Boston which happened while I was in high school, so I don't recall hearing about it then. My spiritual director told me the other day that what we see in Boston may be just the tip of a large iceberg!

The seminary is closing down on Friday afternoon, December 18, for our Christmas break. I'm looking forward to being with Mom and Dad. Paul will only join us Christmas Day. I'm looking forward to the time off. This semester went by so quickly. We return on Wednesday, January 6. Then I will begin my final semester in the seminary.

In closing, you were so transparent earlier when you shared with me how your earlier ignorance of the paradigm of the two halves of life spirituality harmed you. Before you share with me more reasons for your hope or despair about the Church's future, could you share with me how a spiritual roadmap is benefiting you now, personally?

Peace,

Joey

Response to Letter #65
Wednesday, December 30, 2015

Dear Joey,

Thanks for your phone call last Wednesday. I appreciate your concern about my health. Yesterday, I saw a neurologist, and he is concerned about the left side of my face where he noticed a minor change. He said that there is a fairly high probability that I may have another TIA or stroke. My recent stroke makes me aware of my mortality in a very direct way. This intensifies in me the value of each and every moment.

I hope you are having a wonderful Christmas break. As I mentioned to you, I was with my brother Bill and his family on Christmas Day. We spoke about you of course, all of us taking joy in who you are and who you are becoming. I'm so glad that you were able to celebrate Christmas once again with your parents and Paul.

The declaration by Pope Francis of the Jubilee of Mercy began December 8 and will last until November 20, 2016. The biblical theme of the year is "Be merciful, just as your Father is merciful." Pope Francis said, "The greater the sin, the greater the love which the Church must express toward those who convert." The Pope's words well describe a goal in the practice of second half of life spirituality, and specific to our vocation, the central goal of being a good shepherd. In a world marked by so much poverty and violence, advocating and practicing mercy is the path to a more humane world. If God is Love, certainly this is the Way.

I was saddened to read in the latest National Catholic Reporter that Fr. Joseph Girzone died. He wrote two books that I read, Joshua and The Homeless Bishop. Both of his books made me aware of the importance that  forgiveness and mercy permeate life in the Church. I trust that he has now received these gifts from God himself.

You asked at the close of your last letter how a spiritual roadmap is helping me personally. I'll share with you the ways I can think of that a spiritual roadmap is benefitting me:

Benefits of a spiritual roadmap:

1.)   A spiritual roadmap provides me with new insights on ecumenism:

When I was a student in the seminary, I was taught that Jesus intentionally founded the one and only Catholic Church. Thus, our church hierarchy takes as its starting point the assertion that Jesus intended there to be just one Church, the very church the hierarchy now leads. The objective of this Church since the Reformation, pursued through prayer, admonition and dialogue, is for the separated Christians bodies (of which there are hundreds), to reunite with the one Catholic Church. The Catholic Church's approach is not one that I would describe as equitable, but rather takes a position akin to, "Accept what we teach and then there will be unity." To bring about this unity, for many years the Catholic Church has dialogued with different denominations regarding doctrines, interpretations of the Bible, and moral teachings.

I have found that the spiritual roadmap we have been discussing in our letters offers a different viewpoint about the meaning of the diversity of churches. The assumption that our Church brings to ecumenical dialogue, that everyone must agree on doctrines as the foundation of unity, strikes me as dualistic and a sign of the practice of first half of life spirituality. The practice of second half of life spirituality on the other hand assumes that a more profound unity is to be found in agreement upon the deeper truths that fall outside of doctrines that are human constructs. Unity comes when there is more concern about love and less desire for power. Unity could be obtained if there was more emphasis on humility and an attitude of respectfully accepting the worth of other religions with their traditions, doctrines, and moral teachings. Saint Augustine observed that we cannot understand unless we love, and we cannot love unless we understand.

I shared with you earlier my experience with Promise Keepers and the precious time spent with pastors of the First Alliance Church. The prayer and dialogue we shared opened up for me a whole new world of gratitude, appreciation, and respect for differences in the religious convictions of others. I realized that if I fail to listen, love, dialogue, accept differences, and even serve those who share different beliefs, I risk becoming moralistic like the Pharisees in Jesus' day. I don't agree with all of the political convictions and religious beliefs held by the leaders of different religious bodies, but by being knowledgeable and respectful of what others think, I am becoming less dualistic (right/wrong; good/bad). This has led me to the place where I can now respectfully dialogue with others without the underlying motive of "converting them." I think that we need to celebrate diversity rather than fear diversity and we need to avoid blatantly expecting others to view life the way we do.

2.) A spiritual roadmap helps me to love God more:

Until I attended Fr. Richard Rohr's Conference on "Loving the Two Halves of Life," I was unconsciously and uncritically influenced by my first half of life images of God. This conference opened my eyes and provided a spiritual roadmap that has helped me to be aware of different experiences in my own life that are introducing me to new images of God. For example, through doubting and questioning, and opening my eyes to wonder, I discovered an Incarnate God that has convinced me of the reality that I may find God everywhere, in all objects, persons, and places.

As a consequence, I love God more now because a spiritual roadmap encourages me to let go of constraining images of God as Exclusive, Vengeful, Preoccupied with Sex, Demanding Perfection, and exclusively Male. Through contemplative prayer, I am seeking to let go of all my constructed images of God and just simply open myself to the immediate experience of God's presence. It's a wondrous journey where less is indeed more.

A spiritual roadmap is helping me in very practical ways. It is leading me to discover greater wholeness, fulfillment, compassion, inner-peace, forgiveness of others, and charity. The images of God that are newly emerging, Inclusive, Incarnate, Loving, Forgiving, are inspiring me to reflect these qualities of God. Remember, we become what we adore. These new images of God are assisting me to also become aware of and appreciative of the Gifts of the Holy Spirit: wisdom, understanding, counsel, fortitude, knowledge, and piety. I now see these gifts as available not for a chosen few, but for all those, Christian and non-Christian, who seek to know and love God.

When I was practicing first half of life spirituality, I was obedient to the Commandments more out of fear of God rather than the love of God. As I mentioned in an earlier letter, the poet T. S. Elliot warned, "The last temptation that's the greatest treason is to do the right thing for the wrong reason." In short, what matters is the intention, the disposition of the heart. I believe a spiritual roadmap is helping me to discover new images of the divine that enable love, not fear, to guide my journey toward God. In short, I am loving God more because I am finding God in more persons, places, and things.

3.) A spiritual roadmap stimulates my growth in faith:

I was trained as a seminarian to think I had the answers to

almost every question. Thus, in times of doubt, I would just refer to what the Church teaches. Now that I have a spiritual roadmap, I realize this practice of simply deferring to authority, over time, stunted my spiritual growth. Instead of seeking quick, second hand answers, I now realize that seeing the bigger picture and realizing there are not always right and wrong answers helps me grow in faith because it leads me into an unfolding world of mystery with "answers" that liberate and enlarge.

Thomas Moore, an American psychotherapist, in his book, A Religion of One's Own, stresses that when traveling our own spiritual paths, led by the Spirit, we may expect doubt and wonder to be our companions. He says, "The discovery or creation of a religion of your own is not an option. It is a necessary step in your spiritual unfolding." All of this means to me that whether within the Church or outside, the inescapable fact is that we need to leave our childish ways and develop our own adult relationship with God.

So this spiritual roadmap is helping me to discover my own true identity. Through a process of letting go of my false self, I now believe God lives in me not only as the Creator of my soul, but also as reflected in my true self. St. Paul said, "I live, no longer I, but Christ lives in me...I live by faith in the Son of God who has loved me and given himself up for me" (Galatians 2:20). Now that I better understand on a deep level who I am, my faith is stronger because I not only believe, but in some sense "know," that God loves me despite my own unworthiness, imperfection, and inabilities. Paradoxically, this allows me, naturally and spontaneously, to have great joy and gratitude for who I am and the role I may play in God's great and grand creation.

In sum, a spiritual roadmap has helped me grow in faith because I now rely not only on church teaching and tradition to guide me, but also I trust God to lead me through promptings of my heart and inner moral compass.

4.) A spiritual roadmap helps me to better love my neighbor:

In Chapter 10 of Luke's gospel, there is the beautiful and instructional story of the Good Samaritan. Why was the Samaritan the only one to stop and help the wounded man? (Remember, the predominant Jewish mind-set of the day was that the Samaritan was a second class citizen.) Perhaps the temple priest and Levite who had passed by the wounded man were practicing first half of life spirituality and caught up in rules, propriety, and fears. They were concerned about what would happen to them, their safety, their reputations, if they stopped to aid the stranger. The Samaritan man on the other hand may have been practicing second half of life spirituality listening to his heart and seeing beneath the surface. He was more concerned about the human suffering before him, stranger or not, than he was about tribal taboos and himself.

When I was in the seminary, now long ago, the emphasis of my training was on my holiness, my piety, my obedience to church authority, my acceptance of church teachings, my restrictive spiritual reading, and my relationship with My God Alone. At the time this process of formation seemed good and necessary. I erroneously thought that the seminary formation program had transformed me into a holy person. It was all quite flattering. But now with a spiritual roadmap, I am aware that I must continually change and be open to new ideas if I am going to fulfill the command not only to love God but to love my neighbor as well. Loving my neighbor at times requires that I put others before myself.

At the Last Supper, we read that Jesus told his apostles, "Remain in my love" (John 15:9). What does this mean? I believe we remain in Jesus' love when we invite his Spirit to abide in us. A spiritual roadmap offers us new images of God, for example an Inclusive God, an Incarnate God, a Forgiving God, and an Unconditionally Loving God,  that help this transformative process of God abiding in us and expressing the love of God through us. And when filled with this Spirit, we come to understand that Jesus' command to love one's neighbor (and the stranger) is more important than the illusion of being perfect, of striving to amass more material possessions, of being in control, or of habitually competing to be "number one." Jesus taught us by his life of service to others what is best for us to seek and to become. Jesus' focus was on seeing and responding to the needs, sufferings, crises, and hardships of his neighbor. And through Jesus' eyes, all of humanity, including the stranger, must be counted as neighbor.

Bishop Spong speaks to this issue of our common humanity in his book, This Hebrew Lord. In the chapter entitled, "I am the bread of life," he discusses how all of us are lonely, separate, and insecure to varying degrees and in different ways throughout our lives. We all hunger for a wholeness that is not yet realized. Wealth and power and fame cannot satisfy us. And so Spong urges us to feast our eyes on Jesus, the "bread of life," who is most readily found in the love and affirmation we receive from other people. Our experiences of receiving the "bread of life" from others enables us to truly love ourselves, accept ourselves, feel secure, feel whole, and know that God unconditionally loves us and all others too.

As I become more aware of the many ways the "bread of life" feeds me daily, I realize my responsibility, my desire, to feed, affirm, forgive, unconditionally love, and accept others as they are. I am more aware, as Bishop Spong says, that my baptismal call invites me to be taken, blessed, broken, and given so that I become, through the love of Jesus abiding within, a sacrament to others, the "bread of life" for others.

5.) A spiritual roadmap helps me to grow in humility and wisdom:

Hinduism teaches there are four major stages of life:

1) The student
2) The householder
3) The forest dweller (the "retiree")
4) The wise or fully enlightened person.

In our society, as well as in the Church specifically, we emphasize the value of being a student and later a householder focusing on social, biological, and economic contributions. Little emphasis is given to the spirituality involved and the positive role that retirement may play in the life of the Church, the family, and society at large. And almost no attention is paid to the opportunities afforded by retirement to enter the fourth stage of life, i.e., becoming a mentor serving the spiritual needs of others. A spiritual roadmap makes us aware of the many new opportunities in these last two stages of life to journey toward wholeness, to better fulfill God's plan for our lives, and to give back to the world practical wisdom which is sorely needed.

In the Catholic Church, most retired priests and nuns need money (beyond their pensions). So they offer their time "helping out" in parishes, simply repeating and sharing with others what they have learned earlier in life when they themselves were of the householder age. For all practical purposes, this means that most retired priests and nuns are stuck in the second stage of life, the householder stage, and never minister from the third and fourth stages.

Earlier, I shared with you some of the benefits to one's spiritual development during the retirement years. During the third stage of life, it is possible to create the time and space to discern important lessons learned in one's life. It is possible to go back in time and learn from past mistakes. We can perceive times when God helped us to bring good out of bad. We can better understand the role of grace, forgiveness, and of courage to become a more fully developed person and a better shepherd. This process of reflection and honest assessment is at the heart of living wisely. As George Santayana said, "Those who cannot remember the past are condemned to repeat it." It is important to be humble by taking time to re-learn much of what we learned in the first half of life. With the experience of living and learning anew, we can interpret the deeper meanings hidden from us earlier in our lives.

In my own life, I assumed for so many years, while in the householder stage of life, that I was more knowledgeable and far wiser than most people regarding the spiritual life because of my ten years of seminary formation. I had read many books on religion. I had tried so hard to be spiritually perfect. I listened to so many lectures and watched so many DVDs. I have read all of Richard Rohr's books. In my years of retirement, I began to realize that so much of my book learning actually separated me from the real issues of life. Too much head, too little heart. For example, I spent years learning Latin, Greek, and Hebrew and yet no one in all my ministry has ever asked me questions involving these languages nor have they been useful in helping people in their time of need.

In contrast to reading so many books that were remote from life, so many of my lay friends have taught me profound truths. They have faced the difficult life-challenges that came with their marriages, loved-ones dying, childbearing, working, financial stress, conflicts, and broken relationships. For example, your Aunt Rose has lost three children and her husband, and yet she still has a deep trust in God. She attends mass with a spirit of gratitude. She witnesses to our family a spirituality that is amazing and humbling to contemplate! She conveys a deep and real wisdom, born from sorrow, that has marked her journey in faith. Your Aunt Rose had to trust God so many times when she did not know how she could cope with her tragic losses. Over the years, I have come to know many lay people who appear to have arrived at the fourth stage of life through their suffering and  the loving hand of God. They have been humble and wise in the most unassuming ways.

We can ask, "Do we as a Church recognize the humility, holiness, and wisdom of so many of our married members in the Church?" As I mentioned before, nearly all the declared saints that we admire in the church calendar were virgins and celibates while few were married. It seems that sexual activity precludes holiness or sainthood. The Church gives the impression that the celibates in leadership positions ("the first") are humbler, wiser, holier, and more fully enlightened than those that they teach ("the last"). Paradoxically and instructively, Jesus said in Matthew 20, "The last will be first, and the first will be last."

6.) A spiritual roadmap helps me appreciate
different theological perspectives:

A spiritual roadmap helps us to appreciate different theological perspectives by opening our minds to new ideas. This has a salutary effect. For example, we may come to see that throughout church history, theologians have not only offered positive formulations of church doctrine, but theologians have also provided the invaluable service of questioning and even denying some of the basic teachings of the Catholic Church. They have done so to understand the realities of life in God's complex and abundant creation. These criticisms of orthodoxy are themselves then assessed for truth and error. In this manner my faith, and the theologies and practice that underpin my faith, have been refined and given solid footing.

As an example of this critical thinking, some spiritual writers have examined the Nicene Creed (adopted by the Council of Nicaea in 325 CE) and attempted to articulate it in concepts and language which are more respectful and meaningful to the realities of our time. By this I mean that the Apostles' Creed, and later the Nicene Creed, reflect a dualistic three-tiered view of the universe that is no longer plausible. Sadly, institutional religion too often seems fearful of inquiry, expelling its most creative thinkers, such as Hans Kung and Michael Morwood. These two thinkers attempt to explain basic Catholic teachings in a new way, compatible with the findings of rational inquiry and empirical experience.

In the book, Perennial Wisdom for the Spiritually Independent, we notice that the great sages and mystics in Christianity, Buddhism, Hinduism, Islam, Judaism all follow the Golden Rule, "Do to others whatever you would have them do to you. This is the law and the prophets" (Matthew 7:12). While using different words, they all agree that one's moral compass always points toward justice and compassion. By noting the similarities and differences in different theological perspectives, I find that I have a deeper appreciation for Jesus' teachings.

The case of Michael Morwood is instructive. He was a former priest with the Missionaries of the Sacred Heart. He worked in the field of Adult Faith Education. In 1998, Australian Cardinal George Pell told Morwood that he was unfit to speak on certain topics. His case caused considerable controversy at the time in Australia and beyond.

In his book, written after he left the priesthood, Is Jesus God?, Finding Our Faith, Morwood challenges his readers to question the nature and role of Jesus in salvation history. He suggests that salvation is not about Jesus getting us into heaven but about Jesus setting us free from darkness and ignorance so that we can experience light, trust, and insight.

Michael Morwood in his book, In Memory of Jesus asks other provocative questions, and he advocates for a revision of our relationship with Jesus in ways that are admittedly challenging. For example, he maintains that Christianity must return to focusing on the human Jesus and his message for our lives. Morwood believes this provides a counter view to the view of Jesus as someone who doesn't really seem to be human and is miraculous and magical. Morwood also questions whether Jesus himself knew of his divine identity. He suggests that Jesus faced death with a courageous act of faith in the God in whom he trusted, and it is at that point that the human-divine mystery is most evident.

By being exposed to new ideas, a spiritual roadmap encourages me to reflect on what I actually believe about Jesus. The result of this is a faith more securely grounded, more flexible, and more open to unfolding truths. At this stage of my life, I am more appreciative of mystery rather than assuming, as I did earlier in my life, that my theological convictions were all-knowing and for all persons.

At bottom, internalizing a spiritual roadmap does mean that I do not view opposing ideas as a threat to my faith-life but rather as blessings that invites us to do "inner work" so as to better discover and form my own mature belief system. In the Hindu paradigm of life stages, in the second stage, the House Holder, we pass on what we knew to the next generation without too much reflection. In this way social and generational continuity are ensured. In the third and fourth stages of life, the Forrest Dweller and the Wise Person, we realize our faith grows when we are challenged by new ideas. Through these encounters with new ideas, we are encouraged to search and reflect upon our rich tradition in creative interplay with the      traditions and theological perspectives of others.

Joey, my letters to you are not meant to judge or advocate positions that differ from the official teachings of the Catholic Church. Rather, I present the value of being familiar with different theological perspectives in order to affirm the need for respectfully dialoguing within the Church. In this way, individuals who dare to challenge a way of thinking do not feel separated from the Christian community, the Body of Christ.

One last thought on this issue, Dr. Daniel C. Maguire dedicated his book, Christianity without God to the "American Association of University Professors which stands tall as the defender of academic freedom and integrity." Reading between the lines, this dedication tells me that some of Maguire's views are not in accord with dogmas and even traditional Catholic scholarship, and he is deeply appreciative that this professional association provides him with a secure home where freedom of thought is encouraged and defended.

If we are going to be good shepherds who are willing to listen to others, it is important to be aware that different world views not only help us to see reality differently, but they challenge us to clarify our own viewpoints on different topics. When you think about it, Jesus himself represented a dramatic departure from the dominant world-view of his day. It was only through an openness to the Spirit of God, manifold in the life of Jesus, that those around him were born again. So it ever is.

7.) A spiritual roadmap helps me to enter into the mysteries of the liturgy:

A spiritual roadmap helps us to see that early Christian understandings of Jesus, who he was and what he did, rested upon their society's prevailing images of God that preceded the life of Jesus. For example, they had internalized the image of God as a heavenly king, mirroring the very real earthly kings they knew and feared, giving rise to an image of Jesus seated at the right hand of the heavenly throne. This mythic portrayal assumed that the universe was a kingdom, hierarchal and absolute. Human beings were thought to be simply subjects who obeyed and served their king, sometimes out of love, often out of fear. This view of the universe still distorts our understanding of the historical Jesus. From the scriptural accounts we have, it is apparent he was more interested in love, forgiveness, and spiritual integrity than power, judgment, and punishment. In whatever way Jesus was related to the divine, and in whatever way he returned to God in heaven, it is doubtful to many people that a kingly throne captures the essence.

Another example: a spiritual roadmap makes me aware that the Easter liturgical celebration is not only about the raising of Jesus from the dead, but the Resurrection may be applied to our own lives as well. The Resurrection can apply to the death and rebirth of our images of God. Coming out of darkness into the light may be applied to the letting go of our previous understanding of scriptural stories about the post-Resurrection appearances. Change may be felt as threatening and seen as a loss. But as one pursues this path, broad meaning may arise and the truth of the gospel message becomes real in this lifetime. Then a new understanding of the liturgy enables us to enter into and embrace the truth of liturgical mystery. When this is experienced, true freedom and great joy may follow.

We will never know exactly what happened historically regarding the events we celebrate as Easter. A spiritual roadmap once experienced and known as leading to the truth diminishes the importance of the literal, historical question. A spiritual roadmap helps me to grasp the truths of metaphor and mystery, as opposed to clinging to a literal and historical understanding of events. Paradoxically, the result is a sturdier and more solid faith and a resulting capacity to love more fully.

In his book, Immortal Diamond, Fr. Richard Rohr says, "Up to now, it has been common, with little skin off anyone's back, to intellectually argue or religiously believe that Jesus' physical body could really 'resurrect.' That was much easier than to ask whether we could really change or resurrect. It got us off the hook; the hook of growing up, of taking the search for our True Selves seriously." This speaks to me and my life experiences.

On Easter Sunday, the disciples were newly aware that Jesus was no longer among the dead but among the living. Jesus was alive within and among the people his disciples had met. Following a spiritual roadmap into the practice of second half of life spirituality is helping me to be aware of the continuing reality of the Resurrection, enabling me to see and feel the presence of the divine in all the people, places, and things around me. Praise be!

8.) A spiritual roadmap helps me to challenge my assumptions:

In an earlier letter to you, I shared that the initial goal of second half of life spirituality is "to question." When we question things, we open ourselves to new information, possibilities, and insights. When we question, we challenge our assumptions that serve to constrain our thinking and openness to reality. For example, through practical questioning, I now no longer assume that the best way to engage new experiences and information is by thinking dualistically. I am now aware that my mind wants to categorize things as black/white, true/false, good/bad. But this reflex often shuts out the full reality of things, diminishing the glory and fullness of creation. And, importantly, this dualistic thinking can make me self-righteous as well as ignorant.

Hence, I now consciously try to think non-dualistically so as to allow a both/and approach to life. Questioning our assumptions opens us up to the Life of the Spirit, the Gifts of the Spirit, as we seek Wisdom and Understanding. Questioning our assumptions makes possible the healing of our sexism, racism, clericalism, and makes us aware that we live in a conflicted yet gloriously imperfect world. Questioning our assumptions helps us to know who we are and the world we live in, motivating us to build our lives on the true self instead of the false self.

When we begin increasingly to think for ourselves, we become aware that so many of our beliefs and behavior patterns flow, not from our own experiences in life, but from what others have told us. The ethics, rules, norms, laws, beliefs that we follow have come to us from outside sources, especially from our parents, church leaders, and teachers as is right and proper at this time in our lives. When we practice second half of life spirituality, we become more aware of, and listen to, our inner moral compass, our own sense of morality. This listening is a form of prayer. For example, when we develop an interest in the deeper mysteries of life (suffering, beauty, and happiness), we are willing to challenge our assumptions and think. I am not suggesting an ethic or spirituality of individual subjectivity, but rather the development of an authentic faith where established truths and practices, learned in our younger days, become tested and real in our own life. Remember, Jesus came not to discard the Law, but to fulfill it. I hope this all makes sense, Joey.

In my many letters to you, I have encouraged you to learn the rules of society and the Church but also to listen to your own inner moral compass and to be aware of your guiding assumptions. But remember as an institution, I believe the Church is a first half of life spirituality structure. This means that church leaders will not be very pleased if you challenge too many of your (and their) assumptions and think for yourself beyond certain parameters. The roadmap we are discussing is a narrow path, but one that I am sure you are capable of walking.

So yes, we all bring assumptions to the full range of topics before us. Maturing into adulthood and becoming a spiritual doctor and a good shepherd involves subjecting these assumptions to challenges. By doing so, we have a chance to become fully human and fully alive. Let me now get specific, and less abstract, to illustrate what I have been trying to convey. Here are a few examples of how we may challenge prevailing assumptions promoted by Church and society at large. I'll list a few assumptions that people have questioned.

a.   During the Vietnam War, several hundred thousand men refused to serve in the military. They were often regarded at the time as being disloyal to this country. Yet in hindsight, more people challenged that accusation, this simple assumption of disloyalty. They now ask the more difficult question of whether conscientious objectors were acting on a different, deeper form of loyalty.

b.  Most people assume that the Church treats with great respect its own priestly work force, active, semi-active, and retired, since the Church preaches fair labor practices and, of course, justice and compassion towards all. Many assume that the Church walks the talk. Yet some people now challenge that assumption, based on direct experience, and ask "Does the Church treat her priestly labor force with respect when in most dioceses the pension plan is inadequate to sustain a life of modest dignity?"

c.   Most people in the Church assume that a priest caught in homosexual activity is solely responsible for his actions. Yet following decades of exposure to wide-spread institutional dysfunction, some people challenge that assumption and ask, "Should mandatory celibacy and clericalism be considered underlying factors in a priest's misguided sexual behavior?"

d.  Most people assume that priests are psychosexually mature since priests have had so much formal education and the Church lifts them up as wisdom figures. Yet, the sexual abuse crisis in the Church increasingly makes people challenge that naive assumption. Once someone becomes skeptical of a priests psycho-social development, certain behaviors that were once charming may become a cause for concern if, for example, they observe that a priest relates better to children than to adults his own age.

e.  Many people hold the assumption that a terminally ill person should be kept alive as long as possible. This includes the use of extraordinary interventions regardless of the suffering this may entail on the patient and the patient's family. Some people assume a patient commits a grave sin if a decision is made to opt out of treatment for terminal and non terminal cancer and let nature takes its course. Some people challenge these assumptions and ask, "Shouldn't exceptions be allowed in certain cases?"

I hope these examples make it clear that challenging one's assumptions has to be done with great humility so as to give the necessary respect and attention to ethical norms, church teaching, the discernment of others, and one's own life experiences. This is of course difficult, but the other option is to remain fixed in what one has been taught to the exclusion of unfolding truth.

9.) A spiritual roadmap helps me to become fully human and fully alive:

In Anthony de Mello's book, Awareness, he shares a story that could apply to many of us, especially if we continue to rigidly practice first half of life spirituality even as we age chronologically. I'll simplify his story for you.

There was once a man who found an eagle's egg, and he placed it in the nest of a barnyard hen. The eaglet hatched and grew up with the chickens, and he thought he was one of them. One day he saw an eagle flying above him. He asked another chicken what that was, and he was told it was an eagle. Since he thought he was a chicken, he never learned to soar.

The message here is transparent. Though we each are born to soar, if we are only surrounded by those who tell us otherwise, then we likely never even flap our wings! We will never realize the fullness of God's plan for our lives, the joy we may feel, the gifts we may give. This spiritual roadmap that I have been suggesting to you is a means of helping us to flap our wings, to be fully human, to be fully alive.

This metaphor of chickens and eagles is talked about in more serious language by the mystics, using terms such as "humanity" and "divinity" and their possible union. A trio of extraordinary mystics in the thirteenth century, Saints Mechtild of Hackeborn, Gertrude the Great, and Mechtild of Magdenburg, used such language and imagery. St. Mechtild of Hackeborn had great devotion to the humanity of Christ. She said this humanity was the "door" by which human beings and all creation entered into union with the divine.

In my own way, a spiritual roadmap helps me, paradoxically, to have a greater appreciation and acceptance of my humanity while at the same time keeping me aware of the divine presence both in me and my neighbor. This awareness and mutual embrace open my heart and mind to the presence of God.

A spiritual roadmap makes us aware that an exclusive worship of an exalted king negates Jesus' humanity and perpetuates an alienating dualism between the human and divine, within Jesus as well as in ourselves. This dualism is transcended when we come to know that it is when we are fully human and fully alive that we may share in divine life most fully. It is then that we are using all of our human gifts and talents. In this way, we may witness to others the presence of divine life as demonstrated by the Gifts and Fruits of the Holy Spirit that I mentioned earlier.

Without a spiritual roadmap, we could easily believe that Christianity's major theme is the avoidance of sin and evil and that the body and the created world are essentially bad. Through this mind set, we can believe that we are poor miserable sinners. As a result, many of us pray the Chaplet of Divine Mercy that emphasizes how wretched we are rather than how blessed we are. A spiritual roadmap provides a balance. We are good by nature, but at times we sin. This provides a much more constructive way to live life, since our spiritual problems are rarely solved on their own terms, but instead are outgrown aided by friendship, unconditional love, compassion, and self-acceptance.

A spiritual roadmap provides us with a new understanding of Original Sin that better helps us to stay fully alive because we come to know that we are never separated from God, most basically, because we are an expression of God. I believe a spiritual roadmap helps me to know that my true self is of, in, and through Christ. As Jesus said, "The Father and I are one" (John 10:30), and "On that day you will realize that I am in my Father, and you are in me, and I am in you" (John 14:20).

By following a spiritual roadmap, I am helped to understand new outlooks, new metaphors, and to re-learn so much of what I learned earlier, all of which help me to be more human and more fully alive. I am beginning to understand Jesus' words, "You will know the truth, and the truth will set you free" (John 8:32).

In his book, In Memory of Jesus, Michael Morwood says the Church must do what Jesus did: "Affirm the divine in all people, respect the divine in all people, listen to the divine in all people, and challenge everyone to create a better world in which the divine would be clearly manifest in our religious, social, political, economic, and environmental systems."

In my humble opinion, a spiritual roadmap, if better known, could do so much to make our religion more relevant to both practicing and non-practicing Catholics, and in so doing make more real in our day the ministry of Jesus.

Peace,

Uncle Matthew

Letter #66
Friday, January 15, 2016

Dear Uncle Matthew,

The time I spent at home for the Christmas break was wonderful. Paul and I took a long walk together after dinner on Christmas Day, and I shared deeply some of my conflicts and fears regarding my future. Hearing Paul's views on things, both similar and dissimilar to my own, was helpful. I believe that his ability to "connect the dots" is a sign of an innate practical wisdom. Paul confirms for me that a person doesn't have to have a degree in theology to have a rich spiritual life. I believe that anyone can grow wise if there is an openness to the Gifts of the Spirit, a sign of one's faith in the Christ within, combined with courage and humility. So often I find myself putting priests on pedestals while missing the wisdom that is right in front of me, in my brother, in other members of my family, in friends, and in strangers.

My spiritual director keeps telling me that I need to listen more to the Spirit (the divine) within when I experience fear and when I need to make important choices. He reminded me of Samuel who heard God speaking to him when he was trying to sleep. I believe God does speak to me when I am quiet, yet I find my seminary experience with its emphasis on rational, analytical thought, and deference to external authority, actually makes it harder to hear this still, small, voice within. Perhaps in times of internal confusion, God speaks to me both through those I encounter in my daily life and when I am prayerfully listening to God speak to me.

You give me increased hope for the future when you share the many benefits that a spiritual roadmap is providing for you. What I hear most is that a spiritual roadmap is helping you to be motivated by love rather than fear, reflecting your discovery of new images of God. But I wonder, which comes first, the discovery of new images of God or the willingness to change and seek new insights.

I must admit that I am fearful of appearing to be unorthodox to my classmates since I suspect that my classmates are practicing first half of life spirituality. And yet I find myself drawn to the practice of second half of life spirituality. I believe my calling is to seek to be mature, in body, mind, and spirit, to become the person I want to be and believe I am called to be. This means more to me than just developing intellectually, but means being real and truthful about who and what I am as an embodied, emotional, and amorous being. If I set as a goal being fully human and fully alive, I want to mean it. In the end, I believe becoming a holistic person benefits not only myself, my seminary colleagues, and future parishioners, but will be of some service to God and the Church as well.

I am concerned about your health. Please take care of yourself. I guess that living alone causes you to have some anxiety, understandably, in case you were to have another stroke and not be able to communicate for outside help. You mentioned in our last phone call that your wonderful neighbor, Jimmy, checks in on you daily. That is good, but I find it sad and unacceptable that your diocese doesn't provide retirement options that include independent living, memory care, assisted living, or full nursing care. Religious order priests are cared for until the day they die. Why aren't priests in your diocese given the same care? You gave your life to the Church, and now you have some fear of being forgotten and abandoned as your health declines. Do parishioners understand this? This makes me realize I should check on what kind of a retirement plan is provided in my own diocese.

In an earlier letter, you shared with me that you are hopeful about the Catholic Church's future because (1) positive change is taking place in the hierarchy, and (2) the laity is demanding change. Do you have any further reflections on the Catholic Church's future? I don't want to miss a word of what you have to share. But at the same time, if it is a burden to write, I understand. I already have in all the letters you have written an immeasurable gift to help me along the way. I do love you, Uncle Matthew.

Peace,

Joey

Response to Letter #66
Saturday, January 30, 2016

Dear Joey,

Since you asked, my health is about the same as last reported.
Thank you for asking. I hope that when I die, my passing will not
be prolonged and I will go quickly like my dad who passed
quickly with his heart disease. I was there, now long ago, alone
with my dad, when he took his last breath at the Medical Center.
I shut his eyes and said, "Dad, you made it!" It was a moment of
blissful acceptance of life and death, of all that is.

I am finding now that I need more rest, and I neither drive at
night nor drive out of town. I guess I'm just getting old in body
which impedes the spirit at times. Awareness of my aging
reminds me of a saying from two thousand years ago by Seneca,
the Roman Stoic, who said, "Throughout the whole of life one
must continue to learn to live, and what will amaze you even
more, throughout life one must learn to die."

Writing to you, a young man on the cusp of a fruitful life of public
ministry,  is giving me a real purpose in life these last few years.
You have made me aware, through our letters, the many
opportunities retired priests have, if we so choose, for learning
and re-learning, making new friends, growing wiser, and
hopefully blooming into fully alive human beings who have a

wise message to share with others. The great challenge for all of us as we age is not simply recede into easy ruts of habit and conformity, but to continually question our assumptions, labels, and stereotypes. In this way we may remain youthful, not in body, but in disposition and spirit. I can even say that aging has a positive function to help us to be aware of our true nature, to better appreciate God's unconditional love for us, and to finally better understand the real purpose of life.

Our letters bring to mind a related insight shared by Robertson Davies, the Canadian novelist, who wrote, "One always learns one's mystery at the price of one's innocence." When we are born, we come into the world as innocent babes. In our youth, most of us quickly lose our innocence as we realize that life is not only full of wonder and joy, but it is at its heart full of difficulties as well. We come to realize that we will sink if we do not learn to swim, if we do not find ultimate goodness in a role full of suffering. When we move away from home, we are exposed to many discoveries and temptations that usually further erode our innocence. As our awareness of the complex realities of life grows, our spiritual lives, our understanding of God, must grow in parallel or a dangerous rift may emerge. Our experiences of the world and God go hand in hand. If we keep one small, it constricts the other. Or, preferably, they both become bigger, more abundant, without end.

For instance, when we study the Bible, we are likely to find that as our knowledge of life expands, we can no longer innocently claim that everything we read is literally true. Something supposedly as straight forward as the Bible in fact has many layers of meaning, many literary forms, many mysteries for a life-time of discovery. And so, like the Bible, life itself is layered and wonder-filled beyond our controlling grasp, meaning that in all the choices we make, both good and bad, we discover our mystery. I am so grateful to have been able to have this rich opportunity of dialogue to discover my own identity, my own mystery. I am, as you are, a child of God. We were created to love like our Creator. Christ lives in us and we within Christ. Our letter writing has been a part of this unfolding life for me.

Shifting gears now, you asked me, if I have any more reflections on the church's future. In an earlier letter, I shared two basic reasons why I am hopeful about the days ahead. First, change is taking place in the hierarchy. Second, the laity is demanding change. The Spirit is alive. So let me share a few other reasons why I am hopeful about the church's future. And then, alas, I will share with you my sense of pessimism about the church's future. Which outcome will prevail, which spirit will triumph, which travails must be borne, only God knows. But my individual path, my calling, my role, has been made clear to me.

More reflections on the Catholic Church's future:

3. Paradigms on spirituality:

As I mentioned in my very first letter to you, going to Fr. Richard Rohr's Conference on "Loving the Two Halves of Life," in January 2011, was by far the best conference I had ever attended to date. I was blessed throughout by the presenters: Fr. Richard Rohr, Fr. Ronald Rolheiser, and Ms. Edwina Gateley. If you want to get a second-hand sense of what I experienced, I suggest that you read Rohr's book, Falling Upward, a spirituality for the two halves of life.

Rohr's paradigm on the two halves of life spirituality is thankfully becoming well known and deservedly so. If more people knew about this paradigm, and embraced its implications, positive change would take place in the institutional church more quickly. Society, underpinning and permeating the Church, is changing at a rapid rate. If we as an institutional church do not continually make an effort to speak today's language, our Church will become irrelevant. We must not put the new wine in old wineskins.

I am also hopeful about the future when I read Fr. Ronald Rolheiser's books on spirituality. He offers a three-fold paradigm of the spiritual life: Essential Discipleship, Mature Discipleship, and Radical Discipleship. His first book, The Holy Longing, deals with Essential Discipleship while his second book, Sacred Fire, deals with Mature Discipleship. He is planning on writing on Radical Discipleship in a future book. I think you will find him to be an outstanding writer. Many people are reading his relevant books on spirituality.

As a result of these easy-to-understand paradigms on spirituality, two halves of life, evolving discipleship, etc., many people today are learning to appreciate the stages of spirituality not only for themselves, but for people both in the Church and outside the Church. These dynamic paradigms of spirituality stress inclusivity regarding the love, respect, and appreciation of others. People are learning to dialogue with others with a deep respect because they have come to believe in, and to know, the "Cosmic Christ" that offers salvation to everybody here on Earth. People realize their prime task is not to judge others but to accept others as they are. Love precedes understanding. More people today are realizing through these paradigms that their tasks in life are simple, to live fully in a way that allows the Christ to be alive in themselves, and to see and appreciate the Christ in others. "Do you not know that you are the temple of God, and that the Spirit of God dwells in you?" (1 Corinthians 3:16). This basic way of seeing and living fulfills Jesus' Great Commandment and informs the Golden Rule.

4. "Cafeteria Catholics":

This may surprise you, but I am hopeful about the future of the institutional church precisely because so many people, young and old, are willing to say that they are "cafeteria Catholics." Many people are not ashamed to say that they have difficulty accepting everything as believable in the Catechism of the Catholic Church, and therefore seek and find truth elsewhere as well. When we prayerfully consult our conscience, thoughtfully question our assumptions, judicially seek other opinions, and carefully study the tradition found in world religions (Hinduism, Buddhism, Judaism, Islamism, as well as Christianity), we become more broad-minded and discerning.

This issue of seeking the truth speaks not only to the breadth of sources to which we avail ourselves, but also what we choose to focus on with what is presented. Consider the Sermon on the Mount, the message that Jesus chose to give before the crowds. What did he speak of? Jesus was preoccupied with the issues of non-violence, love of enemies, and respect for all life. And yet so often the Church focuses on the issues of abortion, birth control, same-sex marriage, and homosexuality. Is it any wonder that many of our brothers and sisters seek spiritual nourishment from a broader menu in a bigger cafeteria. Hunger cannot be denied.

5. Prophets of today:

I am also hopeful for the future of the Church because the gift of prophesy is alive and well today. We tend to think of prophets as rare individuals who existed in Biblical days when we read the Major and Minor Prophets in the Hebrew Scriptures. But if we believe that God is actively with us today, then prophetic voices are still speaking. It is up to us to have the ears to hear. What follows are a few examples.

We have wonderful prophets like Fr. Richard Rohr whom I have known since he was a young high school seminarian at St. Francis Seminary in Hamilton, OH. His many books, his leadership at the Center for Action and Contemplation, and his speaking engagements at many national conferences have given hope to so many for the church's future.

And then there is Edwina Gateley, a poet, theologian, artist, writer, and lay minister. She has been described as a modern day mystic and prophet. She gives talks, conferences, and retreats in the United States, as well as internationally while continuing to reach out to women in recovery from drugs and prostitution. She offers a compelling voice for the need to continually grow spiritually throughout one's life.

Another prophetic voice is found in the Benedictine Sister Joan Chittister who lives and acts out of a deep contemplative tradition. She is a nun, theologian, author, and speaker. She has authored over seventy books. She has served as prioress, president of the Benedictine federation, and president of the Leadership Conference of Women Religious. She has provided guidance to millions by making the scriptures, contemplative prayer, and the Rule of Saint Benedict come alive.

Many people today discern that these writers and speakers, along with so many others, are gifted with a passion that flows from God's living Spirit. A common theme of them all is that God's unconditional love is free and accessible to everyone, and that it is an error to deny this. This conforms with the prophets of old who not only affirmed God's mercy and justice but also criticized society around them. They often focused on the people's arrogance before God, leading them to both reject for themselves and deny for others God's mercy. I think of Micah 6:8 in this regard. "You have been told what is good, and what the Lord requires of you: only to do the right and to love goodness, and to walk humbly with your God." And yet some leaders in today's Church attempt to marginalize these prophetic voices of compassion. They have been banned from Catholic properties in numerous dioceses. Many people ask, "Why are we denied the opportunity to hear these and other gifted speakers in our dioceses? What is there to fear?"

Rohr, Gateley, and Chittister, and many other witnesses, give people hope about their own lives and the world at large. They make their listeners excited and newly aware of how God is alive and present in their lives. These courageous, Spirit-filled persons, question many assumptions. They stir the pot. They make people think. They quicken the mind and awaken the heart. They touch the soul. And I believe they do so because many more people are seeking opportunities to know about and personally experience the Christ within. It is this that makes faith real. And to deny these voices seems to me to be more about power and control than serving the living God.

I have discovered in my own life that the prophets of today may be found in the most unexpected of places, even in one's own circle of friends. Prophets are found not only among priests, practicing Catholics, and other Christians, but also among the unchurched and atheists. All can serve as vehicles for God. For example, I am blessed to share reflections on the daily readings with two women, neither of whom regularly attends church. The three of us email one another every day, exploring how the gospel applies to our own lives and the world today. When I read and ponder their wisdom and goodness that often characterizes their reflections, I am saddened that the Church fails to recognize the spiritual gifts in lay persons, denying them the privilege of preaching at mass while denying parishioners the benefit of hearing them (unless they are asked to preach about giving money). These two ladies, without any theological training, write with a depth that places them in the category of modern-day prophets! How many voices remain unheard!

The prophets of today, at least those I have encountered, have learned to forgive, to show mercy, to accept the worth of different viewpoints, to serve others, and through it all, to be humble. Like prophets of old, they convey authority not because of title or rank, but because of a clarity of message and a demonstration that God's spirit fills their lives and work. They embrace the theology of Meister Eckhart who said, "The best name for God is compassion."

In short, I believe a new Spirit is working in these contemporary prophets that encourages all of us, as People of God, to appreciate and practice an adult spirituality. We naturally desire, in our heart of hearts, to change, God willing, when we encounter individuals who witness through their words and actions the presence of an Incarnate, Merciful, Inclusive, Forgiving, and Unconditionally Loving God.

6. The "fire"

Before I leave you with the impression that I and many of those who practice second half of life spirituality believe the church's future looks fully bright, I'll share with you some profound concerns regarding what may lie ahead for the institutional church.

Let me convey these apprehensions by way of a story. There is a tale about the gift of fire in Anthony de Mello's book, Discovering Life, Awaken to Reality. I'll abbreviate the story (but I do suggest reading his book when your schedule allows). Once upon a time, a man invented fire. He shared this new knowledge with some local tribes, and they benefited from this new knowledge. But before they could thank the man, he had disappeared. He had gone to another tribe and had again shared his new invention. The priests in this area began to realize that this man of fire was becoming so popular that their influence was diminishing. So they decided to poison him! But to dispel suspicion, they painted a huge portrait of the man and put it on the main altar of the temple. They devised a liturgy to honor the inventor and this ritual was faithfully observed. What better way to conceal their crime than to publicly proclaim adoration of its victim. But as a result, there was soon no fire, only ritual, remembrance, expressions of gratitude, and acts of veneration.

Some people see parallels in this disturbing story with the structure and practice of the Church today. The church's stress on clericalism, hierarchy, patriarchy, inflexible laws, and numerous rituals that fail to be pastoral, all combine to diminish our awareness that the "fire" is a free gift available to all and at all times. And yet, for many within the Church, accessing the "fire" has been made so difficult because of the many demands put on us by the hierarchy. These demands make us question our worthiness to receive the fire. These demands cause us to doubt that God wants to freely give the "fire." These demands obscure from us the fact that the "fire" already burns if we could but see. The Church too often seeks to control, rather than spread the "fire," by controlling the availability of our sacraments.

For example church officials establish demands of who may or may not receive the "fire," the Eucharist, that Jesus shared as a free gift. This is no small matter for the freedom of our new life in Christ, a life full of "fire," is nothing less than the center of the message proclaimed by Jesus (John 8: 32-36) and St. Paul

(Galatians 5: 1-26).

Many of those who practice second half of life spirituality have serious doubts about the church's devotion to spreading the "fire," to its willingness to change, when something such as divorce excludes so many Catholics from sharing at the table of the Lord. Rather than receiving compassion, many divorced Catholics have been shamed into feeling they are unworthy of receiving the "fire."

And tragically, the many gifted and loving people who fall under the LGBTQ umbrella are rejected, if not shunned, because of who and how they love. As a result, they abandon the Church that tells them they are unworthy of receiving the "fire."

And fully half of humanity, women, is excluded from the institutional diaconate and priesthood simply because they are not males, and are thus told that they are unworthy of both receiving the "fire" and sharing the "fire" with others.

In sum, many are concerned that a culture has been created where accepting the hierarchy's teaching on doctrinal and church decrees seems to be more important than the transformative power of intimacy with Jesus. When we are taught, repeatedly, that God abandons us when we commit any number of sins, and that only a priest can restore us to friendship with God, we may indeed come to think that the "fire" is no longer for us, with us, or in us. It is in this way that the "fire" of God is dampened. But the "fire" of God, the light of God, cannot be put out, and will always find new ways to burst forth into our darkened world. "The light shines in the darkness, and the darkness did not overcome it" (John 1: 5).

I pray along with those who practice second half of life spirituality pray for a Church in the future that better proclaims Christ's inclusivity so that everyone can experience the "fire." This desire for a focus on service and love directly confronts the temptations of power and authority that holds sway over too many in the Church. Clericalism, hierarchy, patriarchy, and sexism within the

Church, all of these structures, both reveal and support this failure to fully live the gospel. These underlying concerns need to be addressed, and major reform taken, if there is to be hope for a vital and relevant Church in the future.

Conclusion:

One of the great Christian theologians of the twentieth century, Karl Rahner, wrote in his Theological Investigations, "The Christian of the future will be a mystic or will not exist at all." What does he mean by this? How does this speak to the great issues we have been discussing, the Church, spirituality, the many images of God, the formation of conscience, courage and conformity?

Most of us who are older priests had no spiritual roadmap to assist us on our spiritual journey when we were ordained. The status quo reigned. We were unaware of the many new and old paradigms offering an adult spirituality. The only paradigm that I heard about, that suggested a potential progress of the soul, was the three basic stages through which the Christian may pass: the Purgative, Illuminative, and Unitive stages. But even with that framework, we were not encouraged to stretch our beliefs to include new theological perspectives. We were not told that change, a letting go, would be necessary. Instead, we were warned not to read "restricted books" that were locked away in the seminary library or to view films that church officials condemned. Control, through fear, prevailed. We hesitated, myself and everyone I knew, to break with the past because that was all we knew. Before us was only a void if we dared to venture forth. We were discouraged to be open to new revelation. And on the most practical of matters, we didn't have priests in the seminary who shared with us how they dealt with loneliness, celibacy, chastity, and authentic prayer. This denial of the common experiences served to alienate us from ourselves and one another. St. Paul said, "When I was a child, I used to talk as a child, think as a child, reason as a child; when I became a man, I put aside childish things" (1 Corinthians 13: 11). And yet, unaided and not encouraged, too many of us remained as spiritual children. We needed a spiritual roadmap to validate, and thus practice, an adult spirituality. How blessed we are today to have ready access to the paradigm of the two halves of life spirituality. How fortunate we are to be able to more readily learn from history and especially from those courageous men and women who witness God's Spirit by demonstrating the transformation of self into fully human and fully alive individuals.

And so, Karl Rahner's provocative claim that we all, as Christians, need to be mystics, is to be heard not as a requirement but as a blessed invitation. An invitation into the wide open world of God's infinite love. To be a mystic means to seek and welcome new and direct experiences of an Incarnate God in our own life, wherever we may be, however we are made, and whoever we may love. Taken together, the many new mystics of today may yet breathe new life into our ancient and venerable church, a vessel, frail and faulty, but blessed and beautiful, for God's unfolding life.

And so, the world today needs good shepherds in families, in the domain of politics, and in church communities of faith. We need leaders to tell us how to be freed from old myths and restraints so that we can be filled with the Spirit of God, experience the "fire," and thus become fully human and fully alive like Jesus. There are enormous possibilities for the future of the Catholic Church, but these looming obstacles and inherent dangers, of which we have written, are also present. Which path will the People of God choose?

Joey, since you are facing and will face many temptations and obstacles as you journey through life as a good shepherd, just remember that Jesus calls you not to be afraid as you journey with him and toward him. He reminds us that, "God is with us" (Emmanuel) as we learn about our true identities, shedding our innocence, while embracing the many mysteries and discoveries of life with God. It is a shared walk, what we have been calling second half of life spirituality, that will lead your transformation into a man who is rich in compassion, learned in communication skills, and strong in creativity. Then you will be fully human, fully alive, transformed into the living presence of Christ, a wonderful expression of God's love here on earth.

Alfred Tennyson (1809-1892; poet laureate of Great Britain and Ireland), in Ulysses, writes, "My friend, 'Tis not too late to seek a newer world." You, Joey, have arrived in the nick of time.

Peace Always,

Uncle Matthew

P. S.

One last thought, I watched a movie last night, The Mission, that is about the experiences of Jesuit missionaries in South America in the 1750s. The Spanish Jesuits had converted and socialized, by building several missions, a tribe of remote indigenous peoples. At first, the Jesuit missions were relatively safe because they were formally protected under Spanish law. This did not, however, fully prevent slave traders from raiding upon them. But matters became much worse when a treaty, brokered by the Vatican, reapportioned that region to the Portuguese who allowed and condoned slavery. Rome sent a Cardinal to survey the situation in order to render a decision about the fate of the missions and the protections they had provided. Bowing to political pressure, trying to protect the power of the Church in Europe, the visiting Cardinal agreed to the destruction of the missions and the related killing of the converted indigenous people.

The Cardinal, although showing signs of inner conflict and bouts of conscience throughout the movie, in the end proved to be hypocritical. Though he had seen with his own eyes the work of God on earth through the missions by way of love, he chose to follow a different God. In the end he adored a god of power and conquest, the god that gave him fine clothes and perks of privilege that he was unable to let go. He, like all of us, became like the images of God that he adored.

The movie concluded with a mournful scene. After the missions had been destroyed and many had been killed, with the soldiers now departed, naked children came to look for anything of use to take with them to their new home deep in the jungle. I perceived their nakedness as symbolic of their return to nature's ways, having witnessed the utter failure of Christianity to manifest love of thy neighbor. So the children returned to their native ways and abandoned what for them was now the fraudulent practices of Christianity. One of the native girls saw a church candelabra and a violin in the shallow waters of the river, and she chose to take the violin with her into the canoe. She left the candelabra. This choice was full of meaning for me. The music which the Jesuits had brought with them by way of flutes and violins, had given joy and life to the children. They experienced the music as an expression of the god that though unseen is in fact everywhere and anywhere. The candelabra, on the other hand, though made of precious metals that the world would value, was for the children worthless, or worse, following the assault by the soldiers and the known complicity of the Cardinal. Unlike the free gift of music, which, like the wind, may stir the waters and blows where it will, the heavy candelabra was like a bludgeon of dominance and power-over. Who could blame the children for their choice?

Today, Joey, so many former Catholics have left the active practice of their faith within the confines of the Church. Many of us, perhaps all of us, know that many of our children, siblings, peers, and friends no longer attend church on a regular basis. Could it be that for so many people the Church is no longer relevant? Or worse, it has become for some a bludgeon. Could it be that what we learned as children no longer suffices to guide us as adults? Is Bishop John Spong expressing a hard truth when he titles one of his books, Why Christianity Must Change or Die? These questions beg an answer from you and your peers. Remember, above all, that with God all things are possible.

# RESOURCES

The following resources were helpful to me in my quest to deepen my understanding of religion and spirituality.

Allen, John, Jr.; *National Catholic Reporter*, "Evangelii Gaudium amounts to Francis' 'I have a dream' speech," November 26, 2013.

Bell, Rob; *What We Talk About When We Talk About God*. New York: HarperOne, 2013.

Borg, Marcus J.; *Convictions—How I Learned What Matters Most*. New York: HarperCollins Publishers, 2014.

—————. *JESUS—Uncovering the Life, Teachings, and Relevance of a Religious Revolutionary*. New York: HarperCollins, 2006.

—————. *The God We Never Knew—Beyond Dogmatic Religion To A More Authentic Contemporary Faith*. New York: HarperCollins Publishing, 1997.

—————. *Reading the Bible Again for the First Time*. New York: HarperCollins Publishers, 2001.

Bradshaw, John; *Healing The Shame That Binds You*. Deerfield Beach, FL: Health Communications, Inc., 1988.

—————. *Homecoming—Reclaiming and Championing Your Inner Child*. New York: Bantam Books, 1990.

Brown, Brene; *The Gifts of Imperfection—Let Go of Who You Think You're Supposed to Be and Embrace Who You Are*. Center City, MN: Hazelden, 2010.

Brown, Raymond E., S.S. *An Introduction to the New Testament*. New York: Doubleday, 1997.

Brunsman, Fr. Barry; *New Hope for Divorced Catholics, Annulment—A Concerned Pastor Offers Alternatives to Annulment.* New York: Harper and Row, 1985.

Butterworth, Eric; *Discover the Power Within You—A Guide to the Unexplored Depths Within.* New York: HarperCollins, 1968.

*The Catechism of the Catholic Church.* Liguori, MO.: Liguori Publications, 1995.

Cahill, Brian; *National Catholic Reporter,* "Church on track to become a shrinking cult," September 12-28, 2014.

Chittister, Joan; *The Gift of Years—Growing Old Gracefully.* Katonah, New York: BlueBridge, 2008.

Christiansen, Drew, S. J.;*America Magazine*, "Changing Hearts —Four Ways Pope Francis is transforming church life," May 4, 2015.

*Code of Canon Law*

Coleman, William V.; *Everyday People.* Weston, VT.: Growth Associates, 1987.

Congregation for Catholic Education (approved by Pope Benedict XVI); *Concerning the Criteria for the Discernment of Vocation with Regard to Persons with homosexual tendencies in View of the Admission to the Seminary and Holy Orders*, November 4, 2005.

Crosby, Michael H.; *Celibacy—Means of Control or Mandate of the Heart?* Notre Dame, IN.: Ave Maria Press, 1996.

Curran, Charles; *Conscience.* New York: Mahwah, N. J.: Paulist Press, 2004.

Cutie, Albert; *Dilemma, A Priest's Struggle with Faith and Love.* New York: A Celebra Book, 2011.

Darwin, Charles; *On the Origin of Species*, 1859.

Dear, John; *The Questions of Jesus—Challenging Ourselves to Discover Life's Great Answers.* New York: Image Books, 2004.

de Mello, Anthony; *Awareness-The Perils and Opportunities fo Reality.* New York: Doubleday, 1992.

—————. *Rediscovering Life—Awaken to Reality.* New York: Center for Spiritual Exchange, 2012.

DeBernardo, Francis; *New Ways Ministry*, "Two Catholic Schools Approach Employees' Same-Gender Marriages Very Differently," July 15, 2015.

Dick, John A.; *National Catholic Reporter,* "Bishop backs recognizing gay relationships," January 16-29, 2015.

Dyer, Wayne W.; *Your Erroneous Zones.* New York: Avon Books, 1976.

Editorial Staff. *National Catholic Reporter,* "Bishop's exorcism stunt mocks and offends," December 6, 2013.

Fares, Ego; *America Magazine.* "Pastors not Princes," July 6-13, 2015.

Fiedler, Maureen, and Rabben, Linda, editors; *Rome Has Spoken, a Guide to Forgotten Papal Statements and How They Changed Through the Centuries.* New York: A Crossroad Book, 1998.

Filteau, Jerry; *National Catholic Reporter,* "Bishop: Synod questionnaire shows most reject teaching on contraception," February 24, 2014.

Finley, James; *Merton's Palace of Nowhere.* Notre Dame, Ind.: Ave Maria, 2003.

Fox, Matthew; *Christian Mystics—365 Readings and Meditations.* Novato, CA: New World Library, 2011.

—————. *Meister Eckhart—A Mystic-Warrior for Our Times.* Novato, CA: New World Library, 2014.

—————. *A New Reformation—Creation Spirituality and the Transformation of Christianity.* Rochester, VT: Inner Traditions, 2006.

—————. *Original Blessing: A Primer in Creation Spirituality.* Santa Fe, NM: Bear & Company, 1983.

—————. *The Pope's War—Why Ratzinger's Secret Crusade Has Imperiled the Church and How It Can Be Saved.* New York: Sterling Ethos, 2011.

Gawande, Atul; *Being Mortal—Medicine and What Matters in the End.* New York: Metropolitan Books, 2014.

Girzone, Joseph F.; *Joshua, A Parable for Today.* New York: Simon & Schuster, 1983.

—————. *The Homeless Bishop, A Novel.* Maryknoll, New York: Orbis Books, 2011.

Helminiak, Daniel A.; *What the Bible Really Says About Homosexuality.* New Mexico: Alamo Square Press, 2000.

Hernandez, Will; *Henri Nouwen: A Spirituality of Imperfection.* New York: Paulist Press, 2006.

Johnson, Elizabeth A.; *CORPUS REPORTS*, "Jesus and Women," July/August 2014.

Jung, C.G.; *Memories, Dreams and Reflections.* New York: Pantheon Books, Random House, 1963.

—————. *Modern Man in Search of a Soul.* New York: A Harvest Book, 1933.

Philip S. Kaufman. *Why You Can Disagree and Remain a Faithful Catholic.* New York: Crossroad, 1995.

Kempis, Thomas A.; *The Imitation of Christ.* Notre Dame, IN: Ave Maria Press, 1989.

Kinsey, Alfred C.; *Sexual Behavior in the Human Male.* Bloomington, IN: Indiana University Press, 1948.

Kosicki, George W.; *Tell My Priests.* Stockbridge, MA: Marian Press, 2002.

Kurtz, Ernest, and Ketcham, Katherine; *The Spirituality of Imperfection.* New York: Bantam Book, 1992.

Lakoff, George; *Don't Think of An Elephant!—Know Your Values and Frame the Debate.* Wild River Ruction, Vermont: Chelsea Green Publishing, 2014.

Lawler, Michael G., and Graff, Emil;. *America Magazine,* "Following Faithfully," February 2, 2015.

Lowe, Robert; *Stories I Only Tell My Friends: an Autobiography.* New York: Henry Holt and Company, 2011.

—————. *Love Life.* New York: Simon & Schuster, 2014.

McClory, Robert; *Faithful Dissenters—Stories of Men and Women Who Loved and Changed the Church.* Maryknoll, NY: Orbis Books, 2000.

McElwee, Joshua J.; *National Catholic Reporter,* "Mercy Sisters support Roy Bourgeois." November 30, 2012.

_____. *National Catholic Reporter,* "Francis: Discern sexual morality case-by-case." October 21-November 3, 2016.

Maguire, Daniel C.; *Christianity Without God—Moving Beyond the Dogmas and Retrieving the Epic Moral Narrative.* New York: Sony Press, 2014.

—————-. *Sacred Choices- The Right to Contraception and Abortion in Ten World Religions.* Minneapolis, MN: Fortress Press, 2001.

Manson, Jamie; *The National Catholic Reporter,* "Synod on the family proves that father still knows best," November 21-December 5, 2014.

Martin, James, SJ; *Becoming Who You Are—Insights On The True Self From Thomas Merton and Other Saints.* Mahwah, New Jersey: Paulist Press, 2005.

Mellody, Pia; *Facing Codependence—What It Is, Where It Comes From, How It Sabotages Our Lives.* New York: HarperOne, 1998.

Merton, Thomas; *New Seeds of Contemplation.* New York: New Directions, 1972.

—————. *Thoughts in Solitude.* New York: Farrer, Straus and Giroux, 1958.

Mickens, Robert; *National Catholic Reporter,* "Disasters of the old boy's network," July 17-30, 2015.

Miller, William A.; *Make Friends with Your Shadow—How to Accept and Use Positively the Negative Side of Your Personality.* Minneapolis, MN: Augsburg Publishing House, 1981.

Moore, Thomas; *A Religion of One's Own, A Guide to Creating a Personal Spirituality in a Secular World.* New York: Gotham Books, 2014.

Morwood, Michael; *From Sand to Solid Ground.* New York: A Crossroad Book, 2007.

——————. *God is Near.* New York: A Crossroad Book, 2002

——————. *In Memory of Jesus.* Sunbury, Victoria Australia: Kelmor Publications, 2014.
——————. *Is Jesus God?* New York: A Crossroad Book, The Crossroad Publishing Company, 2001

——————. *It's Time...Challenges to the Doctrine of the Faith.* Sunbury, Victoria, Australia, Kelmore Publications, 2013.

——————. *Tomorrow's Catholic—Understanding God and Jesus in a New Millennium.* Mystic,CT: Twenty-Third Publications, 1997.

Nolan, Albert; *Jesus Before Christianity.* Maryknoll, NY: Orbis Books, 1976.

——————. *Jesus Today.* Maryknoll, NY: Orbis Books, 2006.

O'Murchu, Diarmuid; *Catching Up With Jesus-A Gospel Story for Our Time.* New York: The Crossroad Publishing Company, 2005.

O'Neill , Patrick;*National Catholic Reporter,* "Daniel Berrigan, priest, prisoner, anti-war crusader, dies," May 2, 2016.

Padovano, Anthony; in *CORPUS REPORTS.* March/April, 2013.

——————. *Hope is a Dialogue.* Mequon, WI: Caritas Communications, 1998.

*Pastoral Constitution of the Church in the Modern World.*

Peck, M. Scott; *The Different Drum-Community Making and Peace.* New York: Simon & Schuster, 1987.

—————. *The Road Less Traveled-A New Psychology of Love, Traditional Values and Spiritual Growth.* New York: A Touchstone Book Published by Simon & Schuster, 1978.

—————. *People of the Lie—the Hope of Healing Human Evil.* New York: Simon and Schuster, 1983.

Pope Paul V1. *Gaudium et Spes, The Pastoral Constitution on the Church in the Modern World*, Vatican II.

—————. *Humanae Vitae*, July 25. 1968.

Pope John Paul II. *Ordinatio Sacerdotalis.* May 22, 1994.

Pope John Paul II. *Veritatis Splendor, The Splendor of Truth, 1993.*

Pope Francis. *Evangelii Gaudium, The Joy of the Gospel, 2013.*

Powell, John; *A Life-Giving Vision, How To Be Christ In Today's World.* Allen, Texas: ThomasMore, 1995.

—————. *Happiness Is an Inside Job.* Valencia, California" Tabor Publishing, 1989.

—————. *The Secret of Staying in Love, Loving Relationships through Communication.* Allen, TX: RCL, Resources for Christian Living, 1974.

Rahner, Karl; *Theological Investigations.* New York: Herder and Herder, 1971.

Robertson, Robin; *Beginner's Guide to Jungian Psychology.* Lake Worth, Florida: Nicolas Hayes, Inc., 1992.

Rohr, Richard; *Everything Belongs.* New York: A Crossroad Book, The Crossroad Publishing Company, 1999.

—————. *Falling Upward: A Spirituality of the Two Halves of Life.* San Francisco: Jossey-Bass, 2011.

—————. *Immortal Diamond: The Search for Our True Self.* San Francisco: Jossey-Bass, 2013.

—————. *YES, and... daily meditations.* Cincinnati, OH: Franciscan Media, 2013.

Ronald Rolheiser. *Forgotten Among the Lillies-Learning to Live Beyond Our Fears.* New York: Doubleday, 2005.

—————. *Sacred Fire-A Vision for a Deeper Human and Christian Maturity.* New York: Image, 2014.

—————. *The Holy Longing—The Search for A Christian Spirituality.* New York: Doubleday, 1999.

—————. *The Shattered Lantern—Rediscovering A Felt Presence of God.* New York: The Crossroad Publishing Company, 2001.

Ross, Dennis S.; *All Politics Is Religious—Speaking Faith to the Media, Policy Makers and Community.* Woodstock, VT: Skylight Paths Publishing, 2012.

Ruhl, Jack; *The National Catholic Reporter,* "Survey finds serious flaws in diocesan financial management," February 24, 2015.

Saint-Exupery, Antoine de; *The Little Prince.* New York: Reynal & Hitchcock, 1943.

Salgado, Soli; *National Catholic Reporter,* "Jesus made deathbed call for women's ordination," March 23, 2015.

Sanford, John A.; *Evil—The Shadow Side of Reality.* New York: Crossroad, 1981.

Schwab, Klaus; *The Fourth Industrial Revolution.* Cologny/Geneva, Switzerland: World Economic Forum, 2016.

Senior, Donald, editor; *The Catholic Study Bible.* New York: Oxford University Press, 1990.

Shapiro, Rami; *Perennial Wisdom for the Spiritually Independent —Sacred Teachings—Annotated & Explained.* Woodstock, VT: SkyLIght Paths Publishing, 2013.

Silverstein, Shel; *The Giving Tree.* New York: HarperCollins*Publishers*, 1964.

Simsic, Wayne; *Praying with Meister Eckhart.* Winona, Minnesota: St. Mary's Press, Christian Brothers Publications, 1998.

Sipe, A. W. Richard; *Living the Celibate Life—A Search for Models and Meaning.* Liguori, Missouri: Liguori/Triumph, 2004.

—————. *"Frequently Asked Questions."*

Schaef, Anne Wilson; *When Society Becomes an Addict.* San Francisco, CA: Harper and Row, Publishers, 1983.

Schenk, Christine; *The National Catholic Reporter,* "Free Mary to be herself," October 21-November 3, 2016.

Spong, John Shelby; *Born of a Woman-A Bishop Rethinks the Virgin Birth and the Treatment of Women by a Male-Dominated Church.* New Work: HarperOne, 1992.

—————. *Eternal Life: A New Vision Beyond Religion, beyond Theism, Beyond Heaven and Hell.* New York: HarperOne, 2009.

—————. *Jesus for the Non-Religious-Recovering the Divine at the Heart of the Human*. New York: HarperSanFrancisco, 2007.

—————. *Liberating the Gospels-Reading the Bible with Jewish Eyes*. New York: Harper Collins Publishers, 1996.

—————. *Living in Sin-A Bishop Rethinks Human Sexuality*. Morristown, NJ: Harper One, 1988.

—————. *A New Christianity for a New World—Why Traditional Faith is Dying & How a New Faith Is Being Born*. New York: HarperSan Francisco, 2001.

—————. *Re-Claiming the Bible for a Non-Religious World*. New York: HarperOne, 2011.

—————. *The Sins of Scripture—Exposing the Bible's Gets of Hate to Reveal the God of Love*. New York: Harper Collins, 2005.

—————. *This Hebrew Lord*. Morristown, NJ: Christianity for the Third Millennium, 1988.

—————. *Why Christianity Must Change or Die*. San Francisco, CA: Harper, 1998.

Stevens, Anthony; *Jung, A Very Short Introduction*. Oxford, England: Oxford University Press, 1994.

Stoltzfus, Kate; *National Catholic Reporter*, "A legacy beyond Catholicism," August 1, 2015.

Weakland, Rembert G.; *A Pilgrim In A Pilgrim Church—Memoirs of a Catholic Archbishop*. Grand Rapids, Michigan: William B. Eerdmans Publishing Company, 2009.

Wills, Gary; *The Future of the Catholic Church with Pope Francis*. New York: Penguin Group, 2015.

————. *What Jesus Meant.* New York: Penguin Books, 2006.

————. *Why Priests?-A Failed Tradition.* New York: Viking, 2013.